PAULE MARSHALL

THE CHOSEN PLACE, THE TIMELESS PEOPLE

Paule Marshall was born and raised in Brooklyn, New York. After graduating from Brooklyn College in 1953, she worked as a magazine writer and researcher and began work on her first novel, *Brown Girl, Brownstones*. She is the author of two other highly acclaimed novels, *Praisesong for the Widow* and *Daughters*, as well as a book of novellas, *Soul Clap Hands and Sing*, and a collection of early writings, *Reena and Other Stories*. Paule Marshall has taught at several universities, and is now Professor of English at Virginia Commonwealth University in Richmond, Virginia. In 1992, she was the recipient of a MacArthur Fellowship. She divides her time between Richmond and New York City.

THE CHOSEN PLACE, THE TIMELESS PEOPLE

PAULE MARSHALL

VINTAGE CONTEMPORARIES

VINTAGE BOOKS · A DIVISION OF RANDOM HOUSE, INC. · NEW YORK

Vintage Contemporaries Edition, October 1992

 Published in the United States by Vintage Books, a division of Random House, Inc., New York, and simultaneously in Canada by Random House of Canada Limited, Toronto. Originally published by Harcourt, Brace & World, Inc. in 1969.

Library of Congress Cataloging in Publication Data
Marshall, Paule, 1929–
The chosen place, the timeless people.
I. Title.
[PS3563.A7223C5 1985] 813'.54 92-81673

ISBN-13: 978-0-394-72633-5

Manufactured in the United States of America
27

"Once a great wrong has been done, it never dies. People speak the words of peace, but their hearts do not forgive. Generations perform ceremonies of reconciliation but there is no end."

From the Tiv of West Africa

BOOK I

HEIRS AND DESCENDANTS

CHAPTER 1

The lower section of the road the woman was traveling, the winding stretch that lay at the very bottom of the old, soaring cathedral of a hill, had washed away as usual in the heavy, unseasonable rain that had fallen the night before. The woman hadn't been told this, though, and in her impelled and reckless way she nearly sent the car she was driving hurtling onto the empty roadbed where it would have been hopelessly mired, for days perhaps, in a thick bog of mud and broken marl.

"Oh, crime, not again!" Braking sharply, she brought the car to such a violent halt both she and her companion, a much older woman seated to her left, went pitching forward almost onto the dashboard. Quickly thrusting her bare feet into a pair of open-back shoes lying turned over on their sides on the floor amid the pedals, the younger woman slammed out of the car and, leaving the door yawning open behind her, marched up to where the unnavigable mud slough began just short of her front bumper and stretched out of sight around a bend a good distance ahead.

Visibly annoyed, close to anger, she stared at the washed-out road as though she would will it into place again, conjure it back. And she might have possessed the dark powers and art to do so. For her eyes, as she snatched off her sunglasses, gave the impression of being lighted from deep within (it was as if she had been endowed with her own small sun), and they were an unusually clear tawny shade of brown, an odd, even eerie, touch in a face that was the color of burnt sugar.

She waited, confident, it seemed, that the road would reappear, one short blunt hand at her hip, the other feeling blindly for her cigarettes in the wide pockets of her dress. Beside her, the motor of the car, which she had left running, drummed feebly in the tropical noon stillness and heat.

The car was an old but ageless Bentley which, from all evidence, must have once served as the state car of a colonial governor. The small staff that had borne his flag stood intact at the prow of the hood, although the flag itself was gone. But the car had been badly used since then, and was now little more than a wreck. And it appeared to have been deliberately abused, willfully desecrated. Someone, perhaps the woman herself, might have taken a sledge hammer and battered in the huge front fenders which swept forward with all the controlled drama of a wave curving in on itself, then scraped off the black paint from the body in great ugly patches that resembled sores, and, as a final insult, driven it head-on into a wall, caving in the high grille that was its trademark.

Standing beside the ruined but still regal old car, the woman looked shorter than she was. And she was no longer young. Her body had already begun the slow, irreversible decline toward middle age. The flesh that had once been firm on the bone and evenly distributed over her compact frame was beginning to slacken and lose hold. Under the bodice of her dress there was the slight weary telltale droop to her small breasts, and the flesh of her upper arm, scant though it was, shuddered now whenever she gestured strongly. But her legs were still those of a young woman, slender and thoughtfully shaped at the ankle and arch and with a lovely tension to the black skin and muscle beneath.

And she was dressed like a much younger woman, in the open-back shoes which featured some rather fanciful, embroidered scroll-work across the instep and raised heels to give her height, and a flared print dress made from cloth of a vivid abstract tribal motif: cloth from the sun, from another cosmos, which could have been found draped in offhand grace around a West African market woman. Pendant silver earrings carved in the form of those saints to be found on certain European churches adorned her ears. The saints, their tiny faces gaunt with piety, their eyes closed in prayer, were trembling anxiously from the force of her annoyance. Numerous bracelets, also of silver, bound her wrists. But these, unlike the earrings, were heavy, crudely made, and noisy. They lent a clangorous, unsettling note to her every move. Even when she was quiet their loud echo lingered. It sounded now above the shrilling of the daytime insects in the cus-cus grass bordering a nearby field of sugar cane and the Bentley's labored breathing. She moved always within the ambience of that sound. Like a monk's beads or a captive's chains, it announced her.

All this: the dress with its startling print, the strange but beautiful earrings that had been given to her years ago in England by the woman who had been, some said, her benefactress; others, her lover; the noisy bracelets, the shoes—all this could be easily taken as an attempt on her part to make herself out to be younger than she was. But there was more to it than that, one sensed. She had donned this somewhat bizarre outfit, each item of which stood opposed to, at war even, with the other, to express rather a diversity and disunity within herself, and her attempt, unconscious probably, to reconcile these opposing parts, to make of them a whole. Moreover, in dressing in this manner, she appeared to be trying (and this was suggested by those unabashedly feminine shoes) to recover something in herself that had been lost: the sense and certainty of herself as a woman perhaps. There was no telling. But her face, as she stood breathing angrily down at the muddy swill at her feet, attested to some profound and frightening loss.

Framed by the tremulous earrings, dusted over lightly with talcum powder that gave it a whitish cast, it was a face that might have been sculpted by some bold and liberal Bantu hand which had deliberately ignored all the other strains that had gone into making her. And it was handsome in its way, with a firm line of bone beneath the skin, a strongly arched flared nose, and a mouth that was full, with a shallow cleft like a small valley above the upper lip, and warm. But it had been despoiled, that face, in much the same way as the worn hills to be seen piled around her on all sides had been despoiled—stripped of their trees centuries ago, their substance taken. Her face, especially in repose or when she was silent (which was seldom), confessed that something of great value had been taken from her. It looked utterly bereft at times. What saved it (and this only in part) was the inner sunlight her eyes gave off. This said some vital center remained intact. And this duality, this sense of life persisting amid that nameless and irrevocable loss made her face terribly affecting, even beautiful.

"But you know," she said, looking up finally from the empty roadbed, "this whole damn place needs to wash away, never mind the old road." And her swift cutting glance took in not only the ring of shabby low-lying hills, whose slopes were green in some places with sugar cane and pitifully bare in others, despoiled, the soil eroded down to the rock, but the few trees as well scattered about, mostly breadfruit and slender long-limbed coconut palms, and the one or two small, unpainted, sun-bleached wooden houses that could be seen clinging like burrs to the mangy flanks of the hills. Her gaze reached up to the incredibly blue, flawless sky (even when it rained you could sense it waiting blue and unclouded, unmoved, behind the overcast). In their sweep upward, her eyes clashed briefly with the single hot eye of the sun. It returned her a look of monumental indifference, and she hastily put her sunglasses back on.

"Just wash away. The whole bloody show!" But she was almost smiling now, her annoyance giving way to a resigned half-smile which said that in spite of everything she loved the place.

"Mr. Douglin," she called to the bent figure of a man busy trimming the grass at the edge of the roadbed up near where it curved out of sight. The man, dressed in patched and faded denims and wearing a frayed, wide-brimmed straw hat against the sun, had taken no notice of the car when it drove up, or of the woman, but had continued wielding his cutlass in slow and loving strokes over the grass on the shoulder. He raised up, though, as she called his name, and under the protective brim of the hat he was an old, old man, his black skin sucked in upon the skeletal frame of his face and his eyes like two cleanly bored holes that had been blasted out of the skull with a gun.

He lifted his cutlass in salute, his manner deferent yet familiar.

"What did you do with Westminster Low Road, please, Mr. Douglin?"

His toothless smile was a raw wound against his blackness. "I sent it so this time." He pointed with his cutlass to a place several hundred yards away, where the almost level stretch of ground upon which they were standing sloped sharply down into a gully.

"Well, go and get it for me, please, and put it back and know I've got to be at the airport in half an hour's time." Laughing now, she turned and walked back to the car.

Once inside she began rummaging on top of the cluttered dashboard for the cigarettes which she had failed to find in her pockets, all the while damning them along with the vanished road and the heat that had accumulated inside the car while it had been standing, and then the car itself as it resisted her efforts to put it in reverse.

Kicking off her shoes, she fought it, her bare feet working the pedals as though they were those of an organ, her hands busy as a juggler's with the gear stick, the clutch, the steering wheel, then the matches and cigarettes which she finally unearthed. Each gesture was loud with the ring and clash of the bracelets crowding her wrists, and she was still calling to the old man, her head out the window.

"And when are you going to bring the mold for the garden I've been asking you for ever since, Mr. Douglin?"

"I bringing it soon."

"Soon!" She gave an utterly cynical snort. "I know your soon. My bones'll be mold by then. And now the crop's started I know I won't see you. It's the same every crop season. You can't find a soul to do a thing for you. Everybody's cutting canes. Look at the painter I hired the other day. The man walked out on me flat when he heard the crop had started. Left the bucket of paint right in the middle of the dining room now! And the room only half done. And guests coming. The first I've had in months. Bournehills people! Deliver me from them. How are the canes looking?"

"Well," the old man called calmly across to her, "they're not looking so good. They wanted more rain."

"And all the rain we had last night and it's supposed to be the dry season! I tell you, even nature has turned against us in this place."

"And I hear they're talking about closing down Cane Vale sugar factory." His voice in the sunlit air was like the tolling of a funeral bell.

"Oh, that again!" she cried, and in her renewed anger almost got back out of the car. "They're starting up that old talk again, are they? And what would the small farmers around here do with their canes, tell me? Grind them between their teeth, maybe?" Her voice had risen dangerously, and now, as abruptly, it dropped. "Look, don't start me this morning. Close down what? Hear me good, Mr. Douglin, they can't close a blast!"

With that the car bounded forward, then back, the reverse working at last, and with a wave to Mr. Douglin she swung it around and started back up the hill. She was still talking, her audience now the old woman, nearly as old as Mr. Douglin, seated in silence on the worn leather seat to her left.

"Did you hear that, Leesy?" she said, her eyes on the road, the outrage still in her voice. "They're starting up the old tune again. But I'm not going to let them upset me this year with that old business. Oh, no. Besides," she said, with a laugh that was clearly forced, "it's as you yourself once said: whenever they begin the crop season by threatening to close down Cane Vale, it just means that we're going to have a good crop for a change."

The woman Leesy said nothing. She did not even glance her way. Nor had she shown any interest in the missing road earlier or in the exchange between the younger woman and the man. Instead, she had sat there the whole time contained and inaccessible behind the high wall of her silence, her gaze distant and incurious throughout.

She was slight and dry, a mere husk but for her hands, which were as large and work-worn as a cane cutter's. Since she was on her way to town she was wearing what she called her "good clothes": a severe white dress that might have belonged to some nineteenth-century missionary's wife, high at the neck, long at the sleeves and with a straight skirt that reached almost to her shoes, a pair of sturdy schoolgirl's brown Oxfords. A dowdy felt hat, the same earth brown as her face, crowned her head. And she had carefully arranged her hands for the trip to town. The one on her lap was closed tightly around a flowered handkerchief, which contained her money, a few coins, tied in one corner; while the other was gripping the window ledge beside her in profound distrust not only of the other woman's driving, but of the car itself.

"Leesy . . . ?" the younger woman said, glancing her way. "What is it? Are you vexed because the road's gone and you won't be able to get to the Labor Office today? Oh, woman, rest yourself, will you? You've been going to that office every week for the last two months and they still haven't told you when Vere might be back. He might not even come back. You know what happens to some of these young fellas when they go to America on the labor scheme. They forget all about a small island like this. They want the big time, the big lights. Why, we might never see Vere again. . . ." But she must have thought better of what she had said, because suddenly reaching across, she apologetically touched the hand clenched around the handkerchief. "Don't listen to me," she said. "He'll be back. And any day now, you watch. I miss him, too, you know. He was the only one who knew how to keep this old car running properly. One thing, let's hope that when he does come back he won't go and put himself in trouble again with that foolish girl from up Canterbury."

There was still no word from Leesy. Only after the younger woman had been silent for a time, and the breeze at the open windows had cleared away most of the smoke from her cigarette did she finally speak, and although there was something of the old man's deference in her voice and manner, it was tempered, and delicately, infinitely balanced, as his had been, by the weight of her own authority.

"Every time the least little rain falls these days Westminster Low Road's got to pick up itself and walk away," she said, the words as expressionless as her face, as her eyes which, yellow and clouded with age, were fixed, unseeing, ahead. And then, in the next moment, without her face changing, her voice rose thin with a kind of triumph. It was as though some prophecy which she had voiced long ago, which others had dismissed, was at last coming to pass: "I tell you," she cried triumphantly, "everything's going down down to grass. We're seeing the last days now."

The other woman suddenly became more than just silent. Her entire body seemed to give way momentarily to an exhaustion she could no longer resist. For an instant her hands went slack on the steering wheel so that the car, which she was having to goad up the steep rise, began sliding backward. "Oh, Leesy, it's true, you know," she whispered in a drained, frightened tone. "It's true. Everything's going down. Lord, lemme telephone Lyle."

The one telephone in this part of the island was located in the police substation, one of a complex of low, white stone public buildings, consisting of a small local court, a parochial office (which housed the district's records), and an almshouse, situated at the top of the hill they were climbing. The hill, named Westminster because of two tall, jagged, uneven peaks which rose like the crude spires of a church from its summit, was the highest in the district and boasted great spurs that reached out in all directions. From where it stood at the northeastern edge of the land near the sea, it commanded all the lesser hills and valleys lying crowded between it and a high curving ridge, whose outline, on a clear day, could be seen rising in the west like a wall separating this district from the rest of the island.

Ruthlessly spurring the flagging car up the last winding stretch of road to the top, the woman turned in at the almshouse, a long rectangular structure of dazzling white coral stone which called to mind an unadorned sarcophagus. It was the largest of the buildings, and served not only as a refuge for the poor and indigent of the area, but as a local clinic, hospital, orphanage, old-age home and mental asylum for less violent cases. She passed one of the mental patients at the gate, a young man with the transfixed expression of a mystic, who stood gazing up at the blinding noon sun with wide, unblinking eyes.

"Seifert!" she hailed him, but though the breeze she created as she drove past ruffled the long, faded blue regulation smock he wore, his eyes remained on the sun.

A huge silk-cotton tree, whose roots had reached up out of the earth over the centuries to snake around its trunk and out along its thick branches, dominated the bare yard, and the woman pulled up under this. Leaving her companion behind, she hurried into the almshouse, into a smell of harsh soap and scrubbed stone, saltfish from the main meal eaten just an hour ago at eleven o'clock, disinfectant and despair, calling familiarly to the nurses and patients as she went, to the orphaned children, telling them all what had happened to the road at the foot of the hill.

Without breaking her stride she swept out a side door and on toward the police substation across the way. The heel of her foot slapped loudly against the open heel of her shoe with each step she took. The hem of her dress flickered about her knees. Once inside the substation she waved to the officers who, their heavy blue serge uniforms in order, the jackets buttoned to the throat, were idling away yet another hot uneventful day playing dominoes in the orderly room. Their spotlessly white cockaded hats stood in a neat row on a nearby shelf. She informed them of the missing road; unperturbed, they called back that they knew and word had been sent to the road works department in town. Then, alone at the sergeant's desk which held the telephone, she placed her call, her hands once again performing their juggler's act with the old-fashioned telephone (which first had to be wound), her cigarettes, and matches. Waiting for the operator to put through the call, she clung to the receiver as though she believed it could somehow steady and save her.

"Lyle?"—her voice rushed into the mouthpiece—"Are you there? Merle here. Can you hear me? This miserable telephone! Listen, love, Westminster Low Road's gone again, down Spring Gully this time, and it's too late for me to go by M'Lord's Hill and, as you well know, Drake's can't be trusted after a rain. Besides which the car's giving trouble. I can hardly get it in reverse and I'm too damn tired to contend with it because I was up half the night painting. Did I tell you the painter walked out on me flat the day he heard the crop was starting? So, love, do me a favor, yes, and go meet Allen and the others for me. . . . Lyle, are you there? What's wrong? Have you gotten so great you can't do a favor for an old girl friend? Case! What case? Look, don't form the fool, man. Have it put off. What case in Bourne Island could be that important? Somebody steals somebody's chicken and eats the evidence? Somebody sweeps dirt in their neighbor's yard and they come to blows? That's all the cases we have about here, so don't try to play Mr. Big with me because you know what I think about all you legal luminaries with your duppy nightgowns and musty wigs: leeches, the lot of you. And as for you lawyers-turned-politicians! . . . All right, finish for now, but remember, I've had to pay with my sanity for the right to speak my mind so you know I must talk. Love, go meet the people for me, yes, and for God's sake, tell Allen what happened with the road and the old car because he'll be disappointed that I'm not there to meet him. Tell him I'll definitely be down, though, for the reception for them at your place tonight. I'll rest the car this afternoon and try to finish painting the dining room. By the way, they're spending tonight at the Banyan Tree so take them there. I thought they might as well see the best the island has to offer before they see the worst. Now, about the reception. See to it that that so-called expert who's here from England helping you people in government cook up the new development plan comes. I'm sure they'll want to talk to him. And I suppose you'll have to ask the Honorable Member for Bournehills, even though as far as I'm concerned we could do without him. And you had best invite one or two chaps from the Opposition, as hopeless as that is, so they can at least have their say. And don't forget to tell your wife, that dear distant cousin of mine, not to make people wait a half-hour between drinks. And, oh, Christ, man, see to it that the men don't go off by themselves as usual and leave the women sitting alone in a corner someplace like they're in purdah. . . ."

Still talking, her voice caught up in what seemed a desperate downhill race with itself, she began backing toward a window close by, drawn there by a sound that could have been the low, unremitting whirr of the heat slowly rising, now that it was past noon, to a new and ominous high. "Oh, crime, the plane! Lyle, you've got fifteen, maybe twenty minutes to get to the airport. *Move!*"

CHAPTER 2

The small two-engine plane, empty but for its crew and four passengers after the long interisland run, had begun the gradual descent toward the last of the islands in the distance. The first deep drop sent a shudder over the plane's light hull, and Vere, feeling that sudden drop and shudder in the pit of his stomach and knowing it spelled the end of his journey and home, leaned across the empty seat between himself and the window and for the first time since changing planes at Puerto Rico looked out.

He had kept to his seat on the aisle for the entire flight, not even getting off with the other passengers during the brief stopovers at the islands along the way. Those other places had held little or no interest for him. He had scarcely glanced out the window while the plane was on the ground. Instead, his head bent, he had continued to study a ragged well-thumbed manual on the repair and reconditioning of used cars while waiting for the flight to resume—sitting there, a dark young man of about twenty in an out-of-date powder-blue zoot-style suit with large lapels and trousers that ballooned at the knee, new shoes that were slightly too long at the toe; and with a broad-featured yet undefined boyish face, a man's body at its prime, and powerful hands which looked as if they had been worked in stone.

The island that had finally claimed his attention was essentially no different from the others he had flown over since leaving Florida at dawn. From this height it was simply another indifferently shaped green knoll at the will of a mindless sea, one more in the line of steppingstones that might have been placed there long ago by some giant race to span the distance between the Americas, North and South. Like the others, it was small, poignantly so, and vulnerable, defenseless. At any moment the sea might rise and swallow it whole or a hurricane uproot it and send it flying. Like all the rest, it seemed expendable: for what could it be worth to the world, being so small? Unlike the others, though, which followed each other in an orderly procession down the watery track of the Caribbean, the island below had broken rank and stood off by itself to the right, almost out in the Atlantic. It might have been put there by the giants to mark the eastern boundary of the entire continent, to serve as its bourn. And ever mindful of the responsibility placed upon it in the beginning, it remained—alone amid an immensity of sea and sky, becalmed now that its turbulent history was past, facing east, the open sea, and across the sea, hidden beyond the horizon, the colossus of Africa.

The young man, Vere, noted the white line of beach, like a line drawn in chalk by an unsteady hand, which defined the irregular shape of the island. He could just make out far to the southwest the jumbled red-faded tin roofs of the main town of New Bristol crowded around the largest of the bays that interrupted the coastline, and stretching back beyond this to cover the entire island, the endless fields of sugar cane.

Leaning close to the window across the empty seat, he studied those fields, his practiced eye quickly separating the strong primary green of the ripened canes, which were due to be harvested now that it was the crop season, from the mild tenuous green of the young, newly planted canes which would wait until January of next year. His gaze shifted again to the town of New Bristol which, as always, was partly obscured by a pall of haze that not even the noon sun could ever completely burn away. And a frown creased the smooth skin of his forehead, because although he knew this to be Bourne Island and home, he could not think of the part of the island within his view as the place to which he belonged, as having the familiarity of home. And then, happening to glance beyond the wing of the plane just outside his window he saw, away off in the distance, his eye drawn to it against his will, the high ridge at Cleaver's, and it was all suddenly, painfully, familiar.

Winding down from the northern tip of the island like the deformed spinal column of some huge fossil buried there from prehistoric times, the ridge, called Cleaver's High Wall, described a crude semicircle along the northeast sector of the land before curving in and disappearing into the sea halfway down the east coast. Rearing up out of the land, the ridge divided Bourne Island into two unequal parts. To the west stretched the wide, gently undulating plain with its neatly ordered fields and the town poised at its southern edge. To the east and sealed off from that bright green world lay a kind of valley which occupied less than a quarter of the land space on the island. Viewed from the plane, it resembled a ruined amphitheater whose other half had crumbled away and fallen into the sea.

And it was a valley of hills, for the hills began here, starting up out of the eastern wall of the ridge like the knuckles of an angry fist and then racing over the valley floor toward the sea like a pack of large, low-slung animals with menacing shoulders and scarred flanks, that had thrown back their heads to low at the sun as they ran. A few of the hills were fairly high, but none of them, not even the one called Westminster at the far end, reared higher than the ridge that enclosed them all.

Straining forward, Vere could just make out the old hill with the two craggy peaks rising like steeples from its crest. Hidden below to the left, where Westminster's long northern spur flattened out to almost level ground, was Cane Vale sugar factory, he knew. Cane Vale! where every morning as a boy he had taken his great-aunt Leesy's husband his eleven o'clock breakfast of rice and saltfish, before the latter had fallen into the deep pit which housed the rollers used to extract the juice from the canes, and been crushed to death. Out of sight also, between the broad foot of the hills and the sea, lay the small village which its inhabitants insisted on calling a town: Spiretown. It was there he had been born and his mother had died giving birth to him. . . . Suddenly, sitting there with his face pressed like a child's to the plane window, he realized beyond word or thought how fixed and inevitable had been his return, how inescapable. The distances he had traveled, the different places in which he had lived and worked—all the things he had seen and done his three years in the States were as nothing suddenly in the face of that dark steepled hill and the village obscured at its foot. They had awaited him the while.

Something vague and nameless troubled his face, and he sat back in his seat on the aisle. Taking up his hat he carefully fitted it on his head. It was a high-crowned, wide-brimmed sharpie's hat of blue velour, the same light powder-blue as his suit. He had seen it advertised in *Ebony* magazine and written away for it. Planted firmly on his head, the blue crown reaching above his seat back, the hat settled him. Quickly he returned to the automotive manual he had been reading all along, and to the daydream, comforting and familiar, which in the last year had come to serve as the antidote for everything that troubled him.

In the dream he was driving his own car in the Whitmonday Motor Race held every year in Spiretown, something that had long been an obsession with him. (And one of the first things he was planning to do now that he was home was to buy a car with the money he had saved while away. He would take his time and look around for a good used car, an American make preferably although these were rare in Bourne Island; then strip it down, and again taking his time, slowly rebuild it according to the instructions in the manual.) Thinking of the car and of the Whitmonday Race he smiled. And it was as though someone had struck a match and held it up to his face, for his smile was like a sudden light which discovered qualities in him that otherwise went unnoticed. The smile lingering, he brought his foot down on the accelerator of his imaginary car, pressing it by slow degrees to the floor. His hands closed strongly around the steering wheel, and sitting quietly there in his aisle seat toward the front of the plane, oblivious of the other three passengers behind him, he felt the power of that invisible motor rise up through the floor of the car to charge his blood, becoming his power as he sped cleanly ahead of his competitors in the race. And as always in the dream everyone in the village had turned out to see him, including Leesy, who customarily remained indoors on Whitmonday in protest against the race. Even the girl from up Canterbury who had wronged him was there. He glimpsed in passing her thin, near-white face, and the astonishment mirrored there was sweet revenge for all he had suffered at her hands. She quickly vanished, and then there were only the dark friendly throngs reaching down the length of the roadway, their faces a featureless blur as he roared by, their proud cries of "Vere! Vere! But look a' Vere!" rising like a hosanna behind him.

Several seats behind, Allen Fuso saw the blue hat go up and with his Aristotelian fondness for putting everything, including people, in their proper categories, promptly placed Vere in the file in his mind marked "Farm Labor Scheme." The man, Allen was certain, was one of those young laborers recruited from the islands to pick shade tobacco in Connecticut, cut canes in Florida, or work on the truck farms of south Jersey, and he was returning home now that his contract was up. Allen speculated as to which of the three places the man had worked. He wondered if by any chance it had been Jersey, where an uncle of his had once owned a small produce farm, which he had loved visiting as a boy.

At the same time, his thoughts overlapping, the sight of the hat roused a memory from his childhood he had hoped he had forgotten, that of a Cadillac car which had been the same bright powdery blue in color. He and his best friend, Jerry Kislak, had been idling away the hot empty summer Sunday afternoon on the overpass above the highway through the north Jersey town where they lived when they had seen the car sweeping toward them down the straight ribbon of road, bound for the cool mountains of the Catskills. Suddenly Jerry, his flat-boned, good-humored Polack face going white with rage, had leaned out over the stone parapet and with a skinny finger pointing had yelled, "Hey, Al, here comes one of 'em, I betcha. Here comes one of them dirty Jew cars, I betcha any money. . . ." Then, as the car, with a glimpse of two children playing happily on the back seat, shot out of sight beneath the overpass, he had whirled and dashed across to the other side to scream after it, his voice straining under the weight of his inexplicable rage, "Yah, yah, yah, Jew car, Jew car! Yah, yah, y-a-a-h . . . !"

After glancing nervously around to see if anyone was watching, Allen had added his own loud, uncertain "Y-a-a-h . . . !"

Feeling something of the uneasiness he had experienced then, he looked across the aisle at his boss, Saul Amron, and wondered what he would have said had he known. He would probably let him off lightly, Allen thought. The worn, heavy eyelids, which always made Allen think of the curtains to the confessional that had dominated his Catholic boyhood, would fold wearily over the eyes, which looked almost colorless they were so pale. The man would give his characteristic shrug, his large shoulders lifting in what could only be a philosophical acceptance of the cruelty man was capable of as well as the good. Then, with a smile that like the collar of an old shirt was slightly frayed at the edges, he would probably dismiss the incident with something like, "So you're the little snotnosed goyim on Route 3 who hurt my Uncle Herbie's feelings by laughing at his brand new super-de luxe, Capri-blue Eldorado Special with the Hawaiian-red upholstery. Shame on ya."

He was asleep in the aisle seat, or appeared to be—Allen wasn't sure—his loose, oversized body in which no two bones seemed to fit properly, propped up beside his wife, Harriet, whose face was to the window. Allen's gaze took in the nose, rising like the curved blade of a scimitar out of the pale, somewhat fleshy face, the forehead that in its breadth and height looked vaguely hydrocephalic, the hair, coarse and rust-colored (nigger hair, Allen's mother would have called it) which was beginning to recede at the temples.

He had lain like this, shamelessly on view, offering, without apology, himself and all his physical flaws to anyone who cared to look, since their last stop, where, during the brief twenty-minute stopover, he had somehow managed to sample the local rum, chat about hurricanes with the airport meteorologist whom he met in the bar ("The son of a gun's working already," Allen had muttered to himself as he stood on the edge of their talk, drinking a beer which he should have known would have been warm), as well as purchase a straw hat with a wide, turned-down brim for his wife, which he took his time selecting.

He never lets up, the bum. With a smile that reflected the peculiar mixture of affection and exasperation, envy and respect he felt for him, Allen turned back and, bending over, began putting away the papers he had been reading—most of them containing statistical information on Bourne Island—in an overstuffed briefcase at his feet.

Bent there over the briefcase, Allen Fuso looked more the athlete than the scholar. He had the thick, stocky, aggressive body of certain soccer players, with a suggestion of tremendous power in the arms and legs, shoulders and back. But this strength, all the force and passion hinted at in his build and in his strong Mediterranean coloring, lay unused. One had the sense of its quietly atrophying within the bulky professorial tweeds he always wore.

It was as though there had been a concerted campaign from the time he was born to subdue this part of him. "He might look like his father's side of the family, but thank goodness he's got my family's brains," his mother used to say to company, with his father sitting right there. All the various strains that had gone into making him (and between his parents these included the whole of Europe from Ireland to Italy) might have been thrown into one of those high-speed American blenders, a giant Mixmaster perhaps, which reduces everything to the same bland amalgam beneath its whirring blades.

Allen had emerged from this ordeal an altogether bright, personable young man, who talked easily and well when he had to and contributed his little joke when this was called for, who took an occasional beer and even swore mildly when provoked, but who, withal, remained curiously undefined, hard to know. Behind the rimless glasses he wore his hazel eyes kept their distance. But nothing harsh or condescending lay at the heart of his detachment. People sensed this and forgave him. Besides, his smile, when he forgot himself, was openly boyish and warm, beautiful even in that it restored, for the moments it lasted, that part of him, his true self, which the blender had sought to destroy.

He snapped shut the briefcase which he held tightly cradled, as if it were his most priceless possession, between his feet on the floor, and sitting up consulted his watch, a large moonfaced instrument which resembled a computer, with its various dials and slots. The watch not only gave the time and date but had been specially fitted with a tiny alarm so that he wore it to bed to wake him in the mornings. Thinking now of the development project that was taking him back to the West Indies, he looked down at the island below, which was their destination, and which someone, who was it?—Merle probably, it sounded like her—had once described as "a hundred-and-seventy square miles of sugar cane stuck in the middle of nowhere." It was familiar to him. A little over a year ago he had spent some months there carrying out a short-term demographic survey under the joint sponsorship of the University of the West Indies and Penn State, where he had gone to teach after completing his doctoral dissertation on "The Quantitative Approaches to the Analysis of Social Anthropological Data" at the age of twenty-three.

He had taken a liking to the island and remained longer than necessary, living in the hill country in the one dilapidated guesthouse to be found there. He remembered the small kitchen garden he had planted in the lee of the building and wondered if Merle, who owned the place, had kept it up. Merle! He had missed her. Like the man, his boss, asleep across the way, she always evoked the most contradictory feelings in him: on one hand, a helpless affection and regard, but annoyance, on the other, that he should feel such closeness to anyone, especially a hopelessly muddled, mildly psychotic, middle-aged colored woman who talked incessantly. But without ever quite admitting it to himself, he had missed her over the last year and more, and would be glad to see her again. And then suddenly he began to worry that she would not be at the airport to meet them. She might have failed to receive his cable in time. Or her car might have broken down again. Or worse, something might have happened to upset her and she had withdrawn into one of those long, dramatic, cataleptic silences of hers during which she remained shut in her room for days. Lord, he hoped to goodness she was all right, because wasn't she, as reluctant as he was to admit it, and in some way he couldn't even explain, the first real friend he had had since Jerry Kislak long years ago?

Out of the four on the plane only Harriet had kept watch. She had been the first, in fact, to sight Bourne Island when it had been nothing more than a small green wen on the absolutely smooth, stretched skin of the sea. Long before it was even due to appear, when all that could be seen down through the deep cloudless well of air was the sea, she had been quietly waiting and watching for it, her head with its disciplined cowl of wheat-colored hair framed by the oval-shaped window, her trim, tall, pleasantly angular body poised lightly on the seat. Despite the long flight, her beige linen dress looked as if it had just been put on fresh. A slender wedding band was her sole jewelry.

She had been thinking during her wait, going over it in a leisurely fashion in her mind, of the many events that had led to this journey. It went back, of course, to the day, more than three years ago, when she had first met Saul Amron, her husband now of a year. It had been at a meeting called by the Philadelphia Research Institute, with which she was associated as a voluntary fund raiser, to announce its plans for a new overseas aid-and-development program. Saul Amron, as one of the pioneers in this field, had been invited to give the main address, and he had flown in from Stanford, where he was teaching at the time, arriving somewhat late, she remembered, because his plane had been delayed.

As he entered the Institute's oak-lined auditorium that spring day and she had seen him, her eye taking in all of him at a glance, she had given, she recalled, a little amused, interested start, because with his large disheveled body, lidded eyes, with that clear startling sweep of forehead and the hair that looked as if it had been singed in a fire, he had made her think not of a social scientist but of some pale, rumpled Rabelaisian poet who stayed up nights writing ribald verses in an airless room.

During his talk she had studied him closely, taking note, for instance, of the way he would from time to time abruptly, without warning, raise his sword of a nose high into the light while speaking, as though to proclaim his heritage to all there. It added to him, she thought; she found it a not too extreme exotic touch.

Later, at the reception in the Institute's garden, she had waited patiently on the edge of the crowd surrounding him, again taking careful note in between the baldish heads of the men and the flower-laden spring hats of the monied Philadelphian matrons who supported the Institute, of little things about him, of how, for example, when he raised the Manhattan he was drinking to his lips, his pale eyes reflected the deep red of the cocktail like a mirror. And she had noticed something else, seeing him at close range, piecing the meaning of it out of the worn smile with which he acknowledged their praise and the numbness she sensed behind the smile, out of the way his heavily creased lids came down briefly over his eyes from time to time as though to shut out the faces around him—simply, that something in him had gone badly awry and needed setting to rights.

When the crowd had thinned she had stepped up and offered him her firm, slender hand, her steady direct gaze and, with a lift of her chin, her face, with its precise, quietly stated features and almost dazzling look of health: the evidence of her well-nurtured childhood —the milk, the morning walks with her brothers in the woods near their summer home on Delaware Bay, the twice-daily swims, and she had said, smiling self-assuredly up at him, "Dr. Amron, I'm Harriet Shippen, a kind of hanger-on here at the Institute. We're going to steal you from Stanford."

Recalling the faintly quizzical look he had given her she smiled to herself and turned her attention to the island over which they were now flying. She followed the tiny shadow of their plane as it flitted swiftly over the neat, restful green fields spread below. They reminded her, those fields, of the gently sloping lawn outside the house in Delaware long ago. Occasionally, as a child, when she was overcome by a desire to know more about the world beyond hers, she had thought of that broad lawn as a sea and their house as an island in its midst upon which she was marooned. Once, she had led her two brothers, who were younger than she was, in an abortive escape. At her prompting they had made a flag out of a pillow slip and a broom, which they had then waved as a distress signal from the attic window. But no one had come to their rescue, the public road being almost a mile away and hidden by the woods which ringed the house. And when the ruined pillow slip had been discovered she had been punished.

Although the memory was innocuous enough, she was irritated with herself for having allowed it to slip past her guard. She disliked having her childhood intrude. Then, before she could quite recover from her fleeting irritation, the plane veered sharply left, headed for the airfield in the southeast corner of the island, and gazing out beyond the canted wing she saw in the near distance the ravaged sea bottom that was Bournehills.

It struck her as being another world altogether, one that stood in profound contradistinction to the pleasant reassuring green plain directly below; and she wondered, gazing intently out toward those scarred hills, how an island as small as this could sustain such a dangerous division. To add to matters, the hills were filled with shadows even though it was noon and the sun stood at its zenith. Because of the shadows Bournehills scarcely seemed a physical place to her, but some mysterious and obscured region of the mind which ordinary consciousness did not dare admit to light. Suddenly, for a single unnerving moment, she had the sensation of being borne backward in time rather than forward in space. The plane by some perverse plan might have been taking her away from the present, which included Saul and the new life she was about to begin with him, back to the past which she had always sought to avoid.

The unsettling impression lasted less than a second, and then, in that way she had of dealing with the unpleasant, she firmly put it from her mind. Turning away from the window she began sorting out the articles on her lap. These included her handbag, the straw hat her husband had bought her at the last island, a novel she had been reading off and on, their passports, hers and Saul's, and the numerous landing papers and forms for them both which she had already filled out. Saul hated doing such things, which was one of the reasons she loved him. The times before their marriage, for instance, when they had gone away together, she had always been the one to make the arrangements. And she knew he would leave the practical details of getting settled in Bournehills to her. From what she had glimpsed of the place just now and from what Allen had said about conditions at the guesthouse, where they would be staying for the time being, she was anticipating the worst. But she didn't mind. It would prove a small challenge in a life which, to her dismay, had been sorely lacking in the larger ones.

The landscape below had become sharply differentiated meanwhile. She saw a clutch of tiny weatherbeaten houses with steeply pitched roofs: a village buried like a bird's nest amid the dense canes; and she could even make out now what looked to be an occasional human figure—very minute and insignificant and black—walking along a thin strip of road. Then suddenly the fields and roads and people, the houses were rushing up to meet the plane at the same helpless speed at which it was plunging downward. A large stand of coconut palms leaned in close, their fronds slapping frantically in the down-draft from the plane, but just as the wings were about to shear off their tops, the trees vanished and there stood the runway, bounded on each side by a cane field.

"Saul," she said and touched his knee.

His eyes opened instantly, but he wasn't really awake yet. For some moments longer he continued to stare quietly ahead, his eyes filmed and slightly inflamed, preoccupied with some other vision. He might have been watching the conclusion of his dream. Turning finally, his eyes clearing, he gave her a sleepy smile.

"Where the hell are we now?"

She laughed. "You know perfectly well," she said. "We're here. Bourne Island," and leaned back so that he could see past her out to the small but rather extravagantly modern palm-shaded terminal building they were approaching down the runway. An American jet liner that easily dwarfed their plane stood to one side of the apron busily disgorging a load of tourists. And beyond the airfield, where the land stretched level to the sea, they could see the gaudy, striped red-and-white beach *cabañas* belonging to the airport hotel—also a kind of ersatz modern in design—situated there.

"It looks a little like Miami after Uncle Herbie and his crowd took over."

"Saul!" She laughed again, in mock disapproval this time; then, welcoming the weight of his body against hers as he leaned closer to get a better look, she said, "I missed you when you were asleep just now."

With his gaze out the window he pressed a hand to her knee. "It's the rum I had back at the last place we stopped," he said. "It knocked me out."

"Yes, I thought I had better let you sleep it off," she said.

"How does the island look from upstairs?"

She thought a moment. "Different from the others," she said. "It doesn't have the lushness of—which one was it?—Dominica, I think, and it's not at all mountainous like some of the others we saw. In fact, most of it puts you in mind of somebody's big front lawn because of the cane fields everywhere. It's really very lovely and peaceful looking. You get the impression it doesn't have a problem in the world—that part of the island at any rate. . . ." Then, frowning slightly: "And then off by itself in a corner there's Bournehills, if I have my directions straight. It's only just a few straggly hills, but they manage to look pretty forbidding. And *it* gives the impression," she said with an attempt at a light laugh, "that it has all the problems there are."

"That must have been it, all right," he said. "Bournehills. Bournehills reborn once we're through with it . . . maybe. . . ." He sat back heavily in his seat.

"Oh, Saul, you're really worried, aren't you?" she said.

"Worse," he said. "I feel like a goddamn graduate student setting out on his first field trip. Oh, I'll be all right," he added after a moment, giving his characteristic shrug. "It's just that I've been away from field work for so long I'm probably rusty. More important, I'm not sure I'm up to handling anything as big as this project."

"Well, I'm sure," Harriet declared. "You'll do a wonderful job. I consulted the oracles before we left Philadelphia"—she smiled—"and they told me."

And she did seem to know in a way that was beyond all questioning. Her certainty was reflected in her eyes, which were blue at the same time that they were faintly gray, the tone and texture of a winter sky as the first snow gathers. It was part of the larger certainty which served as her rock, that she had taken in with her mother's milk.

"Here," she said, handing over the passports and landing papers. "I never know just which one they're asking for. And whatever am I to do with this?" She held up the straw hat with the wide turned-down brim he had bought her. "Don't get me wrong, darling, it's a lovely hat, but I'm not the type. Besides, I'm sure to look like one of those awful seventeen-day excursion tourists in it." Planting it at a comical angle on her head she modeled it for him.

Laughing, he brought his face up under the brim and, in the wide shadow there, kissed her. "Wait'll that sun outside gets hold of you, my girl, you'll be glad to wear it no matter how you look," he said. Then, clapping his hands once and straightening up with a gesture that sought to tighten the ligaments that strung together his loose bones, he said, "Okay, let's to work. There's no avoiding it any longer. First, what's the name again of the woman who's supposed to be arranging everything?"

"Mrs. Kin—something," she began. "Wait, I have it here." She started opening her handbag.

But he had already turned and was calling across to Allen, "Say, Al, what's your friend's name again, the one who's meeting us?"

Both Allen and Harriet answered at the same time, their voices converging on the name "Merle Kinbona." The sound of it filled the sudden silence in the plane as the last engine died. And for a moment it was almost as though another passenger had joined them in the cabin. At the familiar name the dark young man in the blue hat seated up ahead glanced briefly around; then slowly rolling up the dog-eared manual he had been reading and stuffing it in his back trouser pocket, he rose to leave.

CHAPTER 3

"Leesy."

"Who the person is?"

"Vere."

"The Lord!"

At that, he dropped the other small stone he was about to lob like a cricket ball against the side of the house. In the darkness the stone seemed to fall a long way before it struck, giving the impression that the earth had given way underfoot, and that he and the house, which he could scarcely discern in front of him, and the village in which it stood, as well as the hills over which he had just traveled by car, by lorry, by donkey cart and finally by foot were not fixed on solid ground, but suspended, weightless, in the vast warm womb of the Bournehills night.

He waited, hesitant as a stranger, on the low embankment leading down from the road into the yard surrounding the house. It would be some time, he knew, before she came to the door. She would first have to dress. As carefully as though it were morning and she was dressing for the day, she would put on her flannel undershirt and long drawers (her vest and trousers she called them), then the innumerable layers of slips and petticoats she always wore, and finally the dress, attaching weights to the dry husk of her body lest the wind take it. Afterward, standing before the dim mirror in her bedroom, she would slowly and with a trace of vanity tie a white cloth around her head.

The sheep tethered under the house stirred, and at the same moment a few, very thin strips of yellow light, like lines drawn with a quill across the darkness, betrayed the cracks in the bedroom wall. She had turned up the oil lamp she kept burning at a low flame all night. She was ready, and Vere vaulted lightly over the embankment down into the yard to meet her.

The small board-and-shingle house had been built with one blank windowless wall to the road to frustrate the curious. The front with its narrow double door and Demerara windows faced a side yard that was also partly hidden from those passing by a large mango and a calabash tree. A little beyond the trees a listing fence of frayed galvanized iron separated Leesy's yard from that of her neighbor, whom she hadn't spoken to in three years because of an argument over a pig belonging to Leesy which had been caught foraging next door. Over on the far side of the yard, and pressing so close up against the house you could hear them running their long fingers over the wall whenever there was a breeze, stood Leesy's pride: the tiny half-acre of canes she owned outright.

Vere made his way through the still-life clutter in the yard, dodging the pigpen, the fowl run, the donkey asleep on its feet beside the cart, and the low-slung branches of the mango and calabash trees which were hung with the night as with some dark and heavy fruit. Without even having to think about it he instinctively slowed down as he approached the place where a root of one of the trees arched up out of the ground—and stepped over it.

Upon reaching the front of the house he found to his surprise (making it out in the lamplight from within) that Leesy had replaced the old half-rotten wooden jalousie panels set in the door with ones of flowered glass. And suddenly it was as though the glass panels had been put there for him, to celebrate his return. He smiled, ready to believe it, and his smile, together with the sudden rush of light as Leesy opened the door, drove back the darkness.

"Oh, he's laughing, the vagabond," she cried severely, and as severely embraced and drew him inside. "Come pelting rock-stone at the old house, come calling out my name in the night like some duppy or the other, and he's laughing. How did he find his way back here anyway after all this time he's been away? Who sent for him? And where did he get the fancy suit and hat he's wearing and those long toe shoes? Oh, God, look how this boy has fallen away in his skin!"

He stood smiling shyly in the center of the tiny front room, pleased, posing a little for her in the clothes, truly the boy. But Leesy, after the first long scrutinizing look she dealt him scarcely seemed to notice him further. Instead, moving briskly around the room, in and among the shadows that stood like silent members of the household everywhere, she quickly set about putting their life together in order again, all the while sounding the welcome that was like one long reproof.

". . . And don't think I didn't know he was coming," she was saying as she busied herself, addressing the shadows, ignoring Vere. "I had the sign after all. Oh, yes"—she gave a little nod that was like a nervous tic—"Two months ago his mother-self who died in baby-bed having him came to me as I was out in the ground weeding. Just so. Standing there in front of me as good as he is now. She was dressed all in scarlet. The hat and all was scarlet. And she said, 'Dear aunt, I'm not resting easy these days. I'm studying Vere too bad. I beg you, go down to the Labor Office in town and ask them when he's coming back.' And quick so, I bathed my skin, put on my good clothes and I gone. The morning bus had already left so I start walking. The sun warm but I'm walking. All up Westminster till somebody came along in a motorcar and give me a drop to town. And every week God sent I was down to the Labor Office asking them for him. Today and all I went, even though I never reached there because the old road had wash away again. Yes, bo," she said, speaking to him directly for the first time, "I knew you was coming. I had the sign.

"Come," she said, pausing at the table which she had set with the remains of her supper. She held a chair for him, a new secondhand Bentwood with the skittish legs of a foal and a nosegay of flowers printed on the backrest. "Come sit and have little something to eat—or are the clothes you got on too pretty to sit in?"

He laughed. "No," he said, "it's just that things look kinda different. . . ." And he meant not only the chair and the glass panels at the door, but the subtle alteration that had taken place in the old and familiar objects as well during his absence. The house with its warped walls, smoke-blackened shingle roof, and familial shadows had shrunken, it appeared, grown smaller. During the three years he had been away more of the color had faded from the magazine photographs of Pearl Bailey and the Queen pasted to the wall and from the picture of the pale suffering Christ on the calendar, which still read May 1950, the month and year Leesy's husband had slipped into the roller pit at Cane Vale and been killed. And the faces of their numerous relatives who had either died or emigrated to England or America had withdrawn deeper into the brown obscurity of their photographs, which were neatly ranged on top of the food larder in the corner.

One thing had remained the same though: the silverplated plaques inscribed with the names and dates of the family dead, which Leesy appropriated from the coffins just before they were lowered into the ground, hung in orderly rows on the wall and polished without fail once a week. These were the same. And the smell of the house was unchanged. A settled effluvium of wood rot and mold, the smoke of long-dead fires, the mild stink of the saltfish cooked nearly every day out in the adjacent shed-roof kitchen, and the bit of camphor Leesy wore in a sachet pinned to her undershirt both as protection against a variety of ills and, even more important, as a phylactery against imagined evils.

"Yes," he said, "things've kinda changed up," and sat down.

It was her turn to laugh. "Don't let a little chair and thing fool you, bo. You should know nothing ever changes in this place," she said, and sat down some distance from him. Something in her manner, in the careful, almost wary distance she had set between them, suggested that in spite of the welcome she had given him and the table of food she had prepared, she was not altogether convinced it was Vere. It was as though she feared he might be a duppy after all, a ghost, who had assumed the form of Vere and roused her from her sleep. With eyes that were like shards broken off from some dark volcanic rock beneath their yellowish film she watched him almost distrustfully as he raised the first forkful of rice to his mouth and slowly chewed it.

"Ah," he said, turning to her with the smile that was a light blooming in his face, "it's too sweet to my mouth."

With that she gave the characteristic snap of the head and sat back, convinced apparently that it was Vere in the flesh. After silently watching him for a time, she folded her arms on her flat chest and said, "So tell me, how did you find it in that place? Some the fellas that came back before you said they smelled hell down there."

He considered this a moment, his fork poised midway to his mouth, and then he said almost casually, "No, it wasn't so nice, come to think of it. Especially Florida. New Jersey, where I worked once picking fruits and so, wasn't s'bad. The money was slight but the man who owned the place there was a person something like me in that he loved a car. He used to race every Sat'day and Sunday in something they call the stock-car races. Man, you ought to see those old cars go!" He laughed reflectively. "Well, the man took a liking to me when he saw I also knew a thing or two about cars. I learned a lot from him. . . .

"But that Florida," he said after eating in silence for a time, "was no joke. For one thing they put us to live in a barracks way out in the woods, away from everybody, like we was criminals. Nothing but bush and a lot of trees when you looked out, and there was all kind of alligators and big snakes 'bout the place. And they gave us a lot of rough food to eat. You think I ever had rice tasting this good there? Never, man. And the weather wasn't so nice, neither. The sun hot like fire all day and bitter cold at night. Some the fellas got sick from it, but not me. And the cracker bosses we had there weren't so sweet, either, but I just did my work and kept myself to myself."

"And how did you find the work?"

He laughed, proud and superior suddenly. "How you mean? The work hard, man! Canes! You think you see canes here on this island?" He sucked his teeth disparagingly. "Man, in Florida it's like the whole world is planted in them. And they grow theirs different to us, you know. They plant them in rows so when they spring they spring thick. And they have to burn the fields before they start cutting because of the snakes I told you about and the lot of trash on the canes. The ground would hold that heat for days at a time sometimes—and do you know those crackers would want us to go in and start cutting before it even cooled down good. Some the fellas refused to go, but I nearly always went. Some them got so disgusted with the bad conditions they broke their contracts and came on home. Some them ran off to New York and the authorities haven't found them yet."

"That's what I thought you had done when I stopped hearing from you," she said.

"I tried," he said, his voice going suddenly flat, "but I didn't meet with a success."

For a long time he said nothing more, simply ate, the muscles of his jaw working smoothly under the burnished skin. Finally, he put down his fork and speaking slowly, in a matter-of-fact voice from which all emotion had been drained, told her that while working on the truck farm in Jersey he had decided to run away and on his weekend off had sought out a relative of theirs in Brooklyn. "So I asked Uncle Seon if he would let me hide out there," he said in the impersonal lackluster voice. "But he said he would be taking too much of a risk and if the authorities found me he might lose everything. And he had plenty: a big house and two cars, and his children were all big shots. But he said he knew of a way for me to stay legal and he would get his lawyer to fix it up and write me at the place in Jersey. Well," he said, and picked up his fork—the silver, old and tarnished, shone dully against his dark hand—"I never heard from him. And do you know something," he added quietly after awhile, "when the work in Jersey was over and they shipped me back to Florida and I still didn't hear from him, my mind kinda turned from America. I just gave up on the place altogether. So I made out I was sick and couldn't do the work and they put me on a plane and I came on back where I had to come. I left there early this morning and reached back here this afternoon-self."

He resumed eating, his face closed and now immune over the plate.

And it had remained immune, you sensed, through all that had happened to him. His three years in that distant land, in those alien fields which had scarred and swollen his hands and hardened his body prematurely, which had refused him asylum and turned him out with a parting gift of an outdated slickster's hat, suit and shoes had not been able to shake the essential immunity of that face. Flat, the features merely roughed in, his face appeared unfinished. It was like a piece of sculpture upon which only the initial work, what's called the boasting, had been done. Only his cheekbones were defined and these overwhelmed the face. You knew looking at them that as he aged and his flesh thinned, those broad bones slanted high under his eyes would fill with shadows underneath, so that by the time he was forty-five or fifty, an old man already playing dominoes in the rumshop and drinking his finger of rum with pursed and trembling lips, those deep hollows under the bone would have become the repository of his dead dreams.

For a long time the only sounds in the room were the scrape and tap of his fork against the plate and the canes scratching away at the walls of the house outside as the wind broke in warm waves over the roof. With each gust the meager lamplight threatened to fail altogether and the shadows made little joyous incursions in and around the table.

Finally Leesy said very gently, "And where was you all today, Vereson, if you say the plane got in this afternoon?"

"About in town," he said.

"Doing what?"

"Just walking about and looking."

"Looking at what? Where?" she asked, puzzled.

"Oh, Whitehall Lane. Mayfair Alley. About in there." He kept his head bent over the plate.

"Whitehall! Mayfair! The worst places they got in town, where all those sailor clubs and rumshops are? What were you doing there?" she cried. And suddenly she knew. "Oh, no, don't tell me the first thing you did as soon as you got off the plane was to go looking for that girl? Don't tell me you're still thinking about her! She's gone. Didn't I write and tell you that over a year ago? She's gone and the money you sent her is gone and the child she had for you is dead and there's nothing you can do about it. What would you still want with somebody like that?"

The face he turned to her was expressionless, but something had hardened in his eyes. "I wish to ask her a question," he said, and there was the same hard edge to his voice.

"You wish to put yourself in trouble, you mean! But what is it with you and that girl, anyway?" she cried in profound bewilderment, and waited. But he said nothing, only gave her a patient, unperturbed smile that with the hardness behind it made him seem suddenly older and more knowing than she.

In despair she turned to the shadows in the room. "What is it with him, I ask you?" she asked them. "Why can't he forget her? He's not the first man ever had a woman do him a wrong. Why's he so bullheaded? But what to do, yes? He was always that way. Once he set his mind on a thing he can't let go, not even if it means his death. Take this business of going to Florida. He wasn't of age. But once he got it in his head to go, there was no stopping him. He put up his age and he went. Playing the man. That's all it was. And the same with the girl. What right a seventeen-year-old boy had keeping a woman? And somebody like that. She wasn't no quality or class for him. Those red people from up Canterbury are all cross-bred and worthless. They might have little color and think themselves better than us because of it, but they ain't got personality. Oh, don't think I didn't see her in town the other day styling in more can-can petticoat and wristwatch. A real sports. But she can afford to be a sports now she took the money the boy sent and killed his child. Yes, killed it," she declared shrilly, in a voice that time had worn to a single, thin, dangerously raveled thread. "Bare murder!"—the force of the word swung her head back to him—"And a nice boy child, everything like you. But she didn't want it, said it was too black. And I know it didn't live six months. Every morning she had it in a hot hot bath, like she was stewing it, and she would leave it alone in the house all day without little tea. And as soon as it died she upped and went to live in town with those other wild ones like herself. She's a wicked something you see her there. And now here you come back looking to put yourself in trouble with her again. Oh, God," she cried, her bewilderment at its height, "didn't Mis-Merle say you would do as much upward to today!"

"And how's Mis-Merle?" He spoke in the same pleasant, unruffled manner.

"Haven't you heard what I said about the girl?"

"I heard," he said. "But I've heard it before. You wrote and told me all that in the letter."

"Yes, and you stopped writing after that," she shouted, aggrieved. "Only sending the money for me to save for you, but never a word after that, like you was vex with me instead of the girl."

"I asked you for Mis-Merle," he said patiently. "Has she still got that old car? I heard some white people on the plane today calling her name so she must be getting guests. How's she keeping?"

"She's there, yes," she at last answered curtly, annoyed with him still. "She's better now."

"How you mean?" he asked, pushing aside his plate. He had eaten most of the food.

"She had a little trouble some weeks back and it kinda set out her head. But she's herself again."

"What happened to her?"

She made him wait. Then: "Well, she had taken a job at the new high school in town because the guesthouse wasn't bringing in any money. She was teaching history or one of them big subjects. But it seems they didn't like the way she was teaching it. She was telling the children about Cuffee Ned and things that happened on the island in olden times, when the headmaster wanted her to teach the history that was down in the books, that told all about the English. But she refused, saying that way made it look like black people never fought back. Well, they fired her in no time flat. And I hear tell she performed something terrible down there the day, told them all where to get off at, even cursed the headmaster-self. You know Mis-Merle. She says what she feels to.

"But the thing had her so upset her head went clean out again. They had to run and call me the night. And when I got there she was like somebody that had suffered a passover. She didn't know a soul. She couldn't do a thing for herself. She had come like a child again. Why, Mis-Merle couldn't even talk. Well, I clapped her and 'nointed her down and I said, 'Lord, increase my faith.' But she stayed like that for days. Like a dead. Not a word. Only staring at you with those eyes that make a person feel she can read his life with a look. . . ."

She lowered her head, remembering, and with it bowed, said, "But that woman has been through enough to set out the strongest head, you see her there. Look, how when she was only a two-years child, the woman her father was married to shot and killed her mother right before her eyes. It was the worst thing to happen in Bournehills since they killed Cuffee Ned long years ago. I remember Mis-Merle's mother good. Clara, she was called. She was only sixteen but fat and pretty in her skin and black like a real African when Ashton Vaughan took a liking to her and bred her. Mis-Merle came looking everything like her except for those Vaughan funny eyes. And look how when she got to be a young lady and the father sent her to England to study, all the things that happened to her there: the wild people they say she took up with, and how the man she married walked out flat on her one day taking her child with him. The poor woman still can't bring herself to talk about it. Yes," she said in conclusion, "she's known what it is to suffer."

"Is true," he said, his own head bowed in deference perhaps to that suffering. "Mis-Merle hasn't had it easy. One thing though she always has a joke for you. I must go and see her first thing tomorrow.

"And what about the crop?" he said after a pause. "Has it started yet?"

"It start," she said. "But it might not finish."

"How you mean?"

She swung aside, again refusing him an answer for a time. But then, taking a deep breath, straining the ancient lungs, she gathered together the frail wreckage of her body to speak. The face she turned back to him was deeply scored, and the features—the fey yellowed eyes, the tuckered mouth, the little broad-winged nose with its arched nostrils—were lost amid the hopelessly scrabbled lines, negligible, mere apertures through which she breathed and spoke and kept her close scrutiny. And whenever she spoke of the crop as she was about to do now, her face assumed an expression of infinite complexity. It revealed a single-mindedness that reduced everything else to insignificance, an arrogance which said she alone knew all there was to the growing of canes, a pertinacity which declared she had set her life upon the narrow cart road that bisected her half-acre plot outside and she would not be moved; and a vast durable love for that patch of ground which asked nothing in return.

"Well, for one," she began, "they're talking again about closing down the sugar mill."

He dismissed this with the comment that was standard in Bournehills, which she herself had coined years ago as a kind of talisman to ensure its never happening. "But you yourself know that only means we might have a good crop for a change," he said.

She quickly averted her face in a gesture which said she no longer wanted to be held responsible for that statement. "Let's hope so, yes," she said. "But you can't tell anymore. They keep saying they're losing money keeping it open. They're always complaining that the canes the small farmers grow ain't worth the trouble. And that's not the worst of it. It's got so now that the old people like myself can't even find anybody to help us get out our few canes. If you hadn't come back I don't know what I would have done this year. The thing had me so worried I got pressure and had to 'tend the doctor. He told me to stop humbugging myself with the piece of ground and either rent it or sell it. But how could I do that? Because then when our family comes back what . . . ?" (And she was talking to herself now, her eyes clouded over, Vere forgotten.) "When the work in England or America gets slight or they fall sick or get old and have to come home, what? No, bo, I have to look after it for them, so when they come back or their children come (and even your Uncle Seon might be back here never mind how much big house and car he's got now), they'll at least be able to work the piece of ground if nothing else, and have money to buy rice."

It was the belief by which she had ordered her life, which had kept her alive beyond her time. It was as old for Vere as his first memory, as familiar to him as the dusty wax antirrhinum lilies in their vase on the small round center table and the calendar that had brought time to a standstill in the house. Hearing it again after the long absence, the words unchanged and spoken in the same spare, inflectionless manner as a plain-song, he felt the old life close round him. She had been right before. Nothing had changed. He had been foolish to imagine that it ever could, this being Bournehills. Worse, it was as though he had never been away. And this feeling, along with the food lying warm and heavy in his stomach and the exhaustion of the long day, was a weight which slowly bore his head down in sleep while she was still talking.

". . . Yes," she declared in closing, "I must care it for them." The cloud over her eyes lifted and she saw Vere, the baggy trousers fallen in tired folds around his ankles and his drooping head resting like a huge wilted boutonniere on the oversized lapel of the suit. "Ah," she said, "his belly's full and he's sleeping," and rising with a sudden movement that sent the shadows scurrying back to their corners, she made preparation for the night. Then, when Vere had been put to bed in his small cubicle of a room next to the kitchen, and the blue suit and hat carefully hung on the door, Leesy paused before the dresser in her bedroom, and before turning down the oil lamp there she gave the little knowing flicker of a nod. "Yes," she said, "I had the sign. Now come tomorrow, God willing, we'll see to the few canes."

CHAPTER 4

CASR, the Center for Applied Social Research, which was sponsoring the development project to be carried out in Bournehills, or simply the Center, as it was called, was the agency created by the Philadelphia Research Institute to administer its new overseas program. The Center functioned more or less independently of the Institute, having its own staff and building, a small Philadelphian town house belonging to Harriet Shippen, which she had given over for its use. But final decisions on important matters still rested with the parent body's powerful board of directors, some of whose older, more conservative members remained skeptical of the new venture.

The Institute, along with private contributors, also provided part of the money needed to run the Center. But this was a relatively insignificant amount. The bulk of the funds came from several major business corporations in the state, for whom the new Center, with its emphasis on uplifting the impoverished of the world, served as a fitting public expression of their quiet humanitarianism and concern, and as a means, although this was seldom mentioned, of saving substantially on government taxes by being intimately connected with a nonprofit, tax-exempt foundation.

The largest contributor to CASR and, in a sense, its virtual creator through the Research Institute which it controlled (nearly all of its board members also sat on the Institute's board) was the United Corporation of America or Unicor, with main offices in Philadelphia and branches throughout the nation and world. Unicor represented a merger of most of the old family businesses in Pennsylvania, including that of Harriet Shippen's family, and so had its roots struck deep in those homey products that had created the state's first wealth: such ordinary staples as cornmeal and flour, salted meat and fish, lumber, candles and cloth. All these, in the beginning, had been shipped mainly to the West Indies. Early in its history, one of the family businesses that now made up Unicor had also gained a controlling interest in the Newfoundland cod industry which supplied the dried salted cod still eaten almost daily in places like Bourne Island. The merger of all these various enterprises had, in turn, provided the base for expansion into other areas. So that out of them had come, like endless sproutings over the generations, huge sugar refineries, a soft drink popular the world over, mammoth flour and paper mills, as well as major interests in other, more impressive, industries: iron, steel, oil, the large-scale manufacture of munitions, uranium mining, banking. . . . And over the years Unicor had reached out to link up with other great trading and industrial empires abroad, including Kingsley and Sons, Ltd., with its vast holdings in Africa, Asia, and smaller places like Bourne Island. Thus, Unicor was now part of that giant commercial complex which, like some elaborate rail or root system, endlessly crisscrosses the world, binding it up, until the world almost puts you in mind of one of those high-bouncing balls children used to make years ago by twisting layer upon layer of rubber bands around a toy marble.

CASR had chosen as its special area of interest the English-speaking islands of the West Indies, the feeling being that these would be good places to try out the new program. They were small, as yet politically stable, and their problems, though acute, had so far not reached the inflammatory stage. Moreover, they had been almost totally neglected by the big showy development projects undertaken by the government and the larger private foundations. And there was also some small measure of sentiment involved in the choice born of the close commercial ties with the islands in the beginning. An early forebear of Harriet Shippen's, for example, the widow Susan Harbin, had launched the family's modest wealth by her small-scale speculation in the West Indies trade, which in those days consisted of taking a few shares in a number of sloops making the twice-yearly run between Philadelphia, the west coast of Africa, and then back across the Atlantic to the islands. In a stained, faded ledger still to be seen in a glass display-case at the Historical Society, the widow had kept careful account in a neat, furbelowed hand of the amounts of flour and salted cod, cornmeal and candles that went out on the sloops, the number of slaves taken on in Guinea and then just how much her portion of that cargo, both human and otherwise, had brought in crude sugar, rum and molasses in the islands. A portrait of the widow hangs directly above the case containing the ledger, and reveals a pair of calmly avaricious eyes beneath a frilled cap and a face whose missionary mien and pallor triumphs over the obfuscating gloom of the painting.

Harriet, descendant of that long line, heir to the widow's questionable legacy, had supported the idea of the new Center from its inception. By then she had been associated with the Philadelphia Research Institute for some time as a member of a small layman committee, whose job was mainly fund raising. She would drive up for committee meetings regularly from Maryland, where she lived with her first husband, Andrew Westerman, a physicist at the atomic Proving Ground at Aberdeen.

Her interest in the Institute had been due largely to Chester Heald, a member both of its board of directors and Unicor's as well as the head of a well-known Philadelphia law firm. Chester Heald was a long-standing friend of the Shippen family, and he had known Harriet from the time she had been that quietly rebellious, seeking little girl, tall for her age, in long white stockings and a bow, who had led the attempted escape from the attic window. She had always considered him something of a surrogate father, especially after her own father had suddenly, one day when she was twelve, abandoned his law practice, nearly ruining them financially, and shut himself away in the downstairs study to devote the remainder of his life to a long scholarly biography of Lorenzo de' Medici, which he never completed.

It had been Uncle Chessie, as she called him, and not her father, for instance, who had taken her part when she refused any longer to attend the fashionable finishing school her mother had chosen for her, and he alone had supported her during the family crisis brought on by her first marriage, because, although Andrew Westerman had the right name, he had had even less money than they at that juncture. Over the years Chester Heald had remained her close friend and mentor; and when her parents died—her mother from what Harriet was convinced was a protracted form of suicide, her father at his study desk—she had handed over all her affairs, including the managing of her modest inheritance, to him.

By the time Saul Amron spoke at the meeting to launch the Center, she was once again Harriet Shippen, having just divorced Andrew Westerman and resumed her maiden name. She could not have said for certain why she divorced him. Theirs had not been a dramatically unhappy marriage and she had never, even toward the end, really disliked him. It was just that once he had become firmly established in his field (and he was considered one of the country's leading young nuclear scientists), their marriage had gone flat for her, had become hollow at the center. She would find herself longing for the years when he had been the poor but brilliant graduate student, whose career she had helped shape and secure with the little money left her and her family connections, with her love and support. And she had loved him, since love with Harriet was intimately bound up with the need to *do* for the beloved, to be more than just a wife, and this, in turn, was part of an even larger need, present in her from a child—and innocent enough then—to wield some small power.

Toward the end with Andrew she had developed, she remembered, an odd sensation in her hands. She would be holding something—flowers for the table, a fork, a glass, her hairbrush—and she would not be able to feel either the weight or shape of the object. Her hands would feel utterly, unbearably empty. It was around this same time that the nightmare started. In the midst of the most innocuous dream there would suddenly be an explosion so massive it seemed the molten center of the earth had erupted, and in the searing light that followed, a great cloud shaped exactly like the toadstools she had often uprooted as a child on her morning walks in the woods would slowly and majestically rise in the final silence. And then one morning she had awakened from that recurrent nightmare only to realize, to her horror, that it was not, as she had believed all along, only Andrew's hand on the lever which triggered the holocaust, that mass suicide in which its creators would be the first to go, but that her hand was also there, resting lightly on his, guiding it. . . .

She left him shortly after that, on an April morning with the lawn outside the breakfast room in which they were sitting turning softly green and the three-hundred-year-old oak tree which she loved in new and tender leaf. She had happened to look from the tree just beyond the window to Andrew across the table, and seeing his sealed face and the distant gaze which she knew meant he had already driven the ten miles from their house to the Proving Ground and was at work in the huge secret laboratory he directed, she had felt, with a chill, how fundamentally opposed he was to the spring day, to the budding tree. If given the chance he might well destroy them. He had surely already contaminated them, just as he had, she wanted to shout at him (she who had never shouted in her life), contaminated the house they lived in, the food they ate, their beds, even her body so that she no longer conceived—and when she had, twice in the twelve years of their marriage, she had lost both babies. And remembering the pain as her womb relinquished the bit of life embedded in its wall, she leaned across the poached egg on her plate, and her face composed, her voice calm, said, "Andrew, I've decided to leave you, dear."

The divorce had been amicable. Before leaving she had helped him close up the house and move to an apartment nearer the Proving Ground. Moreover, she found, after being back in Philadelphia for a time that she could scarcely remember anything about the house in Aberdeen aside from the lovely old tree outside the breakfast room window. She even found it difficult as the months passed to call Andrew's face clearly to mind, except for the closed, top-secret look to it. After awhile it was almost as though she had never been married to him, and was therefore no longer responsible for what he had become or, more important, implicated in, the awesome destruction of the lever.

With that phase of her life over (and she regretted having given so many years to it), Harriet's thoughts turned to Saul Amron, and in the weeks following their first meeting she set out to learn as much about him as possible. She discovered that up until three years before he had worked almost exclusively outside the country, carrying out various small-scale community development projects in South and Central America, and that he was a highly regarded though controversial figure in the profession. Early in his career he had written two books on his work among the Quechua-speaking Indians of Peru, one a much praised straight anthropological study which was considered a classic, the other a moving personal account of his two years there, which had established him as something of a creative writer as well.

Harriet read them both, as well as all the articles and studies he had published over the years in the professional journals. She could not, of course, understand most of the technical terms used, and as always happened when she found herself in the presence of someone who had definite work, a career, she felt her own lack, and resented again, as she had many times before, first the fashionable education she had received which had prepared her to be little more than another attractive appointment, like an expensive Waterford chandelier, all cold faceted crystal, in some well-to-do man's house, and then the person responsible for this: her mother, that hopelessly superficial latter-day Southern belle (she had come from Virginia) whom Harriet believed her father had married in a moment of weakness and then promptly forgotten.

Saul Amron had also been, she learned, one of the early pioneers in the field of applied research who had insisted that sciences such as anthropology move beyond mere research and use their knowledge, whenever possible, to help improve the lives of the people under study. To this end he had designed a number of large-scale projects for the places in which he had worked, but he had been unable to get them financed since the concept of direct aid had been new and therefore suspect at the time.

In talking about it later to Harriet, he said, "It was still pretty much research for research's sake back then, I'm afraid, and I got exactly nowhere with those projects of mine. Admittedly, they were somewhat grandiose. I used to think big in those days, but they would have worked, given the time and money. But it was no go. To make matters worse, some of my colleagues started implying I was nothing more than a bleeding heart. They had always felt I became too involved with the people in the places I worked. Their approach to field work was to rush in a place, collect their precious data and rush out without stopping to realize it was flesh-and-blood people they were dealing with and not so many statistics for their charts and tables. The bastards." But he said it almost fondly. None of it could touch him anymore.

"Anyway," he said, "I finally had to give up trying to find sponsors for my dream projects. And just look at what's happened since. There're more agencies and money around for that kind of thing than you can shake a stick at. It's gotten to be A-I-D in capital letters with everybody, including the goddamn government and Henry Ford, getting into the act."

In later years he had worked for one such agency, the huge Moran Research Corporation in California, where he had been one of a team of specialists hired to carry out a sweeping rehabilitation project in

Chile. But the Moran people had suddenly, without explanation, dropped the project just as it was getting underway. Disillusioned, he had returned to the standard university-sponsored research and had done this up until three years ago when his first wife, whom he had met in Poland after the Second World War (she had been a survivor of the death camps), had died following a miscarriage while with him on a field trip in Honduras. Shortly after that he had announced his retirement from field work—abruptly abandoning both the study he was conducting in Honduras and the book he was writing—and gone to teach at Stanford.

Having learned all this about him Harriet was not in the least surprised when he turned down the Center's offer to join their program-planning division. He wrote briefly from California saying he had no desire to leave teaching. But he did subsequently agree to serve as a consultant and, from time to time, when his schedule permitted, would fly to Philadelphia.

It was on one of these trips east that he and Harriet began the affair that was to continue, despite the frequent interruptions, for well over two years.

From the beginning it was a discreet and casual arrangement which did not appear to commit either of them in any way. He had been involved, though not seriously, with a woman colleague of his at Stanford and he continued to see her with Harriet's knowledge when out on the coast. Harriet, for her part, did not ask for more than the occasional evening or weekend the times he was in town—and she was careful to conceal the full depth and determination of her love.

Except for their first time together. She had been overwhelmed then by his touch which had roused passions in her she had not known were there and she had, in turn, overwhelmed him. His large hands with their long, loose-jointed fingers which seemed made for casting shadows on a wall to amuse some child: rabbits and donkeys with long ears, had discovered her body as if she were a virgin he was gently initiating. There had been great thoughtfulness in his touch and restraint. He had even paused at one point, and lying like a ship becalmed within the narrow cove of her body, had traced repeatedly with the same fingers the line of her chin down to where the winged bones of her collar almost met at the base of her throat, smiling to himself the while. It was almost as though this part of her appealed to him the most, and this one small act afforded him more pleasure than all the rest.

But at the same time there had been a strange hesitancy in his touch. In the midst of the deep, abstract, almost impersonal pleasure her body brought him, something in him held back. Part of him was clearly reluctant to assume again the responsibilities and the burden of love. Harriet sensed this; she saw it in his barely perceptible frown, in his averted eyes, and fearful that he might suddenly end it, withdraw, abandon her, she began caressing him, doing so with a wildness that seemed to come from someone other than her. And under her hands, her mouth, her tongue, at the soft fierce pleas she whispered into his ear, he yielded. With a cry his arms closed almost angrily around her and the ship that was his body began moving in her again.

She had remained half-kneeling over him afterward, her head bowed like a suppliant's over his chest and her bright cap of hair, each strand of which was always in place, falling wildly forward, screening her face. Through it, she had gazed down at him lying there, with his eyes closed, his blood subsiding, and the faint grimace that had pulled his face tight as he gritted his teeth at the end and came slowly easing, giving way to a secret indrawn smile. And suddenly she had thought of Andrew Westerman, whom she almost never thought of anymore; and remembering the equable embrace that had passed for passion between them she hated him for the first time ever, despised him for having known her body when it was young, unimpaired by time, the breasts firm, the skin on the insides of her thighs smooth and taut, and for having used it so badly. She would have liked to have offered that young body to the man lying beneath her, to have given over to him in a single profligate act all that she had been then.

Saul had opened his eyes just at that moment and looked at her. And his expression had been the same as on the day she had come up and introduced herself at the reception in the Institute's garden, a trifle taken aback, but somehow indulgent, paternal, almost as if he glimpsed in her the quietly strong-willed child she had been. Taking up one of her hands he had examined the palm like a fortuneteller seeking to divine its meaning, then slowly replaced it. Reaching up he had lifted her fallen hair to look at her face. And his eyes had closed again. It was a thoughtful, courteous gesture; the lowering of the confessional curtain, Allen Fuso would have said. He wished simply to spare her the reflection of herself in his clear mirrorlike gaze. For revealed there on her face was all that had brought her to his bed, her love first of all and the wide frightening need it encompassed, then the fear, with her from a child, that she would somehow end up like her mother, useless, alone, a slow suicide; and finally the way she had lived for the greater part of her life, with the mild but persistent dysphoria, the better part of her in disuse, with her hands gone numb. . . .

And lying beneath her on the bed, his own hands had started up in a gesture that said there was little he could do to make up for that waste, that what she was asking of him, seeking in him, was too much and he could not fail but disappoint her; and finally that he came to her as burdened and with as great a sense of loss.

"All right, Harriet," he had said, and without opening his eyes had wiped the tears from her face with the edge of the sheet. This done, he had slowly let fall her hair. "All right. We'll do. Only it'll have to be the other way around—" and reaching up again he had slowly drawn her down so that she lay beside rather than on top of him.

Aside from intercessions and holidays and the long summer breaks which they spent together, usually taking a house somewhere, there were only the brief visits during the rest of the year for her to look forward to. And she contented herself with them, making no protests, no demands. Moreover, in all that time she never once brought up the question of his leaving Stanford to work for the Center, although this was her hope. In loving him she envisioned the day when he would head up the Center's program-planning section, a position which would give him the chance to carry out the kind of bold, imaginative projects he had dreamed of years ago. But before this, she wanted to see him return to doing field work, because although he insisted that he had no wish to leave teaching and had flared up and shouted at her once when she had suggested otherwise, she knew how much he disliked being what he called "an armchair anthropologist." And he would relent, she was convinced, if offered the right kind of project. Something about the way he occasionally spoke of those remote villages where he had lived and worked over the years and the people he had known there, the affection and longing in his voice, revealed to her his desire to return to his real work.

And the right project would come along, she was certain. It was only a matter of time. And she was willing to wait. Waiting was nothing for her. She had come after all from a family that had always measured time not in years but in generations. She remembered how her great-uncle Ambrose Shippen, who had been affectionately dubbed the robber baron of the family because of certain of his business practices, used to speak of the widow Susan Harbin in the present tense, as if she were still alive.

Around that time Allen Fuso, recently returned from his first trip to Bourne Island, came to work for CASR. At his recommendation the Center decided to undertake its most ambitious project to date in the Bournehills Valley District of the island. Immediately upon learning this, Harriet spoke to Barney Cole, a member of the Center's professional staff and a close friend and colleague of Saul's for many years. She followed this with a long visit to Chester Heald on the Research Institute's board, which had final word on all appointments. Both men agreed with her that Saul Amron would be the ideal person to head up such a project. The decision to approach him was quickly reached once Chester Heald spoke to certain key board members, and a letter carefully stressing the size and scope and long-range possibilities of the project for Bournehills, as well as the challenge it would offer the person directing it, went out to California.

They did not hear from him for some time aside from a brief note acknowledging their letter, and as the days, then weeks, passed, doubts began to grow that he would accept their offer. Only Harriet remained unworried. But then she knew him well enough by now to know what his silence meant and to be encouraged by it.

Finally, as she had expected, he wrote saying he would direct the project if they were willing to wait at least a year until he had fulfilled his commitments out on the coast, and only if certain conditions were met on their part: first, that the money for the project be absolutely guaranteed and forthcoming as needed; second, that he be given a completely free hand, especially during the initial stages of the work; and finally, that he have the option of withdrawing from the project once the preliminary study was done if he thought it best. All this was agreed to, and two weeks later he flew in from Stanford for the formal acceptance.

Harriet went out to the airport to meet him and, standing on the observation deck of the terminal building, watched him slowly make his way from the plane. He walked as though still debating with himself whether he should have come, his legs pulling back even as they propelled him forward. She saw the troubled set to his shoulders; sensed a reluctance akin to that which she had caught on his face their first time together as lovers: the unwillingness to begin again, in the slight droop to his head. But then he looked up, searching for her amid the crowd at the high railing, and something in the lift of his head and in his pale rueful face—a faint, almost boyish anticipation and hope that had managed to struggle through his unwillingness and doubt made her start pleasurably. Catching sight of her he smiled and, raising his arm, playfully shook his fist up at her —and she loved him.

"All right," he said when they met downstairs, "come clean. How much of this was your doing? Don't answer. All of it probably. You along with that rich buddy of yours on the Institute's board. Jesus Christ, Harriet, I'd hate to have you not on my side." He kissed her.

They were married shortly afterward, during that same visit.

"I don't know if this is the wisest thing for us to be doing," he said, his smile teasing her a little; but his eyes under their deep hoods were somber and his uncertainty had caused a frown to gather above the abrupt bridge of his nose. (It was the night before the ceremony and they were together in the living room of Harriet's apartment.) "I guess you know we're something of an odd match," he said. "Here I am what my father used to call even after we moved out to the coast and had some money a poor little *pitser* from New York. And here you are strictly Main Line Philadelphian."

She held up a hand. "Not true," she said. "Not altogether, anyway. My mother spoiled it by being a Southerner, and remaining one all her life. Nor did we have the money really to qualify after my father turned his back on all such worldly matters."

"And then there's that weird family of yours, now that you mention it."

"But I never see them!" she laughingly protested.

(It was true. Both her brothers worked for Unicor, had large families and lived out in the country, and she seldom visited them. The host of aunts, uncles, cousins, and the like who staunchly upheld the familys' ways, she almost never saw.)

"I know," he said. "You never even talk about them."

(Which was also the case. Whenever he tried getting her to talk about her relatives, her childhood, her marriage to Andrew Westerman, wanting to have more of an idea of what her life had been before they had met, she would very skillfully, without appearing to, evade his questions; and he found that privacy of hers, which almost seemed to him at times a desire on her part to blot out her past, to treat it as though it had never happened, vaguely disturbing.)

"But what's there to say about them?" she cried with the laugh.

"They're no better or worse than most people's families, I suppose. They never really approved of me, of course, especially after I married Andrew, and they'll probably disown me altogether now that I'm marrying you, which is perfectly all right with me. Only dear old Uncle Chessie has always gone along with whatever I've done, whether he's approved of it or not. He's my only real family."

Then, with a sudden despairing cry that seemed less directed at Saul than at some other presence, visible only to her, seated in silent judgment in the room, "Must I really be held liable for them?" she cried. "For all those Harbins and Shippens and what they did and didn't do, for all those great-aunts of mine who love nothing more than sitting around all day talking about the family with a capital F. Well, I refuse. They're too dull." She had recovered and was laughing again.

The two of them were next to each other on the sofa and he leaned over and kissed her. "I'm sorry, Hatt," he said. "I didn't mean to give you a hard time about them."

Then, leaning close, his eyes reflective, still uncertain, he went on, "The other thing is that I don't know if I'm fit material for a husband right now. There's so much that happened before we met which I still haven't gotten over. I can't even talk about half of it yet, not even to you. . . ." Which was true; he had never, for example, really spoken to her about his wife's death or, in any detail, of his experience with the Moran group in California which had so disillusioned him. "I can't help feeling," he said, "that I should at least try to clear away some of the dead weight so to speak, resolve those things in some way, before—how to put it?"—he gave the dog-eared smile—"venturing forth again."

She caught his face between her hands. "That will all clear up of itself, darling, once we're together." She spoke out of the confidence that was her rock. Then, with a playful smile, "Do you know what I think it is with you, Saul Amron?" Her eyes were very blue and clear, with not a trace of their customary gray. Her hair in the lamplight was a warm cowl, the proper frame for her face.

"No, what?"

"I think you've got a mild case of premarital jitters. But never mind," she said, touching the uneasy frown that persisted above his nose, seeking to smooth it away, "you'll be fine once tomorrow's over."

The following day with its brief civil ceremony came and went, as did the first year of their marriage during which Saul completed his work at Stanford and Harriet, living with him in Palo Alto, waited somewhat impatiently for the months to pass and the trip to Bourne Island to begin. The question of whether or not she should accompany him there had come up from time to time over the course of the year, and the discussion invariably brought on a quarrel. Saul, remembering his first wife and the tragic events in Honduras, was against her going. Harriet, on the other hand, was determined, and over the months she managed to prevail.

"I still don't know if it's a wise thing for you to come along," he said gloomily.

The year in California was over, and they were back in Philadelphia for the final round of talks and conferences preparatory to their leaving for Bourne Island.

"We're not to talk about that anymore, remember," she said. "It's too late, anyway. My bags are packed—" she motioned toward their suitcases standing packed and ready near the door in the living room of her old apartment. "Oh, Saul, don't scowl, I'm so looking forward to it."

But he persisted. "I still think it would be better if you stayed behind or at least waited until I got things underway down there before coming. Because I'm likely to be so busy the first few months just getting my bearings I won't have much time to spend with you. The other thing is that it's sure to be rough on you living there. You have no idea of how bad conditions can sometimes be in such places."

She was shaking her head with an unworried smile. "You're wrong, darling," she said. "First off, I'm not some hothouse flower who will expire at the least breath of ordinary air. Second, I'm not completely ignorant about how bad things can be in a really poor place." She explained: "Some years ago the Institute opened a large recreation center in North Philadelphia which, as you know, is close to being the worst slum in the world, and I made a point of going out there as often as I could, mainly to help out, but also because I wanted to see for myself how the Negroes there lived. And yes, I did find it rough at times, to use your word. I would come away utterly demoralized some days, just sick with guilt and anger that people had to live that way. But I always went back. I managed, in other words. And I'll manage where we're going."

It was his turn to shake his head. There was a truly unhappy expression on his face, in his veined eyes. "It's not the same, Harriet. It's true you might have gone out to North Philly but you always came home to this after each visit"—his hand took in the tastefully furnished, softly lighted room in which they were sitting—"but there won't be any coming 'home' at the end of the day in Bournehills. That will be home—and for quite some time at that. Besides, you'll probably be bored to death after being there awhile since you won't be directly involved in the work of the project."

"I'll find ways to keep busy," she said. "And I had thought I might be able to lend a hand with the work. After all, you might need someone to type up field notes or sharpen pencils or empty the wastepaper basket. I can do that."

"Oh, for God's sake, don't sound so offended." He had caught her injured tone.

"No one likes being told they're useless."

"Who the hell said that?"

"You implied as much."

"Jesus Christ, I did not!"

"We're quarreling again," she said at his loud cry, and then seeing the way his somewhat heavy-featured face became swollen whenever he was angry, almost like a boy with mumps, she laughed. "I must say this isn't a very auspicious beginning to our trip, is it?"

"But who said that? You've got a thing about this notion of being useless which really bothers the hell out of me."

He waited, but in the face of her silent refusal to go on with it, and her smile, his anger subsided and he said—and he was suddenly very gentle with her—"Don't worry, Hatt, there'll be plenty for you to do besides sharpening pencils. I'll talk to you about that later. One thing though, I had better warn you now—and I'm dead serious about this —that you're never, under any circumstances, to interfere in the work . . ."

She started to protest and he held up his hand.

"No, I mean that, Harriet," he said. She had never heard him sound like this before. "You're never, in other words, to act on your own in anything connected with the project. Always check with either me or Allen first." (It had been decided, at his insistence, that he would conduct the first exploratory phase of the work alone, with only Allen to assist him.) "Because sometimes, dear Hatt"—his tone had changed and he spoke now so as not to offend her again—"in your eagerness to come to the aid of this half-assed anthropologist whom you've decided, for God knows what reasons, to rehabilitate, get moving again, and who loves you for it, never mind he shouts at you every so often, you tend to go overboard. So just watch it. Don't interfere. Because it could really foul up everything. And neither one of us, I know, wants to see anything go wrong with this project. It means too much—not only to me and the Center, but, most important, to the people in Bournehills."

CHAPTER 5

The proposed plan for Bournehills, as outlined during the talks at the Center prior to their departure, was to be done in three stages. There would be a preliminary study of six months to a year to obtain a general picture of life in the district as well as to discover why a number of other projects previously attempted there had all failed. Once this was completed, the second or action phase of the work would begin with an expanded research team and one or more demonstration projects. Out of these would eventually come the large, long-range programs which hopefully over a period of years would see life in Bournehills vastly improved.

Saul Amron was explaining this in part now to the group of men gathered around him on the veranda of Lyle Hutson's imposing white stone house, where the reception for them was being held on this, their first night on the island. Out beyond the veranda, down through a well of darkness separating the house, which stood on its own private rise, from the town of New Bristol below, he could see, whenever he glanced over his shoulder, the scattered lights of the town lying there like a small constellation of stars that had fallen and taken root, or flares that had been set within the darkness of sea, sky, and land to point the way for the ships and planes seeking the island. And he could feel the almost human presence of the tropical night waiting just beyond the reach of the lights from the house. It appeared to be listening to him more closely even than the men in his audience.

Bournehills, on the other side of the island which he had not as yet seen, seemed very far away.

Farther along the high-ceilinged veranda which embraced the house on all sides, past the other guests drinking and chatting under the globed light, Allen stood talking with another group of men near the broad fan-shaped steps leading down to the driveway and the formal gardens surrounding the house. Dark head tilted to one side, thick arms folded on his chest and his legs slightly apart, he had assumed what was for him a characteristc pose: a little as if lecturing a class. From time to time, all the while he was there, his hazel eyes would drift out to the floodlit circular driveway below, and from behind his glasses he would follow its path to where it gently sloped down the rise between two rows of royal palm trees and disappeared in the darkness below. He was watching, waiting for Merle.

Harriet could be glimpsed inside the large formal drawing room which opened off the veranda. Most of the other women were also there with the exception of a few of the younger ones who had joined the men outside. Harriet, poised lightly in her seat, her hair warming to the light, was listening to the talk around her with an attentive, interested air, and occasionally she spoke herself, turning as she did from one to another of the women nearby with a movement of her head which made her seem incapable of a single false or awkward gesture. Seeing her, you would not have thought that any of this was new to her.

Outside Saul was talking about the project only in the most general terms. But he was having difficulty, because some of the men in the group around him, especially the editor of the local newspaper, kept pressing him to be more specific and, above all, to state how much money was likely to be involved.

The editor was an Englishman of perhaps thirty-five called George Clough. He was an openly supercilious man, with a blandly handsome, store manikin's face, inanimate eyes and a set of very small, fine, absolutely even, absolutely white teeth which he bared from time to time in something that passed for a smile. Saul had learned earlier in the evening that Clough had been sent out the previous year to overhaul the local paper by the large English newspaper chain which had taken it over just shortly before Bourne Island had been granted its present quasi-independent status.

Aside from the editor and himself there were only two other white men present, one a big, square, taciturn Australian named Bryce-Parker, with a weathered face and vague kind eyes, whom Saul liked immediately. He was the chief soil conservation officer for Bournehills. Then there was Waterford, a seemingly hearty but remote man, who was the specialist in economic planning sent down at the request of the Bourne Island government to advise it on its new five-year development plan.

All the others were native Bourne Islanders, and black men—but black that for the most part had been passed through the white prism of their history and been endlessly refracted there, altered, alloyed. So that the faces surrounding Saul Amron presented him with a shade and color spectrum which ranged from the soft, deep-grained black of the Honorable Member for Bournehills at one end, a stout ill-at-ease man named Deanes, with a nervous habit of glancing over his shoulder as if he were being pursued, to, at the other, the near-white skin and slate-blue eyes of a permanent secretary in the government.

Like this man and Member of Parliament Deanes, nearly all the men there were senior civil servants and high-ranking government officials. The rest were members of the professions, which in Bourne Island were largely taken to mean only medicine and law. And they were very much of a type. They were all, to a man almost, drinking imported whisky, scorning as a matter of status the local rum, which was excellent; all wearing dark-toned, conservative, heavy English suits in spite of the hot night. Some, like the pale, austere permanent secretary, had on matching vests, and a few wore their old school ties.

And their manner, as they stood there listening with carefully controlled expressions and neutral eyes, was in keeping with their dress. Reserved, almost formal (one or two of the older men called to mind some slightly outmoded, upper-class Victorian gentlemen of the turn of the century), their demeanor was marked by a surface ease and charm that did not quite mask a subtle tension beneath. And uncertainty. This—more pronounced in some than others—suggested that in spite of their secure air, they were not altogether sure that the relatively new affluence and position they had come into were truly theirs.

Down below, along the sweep of driveway, were parked the large, late-model English and German cars they drove. And Saul, assessing these men under his partly drawn lids as he spoke, as they were him, was certain that they all probably lived in houses similar to this one—not as lavish perhaps but essentially the same.

The house as you approached it up the drive looked to be modern, although it had been built out of the remains of an old Georgian estate house that had once stood on the site. And it had retained, you saw as you drew closer, many of the features of the old house, and the most unattractive ones at that. The thick, square graceless columns supporting the veranda, for example. And the heavy stone balustrade around it. As well as the ponderous, tightly shuttered look to the façade. To this had been added a profusion of modern touches that were suspect: flat, sharply canted roofs that soared off in all directions from the various wings, with on top of the roofs an elaborate television antenna that resembled a sculptor's construction. New imitation stone had replaced the lovely old coral stone of the original house, which had been allowed to crumble away, and a good deal of fanciful iron scrollwork was to be seen covering the already deeply shrouded Georgian windows.

The house was a failure, although this was not immediately apparent, and most people thought it handsome, progressive and new. But the designer, in trying to blend the old and the new, had failed to select the best from each—those features from the past and present which would have best served his end. Instead, in his haste perhaps, he had taken the worst of both architectural styles, so that although the house stood high on its private rise above the town, and was graced by the avenue of royal palms in front and breathed upon by the flowers in the gardens spread around it, it still could not rise above the profound error and confusion in its design.

"Frankly, all we'll be doing for the next few months is trying to learn as much as we can about Bournehills, but nothing more ambitious than that," Saul was saying in answer to someone's question. "By that I mean we want to know what life is really like in the district, the attitudes and aspirations of the people there, as well as what they feel to be their problems. But this is pretty much all we'll be doing for the time being. It's fairly standard procedure, but important since it will serve as the basis for the real work later on."

"Can't you tell us, though, what you have in mind to do down there once you've finished with this so-called preliminary study?"

The question was asked somewhat suspiciously by the very dark man, Deanes, the Member for Bournehills. It was clear from his heavy accent and uncertain speech that he lacked the formal education of the others.

And again, very patiently, Saul explained what would probably follow the initial survey: a more in-depth research study and one or more pilot projects. "But all that's very much in the future," he added. "Right now, as I said before, we're just here to learn. And to find out whether a project is even possible. Because it might not be, since I understand there've been any number of development programs tried out in Bournehills which haven't worked. One of the things we'll need to know before we begin is just why they failed."

It was clear from the expression on Deanes' face that his answer had proved unsatisfactory, and realizing this Saul said, "You'll have to forgive me, Mr. Deanes, for speaking in what must seem such vague terms, but it's impossible to be any more specific at this point. In fact, I feel I'm being presumptuous in saying what little I have. After all, I've only been on the island—what?—no more than eight hours and haven't even gotten my first look at Bournehills yet."

"But if I might get back for a moment to the question of the money for this proposed scheme of yours, Dr. Amron. Surely you can at least give us an idea as to approximately how much your organization is planning to spend."

It was George Clough, the editor, speaking impatiently through the tightly closed milk teeth, insistent still. His wife had joined them meanwhile, and stood with her arm linked through his. She was a small, youthfully pretty, fair-haired woman with thin, very fine English skin and the practical, pleasantly level-headed air of a young London matron. She was smiling sympathetically across at Saul.

Saul spread his hands; unperturbed, he said, "I'm afraid I can't, Mr. Clough. As I said before, the amount of money will depend on the kinds of programs we set up—and there's just no saying right now what those will be. But let me again emphasize that the money will definitely be forthcoming. We've been guaranteed that. But just how much it will be over the long run I can't say."

He not only sensed a general dissatisfaction with his answer, but something else which he had been vaguely aware of all along, and which had puzzled him. Behind their neutral, attentive silence, behind the questions they had put to him, he had sensed all of them waiting, biding their time, to make what he was sure would be some telling comment on everything he was saying. He had felt this unsaid thing circling the air above their heads like the moths and small night-flying insects circling the light globes set high in the veranda's tall roof. From time to time he thought he saw a veiled, knowing glance flit swiftly among them although their eyes did not leave his face. And he had wondered, talking the while, what this unstated thing might be.

Now, in the face of both this and the insistent silence that had fallen, he heard himself saying—and he spoke against his will, "I'm sure, though, that all of you here realize that a project as large as the one we have in mind could run well into hundreds of thousands of dollars, into millions for that matter. But I definitely wouldn't want to be quoted on that."

He was looking directly at George Clough as he said this, to impress it upon him, and so did not notice for a moment the change that took place among the others at the mention of the word millions. The thing he had sensed circling unspoken overhead had suddenly dropped and burst like a shell in their restrained midst, releasing them, and one of the barristers who had been questioning him closely all along, a younger man named Hinkson with a pale amber-colored face and the crimped dark-blond hair typical of the Bourne Island colored-whites as they were called, suddenly laughed. It was a loud cynical outburst, and half-turning away in disgust, he declared, "Well, good money gone again!

"Gone!" he repeated in the same abrupt manner, addressing not only Saul, who had turned questioningly to him, but the others as well, challenging them to disagree with him. "Bournehills! Man"—this to Saul—"you don't know that place. There's no changing or improving it. You people could set up a hundred development schemes at a hundred million each and down there would remain the same. Tell him"—he turned to the others—"about the money that's been wasted on that place. Tell him, for instance, about what happened to the small farmers' co-operative government tried starting there a few years back. . . ." He waited, but when the others held back, looking uncomfortable in the extreme, he said, "All right, I'll tell him. He'll soon find out anyway." And in the same half-laughing but disgusted tone, declared, "It nearly caused war down there, that's what. Work their crops together? Share with each other? Not those people. The poor co-operative officer had to run for his life.

"Then there was the housing scheme government built with the help of that Canadian company," he continued. "My good sir, those people refused to go near it. Decent houses now with water run in and a proper toilet. They preferred the old shacks they live in. Why? Hear them"—and he suddenly lapsed into the strong island accent, parodying it—" 'Because it's we house and we land.' "

With that the laughter broke and as it rushed out into the darkness beyond the veranda it seemed to take with it a large measure of their formality and restraint, so that others in the group now joined Hinkson, their voices closing in on the subject of Bournehills like hounds around a trapped quarry. And they were soon talking among themselves, Saul and the other outsiders—George Clough, his wife, Waterford, the economist, and the soil conservation officer, Bryce-Parker—forgotten.

". . . Remember the crop diversification scheme to get them to grow bananas instead of the few sickly canes . . . ?"

"Good money gone again!"

"And the irrigation system that farming group from America installed for them awhile back . . ."

"I know they allowed the pipes to rust in the fields."

"And look at how they're sabotaging the soil conservation program. Ask Bryce-Parker here."

And in a body they turned to the large, silent Australian who, a drink in hand, had stood all evening looking as though he was not altogether sure whether he was in Australia still or Kenya, where he had worked for many years, or Bourne Island. At their urging he spoke—but obviously with great reluctance. "Well," he said, "I don't know as you can quite call it sabotage. It's just that they don't like it when we have to raze one of the smaller hills to try and stop the slippage. And to get back at us I suppose they put their sheep out to graze on the new grasslands at night and cut down the casuarina trees we plant to hold back the soil. For firewood you know. It's strange but it's as though they don't want to see a stone moved in the place. . . ."

He had scarcely finished before the voices rushed in once again. "And what did they say to Lady Stanley when she went to speak to them about family planning? Didn't one of them shout out at the meeting, 'What, woman, you mean to say you've come to take away our only sport?' I hear poor Lady Stanley nearly died of mortification."

Amid the laughter, the medical officer for Bournehills, a handsome, heavy-set man named Miles Wooding with a subtle reddish cast to his dark-brown skin, drew near to Saul and, laughing, said, "It's true, you know, Dr. Amron. The Governor General's wife now! They literally ran her out of the place and they're down there breeding faster than ever, adding to the overpopulation. But then they're a hardy type," he said with a proud air that suggested he was somehow responsible for this fact. "You don't get much sickness in Bournehills. A little high blood pressure, yes. A few cases of worms, yes. From the rice. Every grain of the blasted stuff is a worm I tell them. Eat cooked green bananas I tell them. At least they'll be getting some iron that way. 'Yes, Doctor,' they'll say, 'we'll start with the bananas today-self,' and then go right home and put on a big pot of rice to boil. Bournehills people!" He gave a resigned, indulgent shrug. "There's nothing to be done with them. But they're a hardy lot. It's the sea air down there. The damn place is a natural sanatorium."

". . . And look at what happened to the pottery factory my Ministry built there to give them work making little souvenirs and things for the tourists," a tall dark man, darker even than Deanes and with the same lovely bluish cast to his skin in the light, was saying. He had been introduced earlier to Saul as the Minister of Trade and Development. "Why, those scoundrels refused to work in it," he said. "And we had to abandon it."

"I tell you, Bournehills is like someplace out of the Dark Ages." It was the young lawyer, Hinkson, again; and his voice was rapidly losing its joking tone, becoming thick and hard. "Even when you try to brighten up life a little for them, they don't seem to want it. Look how they refused to have in Rediffusion even though government was willing to install it practically free of charge . . ."

". . . And the television set that British firm gave them for the social center played one day and then mysteriously broke down . . ."

". . . The jukebox from America didn't last a week . . ."

". . . There's no understanding those people, I tell you!" someone else cried. "Why, they even refused to have anything to do with the independence celebrations. Not one of them came to town for them. . . ."

The voices swiftly mounted, becoming an increasingly loud fugue as the men, joined by others on the veranda, vied with each other to be heard; and an unmistakable note of anger and outrage, born of a profound bewilderment, began to underscore the words and the volleys of laughter.

"Those people? They're a disgrace!"

They might have been speaking about a people completely alien to themselves, who did not even inhabit the same island, Saul thought. But then who, he reminded himself, can speak calmly of the brother who shames him? Because listening to them he had suddenly remembered, to his own shame, how, as a boy, he had fled his brothers, those with the sallow, long-nosed look, sloping shoulders and side curls, whose bodies always appeared to be cowering out of the way of an impending blow. The Ashkenazi look he had called it as an arrogant young man who had taken pride in his large, straight-shouldered build—the look of the long persecuted; and while maintaining his allegiance (for they were his people after all) he had still, at the same time, often been impatient, even angry, with them.

Looking around he noticed that most of the older, more reserved of the men had quietly slipped away, leaving the noisy field to the younger and bolder ones like Cecil Hinkson. Deanes, the representative for Bournehills, had disappeared, for one. Earlier, when Hinkson had first spoken out, a look of acute dismay had come over his round anxious face, and something in his eyes had pleaded with the young lawyer to forbear. Then, as the others had joined in, he had kept glancing nervously over his shoulder out toward the dark end of the driveway as though expecting that shameless horde who were his constituents to come rushing up the rise to further embarrass him. Finally, with a pained look Saul Amron's way which was meant, it appeared, to absolve him from any responsibility for them, he had edged away.

". . . But worst of all is what they're doing to carnival!" Hinkson was almost shouting now, his amber-colored face white with a rage that went beyond Bournehills to include, it seemed, the thing in himself that joined him to those irredeemable masses on the other side of the island.

"Oh, Cecil, man, don't even bring that up," someone cried in angry despair. "Why, those brutes have changed the whole meaning of carnival with their foolishness."

And again Miles Wooding turned to explain to Saul. "You see, every year we have a little carnival. Oh, nothing much. We're not a people who go in for a lot of feting. We put it on mainly for the tourists, who like that sort of thing. And every year those people from the hills do the same masque about some blasted slave revolt that took place down there long ago. It was all very well for a time. A bit of history, you know, and they do it surprisingly well. But it's become too much. And what's the point of it? Who wants to be reminded of that old-time business? What are they trying to prove? Worse, it's beginning to embarrass those of our visitors who come to carnival every year."

Around them the voices continued to rage:

". . . The carnival committee should ban them from town, the brutes."

"I tell you"—a voice raved above the others—"sometimes I wish that whole blasted place would just disappear—wash away in the sea or some damn thing. You'd wake up one morning and hear that it's gone. . . ."

"One good hurricane across that end of the island and finish with them!" It was a trembling and livid young Hinkson shouting again.

"Gentlemen, gentlemen, less heat I beg you." A calm, admonitory voice suddenly sounded at the rear of the violent circle. "There's no need to drag the family skeleton out of the closet and cane him so unmercifully before our visitor from America. What will he think?"

Lyle Hutson, their host, came and stood between the newspaper editor, George Clough, and the angrily trembling Hinkson. Placing his hands on their shoulders as if they were the pillars to a triumphal arch through which he was about to pass to take command of the group, he gently chided them all, including Saul, with his smile. Which was not so much a smile as a careful arrangement of the small muscles around his lips, a fixed enigmatic expression that had little to do with the man within, who, you suspected, seldom if ever smiled.

He was about forty-eight, Saul's age, and his tall, lightly fleshed body was still fit and youthful looking. The custom-made suit and vest he wore were even more uncompromisingly British than those of the others. And he had more than perfected the poised, almost courtly manner all the men there exhibited in varying degrees. With him it seemed completely natural, something he had been born to. And perhaps because he had learned the style so well and even, at times, exaggerated some of the mannerisms, he had achieved, without knowing it, a subtle saving irony which lent everything he did or said a faintly self-mocking note.

Lyle Hutson was, to begin with, a leading barrister, perhaps the most successful and popular on the island. The courtroom was always packed for his cases, and the smallest child on the roads knew the license number of his large silver-gray Humber Super Snipe and would shout his name as he sped past. He was also a senator in the legislature and a member of the powerful clique which ran the government for the Prime Minister, a mild nondescript man who had been chosen as a compromise between warring factions of the party. In addition, he was something of a businessman, and was in the process of building a small yacht basin and club for those like himself who still could not, because of their color, gain admission to the venerable Bourne Island Yacht Club, one of the last preserves of the old white and near-white families on the island.

And the remarkable thing was that Lyle Hutson had accomplished all this despite having been born the son of an obscure village tailor in a remote section of the island. He had done all this in a place where, especially when he was a boy, a very high premium had been placed on being the right skin shade and of the right family in establishing a career. But he had been bright and ambitious even then, and had won a scholarship to the elite boys' secondary school in town. He had stood among the sons of the island's leading families flawlessly reciting his Latin—"a small boy" from the country in a clean, starched, but slightly threadbare uniform, school tie and garters, his thick bush of hair brushed flat, his knees greased, and a hint of his mother's talcum powder lightening the strong, dark-umber of his face.

Later, he had been a Bourne Island scholar and gone to England to study, first to Oxford (and there could be a fine Oxonian thrust to his speech when he so chose), then the London School of Economics, and finally the Inns of Court. And he had been something of a radical his years in England, due largely to Merle Kinbona, who had also been there studying at the time. They had been lovers briefly. Along with her and the other West Indian students he had shouted socialism and revolution at the heated parties they attended. He had talked of nationalizing the sugar industry at home and driving Kingsley and Sons from the island. But once he had returned home and married into the famous Vaughan family, once his law practice had grown and he had entered politics, he had gradually started speaking about the need for change in less radical terms. He had begun to caution moderation and time.

He stood in their midst now, framed by George Clough and Hinkson, the one, white; the other, near-white, his hands resting easily, and with a mocking familiarity directed solely at them, on their shoulders. The noisy argument had immediately subsided at his appearance, and in the silence that had fallen he turned with an apologetic bow to Saul.

"My dear Dr. Amron," he said, "I trust you will forgive this rather emotional display. I assure you, we are not a people given to such outbursts as a rule. We're much too British for that. But the subject of Bournehills does tend to evoke a strong reaction on the part of some like my young friend and colleague here"—he playfully shook Cecil Hinkson's shoulder. "They're a bit sensitive about it. We all are. Bournehills, you see, is the thorn in our sides, the maverick in our midst, the black sheep of the family, if you will, which continues to disgrace us in spite of all our efforts to bring it into the fold. In other words, while we have been making quite considerable progress on this side of the island it has remained a backwater even with the large amounts of money that have been poured into it. The place is really quite unique in that respect. I don't believe you could find another like it in the whole of the West Indies or the world for that matter. In any other place, no matter how formerly backward or remote, one can still, I'm sure, see some small sign of things moving ahead. But hardly in Bournehills. And it's not, you know, that it can't change, but rather, one almost begins to suspect, that it chooses not to, for some perverse reason. These are very subtle points, I know, to be offering a stranger his first night on the island, but you will soon appreciate them for yourself. All I hope is that we haven't caused you to lose heart before you've begun. Because in spite of our remarks, we welcome your interest in us. We're flattered that your organization has chosen our little island for so grand a scheme. And I for one am optimistic, since I know you Americans"—his cold smile widened slightly—"are famous for working miracles—and surely this is what Bournehills needs. It's just that these good gentlemen felt it their duty to warn you of some of the difficulties ahead in much the same spirit, say, as the family of a bride-to-be might feel morally bound to inform the prospective groom that his intended suffers from some rare, incurable disease and is, moreover, decidedly unbalanced."

"Small faults," Saul said with a laugh. "I shall love her the more for them."

"Let's drink to the love match then!" Lyle Hutson said, laughing in return, and clapped for the servant, his screened, unsmiling eyes fixed on Saul's face.

The servant, a white cap perched atop her thick braids, a young, closed black face beneath, appeared almost immediately with the tray of drinks; and at the same moment, as if also in response to Lyle Hutson's clap, the headlights of a car—four feeble unsteady cones of light—appeared in the darkness down the palm-lined driveway. The sound of a motor that seemed about to breathe its last carried to the veranda, and someone in the group around Allen said, "Well, it looks like Merle finally reached."

But Allen already knew. He had recognized immediately those faint wavering lights and the asthmatic sound of the motor. He had been seeing and hearing them all evening, he realized, imagining them in his mind's eye and ear all the while he had been standing talking. Excusing himself he went over and stood at the top of the steps, feeling relieved, on the one hand, that the long wait was over, but annoyed, on the other, that she had taken so long.

Sweeping past the cars lining the driveway, Merle parked the shabby Bentley with its mangled front grille and battered body in the middle of the driveway directly in front of the house, and got out.

She was wearing the same open-back shoes, vivid print dress, earrings, and bracelets as earlier in the day; and to this she had added, now that it was evening, a long stole made from the same colorful cloth as her dress. This lay draped offhandedly across her shoulders and down her arms.

Allen smiled at sight of the dress, his annoyance vanishing. Because it was the same one—or so he believed—that she had worn the day he had left over a year ago. It was as though she had put it on to assure him that nothing had changed and she was the same. To confirm this all the more he saw that she was as usual talking to herself as she got out of the car, and from the way she slammed the door and the angry hieroglyphic the red tip of her cigarette described against the darkness he could tell she was castigating the Bentley, her favorite target for abuse.

"Into the sea," she was saying as she came down the path through the flowers spread in a rich feast in front of the house. "I'm going to pitch it straight into the sea one of these days, mark my words. It's no use. A car that can't climb an anthill! That creeps along at ten miles an hour! It's not worth the petrol you put in it. . . ."

Then suddenly she stopped short, her attention caught by a thick mass of golden zinnias in a star-shaped bed near the steps, and with a soft awed cry she gazed at them. And she was utterly still for a moment, her whole being given over to the sight of the flowers. Even the saints on her silver earrings who never ceased their anxious dance were still, as were the many bracelets on her arms. Finally, with her odd off-brown eyes retaining the yellow flame of the flowers she looked up from the bottom of the steps and saw Allen.

"What the heck happened to you?" he said. He was grinning like a schoolboy. "How come you're so late?"

By way of an answer her arms with the stole draped over them opened, her shoulders lifted and her entire body shaped a slow, eloquent shrug. (It was the gesture of a Jew, Saul thought, glancing down at her from where he stood with Lyle Hutson and the others. Prayer shawl and all. Full of that almost indecent love of the dramatic.) With the gesture she simply offered herself in explanation for her lateness: the face that was like the portrait of some young and handsome woman which had been defaced by vandals; the eyes with their mysterious sunlight, and the aging forty-year-old body which she disguised beneath the flared, one-piece dresses she made herself.

Still without speaking she quickly mounted the steps and coming up to Allen raised her hands, took his face between them and brought it down to rest maternally against hers for a long silent moment. Then, stepping back, she said, "Allen-love, hear me. Only God in his infinite mercy has seen me through this day. Everything went wrong. Westminster Low Road ran off in the rain last night. The old car started giving trouble first thing this morning. The painter walked out on me flat and I had to finish doing the dining room myself. Then, this evening before coming down here I thought I'd take a little nap and slept longer than I intended. But you'll forgive me. My dear, you'll be all forgiveness when you see how I've kept up your garden. Did you know that Allen could grow carrots out of stone?" She turned with the question to Saul as he came up.

"No," he said, startled by her abruptness, but recovering quickly. "Although I must say I'm not surprised."

"Well, you should be," she said. "Miracles are hard to come by these days. You should have seen those lovely little loose heads of cabbages he would grow, those carrots no bigger than my thumb"—she held up a stubbed thumb, a resolute brown on one side, beige on the other.

"You ate them, one thing!" Allen cried, pretending an injured tone.

"Ate them! How you mean," she exclaimed. "I loved them. Do you know what it meant to see something live come out of that stony ground? I can still see you out in the yard at the crack of dawn coaxing the damn things up out of that stone and singing like Caruso. Why, I think I even have an old work pants of yours somewhere around the place. I knew you'd be back, you see. So did everyone in Bournehills, for that matter. We're psychic down there, you know.

People in the village would stop by the guesthouse and ask, 'Have you heard from Mr. Allen? When did he say he'll be back?' But tell me, how're you keeping?"

And again falling silent she studied his face with the eyes the old woman Leesy claimed could read a person's life with a look. And her gaze did appear to penetrate the rimless glasses which served Allen as a kind of psychologist's one-way screen in that he could look out, analytically, upon the world but the world could not look in. Piercing the shield her gaze reached all the way in.

"You've lost all your little color," she said. "You need some sun. Some good strong Bournehills sun. You could do with some, too." She had turned to Saul. Then, with a light complex laugh which said she knew how she must appear but didn't care, she held out a hand. "Hello, I'm Merle, the London landlady of the guesthouse where you'll be staying until you find a suitable place in the village. I hope Allen has warned you about me. I'm a talker. Some people act, some think, some feel, but I talk, and if I was to ever stop that'd be the end of me. And worse, I say whatever comes to my mind and the devil with it. But I'm harmless. And I mean well. Ask Allen. He's my good friend. . . ."

Pausing a moment she appraised Saul with the same close proprietary look she had given Allen moments ago. He, too, might have been someone who had once visited the island, then left only to return again after a year's absence, and she was inspecting him to see if he had changed while away.

"I guess you've been hearing the worst about my end of the world," she said, continuing to assess him with the penetrating gaze. "How impossible we are. How much money's been wasted on us. Oh, I know this bunch down here. Bournehills, sex, cricket, and politics are all they ever talk about. But don't mind them. You'll like Bournehills, as hopeless as it is. And we'll like you if you're anything like Allen. I'm not exactly clear as to what you have in mind to do—and don't tell me now because I won't remember a word my head's so turned around from all that's happened today—but I can tell from your face (you've got a decent face) you mean to do your best.

"Lyle, you rich rascal, come over here." An imperious forefinger ordered Lyle Hutson, who was approaching them through the crowd, to a spot directly in front of her. "What've you brutes been telling this nice gentleman from America about us in Bournehills? You want him to take the next plane out? And who told you to build this house so high up when you know my car's no use anymore. And I see," she said, glancing toward the drawing room, "that most of the ladies are in purdah as usual. . . ."

While talking she had lifted her face for his kiss, and despite his laugh as he bent to her, there was something almost deferential in the way he touched her cheek with his lips. "I see I'm in for your customary tongue-lashing this evening," he said.

". . . And where's a drink?" She had not paused. "All these servants you've got running about the place and people still can't get a drink. Go fetch one for me, love. You know I can't take this town crowd otherwise. Rum and water," she called after him as he obediently went in search of the servant. "None of that fancy stuff you people down this end drink for style.

"Dear Lyle." Her eyes rested fondly on his retreating back. She spoke only to herself. "With those blasted suits of his from Savile Row and his quotations from *The Aeneid* when he's had in a few grogs. What the years do to us all, yes.

"Allen"—she turned abruptly back—"did I write you that Glen Hill is gone? Remember it? The little one near Cane Vale factory where we used to find those lovely cashews. Bryce-Parker pulled down the last of it some weeks back. To stop the slippage, he says, even though it won't, of course. I can't tell you how it hurt to see that hill go. And do you know that Delbert got his leg broken and is running the shop from a bed behind the counter these days? And did I tell you what happened to the television set they gave us free for the social center? My dear, it didn't last the day. All of a sudden the screen just went blank. The whole thing was very mysterious. And yours truly is a working woman again. How's that for news? I didn't last any time at the new high school in town as I wrote you, but I've managed to get another job since doing what you might call a little social work at the almshouse up Westminster. I got it through Lyle. Who says it doesn't pay to have friends in high places?" Her laugh struck the air a derisive blow. "And Stinger's Gwen is expecting again. Don't ask me which one this is. All of us in Bournehills lost count long ago. And did I tell you . . ."

The flow of words continued unchecked, the voice rushing pell-mell down the precipitous slope toward its own destruction. And she was talking not only to Allen, who stood like someone transfixed before her, but to Saul as well. He might have known the people, places and events of which she was speaking. And when Lyle Hutson returned with her drink she slipped her arm through his, holding him to her side, forcing him to listen, also.

Saul studied her face; he listened to the desperate voice, and suddenly he recalled how the man Deanes had kept glancing nervously over his shoulder during the loud condemnation of Bournehills as though he feared his constituents were about to descend on him. And it struck him that this woman who shrugged like a Jew and insisted whenever she glanced his way that he had been here before, had brought the entire spurned and shameless lot with her onto the veranda.

". . . And naturally, now that the crop's started, word's out that Cane Vale will be closing down soon. The old Damocles' sword is still hanging over our heads, in other words." But her laugh as she said this was forced, worried. She turned to Lyle Hutson. "Have you heard anything about it, Lyle?" Then, almost angrily withdrawing her arm from his— "But what's the use of asking you. You probably wouldn't say if you had. After all, you're in league with Kingsley and Sons, even though you might not know it. Judas," she declared, and he laughed, his head flung back. She watched him a moment, scowling, then suddenly broke into laughter herself. "But never mind, love, you can't help it," she said. "They put you so. Those English were the biggest obeah men out when you considered what they did to our minds. Where's Deanes? Maybe he's heard something. Where's the Honorable Member for Bournehills, who never comes near the place except around election time? Deanesie!" she called, looking around her. "Where're you hiding? He always makes himself scarce when he knows I'm around." This in an aside to Saul. "He's frighten for my tongue. Deanes! Where's the rascal, anyway? And where's your wife?" she asked him, and then didn't give him time to answer. "I know, inside keeping the wake with the rest of the ladies. I'll go rescue her. Allen, love, we'll old talk some more later. Lyle, come help me find Deanesie. Dr. Amron, I'm going to give you a chance to say something tomorrow."

She was gone, taking Lyle Hutson with her and leaving behind a silence that continued to hum and jar for long moments afterward with her voice and the scarcely suppressed hysteria behind it.

"Does she go on like that all the time?" Saul asked with an amazed laugh when she was out of earshot.

"Pretty much," Allen said. He spoke as though he found nothing wrong with it. "That's just Merle. She never lets you get in a word if she can help it."

"I see," he said, and turned to watch her as she rapidly made her way along the crowded veranda. He heard, despite the loud blend of voices and laughter, the sharp staccato rap of her heels on the tiles and the light slapping sound the heel of her foot (bisque-colored in contrast to the rest of her dark legs, he noted) made against her shoes at every step. Her body appeared to be wavering uncertainly on the raised heels, and seeing this something in him instinctively reached out to catch her lest she fall.

Without seeming to pause in her swift course along the veranda she managed to give everyone there the same elaborate greeting. Lifting her face she offered them her dark cheek to be kissed. And she insisted upon the kiss. The cheek would remain at its high angle until the person bent to it. It was as if she considered the kiss an obeisance due her, an acknowledgment on everyone's part of the wide suffering—wide enough to include an entire history—which her face reflected.

Passing the Australian, Bryce-Parker, she shook a playful finger in his face, "All right, Parkey," she cried. "This is the last warning. When I get up tomorrow I want to see Glen Hill back where it belongs, you hear—or else!" Laughing, she swept ahead, her every step accompanied by the ring and clash of the bracelets at her wrists, and finally disappeared still calling aloud for Deanes and announcing like a town crier to all she passed, "We're still there, everybody. The rain last night only washed away the old road, but the rest of Bournehills is still there. . . ."

Inside the drawing room, a large, formal high-ceilinged chamber filled with an uneasy assortment of heavy Georgian as well as modern furniture, and presided over by a huge glaucous-eyed television set, Harriet sat listening to her hostess, Enid Hutson, who was telling her about Bournehills. It was just moments before Merle was due to enter.

Enid Hutson, at thirty-eight, had a full, still shapely figure which she had encased in flowered silk for the occasion, a pretty but blurred face and slow, somnolent eyes that in spite of their slowness still managed to keep a close check on the servants in the room. Although she was perhaps a year or two younger than Harriet she had already assumed the set, complacent air of the older matrons ranged like so many middle-aged wallflowers around the room. The women, holding small glasses of sherry or Coca-Cola in their laps, their corseted thighs easing gently over the seats of their chairs, had spent the entire evening inside, alone, with little else to talk about but their children, the latest American fashions, and their servants.

Enid Hutson was a distant relative of Merle's, and shared with her the same maiden name, Vaughan, and the same arresting, see-through clear brown eyes. But the resemblance ended there, since Enid was as white as Harriet seated beside her except for the mildest hint of saffron to her smooth scented skin. She and Merle had a mutual forebear in the English planter, old Duncan Vaughan, who, long ago, had owned one of the largest sugar estates in Bournehills. The old man was something of a legend on the island. People still talked about how he had sired the last of the forty children he had had from the black women who worked on his estate at the age of seventy-five and then died six months before it was born sprawled in the planter's easy chair he slept in at night, his gout-swollen legs cradled in the chair's canvas sling.

In his will Vaughan, who had never married, had stipulated that the estate be divided among his many offspring, so that his sons, despite their illegitimacy, had become, most of them, owners of their own small estates. Their children, in turn, had become civil servants, merchants, professionals, and the like who had scattered throughout the island to establish new branches of the family. They had sought over the generations to whiten and legitimatize the line and had succeeded—with the possible exception of Merle's father's small section of the family, who had remained in Bournehills and more or less carried on in the manner of Duncan Vaughan. (Merle's father, Ashton, for instance, a great-grandson of old Vaughan, had had her by the young weeder on his estate, Clara, although it had been 1924 then, a time when such practices should have long been past.) But some of the most prominent figures on Bourne Island were Vaughans and the name was respected throughout.

Enid was from a branch of the family that for some reason had remained relatively poor and obscure, on the edge of acceptability. ("They got color but no personality," Leesy would have said.) Her father had never risen above the position of senior clerk in the Water Works Department, and in contrast to Merle, who had attended the formerly all-white girls' school in town and then gone on to study in

England, Enid had been educated at one of the lesser secondary schools and had never been out of the island. Thus, all she had to offer a prospective husband by way of a dowry was her highly respected family name, her saffron-tinted white skin and a lush, somewhat sluggish sexuality. And she had shrewdly waited for someone to whom these things would matter and who could pay the bride-price. They had mattered to Lyle Hutson, even that unresponsive pale yellow body of hers which he would spend himself at times trying to rouse. And he, for his part, had been more than able to meet the bride-price by the time he returned from England and established his law practice: the huge white stone house overlooking New Bristol, with its formal gardens and expensive furnishings, the crowd of servants to the back, the silver-gray Humber out front, the two children in the island's best schools, and the never-failing invitations to the Prime Minister's and Governor General's homes. The contract had been well kept, so that when reports of Lyle's infidelities reached Enid she would give a loud indifferent suck of her teeth.

"Not me. You'd never get me to live down there," she was saying to Harriet in a voice that refused to be hurried, but made its slow uninflected way through everything she said. "Bournehills! Why, that's no place for decent people. I can't believe you're actually thinking of living there. Even if your husband has to stay down there because of his work you should come live in town. Take a house here. But don't stay in Bournehills. You don't know what it's like down in those hills. And those people are another breed altogether. You can't figure them out. They're like they're bewitched or something. To tell the truth, I don't even like to think the place exists . . ."

Suddenly she broke off, and her body stiffening, she turned toward the door as the sound of Merle's heels, clattering away like small hoofs on the veranda tiles, drew near. With a look of acute dismay, Enid rose to await her.

Merle entered briskly, still calling over her shoulder to those outside. But as she swung round to face the room she stopped short. For an instant something in her visibly faltered at the sight of the women arrayed on the chairs as though they had been left sitting there since their youth.

"Ladies, how?" she said, and despite her wry, mocking tone, there was sympathy, sadness, and genuine affection in the smile she sent round the room. "How goes it? Still dancing attendance on those unfeeling brutes outside?"—she waved toward the veranda and their husbands. "Daphne, how're you keeping? Millicent, love, I can't ever see you unless I take my life in my hands in the old car and come over this way. Lyris, did you hear we nearly got washed away in the rain last night? But we're still there. Is that Doreen? Why, girl, I thought you were still in America on holiday. . . ."

Speaking in the exaggerated island accent she purposely affected, her voice loud in the dismayed, apprehensive silence that had swept the room, she greeted each of them in turn. And as she had done with the men outside she bent her face for the women to kiss, holding it near to their faces until they reluctantly touched her cheek with their lips. "Don't mind the smell, Beryl," she said to a ruddy-skinned woman in a pink dress who shied away as she brought her face close. "It's only turpentine. I had to turn painter today to get the place ready for my guests."

Standing upright again she chided them, "Do you see," she said, "how people come all the way from big America to stay at my guest-house and I can't get you ladies to come down for even a day. But never mind. I forgive you. All I hope is that you haven't been trying to sabotage my little establishment behind my back by telling the lady from America about the bats and centipedes and the damp, and how when the water is running downstairs you can't get a drop upstairs. I hope you haven't been telling her all that.

"Enid!" she cried, spotting Enid Hutson nearby. "Cousin far removed! The zinnias are lovely."

Her arms opened as though to embrace Enid, she rushed toward her, saying, "You must give me a few to take home with me. We can't grow anything that beautiful in that tired-out Bournehills soil. . . ." Then, coming to a halt just inches away, she dropped her arms with a great clatter of bracelets, and with the cutting yet tender smile, she said, "Oh, love, there's no need to look that way. You won't have to have one of your Merle headaches tonight because I'm going to be on my best behavior out of respect for the lady from America. Where is she hiding, anyway?"

She had glanced quickly across at Harriet upon entering the room, but now she turned and faced her directly, and again she appeared to falter momentarily. She gave what almost seemed a start of recognition. "Why, if you don't put me in mind of someone I knew in England years ago," she said in a wondering, strangely uneasy tone. Then quickly checking herself, she held out her hand. "But you couldn't possibly be anyone else, could you, since you're the professor's wife from America."

Rising, Harriet took the hand thrust at her. "Yes," she said. "That I am. And you must be Mrs. Kinbona."

"Yes," she said, "but don't worry with that Mrs. Kinbona business. That's just a little something left over from my African campaign, the one I lost, and I really shouldn't even be using it anymore. The name's just Merle. And soon it won't even be that. No names. No tags or titles. Just anonymity and silence," she said, speaking so rapidly most of the words were unintelligible and the sense of what she was saying was lost. "Ladies, I'm going to steal the professor's wife for a few minutes. It's all right, she'll be perfectly safe. There's a lovely night outside I think she ought to see. No moon, not a star to be seen, but lovely—soft and black and with a cool wind blowing. I would invite you ladies to come along but I know you have to wait until you get word from the gentlemen outside. Oh, don't worry"—this to Harriet with a laugh—"the ladies don't take me on. They're used to me and my gaff. We were all girls together once. Come, my dear."

Talking the while, she led her from the room and through the crowd outside around to a deserted part of the veranda to the left of the house. Drawing over two chairs, she said, "I hope you don't mind. I just thought you might like to be rescued."

"Not at all," said Harriet. "In fact, I'm very grateful. And it is a lovely night."

They stood quietly for a time at the stone balustrade, gazing out into the darkness that was like a black tent raised high above the house, with its canvas walls blowing gently in the wind and the thick ropes that held it down tugging at the driven stakes. They could smell the mixed fragrances of the flowers in the garden below and, faintly, the rich fecund odor of the soil that fed them, and the smells were those of the night itself, the exhalation of its breath.

"Yes," Merle said, breaking the silence, "it is lovely. This is what we call 'dark night' in Bournehills." Then, taking her seat, she began, "Now about my place. I hope you realized all that talk about the bats and such was mainly for the ladies. They've come to expect that sort of thing from me and I don't like to disappoint them. But the place isn't half bad. Of course, it's not the Banyan Tree Hotel where you're staying now, but at least the sheets are changed twice a week, the food's edible though nothing special, and there's always a drink to be had. There's not much in the way of extras though, unless you count the view of the sea from the house, which is quite breathtaking—although some people find the noise a bit much, and the sea air which is said to cure whatever ails you. But that's all, I'm afraid. Anyway, it should do till you find a place of your own in the village."

"I'm sure we'll be able to manage," Harriet said. "I just hope we won't be taking up too much space. You see we'll probably need one or two extra rooms in which to work."

"Rooms!" she cried. "My dear woman, all I have is rooms! Hardly anyone comes to stay at the place. The local people like the ladies inside feel it's not good enough and the tourists keep to this end of the island and the posh hotels, thank God. Oh, I have a few odd birds who swear by me. There's an old couple from England who come out every year after carnival and some of the minor civil servants who can't do better might spend their holiday there. But most of the time I'm empty, as I am now. In fact, you can rent the whole place if you like and I'll come and live royally in town on the money." At her laugh the saints on her earrings promptly began their stiff dance. "Seriously, I thought I'd let you people have the south wing, which is like a separate house. You could set up shop on the ground floor and live upstairs. Allen I know will want his old room near the garden. And I guess he's told you there's no electricity. But I've got pressure lamps which are almost as good. And there's a kerosene fridge so you can have ice in your drinks. I know you Americans insist on that. Now about the meals . . ."

Harriet's calm remained unshaken throughout the barrage, and giving the woman her carefully drawn, attentive smile, she studied her: the face which struck her as being as dark and impenetrable as the night beyond the balustrade and the rather odd way she was dressed. And she was more than aware of the woman studying her, for she did it quite openly. From time to time she would actually turn completely around in her chair and while still recklessly talking stare at her with the unnerving irritating directness of a child. Those eyes probed her face with such intensity Harriet almost had the impression after a time that the woman was searching for someone else, some other face she sensed lurking there.

"Darling, did you by any chance get to meet the woman who runs the guesthouse in Bournehills?"

It was much later, the reception for them was over, and Lyle Hutson and Enid were seeing the last of the guests to their cars. Harriet as she asked the question was standing alone with Saul at the balustrade on the empty veranda, her arm through his. They were waiting for Lyle to drive them back to their hotel.

"I did," he said.

"Saul, what do you think?"

"I think she needs a goddamn ducking stool, that's what." He spoke harshly, but he was smiling.

"Whatever's that?"

"Oh, an ingenious little device your Puritan forebears invented to deal with the likes of her. It was a chair attached to the end of a long plank. They would strap the local scold in the chair and then dunk her up and down in the village pond till she quieted. Sometimes if she continued to rave like our friend here they'd just leave her down in the water long enough so it didn't matter anymore."

"Oh Saul, that's unkind," she said, laughing.

"Well, you asked me what I thought." At that moment his gaze fell on Merle in the garden below. She was squatting beside the star-shaped bed of zinnias busily cutting a few of the flowers and handing them, tenderly, one by one up to Allen, standing at her side. "You're right," he said and all trace of his smile had vanished. "It was a poor attempt at a joke. Besides, I liked her. She was a refreshing change from the others. God, the middle class is the same the world over. Come on, I see Mr. Hutson waving to us. By the way, he and our garrulous landlady are stopping off for a nightcap with us at the hotel. People around here don't seem to go in much for sleep. Lord, it's been a long day"—and his eyes and the tired droop to his shoulders registered his fatigue—"and from the look of things it isn't over yet."

CHAPTER 6

The large, open-air bar and restaurant of the Banyan Tree Hotel took up the entire ground floor of the building, while the hotel itself, an airily modern glass structure suspended above, appeared to be floating, brightly lighted but insubstantial, somewhere high amid the branches of the magnificent old tree at its entrance from which it had taken its name. In approaching the hotel, which bordered on the sea, one passed through what seemed to be a grove of young trees, saplings with odd twisted trunks. But these were really part of the larger tree: outgrowths that had sprouted long ago as thin brown tendrils from the wide-spread limbs of the banyan, and reaching down over the centuries to take root on their own had lashed themselves together to form slender trunks. The newer sproutings, long tangled tresses that had not as yet reached the ground, hung from the branches like the hair of an old harridan.

The small party from the reception—Merle, Allen, Saul, and Harriet, with Lyle Hutson leading the way—passed through the labyrinth grove. Unnoticed in the distance beyond the tree stood a small crowd of local people—young people for the most. They were watching from behind the tall split-bamboo fence which secured the hotel from its surroundings the activity inside the bar, the dancing and drinking, and listening to the music—standing there invisible, their black faces part of the greater blackness of the night, although from time to time the lights from the hotel caught the white of an eye or the ragged edge of a shirt. "Mr. Hutson!" one of them called in a loud whisper as Lyle and the others passed; and startled, he turned and waved toward the fence.

They were met inside the hotel by the manager and part-owner, an American named Hamilton, a large flaccid man with a deeply tanned, lined face, dyed thinning hair, airy gestures and a foulard scarf artfully arranged at the throat of his cream-colored linen sports jacket. In addition to the Banyan Tree, Hamilton also managed another hotel in the exclusive Crown Beach Colony some miles up the west coast, where the wealthy expatriates from England, Canada, and the United States had their villas, and where he also lived in a seventeenth-century Jacobean manor house which he had had completely restored.

He came hurrying over, his broad flat hips swaying lightly, his arms extended to Lyle Hutson, his smile wide, effusive, and false. "Ah, Mr. Hutson, my very favorite barrister, how nice to see you!" (A few years ago Hamilton had retained Lyle in a case he had brought against one of his yard boys whom he had accused of stealing a gold antique clock from his manor house. The boy had admitted the theft, but had insisted he had taken the clock only because Hamilton had withheld his wages when he had spurned his advances. The case, which Lyle had won, had packed the assizes in New Bristol and dominated the front page of the paper for days. The boy had been given three years.) "You've been very naughty of late, my dear Senator," he said, wagging a finger at Lyle, "and haven't been dropping in as often. And I see you've got Dr. and Mrs. Amron in tow. And Dr. Fuso." Turning to them, he said, "You should consider yourselves very lucky to have met one of the prime movers and shakers of our little island world your first day here."

Signaling for the waiter, he escorted them through the noisy crowd of tourists over to a table at the far end of the bar, where the huge room opened directly onto the beach and the mild Caribbean sea which bounded this side of the island. They could not see the water in the darkness, but they could hear the measured strophe of the waves against the white sand just beyond where they sat.

They had been there only a short time when Dorothy Clough, the wife of the editor at the reception, joined them. "Ah, there you are," she said, making her way toward them through the crowd and going directly over to Lyle Hutson. "For some reason I thought you said you were all going to Sugar's place and I went there first. But you did say the Banyan Tree, didn't you?"

"I did," he said, rising and holding the empty chair beside him for her.

She sat down, and leaning forward greeted the others with her pleasant, open smile. Her face had the same careful detailing as Harriet's, and in this they vaguely, only vaguely, resembled each other, but Dorothy Clough's eyes had more blue to them and her skin and hair were fairer.

"How goes it?" Lyle Hutson said with the smile that seemed affixed like a stamp to his dark face and therefore not really part of it. "Everybody tucked in over your way?"

"Just about," she said. "The children have been in ages ago, of course, and George was just about to turn in when I left. Little Catherine was up though, the nanny tells me, all the time we were at your house. It seems she's coming down with another cold. I shall have to take her in to see Miles Wooding first thing tomorrow. I know you think me silly, darling, but I still can't quite reconcile myself to the fact that people catch colds in the tropics—but there you are. I think I'll have a brandy."

"A brandy it is," he said, and clapped for the waiter.

"By the way, Dr. Amron," she said, turning to Saul her clear gaze, "I must warn you about my husband. He sometimes does very naughty things in that paper of his with what people say, so don't be too surprised at what you might see there in the next day or two about your project."

"Yes, I was afraid of that," he said with a frown. "Thanks for the warning."

"It's just," she said, "that he tends to overstate things a bit, and he loves putting everything in big headlines. He says it helps circulation—which I suppose it does. And I also wanted to tell both you and Mrs. Amron"—she included Harriet in her smile—"that Bournehills isn't nearly as bad as people down this end make out. In fact, I'm enormously fond of the place, even though one doesn't dare say that too loud around here. But whenever I get the chance I pile the children in the car and we take off for the hills and a swim and tea at Merle's. Oh, by the way, Merle, I told Sugar you were in town and he seemed terribly hurt that you hadn't stopped in to say hello."

Merle, sitting with Allen at one end of the small table, had been strangely subdued ever since they entered. She hadn't ceased talking, it was true. But it was in a low undertone, and only to Allen. While talking she had kept her gaze on the tourists—most of them, tonight, Americans—watching them with flat, dull eyes. Her face set, she had listened to their loud, overly gay voices and the laughter which made it seem that they had usurped not only the room and the hotel floating above for their amusement, but the entire island as well. Once, straining forward in her chair, she had peered out the open wall of the bar toward the distant bamboo fence as though seeking the hidden onlookers there, then sat back heavily, the tight look on her face.

Now, at Dorothy Clough's mention of Sugar, she slapped her hand hard on the table and rising, said, "Yes, let's to Sugar's. To hell with Miss Hamilton and his Banyan Tree. Besides"—she turned to Saul and Harriet—"you people aren't officially on the island until you've met Sugar and he's passed on you."

"What is it, some kind of nightclub?" Saul asked.

"You can call it what you like." Her voice was short. "Let's just say it's the one place where in the space of one evening you can see how things stand on this side of the island. That should interest someone setting out to do a study of us, shouldn't it?"

"Yes, I suppose so," he said, doubtful but intrigued.

"Okay, then, let's be off."

Harriet was the first to rise, and something about the way she stood up kept the others in their seats. She had been feeling ever since leaving the reception that the evening had gone on too long, and with the appearance of Dorothy Clough and the exchange between her and Lyle Hutson she had felt this all the more strongly.

"You'll have to forgive me," she said. "But I couldn't possibly go anywhere else tonight. It's been a very exciting and interesting but a very long day and I'm afraid I'm beginning to feel the effects of it. But Saul, you go"—she bent with a brief kiss to Saul beside her—"especially since Mrs. Kinbona thinks it's important that you see the place."

She was about to step away when Lyle Hutson on her other side suddenly reached up and placed his hand lightly on her arm to detain her. "Come now, Mrs. Amron, you can't possibly do this to us," he said, looking up at her with the smile that in its cold sealed quality was, she found, vaguely, disturbingly familiar—whom, she fleetingly wondered, did it call to mind? "We won't permit it. Why, no one ever runs out on a party in Bourne Island this early. And we never end a night out without stopping off to pay our respects to Sugar. Isn't that so, Dorothy?"

"He's right, Mrs. Amron. Do stay."

"Besides," Lyle said, "you're sure to find the place most fascinating. Sugar's, you see, is perhaps the one truly egalitarian institution we have on the island. That is, all types go there. From the P.M. down to the lowliest yard boy. And all shades and colors, castes and classes. All the little distinctions and snobberies that beset us here in Bourne Island are set aside there. It's a place, in other words, Mrs. Amron, where the cats can look with impunity on the kings; and the kings, no matter how badly they misbehave, can come away with their reputations intact."

"It does sound fascinating," she said with a laugh. "But I think I'm still going to forgo it tonight"—and with a movement so subtle it went unnoticed she slipped her arm from his hold.

He gave a resigned wave. "You're determined to desert us, it seems. But one last thing before you dash off," he said, and rose to face her, impeccable in the vested suit, his darkness geting in the way of the light. "You're sure to find life in Bournehills rather difficult to take and will want a rest from it now and again, so please remember that my house is here and that both you and Dr. Amron"—he inclined his head toward Saul—"are to come and spend time with us whenever you like. We have more than enough room as you saw, and Enid loves having guests. Or if you prefer I have a beach house a little farther up this coast which you're welcome to use any time."

"Why, thank you," she said, but she was unreasonably annoyed by his offer. "That's very kind of you. I'll certainly keep it in mind, although I don't anticipate finding life in Bournehills difficult. I'm sure I'll be able to manage." The smile she gave him left no doubt of this. "Darling." She turned to Saul.

"I'll take you up," he said.

"Oh, there's no need. I can find my way."

"Sleep for us both, Hatt," he said.

"I will," she said, and with an impartial nod to the others she left.

"I think maybe I'll turn in, too," Allen said and started up from his chair.

"Oh, no, you don't. Not another soul is leaving till I leave." It was Merle, speaking almost angrily, the tightness still in her face. "But you know I don't understand you sometimes, Allen. When you're in

Rome you do as the bloody Romans do, you know that. You don't go prancing out on people, tired or not tired. The professor here understands that. He hasn't tried to run out on us even though he's probably as tired as any of you. Besides, how do you think Sugar would feel knowing that you were back in the island and hadn't dropped in to say hello. For shame. If you're sleepy, you can sleep there."

Which he did. Seated between her and Saul at a cramped table in a dim corner of the nightclub, he slept, his face inexcusably innocent in sleep, his dark head resting against a large life-size photograph of Sugar Ray Robinson with his gloved fists cocked, every strand of his slicked-down pomaded hair in place and his body bent in the classic prize-fighter's crouch, hanging on the wall behind.

Across the room in a scrap of space that served as a dance floor Lyle Hutson was dancing with Dorothy Clough to the music of a steel-band. The young men in the band, dressed in flame-colored satin shirts that clung to their perspiring bodies like a second skin, were sending the mallets so swiftly over the tuned surfaces of the drums they scarcely seemed to touch. And the music itself merely skimmed the surface of the songs they were playing. Quick, light-hearted, frivolous, then sad and haunting in turn, but always unabashedly romantic, the music reflected the warm enveloping night outside, the murmurous sea and the palms fingering the black sky. Yet, it was somehow hollow at its center, repetitious, a lesser version of some richer, fuller sound.

An assortment of dancers crowded the small floor and spilled over among the tables at its edge. There were sailors from what appeared to be every port in the world; tourists from the Banyan Tree and elsewhere, their eyes unnaturally large and bright, even somehow demented-looking because of their hastily acquired sun tans; young soldiers and technicians from the small air base and missile-tracking station the United States maintained on the remote northern tip of the island—fresh-faced boys, the down still on their cheeks, the milk at the corners of their mouths; and their officers, as well as the officers' wives and daughters, who called to mind Harriet with their bright hair and that extraordinary, clear-eyed wholesome look which made them appear immune to the ills that plague ordinary mankind. Some of the younger women in their efforts to follow the complex rhythms of the dance, were spurring their bodies on in a kind of self-flagellation, their movements forced, desperate, touching, and obscene. Dancing among them with great expertise were the dark girls of

Sugar's, who took up their stations every night at the back tables in the room to wait for the trade.

Rough stevedores from the docks were also to be seen on the jammed floor—huge fellows, their dirty sweat-stained caps pulled low over their eyes and their muscles moving as if oiled beneath their black, glazed skin. And the saga-boys of New Bristol, the touts, pimps, and petty thieves of the town, were everywhere in evidence, dressed in their colorful "hot shirts" which they wore opened down to their navels. Not to be excluded was the more respectable element of New Bristol society, the civil servants, teachers and the like. Even those whom Lyle Hutson had dubbed "the kings," the politicians and professional men like himself, could be glimpsed on the floor, a few of them, at any rate.

Because of the small space and the large numbers of dancers it was almost impossible to tell who was dancing with whom. To someone looking on, it appeared that there were no separate couples or partners, but that all the different bodies, black, brown, white, and the endless variations in between, had merged into a single undifferentiated mass, and the dancers were really one body, the inseparable parts of a whole.

The lighting fixture directly above the dance floor added to this impression. It was one of those large, ornate, multifaceted glass globes usually found in a ballroom which send a series of different-colored lights rippling over the walls and the dancers in a never-ending procession. This one, creaking with the regularity of a metronome as it spun on its axis, swept the dancers below with a phantasma of color: reds like the flame of the votive candles in their ruby-glass holders in a Catholic church, deep cool blues that at times became a primordial black, the tarnished yellow of sunlight trapped in dusty rooms, a macabre smoke-white like the gas that comes drifting off dry ice, and a dark smoldering amber that one imagined could be found only at the heart of a conflagration that had consumed the world. The globe sent these various lights wheeling in a mad round over the dancers on the floor, changing the color of their faces at will and imbuing them, it was to be seen as the evening progressed, with something of its madness.

The room which housed the nightclub was a long, high nave, whole areas of which were lost to the shadows dwelling beyond the reach of the touring lights. It occupied the second story of a former sugar warehouse. The thick stone walls still breathed of the crude sugars and muscovado that had been stored there. Previous to this, long, long ago, the building had been, it was claimed, one of the most famous barracoons in the West Indies. The rusted remains of the iron manacles that had been fitted around the ankles and wrists, around the dark throats, could still be seen, some said, in the walls of the cellar. It had all begun here.

The building stood at the very end of Whitehall Lane, a narrow cobblestone street of cheap, neon-lighted sailors' clubs, rumshops and whore houses which ran the length of the long finger of land that formed one of the extremities of New Bristol's deep bay. The town itself had been so laid out that all its cramped winding streets led eventually to Whitehall and down to the former barracoon-turned-nightclub at its foot. Beyond it lay only the sea and the overarching sky and these were one now in the darkness.

The part of the room within reach of the lights presented a curious spectacle to the visitor to Sugar's for the first time. It resembled a junk shop rather than a nightclub, so filled was it with an assortment of odds and ends. It could have been the dumping ground of the world. All the discards of the nations, all the things that had become worn out over the centuries or fallen into disuse might have been brought and piled in a great charnel heap here.

The rotting beams, the crude shelves set high on the walls, sagged under a vast collection of objects which had either been forgotten or left behind as mementos by former patrons of Sugar's. For the most part they were the things people usually forget at such places—handkerchiefs, summer shawls and stoles, jewelry, wallets, keys, eyeglasses and the like. And all of them had been left strangely unmolested, even though many of the regulars of the club were known thieves. But there was the unexpected also. A plump Buddha, the fat draped in oily folds over his belly, sat unperturbed amid the clutter on a high shelf. Another shelf was crowded with a profusion of cheap religious statuary—virgins and saints and mute suffering Jesuses—in the midst of which lay a broken ram's horn and a toy model of a mosque. A huge Teddy bear like the kind given as prizes on a carnival midway did a clumsy jig from a rafter while a large stuffed bald eagle hovered in mid-air, its spread wings casting their shadow over the entire room and its great hooked beak gleaming blood-red in the ruby-colored light from the revolving globe.

In the shadows high above the patrons' unsuspecting heads a giant kite shaped like a dragon coiled and snapped with each breeze that came drifting off the bay through a line of doors opening onto a balcony. And turned over on its side on a nearby shelf lay a richly carved and painted talking drum, silent now, waiting for a drummer to give it voice.

As to be expected, the walls of the nightclub were decorated with the usual magazine photographs of nudes and pin-up girls. The breasts of the latter, brimming over their scanty bras, mocked those of the hostesses in Sugar's, who were mostly young girls of about sixteen (some looked younger) with small negligible breasts and slight sexless bodies beneath the costumes they wore. The costumes, short, loose, gossamer-thin shifts, appeared to float off behind them as they flitted among the tables with the loaded trays, leaving them bare. In addition, the walls were papered with thousands of letters and cards from patrons who had written to thank Sugar for his hospitality and to ask him to remember them. And the usual graffiti were to be seen scrawled in and among the messages, the obscenities hurled like clods of dung against the crumbling stone. And there were the inevitable drawings of hearts pierced with arrows, and crudely rendered genitalia. In their sweep round the walls the lights even discovered snatches of poems and prayers. Someone had started the Nicene Creed in a drunken hand but had gotten no farther than "I believe in—"

The colored lights passed on, reaching across the thronged dancers to the entrance to the club and the dark stairs leading down, to the bar situated nearby, with its rows of rum and whisky bottles, and, on the plate glass behind the bottles, hundreds of photographs past customers had taken, posing with Sugar—and finally to Sugar himself, the smoking white cone of light singling him out for a moment as he sat before a large, old-fashioned cash register behind the counter.

He could have been an aging sexton in a Negro Episcopal church, some mild, faceless functionary who goes unnoticed in his pew at the back during the Sunday morning service. He could have been a bored banker in a gambling house where no one ever wins. Pitifully small, wizened, his body shrunken, it seemed, by the same mysterious method certain primitive people once used to shrink the bodies of their enemies, he sat like a mummy, a gnome, upon a high stool before the oversized cash register. His tiny ageless face was a neutral, indeterminate beige (all the colors known to man might have come together and been canceled out in him), and it was almost completely hidden under a large green eyeshade he wore. And it was utterly without expression, that face, without features even, and his eyes, what little of them could be seen under the eyeshade, seemed to be contemplating some nothingness that absorbed him totally.

He hardly ever moved. Only when those leaving paused to pay their bill, placing the money before him on the counter, would his abbreviated little arms reach out and, like a croupier's stick, rake in the dollar bills and coins. And he was silent. The room raged around him, the laughter and voices stayed at a pitch, the music leaped from the segmented surfaces of the drums, the glass globe creaked loudly overhead, but Sugar said nothing. Or almost nothing. Because occasionally when someone came up the stairs and greeted him or when one of the customers came over and, leaning across the bar, whispered some request in his ear, he would, without looking at them or stirring on his high stool, utter a deep, hoarse, thrilling "Yeah!" It was the exclamation a jazz musician utters when deeply moved; said the same way—a word, a sound, charged with meaning, encompassing every emotion.

"He's an American, you know," Merle was saying to Saul across Allen, asleep between them at the table. "At least we think so. He's never said. But only an American could say 'yeah' that way. Did you hear him when I introduced you? Isn't it beautiful? He manages to say more with that one word than I do with all my millions. Dear Sugar . . ." Her gaze reached through the smoke and dimness and ever-changing lights to rest fondly on him. "He's one of the few people in this world I truly respect. He's so wise. He knows everyone's little needs, better than they do themselves. And he can arrange anything, you know, no matter what your tastes run to," she said with a smile Saul's way that made him think of a pocketknife snapping open. "Just whisper it in his ear, he says that glorious 'Yeah' and it's done.

"Not that you don't have to pay through the nose! But then he's not like me; he knows how to run a business properly, even though it's rumored that our friend Hamilton over at the Banyan Tree actually owns the place. Ah, Sugar. People tell me (I was in England at the time) that he simply appeared out of nowhere one day with this picture"—she indicated the life-size portrait of Sugar Ray on the wall behind them—"rolled under his arm and not a word about where he had come from or who he was. But I'm certain he was into something illegal. What you Americans call the rackets. Anyway, he came among us. But without even a name, so we decided to call him Sugar after his idol here and because he himself is so sweet and understanding—and also, of course, because that's our one and only natural product, the thing that keeps us going in Bourne Island, that runs in our veins . . . Prick me!" She thrust a dark arm across at him, and as he started back in surprise, she laughed. "Sugar," she cried. "That's what you'd find, Doctor. Not a drop of blood, only a little sugar water. I'm a damn diabetic, and so is everybody else in the place. A nation of diabetics. Every last one of us. Take for example that young miss yonder. A diabetic!" She pointed to a tall, thin, indifferently pretty girl in a colorful skirt puffed up by a score of can-can petticoats, who was sitting with a young officer from the tracking station some distance away. She had hair almost the color and texture of Saul's and skin that was as pale as his except for a rough reddish cast which made it look somewhat chapped.

"She's from a place called Canterbury. You'll see it tomorrow. Everyone up there has the same name and looks the same. We call them Backras, meaning more white than black and poor as the devil. This one had a nice boy liking her, but when he went to America on the labor scheme she turned wild. She wouldn't even take care of the child she had for him and it died.

"And there's old Linton, a diabetic if you ever saw one! Rum has turned every drop of his blood to sugar." Her blunt forefinger singled out a handsome, well-groomed man of about fifty with the bemused unfocused eyes and scarcely perceptible tremor of the quiet alcoholic, drinking alone in a corner. "He was brilliant as a boy," she said, "but had no background as we say, meaning no money or family name to help him, and as luck would have it he missed out on an island scholarship by a few points. Lyle got it that year. Ever since then he's been a collector of bad debts for the big Kingsley department store in town. He comes here straight from work and only goes home in time to change his clothes for work the next day. For every Lyle on this side of the island there's more Lintons than you can bear to think about.

"Ah, and there's young Bertram and his patroness!"

Saul, following the line of her finger to the edge of the dance floor, saw a stout, barrel-chested young man with the suspiciously pampered look to him of the kept man. He was dancing with an intense, auburn-haired woman who was considerably older than he and as white as he was black. The woman, her arm slipped inside the opened front of the shirt he was wearing, was straining him to her on the floor; and as obviously skilled as he was in the intricacies of the calypso they were doing, she was nonetheless leading him through the steps of the dance.

"Young Bertram considers himself our leading Marxist," Merle was saying. "He can quote you more theory than in the whole of *Das Kapital*. He's forever talking about the proletariat taking over and throwing out the foreigners who're sapping our strength as he puts it. He's supposed to be starting his own political party—with money, I guess, from his lady friend, who's got enough to burn I hear. Anyway, that's the present sad state of radicalism over this side. The lady's Canadian, by the way, another one of the expatriates from north of here, up your way, who've decided to throw in their lot with us. We had hoped they would have helped to relieve our diabetic condition, but they've only made it worse.

"There's another one"—the finger shot out. "She's just bought and restored the biggest estate house on the island. That's all the fashion with them these days. They love playing the lord and lady of the manor. This one's dead husband made a fortune in nail polish or some such nonsense and left it to her."

The woman with elaborately dressed lacquered hair and a wealth of heavy gold jewelry heaped upon her aging flesh, whom she indicated, was none other than Uncle Herbie's wife, that mythical character who embodied for Saul the worst that had happened to his people in their eagerness to enter the gaudy, gimcrack dream that was America. Uncle Herbie with his mohair suits, white-on-white shirts, diamond pinky ring, and the thing in his eye which remains ever on guard against the jokes about Moishe and Abe, the insults, the slights; Uncle Herbie with his trafficking in old-law tenements, tainted meats and Florida real estate. Merchant of the shoddy and overpriced. Those who had acceded to doing the goyim's dirty work, thus betraying the history that had spanned centuries, and bringing down on the entire race the wrath of those they were ill-using. He had despised them when there had been passion enough in him to feel that strongly. It had been they, the betrayers, seeing them in New York and, to a lesser degree, L.A., almost as much as America itself, who had driven him out, set him wandering.

"Oh, and you're in luck tonight, Dr. Amron"—he had forgotten the woman, and her voice, crashing in upon his thoughts, jarred him —"because I see one or two of the really big boys here tonight, the chaps who run the banks and businesses, and who, consequently, still run us, even though Lyle and his friends in Legco are supposed to be in charge. They're the real 'kings' if you ask me, although Lyle doesn't like to hear me say so, and the ones directly responsible for the high sugar content of our blood."

He saw them, the solid, moneyed men, their faces flushed from the whisky they were drinking and the heat in Sugar's, which was intense. They were all of them white, some foreigners, but mostly, Merle informed him, Bourne Island whites. Talking steadily, she pointed out a heavy phlegmatic man with skin like scar tissue seated among them. He was, she said, the local representative for the vast Kingsley holdings on the island.

"His name's Hinds," she said. "You're sure to have to meet him since Kingsley owns nearly everything in Bournehills. Nobody can quite figure out how Hinds got such a big job he was such a dunce in school. But then his father, old Neville Hinds, had an 'in' with the Kingsley people."

He noticed then as she went on to describe others at the table that the best seats, those that ringed the tiny dance floor and were directly under the revolving globe, were occupied solely by these men, along with the wealthy expatriates like the bejeweled old woman, the tourists and the military. (He saw—and had to quickly look away from—the commander of the missile-tracking station, a bulky, thick-set, very drunk colonel in full uniform, his war medals winking in the circling lights, who was sitting with one large, freckled hand on the shoulder and trailing down near the breast of one of the hostesses, whom he had pulled to his lap as she was passing with a tray of drinks.) Everyone else, including even those local people of Lyle Hutson's standing, were seated as if by tacit agreement or long tradition in the area beyond the choice seats.

"As for that bunch out on the balcony," she was saying, and her voice, as well as the unrelenting smile she kept fixed on him, had tightened. The mood that had come over her in the hotel bar had taken possession of her again. "Not a boy child over the age of three is safe since they arrived on the island."

He had no need to look where she was pointing. He had already taken in the scene on the balcony of the nightclub, which stood out over the darkened sea and the rocks shoring up the building below. It was crowded with men, most of them from the exclusive Crown Beach Colony. The younger ones had the lean tensile look, some of them, of finely bred racehorses and flawless sun tans that might have been produced by a sun lamp rather than the sun; the older ones were more or less versions of the man Hamilton at the Banyan Tree. And they had the overstated gestures of their kind, as well as the unnaturally high voices that called attention to themselves and the laugh that was as shrill and sexless as a eunuch's, and which never ceased. It issued from the balcony in a steady, terrifying, utterly mirthless obbligato to the music within and the lisping of the water on the rocks below.

"And just look at my girl playing Cleopatra to that old Caesar over there. *Look!*" she cried, her voice taut with a rage she could no longer contain as his gaze remained bent on his glass. And he obeyed after a moment, glancing over—but again only briefly—at the bemedaled colonel who, his hand still on the girl, had forced her, still holding the tray of drinks, onto the floor at his feet.

"Another diabetic! Both of them if you ask me, because the disease has a way of infecting those of our visitors who remain with us any length of time. His wife, by the way, sleeps regularly with a chap in the steelband. Tit for tat. As for the young miss, I knew her when she was no higher than so. She comes from . . ."

He would have stopped her here if he thought it possible and told her, if he believed for a moment that it would have made any difference, that he was no stranger to such scenes, no innocent, no Allen asleep between them. He had seen girls younger than these, virgins, literally sold into brothels in Latin America to help earn the family bread; and he knew only too well how his countrymen, with whom he felt no kinship whatsoever, could behave when away from home. He would have liked, in other words, to spare her the pain of saying all this, for he could see how that pain and outrage had laid waste to her face. He would have advised her, if he thought for a minute she would listen, that it was sometimes necessary to seal up the heart as he had done and live as best as one could in the midst of it all. He was even willing at this point to raise his hand and assume responsibility for the ugliness taking place in the room; to say, if it would silence her, that no, he was no different or better than the colonel, and that before, at the reception when he had happened to glance into the drawing room and had seen some of the younger women there, their skins, that incredible range of rich browns and blacks with the undertones of red, yellow, and tan which the bright lights brought to life, he had felt briefly, fleetingly, the all-too-familiar stirring within him, that sensation as of some weighty creature he harbored in the hollow of the groin, turning over voluptuously in its bed there, beginning to rouse, and for a moment he had been swept by the old aimless desire and lust, the longing to touch and penetrate, which was never far from his thoughts. He was willing, in other words, to confess his part in it all.

But that would do little good, he knew. There was nothing he could say that would satisfy and silence her. The finger would continue to stab round the room, impaling both stranger and kinsman on its stubbed end. Thrust forward across the table, the silver earrings setting off her blackness, her eyes reflecting each of the lights in turn, she would continue to tell him about them in the voice that seemed committed to its own end, and to flash at him the wide white smile that pressed up against the soft flesh of his middle like a knife.

And it didn't appear that she could help herself. She might have been condemned to tell the tale—and something in her eyes, a doomed, obsessed glint, did put him in mind of the old mariner in the poem he had read as a boy. She, too, might have been witness to, victim of, some unspeakably inhuman act and been condemned to wander the world telling every stranger she met about it. He was simply the wedding guest she had accosted for tonight. There was nothing for him to do then but play his part and listen. And he continued to do so, attending to her with a scrupulously objective, professional air which he could see galled her and fed her scarcely suppressed anger; dutifully he followed her finger around the room but remained outwardly unaffected, unamazed, no matter what he was shown. And from time to time he drank deeply from the rum in his glass to blunt the thrust of her smile.

The floor show had begun meanwhile. The slight hostesses, looking like children who had been kept up past their bedtime in their filmy shifts, their faces bored and childishly sullen, their eyes without expression, fixed, like Sugar's, on the same nothingness, were performing out on the cleared dance floor under a beam of white light from the globe, which had come to a halt overhead. They were doing their own derisive version of the latest American dance craze and as they twitched and wiggled to the music and bumped and ground their bony torsos, the sheer costumes slowly fell away to reveal the strippers' spangled discs pasted onto the nippleless cones of their tiny breasts and the scrap of V-shaped cloth tied across their narrow hips, back and front.

With the shifts lying in little gossamer heaps at their feet, they suddenly rushed out into the room squealing like schoolgirls at dismissal time, and began dancing in the cramped spaces between the tables, their lean, as yet unformed bodies twisting and gyring, their eyes enormous and empty in their impassive faces. "Do you want this or do you want that . . . ?" they chanted in unison from every corner of the club, and their flat, singsong voices turned the offers they were making of their various parts into a mockery. "Touch me here, touch me there, touch me everywhere!" they screamed tonelessly, and eager hands reached out to sample the dark flesh only to find it gone. "Post post your letter in my pouch!" they shrilled as in some child's game and holding open slightly the strip of cloth across their hips they presented the customers—in what was a scarcely veiled insult—with their behinds which were as small and tight and tucked in at the cleft as young boys'.

"You wish to post a letter?" a girl snapped at Saul over her shoulder.

He mutely shook his head. He could not even bring himself to glance up at the thin face with its look of undisguised insolence thrust at him over her shoulder. With a suck of her teeth the girl flounced on to the next customer, and on the other side of the sleeping Allen, Merle, who had been watching him with the smile all along, threw back her head and laughed.

Angry then, he wanted to turn and tell her, to shout it at her, that he preferred his strippers, if he had to have them at all, to be large standard blondes—Aryans—with ripe, used bodies and some degree of professionalism, and that he found nothing to arouse him in these sullen-faced, undernourished adolescents. He had no daughters he desired. What would have been a daughter, whom he might have obscurely, unknowingly, desired when she was the age of these girls, had issued dead and barely formed—a bloody mass of tissue and soft bone—from its mother's womb months before its time, and, in its abortive birth, had caused the mother to die also. . . . And as always happened when he allowed his guard to drop and thoughts of that dead wife and child and all that had died with them came rushing in, he felt utterly weary, used up, an old man with no real proof that he had lived.

He wanted to leave, to rise abruptly and without a word walk out —out of the room and its ugliness and, above all, away from this woman who had not learned how to live with her bitterness and pain, how to control and disguise her rage; and who, moreover, insisted on holding every stranger accountable. He wanted the hotel room and

Harriet, his rare find of a wife—poised, contained, beautifully self-assured—whom he would always be a little in awe of; and, if she was awake when he came in, love in a strange bed with all the lights on, release within her white slender loins. And then sleep, a blank sleep that like a line drawn through a sentence on a page would cancel out this night.

As if she had divined his wish the woman suddenly leaned across and, clamping a hand on his arm, called his attention to a boy of perhaps eighteen, his black body greased so it glistened, his handsome face a heavily made-up mask, his eyes rimmed with kohl, who had joined the girls cavorting around the room. Dancing with considerably more restraint, he wove among the crowded tables, making the same offers as the girls but with an arch, inviting smile, and all the while swinging the short ballerina skirt he was wearing, which scarcely hid the instrument of his manhood dangling limp and perverted there, almost in the face of the customers as he whirled by. He vanished out onto the balcony, and the ecstatic howl that went up threatened to send the shaky wooden structure crashing down onto the rocks. As he danced back into the room the men outside rushed in a body to the doorway to pelt him with coins.

Through it all Sugar sat on his high stool at the bar, silent, apart, totally uninvolved with the goings-on in the room, absolved. Lyle Hutson had returned meanwhile (he had left the club some time ago to take Dorothy Clough home) and was sitting drinking steadily beside Merle. Raising his glass to Saul at one point he said, "Ah, Dr. Amron, you're still with us, I see. You haven't allowed Merle's tongue to get the better of you. Good show!"

And Merle, determined, it seemed, to send him fleeing from the room with his hands clapped over his ears, did not relent. She was giving him now the life history of the young man in the flared skirt: ("I remember him when he was just a small boy from the country") and her voice, whipped on by her laughter which came in short stinging bursts, pursued its fatal downward course, seeking to take him with it.

By now the music of the steelband had reached a furious pitch as the players sent their mallets racing in a blur over the converted oil drums; and the huge globe of lights which had started spinning again when the girls broke for the room was racing also, the varicolored lights careering over the walls at breakneck speed—now red, now white, now blue that was at the same time black, now the crazed fiery amber that would spell the end. Spurred on by the music and the whirling lights, the dozen or so girls and the one youth began dancing with greater abandon, the girls staging what looked to be an adolescent riot in the room as they leaped onto the tables to dance, spinning like dervishes there for a second or two, and then bounded down again, leaving a trail of spilled drinks and overturned ash trays in their wake. And they didn't spare the customers in their wild leap from table to table, but clambered over them at will, savagely trampling their feet and poking their bony elbows into their eyes, openly assaulting them, and the delighted customers pleaded for more, begged them to come back. Soon, nearly the entire room had joined the mauling dance, the tourists, the technicians and soldiers from the tracking station, the saga-boys and whores of New Bristol, the sailors bellowing drunkenly, the clear-eyed, pink-skinned officers' wives and daughters cleaving to the black, sweating bodies of the stevedores—all of them rampaging through the nightclub at the same frenzied speed as the music and the insanely flashing lights. And it had lost all semblance of a dance. It was more even than one of those spectacular brawls sometimes to be seen in such places. The locked, writhing bodies appeared caught up in violent combat, with the room, divided as it was between great areas of shadow and light, serving as an arena the size of the world.

Outside on the balcony the screams of laughter had been taken to a new and terrifying high, and sounded now like the cries of the lost and anguished ringing through an empty cosmos, addressed to someone who had long since ceased to listen. Inside, Merle's voice and her own anguished laugh were fists striking at Saul's heart, demanding that he open it again, and at his eyes—the strangely numb, deeply hooded eyes which in their colorlessness looked almost blind at times —demanding that he open them also.

And then at the very height of the uproar, when there was no greater level to which the noise could be taken, Lyle Hutson slowly raised his glass and, with his sealed, self-mocking smile in place, sonorously began intoning the stately opening to *The Aeneid* against the din: " '*Arma virumque cano,*' " he quoted, his gaze a little blurred, so that he vaguely called to mind the man Linton quietly drunk in his corner, " '*Troiae qui primus ab oris . . .*' "

BOOK

II

BOURNEHILLS

CHAPTER 1

It was odd what happened to their sense of distance on the trip out to Bournehills. The island, which had been nothing more than a tiny blemish on the smooth, tight skin of the sea when Harriet first sighted it from the plane, a place to be covered on foot in less than a day, seemed almost vast now. Perhaps it was because the road they were traveling, a narrow winding corridor cut through the endless cane fields covering the breast of the land, not only appeared to be lengthening as they advanced, but to be taking them deep into the dense green heart of the island, into another time. Or because the canes themselves, bright lances brandishing in the wind and so tall, now that they were ripe, those in the car could not see over them, gave the impression of stretching endlessly away on both sides of the road. The entire world, as Vere had said speaking to Leesy of Florida, might have been planted in them.

"Humph, they're going to have a good crop over this side," Merle said, glancing out the window to her right. She had interrupted herself, for she had been talking in her usual helpless fashion, which seemed somehow necessary: it was the talk, you sensed, which alone sustained her. Saul had come to understand this in part the night before when, with dawn separating the sea from the sky beyond the balcony and Sugar busy counting the night's receipts in the emptying club, her voice had slowly run down into silence like a Victrola that needed winding and she had fallen asleep, her head coming to rest beside Allen's on the giant photograph of Sugar Ray on the wall. He had seen in her face then clear evidence of the fact that she was almost to the edge. Perhaps all that was keeping her from giving way completely was that steady verbal outpouring. ". . . And if I was to ever stop talking that'd be the end of me." She had said it. And seeing the truth of this in her sleeping face he had silently asked her forgiveness for the joke about the ducking stool at the reception and for wanting to walk out on her at the night club. Reaching over, he had slipped the lighted cigarette from between her fingers and then along with Lyle Hutson had half-carried, half-led her from the room, with Allen following sleepily behind. Once in the car she had awakened and her voice had promptly taken up where it had left off.

It filled the shabby Bentley now, adding its weight to the heat and the strong, cut-grass smell of the canes pouring in at the windows. She was ostensibly talking to Allen, seated next to her in front, still bringing him up to date on events in Bournehills: (". . . and did I write you, Allen, about the jukebox from America they installed in Delbert's shop which only lasted a day? And the Oxford debates are on there every night as usual, with our old friend Fergy holding forth about Cuffee Ned when he's had in his grogs. Delbert's expecting you and the doctor to come over tonight, by the way. And did I tell you . . .") but her voice also reached back to include Saul and Harriet behind, and occasionally, craning her neck, she glanced at them in the rear-view mirror to make sure they were listening.

Harriet had carefully divided her attention between Saul beside her (she was concerned that he had gotten no sleep last night), Merle in front, the green fleeting landscape outside, and her own thoughts. She was quietly going over in her mind the night that had just passed, puzzling over it a little. She had gone immediately to bed after leaving the others in the hotel bar and had slept soundly, only to be awakened near dawn by what she thought was a hand resting lightly on her arm. Thinking it was Saul she had turned, smiling languorously in the direction from which the touch had come, her arms opening to receive him. But she had found the place beside her empty, and when, startled, she had leaned over and turned on the bedside lamp, she had discovered that the room was also empty. And she had remembered then Lyle Hutson placing his hand on her arm in the bar to detain her, and how when she had glanced down somewhat disconcertedly (she was not used to having comparative strangers touch her) at that black hand, she had had the impression, strange and fleeting and scarcely conscious, that it was not his hand resting on her, or any part of him, but rather some dark and unknown part of herself which had suddenly, for the first ever, surfaced, appearing like stigmata or an ugly black-and-blue mark at the place he had touched.

Turning off the light she sat up in the bed, her hair falling instantly into place as she did so. And alone in the predawn room which appeared to be nesting in the branches of the banyan tree just outside the window, she had, in her typical way, emptied her mind of all thought of that hand and of the odd, unsettling impression it had evoked. A short time later Saul returned, and her voice as she called across to him at the door was light, playful, completely herself.

"Well," she said with a laugh, "that's my luck, a night owl for a husband. I was just thinking, darling, of getting dressed and rejoining the party."

"Go ahead," he said grumpily, making his way over to the bed in the half-light. "It's still going strong. When I left, they were on their way over to Lyle Hutson's beach house for breakfast and a swim, dragging poor Allen along with them." He dropped onto the bed with a groan.

"Oh, no!" she cried. "How do they do it? Don't they need to sleep like ordinary human beings? Poor Saul. I should have insisted that you leave with me."

Moving over to where he sat with his back to her on the edge of the bed, she slipped her arms around him. She held him against her for a long time and then, very quietly, asked, "And what was the indispensable Sugar's all about?"

"Oh, just some damn miserable dive that seems to be the 'in' place around here."

"What do they do there?"

He started to tell her. He even drew his breath to speak. But remembering the scene in the nightclub, recalling the way the woman's finger had swung round the room like the restless needle of a compass, hearing again her helplessly enraged voice, the breath collapsed inside him. Turning to Harriet, he brought his face down into the warm, scented cleft between her breasts. "Don't ask," he said, shaking his head as if to rid it of the memory. "Don't ask."

After a time he touched her, her face first, his fingers slowly searching out each feature as though he needed to be reassured that it was she; then, as slowly, he traced with the backs of his fingers the line of her chin and throat down to her breast. His hand came to rest there. "Is it all right?" he asked. "I'm more than a little drunk and I probably smell to high heaven of that place."

"Yes," she said. "You know it is."

"You'll have to do most of it," he said. "I'm too beat."

"Yes. Oh, yes."

"Turn on the lights then. I want to see you."

"Thank you," she said, turning to him now in the back seat of the Bentley, "for the hat." She held up the straw hat he had bought her. But he understood her other meaning, saw in her gaze the memory of that early morning embrace with the lights on, and smiled. "You were right," she said, speaking below the racing surface of Merle's voice. "I am going to need it in this sun. Oh, Saul, you're exhausted!"

"Yep," he said, "I guess I could do with a little sleep."

"Sleep? Sleep? Who's that back there complaining he's sleepy?" Merle said, straining up to look at him in the mirror. "You see that, you should have come with us to Lyle's for a swim and breakfast and I bet you'd feel now as if you had slept the night. I do. Don't you, Allen?"

Allen, his overstuffed briefcase nestled between his feet on the floor and holding on his lap, in a jar of water, the zinnias she had picked from Lyle Hutson's garden, said, "Not exactly, but the swim helped." He had exchanged his bulky professorial tweeds for a short-sleeved white shirt open at the throat, and a pair of rugged Bavarian-style shorts—and he looked suddenly free, unbound.

"How you mean!" Merle cried, her gaze still on Saul in the mirror. "Of course, it helped. A swim, some breakfast, a rum punch or two afterward and you come like new again. That's how we keep going in this place, Dr. Amron."

He said nothing, simply returned her look in the mirror. But she must have glimpsed his annoyance for she said, sheathing her smile, "Look, don't mind me. You've got every right to be tired after the night you put in with those half-mad people at Sugar's, yours truly included. And you did all right for yourself, you know. You held up better than I thought you would. So sleep, soul," she said, and for a second her dark strained face, her eyes, betrayed an exhaustion far more profound than his. "Sleep. We'll be there soon and you'll be able to get a proper rest."

With that she sent the car swerving round a sharp turn in the road, and through a sudden break in the high wall of canes they saw that they had been climbing all along without being aware of it. The broad sweep of open country through which they had just traveled, with its neat orderly fields, tiny villages and great sugar mills, with New Bristol moored at its southern end, lay below them in the distance. And now as the cane fields lining the road began to drop back as the land sloped sharply up, they were within view of the sea for the first time. Wide, smooth, reproducing faithfully the unflawed blue of the sky, glittering with gold snatched from the sun, it bridged the two ends of the land and meeting with the sky at the horizon sealed off the island from the rest of the world.

The moment the sea appeared behind them, two royal palms, looking like pylons, suddenly rose up ahead in the fields on each side of the steep road. Tall, incredibly straight, their fronds tossing in the wind like the headdress of a Tutsi warrior, the trees crowned the high ridge called Cleaver's which marked the ascension of the land. As Merle spurred the car up the sheer lift to the top, the palms stepped swiftly toward them, growing taller as they advanced. At the top the road ran level for a brief stretch across the narrow spine of the ridge, then suddenly took a dangerous swerve and dropped—and the plain, that lovely reassuring pastoral, vanished as if it had never been, the two tall palms stepped majestically out of sight behind, and there, without warning, were the hills.

"Bournehills!" Merle announced, and pulled over to the shoulder. "Bournehills Valley District to be correct. 'Sweet Beulah Land.' Anyone know the hymn? Home, eh, Allen?" She tossed him a fond smile. "Dr. Amron, are you awake back there?" Her gaze sought him in the mirror. "Take a good look, then."

The whole of Bournehills could be seen from this height, all the worn, wrecked hills that appeared to be racing en masse toward the sea at the eastern end; and which, from a plane, looked like the crude seats of some half-ruined coliseum, where an ancient tragedy was still performed. And as usual, because of the thick haze which made the landscape waver and lose shape before the eye, and the sunlight spilling down like molten steel from the lip of the sun, the entire place looked almost illusory, unreal, a trick played by the eye.

It looked strangely familiar to Saul. He had gotten out of the car along with Harriet and Allen, leaving Merle behind, and was standing gazing around him on the sharply inclined shoulder of the road—and thinking that he had surely been here before. He was certain he had. Perhaps, he quickly told himself, it was because the place somehow, for some reason, brought to mind other areas up and down the hemisphere where he had worked. It resembled them all, not in physical detail so much, but in something he sensed about it as his eyes, half-closed against the glare, roamed slowly over the patchwork hills to the sea and back again. Bournehills, this place he had never seen before, was suddenly the wind-scoured Peruvian Andes. The highlands of Guatemala. Chile. Bolivia, where he had once worked briefly among the tin miners. Honduras, which had proved so fatal. Southern Mexico. And the spent cotton lands of the Southern United States through which he had traveled many times as a young graduate student on his way to do field work among the Indians in Chiapas. It was suddenly, to his mind, every place that had been wantonly used, its substance stripped away, and then abandoned. He was shaken and angered by the abandonment he sensed here, the abuse. And he felt this in spite of the occasional field he saw lying like a green scatter rug on a slope. These fields only served to make more eloquent those places which were completely bald, where the depleted soil could no longer even sustain a little scrub or devil grass to disguise what had been done to it. Moreover, the place, these ragged hills crowded out of sight behind the high ridge, with the night hiding in their folds, even seemed, suddenly, to hold some personal meaning for him, his thoughts becoming complex, circular, wheels within a wheel as he stood there. Bournehills could have been a troubled region within himself to which he had unwittingly returned.

Harriet had come over to stand next to him, and taking her arm he drew it through his and pressed it to his side. He was suddenly not only glad that he had given in on the question of her accompanying him on the trip and brought her along, but grateful as well for her calm, her cool touch, her lovely unruffled air, her certainty. He would need them now that he had decided to have a go at life again.

"It's quite some sight," he said.

"Yes, isn't it," she said, a hand shading her eyes, which were slightly overcast. She was remembering her own disturbing impression of Bournehills from the plane yesterday, of its being some unexplored landscape having nothing to do with a physical place as such. It looked even more so close-up.

"Well, I guess you see you've got your work cut out for you," Merle said to Saul when they returned to the car. And oddly enough it was said quietly and without the usual edged smile.

"Yes," he said. "Looks like it."

The journey resumed. Merle, tensed over the steering wheel, her feet working the pedals, goaded the balky car up the steep lifts, down the sudden drops and, from time to time on the sudden sharp turns in the road, almost sent it colliding head-on (or so it seemed to the others who were not used to driving on the left side of the road) into an oncoming car or lorry. And all the while her voice kept pace with the spinning wheels and the noon sun traveling with them across the clear sweep of sky. One arm out the window, the silver bracelets singing their dissonant tune as she gestured, she called their attention to nearly every tree and stone in the disheartening landscape; she announced the name of every hill they passed—Agincourt, Buckingham, Sussex, Lords, Drake—and she did so proudly, as if despite their near-ruin they were still somehow beautiful to her.

"Pyre Hill," she called out, and, bringing the car to a lurching halt, pointed across a wide, almost level field of canes flaunting their vivid green against the drabness to a hill perhaps a half mile off. It stood a blackened heap against the blue unclouded sky—an awesome sight, which held the eye even when you tried looking away. The hill appeared to have been almost totally destroyed by some recent fire. It might have only just stopped burning. You expected to see the last of the smoke drifting up from its charred sides, from its crest, blurring the air around it; and to feel the heat from it against your cheek. The ground, you were certain, would still be hot underfoot.

"It's something to see, yes," Merle said and her voice held the awe of someone viewing it for the first time. "Cuffee Ned did it. He sent the whole thing up in flames during a little fracas we had down here sometimes back—back," she repeated with a laugh, "in the days when the English were around here selling us for thirty pounds sterling. You wouldn't think it, but one of the biggest estate houses on the island used to be right on top that hill. People say it stood like a castle there. It belonged to Percy Bryam, the man who owned all of Bournehills and everyone in it in the beginning. People used to have to get down on their knees when he passed. Bryam's Castle they called it. But I know Cuffee put a match to it one night," she said. "The entire hill up in flames now! Castle and all. The very sky that night was on fire, they say"—and as she turned to the two in back, her eyes seemed to reflect the yellow edge to those flames. "And do you know that hill burned for five years. That's right," she insisted, at the skeptical look Saul gave her. "For five long years, the books say—long after Cuffee Ned was dead and the revolt put down, the old hill continued to burn."

Then, reflective suddenly, speaking largely to herself: "The Pyre Hill Revolt! There was never anything like it before or since. It's the only bit of history we have worth mentioning on Bourne Island, even though I'm always getting into trouble for saying so. Tell them about it for me, Allen"—and turning back to the wheel she sent the car plunging ahead.

With the blackened hull of Pyre Hill accompanying them part of the way, Allen obediently told them the story of the revolt, sitting half-turned around in his seat and speaking in his scrupulously objective manner. According to the historical accounts, he said, the Pyre Hill Revolt had been the largest and most successful of the many rebellions that had taken place on the island. Under the leadership of Cuffee Ned, the slaves had not only, he told them, fired the hill and the surrounding cane fields and captured Percy Bryam, who had died shortly afterward yoked to the mill wheel at Cane Vale, where he had been tied and tortured, but they had also, with weapons raided from the arsenal atop Cleaver's, driven back the government forces in a fierce battle there and sealed off the ridge—and then for over two years had lived as a nation apart, behind the high wall, independent, free.

"And who again was the brains behind it, Allen?" Merle said the moment he was finished. "Who the instigator, organizer, mastermind, the one who personally marched old Bryam with a knife to his throat to the mill wheel, who sent the regiment high-tailing it back to town, who ran things in Bournehills for upward to three years? None other than Cuffee Ned. The only real hero we've ever had around here. Dear Cuffee," she said quietly. Then: "I'm afraid they got him in the end though. Yes." She nodded, and the saints framing her saddened face shivered. "They took his head off and left it for all to see on a tall pike along Westminster Low Road. I'll show you the place when we come to it.

"You know," she began again after a moment, "sometimes strangers to Bournehills wonder why we go on about Cuffee and Pyre Hill when all that happened donkeys' years ago and should have long been done with and forgotten. But we're an odd, half-mad people, I guess. We don't ever forget anything, and yesterday comes like today to us. You'll see," she said, pulling away just in time as a lorry piled high with a load of freshly cut canes came barreling toward them around a curve.

As they penetrated deeper into Bournehills, people began to appear, and Merle, her hand out the window, waved to them all—to those walking in what appeared slow motion along the road who took their time stepping out of the way of the onrushing car, to the occasional black indistinct figure of a woman or child standing outside one of the listing sun-bleached shacks scattered high on the slopes, and to the seemingly static forms of the men and women working in the fields under the overseeing eye of the sun. And everywhere they returned her greeting. Pausing in the fields or along the road they would slowly raise their right arm like someone about to give evidence in court, the elbows at a sharp ninety-degree angle, the hand held stiff, the fingers straight. It was a strange, solemn greeting encompassing both hail and farewell, time past and present.

"Westminster Low Road dead ahead," she announced and pointed to the place where it was said the dead hero's head had been exhibited on its tall pike. Mr. Douglin, the old man from yesterday, was there, wearing his patched denims and wide-brimmed straw hat, and wielding his cutlass with the same loving care over what looked to be the same square of grass. As Merle hailed him he lifted the long knife in reply and the empty holes that served as his eyes glanced briefly their way from under the hat.

A few yards farther on she again brought the car to a halt, this time in the midst of a work gang that was repairing the break in the road.

"Oh, crime," she said, and switched off the motor. Her hands slid to her lap, and a look of unimaginable despair swept her face and caused her body to slump as she gazed silently out at the men and women working there.

As if unaware of the car parked in their midst they continued at their tasks, the women ferrying over large bucketfuls of crushed stones on their heads from a pile nearby and then sowing them like seed over the prepared roadbed, the men spreading the mixture of stone dust and water used to cement the stones and then sealing down the road with flat, long-handled metal tampers. They went about the work at the same slow, almost dreamlike pace as the figures walking along the road or harvesting in the fields.

Finally, after some minutes, they paused, and flicking away the perspiration from around their eyes, they turned to those in the car faces that were eloquent of their life upon the ravaged land, that evoked for Saul a host of other faces he had known down the years—Indian, mestizo, black—which had held the same look. They were smiling faintly at Merle, the smiles soft against their blackness, beautifully controlled and knowing: they knew, it was clear, what was coming and were prepared. They said nothing, though, nor did they betray any curiosity about the others with her, but simply stood there under the sun, which had come to a halt overhead when the car stopped, their bare feet rooted in the crushed stones and dust.

"Could you tell me, please, just what it is you're doing?" Merle spoke at last, and her voice was so quiet she would not have been heard but for the silence.

They didn't answer, but the smiles widened slightly, taking on a sly, conspiratorial edge.

"Hyacinth Weekes," she called in the quiet tone to a tall broad-shouldered woman who stood with her filled bucket balanced easily on her head and her thick arms akimbo.

"Yes, please," the woman said, looking off.

"What are you doing?"

"To tell you the truth, Mis-Merle, I couldn't rightly say."

There was a mild stir of laughter like a shy wind moving close along the ground. Their eyes remained turned aside.

"Desmond Vaughan, could you tell me what you're doing?"

The gaunt man in a tattered shirt she addressed was one of the many Vaughans in Bournehills remotely related to her.

"How you mean," the man said, not without a touch of impatience. "I'm here trying to fix up this piece of old road so you'll have someplace to drive that big car of yours."

Amid the suppressed laughter she said in the ominously calm voice, "But Desmond, you know better than me this road's not going to hold. The next good rain and it'll pick up and march off like all the others. You've got to use asphalt or concrete or something so, not just a few chewed-up stones and spit. You know that. And you need a steam roller, not just that flatiron I see in your hand. And there should be gabions at the sides to hold it in place. You know that."

"Is true," he said, unruffled. This might have been a familiar exchange.

"Mr. Innis!" She had turned to call to the supervisor of the crew, a drawn, aloof figure of uncertain age, wearing a threadbare bush jacket and plus fours that looked as if they had been handed down endlessly, and a worn cork hat to shield him from the sun. He stood scowling against the glare to one side of the road, his body propped on a gnarled length of wood whittled from the slender branch of a tree which he was using as a shooting stick. He saluted, two black fingers touching his hat brim.

"Where's the asphalt? Where're the gabions?" Her voice was rapidly losing its false calm.

He gave a chiding smile that said she should know better than to ask. "Well, Mis-Merle, we hasn't gotten around yet to those newfangled things here in Bournehills."

She began shouting then, her voice pitched to the high drumming of the afternoon heat and the strident hum of the insects hidden everywhere. "But what is it with us in this place, will you tell me?" she cried. "Who put us so? Is it that we can't change or we refuse to or what . . . ?"

The car leaped forward, the loose stones exploding under its wheels and Mr. Innis and his crew, their hands calmly raised in the solemn stiff-arm greeting that was also farewell, disappeared in a moiling cloud of white dust. Brutally she gunned the Bentley up the steep road to Westminster's summit, her swollen silence replacing the sound of her voice in the car and embarrassing the others so that they kept their gaze out the windows. As they climbed the twisting white marl road, the two crudely fashioned peaks which crowned the hill rose slowly before their eyes like stalagmites that would continue to grow until they had pierced the sky. The public buildings appeared, a blinding Mediterranean white in the noon glare, with the almshouse where she worked part time dominating the others. And suddenly, her mood changing, she laughed, and putting on her sunglasses, said, "What am I upsetting myself about anyway, will you tell me? Mr. Innis and his old road will be here long after I'm gone. Right, Allen?" She tapped his bare knee; then, with a wave to the idiot, Seifert, who stood in his shapeless blue smock at the almshouse gate staring up into the sun, she sent the car plunging down the precipitous drop into the village of Spiretown, wedged between the broad foot of the hill and the sea beyond.

The two in back could distinguish little of the village because of the rapid way she drove through it. They had a fleeting impression of a long, almost unbroken line of small, badly weathered wooden houses that were little better than shacks strung out along an arrow-straight road that appeared to be taking them head-on to the sea about a half-mile ahead. Through the mournful gray dust churned up by the car which set the theme of the land here, they glimpsed occasional figures standing like statues carved out of basalt along the way, their hands raised in the silent, formal salute in answer to Merle's wave. They spied a few brown, pot-bellied sheep grazing on what looked to be barren ground, a pig rooting absently in the open drain that lined the road on each side, and here and there a few testy thin-necked fowl who refused to give way until the car was almost upon them, and then squawking indignantly, quickly goose-stepped out of its path.

Toward the end of the village where the houses began to thin, the stretch of straight road suddenly broke off and veered right and they found themselves jolting over a narrow, unsurfaced track mined with stones and potholes. The landscape here had been stripped to its barest essentials. To their right reared a dark brooding spur of Westminster Hill which had curved around the village in a wide arc to slope gradually to the sea; to their left stood a row of low sandhills thrown up by the wind and covered in sea grape and sedge; beyond these lay the sea itself.

It was the Atlantic this side of the island, a wild-eyed, marauding sea the color of slate, deep, full of dangerous currents, lined with row upon row of barrier reefs, and with a sound like that of the combined voices of the drowned raised in a loud unceasing lament—all those, the nine million and more it is said, who in their enforced exile, their Diaspora, had gone down between this point and the homeland lying out of sight to the east. This sea mourned them. Aggrieved, outraged, unappeased, it hurled itself upon each of the reefs in turn and then upon the shingle beach, sending up the spume in an angry froth which the wind took and drove in like smoke over the land. Great boulders that had roared down from Westminster centuries ago stood scattered in the surf; these, sculpted into fantastical shapes by the wind and water, might have been gravestones placed there to commemorate those millions of the drowned.

"Talk about a sea, yes," Merle said softly and slowed the car to a crawl. "Have you ever seen anything like it?"

For a time they sat silently looking at it through a break in the sandhills. "I had forgotten how loud it is," Allen said, and his hushed tone expressed the awe the others felt. As they watched, a huge white-crested breaker which looked as if it had been gathering force and power and speed across the entire breadth of the Middle Passage broke with the sound as of some massive depth charge on the most distant of the reefs. Saul, feeling the thunderous impact in the chambers of his heart, suddenly remembered how, during the war, he used to feel the earth shudder and recoil under him as the bombs struck. Beside him Harriet thought briefly for the first time in a long time, of the terrifying explosion that had rocked her sleep every night her last year with Andrew Westerman. At any moment the huge cloud, whose searing light made it seem the sun had crashed to earth, might mushroom up. She thought of the hand guiding Andrew's on the lever. . . .

"You don't like it," Merle said. She had been quietly watching her in the mirror. "Too noisy, eh? Well, don't mind, you'll get used to the noise."

"Oh, I'm sure I will," she said, and turned from it.

Moments later they were within sight of the guesthouse, and Allen, sitting forward suddenly in his seat, called out "Cassia House!" in the same relieved and grateful way someone else might have said "home."

Perched some distance back from the beach on a rocky shelf of land that was the leveling out of Westminster's tall spur, the guesthouse appeared to be several houses, some in limestone which the salt spray had blackened over the years, others in wood long weathered by the sun and damp, which had been haphazardly thrown together. The original house, a two-story rocklike structure with thick walls and deeply recessed windows to secure it against hurricanes, had been built as a vacation or bay house by the planter Duncan Vaughan, the common progenitor of Merle, Lyle Hutson's wife, Enid, and the man Desmond Vaughan on the road gang. The various wings and other additions had been built by succeeding generations of Vaughans, including Merle's father. Rambling, run-down, bleak, the house was one with its surroundings, as much a part of the stark landscape of sea and sky as the sea and the dunes and the boulders strewn in the surf. It was one with the hill rising like a sixteenth-century cathedral behind it.

"Don't look at it too hard, it might collapse," Merle said with a bitter laugh as they swung into the large, bare front yard. "It's a fright, I know. No plan to it at all. Just thrown together. But then what could you expect of the man who built it, some riffraff out of the gutters of Bristol or Liverpool, who slept on a chair every night of his life and tried to populate the entire island his one. What could you expect of the likes of him?

"And don't look too hard at this old tree either," she said, pulling up under a lone cassia tree. The tall tree, its limbs raised in mute supplication to the sky, looked as if it had been caught in the eye of a hurricane which had whipped it clean of every leaf, stripped it of its bark, and left it stunned and twisted, near dying or dead.

"It looks about gone, doesn't it?" she said. They had gotten out of the car and were standing—she with her shoes on now and the flared dress lifting around her legs in the wind—gazing up at the leafless tree. "But it'll surprise you in a few months. When you're just about ready to give up on it and chop it down for firewood, it suddenly breaks out in the biggest yellow blossoms you ever saw. Great clusters of them. And it happens practically overnight. You go to bed one night with the tree looking just as it is and wake the next morning to find it in full bloom. It's something to behold. . . ." Then, with a sad shrug: "But the blossoms don't last any time, I'm afraid. In less than a week's time they're gone and then my lady here"—she slapped the tree affectionately—"is just her old half-dead self again."

"Not a thing's changed, Merle," Allen said gently, attempting perhaps to comfort her.

She laughed, and the saints on her ears commenced their ceremonial dance. "Of course not!" she cried. "How could it in this place? Dear, dear Allen," she said fondly, and slipped her arm through his, "Man, I'm glad enough you're back."

Arm in arm with him, she led them across the stony yard to a flight of steps which had been hewn out of the rocky ledge upon which the house stood. The steps led down the south wall of the building to the beach, but perhaps halfway down, at what was the base of the house, they came to a long wide landing, and at the end of this, just where the steps began again, she turned off onto a veranda which ran the length of the several houses that made up the guesthouse, and overlooked the sea.

The veranda sloped dangerously with age, but it was a lovely place—cool, set within the wind's eye and, except in the early morning, out of direct reach of the sun. The ancient floorboards, the railing, the simple columns supporting the low roof, the deep-bottomed wooden lawn chairs lined up neatly in a row had all been bleached the color of driftwood by the salt spray and the sun. And it was an astonishingly quiet place despite the noisy sea down the stretch of beach, a sanctuary for contemplation and repose. An invisible soundproof curtain, lifting and falling gently in the wind, might have been hung from its roof to mute the roar and sob of the breakers.

The young man Vere was there, perched on the railing at the far end waiting for Merle. He was absorbed in the dog-eared automotive manual he was never without, and for a moment did not hear them.

Merle stopped short. "Wait," she said, her eyes narrowing against the light, "is that Vere or are my eyes deceiving me? Vere, is that you?" she cried, her voice lifting above that of the sea, and he looked up. "Oh, Father!" she exclaimed. "It is Vere! He's back. Leesy's vision was right after all. . . ."

The others with her forgotten, she hurried across the veranda, her heels rattling the worn floorboards and her voice rushing ahead to swirl around Vere, who had stood up at her approach.

"But is it you in truth, Vere? When did you get back? How long have you been here? My God, I scarcely recognized you, you've gotten to be such a man."

She embraced him as she had Allen the night before, reaching up to take his face between her hands the way a mother would and resting her cheek against his for a moment.

"I reached back safe," he said, with the smile that was like a warm light issuing from his face. He offered the smile to Merle like a gift he had brought her from America. "And how you been keeping all this time, Mis-Merle?" he said. "How's the old car?"

She laughed, gave the eloquent shrug. "What to say, Vere? We're both still here, only living 'cause we ain't dead, as the old people say." And holding him close to her side she turned and called to the others. "Come and meet Vere. He's just back from your country on the labor scheme."

Saul reached them first, and holding out his hand to Vere as he came up said, "You're the young man on the plane yesterday, aren't you?"

"Why, so he is," Harriet said before Vere could answer, and in what was for her an impulsive gesture she took his other hand, drawn to him by the smile. "You had on a blue hat, as I recall."

Motioning over Allen who, his bulging briefcase in one hand and the jar of zinnias in the other, had paused shyly a little distance away, Merle made the introductions. And for the short time that they stood there with Vere's easy smile like a source of light and strength they could all draw upon, they appeared to comprise a warm, close-knit circle. Their small gathering almost suggested a reunion: the coming together of the members of a family who had been scattered to the four corners of the earth and changed almost beyond recognition by their differing circumstances, but the same still. They might have been searching for each other for a long time, seeking completion. And they had met finally (although it was too late and could only last the moment) here on this desolate coast, before this perpetually aggrieved sea which, even as they stood questioning Vere about the places he had worked in America, continued to grieve and rage over the ancient wrong it could neither forget nor forgive.

They separated shortly afterward, Vere going to look at the Bentley, Allen hurrying away to inspect the kitchen garden Merle had kept up for him, and Merle taking the other two in to see the house.

She ushered them first into the drawing room, a large rectangular antechamber filled with heavy, old-style furniture, all of which had been blotched and whitened by the damp. Beyond this lay an equally large dining room that resembled a refectory. "Yellow," she said pointing to the freshly painted walls. "I finished it only yesterday." Passing quickly on, she led them down a long dim hall which took them into the heart of the house and then through a labyrinth of echoing stone passageways which gave the impression of leading ever inward. Many of the rooms they glimpsed along the way were obviously never used. The sunlight could barely penetrate the salt crust from the sea spray on the windows and the light and air in them seemed left over from another time.

Pausing in the doorway of the kitchen, a vast, gloomy cavern of a room, she called to the housekeeper and cook. "Carrington!"

The tall, full-bosomed, maternal figure who came and stood for a moment without speaking in the doorway seemed less a person than a presence. She could have been one of the massed shadows in the kitchen that had broken off and assumed human form. (And she was to remain a shadowy, indistinct figure to Harriet and Saul all during their stay at the guesthouse. They were never to hear her speak or to be certain what she looked like, since she kept almost exclusively to the kitchen, and whenever there was something to be done in another part of the house she would send her helpers, two young, strong-limbed girls from the village who served as chambermaids.)

"Oh, she's a terror you see her there," Merle said of her as soon as the introductions were over and she had led them away. "She never has a word for you and she'll burn the food in a minute if you so much as look at her the wrong way. But there's no getting rid of her. She goes with the house. You see, she was the last keep-miss of the man I'm to call father and the only one to bury him, so I guess she has as much right to the place as I do."

Moving swiftly she pointed out a door at the end of a long passageway. "Those're my digs," she said. "And Allen can tell you that once I go in there and shut the door I'm not to be disturbed. The house could be on fire—and sometimes I wish it would burn down so I could get the insurance money and go on back to England—don't call me. Call Carrington. She's the one who really runs the place, anyway. And here's your part of the house."

The wing she was giving over to them was simply furnished in contrast to the clutter elsewhere. In each of the upstairs bedrooms there were two spartan single beds painted white, with the mosquito netting for each gathered and looped overhead on a hoop suspended from the ceiling, a large chest of drawers, its varnish erased by the damp but with a clean, embroidered scarf on top and, above this, a small spotted mirror that offered only the dimmest reflection of the face. A wash basin and chair completed the furnishings. The bedrooms might have been cells in a monastery, places for meditation and penance.

Harriet, looking around, noted with approval the bare whitewashed walls, the floors that had been scrubbed white also, the windows opened to the mild wind and the squares of sunlight hanging there like curtains of plain jonquil-yellow cloth. She loved the one indulgent touch of the embroidered scarf on the dresser. The rooms were all she could have asked for. They even made her wonder if there might not after all be something in the woman to which she could respond. For the spare thoughtful way in which she had furnished the rooms suggested to Harriet a longing on her part for a certain order, simplicity, and calm. And turning to her she said, "These are really very pleasant rooms, Mrs. Kinbona. We're sure to be more than comfortable."

"Yes," Merle said, and a softness came over her. "This is a nice part of the house. I rather like the old place, you know, even though I'm always talking about burning it down. It's gotten so I don't even mind if no one comes to stay in it. I just wander through the rooms talking to the duppies—those're ghosts, the place is full of them. They don't mind listening to me and I'm glad for an audience."

She left moments later, calling over her shoulder that she would send them their lunch and admonishing them to sleep during the worst of the afternoon heat.

Saul firmly closed, then locked the door, and leaning against it, heaved a loud sigh of relief.

"She is exhausting," Harriest said, laughing. "She just goes on and on, and with that accent and the odd way she puts things I can't understand half of what she's saying, which is probably all to the good. Anyway, the house is big enough for us to keep our distance, and these rooms she's given us will more than do."

"So you like our new 'digs,' " he said, and drew her to him.

"Very much. Don't you?"

Holding her lightly against him he looked around him once more, then nodded.

After lunch, while the others rested, Allen returned to the small kitchen garden he had started his first visit to Bournehills. It was situated at the north corner of the house not far from Carrington's gloomy kitchen, away from the steady salt drift off the sea. He had begun it as a favor to Merle, who had complained of the high price of vegetables in town, and also because he had always, secretly, from a boy, loved growing things. And so for weeks after clearing the ground and laying in the mold he had literally coaxed the few vegetables up out of the stony soil while waging a relentless battle with the land crabs that came out to feed at night.

He knelt now before his handiwork which Merle had sustained—the few green frilly rows of carrots and root lettuce, the little cabbages that were just beginning to fold in, and the tomatoes on their ragged vines, the herbs—thyme, parsley and dill—and he was smiling deeply to himself, unmindful of the heat and the midafternoon sun which had burned away all the blue in the sky and turned the sea to sheet metal, and of the perspiration that was beginning to stream down his face. He took note of the fresh mold and lime she had recently added and the washed seaweed she had spread neatly among the plants as an additional fertilizer. And this, more than anything else, more than the old work pants she had put away for him, which he was wearing now, said that she had remained confident of his return.

Seeing the garden intact, it was almost as if he hadn't been away. The last year might not have happened. The thought pleased him. He would have preferred that it had never been. Because part of the time he had lived at home with his parents; in the house that might have been lifted straight out of a Hopper painting, with its fake Austrian shades at the parlor windows and its impression of small nondescript lives within. He had slept once again in his old bedroom upstairs with, on the dresser, the photograph of Jerry Kislak, who had joined the marines the day Allen had entered college and died a month later in an accident in boot camp; in the bed, chaste and narrow, that he had slept in as a boy. And in a way, he was still, at twenty-six, the virgin he had been then. Because although there had been a few women, his encounters with them had been disastrous, especially the first one, when in his ignorance, fear and distaste, he had put on, one over the other, all three of the prophylactics in the small packet and fled immediately after he was done. The girl, a high-school classmate, had cried. He could sometimes still hear the muffled sound of her crying in the darkened room.

Moreover, being back this last year he had felt closer than at any time in his life to the discovery of some mysterious and painful fact about himself which he had always fled, a revelation that would bring with it a dreadful fate he had sensed awaiting him ever since he was a boy. He couldn't have said what it was. He didn't even like to think about it. But it was there, he knew, lying in wait for him around a dark turn in his life. Being back in Bournehills was like having been granted a reprieve.

The perspiration had trickled down over his glasses and he took them off. And as always happened when he did, everything at a distance vanished and those objects near to hand loomed larger than they actually were. So that the young tender hearts of the cabbages he was gazing down at looked huge. Indeed, the leaves appeared to be folding in, closing, right before his eyes. And suddenly he thought of the uncle whom he had loved more than his father, the one who had owned the small truck farm in south Jersey. Aside from his friendship with Jerry Kislak, those visits to the farm, which his mother had eventually put a stop to because, in her words, his uncle was "nothing but a common wop" (she was Scotch-Irish, French, "and a little German," she liked to boast), were all that had distinguished his childhood. At one point his uncle had changed over from vegetables to raising poultry and had lost everything—had simply taken a chance, risked himself and lost. For some reason Allen had found this admirable, enviable even. He still did. Once, when his uncle had the truck farm and he had gone to visit him, his uncle had picked a large tomato off the vine and given it to him to eat. The tomato had been so warm from the sun, so ripe and red, he had thought of it, he remembered, as a great heart pulsing away in his palm. It had seemed to him to contain all of life. Because of this, perhaps, he had hesitated biting into it, and his uncle, his head thrown back, the black hair on his chest coiling out of his T-shirt, had laughed like a pagan, and his thick arms pumping, had cried, "Whassa matter? Eat it! Eat it!"

CHAPTER 2

"What's with your friend, Al?"

"Who? Merle?"

"Yes," he said. "What's her story? How did she come by that big white elephant of a house, for example?"

It was much later that day and they were on their way over to the rumshop in Spiretown, where Merle had said they were expected this evening. Dusk had fallen sometime ago, the abrupt tropical darkness rushing out from the folds of the hills where it had been waiting all day to overwhelm the land. It moved now, a sentient, breathing presence, around the two men, almost like another companion who had decided to accompany them into the village proper.

"She inherited it," Allen said. He was lighting the way for them along the unpaved road leading from the guesthouse to the village with his flashlight and he had armed himself with a stick to drive off the dogs that would converge on them as soon as they reached the first of the houses. "Her father left her both the house and what little land was left from the original estate. She kept the house but sold the land in small plots to people in the village—probably just gave it to them since it's unlikely any of them would've had the money to pay her. But she didn't want it to fall into the hands of the Kingsley group, who own practically the entire district."

"How is it she came into everything?"

"She was the only child, an 'outside' child, it's true, as they say around here, meaning outside the pale of marriage, but the only one, nonetheless. Hers is one of those complicated family histories you still find in places like Bournehills."

He went on in his detached clinical way to give the circumstances of her birth, describing how, as was often the case in such liaisons, Ashton Vaughan had provided Merle's mother with her own small house and bit of land. And then one day she had been found mysteriously murdered, shot at close range one morning in the house.

"They never found out who did it, but everyone swears that Vaughan's wife, who was a 'high-colored' from town, meaning almost white like Lyle's wife, Enid, either did it herself or hired someone. No one really knows, though. Merle was the only witness they say, but she was only about two at the time and so, of course, couldn't say."

The child Merle had then gone, he said, to live with various members of her mother's family and had been virtually ignored for years by her father. But when his wife died childless, Vaughan had decided to acknowledge her and had brought her, a girl of thirteen, to live with him and had raised her in keeping with his class, sending her to the fashionable girls' school in town and then afterward to England.

"She remained in England for close to fifteen years, I understand," Allen said. "Just what she did there all that time no one but Lyle Hutson really knows and he doesn't ever talk about it. But there're all sorts of stories. She's said to have run around with a pretty offbeat crowd for awhile. She studied history for a time at London U., that much is certain, although she never took her degree. She also married and had a child, but it seems the marriage broke up and her husband, who was from East Africa, took the child with him when he returned home. Why did she permit this? Again, nobody knows except maybe Lyle, because with all the talking she does, she never, but never, talks about any of this. It's known, though, that she had a breakdown right afterward and was very sick for a time. . . ."

He paused, his voice fading into the darkness, then: "She returned here about eight years ago when she heard her father was dying. But she refused to go and see him. She stayed in town until he died, and then the day after the funeral she came back to live in Bournehills."

"She must have been very bitter against him," Saul said.

"She still is," said Allen. "She's always blamed him for what happened to her mother, and she's never forgiven him for having ignored her all those years. And from what I've heard, even when he took her in he didn't pay much attention to her, and most of the time, especially when she was going to school, boarded her with an old woman in town whom she calls her aunt and goes to see faithfully twice a week."

"She's really had a rough time of it." Saul, thinking of all he had seen in her face as she slept the night before at Sugar's, spoke more to himself than to Allen.

"Yes," said Allen, "she has." Then, his own voice turning in on his thoughts, he added, "Yet, somehow, it hasn't gotten the better of her. Oh, she's a compulsive talker, sure; and once in awhile she breaks down altogether and just disappears for days in her room. But with all that's happened to her—and there's a lot as I say I don't know about—she hasn't gone under. She's still Merle, herself, and kind of special. . . .

"I had an uncle something like her," he said after a moment. Behind his glasses, shining a dull rose in the glow from the flashlight, his hazel eyes were journeying back over the years. Around them the darkness listened and kept pace. "Everything bad happened to the guy," he said. "At one point he lost everything he owned. Yet he never said die. He could still laugh. I can never help marveling at people like that, who hold their own, remain themselves, no matter what. It's a beautiful quality, that," he said.

"Yes," Saul quietly agreed with him, "it is." Then, "Tell me, how does Mrs. Kinbona get along with the people here?"

"Oh, just great," Allen said. "And that includes everyone, from the lowliest weed picker in the fields to the rector of the big Anglican church in the village, who's a great friend of hers. Everyone thinks she's a little off, of course, but they like her all the same. The small elite in Spiretown, the headmaster of the school and the like are always talking about her behind her back, but they still invite her to their dull teas and socials. She's a Vaughan after all, and her father left her that big house and the land.

"As for the people at the bottom of the heap, the Little Fella, as they're called in Bournehills, she can do no wrong. Because although she was 'raised decent,' as they say, and has lived in England and hobnobs with bigwigs in town like Lyle Hutson, she's never put on airs with them. They know she's on their side and really takes their problems to heart. She feels for us, they say. By the way"—the detached note returned to his voice—"she'll be invaluable to us in terms of the project, having access as she does to everyone up and down the line. She's what's called in the books the perfect cultural broker."

"Well, let's hope she sticks around then," Saul said, "because she was saying something today about going back to England."

"Oh, that!" Allen dismissed it. "She's always saying that. But she's not going anywhere. In fact," he said, becoming once more thoughtful, "I don't think she'll ever leave here again, not for any length of time anyway. She's become too much a part of the place. In a way I can't explain, she somehow is Bournehills."

There was a silence broken only by the steady scrape of their shoes on the path and the loud keening of the sea in the darkness beyond the low dunes. Then Saul, with a laugh, asked, "And where did she get that fancy wreck of a car?"

Allen also laughed. "That's a story in itself. It belonged to the last English governor before independence. He was a guy, it seems, who believed in living it up big. When he left she somehow managed to get hold of it through Lyle. Knowing Merle, she probably just bought it to get the goat of people in town. I'm sure it's the only Bentley on the island."

"Where'd she get the money for something like that?"

Allen didn't answer immediately, and when he did he sounded boyish, embarrassed. "Well, the rumor goes she returned from England with quite a lot of money that had been given to her by some wealthy woman she had been—how to put it?—involved with, I guess, for years in London. It was more than just friendship I mean. I told you she ran around with a pretty offbeat crowd over there."

"Oh . . ." he said. Then, with an amazed laugh, "Jesus Christ, your friend Merle is a whole damn research project in herself."

He felt Allen stiffen aggressively, ready to defend her against all calumnies. But he relaxed after a moment and said, "Yes, I never thought of it like that, but I guess in a way she is."

They had reached the village proper by now and at the sound of their footsteps on the paved road the dogs came barking and baying furiously out from under the tiny houses with their steeply pitched roofs and foundations of rough-hewn limestone slabs set at the corners. But they pulled up short, their paws furrowing the dirt in the yards as Allen raised his stick and played the flashlight into their glass-amber eyes. "They're just saying hello," he said with a grin. "They haven't seen me in over a year, after all."

Most of the houses they passed were already dark, the windows boarded over with shutters that were solid barricades of wood, the jalousies in the door panels tight shut like the lid of an eye. The houses looked utterly abandoned, deserted. At the first sign of dusk their inhabitants might have packed up and gone to spend the night in some distant place to which they also belonged. Only here and there along the road could the ruddy glow of an oil lamp be seen under a shutter propped open on a long pole. And that faint bit of light glowing feebly in the immense darkness was like a small fire in a great stone hearth or in the ancestral cave; it could have been the first fire said by the Pygmies to have been stolen from the sleeping mother of God.

With the darkness drowning out everything but the occasional lamplight there were only the sounds to go by; and these, too, had been altered by the night and invested with meanings they would not have had during the day. The few voices that reached them from time to time from under the partly raised shutters seemed to be speaking, all of them, of love, so murmurous were they in the dark. A baby cried in one of the tightly boarded-up houses, a sharp piercing wail as if it had just broken free of the womb; and it was as though all of life were being reborn within the darkened room. A bicycle approached on the opposite side of the road. They heard the gentle ticking of the hub, the meditative whirr of the wheels and made out two indistinct forms. Lovers. The man's long legs akimbo as he slowly pedaled, the girl seated sidesaddle between them and sucking her teeth like a coquette at something he whispered in her ear. A hymn came to them on the wind, and turning, Saul saw the tiny, one-room shack of a church situated at the foot of a rise which sloped up from the main road. Through the open doorway he could make out perhaps a dozen or so old women seated on rows of benches under the glare of a kerosene pressure lamp. Most of them were half-asleep, and he thought of the poem he had always loved: "When you are old and grey and full of sleep/And nodding by the fire. . . ." They slept, and the few who were awake offered up the hymn. "Blessed assurance, Jesus is mine," they sang in flat, quavering, old-women's voices, giving expression not so much to any certainty of salvation, but to the unspeakable loneliness and melancholy of the tropic night. Hearing them, Saul felt the dull stir of his own loneliness, the one that was with him always, which no woman or friend, not even his work, could ever completely assuage, and he would have gone and sat with them awhile.

Farther on, nearer the center of Spiretown, other footsteps besides theirs could be heard on the road, and the soft slur and slap of the bare feet on the marl was an infinitely reassuring sound. It said that others like themselves moved unafraid through the night, bent on what seemed a pilgrimage toward the morning. Everyone in passing called "Good night," and they returned the greeting. Once a woman, recognizing Allen's voice, paused and called across, "And is that you come back, Mr. Allen?"—and she said it without surprise, as if, as Merle had said, no one in Bournehills had ever doubted his return.

"Yes," he said.

"You picked a dark night," she said, and walked on.

"She means," Allen said, "there's no moon."

He then led Saul into the bare front yard of what looked to be in the scant light seeping out from the open top half of a Dutch door, a fairly long, narrow building that sagged badly in the middle. It appeared to be held together only by the sun-faded advertisements for Coca-Cola, Colgate's toothpaste and Andrews Liver Salt decorating its front. Along with the weak light issuing from the opened half of the door came the charged strenuous sound of male voices raised in noisy debate. And laughter struck the air like cannonades, igniting the darkness outside. It was music in its own right. A loud and lusty drinking song, a wassail strong and sustained enough to last out the night and usher in the dawn.

"Well, the Oxford debates are on full blast, I hear," Allen said, laughing. But he appeared to falter at that powerful male sound. Hesitant and uncertain suddenly, he paused on the broad square of pitted limestone that served as a step, and his hand on the closed lower half of the door, remained there for a few minutes, long enough for Saul, just behind him, to get a good look of the shop over his shoulder.

In the negligible glow of a single small electric-light bulb around which the spiders had wound their webs like angel's-hair as if to disguise what it was, he saw a dim, rectangular room nominally divided in two by a low partition on the customers' side of the counter which ran its length. One-half of the room was a general store, with a mere token supply of imported canned goods on the dusty shelves and a few potatoes and onions that had begun to sprout hanging in wire baskets from the blackened rafters. Great casks of pickled meats—the fatty ends of beef and pork, and heavy crocus sacks of rice, flour and cornmeal grown musty from the long overseas journey crowded the space behind the counter. Added to these was crate upon crate of the dry, malodorous salted cod from Newfoundland, the long, almost fleshless bone of the fish—the only part sent to places such as Bourne Island—laid out neatly one on top of the other in the long crates, embalmed in salt.

The other half of the shop, the part they were gazing into, contained the bar. Bottles of white and amber rum lined the shelves above the heads of the men standing three deep at the counter with their backs to the door. Their voices, grappling like wrestlers back and forth across the room, sent the dust moiling, and threatened, with each outburst, to bring the flimsy walls tumbling down.

There seemed to be two main contenders in the debate raging, each with his noisy supporters: one, a short, wiry, resoundingly black man, whose face was drowned in the shadow of a work-stained cap he wore low over his brow. He held a honed billhook—the knife used for cutting canes in Bournehills—in one hand and, occasionally, to emphasize a point, he would bring it sweeping down in a short chopping arc close to the floor. The long single-edged knife which curved out slightly at the end seemed almost part of the man's hand the way he held it, something either grafted on or that he'd been born with: an extra limb nature had bestowed upon him to equip him for his world.

His opponent, and the more vociferous of the two, was a strikingly tall, lean old man whose gangling frame appeared strung together by the veins and sinews standing out in sharp relief beneath his dark skin. Everything about him was overstated, exaggerated. His face, his neck, his clean-shaven skull, had the elongated, intentionally distorted look to them of a Benin mask or a sculpted thirteenth-century Ifé head. With his long, stretched limbs he could have been a Haitian Houngon man. Or Damballa. Behind the thick lenses of the old-fashioned spectacles he wore, his eyes were huge, sheened, far-seeing. And as he talked he danced, a taut, graceful, highly stylized dance full of little menacing leaps and feints. He would leap back a step, his long legs bent like a fencer's, his walking stick, a stout length of wood, poised like a sword, and then lunge forward as though to impale his opponent on the stick's blunt end.

"Be-Jesus Christ, Stinger, you can't tell me a shite different," he was shouting as he lunged forward, his stick at the ready. "I say Cuffee held off the whole damn British regiment for upward to six months. Not a jack-man of them could get pas' Cleaver's High Wall all that time. And all the guns and ammunitions they had didn't count for a blast. Cuffee still had them lick. You think he was making any rass-hole sport? Why man, it got so they was afraid to so much as come near Bournehills."

"Fergy, I don't give a fuckarse what you say," the short man said in a somewhat calmer voice, but the billhook that seemed part of his hand came slashing down dangerously close to the other man's foot. "It wasn't no six months. How could he have held out against a whole regiment that long? It was only two, three months at the most, I tell you."

"Six, I say. Six. It was six!" the other cried, leaping back to spring, his huge eyes like those of someone in possession behind his glasses. His supporters took up his cry, bearing it aloft, and the shop reeled under the impact of the word "six!"

"What the bloody hell shite you know about it anyway?" the tall man cried. "I'm the one after all who went down to the library in town and read the big book there that tells all about him. And it said six. S-i-x." He held up six incredibly long, splayed, bony fingers. "You ever read the book? You ever read *any* book? You, Stinger, a man that didn't get past primer standard, who don't know nothing besides cutting canes and keeping your wife belly full up! But you best hide yourself and know you're talking to someone that's used to reading, who reads the newspapers and knows what's going on in the world, and who has read the Scriptures backward and forward. 'Let there be light,' the Lord said: Genesis one, verse three; and he was talking about the light of knowledge. But he forgot 'bout you, Stinger man, when he was sharing out the light. You's one of them still walking in darkness: Isaiah nine, verse two."

"Fergy, you could quote Scripture till you drop I still say it was only two, three months at the most," the man named Stinger insisted, his billhook flashing dully in the light as he brought it down again.

"Six!"

"What are they arguing about, Al?" Saul whispered. He understood little of what was being said. The men in the shop might have been speaking something other than English, for they had imposed their own stinging rhythms and harsh, atonal accent upon the language, had infused it with a raw poetry, transforming it, making it their own.

"Oh, just about Cuffee and the revolt," Allen said. "They always do when Ferguson has in one too many."

"Delly, will you please tell this nigger man here for me that it was six," Ferguson was saying, and his long arms, stretched in wide appeal to someone on the other side of the counter, seemed to span the length of the shop.

And a calm conciliatory voice issued from behind the massed figures standing in the way. "Well, Fergy, it's hard to say for sure about something that happened so long ago. But one thing certain, old Cuffee held out to the end."

The crowd shifted, and through a sudden opening Saul saw the man who had spoken. He was lying propped up on a makeshift bed amid the clutter behind the counter, a broken right leg in a cast laid out stiffly on the bed. He was huge, with massive limbs. The leg in the plaster cast was like part of a column to some great temple that had fallen. His aging skin, which was the same deep terra cotta as the walls around him, lay on his frame like a heavy garment that was beginning to weigh him down now that he was old. He called to mind a regent grown mellow and a little weary toward the end of a long reign, but in command still. He was the chief presiding over the nightly palaver in the men's house. The bed made of packing cases was the royal palanquin. The colorful Harry Truman shirt he had on was his robe of office; the battered Panama hat, which looked as if the mice in the shop had feasted on the brim, his chieftain's umbrella, and the bottle of white rum he held within the great curve of his hand, the palm wine with which he kept the palaver and made libation to the ancestral gods. And each time he filled the glasses ranged before him on the counter he made a point of first pouring a drop or two of the rum on the floor beside his improvised bed.

He saw the two at the opened top of the door and a bearlike hand with a palm the color of raw veal went up, and in a voice that had his full weight behind it, he called, "Allen, is that you? What you doing standing there at the door like you's some stranger or the other? Come on in, man."

The voices locked in their pitched battle fell apart and the men, some of them frozen momentarily in the violent attitudes of the argument, turned to the door as Allen, with Saul behind him, opened it and entered.

They crowded around Allen, greeting him warmly. And Allen, shaking the black hands thrust at him, kept repeating with a wide boyish smile, "Gosh, it's good to be back." Saul, standing forgotten for the moment on the sidelines, saw how deeply he meant it.

When it was his turn he took the stiff, work-swollen hands they extended to him as Allen introduced him around. He submitted to the brief but telling scrutiny of eyes that were the same reddish brown as the aged walls of the shop, the man Delbert's skin, and the amber rum in the bottles on the shelves. Close up, their faces, with the pronounced cheekbones rising out of them like hills and the hollows beneath like dark valleys, made him think of some spectacularly rugged terrain not unlike Bournehills itself.

As he made his way beside Allen through the crowd up to the counter he recognized one or two of the men from the road crew earlier in the day, the gaunt man Desmond Vaughan for one, and the supervisor, Mr. Innis, who, dressed in his hand-me-down bush jacket and plus fours and propped on his stick, stood drinking off by himself at one end of the bar.

"Amram? Amram? Did I hear Amram . . . ?" the man called Ferguson asked, retaining his hand. His enormous eyes squeezed shut, then snapped open like a window shade being rung up and he gave the little spring back. "Ah, yes! Amram, son of Kohath and father of Aaron and Moses-self!"

"Not quite," he said with a laugh. "Mine got changed along the way. It's A-m-r-o-n."

"Don't mind," Ferguson said. "It's Amram all the same."

At the counter the shopkeeper, Delbert, reached across a large hand first to Allen, then to Saul, the pink-lined palm closing strongly around his. And the man's eyes held him in as strong a hold. Small, almost lost within the lines of age cutting deep into the flesh, and the color of serum in the grudging glow of the one bulb that lit the shop, they looked scribbled over. All the events of his long life, and of a time that long antedated his life, might have been recorded there like a story on microfilm.

"I'm afraid I can't greet you proper, Dr. Amron, because of a bad leg I got here but you're welcome all the same," he said. His gaze, like the woman Merle's, seemed to take in everything about him at a glance, and for a long moment he bent on Saul a look which called to mind the way she had regarded him at the reception: almost as if he was no stranger to Bournehills, but, like Allen, had been here before.

"So Allen, man, you're back with us again, yes," he said, turning abruptly to him.

"I tell you"—Ferguson spoke up before Allen could respond—"Allen comes just like General MacArthur in the second big war.

Remember how the general told the Japanese when they drove him out of some island 'I shall return,' and he did—well, Allen here told us the said-same thing and look he's back. Delly, this calls for a grog. Let's fire one."

And Delbert, first pouring a drop of rum on the floor, filled the small jigger glasses on the scarred counter, adding two for Saul and Allen. They drank, the men tossing off the rum with a deft turn of their wrists and a lovely backward flick of the head. The liquor scarcely touched their tongues going down.

The raw rum was a snaking line of fire down Saul's throat. It brought tears to his eyes. Ferguson, seeing them, laughed. "Don't mind, Doctor, it's that your stomach has to get acclimated, that's all. Why Allen cried like a two-years' child his first drink. Remember, Allen?"

"It's pretty strong stuff, all right," Allen said.

"So tell me, Allen, how long are you planning on staying with us this time?" the shopkeeper, Delbert, asked when the talk and something of the tone in the shop before their entry had been restored. His thick arms were folded on the counter and under his gnawed Panama hat his shrewd, stippled eyes waited.

"For quite sometime, this trip," said Allen. "At least three years or more, off and on. You see, we're hoping, Dr. Amron and myself, to set up one or two schemes in Bournehills that will maybe help to improve conditions in the district over a period of time."

"Well, yes," Delbert said. "Mis-Merle did mention your saying something to that effect in your letter. Maybe you and Dr. Amron"—his glance only briefly included Saul—"can tell us a little more what you have in mind some other day when strong drink isn't raging so about the place. . . ." He motioned benignly toward Ferguson who, along with several others, had retired to a corner of the room and, gathered around a huge, defunct, dust-covered jukebox standing there, was arguing heatedly about which island in the Pacific MacArthur had been driven from.

"One thing certain though," Delbert said over the noise, "we can use any help we can get because things have always been critical down here."

"Critical!" Ferguson had heard him and was shouting across. "Critical's not the word, Delly. Why, Bournehills comes like a nation God has forgot."

"Is true, Fergy," he said. "Things are bad. In fact"—he gave a slight, strange, indrawn smile—"if they get any worse government's going to have to declare the place a—what's the name again they give to a place when a hurricane or a flood or something so comes along and licks down everything?" He turned with the question to Saul, whom he had been virtually ignoring up to then.

"A disaster area," the latter said.

"Ah, yes, that's it." He gave a nod; turned away. "Yes, if things get any worse that's just what they're going to have to do, declare the whole place a disaster area and send for the Red Cross."

For some reason this struck him as funny, and throwing back his head, his massive bulk heaving up in the bed as if he had been seized by a sudden pain, he laughed. The laugh—loud, toneless and ironic, containing, it seemed, some private meaning not even the men in the shop were privy to—began in the depths of his belly and traveled up with a sound almost like that of the sea at Bournehills as it moves in over the reefs, the same charged, muted roar. It exploded, and the frail walls recoiled as if struck by a tidal wave. And its loud echo lingered. Saul thought he heard it all the time he stood amid the men at the counter, listening to the talk and judiciously now sipping the white searing rum. Something of it remained to puzzle him when, an hour later, he and Allen, quietly discussing the evening between them—and they both felt it had gone well—slowly returned the way they had come to the guesthouse at the far end of the village.

CHAPTER 3

"The goddamn Fleet Street bastard!"

He said it in a low undertone, and from behind his clenched teeth so that the words were barely audible. But Merle, her eyes intent on his face, caught the movement of the lips and something of the sound, and she crowed her approval from one of the veranda's slanted-back chairs where she had gone to sit after handing him the newspaper. "Oh, that's good, Dr. Amron, first rate. I couldn't have said it better. Because that's exactly what he is, you know. George Clough would betray his own mother for a headline."

"What is it, Saul?" Harriet said anxiously. She quickly put aside the late morning cup of coffee she had been drinking and in a gesture she often used with him her hand went out to calm and restrain him.

Allen had also started up anxiously and, his gaze moving from Saul's face to the newspaper in his hands, said, "It's about the project, isn't it? What did the so-and-so have to say?"

Instead of answering, Saul simply tossed him the paper and, ignoring Harriet's restraining hand, began striding up and down, his heavy tread shaking the veranda's worn floorboards.

Allen read aloud the headlines which, done in large bold type, spanned the entire front page:

MULTIMILLION-DOLLAR DEVELOPMENT SCHEME FOR BOURNEHILLS

AMERICANS TO THE RESCUE

BOURNEHILLS ON THE RECEIVING END AGAIN

"Those're the headlines," he said in a stunned voice, pausing briefly, "splashed across the whole darn front page. How could he have done something like this?" Behind the rimless glasses his bewildered gaze followed Saul for a moment, then dropped again to the newspaper.

A large American research foundation has announced plans for a massive development program for the Bournehills Valley District which, if successful, could well revolutionize life in the area within the next few years. The huge scheme will call for hundreds of thousands of dollars, perhaps millions, according to Dr. Saul Amron, prominent American social scientist and director of the proposed project, who recently arrived in the island accompanied by his wife and Dr. Allen Fuso, his research associate. This vast sum of money will be pumped into an ailing Bournehills through a variety of programs which Dr. Amron and his associates will develop as they go along, and which are almost certain to transform, in a short time, what has always been the most backward section of the island. The money . . .

"The bastard!"—and he said it out loud this time, his voice cutting across Allen's. "And it's not as if I didn't ask him to go easy on the question of the money." He had come to a brief stop. His eyes were flecked red and the curved spine of his nose had gone very white. "In fact, I asked him to go easy on the whole project until we had had a chance to explain it to people here. But no, he talks about 'revolutionizing life in the area,' 'transforming it in a short time.' Good God, people are going to be expecting the millennium overnight. Talk about cheap irresponsible journalism! The sonovabitch!" For a moment through his anger he saw George Clough, the manikin face, the small, fine, predatory teeth, the inanimate eyes: "I could tell he wasn't to be trusted even before his wife warned me." He recalled Dorothy Clough dancing with her face resting against Lyle Hutson's at Sugar's and muttered, "Serves him right, the goddamn cuckold. Oh, Christ"—he broke into the stride again—"and things had gotten off to such a good start the other night at the rumshop."

"Who's this Clough guy, anyway, Merle?" Allen asked. "He wasn't around when I was here before."

"Who, Georgie?" She shrugged. Before going on, she drew her legs up under her and carefully arranged the wide, floor-length skirt of a maroon-colored tea (or at-home) gown she was wearing over them. The gown, with full sleeves and a Mandarin collar, must have been very beautiful in its day, but was badly faded now. "Oh, Georgie," she said in too light and casual a tone, "is just another one in the pack of advisers, experts and the like from England who are still beating a track to our door even though we're supposed to be on our own these days—free and independent. But it's our fault since in most cases we ask them to come. We might have a local chap who can do the job ten times better, but he's not considered quite good enough in our eyes. Take the new development plan. With all the young bright economists we've got about the place we still had to send for Waterford, who couldn't care less about us, and knows little or nothing about conditions on the island. But we don't as yet really trust our own; we don't really believe deep inside us that we can plan and do for ourselves. I tell you, they colonized our minds but good in this place. In Georgie's case the big newspaper chain he works for bought out the local paper and sent him down to boost circulation. Go thee and sell papers, they said, and Georgie, good automaton that he is (look good at his eyes next time, not a bit of life to them; they're what you'd call machine eyes, bo), is doing just that. He's turned it into a cheap, sensational rag, but he's selling papers. His wife doesn't stay home nights, but Georgie's selling papers. And what does he use for news in a place where there hasn't been any real news since Cuffee burned down Pyre Hill and ran things around here for awhile? Everything and nothing. If our dear old do-nothing Prime Minister so much as sneezes that's cause for a headline: PM SNEEZES IN LEGCO in big print. If a chap falls off his bicycle and skins his knee he's sure to find his picture on the front page the next day—an overnight celebrity! Westminster Low Road marched off in the rain the morning you people arrived and Georgie called it DISASTER IN BOURNEHILLS. So just think when he gets hold of some real news like three Americans coming with their moneybags full. Man, there's no containing him.

"Irresponsible. That was a good word you used before, Doctor," she said, and her suddenly serious tone brought Saul to a halt in front of her chair. But she didn't see him. Her eyes, filled with the sunlight that lay like a soothing hand on the restive sea beyond the veranda railing, were abstracted. The saints on each side of her face were still. "A very good word. But what to expect of Georgie, yes? After all," she said, the smile flicking open bright and razor sharp, "he's only the end product of a civilization that never had a reputation for acting in a particularly responsible fashion, that made up its morality as it went along and to suit its convenience. So what to expect. Take for example when Georgie and company were around here selling us for thirty pounds sterling. They somehow put it right with their conscience by claiming we weren't quite up to standard as the species goes. Go back farther to when Georgie and his crew first arrived over this side. How did they behave toward the people they found here—all those poor red Indians up your way, the Caribs down this end, and all the rest whose beautiful house this was. How, I ask you?" The edged smile pressed hard. "Why, I know they finished them off in double-quick time. Gone! Just so! An entire people. And all done in the name of some bogus progress. Now I ask you, was that any way for Georgie and them to behave? I don't think so. Because when you think of it, they were only, in a manner of speaking, guests in the people's house—and uninvited ones at that. Nobody asked them here. We're all only guests in the Man's house when you think of it. And look at how they got on once they came pushing themselves in. Not only did they do away with their host and take over his house, fighting over it among themselves like the thieves they were, but they then took to importing and selling souls—black ones but immortal, nonetheless—dirt cheap on the open market. The ones who lasted the trip, that is. Because most didn't. They're out there"—she motioned beyond the railing—"long gone and forgotten. You can scarce find a word about them in the books. And when you dare mention them, as I do out of sheer wickedness from time to time, you get your head handed to you. . . .

"Ah, well, ah, history—" She stretched, the heavy silver at her wrists falling with a loud crash as she raised her arms. "Any of you ever studied it?" The look, the smile that held everyone to account made the rounds. "Well, don't if you haven't. I did for a time—West Indian history it was and I tell you, it nearly, as we say in Bournehills, set out my head. I had to leave it off. It is a nightmare, as that Irishman said, and we haven't awakened from it yet."

Gazing around at the three of them, seeing their strained, embarrassed expressions and averted eyes, she laughed, a short, sharp, hollow-sounding hoot which said she knew one wasn't supposed to speak of such matters but that she insisted.

"Look, don't mind me," she said to Saul, standing gazing down at her. He felt as he had at the nightclub: trapped, enthralled, as condemned to listen as she was to speak. "I'm full of irrelevancies. Anyway, if you know what's good for you, you had best do something about those headlines and do it quick, before you have the whole of Bournehills descending on my guesthouse looking for their share of the multimillions."

"Oh, Christ, yes," he said, remembering. He resumed his worried pacing.

"Saul, do you think it might help if you wrote a letter to the editor pointing out how your comments were misconstrued and explaining the project in the right terms?" It was Harriet speaking in a voice that like the hand she had extended to him before sought to restrain him.

"I don't know if that'll do any good," he said. "The damage has been done. Besides, that unprincipled bastard might not even publish the letter."

"Our best bet, Saul, might be to hold a meeting in the village," Allen said. "Maybe we could straighten it out that way."

"Yes," he said, pausing. "I was thinking of that."

"Wait." Merle spoke up. "I know it's none of my business but I'll tell you what. I'm thinking of giving a party in a day or two—oh, nothing elaborate, just what we call a little fete—to welcome back Vere and Allen and because, for the first time in a long time, I feel like a party for some reason—and if you like you could explain about the article then. Most of Bournehills will be here. I always invite everybody, you know, the great and the small. Throw the whole lot in together, I say. And they all usually come, even though, of course, each group keeps to itself. You'll see. Class! It's a curse upon us. But you'll have a chance to meet everybody one time; and since there's always some speechmaking at a fete in Bournehills—we all love to hold forth; I'm not the only offender—you could have your say then. How's that?"

He thought for a time, frowning down at the floorboards, his hands deep in his pockets. "Yes," he said, "that might be a way to do it. We'll see."

As Merle had said, most of Bournehills came to the party she held two nights later. And this included not only a large cross section of the population of Spiretown, the only genuine village in the district, but also people from the tiny settlements—sometimes no more than three or four houses—scattered over the outlying hills. The guests—

the more important ones—filled the shabby drawing room, whose tall doors stood open to the night. The rest were gathered in somewhat tense but noisy groups around to the front of the guesthouse under the shorn cassia tree which had been hung with a tilly lamp, and in the side yard, where Allen had his garden not far from Carrington's kitchen door. They sat on the precipitous steps leading down the south wall of the house to the beach and spilled over onto the beach itself, where they stood in great faceless numbers under the far-reaching shadow of the veranda, while behind them, down the stretch of shingle, the breakers pounded and clawed at the land. The torn spume, soaring up into the darkness each time a wave struck, was a brief, brilliant pyrotechnic display in the light from the house.

But surprisingly, although the guesthouse was crowded both inside and out, the long veranda stood empty—this, in spite of the fact that Carrington's two helpers had set out a table with rum and beer, and the strong kerosene gas lamps glowed a welcome from the overhang to the roof. And it was to remain empty—like some no man's land no one dared cross, until almost the end of the party, even though Merle kept urging those outside, especially the ones on the darkened beach below, to come up. Periodically, she would lean over the railing and plead with them to come upstairs. But to no avail. Each time she called down they would look off, making it appear that she was speaking to someone other than they, gently ignoring her. As the evening progressed and they still held their ground, her voice took on an increasingly exasperated note: "But, oh, crime," she cried angrily at one point, "why won't you come upstairs, yes, and stop acting as though you weren't invited to the damn fete, too?"

Inside the drawing room and separated from the guests outside by the empty veranda, Saul, with Harriet at one side and Merle, who was introducing them, at the other, met "the great people" of Bournehills as they were referred to—the postmaster, the magistrate and clerk of the small district court atop Westminster, the managers of the various Kingsley-owned estates dotting the hills who were, by tradition, mostly white; the parochial officer, the matron of the almshouse, all of them far less affluent and impressive versions of the people at Lyle Hutson's reception.

The headmaster of the grammar school, a tall, black, elaborately correct man, bowed with old-world courtliness over Harriet's hand and invited them both to come and see the rosebushes the Queen had planted in the schoolyard on her last visit to the island. And the manager of the sugar mill at Cane Vale, a large harried-looking man named Erskine Vaughan, with sandy hair and freckles sprinkled over his tan face (he was a third cousin of Merle's), gave Saul permission, when he asked, to visit the factory.

The men were at one side of the long rectangular room, their wives at the other, the women seated in stiff, almost painful decorum. Their hands, as they held them up to Saul and Harriet, felt boneless.

The magistrate's wife detained Harriet; and Merle, wearing one of her bright-figured dresses with a matching stole, her hair straightened and drawn back from her face, led Saul over to the rector of the parish church, a bland, weary-eyed Anglican father with olive-tinted skin and a vast sloping front under his white full-skirted cassock which was soiled at the hem. He held the small glass of rum he was nursing between his hands as if it were the eucharistic wine.

Slipping her arm through his, she said, "Meet my father-confessor, Dr. Amron. He's been after my soul for years, even though I keep telling him it's no use and he's wasting his time, that God doesn't want me."

"Neither does the devil, I'm beginning to fear, dear Merle," the rector said.

She laughed, impenitent, her head back, and her earrings, the ones with the saints which she wore all the time, performed their jig. "Purgatory then, is that it?" she cried. "Is that what's ahead for me? One long endless limbo between heaven and hell? Well, I'm ready. I've been in training for it these eight years I've been back." With that she held her face up to him for the kiss she demanded from everyone as her due.

"The church and the rumshop!" she said in a scathing aside to Saul as they left the drawing room. "They're one and the same, you know. Both a damn conspiracy to keep us pacified and in ignorance. Just you wait, though, come the revolution we're going to ban them both!"

Outside the house, under the lighted cassia tree in front as well as in the yards to the side, Saul met those guests who had not entered the drawing room although the doors stood open to them, and who even refused, until much later in the evening when the speechmaking began, to venture onto the veranda. Almost everyone he met there, men and women alike, "worked in the canes" as it was put in Bournehills, in the fields set high on the slopes or at the mill. And most, he learned, also cultivated their own tiny plots, sometimes no more than a quarter of an acre adjoining their houses or lying on the stony lands north of Spiretown, which they either owned outright or rented from Kingsley and Sons.

They had brought with them the strong, fecund, raw-sugar smell of those fields, and this had become part of their own body smell and heat. And the evidence of their labors out under the sun was to be seen in the faces of even the youngest as they stood about the yard, the men talking in small groups while tossing down the little glasses of rum, the women and children standing quietly aside draped like nuns against the night chill in old shawls and lengths of cloth covering their heads.

Saul saw several of the men from the rumshop, and he chatted for some time with the cane cutter, Stinger, whose billhook had stung the air repeatedly that first night. Sitting beside him on the steps leading down to the beach, he listened as Stinger, in answer to a question of his, spoke of the way in which the crop was harvested. He felt himself drawn to the man by the easy, quietly authoritative way he spoke of his work and his sober, introspective air; and above all, by something he sensed behind the eyes half-hidden under the cap he wore, an obscure sadness, an undefined remorse which was like a reflection of the same emotion in himself. He asked if he might come and watch him work sometime. Stinger looked up at him for a moment, his eyes touched by the dull glint from his billhook lying across his knees. (He was seldom without the knife, Saul was to discover.) Then, slowly, cryptically, he smiled, more to himself than to Saul. "Yes," he said, "you must come sometime, 'cause in a manner of speaking maybe that's what the old place is here for, for people like yourself to come and see what another man's life is like."

Minutes later, standing talking to Allen and the young man Vere, for whom the party was also being held, he spied Stinger's opponent from the rumshop, the tall lean man, Ferguson. He was at the center of a group of men arguing passionately out on the potholed road behind the guesthouse. Ferguson, his thick glasses flashing in the light from the lamp in the cassia tree nearby, was holding forth as usual about Cuffee Ned, his long attenuated body weaving and darting and thrusting like a fencer's as he harangued the others. The curses flew like spittle from his lips.

". . . What the fuckarse you all mean I don't know what I'm talking," he was shouting—and again it was almost impossible to make out the words. "He's goin' come again I tell you. What the shite you all know? Cuffee's goin' come. Ain't any of you ignoramuses ever heard of the second coming? Well, who the bloody hell you think they was talking about if not Cuffee? You think just because they cut off his head and put it on a pike on Westminster Road that that was the end of him? You think maybe 'cause he's been gone a little time that you'll never see him again? 'Oh, ye of little faith!' Matthew one, verse three. Disbelievers all. They couldn't kill off somebody like Cuffee just like so, don't you jackasses realize that? He said as much himself. 'Cording to the book in the big library in town, he laughed when he saw them coming with the ax. He knew there wasn't no doing away with him for good. He's goin' come again I say—or he's goin' send somebody just like him, mark my words. You think he was making any rasshole sport . . . ?"

With Ferguson's voice soaring like that of an Old Testament prophet through the yard, Saul moved on, making his way toward the beach on the other side of the house and the guests there whom he had yet to meet. And he was wondering vaguely as he slowly crossed to the stone steps leading down, stopping to introduce himself along the way, how it was that with all the people he had spoken with so far not one of them had referred, even indirectly, to the newspaper article on the project, not even the man Stinger with whom he had talked at length. They might not have seen it.

Merle, who had disappeared, returned, bringing Harriet, whom she had rescued from the drawing room, with her. "Ah, so you want to meet that bunch down on the beach," she said when she learned where he was headed. "Good. Maybe you can get them to stop their nonsense and come upstairs. But first say hello to these ladies over here."

She led them over to a group of old women standing off by themselves near the steps. Leesy was among them, looking frail and insubstantial except for her tough, work-swollen hands. She was wearing an oversized jacket that had belonged to her late husband. A stained fedora, his also, sat at a rakish angle atop the spotless white cloth she had wound about her head, and her face—what little of it that could be seen beneath the hat—was as expressionless as always, aloof, inaccessible, her rheumy eyes fey and critical. The other women, swathed like her against the chill, were silent also. But they gave the impression of being on the verge of uttering some word, some dark pronouncement which they would intone in prophetic Delphic voices. Under the hats their ancient eyes appeared disdainful of everything around them, of the fete, of the laughter and animated talk filling the yard, of the small glasses of rum they held in their hands, of the house, the night, the sea, everything, including Saul's and Harriet's hands as they held them out.

"Don't mind how harmless these ladies look," Merle said laughingly, embracing each of them in turn. "They don't have a kind word to say about anybody or anything."

"Did you see the headline the other day?" one of them said as soon as the three had left. The woman who spoke was so old the irises of her eyes were slowly being eaten away around the edges. She had been humming an atonal hymn under her breath all along, and it continued even as she spoke, underscoring the words. "Did you see the headline, I ask." She addressed no one in particular.

"You think you's the only body can read a newspaper, Mary Griggs?" Leesy said in her flat, spare way, staring straight ahead.

"I guess it means Bournehills is going to come like Trinidad soon or one of them other big places . . ." the old woman said, still humming.

"Trinidad what! New York, you mean," another woman said.

". . . with plenty money and thing sharing 'bout the place . . ." Mary Griggs continued.

"Ha!" It was Leesy again, and her scathing laugh went beyond cynicism even.

". . . and plenty work stirring."

"Ha!"

They fell silent once again.

It was damp and chilly down on the beach, the heavy night dew that had fallen adding to the salt drift off the sea, and the guests there were even more bundled than those above. It was almost as though they were in hiding under the lengths of ragged cloth and bleached flour sacks with which they had all, even the men, cloaked themselves. They stood in scattered groups over the wide strand, looking, as Merle had accused them, as if they hadn't been invited to the party but, strolling along the beach and seeing the house afloat like some brightly lighted pleasure boat on the sea of darkness, had paused to look on. Something in the set, still poses they maintained, a tableau-like quality, even suggested that they had simply appeared out of the darkness; one moment the beach below the guesthouse was empty, the next there they were, a human still life against the night sea.

Saul had difficulty making out their faces as he and Harriet, with Merle leading the way and talking steadily, moved from one to another of the static groupings. He had a fleeting impression of the harsh high bones that structured their faces and of their deep-set eyes which seemed to be regarding him from the other end of a long dimly lit corridor, whose distance was measurable both in space and time, and down which he was certain he would have to travel if he were ever to know them or they to know him. Moreover, as he occasionally, with Merle watching, leaned in close to repeat his name over the loud crash of a wave, he had the odd feeling that the youngest among them, including even the babies asleep on their mothers' breasts, were in some way unimaginably old.

Offering his hand, saying simply that he was glad to meet them, he sought, in the brief moments he spent with each, to penetrate the tunnel of their eyes, to get at what lay there. And under cover of the darkness he felt them assessing him: his outer self first—his large, somewhat soft white body that had never known real physical labor, the eyes that had gone numb after his first wife's death, the coarse hair that had begun to recede at the temples. They saw even farther, he sensed; their gaze discovering the badly flawed man within and all the things about him which he would gladly have kept hidden: his deep and abiding dissatisfaction with himself, for one, his large capacity for failing those closest to him, his arrogance, born of that defensive superiority which had been his heritage as a Jew, his selfishness—for in everything he did, no matter how selfless it might appear, he was always after raising his own stock. . . .

And they did the same with Harriet. Turning to where she stood at his side, her hair drawing down the light from the veranda above, they bent on her the same veiled, even gaze from under the cloths covering their heads. And it, too, plumbed deep, reaching behind that unruffled surface of hers which made it seem none of this was strange, and behind the smile that deferred to them. The masked smiles they gave her in return held a profound recognition.

"Pleased to have your acquaintanceship," they said with Elizabethan formality, and extended their hands in the same slow eloquent manner as they raised them to wave along the roads, that salute which seemed to make of them witnesses after some fact.

Their faces, what little of them he had been able to see, remained with Saul long after he and Harriet had returned upstairs. All during the rest of the evening, part of his mind, his thoughts, dwelt on them. He found himself wanting to return to the beach and speak further with them. If he could have done it without appearing impolite, he would have liked to probe deeper into those eyes, to understand the meaning of the expression there.

The shopkeeper, Delbert, had arrived meanwhile. They had brought him on his palanquin bed over to the guesthouse in the back of the ramshackle pickup truck he used for hauling supplies from town, and had placed him, still on the bed, out under the cassia. He lay in his loud shirt and chewed Panama hat, the broken leg in its cast. He had been given a water glass half-filled with rum and he drank slowly from this while listening like some gentle, unobtrusive arbiter to the talk around him. And from time to time, for no apparent reason, he would loose the startling laugh that wrenched him like a pain, laughing at the colossal joke that would forever remain private. Behind him, the tall steepled spur of Westminster looming above the house took up the sound and repeated it endlessly.

"I see you was in the paper the other day," he said as Saul, still puzzling over those on the beach, came over to greet him. Delbert was smiling, the smile rearranging the wrinkles that were scored like tribal markings into his flesh; but the stained eyes under the hatbrim were watchful.

"Yes, I know," he began carefully, noting to himself that Delbert was the first to mention the article. It was as though only he had the authority to bring it up. "But I'm afraid the way they wrote about us gives the wrong impression altogether. It makes it look as if we've come thinking we can work miracles, and that we've got the money to do it, which just isn't true. I've been very disturbed about the whole thing and I've asked Mrs. Kinbona if I might say a few words later to try and set the record straight."

"Well," Delbert said, the laugh beginning to rumble like a hunger pang, "you're going to have to speak loud and clear if you want the folks over on that side to hear—" the hand with the pink underbelly waved in the direction of the beach. A look passed swiftly between them and was gone.

The party had grown more lively by now, due mostly to the rum, but also to Merle who, her voice bearing her along, flitted from one group to another, imparting to each something of her special ambience. The speechmaking began shortly thereafter, with a long procession of speakers drawn from every part of the house and yard taking their place on the veranda which was crowded now at both ends with those from outside.

Merle spoke first, and standing there with the stole draped across her shoulders and her eyes giving off their warm light, she looked happy, young. The damaged portrait of the handsome young woman her face called to mind might have been restored. "Well," she began in her abrupt way, her smile taking them all in, "as you see I've got a few guests in the place for a change. Things are looking up. . . ." Then, as to be expected, she went on at length.

The headmaster of the grammar school followed with an equally long speech welcoming "the strangers from America who have taken up their abode in our humble village." His talk was interspersed with literary allusions and Latin quotations, each of which was greeted with a loud "Hear! Hear!" Afterward, a respectful hush fell even among the elite gathered in the drawing room doorway as Delbert, speaking from his litter, recalled those who had gone away from Bournehills for what had seemed forever only to return. He cited among these Vere, Allen, Merle, himself. (He had worked for many years as a young man on the Panama Canal.) "It's like there're some of us the old place just won't let go," he said.

Several speakers later Ferguson gave a slightly drunken but moving account of life in the district during the reign of his hero, speaking of it with a nostalgia that made it seem he had been alive at the time. ". . . Cuffee had us planting the fields together, I tell you," he cried. "Reaping our crops together, sharing whatsomever we had with each other. We was a people then, man; and it was beautiful to see!" Behind his glasses his oversized eyes were filled with the memory.

Vere spoke. Dressed in the blue suit, the rare light flooding his face when he smiled, he told briefly of his experiences while away. But he had often, he said, longed for home, and the floor of the veranda shuddered as the guests stamped their feet in approval. Finally, a flushed and ebullient Allen (he had been drinking beer), his happiness at being back evident in his wide grin, introduced Saul.

As the latter took his place at the railing midway along the veranda he turned so part of him was to the silent crowd on the beach. It was to them, perhaps more than any other group present, to whom he spoke—the holdouts who, in spite of Merle's pleading, cajoling, and bullying continued to stand like so many ghosts washed up by the sea under the great shadow of the house. His face inclined toward their indistinct forms; pitting his voice against the sea's so they might hear him, he spoke to them.

He dealt first with the newspaper article, saying he was sure many of them were probably wondering just how much of it was true. Part of it was true, he said. They had come to Bournehills with the hope in mind of helping to improve life in the district. Unfortunately, he said, the article had overstated matters.

"First of all, we don't have millions of dollars as was stated," he declared. "We have some money, yes, enough to cover our work for the next few months, and we should be receiving more once we have more definite plans. But it's unlikely that it will ever be in the millions of dollars. Nor have we come, Dr. Fuso and myself, believing we can 'revolutionize' life in Bournehills or 'transform' it in a short time. We wouldn't be so foolish. Nor are we 'Americans to the Rescue' as the headline put it. I mention all this because we're very concerned that you not get the wrong idea either about us or how much we can do. Perhaps," he said, "if I tell you in my own words why we've come to Bournehills and what we hope to accomplish while here it might help to clear up any confusion the article might have caused."

Leaning against the railing, part of him to the faceless crowd below, he spoke then of the project, confining himself, as he had done at Lyle Hutson's, to the first phase of the work. And as he talked, pausing occasionally to search for the right word or when a wave broke with a thunderous detonation on the reefs, drowning out his voice, he sensed that everyone was paying only scant attention to what he was saying. They were more interested in him at this point, it was clear, in the kind of man he was. This, rather than the project which they had probably already dismissed as just another vague scheme destined to fail like all the others, was the basis on which he was being judged, and would be judged in the months to come. He wondered how he would fare. His faults, it had always seemed to him, were so glaring. Those on the beach had already, in a moment's glance, seen through to them. But what to do? His faults, his many shortcomings had become like old friends over the years. He would be a stranger to himself without them. All he could hope for at this late stage was that he might prove acceptable despite them. And understanding all this, he felt suddenly uncertain (for he might well fail), and presumptuous: for who was he to be talking about transforming their lives? And painfully conscious suddenly of his white skin and the meaning it held for people like themselves, he very much wanted their acceptance, especially that of the stubborn guests below, whose faces had eluded him even when he stood up close shaking their hands.

". . . We've come to learn," he was saying. "In fact you might say that the next six months to a year will be mainly a period of learning and getting acquainted on both our parts. It will give you a chance to get to know us and decide whether we're the kind of people you'd care to have work along with you in solving some of the district's problems, and it'll give us the opportunity to get acquainted with you and learn about life here. There's a great deal we need to know which you can teach us. We're interested, for instance, in understanding about the crops and would like to spend some time out in the fields and over at the mill seeing for ourselves how the canes are reaped and the sugar made. We want, in other words, to find out firsthand how you go about your day-to-day life in Bournehills. Also, we'd like to hear directly from you what you feel are the main things wrong in the district and what in your opinion most needs to be done.

"Much of our time, then, these first few months will be pretty much spent walking around observing and occasionally asking some questions. We won't, I warn you, look as if we're doing very much, and some of you will probably start asking when are we going to get around to doing something concrete. But we'll be hard at work all the same, even though it won't look like it.

"So," he said, rising, "you should be seeing quite a lot of us in the coming weeks. I hope you won't mind—" his smile reached out tentatively. "As for my wife and I, and I know I also speak for Dr. Fuso, we're very much looking forward to living in Bournehills. I hear you have the best sea air in the world, that it's known to cure whatever ails someone, so I expect to leave here a new man."

Merle was the first to come over when the applause—the light pounding of the right foot on the shaky floorboards which was their way—had ceased. "Well," she said, "you did all right for yourself." Her face raised to his, she was openly reappraising him. Her smile had little of its usual edge, but was speculative and strangely mild. Then, abruptly, she said, "You know one thing, I'm sorry now about the way I got on at Sugar's the other night . . ."

"That's all right," he said with a laugh. "I considered it part of the initiation rites. They're standard in my profession." But he spoke absently, because his attention was once again directed to the crowd below the veranda. They had not joined in the applause, and peering down through the darkness he saw that the beach was completely deserted. They had quietly—every man, woman and child—slipped away as soon as he had finished speaking, disappearing so swiftly and soundlessly up the beach it was as if they had simply merged with the night or returned to the sea. It made him wonder for a moment whether they had even been there.

"But I wonder why these people from Away can't learn, yes," Leesy said, taking off the fedora and then slowly unwinding her headcloth before the mirror in her tiny bedroom. The glass was as dim and mottled as her eyes. "Every time you look here comes another set of them with a big plan. They're goin' do this, they're goin' do the other, and they end up not doing a blast. And they always got to come during crop when people are busy trying to get their few canes out the ground and over to Cane Vale, always walking about and looking, the lot of them, like they never seen poor people before. I tell you they's some confused and troubled souls you see them there. . . ."

She draped a dark cloth over the mirror so that the ghosts of the family dead would not come to look at themselves while she slept, and then slowly and painfully, wearing a long nightgown that resembled a shroud, she climbed the short stepladder to the high bed in which she had been born, and in which she would die when she felt it was time. She lay like a figure carved upon a catafalque on the hard mattress of cus-cus grass, an effigy of someone already dead, utterly still, more self-contained and certain in her way than Harriet even.

"And it's not that the gentleman tonight doesn't look like he means well," she said, addressing the shadows which had also arranged themselves for sleep around the room. In the flickering light of the kerosene lamp she kept burning at a low all night they appeared to nod in agreement. "He talks direct. He's a man, you can see, don't put on no lot of airs like some them who come here calling themselves trying to help. And he's the first one ever said he wanted to go out in a cane field and see for himself how we have to work. You can tell he's a decent somebody. But what's the use? He'll never get to know this place. He'll never understand it. Bournehills! Change Bournehills! Improve conditions! Ha!" Her laugh was full of a secret knowing. "The only way you could maybe change things around here would be to take one of Bryce-Parker's bulldozers from the conservation scheme and lay the whole place flat flat flat and then start fresh."

After a long silence broken only by the sound of her tangled breathing (it seemed about to fail at any moment), she said, "Multimillions!" and sucking her teeth, slept.

CHAPTER 4

In bed also that night under a high white tent of mosquito netting that made her think of an extravagant bridal veil, Harriet quietly went over in her mind her impressions of the evening. Beside her in the mate to the two little narrow, celibate single beds which they had pushed together to form one bed, Saul lay awake, occupied with his own thoughts. Outside the unshaded windows, a tardy moon which had risen just when the party was ending had transformed the entire coast into a moonscape which made her think of the coldly lit surreal world of the sleeping gypsy and lion in the Rousseau painting.

As was her custom with each new experience, she had carefully stored her impressions on the shelf in her mind she reserved for that purpose, until such time as she was alone and could go over them at her leisure. It would take her some days, she knew, to sort out her reactions to all she had seen and heard over the course of the long evening, but her immediate feeling, as she began, was that none of it had been as strange or difficult as she had supposed it would be. The main reason for this, she suspected, was that throughout the evening she had felt like one of those special members of the audience in a Restoration theater, notables and the like, who had been permitted to sit on stage during the performance of a play. She had found herself on stage during the somewhat rowdy but interesting drama that had been the party. But although she had been close up on the action, almost part of it, she had nonetheless, by virtue of her seat on the sidelines near the wings, remained apart, immune. So that she had moved safely through the noise, the heat, the drinking, through the gantlet of outstretched black hands, veiled eyes and faces that in their set darkness were as one face endlessly repeated. Even when the party had grown more turbulent and the voices and gestures of the men arguing out on the roadside had threatened violence, she had remained unperturbed, confident none of it could touch or include her. Because of this the entire evening had seemed easy.

"Tonight went rather well, don't you think, Saul?" She turned on her pillow to him. "Especially your speech. You very nicely, I thought, cleared up that whole business of the newspaper article, as well as explained what the project really hopes to do. You're so good at putting things simply. I'd never have been able to do that. Saul . . ."

She waited, then raising up on her elbow leaned toward him, thinking him asleep. By the moonlight filtering in through the net she saw that he was awake. He hadn't heard her.

"Saul."

He roused, his eyes focusing. She had the sense of his returning from some terribly remote and private place. "Sorry Hatt, I wasn't listening. What did you say?"

"I said I thought everything went very well tonight, especially your speech."

"Yes, I think so, too, all things considered. I'm glad I did as Merle suggested."

"What were you so deep in thought about?"

He moved slightly away. "Oh, I was also thinking about tonight. I still haven't gotten over how fast the folks down on the beach disappeared after my little talk."

"Yes, I noticed that, too. It was odd. One minute they were there and the next they were gone. And not one of them ever came upstairs, do you realize that?"

"I know."

"They just stood down there the whole time watching everything. And looking so pathetic," she added after a moment. "I managed to get a good look at one or two of them when we were being introduced, and their faces were so thin you could see all their bones. And so many had hardly any teeth left—and not just the old people but even those who you could tell were fairly young. Why's that, I wonder?"

"What's there to wonder about?" he said. "It takes money to go to the dentist, which they certainly don't have—so when a tooth goes bad, you just pull it out. It's as simple as that."

"Yes, I suppose so. I don't know why, but I thought it might be some sort of custom with them."

"It's got nothing to do with customs, only economics."

They were silent for a time. Then, her face to the ceiling, her voice hushed and tragic under the frothy canopy, she said, "Yesterday, while you and Allen were out, I walked a little way into the village, just to look around. I managed to get a peek inside some of the houses on what they call the main road." She paused; then, "They were awful, Saul; worse, I think, than anything I ever saw in North Philadelphia. I don't see how they can bear living in them."

He stiffened perceptibly, and then slowly, in the dimness, turned to her with the look he sometimes gave her—which said that even after their long affair and the year and more of marriage he still didn't know her well enough to know how to take some of the things she said.

"It's not as if they have any choice in the matter," he said. "They don't choose to live as they do." His voice was quiet.

"Of course not. Oh, Saul"—she swung sharply toward him—"did I seem to be implying that?"

"I'm afraid it sounded like it," he said. His pale eyes with the numb centers had hardened.

"Oh, no! But you know I didn't mean anything like that, don't you?"

He looked at her for another long moment, then finally gave an uncertain nod.

Reaching across she touched the corner of his mouth as if hoping to evoke a forgiving smile. "Darling, you're going to have to," she said, "teach me how to say these things so they don't come out sounding wrong."

He smiled faintly, in response perhaps to her touch; then, with a sigh, turned away. "I don't know how much of it can be taught, Hatt. There're some things you have to come to on your own, if it's in you to do."

But she had been restored by his smile, and said with a laugh, "All right, if you won't teach me, I'll just have to go around putting my foot in my mouth. No," she added quickly, "I won't do anything of the sort. I'll learn. I really will."

In the long silence that followed, the cloudy tent of mosquito netting drew more of the moonlight down onto the bed, and her hair, spread in an orderly halo on the pillow, shone both the wheaten gold that it was and silver.

Then suddenly she laughed again. "Oh, those speeches! There was no end to them. And to make matters worse I hardly understood a word anybody was saying. I refuse to believe they're actually speaking English."

He laughed sleepily. "Well, they are—or a version thereof."

"And the head of the grammar school with his high-flown Latin. I remember wondering if he knew the meaning of half the things he was quoting. By the way, I'm having tea with his wife on Friday."

"Good," he said, his voice muffled. He had arranged himself for sleep, his back to her. "That's your department."

"You're leaving all the dull work for me, is that it?"

"Mmhuh, that's your end of the research."

"And who was that huge man who also spoke, the one with his leg in a cast? You introduced me to him but I've forgotten his name."

He stirred briefly into wakefulness. "That's Delbert. He owns the shop I went to our first night here. According to Allen he's a real power in the village in that he has the respect of the ordinary people. We're certain to need his acceptance and support if we hope to do anything."

"I see," she said. "Well, it should all prove very interesting. I'm looking forward to the next few months. . . ." Then, her own voice becoming murmurous with sleep: "I'm going to have to ask our landlady for shades or curtains to put up to the windows for when there's moonlight." Then, "And I don't know which is worse, the mosquitoes or this ridiculous bridal veil. . . ." Then, gently, "Saul . . ."

But he was asleep, and remembering how distant he had seemed before, as if off in some remote place that excluded her, she turned to draw close to him, only to find that with their movements back and forth, the two beds had moved slightly apart and there was a thin gulf which reached to the floor between them. She would have to get one of the maids tomorrow to fasten together the metal frames along the sides with a length of strong wire.

CHAPTER 5

In the weeks following the party the first phase of the project got underway. It had been decided as far back as Philadelphia that Saul would devote his time during the initial period to obtaining a general picture of life in Bournehills, largely through observation and interviews, while Allen would concentrate on the more technical end of the research, which was his specialty.

So that, for his part, Allen spent those early weeks amassing a wealth of statistical and demographical data. Some days found him poring over the dusty community records in the parochial office within the complex of public buildings on top of Westminster; other days were spent in New Bristol consulting the innumerable records, reports and studies of Bournehills to be found at the various government offices and ministries, and talking to officials. And everywhere he took copious notes, his broad, tough-looking hands with the black hair bunched between the knuckles jotting down the endless numbers and percentages in his notebook with the same rapid stabbing motion of a blind man writing braille. And he always kept his head bent low over the work, hiding the little sensual smile of pleasure, the scholar's quiet pleasure, which shaped his lips then.

He invariably began his day with a visit to the kitchen garden at the north side of the guesthouse. Often waking before the tiny alarm on his moonfaced watch went off or the one old cock Merle kept crowed the dawn in from the bare cassia tree, where it slept amid its hens, he would pull on the work pants she had saved for him, and, after vigorously brushing his hair, taking out all the rich curl as he had been admonished to do as a boy, go out to the garden.

As he squatted there, his head bent as though listening to the small sounds the vegetables made as they fought their way up out of the harsh soil, the day would break, the morning unfolding, blossoming, around him. And it was always as if a hand had reached down and snatched away the last of the darkness like a dust sheet to unveil a world that, each dawn, looked new. Perhaps it was the extraordinary freshness and clarity to the air at this hour which made for the impression, or the fact that the few props which comprised the spare landscape of sea, sand, and hill stood out then in such startling relief. Whatever, everything had the appearance of having been newly created: the sea poured fresh into its vast bed during the night, Westminster raised stone upon stone in the predawn darkness, the sandhills piled up by the wind only moments ago, the cassia planted whole.

The sun, as Allen turned to watch it rise from the sea, was treasure, a doubloon from some pirate's sunken cache. And it was a spendthrift sun which from the moment it appeared lavished its gold upon everything in sight, including Allen, so that his hazel eyes, which Merle had once likened to the stained-glass rose window in the Anglican church in Spiretown because of their mosaic of gray and green and tawny yellow, came warmly alive, and for those moments, he was in touch with the best in himself.

Later in the morning, wearing the Bavarian shorts and short-sleeved white shirt—his uniform when in the field—and equipped with notebook and pen, he would set off for New Bristol. He usually took the car, a secondhand English Ford which they bought shortly after their arrival, but often, especially in the beginning, he traveled by the one decrepit Bournehills bus, a converted lorry with widely spaced slats along its open sides to prevent the passengers from sliding out as it took the sharp turns in the road, a tarpaulin roof and crude benches nailed to the floor.

The mornings he took the bus it would be crowded with women, their dark faces powdered white for the trip to town and their hair freshly braided under their headcloths. They were the hawkers on their way to New Bristol with baskets of mangoes and breadfruit, and the yams, cassava and sweet potatoes grown amid the canes in the fields. He would sit hemmed in by their thighs and vigorous voices, by their free rough laughter; he was privy to the quarrels that would occasionally send the old bus reeling on the hills. They teased him good-naturedly, saying they had expected him to return with a wife. It was time he married, they declared. It was better to marry than to burn. Celibacy would only set out his head. They vowed to find him a wife: "Some nice schoolteacher in town." He hid from them behind his boyish smile.

The day's research done, he would return to Bournehills in the late afternoon, his notebook filled, his eyes strained from the hours of close work, exhausted but exhilarated. He might treat himself to a swim then, going with Merle, if she had returned from her part-time job at the almshouse, and later, when they became friends, with Vere, over to the place up the beach from the guesthouse, called Horseshoe Pool, where the huge boulders fallen from Westminster long ago had formed a natural breakwater that was roughly the shape of a horse's shoe. The sea within the wide half-circle of rock was almost calm, and it was the only place along this coast of rough water where it was safe to swim.

Sometimes, too, at the urging of the small boys in the village, he would join their late afternoon game of soccer on the large pasture in the middle of Spiretown, which also served as a playing field. At its edge, near the main road, stood the social center for the village, an old-fashioned, pavilion-like hall, with, inside, the television set that had mysteriously gone blank only hours after it had been installed. Allen had never played soccer before coming to Bournehills, but he had loved the game ever since his uncle, the one with the truck farm, had taken him as a boy to see a visiting Italian team. And he was good for someone who had never played before—butting the ball cleanly with his forehead and deftly maneuvering it with his feet across the grass, which the sheep, tethered there during the day, had cropped down to the nub.

Finally, when the sun which had met him in the morning took its leave behind Westminster, and the instant Bournehills dusk came rushing down, he would bring his day full circle by briefly revisiting his vegetable patch; then, if he did not accompany Saul to Delbert's shop, which had become an almost nightly ritual with them, he would work till bedtime on the data he had collected.

So his days went, each one carefully planned, orderly, filled with the work he loved and the few simple pleasures he allowed himself. And what added to them even more (although he could not admit it to himself), what, in fact, made those days stand out as perhaps the most memorable he had ever known, was the beginning of his friendship with Vere.

They had talked for some time at the party Merle had given in their honor. Allen, his tongue loosened by the beer, had recalled with undisguised nostalgia his childhood visits to his uncle's farm in south Jersey; Vere had told of the time he had worked picking fruit in the same area. And then one day driving into New Bristol in the Ford, Allen had come upon Vere headed to town on foot, having missed the Bournehills bus which made only one morning and evening trip, and he had given him a lift. Vere had been on his way into New Bristol to shop around for the used car he intended purchasing with the money he had sent Leesy to save for him his three years away. At first they had been awkward and uncomfortable with each other sitting side by side in the close quarters of the Ford. But gradually Vere, the less shy of the two, had begun speaking of his plans for the car he would buy: of how he intended, first of all, overhauling it completely, using as a guide the automotive manual he had brought with him from the States (and he had shown Allen the worn, lovingly thumbed manual he kept in his back pocket); then, once this was done, how he planned entering the car in the Whitmonday Race held in Spiretown in May and also starting his own taxi service, driving people in Bournehills to town or to funerals or to the airport for a small fee. In that way he hoped to eventually accumulate enough money to emigrate to England or Canada.

And he spoke of all this with the complete assurance that it would be, his eyes confident above the high slanted bones that molded his face.

After that, they often drove to town together—for it was weeks before Vere found just the car he wanted. Once, when Allen went to look with him, he had spotted a secondhand Morris which had seemed to him a good buy and he had said as much to Vere. But the latter had dismissed it with scarcely a glance. "No," he had said, "I'm looking for something special. I'll know it when I see it."

One late afternoon, at the end of a long day of close work on Allen's part in the airless government offices in New Bristol, and on Vere's, searching for a car in one dark, stiflingly hot garage after another, Allen proposed that they take a swim in Horseshoe Pool upon their return to Bournehills. Vere agreed. And so with the departing sun setting aflame the white stone public buildings atop Westminster and sending its fiery glow out to the coast, they swam, just the two of them alone in the heavy, wine-dark sea. They kept pace, their bodies —the one white but growing brown from the sun, the other as dark as the sea beneath its fire-lit surface—attuned to a single rhythm as they repeatedly circled the pool. Allen was the first to tire, and stumbling back onto the beach he sat in the surf, breathing heavily, the black hair matted on his body, his gaze on Vere. Watching him. His body as he strongly rode the waves. As Allen watched, a large wave, sweeping in over the barrier rocks, lifted Vere high and then gently deposited him in its wake as it came racing on toward the shore. It broke in a furious boil of pebbles and torn spume and stinging sand around Allen. He felt the hard-packed shingle under him give way and the receding wave tugging at him, determined to bear him with it back to the sea. And he let it take him—shouting in mock protest, his body a happy sprawl—back to the pool, where a laughing Vere awaited him.

The next morning, and every morning thereafter, he could be heard singing in the garden at dawn.

In contrast to Allen's carefully planned schedule and well-ordered days, Saul gave the impression of working without any schedule or set plan in mind as he went about his part of the research. Most days found him simply wandering the roads of Spiretown and the surrounding countryside, his hands in the pockets of his slightly rumpled seersucker pants, his eyes narrowed against the glare and his head bared to the sun. ("But Dr. Saul, don't you know that walking about without a hat in this Bournehills hot sun will set out your head?" a woman cried in irritable solicitude from behind the drawn jalousies at her door after he had been there some months.)

During those long, seemingly aimless walks he would stop to chat with anyone who appeared willing. It might be a woman drawing water at a standpipe, a man on his way to or from the fields with his billhook in hand, or a child leading a cow or a string of knobby sheep over to the near grassless pasture where Allen sometimes played soccer. It might be the idlers of the village, most of them young men Vere and Allen's age, who spent their days lounging on the tree-shaded culvert wall over a small river, dry now, which traversed the main road at a point near Delbert's shop, and their evenings practicing the steel drums for carnival later in the year.

To his surprise, nearly everyone he approached seemed willing enough to talk with him. There was little of the initial resistance and even distrust he had encountered in other places where he had done field work. Part of it he attributed to the fact that he had come as a friend of Allen's; part to the fact that they were used to his kind. He was only the latest, after all, in a long line of strangers who had come seeking to rouse Bournehills. But there was more involved, he sensed, in the ease with which they accepted him. They appeared almost *eager* to have him observe them at their daily round. Something behind their voices and in their eyes, which even in the daylight seemed to be regarding him from the other end of a long, shadow-filled tunnel; above all, something in the slow smiles they gave him from time to time encouraged him to look on at their lives, to see for himself how it was with them.

Moreover, as the weeks passed, he felt himself being slowly drawn into the life of the place, his day taking on the rhythm and feel of the day in Bournehills—so much so that after awhile, without being conscious of it, he left off wearing his watch and began telling time by the sun like everyone else. And yet, although this was what he was after, this participation and merging, he couldn't help feeling obscurely troubled by the ease with which it was happening.

One of the first places he visited during those early weeks was Cane Vale. The mill, the only one of three left in the district, which meant that it was grossly overworked, was situated just behind the village, at a place where the great northern flank of Westminster flattened out to almost level ground. There, with the permission of the manager, Erskine Vaughan, Merle's tense, anxious relative with the freckled sand-colored skin, he toured the buildings and wandered on his own around the huge yard, talking informally with the men and observing operations.

As the lorries came in laden from the fields they were weighed on a scale set into the ground outside the bookkeeper's office, a small separate building near the entrance gates. Inside, the bookkeeper sat on his high scrivener's stool recording the tonnage registered on the indicator in front of him while Erskine Vaughan hovered worriedly nearby. At times when a donkey cart carrying a small load of peasant canes—those which the villagers grew amid the stones in their tiny plots—would creak onto the scale, he would dash, fussing, outside.

"What, you call these canes, too?" he would cry, snatching one from the load, his annoyance and disgust causing the freckles to stand out across his broad nose. "These few dried-up sticks you got here.

Can't you see they scarce got any juice in them?" And they were, for the most part, pitiful—thin, and with a parched look to them, like canes left over from a harvest that had taken place many seasons ago. "Ain't you people heard that Kingsley and them are going to shut down the blasted place any day now because with all the canes we grind we still don't produce no sugar to speak of. Haven't you heard that?"

And far behind their veiled eyes they would smile at the old threat, recognizing that he said it as they all did, as a precautionary measure, like knocking on wood or making the sign of the cross to ensure its never happening.

Once weighed, the canes were scooped up from the trucks by a giant hoist and swung through the bright dust-laden air over to a chute leading into the factory, or if there was a backlog, as was usually the case, they were dumped in a large storage nest made of steel girders outside.

The first time Saul entered the factory—a low sprawling building in serious disrepair, with a torn, rusted galvanized roof and a smokestack rising above it like a great phallus—he was reminded of the deep hold of a ship. There was the noise, for one—the loud unrelieved drumming and pounding of the machines that powered the rollers which crushed the juice from the canes, and the shrill, almost human wail of the rollers themselves as they turned in their deep pit. There was the heat, for another, which came pouring up through the metal floor from the furnaces below to join the heat and steam flaring off the large open vats and boilers in which the cane juice was boiled till it turned to sugar. And the light in the place was dim and murky as in the hold of a ship, the color of the molasses bubbling away in the boilers. Moreover, because of the dimness and the cane chaff which came flying up from the roller pit to whirl like a sandstorm through the air, the men working there appeared almost disembodied forms: ghosts they might have been from some long sea voyage taken centuries ago.

The tall man, Ferguson, became Saul's self-appointed guide whenever he visited Cane Vale. And it was a sober, businesslike, albeit voluble, Ferguson then. He had worked at the factory since a boy, from the time, he liked to boast, when the original windmill, the one to which the planter Percy Bryam had been bound, in the story of the Pyre Hill revolt which he retold endlessly, had been in use. (The windmill, still to be seen in the yard, was miraculously intact except for some crumbling away of the stone at its base and the missing sails to its vanes.) In his younger days Ferguson had operated the giant hoist outside, but now that he was old he worked as a minor overseer, mainly supervising the women and boys who cleaned and oiled the machines. It was also his job to sound the horn that signaled the change in shifts and whose baleful foghorn blast carried clear to Spiretown and even as far as the guesthouse at times.

Ferguson's great pride was the rollers, and whenever Saul dropped in to see him, he would take him up to the platform over the pit which housed them, and leaning over the railing, unmindful of the chaff flying up in his face and the stunning noise, point to the two huge, slowly turning wheels with an air almost of ownership. He worried over them, for like all the equipment in the factory they were overworked, old, and needed replacing.

"They're on their last legs, you see them there. They might not even see us through this crop. And I know what I'm talking 'cause I'm a man been 'round machines all my life and know them," he said to Saul one day as they stood on the platform gazing down at the rollers. The whites of his troubled eyes were stained brown by the muddy light; the planes of his long, boldly sculpted face looked sharper because of the shadows. "They're only trying their best now 'cause they know we got the crop to get out, but they can't last. Man, they've ground 'nough canes in their time and they're tired out, old. Why, these rollers have been here longer than me and I'm no pup. They've even killed a man. Yes. Neville Walkes, Leesy's husband, God rest him in his grave. He get a slide one day from this said-same platform and fell into the pit and Mr. Roller chew him up like he was piece of cane. You think they used to make any rasshole sport! But they're near finish now. There's no way in this Christ world they can last much longer . . ."

"Does Mr. Vaughan know the shape they're in?" Saul asked.

"You mean Miss Calamity!" Ferguson cried contemptuously against the thunderous pulsing around them. (It was the name everyone called Erskine Vaughan behind his back, given him, it was said, by Merle.) "How you mean! 'Course he knows. He have eyes in his damn head, don't he? But he wouldn't ask the Kingsley people to put in new ones not for Thy Kingdom Come! He's frighten they'll get vex with him if he asks for anything. And if anyone here so much as mentions that the rollers are looking bad, he flies up and says it's because we don't care them proper. . . . No, man, there's no talking to Calamity. But I'm making my plans." His glasses sparked dull red in the dimness as he nodded. "I'm planning on speaking direct to Sir John, the big boss from England-self, next time he comes to visit."

"Do you think he might be coming this year? I'd like to meet him."

"Oh, yes," Ferguson said. "He comes every year—he has a big house over to the Crown Beach Colony where he spends his holidays —and he always visits Cane Vale then, just to look things over." Suddenly he laughed, the laugh baring the few widely spaced yellowed teeth he had left and bending his body like a wind. "Lord, man, you should see Calamity the day Sir John comes; he's near messing in his pants. Yes, I'm going to speak to the big man himself," he said, sobering, "even if I got to have in a few grogs to do it. I'm going to step right up"—and he leaped close to Saul with the lunging step that was part of the dance he performed while talking—"and say, 'Sir John, sir, please to direct your attention to these rollers you got here. They want changing. We been trying our best with them lo these many years but they're ready to kick out any day now, so if you know like me you best put some new ones in and quick too.' Just like that. I'm not going to bite my tongue. You think I'm making any rasshole sport. I'm gonna tell him straight, just the way I'm telling you. Mark my words."

During those early weeks that were so full they seemed like months, Saul also made a point of visiting the sites of the other projects previously attempted in Bournehills, all of which had failed. He saw for himself the pipes for the irrigation system that had never been utilized lying rusted in the tiny fields belonging to the small farmers; he inspected the roofless crumbling shell of the pottery factory that had been unable to open because people in Bournehills refused to work there, and the remains of the little graceless cinder-block houses in the government housing scheme which were overrun with devil grass. In the company of the reticent Australian, Bryce-Parker, he toured the utterly denuded sun-baked lands north of Cane Vale where the soil conservation program was concentrating its efforts. And even as they stood watching the bulldozers and the heavy earth-moving equipment leveling one of the low hillocks nearby, the dry gray soil appeared to be drifting back, piling up again, forming a new hill where the old one had been. Taking Harriet along, he went to see the experimental banana grove the government had started in the hope that the small farmers would start growing them instead of the meager canes. But this, too, had had to be abandoned for lack of interest, and the few banana plants that had not been tumbled by the wind stood lopsided and forlorn like scarecrows who had failed at their job.

The reasons for the failures were not hard to come by for someone like himself who had spent so many years in the field. They were the ones, he discovered, after reading the reports and talking with the officials in town who had been involved, which usually defeated such programs: generally poor planning, the condescending attitude of the people in charge, the failure to include the villagers directly in the project from the beginning—the failure to prepare the way, in other words. All this and more had made for the defeat. And yet, although the reasons were clear enough and answered his questions, he remained strangely dissatisfied, questioning. He couldn't help feeling that something apart from the obvious had also been at play. He couldn't say why he felt this. But vague and formless though it was, the impression stayed with him, and one day, when he had been in Bournehills for a time, he tried, without even knowing what it was he was after, to talk about it to Delbert.

He would often on his walks around Spiretown drop in at the shop. It was his refuge from the hot roads. Its ancient, wormeaten walls and steeply pitched roof, its dimness, kept the heat at bay, so that it was—at least during the day—quiet, contained, and almost cool. Delbert would be there on his bed behind the counter playing dominoes with the village butcher, a dour, laconic old man named Collins, who worked only on Sundays when he officiated at the killing of the sheep or pig which took place before dawn in the yard behind the shop. Down the counter from them, the woman who lived with Delbert would be waiting on the customers in the grocery beyond the low partition which divided the interior in two. The woman, a large, rawboned Backra, was from Canterbury, a hill southeast of Westminster where everyone in the small settlement there was related and shared the same crinkled, snuff-colored hair, rough reddish near-white skin and the same name, MacFarland. Like the butcher Collins the woman seldom spoke, but would dispense the gill of rice, the few onions, the half-pound of salted cod the customers called for with scarcely a word.

The day Saul dropped in she was ladling kerosene oil into a quart can for a small boy in a dirty singlet and ragged khaki shorts, the seat of which had worn away, revealing the dark cheeks of his buttocks. The smell of the oil drifting across to the men in their half of the shop was heavy on the air but not unpleasant.

Delbert and Collins were as usual playing dominoes, and for a long time Saul watched their game in silence. Then Delbert remarked that it looked as if the dry season would be a long one this year, and Saul, remembering the rusted pipes lying in the parched fields, said he wondered why people in Bournehills had never used them. They seemed a good idea to him. Or why, for that matter, they had never taken advantage of any of the improvement schemes started by the government. It made him wonder, he said.

Delbert, a domino poised in one hand, slowly lifted his head and smiled, the smile a precursor of the laugh that shook the walls. The scribbled-over eyes held him in their gaze.

"You can't tell," he said. "Bournehills people are funny, you know. They don't take easy to anything new, even when it might be to their good. Too set in their ways, I guess. Another thing is the kind of schemes government starts. Most of them don't suit conditions here. Who told them we could grow bananas on this stone we have for soil? And who told them we're a people used to living in any concrete box in a housing scheme . . . ?"

"But there was nothing wrong with the irrigation pipes," Saul said. "They would have helped."

"Is true," he conceded. "Although only a few of the small farmers got the pipes, which wasn't right. If you give one, you must give all. But as you say, they would have helped those that had them. What to say, yes?" he shrugged. His aged massive shoulders were scarcely able to lift. "Maybe Bournehills people just want the old place to stay as is for some reason. I don't know. One thing certain, these people in government and the ones like yourself from Away need to study their facts better before starting up their big schemes. They need to do like you, man, and come live in the place and speak directly with the people and find out firsthand what's what." Then, his gaze taking the other's measure: "I heard you was out to the fields with Stinger a few days back."

"Yes," he said. "And I'm supposed to go with him tomorrow, and this time spend the morning if I can manage the heat."

"Good," Delbert said. "That's good. Maybe the more you walk about and see for yourself how things stand with us, the better chance you'll have of understanding the place one day. 'Cause Bournehills isn't easy to know. It might seem so, and it fools a lot of people. But it's not."

He resumed the game. Across the counter from him, next to Saul, Collins hadn't once looked up from studying the configuration of dominoes on the scarred wood.

He was never to forget the morning he spent in the fields the following day. He had been there, it was true, several times before. In fact, the greater part of those first weeks had been spent out on the high slopes observing the harvesting in the company usually of Stinger, whom he came to know and like so much that after awhile he found himself seeking him out not only for information but for companionship as well. He found himself increasingly drawn to the man, as he had been on the night of the party, by his quietly self-assured, reflective air and the subtle sadness (or was it remorse?) which mirrored something in himself.

He went to visit Stinger, taking Harriet along, in the cramped house just up from the main road, where he lived with his common-law wife, a lively young woman of great wit who was always said to be pregnant (she was now), their numerous children (no one was sure of the exact count) and one sway-backed cow, gone dry long ago, which they kept tied out back. Every dawn without fail, Stinger, his billhook in hand, would lead the cow on a long journey that took them down the beach past the guesthouse, south to where the sandhills gave way to a high palisade called Plover Cliff. The cliffs, a way station for migratory plovers long ago, boasted a network of inaccessible caves hollowed out by the sea below, and a little grass growing like stubble on top. Stinger would tether the animal there and return for it at dusk. Sometimes, rising earlier than usual, Saul would accompany him out to the cliffs; and returning they would stop off at the guesthouse for a cup of coffee together. After awhile Stinger often dropped off on his way back to see whether Saul wished to go with him to the fields. If so, they would walk over to the village together, with around them the dawn mist rising to meet the smoke of the morning fires just beginning to drift from the houses.

Usually, he would spend no more than an hour or so out in the cane lands with Stinger. He had often wanted to stay longer, but had found the heat (especially in the beginning) overpowering, and the steady climb up the slopes too much for his badly out-of-condition body. Then, too—and far more discomforting than the heat—was the feeling that he had no right to be standing idly by watching their ordeal (this was the only word for him that came close to describing what he witnessed in those fields). At times he felt almost like a voyeur looking on from the immunity of his peephole at another's debasement. When overcome by this feeling, he would, with a parting word to Stinger, hasten away.

But this morning he had decided, feeling somewhat more up to it, to spend the better part of the day out with him. But he had chosen unwisely, he was to discover later, for with the dry season fully underway, the sun, by the time they reached the slopes at eight o'clock and the cutting began, was as hot as it would normally be at noon.

Stinger was the boss of his own small work crew which consisted of three other men besides himself who did the cutting, and a number of women, including his pregnant wife, Gwen, called headers, whose job was to gather and tie the canes felled by the men into great bundles which they then bore on their heads down the hillside to the lorries waiting on the road to take them to Cane Vale. Once Saul had tried lifting one of the bundles. It had felt to be well over two hundred pounds. He had barely been able to move it from the ground. Gwen, spotting him, had laughed. "Watch, you don't break your navel string," she had said not unkindly. "Your body ain't use to nothing like this."

As front man Stinger set the pace of the cutting, which even today with the early heat, was formidable. Following him up the steep shoulder of the hill upon which the field lay, Saul was impressed, amazed. All the strength in the man's slight, wiry body had been poured, it seemed, in some highly concentrated form, into his right arm, and with this he slashed away without pause at the canes, his billhook describing the same beautifully controlled downward arc as in the rumshop that first night.

He worked, silent and absorbed, unmindful of the sun that was like a yellow floodlamp trained on his back and of the heat rising in visible waves from the ground at his feet: "The devil's pushing the heat, man," people in Bournehills said—and it was as if some diabolical smith deep in the earth was working a bellows over an enormous, roaring forge. Stinger, his dirt-stained cap pulled low, didn't even take notice of the estate manager who rode by from time to time at a distance. The manager, one of those who had attended Merle's party, was an old Bournehills white named Pollard, with bleached anonymous blue eyes and meal-white hair, his lips galled from what seemed centuries of sun. He had once owned the small estate they were working today but he had sold it to the Kingsley group, who had then kept him on as the manager. Pollard still held to the old ways, and always made his rounds dressed in jodhpurs, polished boots, a cork hat and riding a piebald horse. Seeing him ride past in the distance with his large black sun umbrella raised called to mind some ghost who refused to keep to his grave even during the daytime.

Stinger never saw him. He saw, was only conscious of, the canes ranked like an opposing army before him up the slope, their long pointed leaves bristling like spears in the wind. To these only did he give his attention, and each time he brought one of them crashing down, he would give a little triumphant grunt (the only sound he was ever heard to utter while working), and toss it contemptuously aside.

Behind him Gwen kept pace, gathering together the canes he flung her way into great sheaves which, with an assist from the other women, she then placed on her head and "headed" down to the truck below. And it was a precarious descent, for the ground would be slick underfoot from the "trash": the excess leaves the men hacked off the stalks before cutting them, and treacherous with the severed stumps hidden beneath. One bad slip and the neck could snap. But Gwen moved confidently down, as did the other women, her head weaving almost imperceptibly from side to side under its load (the motion was reminiscent of those child dancers from Bali, but more subtle, more controlled), her swollen stomach thrust high and her face partly hidden beneath the thick overhang.

The morning seemed interminable even with the brief breaks for water and the longer one for the meal of rice with its gravy of saltfish brought, cooked, with them to the fields, which they took at eleven. To add to matters, the sun, instead of rising to its zenith as it should have as they approached noon, appeared to drop closer, so close finally it looked as though the men could reach up and touch it with their billhooks. Also, by now the heat from below had choked off what little air there had been earlier, and shimmering up in thick waves around them gave the entire scene a feel of unreality, of something taking place at a time long passed. Moreover, as Saul, his eyes inflamed by the fallen sun, glanced up ahead to the portion of the sloping field which had yet to be done, it struck him that the canes, while giving the impression of retreating, had all the time been swiftly regrouping, replenishing their ranks, so that there were now as many of them as when the cutting began.

And still Stinger pressed the assault, his drenched shirt cleaving to his back like a second skin under which you could see the play of his smallest muscles and the almost matte finish to his blackness. But although his pace did not slacken, Saul saw him undergo as the noon hour passed a transformation that left him shaken and set in motion his own collapse. For one, Stinger's essentially slight, small-built body, which was further reduced by the canes towering above him, appeared to be gradually shrinking, becoming smaller and painfully bent, old. By early afternoon all that was left to him it appeared were the shriveled bones and muscles within the drawn sac of skin and the one arm flailing away with a mind and will of its own. He saw, too, that every exposed place on his body—his arms, neck, his blind shrunken face, his bare feet—was covered with tiny bits of the tough cane peel which flew up along with the thick dust and chaff each time a plant was felled. They were like slivers of wood driven into the flesh. Saul felt them like splinters in his own flesh. But most telling of all was that the low private grunt of triumph which Stinger uttered whenever he sent one of the cane plants toppling had ceased and the only sound issuing from him was a labored wheeze which came in short desperate gasps—and which, in the klieg-light intensity of the afternoon sun, called to mind a winded wrestler being slowly borne down in defeat by an opponent who had proved his superior.

Then even as he watched Stinger succumb, Gwen passed him on her way down to the lorry. All along she had been carrying on a lively exchange with the other headers, joking and calling out to them as they bent at their work, but now that the morning had crept into noon and that, in turn, into an afternoon to which there seemed no end, she had fallen silent. And suddenly, she appeared less certain of her footing on the steep grade. The almost offhand confidence of the morning was gone, and like Stinger, who remained absorbed in his cutting to the exclusion of everything else, she was only conscious of the dangerous footing down the hill. The set of her back, the way she stepped—first carefully feeling the ground ahead with her foot before placing her weight on it—said she had marshaled her slender forces to see her down.

She passed, and under the waving green forest on her head, Saul saw her face, a face which when she laughed proved she was still a young woman. But in the short time since he had last glanced her way it had aged beyond recognition. A hot gust of wind lifted the overhanging leaves a little higher and he glimpsed her eyes. . . . He tried describing them to himself some days later when he could bring himself to think of them. But he could not, except to say they had had the same slightly turned up, fixed, flat stare that you find upon drawing back the lids of someone asleep or dead.

He fled then, forgetting even to take his leave of Stinger as he usually did. His head pounding, eyes burning, unable to breathe in the choked-off air, he groped his way down the shorn hillside, which, with the dust and smoldering heat and the cane trash lying heaped up like so many abandoned swords, resembled a battlefield on which two armies had just clashed. He stumbled past Gwen, her head weaving in its subtle dance as she meticulously picked her way down amid the debris. The dead eyes didn't notice him.

At the bottom of the hill the jaunty young men whose job was to load the canes onto the lorry waved to him, and he could barely lift his hand to return their greeting; their faces were a black blur. And he could not say in what direction he was headed as he started off down the road, whether east toward Spiretown and the guesthouse which was his destination or toward the high ridge at Cleaver's which sealed off Bournehills at its western end.

But he had not gone far before he had to stop, as the vertigo which he had felt coming on took hold of him completely, causing the white marl road stretched level in front of him to rise up from its bed and undulate before his eyes and the sun to begin spinning like Ezekiel's great flaming wheel in his stricken gaze, blinding him utterly for a moment.

And he was struck then, in that moment, there on the road to Spiretown, by a double memory that had about it the quality of a vision. He saw his mother, that absurd, improbable yet intriguing woman, something of whom—some small trait or characteristic—he had always, without knowing it, sought in every woman he loved. She had had flesh like smooth-churned cream beneath a perennially tanned skin, crimped reddish hair and his same fullness to her lips. She had been a Sephardi, a rarity in the almost exclusively Ashkenazic world of New York Jewry in which he had passed his childhood. But somewhere back in her line certain of her forebears had been Sephardim who, according to the few remaining threads of their story which she, with her flair for the dramatic, had filled in and enlarged upon, had somehow made their way to South America after the Inquisition and then, slowly, over the generations, journeyed north through the countries of the Americas and the Caribbean. There were, she would proudly boast without a shred of evidence to support her claim, tombstones bearing the family name on the island of Jamaica.

She had never allowed them to forget that special heritage of hers, and to see that they didn't she would periodically treat them to a highly colored yet moving account of that ancient flight, privation and wandering, speaking of it, in her gaudy way, as though it were the one outstanding example of all the suffering known to man. And what had been his father's response, he who had been the most ordinary of Jews? One day, after patiently hearing her out, he had, Saul remembered, slowly raised his heavy eyebrows and, his eyes pale against the singularly pale, almost colorless skin he had bequeathed him, had looked at her very quietly for a long time. Then, as quietly: "So that makes you Roosevelt, maybe?" he had said and fanned her down.

But although her story had been suspect and had even ceased to impress him after a time (what difference did it make being an aristocrat among Jews if one were still a Jew, he had wondered at age eight, thus committing his first heresy and beginning his life-long apostasy), it nonetheless came to stand in his child's mind for the entire two-thousand-year history of exile and trial, including the Nazi horror which was still to come when he was a boy. Moreover, her tale, in assuming the proportions of an archetype, a paradigm, in his youthful imagination, also came to embody, without his realizing it (the story working its powerful alchemy on him when he had been most vulnerable), all that any other people had had to endure. It became the means by which he understood the suffering of others. It encompassed them all. It had even, suddenly, reached across the years to include within its wide meaning what he had just witnessed on the hill.

And then before he could recover, her image was replaced by another from that same time, and he saw with the same frightening sharpness of detail the senile old man who used to sit all day in the window above the candy store he had passed on his way to and from school. Wearing a soiled tallith, his tangled white beard stained yellow from the cigarettes he chain-smoked, he was always, whenever the boy Saul looked up, beating his chest with a frail fist. The old man turned every day into Yom Kippur, atoning not only for his sins but, because of the steady light pounding of that fist day in and day out, for those of the world as well. Years later, when Saul and his family moved to California, a relative had written saying the old man had died, and he had wondered, scarcely conscious of putting the question to himself, who would there be to atone for the world now, who to do daily penance for the host of crimes committed by man against man? Who would redeem and reconcile them now that he was gone?

He came to himself to find Merle quietly watching him from the window of the Bentley which she had pulled over to the dusty shoulder of the road. He would not have started so badly had it not been for the state he was in, because he had gotten used to being surprised like this by her. Often, walking along the thin edge of some road, on his way back to the guesthouse (if it was afternoon) to write up the morning's observations, he would hear the car in the distance behind him and turning see it swaying, shabby and abused, willfully desecrated, toward him. She would either be returning from her part-time job at the almshouse or from a visit to the old woman in New Bristol with whom her father had boarded her as a girl. The woman, whom she called aunt, Aunt Tie, had become partially blind in her old age and Merle went twice a week to do shopping and other chores for her. She usually spent the night, sleeping in the room that had been hers years ago, and returning to Bournehills the following afternoon. Most times when she stopped for him, the car would be bright with fruit she had bought at the market in town—mangoes and pawpaws, sugar apples that looked like small artichokes and fat prickly soursop, which Carrington made into a cool milky drink. The air inside the Bentley would be heavy with their smells, the sweetness of them overwhelming the more familiar odor of the hot, worn leather upholstery and Merle's special essence, a distinctive, not unpleasant mix of the strong English cigarettes she smoked, the lightly scented pomade she used on her hair, the talcum powder she brushed on her neck and in a faintly whitish mask on her face, and the Limacol lotion with its subtle fragrance of fresh lime with which she anointed herself from time to time against the heat.

Occasionally, his mind would be so filled with all he had observed over the course of the morning he wouldn't hear the Bentley until it had pulled up alongside him, and startled, he would turn to find her gazing at him from the open window with the bladelike speculative smile he was slowly getting used to. She invariably followed the smile with some remark that was in keeping with it, saying perhaps, "Well, how's the investigating business going? Are you finding out all about us?" But some days, seeing that he was tired, she would, without a word, lean across and open the door on the other side for him, and grateful, he would take his place beside her on the mate to her sagging front seat.

After a time, without realizing it, he found himself listening out for the car whenever he was returning along the roads, hoping to hear her behind him.

"What's it?" she said now. "Don't you feel well?"

"It's nothing," he said, "I'm all right. I just stayed out in the field with Stinger and the others longer than was good for me and got too much sun. It made me a little dizzy, that's all."

Her eyes narrowing, she scrutinized him, and he quickly averted his face, not wanting her to see how shaken he really was. Worse, he was afraid, foolishly so, that she would be able to see, that gaze of hers reaching deep, what had just happened: of how when, for the sake of his own self-preservation, he had fled the scene on the hill, he had been hurled, blinded, back into his past, into those memories that served as his reference to the world. Perhaps she was even able to see the faces of his mother and the old man still superimposed on the retina of his mind.

"Were you on your way home?" she said.

"Yes."

"Then hop in, I'll give you a drop."

He started toward the car, then stopped, knowing suddenly that as badly as he needed the ride, he could not, feeling as he did, take that endless voice of hers—not at such a time.

She gave a tight smile. "You don't feel like hearing me, is that it? All right, not a word. I promise."

The car was a dim fragrant room filled with her presence. It received him kindly, and resting his head against the seat back he closed his eyes. True to her word, she didn't once speak; and though she drove swiftly, she did so without her usual recklessness. Soon, feeling a brightness on his eyelids he half opened them to see the sandhills rising golden in the late afternoon light at the end of the long pure stretch of main road which linked Westminster and the sea.

CHAPTER 6

By the time Harriet finished with their wing of the guesthouse she had transformed it into a comfortable, attractive two-level apartment which not only bore her unmistakable personal stamp but seemed completely separate and apart from the rest of the rambling, cluttered building. The large front room downstairs which opened onto the veranda and also had its own private entrance on the landing to the stone steps leading to the beach, became a sitting room where visitors from the village were entertained; the one behind this, a dining room where she and Saul often took their meals, especially breakfast, preferring it to the cavernous, yellow-painted refectory with its oilcloth-covered tables and Bentwood chairs in the main section of the house; and she turned a good-sized room in the part of the wing which was spared the full brunt of the sea's steady roar—the part facing the potholed road that ran parallel to the guesthouse into the village—into a study, where Saul and Allen could work undisturbed.

She made desks out of the heavy baronial tables, set up a filing system, and kept a calendar to remind both the men of interviews and appointments they had scheduled. She brightened the rooms with flowers—lovely little sturdy mauve-and-white periwinkles and cannas which she found growing wild in sheltered places along the coast. She bought a medicine cabinet in town and stocked it with a few drugs and first-aid supplies to dispense to people in the village. And on top of the medicine cabinet, in a large jar shaped like a fishbowl, she kept candy—hard round sour balls and English toffees—for the children.

They had been the first to come. One morning shortly after her arrival in Bournehills she had gone out on the veranda to find a small group of them—four girls, a tall string of a boy and a fat naked baby whom one of the little girls was carrying astride her narrow hip—standing like characters in a Pirandello play on the beach just below the house. Silent. Their eyes raised unblinking to the veranda, their feet with the small splayed black toes rooted firmly in the sand. Simply presenting her with the fact of themselves: their thin potbellied bodies, the ragged clothing that hung like seaweed washed up by the tide on their thin frames, their closed expressionless faces. Some carried chipped enamel basins filled with sand on their heads, balancing them effortlessly there despite the sand's considerable weight; others, heavy bundles of the broom sage to be found on the spur of the hill behind the guesthouse.

Seeing them there, Harriet almost had the impression they had been standing on the beach all night—and even longer than the night, waiting for her to come out. And they scarcely seemed children to her for some odd reason. Something unnervingly old and knowing lay within their dark gaze and was suggested by the quality of their stillness. They might have been very old people who had lived out their time, and then instead of dying, had resumed the forms of the children they had once been and begun the life cycle all over again.

Moreover—and this was also most odd—they somehow called to mind the many nieces and nephews of the Negro woman named Alberta—Alberta Lee Grant—who had been her mother's personal maid for as long as Harriet could remember. Alberta, with the large industrious hands, the private hum that had been like the sound of her breathing and the impenetrable black skin. (Once, as a very little girl, Harriet had wondered if the fairies hadn't turned her that color because of something naughty she had done.) Harriet's mother had insisted on bringing Alberta with her from Virginia when she came to Philadelphia as a bride, and she had remained with them up until the former's death. She was an old woman past eighty now living off a liberal pension which Harriet, through the family lawyer and her close friend, Chester Heald, sent her every month. As children, she and her two brothers, had always, once a year, sent Alberta's nieces and nephews all the clothes they had outgrown as well as those toys they'd become bored with. Once, though, she remembered, she had refused to part with one of her toys. And it wasn't because the toy had been a favorite of hers. She couldn't even recall what it had been, it had mattered so little to her. It was just that she had felt she was being asked to give too much and had balked. She had been calm, dry-eyed but unyielding, and when her mother, aghast at her behavior, had insisted that she send the toy, whatever it had been, she had quietly threatened to burn it. She had been allowed to keep it finally, but she hadn't ever played with it again. . . .

They had never, she and her brothers, met Alberta's young relatives, had never even seen a picture of them, and yet suddenly, for a moment, it was as though she was seeing them in the children below.

"Why, good morning," she said.

They didn't respond immediately. Harriet had the impression they were waiting for a prompter to stage-whisper the words they should speak, to give them voice. Seconds passed, and gradually, under their unwavering gaze, which though not unfriendly was neither particularly friendly nor even curious, she began to feel uncomfortably, absurdly, like a defendant, the accused, standing in an old-fashioned dock with the children below her silent jurors. It was the veranda railing directly in front of her, with its bleached posts and waist-high bar, and she quickly stepped back. Then, far down the strand a wave broke, sending up a torn curtain of spume, and as the water withdrew and the early morning quiet was restored, the children said, speaking in unison, "Morning."

She went down to join them then, and while their heads, under the basins of sand and heavy faggots, didn't once move, their eyes, drawn it seemed by a muscle they shared in common, slowly followed her along the veranda, then down the steps, and across the beach to where they stood.

"Hello," she said, coming up. "Are you always up and out so early?"

Again there was a wait, but finally the tall boy, whose long colt's legs were covered with scabs from the saltfish eaten almost daily, the sores pale whorls against his blackness, said, "We come for sand."

"Oh? What do you use it for?"

"To spread out in the yard sometimes, and sometimes to use with white lime to scrub down the floor of the house. It have plenty uses." He spoke without expression.

"And sometimes we come for this," a girl suddenly volunteered. Raising a hand she touched the broom sage under which her face was buried. And before Harriet could ask her about it she said, speaking in the same flat manner as the boy, "We use it to sweep round the yard and keep the place tidy."

Harriet smiled, touched by their solemnity. "Well," she said, "I see there're any number of things I'm going to have to learn. Perhaps you'll teach me some of them." Then, as they remained silent: "I'd like that very much."

Still they said nothing, but after a time the small girl with the naked baby who looked larger than she did (it was certainly fatter), propped on her hip, asked abruptly, "You have children?"

"No," she said—and the baby's eyes, two huge black discs in a field of white seemed to demand the reason for this. "But I hope to someday," she added. "Is this your brother?"

"Yes," the child said, and held up the baby's fist which was half-closed around a fruit that looked like a crab apple with a shriveled purplish red skin. "You have these in America?" she asked.

"I don't know," Harriet said. "What is it called?"

"It have a proper name but we call it fat pork. They grow yonder." With her free hand she indicated the tall palisade called Plover Cliff about a half-mile down the coast. "Have you eat them since you been here?"

"No," said Harriet. "Not yet."

"You would like to try one maybe?"

"Yes, I might."

"All right, we'll bring some for you tomorrow."

They turned in a body then and left, and Harriet, smiling to herself at their odd, old manner, watched them go. Maintaining the same close formation in which they had stood, their loads riding easily on their heads, they walked at a brisk, stiff-legged gait which, somehow, as they moved farther away, gave the impression that their legs weren't really moving, but that they were being borne back to the village on a moving platform hidden beneath the sand. And yet not to the village. It didn't seem that they were returning to an actual place, but were slowly disappearing, dissolving, ascending into the salt drift curling in like smoke off the sea, which turned everything at a distance into a mirage. And they never once looked back. But just seconds before they disappeared, vanishing into what struck Harriet as some other time and place from which they had come to assess her, the wind suddenly caught a long streamer from one of the ragged dresses the girls had on and lifted it high, and it was like the child's thin arm raised in the eloquent Bournehills farewell.

Next morning she came out to find them assembled in the same formal grouping in the same spot below the veranda—and again it was as if they had been there all night waiting for her. The only difference was that today the child with the fat baby on her hip had the enamel basin on her head filled with the fruit she had promised instead of sand.

Nearly every morning thereafter they were in attendance on the beach, and as the days and then weeks passed, they slowly and beautifully—their teeth very strong and white in their small dark faces—began to smile in answer to her smile, and she saw, with immense relief, that they weren't so many old people repeating their lives or vanishing spirits, but only children after all.

They were, the children, the first in what quickly became an unending procession of visitors. Because soon, people from the village took to dropping in at their wing of the guesthouse. They were mostly the women for whom there was no work on the estates and their silent children, although from time to time, toward evening, one or two of the men might stop in, and with Saul and Allen gone most of the day it was left to her to entertain them.

Sometimes, before she could complete the work she did in the mornings, typing up Saul's notes and the like, she would hear footsteps on the landing outside or a dark figure would suddenly, like a shadow, appear in the doorway opening onto the veranda, cutting into the sunlight there and startling her—and the first visitor for the day would have arrived. They came to sit, to rest out of the heat, to drink the cool fruit juices she served (she was appalled at the lack of vitamin C in their diets and kept gallon cans of grapefruit and orange and pineapple juice on hand), and to talk endlessly among themselves and to her about events in Bournehills both past and present. And peculiarly they treated the events of the past as though they had only just occurred and treated her, almost from the beginning, as if she somehow knew about them, and was thus no stranger, but part of the place, bound to it and to them in some way.

It interested, amused, and vaguely puzzled her, the manner they assumed with her. It might even have annoyed her had it not been for the feeling that had remained with her since Merle's party, that sense of being a spectator seated on stage during the performance of a play, someone virtually right in the middle of the swirling action yet apart, an onlooker.

This made possible her adjustment to their rather disconcerting ways and, over the weeks, to them in general. After a time it got so their sudden appearance against the sun at the doorway no longer made her start; they no longer seemed to eclipse all the light in the room as they entered. Soon, anyone seeing her in the midst of a voluble circle of women in the sitting room, listening and occasionally joining in the talk, laughing; or busy pouring the fruit juices which she sometimes, at their request "sweetened" with a little rum, or dispensing the few simple drugs in the medicine cabinet: aspirins, cough syrup, dewormer for the children, would have said none of this was strange to her, and she had always lived this way, surrounded by people, in a sea of black faces.

But being an essentially solitary person she demanded some time to herself. So that early in the morning, usually before Saul awoke and the small band of children, her first visitors for the day, appeared, she would go for a swim alone up the beach at Horseshoe Pool. She loved that lonely swim. The sun would not yet be at full strength and the sea would be chill, still cold from the night and slate-gray beneath its sunlit surface, a northern sea, one to which she felt akin. Then, later in the day when the sun had abated, she would, if there were no visitors, take a solitary walk along the beach, usually in the direction of Plover Cliff which shut off Bournehills to the southeast. There, seated on a warm rock, a few bright strands of her hair lifting in the wind and then gently falling into place again, she would watch the departing sun burn away the harsh edges from Westminster's tall peaks, leaving them as smooth as the steeples of a country church. Before her eyes the sandhills would change from the flushed pink-gold of late afternoon to dark rose to mauve, while below her, in the inaccessible caves under the cliffs, the sea keened loudly. She scarcely heard the Bournehills sea anymore though. And it wasn't that she had gotten used to its special sound, that sustained roar of outrage and grief. She never would. Rather, in that way she had of dealing with anything she found truly unpleasant, she had, working at it quite consciously over the weeks, simply closed her mind to it.

Those late afternoon walks of hers became a subject of comment for Merle, perhaps because the latter never walked anywhere if she could help it. She even took the car when going the short distance into Spiretown proper. One early evening, returning from the cliffs with a few of the wild flowers she used to brighten the rooms, Harriet met her at the bottom of the steps hewn out of the ledge upon which the house stood. Merle was setting off for a swim in Horseshoe Pool, wearing an ill-fitting, faded-black bathing suit, a kerchief tied like Leesy's around her head and carrying a glass containing an inch of rum which she always drank like a dose of medicine immediately upon coming out of the water.

"But if you don't put me in mind of Daphne Pollard," she said.

"And who's she?" Harriet spoke absently. Part of her was still sitting on the sun-warmed rocks out at the cliff watching the slow brilliant demise of the day.

"Old Pollard's sister," she said, referring to the aged planter-turned-manager who rode the fields on his piebald horse, his sun umbrella raised. "She's dead now but when she was alive you'd see her walking the beach every evening the same as you wrapped in a shawl like it was the dead of winter and wearing her facecloth."

"Her facecloth?"

"Not the one you wash with," she said. "This was a sort of fine linen mask the great ladies around here used to wear over their faces years back to protect them from the sun. Miss Daphne used to wear hers pulled all the way down. You never saw what she looked like. And the facecloth still wasn't enough. She would have a servant walking along holding a big parasol over her. That woman was frightened for the sun, yes! And she was a great collector of flowers like yourself—what few there are around here. She was always stopping and picking. You couldn't keep one in the place for her."

Harriet laughed. She had, very early in their stay, decided that the only way to deal with someone like Merle was very politely but firmly to ignore those things about her which were irritating. The smile for one. The sharp, sad empty hoot of a laugh for another. The voice that seemed caught up in some desperate race against both time and itself. And above all the disconcerting, ill-mannered habit she had, which she did only with her, of suddenly, at times, leaning close and, with the odd, off-brown eyes, searching her face as if seeking someone other than herself there. (She was gazing at her now, Harriet thought, as if she spied Daphne Pollard lurking somewhere behind her features.) All this Harriet ignored, and instead, most of the time, treated her as though she were an altogether rational, coherent human being.

"Well," she said with the unperturbed laugh, "I assure you I'm not Miss Daphne come back to life. After all, I don't go around wearing a shawl or a facecloth and nobody trails me with an umbrella. I'm really not that bad. And," she added, holding up the few periwinkles in her hand, "I'll put back the flowers if you like."

Merle gazed hard at her for a moment; then laughed. "Keep them," she said. "They're nothing but weeds, anyway. Wait till the cassia blooms and you'll see some real flowers. These purplish ones are nice, though," she said, and reaching out touched one of the little mauve open-faced blossoms. Her voice was suddenly soft. She held the small petal tenderly between her forefinger and thumb, sampling it the way one would fine silk. Harriet, hearing the softness in her voice, remembered how, on that first day, seeing the simple manner in which she had furnished their wing, she had sensed in the woman a muted longing for order, simplicity and repose, and, above all, for an end to the talk.

"Yes," she said, addressing that part of her, "they are nice. The sandhills are the exact same shade of mauve when the sun's just about to go down."

"Are they?" Merle cried. "Imagine I've lived here all this time and never noticed that. Harriet, you should paint. You've got the eye." She started to leave, then turned back. "By the way, I saw our rich friend Lyle in town today and he asked for you. He wanted to know how you were bearing up under the strain of life in Bournehills. He doesn't seem to feel you'll be able to stick it."

"Yes, I know," she said with a laugh. "He said as much in the hotel bar that first night. It really seems to worry him. I hope you told him I seem to be managing and that the strain, if there's any, isn't visible yet."

"Yes, I said you were doing all right. More than all right." It was said with grudging admiration and she began moving away again. "In fact, I told him you've taken so well to the place and to Bournehills people, and they to you, it doesn't seem you've only been here a few weeks. Your part of the house is always full up with visitors, I told him. And he couldn't believe it"—this in a loud voice over her retreating back—"when I said you've even started dropping in to see the Little Fella in his little two by four house."

Which was true. In addition to the stiff teas at the headmaster's, the rector's, and others of the Spiretown elite which she dutifully attended, she had also started, at Saul's suggestion, returning the visits of the women who came with their barefoot children to crowd their living room every day. At least twice a week she could be seen moving around the village from one incredibly small, listing, gray board house to another, paying calls. And seeing her walking along those hot, marl roads, dressed in an oatmeal-colored linen skirt which flared slightly to free her legs, sensible low-heeled shoes and a white blouse, the material of which might have been treated with some special chemical that kept it permanently fresh, one had the impression of someone who had been inoculated against the effects of the sun, heat, dust, and glare. She appeared immunized to all that as she made her way with a light but purposeful step and a smile that in its graciousness declared she had set aside herself entirely for the person she was greeting.

And being Harriet, she made the visits seem effortless, something she had done all her life. She had been instructed by Saul to take mental note of any information she thought might be useful to the research, and she did so, taking in everything said in the hot, close drawing rooms where she was entertained, that were no bigger, most of them, than the walk-in closets in her old house near the Proving Ground in Aberdeen. And as Saul had warned her before coming to Bournehills, she made certain not to do or say anything that might be considered interfering in the work of the project. Except once at the home of Stinger and Gwen when, without even stopping to question her actions so certain was she that she was doing right, she had taken matters into her own hands, and as a result, had been severely taken to task by Saul later.

She had gone that late afternoon to the hopelessly overcrowded house on the dusty rise up from the main road where Stinger and Gwen lived with their innumerable children, for Gwen had been next on the schedule of return visits she carefully kept. She arrived to find that Gwen had not yet returned from the fields although it was past five, and the children, left alone in the house all day, had had nothing to eat since the midmorning meal at eleven. She could barely make out their individual faces in the interior dimness of the two tiny cluttered rooms, and like most people in Bournehills she could not have said just how many of them there were, although they seemed to take up every inch of space in the house. But she could sense their hunger, almost see it. It was like something that had detached itself from their potbellied bodies and round quiet eyes, and assumed an awesome form all its own. And this creature (for that's what it seemed to be to her) had none of their silence and restraint, their resignation, but prowled angrily up and down, its footsteps shaking the weak floorboards, its fists pounding the walls, demanding to be appeased.

It had even, it seemed, barred the door behind her as she entered, shutting her in with them. She was suddenly as trapped as the children amid the squalor and the smells of too many bodies crammed into too small a space; she was as much at the mercy of that palpable hunger as they were. And she would not gain her release, she knew, until she had in some way satisfied their mutual jailor.

The oldest child, a girl, had been left in charge, and Harriet, drawing in a determined breath, some resolve coalescing in her, called her over. She came, a frail hesitant girl of perhaps twelve, her breasts just beginning to bud under the rag of a dress she had long outgrown.

"Isn't there anything at all to eat, Brenda?" she said. She could not bring herself to look at her.

The child also kept her gaze averted. "No, please," she said.

"Are you sure? Isn't there perhaps something left over from this morning?"

"No, please. We've eaten the last."

But there was nothing in Harriet that could comprehend such a fact, and on sudden impulse she turned from Brenda and made her way out to the shed-roof kitchen, a smoke-blackened lean-to one step down from the house, with a dirt floor, a one-burner kerosene stove on top of a waist-high stone hearth and the walls above the hearth made of evenly spaced slats to let out the smoke.

She remained for the longest time in the middle of the kitchen gazing with a kind of numb fixity at the soot-covered pot in which the day's rice had been cooked. It had been scraped clean. Even the burnt part at the bottom had been eaten. Dusty bars of sunlight rained in through the slatted wall, adding to the staleness and heat, and even, oddly enough, to the sense of dimness there. Outside the doorway to the back yard a young cock reared up and crowed thinly. With her resolve hardening the blue in her eyes she might have well killed and cooked him had she known how.

And then she saw them: a half-dozen brown-speckled eggs in a cracked bowl inside the otherwise empty larder. Never thinking to ask herself why they had been left there unused, she strode over to the larder, opened the wire-mesh door, giving it a little yank as it resisted her, and took out the bowl.

The eggs were scarcely pullet size, but her disappointment at their smallness only brought her lips together in a more determined line.

"Brenda."

The child came noiselessly to the doorway behind her, but did not step down into the kitchen.

"Yes, Miss Harriet?"

"Is there a frying pan?"

She didn't turn to look at Brenda as she spoke, or at the other children who, curious and intrigued (as much as they would permit themselves to be), had slipped silently up behind their sister, filling the doorway.

"Yes, please," Brenda said.

"Would you bring it for me, please."

The child held back a moment, her troubled eyes on the eggs, wanting to say something but not bold enough; and then brought her the heavy iron skillet. Its bottom and sides were burnt and encrusted but the inside had been scoured clean.

Harriet then asked, one by one, for the other things she needed, and Brenda, hesitating briefly each time, brought them—the salt and pepper, a fork, the melting lump of strong-smelling, orange-colored butter from New Zealand in a brown paper square that had soaked through, a clean plate. There was no milk, and the thought of that gaunt, dry cow which Stinger faithfully led out to the cliffs each morning brought on a wild momentary despair born of the futility of his devotion and her failure to understand it. Her hand began to tremble slightly, and picking up the fork she dealt the first egg a sharp little whack that broke it cleanly in two.

At that Brenda, who had returned to stand in the doorway with the others after lighting the kerosene stove at Harriet's request, uttered a near-soundless, quickly stifled cry of protest or dismay—it was impossible to tell, and then silently bowed her head. Harriet brought the fork down a second time.

When all the eggs lay free of their shells in the bowl—the intact yolks like weak suns in an albuminous sky, she added the salt and pepper, then some water in place of the milk, and began beating them with the fork. Her mouth set in its tight grim line, her back to the children, she beat the eggs as if trying to swell them into a greater portion, and until large air bubbles formed. Her forehead became moist and the sunlight striking her hair made it appear a bright helmet she had donned as part of some battle gear.

Her most severe test came during the actual cooking, when she had to struggle with a nausea that threatened to defeat her at the sight of the littered, food-stained hearth, the grease-encrusted pan she had to take by the handle and the suspiciously rancid smell of the butter as she heated it. At one point as she was folding in the omelet, the fitful kerosene flames, an ugly yellow at their edge, suddenly blazed up around the pan, and before she could snatch away her arm the heat caused a slight burn on her wrist. It was negligible and left hardly a mark. But the fleeting pain, added to the upheaval in her stomach, along with the knowledge that with all her efforts there would still not be enough to go round, made her, for an uncontrollable moment, want to abandon the entire project and flee.

But finally there lay the finished omelet—a little too browned on one side, stained orange by the butter and woefully plain (so unlike the ones she occasionally liked to make with diced meats, herbs and sometimes a little wine), but an omelet nonetheless. She was suddenly inordinately proud of it. There was something of a miracle about it almost; the fishes and loaves. Above all, she felt an immense relief. She had done her part, she told herself, gazing down at it steaming gently on the plate, to quiet that ravenous presence charging up and down the two rooms.

She turned then, and for the first time since entering the house really looked at the children. And she was smiling tentatively, and hoping, with a certain wistfulness, to elicit a similiar response from them. Their pleased smiles would have been a small reward. But they continued to regard her with the same flat, noncommittal curiosity, the same quiet refusal to be grateful, impressed or moved, and Brenda stood as she had all along with her head bowed mournfully in their midst.

But Harriet wasn't overly dismayed by their lack of enthusiasm. She was getting used to the manner of children in Bournehills, their almost frightening reserve, the old way they had about them. Besides, she reminded herself, she had done her part; the omelet, if no more than a token gesture, was there. It would hold them until Gwen came.

"Brenda, I'm leaving it to you to see that everyone gets his share," and she tried not to think of how little that would mean for each.

"Yes, Miss Harriet," Brenda said without raising her head.

She left then, and rather than pass through the close-smelling rooms to the front door, hurried out the back and around the side of the house to the road.

She described the afternoon's adventure later that evening in a letter to her old friend and member of the Institute's Board of Directors, Chester Heald. (She wrote him at least twice a month, long chatty letters full of her reactions to life in Bournehills which served her as a kind of diary.) She was just completing the letter when she heard over the somewhat reduced voice of the night sea the sound of their car turning into the guesthouse yard. She glanced at her watch, surprised. She had not expected Saul back so early. He had spent most of the day at a house-raising, where a group of men, well supplied with rum to make the work seem less, got together to put up one of the little boxlike houses of raw Canadian pine and galvanized iron for a neighbor, and she had supposed he would be stopping off at Delbert's shop, as he did nearly every night, before coming home.

She quickly rose to start the coffee which they always drank upon his return at the end of the day. The coffee was a nightly ritual with them, and Harriet prepared it with something of the care and ceremony that attends a ritual on the one-burner kerosene stove they had bought for their private use when they had discovered, shortly after their arrival, that neither of them could drink Carrington's coffee. She treasured this period at the close of the day. The last of the visitors would have left hours ago, Saul's work would be over, around them the old house would be quiet: Merle and Allen off in their distant wings, and they would be alone together perhaps for the first time all day. Over the coffee which they both took black and without sugar, they would discuss their respective days—Saul, relaxed in one of the Morris armchairs with which the large front room was furnished, musing aloud about the progress of the work, she telling him who had dropped by and what had been said. And also telling him, each evening, behind the words, that she did it all for him. Every glass of fruit juice she poured for the visitors, every aspirin she shook from the bottle and offered them in the palm of her hand, every scrap of information she carefully stored to pass on to him later, was done for him. To help right the thing in him which she had sensed, on the day they had met over three years ago, had gone awry. And to restore him to the image of him she held in her mind. And to secure their marriage. That hour or so in the late evenings was an important time.

Tonight she could tell from the ring of his footsteps on the stone landing outside that something had happened to annoy him, and as she turned toward the door her hand instinctively went out in that lovely gesture which always, at such times, sought to check and restrain him.

"Could you please tell me just what the hell you thought you were doing over at Stinger's today?"

For a moment she couldn't imagine he was speaking to her, and she actually started to look around to see if there were someone else with them in the room. "What did I think I was doing?" Her voice, her frown, expressed her bewilderment. "I don't understand. I dropped by this afternoon to pay Gwen a visit; she wasn't there; only the children; and they were starving, poor things. So I made them an omelet with a few eggs I found in what they call the larder. That's all. I was going to tell you about it when you came in. . . . Oh, Saul, don't tell me I did the wrong thing!"

In the face of her distress he turned aside, ashamed of his anger, and went and sat heavily in one of the Morris chairs. "Oh, Christ, Hatt, I know you meant well," he said. Most of the anger had dropped from his voice. "But if only you had thought to ask somebody first. . . ." Then, slumped in the chair, he told her what had happened as a result of her using the eggs. On his way back from the house-raising he had stopped off at Stinger's, thinking to accompany him on his nightly visit to the rumshop, only to find Gwen quarreling and the child Brenda in tears. Gwen, it seemed, had a long-standing agreement with the Spiretown postmaster to sell him all of her eggs. This money was then used toward purchasing the family's weekly supply of staples. It was a very carefully worked out arrangement of which Gwen was proud.

"Gwen's not mad at you for having cooked the eggs," he said. "She understands why you did it, but she blames poor Brenda for not speaking up and telling you who they were for. I'm afraid she gave her quite a thrashing."

"Oh, no!" she cried, and her mind wheeling back she saw Brenda standing bowed and silent amid her sisters and brothers in the doorway; she had been resigned even then to the punishment that had followed.

"Well, it'll all blow over, I guess," he said. "We have to be grateful it was Stinger and Gwen and not someone we haven't gotten to know as well or we might've really been in trouble. . . ." Then, his annoyance with her returning, he said, "If only you would stop and ask, Harriet, before taking things into your own hands! I'm sure it never even occurred to you to find out if the eggs hadn't been left there for a reason. I don't know," he said, slowly shaking his head, "there's this thing in you which makes you want to take over and manage everything and everybody on your own terms. It really worries me. And it's not to say you don't mean well most of the time, but it still makes for complications."

"But they were hungry!" Her voice was sharp and emphatic; she had not permitted herself to hear what he had just said. "Besides, it doesn't make any sense to sell perfectly good, nourishing eggs to buy that awful rice they all eat."

"It might not make sense to you," he said—and the harshness had returned to his tone and to his pale, mirrorlike eyes, "but it obviously does to Gwen. She's probably discovered she can feed more mouths doing it her way. I don't know. What I do know is that you can't go around ordering other people's lives and trying to make them change long-standing habits overnight—especially food habits which are always the hardest to give. Everybody doesn't live by your standards. Your values aren't necessarily the world's. Why, the kids didn't even eat the goddamn omelet."

"They didn't eat it?" And she was perhaps more stunned by this than anything else he had said.

"No. It was still there when I dropped by."

"But why?"

He shrugged. "Maybe they don't like their eggs that way. Or they were afraid they'd really get it from Gwen if they had. I don't know. Anyway, they didn't touch it."

"They didn't eat it . . ." Her voice was suddenly drained, hollow. "Perfectly good, nourishing eggs . . . I don't understand . . ."

She sank slowly into a chair, and for a time sat there bewildered, silent, crushed, the day that had been so bright with her small triumph lying shattered around her. Her limp arms had fallen open in her lap, revealing the place, just near her right wrist, where the heat from the flames that had flared up around the pan had left a tiny mark. She stared numbly at it. She thought of going over to him and holding out her wrist, silently offering the burn as testimony of her good intentions. At the same time she wanted to thrust it angrily under his nose and shout, "See, I even burned myself fixing it for them!" But instead, her head dropping, she simply covered the spot with her other hand.

"I don't understand," she said.

"Hatt, do you think you might like to go and spend a few days with the Hutsons in town?" he said. "Remember Lyle said you could come any time you liked."

Her head came up and she looked at him with both a child's hurt and an old woman's severity. "I don't need a rest," she said. "Things aren't getting too much for me."

He started to protest, but instead, his impatience with her getting the better of him he jumped up and strode across to the small kerosene stove on its table on the other side of the room. She had only just started the preparations for the coffee when he entered and he noisily completed them now, standing at the stove with his back to her and his tight shoulders shutting her out.

When it was done, he brought a cup of the coffee over to her. His face as he held it out was somber and closed, and when she sought his eyes, wanting to express her remorse, to make apology, she found them veiled, distant.

"I suspect you're thinking you were right after all and it wasn't such a good idea to bring me along." She spoke after a long silence.

He made no answer, only sat frowning down into the small black pool of coffee in his cup which he held cradled between his palms as if he needed its reassuring warmth.

"How was the house-raising?" She spoke after another silence.

His head remained bent a little longer over the cup, and then he said, "Hard work but fun, and very beautiful in a way. The house is only one room scarcely bigger than a closet, but a house nonetheless. The man to whom it belongs, a fellow named Cox, who works with Stinger, was years accumulating the money just to buy the lumber. The next thing he's planning to do now that it's up is to get married. He's been going with a woman from Drake Hill who has a couple of kids for him and they'll be getting married now."

"That's slightly the reverse of things, isn't it," she said with a cautious laugh. "First having your family and then getting married?"

"I guess," he said. "But in Bournehills a man doesn't believe in making it legal until he can at least offer his wife a house of her own no matter how small. It's their way, and as valid, in the final analysis, as any other. . . ." He paused, a slow smile taking shape. "You should have seen Cox! He was so happy, poor guy, especially when he saw the roof going up, that he drank too much and passed out on us. We put him to sleep it off in his new house." Then, the smile giving way to the subtle sadness and irony that was so much a part of him, he said, musing it aloud, "It's so little for a man to ask of life—a closet of a house that'll start falling apart on him in no time, yet it's the world to someone here. So that things being relative, Cox could see himself as a man who had succeeded at his life. And he did—at least for the time the house was going up. I saw it in his face, and I'm afraid I also got a little drunk as a result.

"Oh, Hatt," he said, his tone, his smile setting all to rights between them again, "I know I shall probably fall victim again to my emotions and get too involved—a defect I'm known for—but I'm beginning to feel so at home here in Bournehills. It's as though I've lived in the place for years. And I so like Bournehills people."

Harriet heard this not without a twinge of resentment she was helpless to suppress. "And I so love you," she said.

CHAPTER 7

After having looked for weeks, Vere at last found the car he wanted. It was a much used but fairly late model Opel Kapitän, the car made by the General Motors subsidiary in Germany, which combines features drawn from both countries: on one hand, a high-powered German motor, on the other, a long, sleek, low-slung American body that in motion, going very fast, looks like some powerful animal leaping forward to strike. It was the body, perhaps more than anything else, that decided Vere. The Opel had been badly damaged in an accident and with its crumpled fenders and generally battered hull looked fit only for the scrap heap. But Vere, his head cocked thoughtfully to one side, examined it with an expert's eye; he tried the motor, sitting tensed forward over the steering wheel listening to it as he fed it the gas. When it shuddered feebly into life he gave a nod and purchased it on the spot.

He brought it like a bride home to Bournehills. With Allen behind in the Ford giving him an assist on the upgrades and nudging him into motion whenever the motor failed, he gently coaxed the Opel over the hills to Spiretown and finally down the low embankment into the yard adjoining Leesy's house. Near wreck that it was, it immediately became part of the ancient wreckage in the yard, including the ragged mango and calabash trees, the torn galvanized fence, the wattle-and-daub pen that housed the sow Leesy was planning to have butchered at carnival, and the ramshackle cart she used for hauling her canes to the factory. It was instantly at home with the bad-tempered fowls who fought each other over the scraps tossed them from the doorway, and the donkey standing, abject and morose, near the cactus bush where the wash was hung to dry.

The day Vere brought the Opel home the donkey had slowly raised its head and, its blank eyes filled with the sunlight, its tight gray belly working, had emitted a series of deep sucking groans that were like sounds uttered during some protracted and painful coitus. The cry ended, it had resumed its pose of profound dejection and never again acknowledged the car.

Nor did Leesy ever really acknowledge it. She never went near it, but would move about the yard at her chores as if unaware of its presence. During the day when she came to the doorway to check the sun or feed the fowls she refused to let her glance as much as pass over it. And in the mornings she would fling the water from her washbasin in a bright arc that fell just short of it.

And she never spoke of the car to Vere, and he, feeling the chill wind of her disapproval, thought better than to mention it to her. Only once did she permit herself to comment aloud. It was the day he began the long job of overhauling it. Opening the door a crack she had looked out at him lying sprawled under the car with only his legs showing. Then, her eyes as hard as rock she had looked at the car itself, gazing at it openly for the first time. And as she did so an expression of the most deep-seated distrust, enmity and fear came over her face.

It was as though she believed beyond question that all such things as cars, all machines, had human properties, minds and wills of their own, and that these were constantly plotting against those whom they served. They were for her the new gods who, in a far more tyrannical fashion than the old, demanded their sacrifices. Something in her gaze as she stood there peering out, her face as reamed and eaten away by time as the wood of the door, said she feared and detested the Opel straddling Vere as much as she did the rollers at Cane Vale which had crushed and killed her husband years ago. She would have reminded Vere of this; she even drew a breath to speak, but then in the next instant her resolve gave way, and closing the door she turned back into the room, muttering scathingly to herself: "He and all got a car now! All the little money he made in Florida gone on some old wreck! Instead of him using it to buy himself piece of ground or build a house so when he finds himself a woman he'd have someplace decent to put her, every penny of it's gone on a car. He don't realize that when a person's just starting out in life he's got to put first things first and not let a lot of foolishness turn his head. And the first thing a man needs to do is make provision to feed himself so he don't have to look to nobody and to put a roof over his head. His own roof. Then he's his own man, what you'd call an independent person." She gave the nod that was like a nervous reflex. "Then if he likes he can start thinking about motorcars. . . .

"And it wouldn't even hurt you so if the car was a decent something!" she suddenly cried, coming to a halt in the middle of the room, standing there small and dry and outraged, giving vent at last to the anger she had contained since the arrival of the Opel. And she was speaking not only to the shadows that shared the house with them, and the faded photographs of Pearl Bailey and the Queen, but to the painted Christ on the calendar left unchanged since the date of her husband's death and even the silver plaques inscribed with the names and dates of the family dead mounted on the wall. "But no! He had to go and throw away good money on some old thing the white people in town didn't want anymore, that they had done run through and lick up and figured they could use now to turn his head. They saw him coming. Because that car'll never run decent—no matter how much fixing he does. He would have done better to try and build his own car from nothing instead of bothering with that one out there. Why you can tell just from the looks of the thing it don't mean that boy no good. But what to do?" Her hands opened in a gesture eloquent of her helplessness. "You couldn't say anything to him. It was his money to do with what he pleased."

Leesy wasn't the only one who doubted Vere's wisdom in buying the car. The idlers of the village who whiled away the day on the culvert wall above the dry riverbed along the main road were also convinced that the Opel was beyond repair. Occasionally they would bestir themselves and, leaving the shade of the tamarind tree which stood next to the culvert, stroll over to watch him from the embankment just above the yard—impressed, envious, but convinced of the futility of his efforts. They teased him:

"Vere, man, I see you got yourself a big-time car there."

"But tell me, what junk heap in town did you go to to find that thing, boy?"

"How much you think she'll do when you're through with her,

Vere? 'Bout five per maybe? Well, if she does that much she'll be doing a lot, lemme tell you."

"Vere, love, I hear you're planning on entering that vehicle in the Whitmonday Race this year. But take my word, she'll never leave the starting line."

Vere seldom took them on, but once in a while as their taunts continued to ring through the yard, he would slowly wiggle out from beneath the chassis or raise up from the motor under the hood, and his face, arms, the palms of his hands covered with grease and dirt, smile at them. It was the same patient, quietly superior smile he sometimes gave Leesy when she tried lecturing him, which always made him seem the older and wiser of the two.

"But you know," he might say, leaning casually against the Opel, "you all sound just like what you are: fools who don't know nothing but sitting under a tamarind tree all day and playing a steel drum all night. Ignoramuses. But you wait. This car's going to pass you going bird-speed down the main road one day and you all goin' be running after it begging for a ride."

Ferguson dropped by the yard one afternoon to inspect it. The long stick he used like a sword in hand, his eyes wary behind the thick-lensed glasses, he slowly circled the Opel, dubiously shaking his head.

Vere laughed. "Don't mind how she looks now, Mr. Ferguson," he said. "She's going to come like new time I finished with her, like something I built myself. In a way"—his eyes became thoughtful—"I don't even think of it as a car that ever belonged to anybody, but as one I'm putting together myself from some parts I bought in town . . ." Then, breaking off with an abashed but certain smile, "She's goin' run, Mr. Ferguson—and soon, mark my words."

"Well, bo, I thought I was a man knew a thing or two about machines, but if you can get this one here to work you got me beat," Ferguson said.

Even Allen had his doubts. By the time Vere had acquired the car, Allen had completed the research he had been doing in New Bristol and had started on a fairly large-scale household survey in the village which was to occupy him for the next months, and he had taken to dropping by Leesy's yard nearly every afternoon, once his interviewing for the day was over, to see how Vere was progressing with the car. They said little during these visits. Vere would either be half-buried under the hood or sprawled like a pinioned Gulliver beneath the chassis, while Allen would squat in the dust near his feet with the long questionnaire forms he was using in the survey lying across his knees and his watch and glasses reflecting the late afternoon light. But there was an ease and intimacy between them despite their silence. The steady muffled tapping of the tools Allen handed Vere from a pile lying nearby, a pleasant sound in the stillness of the dying day, was like a gentle exchange they were carrying on with each other.

"How's it going?" Allen would ask somewhat worriedly from time to time, as full of doubts as the others. "Do you think she'll make it?"

And as with Ferguson, Vere would give the confident laugh. "How you mean, man? She's going to run, I tell you. I'm going to have her on the road by carnival—before that even—if I have to work on her day and night."

And he did devote almost every free moment to it. Sometimes long before Leesy had awakened in the morning or the sky had fully cleared he would be out in the yard, working away in the half-light. In the afternoons he hurried back to it from the job he had gotten since his return as one of the young men who helped to load the estate lorries with the canes the women headed down from the hills.

But at least twice a week he took off an evening from working on the Opel and went to town. Returning from his job he would bathe out in back of the house, where the canes in Leesy's half-acre plot, pressing up against the house, hid him from view; then, putting on one of the colorful hot shirts he had bought in Florida and brushing the cane dust from his hair he would take the evening bus into New Bristol. He never went to town without taking with him a very slender, supple, notched Malacca cane that had belonged to Leesy's husband. Leesy had used the same cane to whip Vere with as a boy. But for years it had stood forgotten in a corner of his cubicle of a bedroom off the kitchen. And then one day shortly after his return he had taken it and very carefully cut off perhaps twelve inches from the bottom, and now each time before setting out for town he would slip the foreshortened walking cane down inside the back of his shirt, hooking its handle over his undershirt so that it lay flat against his spine under his clothes.

"But where are you going with that hook stick down your back, Vereson Walkes?" Leesy very quietly asked him one evening as he was preparing to leave. She was lying frail and stern-faced on a wooden day bed in the small front room where she sometimes rested during the worst of the afternoon heat.

He said nothing, only offered her a faint, noncommittal smile.

"You really intend putting yourself in trouble over that girl, is that it? Is that it, I ask you?" she cried, her restraint giving way.

"I'll be back first thing in the morning," he said. "I'll bring you some mints from town."

And before she could struggle up from the day bed, he was out the door and on his way down the rutted dirt road that led from their house, which stood on the same dusty rise as Stinger's, to the main road below, walking with his back held a little too stiff and straight because of the cane.

It would be dusk usually by the time he reached New Bristol. Only a few of the hawkers who roamed the large central bus stand plying the waiting passengers with candies and fruit, which they sold from big trays carried on their heads, would be left when he arrived, and their flat sing-song cries of "Mints, toffees, nuts, who call?" as they wove in and among the standing buses, their arms swinging free and the trays riding easily aloft, sounded disembodied, forlorn, like the sounds of the expiring day. Over on Queen Street in the heart of the business district the stores would be closed, the smaller ones boarded up tight, while the large department stores, the largest of which was owned by Kingsley, would be ablaze with lights, their windows offering all such as Vere a feast of things far beyond their means. In the tortuous back alleys and lanes behind Queen Street by this time of evening, the women would have already set up their coal pots in the darkened niche between two houses or on the roadside itself and would be frying fish just brought in on the boats—dolphin and kingfish and red snapper—by the smoky light of a soot lamp. The air would be sweet with the seasonings they scored into the flesh of the fish—thyme, pounded cloves and hot red peppers.

Vere never hurried. Sucking a penny mint bought from a hawker in the bus stand or munching a piece of fish purchased right from the pan, he would stroll at a leisurely pace through New Bristol. Savoring it. Past the banks, the air-conditioned offices, the shop windows with their rich displays; then down the cobbled alleys to Harbor Road, a narrow strip fronting the bay and lined with warehouses. There he would watch the stevedores who worked the night shift loading the raw sugar onto the ships. He wandered boldly through the fashionable residential area just outside town where the well-to-do—the politicians, professionals, senior civil servants and the few remaining old white families—had their homes. The houses ranged from the solidly

Georgian to a tasteless, ill-conceived modern, and were set well back from the road at the end of long rows of shade trees positioned like sentries down the drives. To the front, facing the roadway, reared high stone walls with shards of broken bottles cemented along the top to secure them against intruders. Huge dogs rattled the gates to get at Vere as he passed.

Still without hurrying, he would describe a wide semicircle at the end of this section, north to where the ground gradually sloped upward to a low ridge. There, poised like an ever-present threat above the homes of the well-to-do and running parallel to them into the heart of New Bristol stood the area people in town had recently taken to calling Harlem Heights, a vast fetid shantytown of wooden shacks piled one against the other so that it resembled a fowl run, open scum-covered drains and narrow dirt tracks that served as roads amid the squalor. It was another city that had quickly spawned in recent years, attaching itself like a great sore to New Bristol below. Viewed from Queen Street it called to mind a hastily erected camp for refugees, a place for the DP's of the island. And every day, especially since independence, they came, abandoning in droves their little villages half-buried amid the canes, led forth by the wonder and dazzle of the store windows along Queen Street and the promise of the lights at night. "Man, I living in town now, you know," they would boast and everyone would understand they meant Harlem Heights.

The girl who had had the child for Vere lived there in a small rented room to the side of a house that was a pastiche of rotted boards, flattened oil drums and scraps of corrugated roofing scavenged from the town below. Taking his time, Vere would make his way through the crowd and stench of the Heights to the house, and once there station himself in the darkened lane across from her window. The shutters were always partly opened and the cheap plastic lace curtains gathered and tied to one side so that he could occasionally glimpse her as she dressed to go out. And as patiently as he had waited outside on the embankment the night of his return for Leesy to dress and open the door, he would wait in the darkness for the girl to finish dressing and leave the house. The kerosene lamp would dim finally and she would emerge—a tall, thin, sharp-boned girl of perhaps twenty with snuff-colored hair and eyes and the coarse mottled skin typical of those from up Canterbury. Her standard dress was a wide skirt puffed up with layers of can-can petticoats and shoes with heels that were too high for the rutted paths of the Heights.

Vere would follow her at a discreet distance into New Bristol, then through the bright heart of the town, pausing whenever she paused to stare greedily into the shop windows or to examine her face in the lighted glass. Each night she invariably led him down Whitehall Lane past the bawdy sailor clubs and rumshops lining the street to Sugar's at the tip of the long finger of land that marked the extremity of the deep bay upon which New Bristol stood. Her petticoats fussing around her knees, she would quickly disappear up the stairs to the night club.

She would be gone for hours. Sometimes it was almost dawn before she finally reappeared. But Vere would wait out the time, standing in the night shadows thrown up by the sea across the street from the club, the foreshortened Malacca cane rubbing gently against his spine whenever he shifted. She might be accompanied when she left by a sailor or one of the young officers or technicians from the missile-tracking station at the northwest corner of the island. Sometimes she was with one or two of the girls from Sugar's. Occasionally she left alone. Whatever, Vere would fall in behind her as she moved up the narrow cobblestone street. He never followed her back to her room, but at the top of Whitehall Lane, where all the winding streets of New Bristol converged to plunge together down to the sea, he would leave her without so much as a backward glance and, making his way to the bus stand on the other side of town, spend what was left of the night in the empty bus that would take him back to Bournehills in the morning.

It wasn't long before she noticed him. But then he had never made any attempt to hide himself. One night as she lingered before one of the department store windows, her head suddenly snapped around and she looked over her shoulder to where he had come to a halt under a street lamp some yards behind to wait for her to continue on. Her face betrayed no surprise at seeing him there. She had known all along, it was clear, that he had been shadowing her, but for reasons of her own had waited until this moment to acknowledge it. Nor did she speak. She simply stared at him with her flat, tobacco-colored eyes, her chin raised, one bony arm akimbo, ready to brazen it out if he should address her. But he said nothing, only quietly returned her level, unblinking gaze, all the while smiling faintly to himself, his face raised to the lamplight so that she might better see him. They remained like this for a long time, staring at each other across the darkened expanse of sidewalk, until finally, with a little show of impatience, she swung away and, her many petticoats rustling derisively, her high heels clacking loudly, mocking him, walked on.

This became something of a ritual with them. On occasion she would pause in a deserted street, turn to face him, wait a few moments for him to speak but saying nothing herself, and then when he, too, remained silent, flounce on ahead. After a time these silent exchanges took on, oddly enough, a kind of intimacy. Slowly, over the weeks, it was almost the same as if they had spoken or had approached and touched each other.

Then one night she broke the silence. She had come out of Sugar's late, accompanied by a blond, very drunk young officer from the tracking station, who was hanging on her neck and singing in a voice that threatened tears, "Take me home again, Kathleen . . ." Vere had as usual fallen in behind them, when suddenly halfway up Whitehall, in front of one of the sailor clubs, the girl had spun round, and more out of disgust with the drunken officer on her neck than with him had shouted, "But what in hell are you always following me about like some duppy or the other for? I got something belonging to you?"

She gave him time to answer and when, as was his custom, he remained silent, she cried, her voice shrill and weary in the empty street—she had finally grown tired of their game—"Oh, God, man, why you don't say what you have to say or do what you have to do, damn you, and leave people in peace!"

Again he said nothing, but this time, unlike the others, he had not stopped when she had, but had kept on walking so that he was almost upon them. And she stood her ground, although as he drew near she quickly maneuvered the staggering soldier—who was weeping now and calling her Kathleen—in front of her. Using him as a shield, she thrust a peaked enraged face out at Vere as he came abreast and screamed, "You keep it up, you hear. You keep on following me about like I got something belonging to you, Vereson Walkes, and as God is my witness I'm going to put the police on your black tail."

He smiled, the serene little smile which made him appear older and more knowing than most. The eyes slashed in above the jutting bones of his face briefly and with no great interest inspected her in passing; and then he sauntered ahead, his back as straight as a soldier's because of the cane like a second spine under his shirt, leaving her screaming after him in the road.

CHAPTER 8

At Lyle Hutson's touch the Humber shifted smoothly into lower gear, and gathering its full powers swept up the winding road to Westminster's summit as effortlessly as if running on level ground. At the final turn the two uneven peaks that crowned the hill appeared with the departing sun cradled between them and the public buildings, including the almshouse, nestled at their feet. One arm out the window, the elbow sharply angled, he gave the required Bournehills greeting (he too might have been a witness) as he sped past Seifert, quietly, as usual, returning the sun's stare from the almshouse gate. The other inmates, children and adults alike, were wandering aimlessly as usual about the dusty yard in their regulation blue smocks. Lyle both saw and didn't see them.

The almshouse, the sleepy police substation next door with its dominoes-playing officers and telephone that seldom worked quickly vanished, and moments later, just before he took the deep plunge into Spiretown, the whole of the valley with the sea at its head lay before him. And it was as though it had been put there solely for him, for his pleasure. All of it: the village spread at the broad foot of the hill, the clean stretch of road through its center, the low sandhills that brought it to an end, and to the south the guesthouse perched like a small weathered rock on its ledge back from the sea. And the sea itself moving in over the reefs in a succession of long smooth waves that were like welts raised on its smooth surface, each one beautifully controlled, a statement in itself, and soundless at this distance. At this height the horizon appeared a high-tension wire strung between the poles of the land, and the tall clouds banked along its length and purple now with the oncoming dusk could have been the mountainous landfall of another island in the distance.

The day lay behind him, the evening ahead. There would be a swim in Horseshoe Pool with the strong Bournehills sea moving under him like some powerful woman he had roused, and afterward drinks and talk with Merle and the others on the veranda while the air dried the salt from his swim to a fine white dust on his body and pulled his skin taut. And then later, in the large room upstairs looking out over the veranda roof to the sea, which Merle always set aside for him, there would be Dorothy Clough, who had arranged to drive out to Bournehills earlier in the day. A long full night with her. And in the casual way of a man who knows his satisfaction is assured and nothing will be refused him, nothing withheld, he thought of her during their times together, the quality of her passion. It was deceptively strong, adventuresome (so unlike his wife, Enid, in this respect), and direct; and heightened by that faculty she had of making everything they did then seem simply part of their being together. The English. Nothing fazed them. With an idle smile he thought of her thighs arched whitely in the dimness, her mouth ravening with a little girl's greedy delight the parts of his body; her tumbled hair against his skin was an imperial fly whisk wielded by an ever-faithful servant. Kenyatta. (He laughed out loud and reined in the Humber on the steep drop into the village.) He became the old Mzee himself then. And her equally delighted cries as he made free with her body, exploring at will her crevices, driving first gently, then hard, then gently into them as if they were all part of some territory to which he had been granted exclusive right. And as with a man and wife of long and happy standing, everywhere received him gladly.

The night would be a fitting end to what had been a long, productive week.

Lyle Hutson came down to Bournehills at least twice a month, arriving late Friday usually and sometimes staying the weekend. Those at the guesthouse would see the great Humber flashing silver against Westminster's dun-colored spur as he swung onto the unpaved road leading to the house, with the dust rising in a bright plume behind, and minutes later he would make his appearance on the veranda, impeccable in his Savile Row suit, a dull finish to his dark-umber skin, his surface smile affixed.

Dorothy Clough would already be there, having driven down earlier with her three children, two lean, sober little girls of six and eight with wisps of sun-whitened blond hair always escaping from their pigtails to stream across their eyes, and a plump boy of three with dimpled knees. During the hours before Lyle's arrival she would sit on the veranda busy at some form of embroidery—needlepoint or crewelwork design—which she always brought along, while down on the beach her children built castles out of the damp sand at the water's edge. Waiting there, her serene, lightly boned face with its carefully detailed features and thin English skin bent over the square of stamped linen or canvas in the frame, she was in every sense the practical-minded, attractive young matron. From time to time she would rise up a little in her chair to check on her children, a slender hand shading her eyes against the glare off the sand.

Harriet found her disconcerting, and even somehow appalling. And it wasn't because of the affair she was having—married women had affairs after all. Nor was it, she believed, the fact that Lyle Hutson was black. She had been told and, to her surprise, had found it to be true that such considerations counted for much less in places like Bourne Island. It didn't seem quite the same thing here. Rather, it was the woman's manner; pleasant, direct, level-headed, which somehow made everything she did, including putting her three children to sleep in the room adjoining the one she occupied with Lyle Hutson, seem perfectly natural. It was the bright faces of the children at the car windows as she drove up and the bit of embroidery she brought with her, and the way she sat plying her needle while awaiting Lyle, like a wife spending the summer at the seashore with the children awaiting the weekend visit of her husband. It was the dimples on the little boy's fat knees as he squatted in the sand helping his sisters build the castles, and the way the three of them rose to chorus "Uncle Lyle" up the beach when Lyle Hutson arrived. . . . All this she found appalling; impossible to encompass. Worse, she could not as she usually did with such things close her mind to it, and so had taken to avoiding the woman whenever she came to visit.

Lyle Hutson she found even harder to take. There was first of all the lingering memory of his hand on her arm that night in the hotel bar, and her fleeting impression then that it was less his hand than some dark and submerged part of herself, painful aspects of herself she denied existed, which had suddenly surfaced. She could not quite forgive him for that presumptuous touch. Nor, for some reason, could she reconcile herself to the custom-made suits he wore, the large silver-gray car he drove, the Oxonian accent he affected at times, and his proprietorial air: he would stride onto the veranda of the guest-house as though he owned it and everyone there!

Moreover, she discovered, after thinking about it vaguely for weeks, that something in the man's smile, its essentially cold, hermetic quality, vaguely reminded her of Andrew Westerman: his sealed inaccessible face across the dining table and across their separate beds. It was that both men conveyed the unmistakable impression of having accomplished all they had set out to do with their lives, of being complete and therefore no longer in need of anyone's help. There would be nothing, in other words, a woman could do for them. It would all have been done. If a wife, she would simply be part of the established constellation of their life—and not particularly central to it either; a peripheral star, rather. A mistress would merely be the occasional diversion such men consider their due, one of the small spoils of their success. . . . Men like that, whose lives had achieved a finished form, held absolutely no interest for Harriet. She could feel nothing for them.

But perhaps the thing that most galled her about Lyle Hutson was his assumption that she would fail the test of Bournehills. Whenever he came to visit he invariably made reference to that fact, and although she always passed it off with a laugh and remained outwardly unruffled, she would chafe within. Because, in a way, it was like saying she was no better than her mother, that weak, ineffectual woman who had been so easily defeated by everything, and for whom she had always felt such impatience, contempt and fear: fear that she might end like her. Harriet remembered her standing helpless and bewildered outside the locked door of her husband's study after he took up with Lorenzo de' Medici, unable to understand that he had shut her out of his life. Harriet recalled the hours she would spend before the tall cheval glass in her bedroom examining her face, her hair, her small, modish figure, while the maid Alberta loomed like an attendant genie behind her in the mirror. But all this had availed her nothing. The door to the study had remained locked. And even when she had tried taking revenge, first in a series of hinted-at affairs (Chester Heald had been one of the lovers, it was said), then in a long vague illness that kept her rooms smelling faintly medicinal for months after her death, and finally in death itself, Harriet's father had scarcely seemed to notice.

She had not thought of her in years. As with so much of her past, her mother had been excluded from her thoughts. And now, because of a few needling remarks from a comparative stranger, memories of her had begun seeping in like smoke under the door in her mind she kept bolted against her. To have come this far and not to have escaped her! And Andrew! And Harriet didn't just mean the eighteen hundred odd miles she had traveled from Philadelphia to Bourne Island. Her marriage to someone like Saul Amron, the daring, the repudiation of the past it represented, was part of the journey she was speaking of, and the whole new life she had chosen with him so that she would not spend the balance of her days seated across the breakfast table from Andrew Westerman feeling utterly useless and contaminated, made barren, while outside the window a three-hundred-year-old tree stirred with new life, mocking her.

"You know you're really quite a remarkable woman, Mrs. Amron."

"How's that?" she said, turning coolly to him. They had caught her—Lyle Hutson, who had just spoken, and Dorothy Clough—on the veranda, where she had gone after returning from her afternoon stroll to write a letter to Chester Heald.

"The way you've taken to Bournehills," he said. "It's not everyone, as I've told you before, who can bear the strain. But you appear to have adjusted completely to life in a place which someone once very appropriately described as being behind God's back. It's really quite amazing. I was certain you'd need to escape from time to time and we'd be seeing something of you down our end. Enid's always asking for you. She has the guestroom all ready or, again, there's the small beach house we keep near the Crown Beach Colony, where you're welcome to stay any time. But so far you refuse to honor us with even the briefest visit. We don't despair though, since we're sure to have the pleasure of your company at carnival. Everyone comes to town then, even people in Bournehills."

"Perhaps," she said. "But carnival's at least two months away, isn't it?"

"Yes."

"You still have a little wait then, don't you?"

His smile widened but took on no warmth. "Mrs. Amron, I am among the most patient of men," he said.

"Don't believe a word of it, Mrs. Amron," Dorothy Clough said, looking up with a laugh from her embroidery. "He's the most impatient man on earth."

There were only the three of them on the veranda. Harriet, seated a little apart, the unfinished letter on her lap, had thought of making her excuses and leaving, as she usually did, at their appearance. But today something in her refused to concede to them the power to irritate her, and she had remained on. Two chairs away Dorothy Clough was busy working a number of the colored threads through a linen square in a design of tea roses. A mild rum and soda was fitted into the hole on the armrest of her chair made for anchoring a glass, and from time to time she would sip from the drink and, holding it, lean forward to look out over the railing at her children playing far down the beach.

Lyle Hutson, in wet bathing trunks, his own drink in hand, reclined next to her in an old-fashioned planter's easy chair, the only one of its kind at the guesthouse. He always claimed it whenever he came to visit. His long legs cradled in the canvas sling suspended between the chair's lengthy arms, his body very dark against the tan cloth, he was smiling faintly to himself through half-closed eyes, enjoying the aftermath of his swim, feeling still the sensuous heave and fall of the sea under him. Up the beach at Horseshoe Pool, Merle, Allen, and Vere could be seen swimming within the wide half-circle of rock.

Around them the day hung fire with a stationary sun lodged between Westminster's spires as if it had gotten stuck there. A patient dusk waited off in the swollen clouds Lyle Hutson had seen piled the length of the horizon from the top of the hill. There would be enough light for Dorothy Clough to work by for some time yet.

"Do you think you might be playing carnival, Mrs. Amron?" she asked, turning to Harriet her friendly gaze. Her eyes, not having the faint touch of gray to be found in Harriet's, were a clearer blue. She kept at her embroidery while talking.

"You mean actually marching in one of the bands in the streets?" Harriet laughed. "I should think not!"

"Oh, but you should, you know," the woman said. "It's the only way to really enjoy carnival. Isn't that so, Lyle?"

His eyes had closed completely. "She's right, Mrs. Amron," he said. "You must 'play mass,' as we say."

"I'm planning to," Dorothy Clough said, turning back to her. "I'm dressing as a sailor and marching in one of the sailor bands, which are always the biggest because the costume's so cheap, and the rowdiest. It's a bit silly, I suppose, but I'm looking forward to it, especially since this will be my last carnival for some time. We'll be leaving right afterward, you know. George's work here is just about over. It'll be back to dear, sooty old London for us. But I must say it's been a marvelous holiday."

"We shall miss you, old girl," Lyle Hutson said.

"No, you won't, you unfeeling man," she said. Her expression as she looked across at him stretched out, eyes closed, in the planter's chair, was both fond and sad. "Not for long at any rate. I suspect you've already decided on my replacement."

He laughed, and Dorothy Clough, her needle poised above the cloth in its round frame, turned and said to Harriet—and it was impossible to tell whether she was being serious, "Do you know, Mrs. Amron, I think I'd be perfectly willing to throw over poor George, who even though he sometimes does naughty things as a newspaper editor, isn't really a bad sort, if I thought for a moment the gentleman here would have me. But I know better."

"Why not take your chances if you feel that strongly about it," Harriet said. She began gathering together the items on her lap—the letter paper, the air mail envelope, her pen and the clipboard she used to write on.

"Oh, I'm not such a romantic!" Dorothy Clough said. "Am I, Lyle?"

"No, thank God," he said—and they both laughed.

"But getting back to carnival—you must really give it a try," she said after a time as Harriet didn't leave. "It can be quite an experience. I remember my first one. We had only just arrived in the island and I couldn't believe my eyes when I saw all these people dancing in the streets in broad daylight—and on a working day at that! I was shocked to the depths of my solidly middle-class English soul. I remember standing there gaping in the most idiotic fashion for the longest time, and then there was a big commotion in the crowd around me and I found myself pushed right out into the middle of the people marching. I was sure it was the end. But do you know, once I got my feet untangled and saw I wasn't really going to be trampled to death I rather began to enjoy myself. After awhile it seemed the most natural thing in the world to be dancing in the streets in the middle of the day. It made perfectly good sense. I must have gone on for hours. I got horribly sunburnt, of course, and ruined a perfectly good pair of shoes, but I had a grand time. And best of all I met a delightful chap who took me in hand and taught me the proper steps. He was a waiter at one of the hotels and was all dressed up as a Watusi warrior—with a lovely fake lion's mane on his head which he kept tossing about, bells on his ankles and a long spear"—her arms, very slender and white, opened to indicate its length; she gave Harriet her pleasant, good-natured smile. "We stayed together for the entire march. I'm sure if George had seen us he would have put our picture on the front page of the paper as an example of the democratic spirit of carnival."

"'All o' we is one,'" Lyle Hutson said, speaking in the marked island accent. His eyes remained closed.

"That's the saying at carnival," she explained to Harriet. "I think it's beautifully put, don't you? And it's true more or less for the two days carnival lasts. You see all sorts of people, rich and poor, black, white, and in-between, dancing together in the streets, laughing and talking to each other. It's a marvelous sight, and a much needed one, goodness knows, in a world where all of us manage to be so ugly to each other, especially over this whole stupid question of race and color. And matters seem to be getting worse. Even my country's joined in the game now that a few Pakistanis and West Indians have gone there to live. All one can hope is that things don't get as bad as in your country or that dreadful South Africa."

"I don't see how you can speak of the two countries in the same breath. The situations are by no means the same," Harriet said sharply, but she felt a great reluctance to take the woman on. She had always disliked discussing the subject; she even disliked acknowledging to herself that the problem existed, and it was one of the things she had long closed her mind to. "At least," she said, "we're attempting to solve matters in a sensible fashion. There're laws now against discrimination and various government programs . . ."

"Yes, but none of it seems to be half enough, does it, from the terrible trend of things there recently?" Dorothy Clough said. She hadn't missed a stitch. "It's sad to say, but I'm afraid we shall be done in, the great white race, by our niggardliness and bad faith, our refusal to really take down and make room for the other fellow. Anyway, one has to be grateful for holidays like carnival where if only for two days people can behave as though we're truly one. . . .

"And," she added reflectively, putting down her needlework, "one must also be grateful for places like Bourne Island, where it's possible to meet and be with whomever one pleases without all the fuss and unpleasantness one often encounters at home. This isn't to say one doesn't eventually return home and pretty much resume the old life, but it's important, I believe, to have had the experience. I know I shall always be grateful for the year and more we've spent here. Some people like dear old George will never change, of course. But I think it's made me a bit of a better person . . ."

She broke off on the same reflective note, and turning to Lyle Hutson with a tentative smile, said, "Have you been listening, darling? I just gave a little speech."

"I heard you, girl," he said. "I heard you."

Saul had come out on the veranda meanwhile. He had been inside writing up the morning's work in the quiet back room Harriet had converted into a study for him and Allen. He had joined them just as Dorothy Clough was describing how she had been pushed into the midst of the marchers her first carnival. After half-listening to her for a time, seated on the armrest of Harriet's chair with his arm draped lightly around her shoulder, he had wandered off to the other end of the veranda out of reach of their voices so that he had missed the brief clash between the two women. He was leaning forward with his elbows on the railing, going over in his mind the material he had just recorded while absently watching the Clough children playing down at the water's edge.

The two girls, reaching up from time to time to wipe the strands of hair from their eyes, were building an elaborate sand castle right where the waves were breaking, while their small brother stood on his stout legs nearby solemnly watching them. But they were building too close to the edge, allowing no room for the early evening sea. The spume from each breaking wave was already beginning to foam and hiss around the castle and nibble at its base. Finally a wave dark with the oncoming night and swollen by the rising tide suddenly charged up the beach and washing over the castle with a roar reduced it in a matter of seconds to a few indistinct lumps. The little boy immediately plunked down in the retreating surf and began to cry; but his two sisters, after soberly contemplating their ruined handiwork, kneeling there in the wet sand with their arms akimbo, began rebuilding in the exact same spot.

Saul started to motion to them to move higher up the beach, and then didn't. Something in the willful set of their lean, tanned shoulders stopped him. And feeling a strange futility he looked away, his gaze traveling the short distance to Horseshoe Pool. Vere and Allen were still in the water, but Merle, who never stayed in long, was sitting close to shore on one of the flat rocks that formed the pool's protective barrier holding the small glass of rum she always drank right after a swim to warm her. She looked, he thought with a smile, like some dark, squat attendant spirit of the sea, who had clambered up out of her dwelling place to sample the world of men for a time. She was talking. He could tell from her gestures and the way her body was pressed forward—and he substituted her voice for Dorothy Clough's, reaching him remotely from the other end of the veranda. As he watched, a wave came sweeping in low over the rock upon which she was sitting, and he thought of the water circling her waist as a lover's arm. The spume reached up as though to kiss her cheek, and laughing she raised her glass out of the way. He thought he heard the crash of her many bracelets as her arm went up. He was certain he heard her laugh.

A short time later she was standing in their midst on the veranda (Saul had meanwhile rejoined the others) in the shapeless black bathing suit which revealed her body's slow decline. He saw the slight telltale droop to her breasts which were not much larger, he judged, than those of the little bony adolescent hostesses in Sugar's, the wearied flesh of her upper arm which shuddered whenever she gestured strongly, all the slowly slackening, aging lines which she didn't even bother trying to hide with the large beach towel she had draped across her shoulders. Things that would have displeased him, even offended him in another woman somehow pleased him in her. He did not understand it.

"How was the water?" he quietly asked.

And she answered as quietly, turning to him with a soft, abstracted smile, the private sun in her eyes, "Like wine, Saul Amron, like wine. I've never seen the sea so lovely. I hated to leave, and as you can see, Vere and Allen are still in. You should have joined us, but then I've noticed"—her smile took on its familiar edge—"that you don't seem too particular about the sea."

"I'm not," he said. "But had I known it was like wine I might have relented and come in."

"And what about you?" she said to Harriet.

"Not guilty," Harriet said with a laugh, and raised her right hand. "I was in this morning long before any of you were up, and although the water wasn't anything like wine then, it was still pleasant."

"Brr!" said Merle, "I don't see how you can take that cold sea first thing in the morning." Wrapping the beach towel around her she settled into her chair. "Ah," she began, bracing her bare feet against the posts of the railing directly in front and taking up her cigarettes which she had left on the arm of the chair, "What more to ask of life, yes? A sea bath at the end of the day. A drink or two afterward. Some old talk with friends. Small pleasures, but they hold up till the end. Right, Lyle?"

She glanced over to where he lay with his eyes closed and drink in hand in the chair next to Dorothy Clough. "But look at you lying there like some Indian rajah!" she cried mockingly. Her gaze was warm, though, and it lingered appreciatively on his dark, fit body in the bathing trunks. With a sigh she drew the beach towel closer around herself. "You must have had a good week," she said—and a bitterness born of an envy she could not help tinged her voice. "How many bribes did you take?"

He laughed, and raising up briefly, blew her a kiss. "I always have a good week," he said. "With or without the bribes. And why not? I live good, man"—he spoke in dialect. "You know that. As the young chaps used to say, 'I living good, I living right, but muh clothes at muh mother's.' "

"What did they mean by that, Lyle?" Dorothy Clough asked, looking up from her work.

"Well," he said, "when a fellow had a girl friend he might be sleeping at her place every night, practically living with her, but he always made a point of keeping his clothes at his mother's house as a sign, shall we say, that he wasn't totally committed."

"What a perfect scoundrel," she said laughing. "I hope you never behaved in such a fashion, darling."

"What, that scamp lying there!" Merle cried. "That rogue . . . that womanizer . . ." She sputtered to a stop, pretending to be at a loss for words to describe him. "Don't start me on him."

"Well, I suspected as much," Dorothy Clough said with the laugh, and laying aside her embroidery, stood up. "It's getting late, I had better fetch the children."

She left and Merle, her gaze still on Lyle, her expression one of helpless affection, said softly, "You damn rascal. So tell me, what's the latest over in Babylon?"

"Big news, man," he said. "The new development plan is finally ready. It's to be made public Monday."

"Oh?" said Saul, turning his way.

"Yes, I'm going to send copies to you both."

"So, it's ready, eh," Merle said. "All right, tell us the worst."

He laughed. "Dear Merle, you're a born pessimist. Here you're ready to condemn the thing before setting eyes on it. But you won't be able to find fault with this one because, unlike the last, it's a good solid plan—very sound. You might call it the Great Leap Forward, Bourne Island style. Waterford did a first-rate job. I know you don't think much of government for bringing him in, but the chap knows his business."

"What's being stressed in the plan?" Saul asked. He had left where he had been lounging half-perched, a leg dangling, on the railing across from Harriet and gone to stand near Lyle.

"Well," said Lyle, "as Waterford sees it, and I agree, there are only two ways for us to get into the modern swing of things, so to speak. One is to bring in far more investors than has been done to date, not the big chaps: we've neither the size nor the resources to interest them, but the smaller ones. The other is to expand our tourist trade. We want, we need more of those nice fat dollars you Americans spend so freely when you come down on holiday"—he gave the bland smile. "Small industry and tourism then," he said. "Those two are to take precedence over everything else for the next five to ten years."

"What about agriculture?" Saul asked. He was frowning slightly, the lines forming a faint wing-shaped pattern above the strong bridge of his nose.

"How's that?"

"How does it figure in the plan?"

"It figures very high, naturally," Lyle said. "After all, we're an agricultural country—and will be for some time to come. We haven't forgotten that. Any number of changes and improvements are planned."

"Such as?" Then, as Lyle didn't answer immediately and seemed, moreover, disinclined to go into this, scarcely interested, Saul said, his frown deepening, "I ask because one of the things that troubles me about so many of the development plans one comes across in places like Bourne Island is that they tend to go all out for industry and tourism—to see these as the solution to all problems—while agriculture, which is the base of the economy, whatever little lifeblood it has, gets very short shrift indeed. Don't misunderstand me," he said. "I appreciate the need to diversify and find other sources of income.

And I know that under the present setup the options are few. But I'm also convinced that equal if not greater attention has to be given to agriculture. And there has to be, first, a solid land-reform program—it just doesn't make any sense, for God's sake, for Kingsley and Sons to own all the goddamn land in Bournehills except for the little plots belonging to the small farmers; and, second, an all-out effort to produce as much of your own food as possible. That above all else." He spoke with passion. "Even in a place as cramped for space as Bourne Island. Because a country . . ."

"My dear Doctor," Lyle said, interrupting him, "we're well aware of what you're saying, and I assure you that all such matters have been taken into consideration in the new plan. In fact, one of the first things being called for is a full-scale investigation of the entire agricultural picture with an eye specifically to finding ways of increasing food production."

"We had one of those 'full-scale investigations' five years ago, remember?—with the other so-called development plan and not a damn thing came of it. We're still importing everything we eat, and it's killing us." It was Merle commenting, in a voice that was for her strangely subdued.

"Because a country," Saul repeated, insisting on making his point, "first has to be able to feed itself to some degree before it can think of getting into the modern swing of things as you put it, Lyle. It's as simple—and as difficult as that. Merle's right. It is killing, it's crippling for an island like this to be importing the very basics of life."

"And it wouldn't even be so bad if the food coming in was at all decent," said Harriet, speaking for the first time. "But that awful rice and dry, bad-smelling cod which everyone around here eats nearly every day."

"Food fit for a slave, my dear Mrs. Amron!" Lyle bent on her his chill, sealed smile. It shone very white against his blackness in the rapidly failing light. "Foisted upon us long ago by our metropolitan masters. And still with us to a depressing degree, I admit. You've named them well. Saltfish, as we call it. The damn, half-rotten rice. The cornmeal that used to be crawling with weevils by the time it reached us when I was a boy. But do you realize that some people up your way made their fortune in the old days selling us these delicacies? Do you know that . . . ?" He waited; then, as she remained silent, he laughed—and in such a way it almost seemed he knew about the faded ledger in the glass display case at the Philadelphia

Historical Society and the portrait of the widow in her frilled cap, that whole questionable legacy which Harriet had long ago ruled from her thoughts. "Tell her about that, Merle," he said. "You're the historian. Tell her that saltfish, for instance, has been with us for so long on Bourne Island it actually tastes good to us."

"Even I've gotten to rather like it." Dorothy Clough suddenly spoke up. She had returned from the beach with her three children, and had paused with them in the doorway to the house, on her way to take them in for their supper and bed. Allen and Vere had left the water by now and gone together into Spiretown to work on the latter's car. "And the children love it made into those little crisp fried cakes."

"There you are," Lyle exclaimed. "Irrefutable evidence." Then, turning back to Saul, "But you and Merle are right. We've got to break the old pattern of depending on the outside for everything we eat. Government knows this. But it also knows it can't be done overnight. We're certain, though, that once we industrialize on a large enough scale we will then have the means to finance the changes needed in agriculture."

"It just doesn't work that neatly, Lyle," he said. "You can't do one without the other."

The latter shrugged, ignoring his urgent tone. "Everything's a gamble, you Americans say. And so, my dear Doctor," he continued, "even though our approach doesn't seem particularly wise to you, we shall be concentrating our efforts in the years ahead on inducing more of the chaps with money up your way to come down and invest it here. Of course, we have to make it worth their while, and under the new plan we shall be offering them a number of very attractive incentives."

"Such as?" Merle very quietly asked. She sat drawn deep into her chair, smoking steadily, with the towel wrapped tightly around her. There was the same dead calm in her voice as before.

"Yes," Saul echoed her. "Just how much are you offering them?"

And Lyle, relaxed in his planter's chair, his face and the details of his body scarcely visible in the nearly completed dusk, told them—and his voice in the settling darkness had the same impersonal quality as his smile, which was still there, they knew, although they could no longer really see it.

For one, he informed them, the tax-free period for new businesses was being extended from five to fifteen years, and all customs duties for them were also being waived for the same period. In addition, the Bourne Island government was planning to build at its own expense a huge industrial park, so that when an investor arrived he would find a plant awaiting him—and this for only the most nominal rent. ("How much? Give us the figure," Merle said in the dangerously still voice. "Oh, just a token amount, no more than ten or fifteen dollars a year." His own voice remained unruffled.) Finally, under the new plan, anyone from abroad setting up a business on Bourne Island would not only be allowed to send all his profits out of the country, but could repatriate his capital in full should the business fail.

Saul's sigh was loud and unhappy in the near-darkness. "You're certainly giving them a hell of a lot," he said. "Don't get me wrong, I know you have to make it an attractive deal for them, if not they'll take their money elsewhere, but this seems an awfully high price to be paying, given the island's budget, just to bring in a few small plants which, from what I've seen in other places over the years, don't begin to solve the basic problems.

"And why give them such a free hand?" His voice rose; he stood away from the railing against which he had been leaning. "They should be made to invest in partnership with the government so you'd at least have some say in their operations as well as a definite share of the profits. It's your country, after all! In fact," he declared, "all such as Kingsley and Sons and the big trading companies and banks along Queen Street should, at the very least, be owned in part by the government. It should demand a controlling interest in them . . ."

"Whoa there!" Lyle stopped him with a laugh. "All that sounds very suspect to me, Doctor. I didn't realize we had a rabid socialist in our midst. You've been dissembling all along."

"It doesn't matter how it sounds." He spoke sharply. "All I'm suggesting is that even under the present setup some more equitable arrangement is possible."

"And I assure you it is not possible," Lyle said, and from the sudden Oxonian thrust to the words, they could tell his smile had tightened in a small show of impatience. "I see I had best explain our situation here on Bourne Island to you, apprise you of the realities, so to speak, even though I must say I thought you knew them by now. But it's clear you don't. The reality, my dear fellow, is that as far as the world goes we are an insignificant green speck in a relatively small American lake called the Caribbean. Poor. Totally dependent on a single crop that isn't worth a ha'penny anymore on the world market.

Without any resources except perhaps people, and too damn many of them and nowhere to send them now that England has followed the example of your country and barred her door to the nigs. We're somewhat independent, yes. But you and I know that doesn't matter for much. How independent when if England were to cease tomorrow taking our sugar at a preferential price we'd be finished. How when you Americans can plant a missile-tracking station right on our backside and there's nothing we can do about it because the agreement was made long before the present government took office . . ."

He uttered his hollow laugh, stretched languorously in the canvas chair, drank from his glass. "It's indiscreet, I know, to mention such matters," he said. "And I avoid doing so whenever possible. I usually leave such talk to my good friend Merle here and the one or two like her on the island who still cling to the hope of some impossible revolution. But it's obvious, Doctor, you need to be reminded of the realities. You know, very often, people like yourself tend to confuse us with the new, large, potentially wealthy countries in Africa and Asia who have a little something to bargain with, even though at the present they, too, are at the mercy of the giants. We have nothing to bargain with. Therefore, the concessions that strike you as excessive. Now as to tourism . . ."

And without pausing he went on to speak of the government's plans there, citing among other things the new extension to the airport, the big promotional campaign planned in the United States and Canada ("We shall be selling the island as the newest vacation-paradise in the Caribbean," he said in the voice from which some small measure of sarcasm and even rage was never missing, "emphasizing our blue, warm waters, white beaches, palm trees and happy natives, the usual sort of thing . . .") and ending with the announcement that the Hillard Hotel chain, the largest in the world, was interested in having a hotel on the island.

"Of course, we might have to agree to them operating a casino in it," he said. "The Opposition and the church are sure to make a big noise about that, but they'll come round once we assure them that none of the other unsavory business that often goes along with gambling—American gangsters, prostitution, that sort of thing, will be allowed to get started. It's something of a risk, I suppose, but we can't afford to miss out on having one of their hotels here."

"What's the arrangement? Who's to actually build it?" Saul asked, and a kind of depression had taken hold of his voice. They could sense his shoulders drooping in the darkness.

"We are," Lyle said. "That's the usual procedure with those big chains in a place like Bourne Island. We'll build it—and yes, it'll be a strain on the budget, but what to do?—and they will operate it under their name. For a handsome percentage I needn't add. But then that's business. You couldn't very well expect the chaps to come into a place to lose money, could you?"

There was a long silence, broken only by the unintelligible comment of the sea on all he had said, and then Merle, as though musing aloud to herself, said very quietly, "Signed, sealed and delivered. The whole bloody place. And to the lowest bidder. Who says the auction block isn't still with us?"

The glass she had been drinking from in hand, she slowly and almost painfully stood up. (Her joints might have grown stiff from sitting in the damp bathing suit.) Saul heard the intimate sound of the towel being drawn around her body. She must be cold.

"Yes, Lord, you fellas in government are all right," she said in the ominously low voice. "You're doing a good job. You're to be congratulated."

"Now, now, Merle . . ." Lyle said, and leaning up from his easy chair made to touch her as she started past him toward the door to the house.

The hand reaching out to her through the darkness might have acted as a kind of release, because she suddenly snatched away her arm and turning violently on him, cried, "Merle me no Merle! Don't let my name cross your lips, damn you!" And after her long foreboding silence and the dangerously muted tone she had used when speaking before, her anger actually came as something of a relief to the others present. "Signed, sealed and delivered, I say. The whole place. Is that what we threw out the white pack who ruled us for years and put you chaps in office for? For you to give away the island? For you to literally pay people to come and make money off us? Fifteen years without having to pay a penny in taxes! All their profits out of the island! A whole factory for ten dollars a year! Why, man, Bourne Island comes like a freeness to them. And with all the concessions, what? We don't see any benefit as such. It's as Saul said: they don't get at the real problems like providing enough work for people. Remember the plastics factory? How many did it employ altogether?

How many?" she shouted down at him in the darkness. "Twenty," she answered bitterly, "to watch the machines. And over fifty thousand walking Queen Street every day with nothing to do and getting desperate. Man, it's a joke."

She swung away in disgust and as quickly spun back. "And now you're to be giving away even more. Worse, you're ready to let in every crook and gambler in the hemisphere just to have some big hotel. To turn us into another Bermuda with everybody bowing and scraping for the almighty dollar. Is that all that's possible for us in these small islands? Is that the only way we can exist? Well, if so, it's no different now than when they were around here selling us for thirty pounds sterling. Not really. Not when you look deep. Consider. The Kingsleys still hold the purse strings and are allowed to do as they damn please, never mind you chaps are supposed to be in charge. And the Little Fella is still bleeding his life out in a cane field. Come up to Bournehills some day and see him on those hills. Things are no different. The chains are still on. Oh, Lyle, can't you see that?" she cried, and the three on the veranda felt the little rush of air, heard the dull crash of her bracelets in the darkness as her arms went out in appeal to him. "Haven't you fellows in Legco learned anything from all that's gone on in this island over the past four hundred years? Read your history, man!"

And then suddenly her voice dropped, and she muttered obscurely to herself, the words unclear, almost inaudible. "And then you wonder why Bournehills is the way it is. Why with all the improvements you try out down here it still won't change, get into 'the modern swing of things'? Ha!" She uttered a dark weighted laugh that Saul had occasionally heard from others in the district, and which always left him vaguely disturbed, wondering. Then, in an even lower voice, and speaking almost as if she herself was not conscious of what she was saying, she added, "Bo, you don't know it, but Bournehills is the way it is for a reason—that you people in town are too blind to see. And it will stay so, no matter what, for a reason."

Just at that moment Dorothy Clough, who had been inside seeing to her children, came out carrying a lighted tilly lamp. Taking one look at Merle poised angrily above Lyle, she hastily went and hung the lamp on its hook on the middle veranda post and sat down without a word.

In the sudden harsh light, Merle, the others forgotten, bent over the planter's chair, and her enraged face just inches from Lyle's, said, whispering it, "But you know, sometimes I don't recognize you at all. I don't know the person. Tell me, are you the same Lyle I once knew in England . . . ?" Unperturbed, he smiled and shook his head, saying no, but she didn't notice. "The same chap who used to say that things in the West Indies had to be completely turned around in order to favor the Little Fella, that any planning had to be done with him in mind, because it was his country and he had to be made to feel part of it? You used to say that places like Bourne Island needed radical surgery, remember?—that was the expression you always used—the old cancer feeding on us cut away, so we could really build something new. You used to . . ."

"Dear Merle," he said, and the calmness of his voice momentarily silenced her. "Dear, dear Merle. You know what your trouble is?" He waited a moment, the eyes that remained veiled, hidden above the broad nose, in the fixed darkness of his face, lifted to her face, holding her to silence. Then: "You refuse to grow old. At your age—and I know how old you are, remember—you're still full of all that bogus youthful idealism. And you'll remain the idealist to the end. Which is one of the reasons I love you, and come down here every so often and let you give me a good tongue-lashing. You make me feel young again, girl, you and the doctor here, talking all that socialist nonsense they used to serve up to us at LSE. But hear me, all your high ideals are quite out of order in the present discussion, as is your emotionalism—which has always been your worst fault, and I see that I shall have to remind you as I did the doctor of the realities of our situation . . ."

"The reality, blast you"—her cry jarred the air and caused the lamplight within its enclosure of glass to waver—"is that you and others like you have got yours: the big house, the motorcars, the fat jobs, the lot, and it's to hell with the other fellow. You don't even see him. Do you realize that? Do you know the terrible thing that's happened to us on Bourne Island? It's that we live practically one on top the other because the place is so small and yet we don't see each other, we don't ever touch. Instead of us pulling together when we need each other so much, it's every man for his damn self. That's the reality—and the tragedy of us on this island. But I'm not telling you anything you don't know. You understand it better than I do. You're not Deanes or one of those other political hacks down in Legco. But you make out you don't. Oh, God, to know, to understand and to act and live as if you don't. Man, I wouldn't want to be you for a day. . . ."

Then suddenly straightening up, she declared with savage vehemence, "Look, don't come around here anymore, you hear. I don't want to see you. Stay in town where you belong. Finish with you!"

Her hand flew out, banishing him; and afraid perhaps that she meant it and was really through with him, Lyle quickly sat up and caught her by the wrist. And though he was laughing—the mildly chiding, playful laugh he used with her—his manner had changed. "Merle, Merle," he said, and his tone had changed also. "What are you upsetting yourself about? You'll just have another one of your attacks. Let's not quarrel, man. You know as well as I do, even though you'd never admit it, that there're no alternatives for us in this place. Not for the time being at any rate. So just relax yourself. Don't think about it so much. Let's remember the old days. . . ."

And gazing up at her standing over him with the towel wrapped like a great stole or scarf around her, he smiled in an almost tender fashion, some memory stirring in his eyes. "Remember," he said, "that long red muffler you used to wear all winter long in England? It was twice as long as you were tall. You would wrap it around and around your neck and face until all anyone could see were your eyes. You were never without it. People said you wore it as a sign of your politics. You would even put the damn thing on in the house sometimes when it was cold. You even slept in it once, remember . . . ?"

"What's all this in aid of?" Her scream split the air. She tried pulling away.

"Not a thing, girl," he said. His softened gaze remained on her face, his hand around her wrist. And now, like her, he had also forgotten the other three on the veranda. And they, aware of their exclusion, kept silent, their faces turned aside. For the moment all that existed for him, it was clear from his expression, was the memory of that brief period long ago in England when he and Merle had been lovers—a memory which, from time to time, when there were no Dorothy Cloughs and Merle had been alone too long, they renewed —but casually, as no more than a gesture in acknowledgment of their long and difficult friendship.

"Not a thing," he repeated. "I know you've forgotten but I often think of the time we spent together in London. That place, yes!" he laughed. "All that blasted damp and fog. That miserable flat you had once with the gas heater that never worked when it turned really cold. You used to say the English were the only people who could turn their discomforts into virtues. Remember those parties you used to throw with the money from your rich lady friend in Hampstead who wanted to keep you for herself. They would go on till dawn. Every homesick West Indian student in London would be there. You used to make fishcakes and cook up rice. Man, those were the days."

"You bitch," she said. But the fight had gone out of her, and she stood, her hand lax in his, caught, ensnared in the trap of memory he had set for her.

"Remember that long string of a fellow from Trinidad named Richardson? He was with me in the RAF. I used to bring him to your parties sometimes. There was nothing Richy loved more than a fete. But he would refuse to listen to all our talk about the coming socialist revolution in the West Indies. He was always telling us not to be so serious about everything and just go on and enjoy ourselves, that life was nasty, brutish and short. Well, his was, I know. He went down in flames over Germany. I saw it with my own eyes; we were on the same mission. Those Germans shot the plane right out from under him. And remember . . ."

But she had broken free of the hold of his voice, and the hand with the empty glass came up as though to hurl it at him. "What's this in aid of, I ask!"—and again the light in the tilly lamp appeared to dip and recover. The glass hovered just above Lyle's head. And strangely he looked up at it and smiled. This might have been what he had been hoping for. Something in his expression, his eyes, in the way his body was straining up in the chair, urged her to throw it. He both sought and required her abuse it seemed—and not only the customary tongue-lashing she dealt him almost every time he visited Bournehills, but this sharp physical blow as well. It was as if this alone could ease the dull ache of some loss and betrayal of which he was never free.

And she must have understood this because the hand with the glass dropped back to her side and her anger collapsed. And standing there, her gaze bent on him, seeing him both as he was now and as the young man who had once shared her beliefs, her anger, she said in a voice that gently reproved him, "Why would you bring up all that ancient history? Are you looking to lose the only real friend you've got?"

She turned away then, only to start at the sight of Saul standing across from them at the railing. She had forgotten he was there. And seeing him she involuntarily, for an instant, made to step toward him, and he appeared to start toward her. But neither move was completed, and in what was almost the same moment, she had turned and was heading toward the door of the house, moving slow and heavy-footed, the beach towel trailing on the floorboards.

She did not so much as glance at the two women as she passed their chairs; nor did they look at her. Dorothy Clough, who knew better than to interfere in these periodic clashes between the two, kept her head bent over the embroidery in her lap. From the rapid way she was plying her needle through the linen in the frame, she might have been trying to weave the tension on the veranda into the tea roses slowly blooming there. Harriet, gazing thoughtfully down at her unfinished letter (she appeared to be simply thinking of what next to write), might have heard none of what had transpired from her expression. And in a way she hadn't. Because the moment Merle's voice had struck the first angry note, a door in her mind had automatically slammed shut, closing out the sound.

Merle reached the doorway and paused and, her face turned toward the drawing room, said in a voice that struggled to recapture something of her old spirit, "To hell with all of you. To hell with this place. The first real money I lay my hands on I'm making tracks out of here. Gone! To the other end of the world. Japan or some damn place. You watch." Then, staring numbly down at the empty glass in her hand: "I need a drink and a cigarette. And what's happened to supper? Carrington!" she called, but her voice could scarcely lift above the level of her despair. "Carrington!" she repeated and slowly disappeared into the house calling for the old woman.

CHAPTER 9

For some time afterward Saul found himself puzzling over the scarcely intelligible remark about Bournehills Merle had made during the height of her outburst that evening. It had somehow implied that there were other, more profound, even mystical, reasons for the place being as it was. He tried getting her to explain what she had meant, but with no success. First, immediately following her quarrel with Lyle she had sunk into one of the long, numbing depressions that came over her whenever anything happened to upset her—a lingering symptom, perhaps, of the breakdown she had suffered years ago in England, and for several days had remained shut in her room in the section of the house that was off limits to everyone but Carrington. Then, when she had emerged and he had asked her about the remark, she had looked sharply at him for a moment, then declared almost irritably that she couldn't remember what she had said: "You think I know what I'm saying half the time!" and had refused to discuss it.

But it continued to occupy his thoughts, mainly because it seemed related to something he had come to feel more and more about the district. Although the research was going well, and he and Allen were accumulating an impressive amount of data, he could not rid himself of the feeling that something about the place was eluding him, some meaning it held which could not be gotten at through the usual methods of analysis. He could not say what made for this impression.

Part of it, he knew, stemmed from his earlier suspicion that something other, and deeper, than the causes he had discovered had made for the failure of the other projects in Bournehills. Part of it also had to do with the strong, other-century feel to life in the district, which though typical of other places he had worked in was more pronounced here. Sometimes driving past the old man Mr. Douglin, trimming the grass along Westminster Low Road, or catching sight in the distance of the tiny, seemingly motionless figures of Stinger and the others cutting canes high on a slope (and why did it always seem to him the same slope?) or seeing when he dropped over at Cane Vale the ancient windmill standing intact out in the yard, he would be struck by the feeling, too fleeting to grasp, that he had stumbled upon a world that was real, inescapably real, yet at the same time somehow unreal; of the present but even more so of the past.

He tried putti. g the thought from his mind. He was letting his imagination get the better of him, he told himself, seeking more in things than was there, trying to make the work harder for himself, and yet he couldn't help feeling as the weeks came and went vaguely surrounded by a mystery, and he became increasingly puzzled, even annoyed. Something, goddamn it, he swore to himself, about the place was being withheld, hidden from him. And yet not hidden. It was there, he sensed, just behind the carefully measured smiles people gave him, in the look he occasionally surprised in Delbert's shrewd, stippled eyes, in the hands raised solemnly in greeting to him along the roads. But whatever it was came and went so swiftly, and was expressed in such obscure terms, it eluded him. He came to think of it as one of those subliminal messages which slip undetected past the eye and ear to fasten like a nettlesome burr on the mind.

He considered discussing it with Allen, then thought better of it. The whole thing was too nebulous. Allen, with his scrupulously scientific approach to everything, who dealt with life in terms of so many charts, graphs and statistical tables (and it was a valuable asset for someone like himself to have in a research partner), would never understand what he was getting at, and would only be made uncomfortable and puzzled. Even Harriet, when he mentioned it to her, musing aloud about it sometimes during the quiet period they spent over coffee in the late evenings, didn't understand. She attributed his suspicions to the fact that he was working too hard and suggested they go away for a week or two.

To add to matters, this thing he sensed about Bournehills even took on a personal meaning. Because just around that time he found himself recalling events from his own past. Not with any regularity, but often enough to start him questioning. Walking along the roads he sometimes had the impression he was wandering back over the paths his life had taken. Incidents from his childhood and youth, from his early field-work experiences in Mexico and Peru, from the war, where he had served in Europe, and the journey he had felt compelled to make afterward to see for himself the death camps in Poland; memories from his first marriage and his long uneven career —all these, fragments from the past, had suddenly for no reason begun to surface to his mind like flotsam from a submerged wreck.

And faces from the past began to accost him along the roads, rising out of the shimmering heat and haze and the little clouds of white powdery marl dust stirred up by his shoes. Faces of his family: his mother's the day he had clapped his hands over his ears, refusing to listen anymore to that wildly imagined tale of her family's ancient flight and suffering; his father's the time when, in his youthful arrogance, he had scornfully rejected the old man's ambitions for him and declared he would go his own way. He had wronged them both. At times he again saw the senile Jehovah in the upstairs window, he of the tobacco-stained beard and soiled tallith who had daily atoned for the sins of the world. Once, the eyes of the young German soldier he had shot point-blank stood blue and terrified before him, hanging there disembodied in the air; another time he saw with startling clarity the face of the first woman he had ever truly loved. She had been Peruvian—a public health nurse as well as a strong nationalist even back then, who had at first questioned and even resented his presence in her country. But when they became lovers she had begged him to stay on, join their fight, marry her. . . . Remembering her face the day he told her his research was done and he would be leaving, the disappointment, sadness and scorn reflected there, he had to stop and pass his hand over his eyes to clear away the memory. And other faces rose to haunt him as well, as he made his way around Bournehills: the white ones of his colleagues who had condemned what they felt to be the reformer in him, the dark ones of the people among whom he had worked, whose eyes, especially those of the children, reminded him of how abysmally he had failed in his grand designs for them.

Moreover, as the weeks passed, all the faces began to merge, flowing one into another to form one face: that of his first wife; and all the events he found himself recalling began gradually to lead, as if by some natural progression, to a single event: her death—and he was brought finally, after having avoided it for so long, to the fact of that tragedy. He was like a man who had fled the scene of some fateful accident for which he was partly to blame, wanting desperately to put time and distance between it and himself only to find when he glanced over his shoulder that it had followed close on his heels. He had glanced back only to discover her there. Her face as it looked during the last days before her death—fleshless, utterly consumed by the pain and the rapid draining away of her blood that had followed the miscarriage. Her body twisted out of shape and wasted by the fight she had waged to hold onto the child till its term. Her glazed and blasted eyes which grew demented as the end neared. They had accused him, those eyes—not wanting to, but helpless to stop themselves—of her death. And she had been right. He had killed her, as well as the child. For hadn't he, in his absorption in his work, subjected her year after year to the hardship of life in the field, when he knew her health had been nearly ruined by her youth spent in the camps? And how was it she had been able to survive that horror, only to die in what was for most women the relatively uncomplicated act of giving birth. What was the meaning of such a death, of all such senseless deaths and suffering? Her darkening gaze had begged him for an answer; later, when the fever set in and her mind broke, she had screamed at him to tell her; and finally, when the only thing he could do was to sit helplessly by, his bowed head admitting that he had no answer to offer, she had cursed him.

She had come to stand in his mind for all those he had failed. And in her death had been summed up all his mistakes, the wrongs he had committed, his defeats, most of which he had brought on himself. At the end her dead stare had demanded, it seemed to him, that he turn and examine himself, look within. But he had refused; and to spare himself he had simply gone numb. And now here she was back again with the old demand; and worse, with the question of her death which he had closed his mind to. Now, when he had taken a new wife and started to work again, trying like some old vaudevillian to stage a comeback. But her dead gaze welling up at him with unnerving frequency out of the Bournehills heat and haze was insistent. Under it he felt the numbness that had formed a hard protective shell around his heart, a carapace that had deflected all feeling and memory, slowly begin to crack. And as it gave way, exposing the tender places beneath and rendering him sensitive again, feeling returning in little stinging bursts as blood to a limb that's fallen asleep, he found himself slowly retracing the troubled course of his life, seeking the meaning there.

He was wondering idly to himself what it was about Bournehills that should evoke in him such painful memories as he walked over to Cane Vale one morning early, the sun setting fire to his hair which looked as if it had already been singed in a blaze and branding his shoulders through his shirt. Sir John Stokes, the head of the London office of Kingsley and Sons whom Ferguson often spoke of, was due at the factory today on his yearly visit and he wanted to be on hand. He arrived before the visitor to find the usual stir and activity in the yard. The lorries that had returned loaded from the fields stood waiting to be weighed in a line which reached out of the entrance gate and up the road, with here and there among them a laden donkey cart belonging to a small farmer. The young lorry helpers sat enthroned on top of the waiting trucks sucking cane, tearing off the tough peel with their teeth and spitting the chewed pulp down into the dust. They called down to Saul as he passed. Inside the yard the giant hoist that conveyed the canes from the weighing platform to the storage hive was swinging like a great scythe overhead; and off by itself in a corner the old mill stood as if waiting for the wind to set its vanes in motion again.

Erskine Vaughan, more tense and harried-looking than usual, had posted himself outside the weighing office near the entrance gates to await Sir John's arrival. His gaze fixed nervously on the road leading into the yard, he scarcely noticed Saul as he came up to greet him. His voice as he lashed out at the men was as strident as a woman's.

Saul looked in briefly on Ferguson inside the factory, and found him more than ever resolved to speak to Sir John about the condition of the rollers. He had taken a few drinks to give him heart, and as he stood waiting in all his lean tensile grace and authority on the platform above the two noisy wheels, his breath, his whole person, gave off the faint redolence of rum.

Toward noon they saw the car, a black stately Rolls with the look to it of a hearse. It came swiftly toward them through the dazzling sunlight, moving smoothly and without a sound over the stony potholed road past the line of waiting lorries and carts. It didn't appear to be moving of itself. A pair of invisible horses deeply caparisoned in black and with their hoofs muffled might have been drawing it along.

Without disturbing the thick dust and cane chaff over which it passed as it entered the yard, the car drew up outside the weighing office and Erskine scrambled forward.

The man who emerged from the Rolls was one of those small men who succeed in giving the impression of height and size because of the stiff-shouldered, military bearing they affect and a certain impatient, imperious air. Sir John was dressed as if for a safari, in a belted khaki bush jacket with epaulets, shorts, olive-drab knee socks and brown Oxfords. Below the shorts, between them and the socks, his scraggy old man's thighs showed the pallor of the long London winter. In a small show of vanity, the fringe of graying hair to one side of his head had been grown long and then carefully combed up and distributed over his naked skull. The moment he stepped from the car he put on a pith helmet and took his swagger stick in hand.

Sir John was accompanied by the local representative of the Kingsley interests on the island, the man Hinds, whom Merle had pointed out to Saul at Sugar's that first night. Early in the research, he had gone to see Hinds in the air-conditioned Kingsley offices above Barclay's Bank on Queen Street. The meeting had been more unsatisfactory than he had anticipated. Not only had Hinds, like everyone else he'd spoken to in town, immediately condemned the project to failure ("Bournehills! Man, you won't be able to do anything with that place"), but most irritating of all, he had refused to take his interest in the district seriously. His tone, his falsely genial air, the jokes he told in the heavy, exaggerated accent typical of the island's whites, insisted that although Saul might go to the fields with Stinger and the others and drink with them in the evenings, live practically as they lived, and although he, Hinds, neither understood nor approved of such behavior—and moreover, didn't understand or approve of him—he, Saul, was still by virtue of his color one with him.

"American, eh?" Sir John said as Hinds introduced him. "One of those anthropologist fellows, you say." His eyes set deep within the bony mask of his face scarcely acknowledged Saul.

"Yes," said Hinds. "Dr. Amron's here on some sort of study. "Maybe when he's through he'll be able to tell us what's wrong with these people in Bournehills, why they still get on like they're living in ancient times"—this with a bluff laugh.

"So he might, so he might," Sir John said, and with a nod set off at a brisk military stride toward the factory, Hinds at his side and the anxious Erskine following a pace behind. Saul, not wanting to give the impression to the men watching that he was one of their party, trailed them at a distance.

Sir John paused just inside the doorway to the factory, overcome momentarily as was everyone upon entering the building by the noise and heat, the cane chaff whirling in the thick molasses-colored gloom and the strangely disembodied look to the men at work there, who never failed to call to mind ghosts confined to the dark hold of a ship set on some interminable voyage. Then he was off again, his companions at his heels and Saul keeping his distance behind. Like a general reviewing the matériel with which he waged his war: the tanks and mounted guns, the stacked bombs and missiles, Sir John moved briskly through the aisles of machines, boilers and steaming vats, stopping occasionally to point with his swagger stick or consult with Hinds. Under the sun helmet his hawk eye was impatient, sharp, taking in the condition of the machines at a glance but passing without interest over the faces of the men. They might not have been there.

Reaching the metal stairs that led to the platform over the rollers he quickly mounted them, and with Hinds and Erskine Vaughan who had followed him up standing to one side, he went and gazed over the guard rail at the giant wheels in the deep pit, watching them as they closed ponderously over the canes, crushing them dry, while sending up the almost human cry of someone being broken on a rack.

Sir John studied the rollers for some minutes, and down the railing from him, just a few feet away, Ferguson stood waiting to speak to him about them. He had drawn himself up to his full tremulous height, and with his shoulders thrown back and eyes fixed ahead, he looked like a soldier awaiting inspection. Sir John was unaware of him, and remained so for a time. But alerted finally to his presence by the strained quality of his silence which had unsettled the air and the tension one sensed beneath his stiffly held surface, he looked up. Their eyes met and for a moment they quietly regarded each other down the length of railing, Sir John vaguely puzzled, questioning, the little commanding lift to his head challenging Ferguson to speak, and Ferguson straining to do so, the veins and tendons that strung together his limbs standing out in a tangle beneath his skin in the effort. But no sound came. He stood silent. Behind his glasses his eyes were eloquent with the speech he was to have given, that he had rehearsed so often for Saul's benefit, but his lips were as if sewn together. His long pliant body that moved with such passion and force when he declaimed upon Cuffee Ned in the rumshop at night seemed a thing of stone, a dumb effigy of himself. From where he had come to a halt at the foot of the metal steps, Saul saw those sealed lips and stricken eyes—and had to look quickly away. He felt the unspoken words choking Ferguson choking him. He felt the other's anguish and helplessness as intimately as if they were his own.

"Well, I see you're still here, yes. How's it going?" It was Hinds addressing Ferguson in his overly hearty manner, seeking to dispel the sudden uneasiness on the platform.

And Ferguson, sounding unlike himself, answered, the words issuing in a rapid breathless burst from his constricted throat, "Fine sir, thank you, sir." His eyes, tinged amber from the rum he had taken earlier, had fled Sir John's by now and were fixed on the murky gloom above his head.

"This chap's one of the oldest hands in the place," Hinds said, turning to Sir John. "He's been here practically ever since there's been a Cane Vale. What's his name again, Vaughan?"

"Ferguson, sir," Erskine Vaughan said.

"Yes, so it is. I can never remember it," he said, and then along with Erskine Vaughan quickly fell in behind Sir John who, with an irritable flick of his swagger stick, had turned from the rigid Ferguson and started across the platform toward the steps. Saul had, by then, slipped away and gone to stand outside.

The inspection tour over, Sir John paused briefly before stepping into his car which the chauffeur had driven over from the weighing office, and casting a final look around, he said, directing his remarks for some reason to Saul, who was standing, shaken and white-faced, apart near the door—and his tone, his stiff smile were almost friendly. "It's always a bit of a shock, don't you know, to realize that the thing that sweetens your tea comes from all this muck." His stick took in the dust and dirt in the yard, the disorderly mountain of canes in the storage hive, the neglected run-down factory and its outbuildings, the ancient windmill. Then removing his helmet and stooping low as if he were a much taller man, he entered the car and was borne away.

Saul watched the Rolls depart as noiselessly as it had come, and then he followed it, leaving behind him a relieved but still apprehensive Erskine Vaughan. A profound exhaustion slowed his steps as he made his way out of the yard and along the road past the waiting lorries. The noon sun seemed to be pressing his head down into his shoulders. As he passed, the young men seated aloft the trucks started to call to him, perhaps to ask what had transpired inside the factory, but at sight of his face and his blind enraged eyes, they checked themselves.

On his way back to Spiretown he searched the fields for Stinger, although he knew he wouldn't find him. Stinger and his crew were working some miles beyond Westminster, in an area between Pyre Hill and the high ridge at Cleaver's, and they would not return until almost evening. Reaching the village he stopped in at Delbert's, but Delbert, whose leg was out of the cast, had gone to town for supplies. Only his woman was there, waiting on a customer in the grocery half of the shop, and Collins, the dour butcher, drinking alone in the bar and honing the knife he used for the pigsticking on Sunday mornings. Collins invited him to a game of dominoes, but he declined, had a silent rum with him and left.

And then instead of heading toward the guesthouse as he intended, he turned in the opposite direction and, only half-aware of where he was going or whom it was he sought, set off for the steep rise that led to Westminster's summit.

He was overtaken on his way up the hill by a girl of perhaps twelve carrying a neatly stacked pyramid of mangoes on a tray on her head. She hoped to sell them, she told him, at Canterbury on the other side of Westminster. Something in her manner, in her plodding purposeful step, in the small face buried beneath the large tray reminded him of Leesy Walkes. She seemed as old. "This blasted old hill," she said, and sold him a dozen mangoes.

They parted company at the almshouse, Saul turning in and the child continuing on. Passing Seifert at the gate, his blank eyes trained on the sun, he gave him one of the fruit. And then across the bare sunswept yard where a few of the inmates—the old and indigent and mildly insane—could be seen milling about, he saw Merle, whom he had been seeking without wanting to admit it to himself. She was seated on a bench beneath the large silk-cotton tree which offered the only shade to be found in the yard, and grouped around her on the ground were the dozen or so children of the almshouse, the orphaned and abandoned. From her gestures and their laughter it was clear she was telling them a story, one of the things she did as part of the rather loosely defined job which Lyle had secured for her.

She looked up, saw him approaching with the mangoes cradled precariously in his arms, saw his clouded face, his dejected walk, and her eyes narrowed, reading him with a look.

"I come bearing small gifts," he said, hesitating just outside the circle of children at her feet.

She said nothing, but in the same way that she would, when stopping for him in the car on the road and seeing he was tired, simply lean over and without a word open the door, inviting him in, she moved over now on the bench, making room for him. Greeting the children, he sat down; and, again without speaking, she took the mangoes and placed them between them on the bench.

She then resumed her story, and beside her, already feeling somewhat soothed, Saul listened absently, his gaze on the rapt upturned faces of the children. She was recounting another episode in the life of Spider, the wily hero of the Anancy tales told throughout the islands, who, though small and weak, always managed to outwit the larger and stronger creatures in his world, including man, by his wit and cunning. In the fretwork of sunlight and shade under the tree the children's eyes as they listened were enormous, huge wells, reservoirs they seemed to him, which were storing everything she was saying against some future use.

The story done, she distributed the fruit, and the children, tearing at the tough-skinned mangoes with their teeth, the juice spurting saffron bright down their dark chins, drifted away. When the last of them was gone she turned to him. The face which bore witness to her life in its gentle ruin was patterned over with the shadow of the leaves. The saints on her earrings had begun a slight formal dance with the movement of her head, but grew quiet again as she waited.

"The great man was down today," he said.

"I know. His car passed here not long ago on its way back to town. What happened that has you looking so?"

He quickly dropped his gaze. He could not bring himself to tell her about Ferguson. Nor would he ever, he suddenly realized, speak to anyone, including Harriet, about what had taken place on the platform. That failure of nerve which had rendered Ferguson mute, dumb, would remain between Ferguson and himself, unspoken of even between them.

"Nothing really," he said. "He just took a quick look around and went on back to his villa at the Crown Beach Colony. It was me. I just found him and his little visit particularly depressing, mainly because it brought home so clearly what you were saying to Lyle the last time he was down and you two quarreled: how really intact the old order is beneath the shiny new surface he and his friends in town love to point to. Because here was Sir John playing to the hilt the eighteenth-century absentee landlord come out to the colonies to look over his holdings."

"Yes," she said wearily, "the old gentleman's still with us. And in Bournehills you can see him just as he was. Tell me, did he have on his usual getup?"

"You mean the white-hunter outfit? Yep. Complete with swagger stick. You should have seen him waving the damn thing around, lord of all he surveyed. I think the outfit got me more than anything else. Maybe because in most of the places I've worked—in South and Central America—the Sir Johns—those from outside who've come in and taken over—were Americans in business suits or those they kept in power: the patrons with haciendas three and four times the size of Bourne Island or strong-arm generals in uniform. So, for me, Sir John in his safari suit took a little adjusting to. But dress aside, they're the same, all of them. Out to own and control the world, and determined to hold on no matter what means they have to employ. And they behave the same, the arrogant bastards, toward the people they feel they own. Yes," he said, his voice dropping, "perhaps worst of all is the effect their mere presence has on people."

"I know," she said. "I know. I guess poor old Calamity was in a state."

But Saul, his eyes veiled, wasn't thinking of Erskine Vaughan, but of Ferguson, seeing him as he stood struggling to speak but no sound coming. Suddenly his face hardened and his voice, though controlled, rang with fury. "They have to be gotten rid of, the bastards. Thrown out! And in one clean sweep. That's the only way. There's no gradual or polite way for it to be done as Lyle and his friends in town would like to think. I was never more convinced of that than today. Oh, hell, not that I haven't known it all along," he cried, turning part of the anger he felt on himself. "But then, when you think of it, I'm another Lyle, a casualty of the radicalism of my youth, you might say. Another one of those who gave up for one reason or another. But I know what needs to be done."

"Well, then, tell me something," Merle said. "How much good do you think these so-called development schemes and the like, such as the one you have in mind for Bournehills, really do while things remain as they are?"

He looked silently at her for almost a full minute. "You've wanted to ask me that for a long time, haven't you?" he said.

She nodded, causing the design of sunlight and shadow to move up and down her face. "That's right. It didn't just occur to me."

"You really don't approve of my being here, do you?"

"Not you specifically," she said. "It's that I don't approve deep down of any white man, even a decent sort like yourself, coming here from some big muck-a-muck country like America with all sorts of plans for us, even if they are meant to help. I guess you could call it the natural resentment of the have-nots. I'm sure you must have come across it before. But that's neither here nor there. Answer the question."

And he did, after remaining sunk in thought for a time. "Yes," he said, "I think projects such as the ones I've done in various places over the years do some good. They help to a degree. I wouldn't be here, Merle, if I didn't believe that"—his eyes, pale, strained, faintly red, held to her face. "But I know what you're asking. It's a question I've often asked myself. Whether what I do: setting up a market cooperative here, a clinic or field canteen there, a leadership-training program somewhere else, all of them fairly small-scale local efforts at improving life in one place can possibly count for much in the face of what really needs doing, the all-out change you and I know is necessary. Whether anything I do matters so long as Sir John and all he stands for are still firmly entrenched. Yes, I've often asked myself that.

"I've even wondered at times," he said, his face reflecting doubts and questions that had obviously been with him for years, "whether my kind of work might not in a way be indirectly serving their ends, since all these projects, no matter how ambitious, are committed to changing things gradually and within the old framework. Perhaps whether I realize it or not I'm really helping to keep the lid on things for Sir John and his kind, and therefore am as much a part of the system as they are. I never told you, did I, how Hinds treated me the first time I went to see him?"

"No."

"Well, he made it quite clear that no matter what I said about wanting to help out in Bournehills and liking the people and the place, he still considered me on his side, part of the establishment."

"He saw a white face, heard you were an American and couldn't understand how it could be otherwise," she said.

"Yes, that was it." He sighed and leaned forward, his elbows on his knees and his large hands trailing down. "You know," he said, speaking very slowly, his head bent, "although I've always enjoyed my work and honestly feel that what I do is of some value, I've also always felt that I should be involved in a more direct way in helping to bring about the real change. And I've had my chances . . ." He hesitated; then, in a shamed sad voice: "A woman I loved long ago in Peru wanted me to stay and join the antigovernment movement which was only just getting started then. But I didn't. And for years I debated with myself whether I shouldn't return home and do what I could there, take a stand so to speak at the source of so much of the evil I saw in the countries in which I lived and worked. And who knows, maybe that's what I'll eventually end up doing. I've been thinking about it lately for some reason—about that and a lot of other things which also go back years . . . It's odd," he said, gazing out into the almshouse yard which was deserted now, the inmates having filed slowly in for the long afternoon nap, while they were sitting there, "but I somehow feel my whole life coming to a head since I've been here. . . ."

It was the first time he had spoken so openly about himself to her and as he turned, his body still bent forward on his knees, to look at her over his shoulder, embarrassment shaded his eyes. "I hope you don't mind my coming and unburdening myself like this. It's just that I got so angry watching that little runt parading around today like some four-star general I had to talk to someone. No," he said, sitting up abruptly to face her, "not just someone. You. I knew you'd understand how I felt."

Her eyes, a clear sunlit brown against the set darkness of her skin and the straightened blackness of her hair, were noncommittal. But she sighed, gave the familiar shrug. "This was your first encounter with the gentleman," she said, "but how do you think someone like myself feels who's seen him come and put on his little show every year now for the past eight years?"

"I know," he said. "I know how difficult it is for you living here."

"No, you don't," she said. "You don't have a clue." She spoke flatly, simply stating a fact there was no disputing.

"And I also know that you think it's impossible for someone like me,"—with a slight despairing wave of the hand he indicated his face, pale and near-colorless beneath the thin tan he had acquired over the months—"especially from where I come, to understand, but I do. I'm really not as hopeless as you believe."

She turned away, refusing for the moment to argue the point. In the fretted silence under the tree they could hear the idle officers over in the police substation next door slamming the dominoes down on the table in their endless game. Then, her profile to him, Merle said —and she spoke in the same flat, emotionless tone—"No, you have no idea what it's like living here, in a place where you sometimes feel everything came to a dead stop donkeys' years ago and won't ever move again, can't move for some reason; and where some little shriveled-up man in a safari suit still drops in once a year to remind you who's boss. You feel so helpless at times you want to scream like a mad woman or rush out and murder somebody. That's right"—she swung toward him and something in him instinctively recoiled from what he saw in her eyes—"just run out the house one day and throttle the first person you meet. It might even be a friend . . ." Her gaze drifted out to the empty yard, came to rest on the almshouse set like a great blinding-white, limestone crypt against the lowering peaks in the background. "I don't know why I came back to the damn depressing place!"

"Yes," he said, "I often wonder why you did?"

She appeared not to hear him. Her gaze remained on the building. "God knows I never intended to. I tried to plan things while I was in England so I'd never have to set foot on this island again. But then you know what happens to the best-laid plans, don't you?" She attempted her terse laugh, but couldn't manage it. "They sometimes blow right up in your face. Mine did.

"It's almost, you know, as if I was destined to come back here, so that no matter how hard I tried, there was no avoiding it. Maybe, as Delbert once said, there are some of us the old place just won't let go." Her voice in the stillness was low, wondering, awed by the mystery of it. Saul had never seen her so subdued. He sensed a door within her opening a crack, permitting him a glimpse in. He felt privileged.

"Oh, it wasn't so bad when I first got back," she said. "Everything was over for me in England, I had been very sick there, and needed a change. I even thought it might do me good, being back here. It would give me a chance, I told myself, to try and sort out my life and perhaps come to some understanding of myself. Because I don't understand me, you know," she said quietly. "I haven't a clue, for instance, why I lived as I did in England, all the damn foolish things I did there which caused me to lose the two most important people in my life."

She paused; he started to press her, but held back, fearful that if he did the door she had opened partway might close again. "I hoped I might have been able to sort it out once I was back—and not only everything that happened those years away, but when I was a child. I wanted to go all the way back and understand. And I've been trying, really trying, to do just that these past eight years. To come to some understanding! To have it make some sense!" She spoke with ntensity. Then, in a suddenly spent flat voice, "I needn't tell you I haven't made much progress."

She fell silent, and in the partly averted face, Saul could see how the lonely eight-year search for coherence and vision had exhausted her. But he saw other things as well: the blunt strength to the bones beneath the dark skin, the warmth her eyes gave off as if from some inextinguishable source of light within, the chin as smoothly rounded as a girl's.

"Does it ever make any sense?" he said, and he was speaking of his own life as well. "I suspect not. One thing, though, Merle, you've got to stop living like this, shut away from life. I know I have no right to be giving advice, but you've got to do something more with yourself than this"—he indicated the bare almshouse yard. "Not that it isn't a good thing, coming up here and reading to the kids, letting them know they haven't been completely deserted by the world, but it just isn't enough for someone like you. Nor is the guesthouse. You need something more, a real job that will make use of all you have to offer."

She was smiling as she turned to him, and he quickly lowered his gaze, unable to take that wide false smile which she had summoned both as a camouflage and a shield. "You mean you've been here all these months and haven't heard about me?" she said. "I can't hold a job. Hasn't anybody told you that yet? Not any halfway decent job. Everybody around here knows that. Take the last one I had teaching at the new high school in town. It didn't last any time. The headmaster didn't approve of my telling my classes about Cuffee Ned and the like. I thought that was all part of West Indian history, but he couldn't see it. Worse, he accused me of trying to incite the students. To what he never said. Well, we had words and he won, naturally. I was fired in double-quick time. The thing had me upset for weeks.

Maybe you heard about it. It happened just shortly before you people came."

"Yes," he said. "I've heard."

"I thought so. And that's how it's been all along, both here and in England. I couldn't hold on to the few jobs I had there either. In fact, I would say nothing I've tried my hand at has ever turned out well. I must not have lived right in my youth. Why, I couldn't even get through the course in history I went to study years ago. And I can't even run a simple guesthouse so that it halfway pays. Me!" She laughed, the sharp, empty hoot which never failed to jar him—"I'm about as much use as those old people you saw dragging around this yard awhile back. As half-alive as them. No, less so. At least they shuffle around trying to keep the circulation going, but I've stopped dead in my tracks. Paralyzed. People in Bournehills would say somebody's worked obeah on me and put me this way, what you'd call a spell. And they'd be right, because in a way"—her voice again took on the awed, almost frightened note—"I am like someone bewitched, turned foolish. It's like my very will's gone. And nothing short of a miracle will bring it back I know. Something has to happen—I don't know what, but something—and apart from me (because it's out of my hands I'm convinced) to bring me back to myself. Something that's been up has to come down," she cried fiercely to herself; there was a harshness in her narrowed eyes, "before I can get moving again!"

Her talk, her odd look made him uneasy, and he said, "Maybe it might be a good thing, Merle, for you to get away from Bourne Island as you've often said you'd like to do. Perhaps you'd find it easier to make a new start somewhere else . . ."

Her eyes cleared; she once again gave him the false, brilliant smile. "You're a hundred per cent right," she said. "Now where shall I go? You suggest a place."

"Well, there're no end of places," he said. "Perhaps another one of the islands or Europe or Africa . . . I understand from Allen"—and he spoke with great caution—"that your husband and little girl live in East Africa, and although I don't know what the situation is with your marriage, you might like to . . ."

But he got no further, for with a look that had to do with the sudden hardening of the sunlight her eyes contained she silenced him. He felt the door that had opened a fraction slam shut in his face.

"I'm sorry," he said. "I know you never talk about them, but I just thought . . ."

She rose abruptly, jolting the bench as she did. "Well, this has been a very pleasant little chat," she said, "but government isn't paying me to sit around all day running my mouth. Besides, I've work to do inside before I leave. It's not much of a job, as you say, but I can't afford to lose it. After all, there's no telling when you people will find a place of your own in the village and I'll be left with a houseful of empty rooms again."

He stood up. "Forgive me," he said. "The last thing I wanted to do was to make you sad."

But she was already moving toward the entrance to the almshouse and calling to him over her shoulder in a loud voice that seemed to be trying to drive back thoughts which, if allowed to form, might well destroy her. "Tell Carrington for me, will you, when you get back, to make a shepherd's pie for supper tonight out of the meat left over from yesterday," she cried in the overly loud voice. "I forgot to tell her this morning before I left."

CHAPTER 10

Dear Chessie,
You'll be interested to know that I've just agreed, not more than ten minutes ago, to march in costume in the Bournehills band at carnival some six weeks from now. Can you imagine? I, who disliked parades even as a child—the sound of those awful bass drums would go right through me. Once I remember I even refused to go to see the Mummers. I must be undergoing a sea change. But I couldn't very well say no. A delegation of women from the village came over this evening and literally begged me to "play carnival" as they say here. They've been after me for weeks. It seems it would be something of a feather in their cap to have "a white lady" like myself—even though I scarcely qualify these days I've gotten so sunburned—marching in their band. They've offered to furnish me with a costume and several of them, including the woman Gwen whom I've mentioned to you before, have promised to act a; my personal bodyguards during the march to make sure I come to no harm. It seems things sometimes get fairly wild. And so I agreed, although I must confess I'm already beginning to feel somewhat apprehensive about the whole idea. And Saul's not going to like it I know. I shall have to discuss it with him when he comes in later tonight.

I've grown genuinely fond of Gwen, by the way, and we've become quite friendly now that the business with the omelet's been forgotten. She's not only a very warm, outgoing person with a wonderful resili-

ency and humor, but she's also surprisingly bright, I've found, and capable. I don't know how she manages to have all those children, run a household and still put in a full day in the fields, but she does. It's unbelievable how hard the women here work. And she's about to have another child. In fact, she should have had it by now since she was noticeably pregnant when we arrived. I'm beginning to suspect it's not a baby at all but some sort of tumor and I've suggested she go see the doctor about it, but she won't hear of it. Perhaps the most remarkable quality about her is that although her life is almost completely taken up with her children, the house and her husband (they're not really married; very few people here are), she still manages to maintain a marvelous kind of independence. She has her work, which, in its way, is as important as her husband's, her little business dealings with the postmaster, even her own bit of land which she looks after herself on Sundays. You sense she's very much a person in her own right, her own woman, and she'd be able to manage no matter what. It's a quality I find myself almost envying.

Both she and her husband have been a great help to us since we've been here. For example, they've taken it upon themselves to help find us a house in the village, and only tonight Gwen told me they might have come up with one. It seems the old woman, a widow, who lives next to them is planning to move in with relatives in another district and Gwen feels she might be persuaded to rent us her house. It's a fairly large one by Bournehills standards and in relatively good condition and should do. So hopefully we'll be moving sometime after carnival if things work out.

Of course, it'll mean less privacy living right in the heart of the village, but then one of the things one has to accept about field work is that you're permitted almost no private life. Even the time I used to have to myself in the evenings when Saul's at the local pub is no longer. A number of the women have taken to dropping in then, bringing with them, of course, their sleepy children. I try not to mind because they're so happy, poor things, to have someplace where they can come and sit and chat. They have almost no social life. The men at least have the rumshop, but the women virtually nothing. The talk these nights has been about carnival, which is the big event of the year on the island. I don't know if I've mentioned it to you, but for some reason people in Bournehills insist on enacting the same masque or story every carnival, which is against the rules. But they say it's cheaper, because then they don't have to buy new costumes.

And so every year they act out the story of a slave revolt that took place in the district long ago, and which, I might add, everyone talks about as if it happened only yesterday. But then nothing is ever forgotten, it seems, in Bournehills. They're really very strange people. They even speak of the dead as if they are still somehow alive. When a woman leaves her children alone in the house, for instance, she will say—and really believe it—that the family dead will come and look after them for her until she returns. Personally, I don't consider it a very reliable baby-sitting arrangement. By the way, now that the women know I was married before, they've started taking me to task for not having children. They're full of advice as to how Saul and I should go about correcting the situation. Most of their suggestions are unmentionable, I'm afraid. They're very outspoken indeed about sexual matters.

I must confess that after awhile all the talk gets wearing, and I frequently end these highly vocal sessions with a headache and the feeling that I'm slowly drowning in people. But at least I do manage in the process to obtain any amount of information to pass on to Saul—things the women would never discuss with him because he's a man. He says I'm threatening to become a better field researcher than he is. I needn't tell you how hard I've had to work for that compliment.

One or two things have come up since I last wrote which might prove cause for concern, one of them personal, the other having to do with Bournehills. Just recently a top official of the company which literally owns the entire district came down to visit the one sugar mill here. It seems he comes every year to look things over. Saul found him thoroughly objectionable, and for some reason which he won't talk about was very upset by his visit. But then I suspect there's a lot of the old, instinctive 1930's Marxist antipathy toward all bosses still left in my husband. Anyway, two days after the man's visit word came from the Kingsley office in town that the mill will not be accepting any more peasant canes for grinding (these are the ones people in the district grow on their tiny plots) until the entire estate crop has been completed. No reason was given for the order, and no one has the faintest idea what it means, not even, apparently, the manager of the mill, a rather anxious man who is a distant cousin of our landlady. She, of course, being so highly emotional, became very upset at the news. (I never cease being amazed—and appalled I might add—at people like her who give in to their feelings so freely.) And Saul is terribly worried about it. And so in a way am I. It's odd how involved

I've become in the life of this place. Not only do I feel that we've been here much longer than we have, but also—and this is most mysterious—that Bournehills has some claim on me. Isn't that strange? It must have something to do with the fact that living here one begins to feel completely cut off from the rest of the world. That world hardly seems to exist. I sometimes find myself wondering if there is a city called Philadelphia for me to return to. I find it difficult at times to believe that it's actually there or that I will see it again.

The other thing that's happened has to do with Saul. He's working much too hard, Chessie, and badly needs a rest, and I've been trying, but without much success I'm afraid, to get him to take off some time. To make matters worse, he's suddenly started having doubts about the work. He feels he's failing to understand something important about Bournehills. Why he should feel this I don't know since he himself admits the research is going well. And other things as well seem to be weighing on his mind. I'm certain it's nothing more than that he's been driving himself too hard and is exhausted. I've never seen anyone, aside from Andrew (why do I always marry such work-driven men?), who gives himself over so completely to his work. With Saul the Bournehills project comes first and everything else, including his poor wife, has to take second best.

It's been wonderful, though, to see the change in him since we've been here. He's slowly finding himself again, as I knew he would once he got back to field work. I'm pleased, and yet I can't help feeling somewhat uneasy at times, a little frightened even, both for him and for myself. He's become almost too preoccupied with Bournehills and the project, and I find he no longer talks as openly to me about things concerning the work. Part of it is probably my fault, because in addition to the incident with the eggs I've committed one or two other breaches of the rules of good field work—small things to my mind and all in the way of trying to help, but Saul's come down very hard on me nonetheless. He takes everything here so seriously! I sometimes have to remind him, being very careful how I say it, that this place isn't home, after all, or these people, as likable as some of them are, the kind we would normally be associating with, and that once the project's over we'll be returning home to the life and people we know. I find myself regretting at times that we weren't able to persuade him to take the job with the program-planning section at the Center which he was first offered. I know he prefers working outside the country, but that might have been the better thing, because al-

though it would have called for some traveling it wouldn't be this extended stay and involvement in any one place.

But that aside, what's important now is that he get away, if only for a week or two. I know I'll never be able to persuade him to leave the island at this point, but Lyle Hutson, about whom I've written to you, has offered us the use of his beach house on the leeward coast and although I don't particularly like the man and would dislike accepting favors from him, we could go there. I shall have to keep after Saul about it.

As for the business matters you asked about in your last letter—whether to sell or transfer those securities and the details of Mother's tangled estate, I leave them all in your capable hands. I'm afraid I've inherited my father's dislike toward the end of his life for anything having to do with money. Also, I've been thinking of increasing Alberta's pension, and I'd like you to see to that for me. You can decide the amount. She's been in my thoughts a good deal lately, perhaps because the cook at the guesthouse, the one I told you hardly says a word, reminds me a little of her. I remember that awful time years ago when her favorite nephew in Virginia got into trouble with the whites in the town and was found beaten and drowned at the bottom of a pond. She went around for days with the tears standing in her eyes. I remember waiting for them to fall, hoping that they would—I was afraid they would blind her, but they never did. Not in front of us at any rate. It's odd I should think of that after all this time. But then I've caught myself here of late recalling any number of things from years ago. It's both puzzling and annoying because as you know I was never one to dwell on the past. I suspect it's this place. I don't know what there is about it, but it seems to have a way of driving you in on yourself and forcing you to remember things you hoped you had forgotten.

Finally, according to the calendar my eldest niece, Teddy's child, is having a birthday the tenth of this month. Please give her for me that lovely gold pin of Mother's that's among my things. She's old enough now for something like that and I'll never use it.

All such I leave to you.

How comforting to know you're there, dear Chessie.

Love,
Harriet

CHAPTER 11

An improvised ramp of old planks had been placed between the embankment of the road and Leesy's yard. Down in the yard itself, the lumps of heavy limestone that had been used to jack up the Opel had been removed and the car stood somewhat unsteadily on its own four wheels beneath the mango tree. The hood that had remained open for weeks on end was closed, the dust-covered windshield washed, and as Allen, his interviews done for the day, turned in at the yard, he found a smiling Vere standing waiting for him beside the car as if it were a lion he had just bagged.

He stopped short. "You don't mean to say you've actually fixed it!" he cried, and he couldn't help the note of shocked incredulity in his voice. Because although he had come almost every afternoon to the yard and, squatting beside Vere stretched out in the dust, had handed him his tools and pored with him over the dirt-streaked manual, he had not really believed the Opel could be made to run. He was no different from most of the people in the village in this, but where they had blamed the condition of the car, declaring it was beyond repair, Allen had doubted Vere's skill and ability in the face of so difficult a job; he had simply, without thinking about it, taken for granted it would be beyond him.

"I don't know if it is fixed," Vere said. "We're goin' take her out for a little run now and see."

"But do you really think it's gonna run?" he said.

"I said I don't know. But we're goin' try. Come, let's get her up on the road."

But Allen held back, standing strangely unwilling and reluctant at the foot of the ramp, the sheaf of long interview forms folded in a neat packet under his arm. His reluctance, he would have admitted, was due partly to his desire not to see Vere fail. And he was also embarrassed for him, because glancing around he noticed that a group of women on their way up from the standpipe at the bottom of the rise upon which Leesy's house stood had paused to watch. They were pretending indifference as they lingered across the road, the buckets of water planted firmly on their heads and their arms folded high on the cushions of their breasts. But under the heavy buckets their eyes were trained on the yard, on the car—and they were, those eyes, as disbelieving as Allen's. Farther up the road near Stinger's and Gwen's house a group of little boys who had been playing cricket with a broad-bladed palm leaf for a bat, a stone for a ball and three sticks for a wicket had also stopped to watch. And although he couldn't see her, Allen sensed Leesy looking on from within the shuttered house. The gray walls gave off her disapproval, and something else which he himself vaguely felt, an apprehension, an undefined dread.

"The darn thing might not even start," he said almost angrily as, relenting finally, he helped Vere ease the still maimed and battered-looking Opel up the planks.

"She'll start, you'll see," Vere said.

They maneuvered the car onto the road and got in. But Vere didn't try the motor immediately. Instead, for a time, he busied himself adjusting the rear- and side-view mirrors, trying out the pedals and gear shift, and carefully wiping the windshield which was partly shattered in the middle, all the while ignoring the silent onlookers outside and the tense, worried Allen beside him. Finally he slipped the key into the ignition slot and turned it. His foot came slowly down on the gas pedal, squeezing it gently. Next to him Allen felt the muscles in his own leg tighten along with Vere's as he sat waiting for the worst to happen: namely, the car to remain dead, the women across the road to suck their teeth in disdain and walk away, and the small boys up the road to hoot in derision.

There was a faint cough somewhere under the hood and then silence. Vere tried again, using the choke this time, and there was the same feeble response followed by the same final silence. Allen stole a sidelong glance at him only to find his lips shaping the smile that had been confident as far back as the day he had brought the Opel limping home.

"Give her a chance, man. We got to give her a chance to come to herself," Vere said.

With that he waited a long moment before gently pressing down again. This time the faint sputter he elicited deep in the ruptured bowels of the car did not die but tentatively held on, and then, to Allen's amazement, actually began to quicken somewhat as Vere continued feeding it the gas. The faint rumbling as the engine struggled to take hold gradually became stronger, more charged, finally causing the car to shudder convulsively into life around them, and culminating as they suddenly lurched forward in a loud backfire that sent Leesy's fowls sailing briefly aloft and the small boys up the road dancing into the air as if they'd been given a hotfoot. With a shout they came racing in a ragged troupe toward the Opel and followed it shouting and waving the palm-leaf bat as it, very shakily, like someone taking his first steps after a long debilitating illness, made its way down the dirt road past the awed, still disbelieving women, who quickly moved aside.

By the time they neared the bottom of the rise they had gathered enough momentum so that the little boys were left behind and the car was running almost smoothly except for an occasional catch in the motor. They swung onto the main road, and as they were met by that long, absolutely straight stretch of white marl that reached from Westminster at one end of the village to the sea at the other, the car momentarily faltered. And once more, taking his time, his expression and smile unchanged, Vere coaxed it to life again, and after some token resistance it again moved forward, even picking up a little speed at his bidding.

Allen hadn't once taken his gaze off Vere, although he appeared to have his eyes trained on the road directly ahead. And watching the way those hands, which looked as if they could easily snap the steering wheel in two, touched the various controls, the skill, authority, and patience with which he did everything, he suddenly knew the car would run. It might balk occasionally and lose power, the motor might threaten to cut off at times and bring them to a standstill, but it wouldn't break down altogether. It would run. He was as certain of this suddenly as Vere had been all along. Vere had succeeded where everyone, including himself, had been convinced he would fail. He had taken a chance, risked everything, and done it. Out of the corner of his eye Allen studied the dark profile outlined against the slow-moving frieze of bedraggled houses and shops lining the road, and seeing the pleased, proud, utterly self-confident expression on Vere's face, he was suddenly swept by a host of feelings that had begun their slow build-up the moment he had arrived in the yard and seen the Opel standing ready and waiting. And which he couldn't understand. Because in the midst of the admiration and relief he felt he was seized at the same time by an unreasonable envy, even a kind of anger that, for a split second, before he struck it from his mind, made him wonder whether some secret part of himself had really wanted Vere to succeed with the car.

"Well, it looks like you did it," he said. "This thing's actually running."

Vere laughed. "Of course she's running. I told you all we had to do was give her a chance."

They were headed toward the guesthouse to show Merle the car, and as they approached the culvert wall over the dry riverbed which traversed the village, the young idlers started up, open-mouthed, from their shady perch under the tamarind tree. For a moment they simply hung there watching the Opel struggling manfully toward them, then they were rushing, yelling, out into the road, trying to flag it down, their arms waving wildly. Swarming around it they pleaded for a ride: "Vere, give us a ride, yes. Le' we ride too, man."

"Some other time," he called from the window. "She's not able for you all today"—and with a little burst of speed that sent an ominous tremor over the chassis, he left them begging for a ride in the dust of the road behind.

Their arrival in the guesthouse yard brought Carrington and her two helpers peering out of the top open half of the kitchen door. At a signal from her one of the younger women disappeared, and minutes later, Merle came hurrying up the stone steps along the south side of the house. She paused at the top, looked first at the Opel (Vere had left the motor running for her benefit), then at the two of them standing beside it, and her arms opening dramatically she came over and embraced Vere.

"You did it," she said, her arms around him, her cheek against his. "You have fixed the unfixable."

"But you knew I could do it, Mis-Merle," he said.

"Oh, yes," she cried. "I knew. You and I knew." She turned to Allen. "Well, Allen, what do you think of your friend now?"

His hazel eyes shied away behind his glasses. He laughed—or tried to. "I still don't know how he did it," he said.

"My dear, there are things that are beyond us lesser mortals," she said. Then, clapping once loudly: "Come, this calls for a celebration. Carrington!" The large shadowy form in the doorway, defined only by the white cap and apron, stirred to attention but did not speak. "Bring a bottle of rum, please, to christen the car, and send the girls to call the others." Her voice dropped and she frowned slightly. "Saul should be here," she said with a touch of irritation.

Neither Saul nor Harriet was at the guesthouse. Harriet had finally persuaded him to take some time off and they had gone, three days ago, to stay at Lyle Hutson's beach house on the other side of the island. But this being the second Friday in the month, Lyle Hutson had come down (his quarrel with Merle had long been forgotten), and as he occasionally did he had brought along a small party of people. Dorothy Clough had as usual arrived earlier in the day with her three children.

The visitors came trooping out into the yard at Merle's summons, even the children, who had been called up from the beach, where they had been playing. Little clumps of wet sand still clung to their legs. When they were assembled and Merle, blithely leaping over the social barriers, toppling the hurdles in her wake, had introduced Vere around, she went over to the Opel, parked next to Lyle Hutson's great silver-toned Humber Super Snipe and her own shabby Bentley. Raising the bottle of rum Carrington had brought her she first ceremoniously sprinkled a few drops on the hood of the car and then on each of the fenders which, in spite of Vere's painstaking efforts over the weeks to hammer them smooth, were still badly dented. Then, being Merle, she gave a long speech. Going over to Vere, who had been made somewhat uncomfortable by the presence of Lyle and the others—the great people—she slipped her arm through his, and holding him to her side, began a lengthy toast in his honor that went back to the time when, in her words, "he had been nothing but a little boy running about the place in short pants." She described how when she had first acquired the Bentley he would spend hours peering under the hood, studying the motor; and he had been the only one, she declared, who had ever been able to keep it running well. "And without having a lesson in car repairing in his life, mind you," she cried. "But then, that's Vere"—the look she gave him was that of a mother whose son has done her proud. "He's always had a mechanical turn of mind. It's like he was born with an understanding of machines. He has a gift."

She turned it into a grand occasion with her oratory, and beside her Vere stood gazing gratefully down at her. He had come hoping she would put into words all that he was feeling but could never have expressed himself. She had known this—a look had flashed between them when she had mounted the steps and seen him next to the Opel, and she had not failed him. She ended her speech on a note of laughter by offering to swap cars with him. Vere laughed loudest of all.

Later, on the way back to the village, the Opel, exhausted from its first outing, was no longer running as strongly, and Vere said to Allen, who was accompanying him back, "Well, she did all right today, but she's going to need a lot more work if she's to make it to town and back for carnival. And I've got to paint her."

"What color are you thinking of?" Allen asked. His face still reflected in part the complex of feelings that had assailed him earlier. He sat slumped in his seat.

"Red," Vere said without hesitation. "She'll really look like new then, like a car just out the store or one I made myself. And I don't want just any old red. Oh, no." He shook his head strongly. "It's got to be fire red, so when people see me coming they'll know for certain it's me."

CHAPTER 12

Lyle Hutson's beach house on the mild Caribbean side of the island was at the lower end of the long Crown Beach Colony strip where the wealthier expatriates lived and the more exclusive hotels were located. Looking up from the house, past a low jutting line of rock which reached out into the sea to separate Lyle's section of the beach from the Colony's, you could see the gay-colored umbrellas and *cabañas* outside the hotels and here and there, in between the large shade trees which stood in a solid phalanx around them, the brilliant Mediterranean white-and-pink villas and restored eighteenth-century manor houses belonging to the wealthy. Their yachts lay at anchor in the offing.

Lyle's house, a roomy low-roofed bungalow painted white with wide screened windows to let in the light and air, was set within a grove of casuarina trees which came down almost to the water's edge. The tall conifer trees, reminiscent of northern pines, with long feathery limbs rising in tiers like the roof of some fabulous pagoda, met overhead to bar the sun's heat and glare, so that down in the clearing where the house stood it was cool, hushed, almost dim, and the air had taken on the grayish-green of the pine needles.

Saul and Harriet spent hours lying out under the high vault of trees, in the nave of silence which was the same muted green as the leaves and air. With their canvas chairs placed next to each other on the spongy carpet provided them by the fallen needles, they listened behind the words they occasionally exchanged and the books they read to the desultory ebb and flow of the wind through the trees, a special sound in the casuarina. It called to mind for Saul a group of black-veiled Italian matrons he had seen gossiping in hushed but impassioned tones outside a church in Florence on his pilgrimage through Europe after the war. For Harriet it was as if she was being allowed to relive the most memorable of her childhood summers at the house on Delaware Bay. The setting was almost the same. Above, a clear, washed sky and a sun that, unlike the Bournehills sun, was a benign and unobtrusive presence somewhere off behind the gently moving screen. The grove of casuarinas was the deep pine wood that had secured her summer world. And the mild soundless leeward sea which, unlike the one at Bournehills, had no old sorrows to lament, no ancient loss to grieve and gnash its teeth over, was like bay water.

They swam. Several times a day they would enter that mild, hospitable sea, treading lightly over their private strip of beach on the way in so as not to disturb the sand, which, when they came out in the mornings, looked as if it had been taken up the night before, cleaned and sifted, every impurity and footprint removed, and then replaced. The water was shallow for some distance out and the color of the verdigris green on old copper around where there were outcroppings of rock, or low-lying sandbars intervened. A broad, free-form reef that didn't quite clear the surface marked the beginning of the deep water and they would wade out to this, step aboard, cross its pitted floor and then where the rock gave way abruptly and the clear sea began, dive deep.

They swam as much underwater as they could, so that they might treat themselves to the incredible still-life at the bottom. There, down through the quiet sunlit drop, the sand was the same highly refined confectioner's white as on the beach, but warmer in tone and utterly untouched, with the specks of mica which gave it its warmth like gold that had filtered down from the sun long ago and settled. Here and there, where there was rock, could be seen vivid colonies of coral, and shells—the carapaces of a hundred small marine forms, all of them gathered and carefully arranged on the sea's floor as if by a craftsman skilled at such designs. And occasionally they came across schools of minnows, silverfish and jacks swimming in a kind of motionless progression far below or simply suspended like mobiles in the brightness. Secure in their world the fish didn't even move as the large wavery forms of Harriet and Saul passed overhead. Sometimes, surfacing for air, the two would exchange a silent look of wonder at what they were witnessing below, then curving their bodies, their arms out and heads bent sharply, press their way down again. Tired, finally, they would simply let the tide bear their lax bodies back to shore.

In the face of all this, Bournehills seemed remote, a place worlds away. In fact after being at the beach house a few days Harriet had difficulty thinking of Bournehills as a place which actually existed. The thought brought with it a strange relief, the sense of an unpleasant weight having been lifted. Or if it did exist, she told herself —speculating about it sometimes as they lay out under the trees or lazily backstroked to shore after a swim, it was like every other poor place she had heard of but never seen, in that it had no claim on her, could not affect her in any way. Nor could Bournehills, being suddenly nonexistent, affect their new-found sanctuary beside this kindly unassuming sea. Moreover, as the first days passed, it almost seemed possible to remain at the beach house forever, just the two of them alone together, living out their lives apart from Bournehills at one extreme and, at the other, the colony of extravagant hotels and pink-walled villas visible beyond the line of rock; safe from them both, accountable for neither, and as secure under their high dome of trees as the fish in their immutable underwater kingdom. She told herself she was being romantic, wishful, but such a life seemed possible.

She watched anxiously those first few days for the place to work its quiet magic on Saul. And she was rewarded in part, because although his eyes didn't quite clear—some part of him remaining preoccupied with the research and Bournehills, and he worried aloud at times about the Kingsley decision to hold off grinding the peasant canes—he did gradually enter into the mood of the place and begin to relax. Above all, that part of him which, to her dismay and even resentment, she had sensed moving away from her over the past weeks, being given over to Bournehills, had returned. His kiss was no longer as perfunctory as it had become and when they made love, with the sun, if it was during the day, staring in at the window like some round-eyed voyeur who had never witnessed such rites before, he would pause as he used to and with the back of his fingers trace the line of her throat down to her shoulder, her breast—and it was done with the old thoughtfulness. It was as though—if only for the time they were at the beach house—he had been given back to her.

"I'm really a very selfish woman, you know that," she suddenly said with a laugh.

They had just returned from the swim they took in the early evenings and were lounging in their wet bathing suits on the beach. Behind them the low-roofed bungalow looked whiter than it actually was against the deepening green of the casuarinas, and around them their private world stood poised at that moment of the day when the light, a flushed pink and gold emanating from the curved shell of the sky, appears powerful enough to hold off the night indefinitely. Merle had told them to watch for a green flash which was said to occur each evening on this side of the island at the point on the horizon where the sun sank into the sea. At the moment the last bit of its crown disappeared, a little stab of green light, lasting less than a fraction of a second, could be seen she said. Saul swore he had seen it two days ago; Harriet hadn't as yet, and they were watching for it again today.

"What made you come to that conclusion?" he said, and as he turned toward her, smiling absently, his eyes were less overcast than they had been in weeks. His hair shone russet in the light.

"Because I'd like to keep you just like this," she said. "All to myself. In thrall. That's selfish, isn't it? But I would. Right here in this . . ." She thought a moment, her head with the straight, almost severe hood of brownish hair lifted high; her gaze, narrowed against the sun, on the distant spot where the gleam of light was due to appear. She spread her hands, laughed. "This improbable paradise," she said.

"And I'd like to stay like this," he said. "Here, in your keep, on this most kind beach." Leaning over, bringing his head around, he lightly kissed the shallow well at the base of her throat where the flared bones of her shoulders almost met.

But his voice and touch held a sadness which she felt like the first chill of evening on her warm skin. "I know," she said, "it's impossible. There's the world to think about. But it's a lovely thought nonetheless. By the way," she said—and she could not have said why this should have occurred to her at the moment—"I don't think our landlady approved of us going away."

"Oh?" he said. "What did she say?"

"Nothing specific," Harriet said. "But I very definitely got the impression she didn't like the idea of us leaving, if only for a few days. She wanted to know what was wrong, and when I told her it was just that you needed a rest and we both needed some time away together, that it would be something of a second-year honeymoon, she said honeymoons nowadays took place before, not after the marriage, and besides we were too old. Can you imagine anyone saying something like that!" She laughed despite herself. "The woman's not to be taken seriously."

Beside her Saul was laughing with his head thrown back, the sound carrying across the quiet plain of water all the way out to the drained sliver of sun on the horizon. "God, if that doesn't sound like her! I can just see her saying it." His laugh died, but his abstracted gaze retained Merle's image. Her dark face with the split merciless smile might have been projected larger than life on the darkening sky. And the sight of her, the thought of her, both pleased and troubled him apparently, because at the same time he was smiling—a faint private smile which went unnoticed by Harriet—he was also frowning. He remained caught between the two emotions for a time, sitting there with his head back and face turned slightly aside. Finally, he swung back to Harriet, a sudden, almost angry movement as if wrenching himself free of that image, and in the last of the daylight (they had missed the green flash), his eyes were strained, bewildered and somehow fearful. He placed a hand on her knee in that way she understood. "Let's go in," he said.

Later, as they lay on the bed in the dusk-filled room, Harriet's body still holding the impression of his (he might have still been inside her), he said, his voice very quiet in the darkness, "I'm a lousy husband, Hatt."

"Oh, you are, you are!" she said, laughing, and stretched languorously, aware for the moment only of her own feelings. At certain times, like today, when she closed her eyes during their embrace she would feel her body expand to take in all of him—not only his physical self but his other attributes as well: his special strength, intelligence and purpose, the depth of feeling that was his. All these became hers during those moments and, as a result, she felt defined, given shape; she became then the image of him she held in her mind. At such times it was as if the goal that had eluded her a lifetime had finally been seized.

Grateful to him she turned and repeated with the laugh, "Oh, you are, darling. A perfectly lousy spouse," and leaning over kissed him. As she did her hair fell open around them in a soft screen, creating a world between their mouths not unlike the one beneath the casuarinas outside in that it, too, for the moment, seemed safe, inviolate.

Coming out for a swim the following morning early before Saul awakened, she was surprised to see a dark knot of figures some distance up the coast near the projecting line of rock that set them apart from the Crown Beach Colony. The trespassers were approaching their section of the beach, having ignored the private property sign close to the wall of rock, and as they advanced toward her she saw they were children. For a startled moment she almost thought they were "her children" meaning the small band of beachcombers with their basins of sand and broom sage, who awaited her every morning at their fixed station below the guesthouse. They comprised the same threadbare, close-knit group of six or more and were bearing down on her with the light skimming stride which gave the impression they were being propelled along by some power other than their own legs. As they drew nearer she made out the distended bellies and woefully thin arms and legs that in their thinness and blackness always made her think of stick figures. And finally, when they were almost upon her, their faces which, like the children in Bournehills, were old, unnervingly old and knowing, at the same time they were young and guileless. The same watchful eyes loomed up at her out of the clear settings of white.

She could not stem the sudden irritation that swept her at sight of them, and her hand involuntarily started up to wave them off. She wanted to call sharply to them that they were trespassing and point to the sign behind them. One harsh word from someone like herself would send them scurrying away, she knew, and the thing in her which resented their intrusion urged her to speak it. And then, in the next moment, appalled at herself, she was advancing to meet them with a smile.

They had been fishing off the reef. The boys in the group each carried a clear plastic bag containing perhaps a dozen or so of the small fish lying in slippery heaps at the bottom and a few sea eggs they had found clinging to the reef's encrusted wall. They intended selling the fish, they told her, and she bought the sea eggs from them, which Saul liked. Then, at the thought of them diving repeatedly into the chill morning sea with the water making their bodies appear to waver and dissolve as they plumbed deep, seeing their pathetically meager catch, she told them to wait and, going into the house made up a small package of food: five eggs out of the more than two dozen they had on hand, the end portion from their loaf of bread which she always discarded anyway, a few onions and potatoes, two tablespoons of butter. She even included some meat, a little less than a half-pound of ground beef: she and Saul would never use all of it.

Returning outside, she held out the bag of food as though it were alms or an offering or a small harmless bribe to keep them from coming back. Before handing it over she made them promise not to sell any of it, especially the eggs, but to eat everything themselves. They promised, all of them speaking at once. Only then did she give them the bag. They, for their part, took it as if it were only their due, and after thanking her turned in a body and left.

That night they were kept awake by a noisy beach party at the large villa just on the other side of the rocks where the coastline curved out slightly. The wind brought the metallic trilling of the steelbands in a steady current their way; and the laughter and talk reached them clearly across the lake stillness of the sea, becoming louder and more inescapable with each passing hour. They could make out whole sentences after a time. Moreover, the voices seemed to have the same coldly bright, hard-edged finish to them as the lights which they could see strung from the house down to the water. Harriet hadn't heard voices like them in months. Worse, as the wind rose during the night it brought them closer until she could have sworn as she drifted into a fitful sleep that the Crown Beach Colony set had, like the children that morning, invaded their quiet retreat and were holding the party on the beach right outside the bungalow.

She awoke toward dawn to find Saul already up and dressed. He had not slept at all from the way he looked.

"I think we had better be making tracks back to Bournehills," he said.

"Oh, no." (They had not set any time for their stay, but she had hoped they would at least spend two weeks. This was only the tenth day.)

"Yes," he said. "There's no point staying any longer because with carnival almost upon us our rich friends up the beach will probably be throwing a party every night, so we won't be getting much rest. Besides, Collins is slaughtering Leesy Walkes' pig this Sunday, the big one she's been saving for carnival, and I promised Delbert I'd be there. So we really will have to be getting back. And truthfully I've started missing the old place the last day or two."

She could tell from the way he said it that he was as good as back in Bournehills, and she made no further protest, knowing it was no use. Later that morning while they were packing, the fisher children returned. She had been foolish to think they would stay away once she had given them the food. But it didn't matter now, and going into the kitchen she gathered together what was left of their supplies and silently handed the bundle over to them.

CHAPTER 13

'Foreday morning. Merle's one old cock in the cassia tree hadn't even crowed yet and the late rising moon was still high, its light spread over a sea that was like hammered silver in the near darkness. The sun would not rise for at least another hour, but it had already put out a pale feeler of light low to the east, so that the entire coast, including the sandhills and Westminster's dark steepled spur and the guesthouse on its rocky ledge, including, too, the great boulders rearing up out of the surf and resembling ancient ruins in the uncertain light: Zimbabwe, Stonehenge, the huge heads on Easter Island, testimony of man's presence, monuments to his ingenuity and grace, witness of his inevitable passing—all this stood poised between the two, between the blanched fire of the moon and the first subtle suggestion of day. Full moon at dawn, Saul mused to himself, the day and night joined, at one with each other; and for a moment as he made his way over the stony path toward the village and the Sunday morning pigsticking he felt almost at one with himself, almost peaceful, part of the armistice of the morning, calm. And he had achieved a measure of calm during the ten days away. Perhaps whatever it was he was seeking to understand about Bournehills would come clear, he told himself, if he didn't force it, didn't press so hard.

By the time he reached Delbert's cluttered back yard where the pigsticking was held every Sunday at this hour, most of the men had already assembled. They were the regulars from the rumshop—

Stinger; the man Cox, whose new house Saul had helped build; Merle's relative from the road gang, Desmond Vaughan; his supervisor, Mr. Innis, standing a little apart as he always did in his shabby plus fours, and Collins, the butcher—naturally, this being his day—as well as the usual assortment of cane cutters, lorry drivers and workers from Cane Vale, all of them standing around in high rubber boots looking sleepy, cold and slightly hung over. Their voices as they talked and joked among themselves were hushed out of deference to the undeclared morning. Their eyes and teeth shone dull white in the dimness when they laughed.

Ferguson, as to be expected, was dominating the talk. He had been subdued for a time following the incident with Sir John (he and Saul had never spoken about it), but he had recovered and was once again his voluble, argumentative self. Delbert sat listening nearby, enthroned on an old crate that seemed about to collapse under his massive haunches. Beneath the gnawed Panama hat his small eyes had all but disappeared in his sleep-swollen face, but one sensed their alertness, their infinite tolerance. From time to time, he spat, the phlegm streaking bright through the dimness to rout the fowls in its path and the lean dogs that abounded in the yard.

Under Collins' direction the preparations for the slaughtering had gotten underway while it was still night. A fire of dried coconut shells blazed beneath a large iron kettle containing the water that would aid in dehairing the pig later. The fire, bright orange in the half-dark, didn't appear to give off either heat or light so that the character of the predawn morning remained unchanged. The concrete tub in which the dead pig would lie while the men cleaned and haired it stood ready. The crude scaffold upon which the carcass would hang had been raised like a cross with its poles kissing against the barely lit sky. And Collins, humorless and laconic as ever, had already mixed the anticoagulant of salt and water in the calabash that would receive the pig's blood. The knife that would take its life lay honed and sheathed at his waist.

The pig itself, Leesy's great white sow which she had kept penned up in the yard between the donkey and Vere's car, waiting until carnival to sell it, stood tied by a short rope to the leg of the table upon which it would meet its death. It was an enormous animal. In its younger days it had been known throughout Spiretown as a thief and aggressor because of the habit it had of breaking out of its pen and invading other persons' yards, where it would not only set itself up as the supreme authority over the pigs and chickens present, but would appropriate whatever it found there that was edible, battening on it until its stomach sagged. But it was old now, its flesh mostly fat, and its hide the color of the mud it had wallowed in a lifetime. Beneath its gut the mass of bruised pink teats trailed the ground. Above its long snout its eyes were the glass button ones of a Teddy bear.

Tied to the table, one hoof tangled in the rope, it was rooting suspiciously at the unfamiliar ground. Each time one of the men walked past, it would start blindly toward him, emitting a high thin squeal, pleading with him to take it back to its pen in Leesy's yard. And the men, understanding its terror, sympathizing with it, treated it kindly. "Don't follow me, gal," one of them said almost sadly as the pig stumbled after him with the urgent cry. "I can't save you. Your time's up, that's all."

"You know some of them can tell when you're planning to kill them and will run off and hide in the canes and you won't be able to find them for days sometime," Stinger was saying to Saul. They were sitting, the two of them, on the limestone step that led to the back of the shop where Delbert had his living quarters. Stinger, his billhook beside him, his cap pulled low over his grave, quiet face, was gazing thoughtfully across at the sow. "Yes," he said, "they have a way of knowing. They might only be pigs but they got plenty understanding."

"Well, this one understands, all right," Delbert said from his crate. "Because ever since Collins brought her and put her in this yard yesterday she's been performing. She kept me up the night crying and carrying on."

"But, Delly, the poor thing was just saying her last prayers, that's all," Ferguson said, coming over. His thick glasses were filled with the contained orange glare of the fire. "She was just calling on the Lord in her final hour. 'Eli, Eli, lama sabachthani?" he suddenly cried, raising a blasphemous hand, all of him straining to touch the high-riding moon. "That is to say, 'My God, my God, why hast thou forsaken me?' Matthew twenty-seven, verse forty-six. She was just crying out to her maker for mercy. Jesus Christ, man, you're not to begrudge her that. After all, she's got some human feelings."

"All I know this one's not going to die easy," Delbert said.

The water in the pot had started to boil, the steam flaring off its turbulent surface like shreds of morning mist in the coolness, and at a signal from Collins several of the younger men approached the pig. And where it had strained after them before, eager to follow them, it shied from them now. It tried first to bolt and then, yanked rudely back by the rope around its neck, began backing away, its hooves furrowing the soft ground and its loose belly swinging violently as it sought to escape them under the table. But the men seized it easily enough, and after a brief struggle pierced by its terrified screams, flung it not ungently on its back onto the table with its head bent over the edge to expose the throat.

It took six of them to hold it, four for the legs and one at each shoulder, and as it fought them, its mud-caked hooves furiously treading the air, they told it affectionately to behave. Someone tied the snout with the same rope that had served as a tether, and that throttled cry was somehow louder, more piercing, more eloquent of the sow's panic than the high-pitched squeal before. The pig's body appeared to swell with the sound as it thrashed and bucked and writhed in the men's tight hold, threatening to crash in the table.

"Man, look, she's dancing," Ferguson cried, moving his long fluid body in imitation. "She's doing the Harlem jive. Delbert, see if you can get that jukebox inside to work so the old girl can have some music to dance to."

A leg escaped a man's grasp and Ferguson shouted, "Hold the pig, man. Hold her like you held that married woman I saw you with last night."

Amid the laughter Collins quietly stepped up to the table. He had been standing on the sidelines with Mr. Innis, directing operations from there. But he came over now, and glancing down at the sow's heaving belly with the worn teats spread over it like so much exposed viscera, then at its stricken eyes, he said quietly, but not without a touch of impatience, "All right now, stop your foolishness and know you got to die."

And surprisingly enough, the pig obeyed. The wild thrashing and bucking ceased. The clawing hooves halted mid-air. The stifled scream of protest and terror died, cut off somewhere deep in the constricted bowels and the sow lay as if suddenly resigned to its fate on the table, inert and winded. The men holding it could have removed their hands and it would not have stirred.

Collins then withdrew the knife—his German knife he called it for some unknown reason—a long single-edged instrument which he lovingly honed in between his games of dominoes during the week. He never did the actual killing himself but each Sunday would select a different one of the men assembled for the job, wordlessly handing him the knife as a sign that he had been chosen. His eyes passed slowly over their faces now, then paused; he motioned the man over and silently gave him the knife.

This Sunday it was a cane cutter whom everyone called Ten-ton because as a younger man he was known to cut ten tons of cane by himself in a single day—and he still did occasionally although he was past his prime. Like Stinger, he was headman of his own small work crew, but whereas Stinger was short and slight, the strength in his abbreviated arms and legs going unnoticed, Ten-ton was strongly built and the power that sent the canes toppling and had earned him his name could be readily seen in his large, muscular frame. He had been to Florida on the farm labor scheme as a young man Vere's age and whenever he spoke to Saul he affected a slurred Southern speech to show that he had learned, as he put it, "the Yankee lingo." He was a great favorite with the men but Saul didn't particularly like him.

He stood over the pig now, taking the measure of its bared throat with his eyes, then with the knife. Around him the laughter and casual talk had ceased and Collins had once again taken up his position outside the crowd of men at the table. The pig lay supine and still, reconciled apparently to its death. The silence in the yard was broken only by its gentle wheeze, the scratching of Delbert's thin-necked fowl at the bare earth and an occasional report from the encapsulated fire.

Ten-ton made a long gash across the throat. It was not a clean stroke. Rather, he sawed away for an unconscionably long time at the tough skin with its stiff bristles, then down through the fat which appeared endless. Finally a bit of pink flesh could be seen, and a pencil-thin line of blood quickly formed along the length of the incision. At that the pig suddenly heaved up powerfully, taking the men holding it up with it, and the shrill trapped scream tore into the silence again.

Unperturbed, Ten-ton then turned the knife in toward the heart, probing for it within the casing of fat while the sow struggled with the strength of someone drowning, its body raised up off the table with the men, perspiring and cursing, grimly fighting to hold it down. And once more he took his time. His gaze abstracted, his face without expression, he slowly sought the place.

"Watch you don't touch the shoulder," Collins called from behind. "Hit the heart."

"Hit it, man!" Ferguson cried, his face reflecting the animal's pain. "Hit it, damn yuh, and see she's suffering."

He touched it finally, they could tell from the trace of a smile that flitted across his lips. Then, raising up on his toes to bring the full weight of his body to bear, he drove the knife home. And as quickly pulled it out. Stunned by the swiftness of the blow, not realizing yet what had happened, the sow remained poised for a puzzled moment above the table top, still straining away from its captors; then, with the sodden thud of one of the huge crocus bags of grain inside the shop being flung onto the table, it fell down.

It lay quiet for a long moment, already dead it appeared. But soon the first slow paroxysm began, a massive shudder that was pain, yes, but also, oddly enough, what almost seemed a kind of relief. It was as though now that the final blow had been struck and the agony would soon be over the pig did not mind dying. It looked almost content, lying there. Perhaps in spite of all the wild heaving and thrashing, the shrill protests, death might have been what it had desired all along. It sighed, the sound thick and bubbly with the blood rushing up into its throat, and this, too, held a note of contentment and relief.

"She's giving up her life now," Delbert said, and the men at the table stepped back. One or two of them even glanced up as though they could see that life passing dim and indistinct through the air over their heads. The others watched the huge belly with its mass of dugs cave slowly in and then the head fall limp.

"She's gone, yes," Stinger said, and with a nod Collins left where he was standing and re-entering the circle at the table held the calabash containing the salted water to the open wound and the blood poured thick as paint into it.

This done, the men tenderly carried the sow over to the tub into which the boiling water had been poured. As they passed Saul, still seated beside Stinger on the steps, he noted that the animal's eyes appeared to have lost their flat, glass button cast. They looked somehow animated, expressive, alive. And in their suddenly live depths was reflected the change that had taken place in the sky. Glancing up he saw that the night was over and the day declared. The moon was still high but it was wafer thin now, a substanceless eucharistic host, and its pallid light had been absorbed and supplanted by that of the sun which had risen unseen behind the sandhills.

Bathed in the sunlight, dead at the moment the new day was being born, the sow lay on its side in the tub. The scalding hot water had softened the bristles so that the dehairing could begin. And oddly, as the men began pulling off the stiff cutting hairs and the skin emerged, a dead white like the underbelly of certain fishes, their manner toward the animal underwent a startling change. They were suddenly brusque, impersonal, cold, even cruel. Crowded around the raised trough of a tub, the splashing water and their boots churning the ground to mud underfoot, they began tearing off the hair in great savage fistfuls and scraping it off with the backs of their flashing knives, all the while methodically pummeling the sow's inert carcass.

They cursed it for being so unwieldly in voices that were charged with an almost abstract fury. And when they had exhausted it as a source of their rage they cursed the heat from the scalding water flying up in their faces and burning their hands; then the mangy dogs foraging amid their legs. They even fell to quarreling among themselves, but these were brief, minor, clashes which in no way affected their essential unity, as they all, including even those like Delbert, Stinger, and Mr. Innis, who had remained apart during the killing, pressed in around the tub for a chance at the pig.

Pushing his way into their violent center Collins chopped off the animal's tail and threw it in the fire. By the time it had cooked the dehairing was done, the cleaned carcass hung on its scaffold against the sky for Collins to gut, and the jovial mood of the men had been restored. Delbert's ruddy-faced woman from up Canterbury then brought out a bottle of rum and a glass, and as the men stood about in the mud slough discussing the pig's death and speculating on the amount of meat it would give, they passed around the bottle, along with the roasted tail from which everyone took a token bite. The remainder was tossed to the dogs, who snatched it from the air before it neared the ground.

Saul almost gagged on his share of the pork, which was charred and covered with ashes outside but raw inside, around the notched bone at the center. He had to swallow hard to keep it down. What would the old gentleman with the stained beard have said could he see him eating half-cooked pig, he wondered, and smiled despite his nausea. He probably would have drawn the worn tallith over his head and wept—fine, dim, old men's tears, as gentle as a spring rain—at the fall of yet another son of Israel even as he rained down execrations on his head from the upstairs window. He drank, tossing the harsh white rum, which made the rounds repeatedly, over his tongue with the same deft turn of the wrist and lift of the head as the others. And his own tears welled as the liquor burned in his stomach with what seemed to him a greater intensity than the orange fire in the middle of the yard which was slowly going out.

The sun had made its appearance by now above the steeply pitched roofs of the houses out near the sandhills, and as the bells of the Anglican church over on the road leading to Cane Vale announced the six o'clock service, the yard began to fill with women coming to purchase the weekly ration of meat. At their arrival the men retreated into the shop, leaving them to Collins who was hacking away inexpertly at the sow's dismembered carcass, using as a chopping block the same table upon which it had died. Thrusting the cracked bowls they had brought with them to carry home the meat under his nose, the women shouted their orders into his impassive face: "Pound of pork, please, Everett Collins." "Colly, sweetheart, darling, love, pass me piece from the ham part, I beg you." "Look here, man, despatch me, yes, and know I don't have the whole day to stand here . . ." They complained bitterly at the amount of fat on the pig: "Oh, crime, where in hell is the lean? This thing's nothing but fat clear through." And knowing it was Leesy's animal they reviled her: "But Leesy Walkes ought to be jailed for trying to pass off that old thieving sow she's had for years as something fit to eat, and at carnival, too, when people are looking to taste little pork." "She's a tricky, deceitful old bitch . . ."

Their clamorous voices trailed Saul up the main road as he made his way, somewhat unsteadily because of the rum, back toward the guesthouse. He had left alone, taking with him five pounds of the pork in a brown paper bag which Collins was sending for Merle. He could have stayed on, and then, as he usually did on these Sunday mornings, walked back with Stinger or one of the other men. But assailed this morning by a strange set of feelings brought on by the pigsticking, he wanted to be alone.

In the beginning of his stay he had sometimes found the Sunday ritual with its blood, flies, smells and ravenous dogs, its stifled animal screams and contending male voices too much to take and would leave as quickly as possible. But he had gotten over that initial squeamishness, and his feelings this morning were far more complex. For some reason he had been unduly affected by the death of this particular animal, perhaps because its eyes had taken on what appeared to be a kind of intelligence at the end, making him wonder for a fleeting moment whether something human wasn't being offered up on the battered table. And he had been deeply puzzled by the change that had come over the men during the dehairing. The sudden harshness with which they had set upon the pig, the coldly methodical, ruthless way they had laid bare its hide, revealed an aspect of them which he had never seen acted out so graphically before. It suggested forces at their depth which he had not suspected were there. It augured some greater violence, and he wondered what carnival, beginning tomorrow, would bring. Above all, standing off by himself, watching them moil round the tub, deserted by Stinger even at the end, he had been reminded, more acutely than at any other time, of his status among them. He was and would continue to be a stranger in their midst, the outsider, someone from Away. As he had always been, wherever he had worked. He had long ago accepted this as inevitable, yet for a moment walking along the road in the mild early-morning sunlight, he was shaken by a sense of his profound displacement. And he felt strangely thwarted as well. For it suddenly struck him that the search which had sent him wandering half his life up and down the hemisphere would not end in the hoped for discovery, and he would be forced to return for good, as unfulfilled as when he had set out, to the place where he had always felt most alien; which never failed to rouse in him when he thought about it the image of being in a house where the shades had already been drawn, the wreath and crape already hung at the door, and the next of kin were simply waiting for the final word to be brought down from the sickroom upstairs.

And yet, to contradict these impressions, he was at the same time strangely elated. He remembered the light reflected in the sow's dead gaze and how, when he looked up, he had seen it was morning. And in the midst of all the things that had disturbed him about the pig-sticking, there had been beneath the violence of the act an affirmation of something age-old, a sense of renewal, which had left him exhilarated, in a high mood. Part of it was due to his being more than a little drunk, he knew. But drunk in a wonderfully light, airy way. The rum had not only, it seemed, neutralized the queasy bit of pork he had eaten, but had burned away, like a powerful acid, all that was impure in him, leaving him empty but clean inside. He thought of himself as one of the bowls the women had shoved in Collins' face. He was as cracked and chipped, as flawed, but scoured clean, a vessel into which new wine could be poured. This image of himself suddenly dispelled all the other troubling thoughts, and feeling absurdly gay he could have broken out in a dance there on the dusty shoulder of the road, a slightly tipsy hora perhaps, such as he had seen at weddings as a boy. Raising his hand in the Bournehills salute he waved across to a group of children passing by on the other side of the road. They were on their way to Sunday school dressed in their "good clothes"; the little girls in puffy, marquisette dresses whose bright colors shone truer because of their blackness, the boys' legs Vaselined till they gleamed like burnished wood. They returned him a solemn "Morning, Dr. Saul," smiled behind their small hands at his exuberance and unsteady gait, and kept on.

He was approaching the sharp turnoff at the end of the main road which led out to the guesthouse when Merle on her way from six o'clock communion drew up alongside. He had not heard the car behind him for he had been thinking of the children: of how as they came toward him down the road they had appeared to be walking out of the sun directly behind them as if out of the mouth of a giant cornucopia. As he turned, his mind still filled with their small faces, and saw Merle in the fussy hat she wore to church, which didn't become her, it seemed to him that her dark face, thrust at him from the open window, mirrored not only the faces of the children but those of the men and women back in Delbert's yard as well. She appeared to contain them all. So that for a moment, perhaps because he was drunker than he realized, he didn't see her simply as Merle, a difficult, troubled woman whom life had done badly by and who, as a consequence, had hidden herself away, but some larger figure in whose person was summed up both Bournehills and its people. For the moment she was more than she appeared. And it suddenly occurred to him that perhaps he would have to come to know and understand her, really know her, before he could ever hope to know and understand Bournehills; that she was, in the old Biblical sense, the way.

" 'Woe unto them that rise up early in the morning to follow strong drink,' " she called from the window, her chiding smile taking in his slightly wavering stance and bloodshot eyes.

He laughed, and going over, bent down to the window beside her, his folded arms on the ledge, his face close to hers. "You sound like Ferguson," he said, "except he would have known the chapter and verse. How are you? Did you pray for me this morning?"

"Heathen," she said. "If I thought for a moment prayer did any good I'd have prayed for myself."

"Then why are you so faithful?" he cried, indicating the prayer book lying on top of her gloves and purse on the next seat.

"Because I like the way old Mr. Dodds plays the organ, that's why." Her tone was defiant. "And the way the sun when it rises lights up the rose window over the altar. It reminds me of Allen's eyes. Have you ever seen how lovely they are behind those glasses of his? And the smell of the incense. And the way the rector rushes through the service so you can't make out a word he's saying to save your soul. That's why. Does that answer you?"

He silently shook his head, saying no. His eyes on her face demanded that she give the real reason. She refused, turning irritably aside to escape his gaze. But after a time, reaching up to take off the unbecoming hat which she placed on top of the prayer book, she said, "I don't know why I go and sit up every Sunday in the damn drafty place. It doesn't help. Maybe, although I know better, I somehow believe that if I go there often enough and sit looking at that rose window and listening to the mumbo jumbo, a miracle will happen and I'll suddenly find I'm able to do the one thing I must do if I ever hope to get moving again."

"And what's that?"

She turned to face him fully. Her eyes, filled with their special light, were very still and clear. He had the impression he could see all the way into her.

"What you started to say that day up at the almshouse before I cut you off. Go see my child. Just forget about everything that happened and what an unfit mother I am and go see her."

She quickly held up a hand, forbidding him to question her further, pleading with him not to. "You know I won't talk about it, so don't ask," she said. The hand remained raised, holding him to silence; finally, she lowered it and, her mood changing, again looked him up and down with the playful, reproving smile. "Come on." She leaned over and opened the door on the other side. "You'd better ride the rest of the way because to tell the truth you don't look any too steady on your feet."

He looked down at himself, started to protest and then laughed. "You wouldn't be any too steady, either," he said, "if you had had six shots of rum on an empty stomach at five thirty in the morning."

"You're getting to be a rumhead just like those others down at the shop, I hope you know that," she said when he was seated next to her in the Bentley and they were underway.

"It's all part of the research, Ma'am," he said. "All done in the interest of science." He held up the paper bag of meat. It had begun to soak through. "I almost forgot. For you from Collins with his compliments. Five pounds of Mrs. Walkes' prize sow."

"You mean that old thing Leesy's had around since God said come let us make pigs. She ought to be ashamed of herself. How much of the five pounds is fat?"

"A good three and a half I'd say."

She laughed, a sudden warm burst totally unlike her usual sad scathing hoot. Bringing the car to a halt, she sat around in her seat and stared quietly at him for a long time. Outside, Westminster's great spur towered above them to the right; to the left lay the low dunes overrun with sea grape and sedge; beyond these the perennially grieving sea.

"You know something?" she said.

"What?"

"Sometimes you come close to being what we call in Bournehills real people. Yes," she said quickly as though afraid he would deny it. "You almost come like one of us at times. Maybe it's the techniques you have to learn in your business on how to get in with people. But I don't think so. Or perhaps it's because you're a Jew and that's given you a deeper understanding. After all, your people have caught hell far longer than mine. But I doubt it. Because I got to meet quite a few Jews in London: the East End was overrun with them in my time; people were saying they were taking over England"—he found himself laughing despite his sudden discomfort at that familiar old saw—"and although one or two of them became my very close friends, most of them were as bad as the English and had no use for black people. Some of them, in fact, behaved worse toward us than the English. You would have thought they would have been more sympathetic, having gone through so much themselves. But it seems suffering doesn't make people any better or wiser or more understanding. They used to say it did, that it was—how did they put it?—an ennobling experience. Ha! I haven't seen much evidence of that, my dear.

It's a sad thing to say—and let's hope those like myself do better when it's our turn up—but there you are.

"So, it's not that with you," she went on, the voice tumbling down its endless decline. "It's . . . how to say it . . ." She paused, and again inspected him: his eyes which gave evidence of the morning's dissipation, the high smooth forehead, the nose rising like a declaration of something or other out of the rueful face, and the uncertain expression there which said he didn't quite know how to take her comments on the Jews, whether to be annoyed, defensive or simply to accept the harsh truth of much of what she had said.

Then, suddenly she smiled—and in such a way none of it mattered.

"It's just you," she said, her voice intimate in the standing car. "It's what I saw in your face that very first night at Lyle's. I can read people's faces, you know. I would have made a good obeah woman. It's that, like me, you've been through a lot, and you're only now coming to yourself. And that you're trying, really trying, poor fellow, to do your best here in Bournehills."

He laughed at her "poor fellow" but he was deeply moved—and grateful—for he remembered the premonition of defeat and eventual exile home that had assailed him earlier on the road.

"Dear Merle," he said, and thinking of how her face before had somehow embodied for him the whole Bournehills, he reached across and touched the place on her ear where the continuous weight of her earring had pulled the lobe down slightly over the years. "I love you for that," he said.

She looked at him hard for a moment; then with a laugh, lightly struck away his hand. "Damn nonsense," she said.

BOOK III

CARNIVAL

CHAPTER 1

The year in Bournehills was divided in two. There was "in crop" as it was now and would be until as late perhaps as the end of June, with Stinger, Ten-ton and the other cutters slashing away at the canes on the high slopes, the piled lorries careering in a hail of chaff along the winding roads to Cane Vale, and the rollers there sending up the rending cry as the canes fell beneath their treads. During this period there were occasional dances on Saturday nights at the social center on the playing field, and money enough sometimes for a man to replace the worst of the rotted sidings on his house. Then there was "out of crop" from June to the end of the year, with the men idle, the silent factory giving the impression Kingsley and Sons had finally carried out their threat and closed it for good, and the shorn fields looking as brown and sere and permanently barren as the eroded lands visible everywhere on the hills.

But within these two major divisions there were holidays and the like which also marked the passage of the year in Bournehills and by which people dated events, saying, "Yes, it was just before Whitsun last year that I put new shingles on the roof," or, "It was Christmas month, wasn't it, when Delly got his leg broke?" The first holiday in the year was carnival which if Lent fell late, as it did this year, came at the height of the "in crop" season, then Easter, followed by Whitsuntide in May, when the young taxi drivers from town invaded Bournehills on Whitmonday to race their cars along the Spiretown main road. After this, during the "out of crop," came the August First Bank Holiday celebrating Emancipation, which Merle with her talent for overstating everything once described as "the day the brutes decided we weren't worth the thirty pounds sterling anymore and turned us loose to starve on our own." Then, toward the end of the year, in November, came All Souls, perhaps the most faithfully kept of the holidays in Bournehills. On All Souls' night the entire village —men, women and children, as well as people from the tiny settlements scattered beyond Westminster—would pilgrimage in long columns out to the cemetery adjoining the Anglican church. There, they would first clean the weed-choked graves of the family dead, then afterward ring them with lighted candles. Leesy would be much in evidence, tending to her numerous graves, and ever since she had returned from England Merle would go to stand alone at the place where her mother was buried. Her father's grave which was in the part of the cemetery reserved for the important families in the district went unattended, unadorned, except for a single candle placed at the head by Carrington.

Everyone usually stayed until dawn. Gathered around the graves, their faces sculpted into abstract masks by the candlelight, they sang to the dead, throwing their voices against the surrounding hills and the black tent of the sky. And those voices welling up strongly into the night transformed the bleak joyless Protestant hymns of mourning into songs of celebration and remembrance, joyous songs. They made them their own. They sang loudly, as though hoping to rouse the dead at their feet. And it always seemed they succeeded. Because toward dawn when the sky began to clear, the gray shreds of morning mist that could be seen rising from the graves could have well been the ghostly forms of the ancestral dead who, in answer to their summons, had emerged from their resting place to stand at their sides.

After All Souls came Christmas to close out the year.

But it was carnival now. Bacchanal. Big Fete. All work had ceased in the island for the two days—the Monday and Tuesday preceding Ash Wednesday—during which it was celebrated. Over at Cane Vale the rollers had ground to a stop and the estate lorries stood parked and empty in the dusty yard. The fields dotting the high slopes were deserted. Some miles north of Spiretown, at the soil reclamation site, the heavy earth-moving equipment used by Bryce-Parker and his crew—the tractors, bulldozers and power shovels with their mammoth jaws and huge caterpillar feet, stood temporarily abandoned amid the torn earth, looking like so many witless creatures, the dinosaurs of the age.

Back in Spiretown the giant float, built years ago, depicting Pyre Hill in flames, with a model of the planter's estate house at its summit, had been hauled over to the main road from where it stood all year, covered in tarpaulin, at a remote corner of the playing field. It was parked now, its cover off and freshly painted, outside Delbert's shop, ready for the long trip into New Bristol on Tuesday morning and the all-day parade of the carnival bands through the town's cramped streets.

By way of preparation also, people in the village had taken out and aired the costumes that had remained unchanged over the years. They were the same for everyone, a loose-fitting, wide-sleeved tunic of coarse blue-and-white striped Osnaburg cotton, which had been copied from the dress worn in Bournehills during the time of the revolt. The men wore the Osnaburg, as it was called, as a kind of overblouse; the women, in a longer version, as a dress tied loosely at the waist.

The day before Carnival Monday, the Sunday of the pigsticking, Stinger's Gwen and the other women who visited Harriet in the evenings presented her with the Osnaburg costume they had made for her. Later that night when she and Saul were alone she modeled it for him. To go with the costume, the women had loaned her a number of the heavy silver bracelets which were standard in Bournehills, and she had put these on to show him also.

His expression, as he sat watching her parade up and down in the shapeless roughspun Osnaburg with the bracelets like handcuffs on her wrists, was both amused and troubled.

"Frankly, I still don't like the idea of your being in the middle of this thing, Hatt. No one knows what might happen."

"I'm not sure I like the idea, either," she said, coming to a halt in front of him. "But I can't very well go back on my promise now."

"No, that'd never do," he said. "All you can do at this point, I guess, is to be as careful as possible. Stick close to Gwen and the other women. And I'll keep an eye on you even though I'll probably be all over the place. And, as I told you, if things start getting rough as I understand sometimes happens, and you don't see me, just head for the Cockerel Club off Queen Street as fast as you can and wait there for me. Have you got that straight?"

"How could I not help but have it straight!" She laughed. "That's all you've been saying for the past six weeks. Oh, Saul, nothing's going to happen. Or, if it should"—this to tease him—"maybe I'll be lucky like our friend Dorothy Clough and run into some brave handsome Watusi warrior with a long spear who'll snatch me out of the jaws of danger and we'll spend the rest of the day dancing arm in arm through the streets."

He laughed. "Just don't let me catch you, that's all."

That same day over in Spiretown proper Vere completed the finishing touches on the Opel. The two coats of red paint he had applied earlier in the week had dried, and the car, standing parked and ready on the sloping dirt road outside Leesy's house, looked as if it had been washed in the blood of the sow that had only recently shared the yard with it.

The following night, Carnival Monday, he drove it into town for the first time. Sitting stiffly at the wheel because of the foreshortened Malacca cane hooked onto his undershirt in back, he patiently coaxed the car over the hills to Cleaver's High Wall. When it balked on the steep upgrades he spoke softly to it, urging it up; and then as the road dropped downhill again and the Opel started to plunge recklessly down with it, he gently restrained it. But occasionally he gave it its head on the deep plunges down, so that the night wind and the smell of the land (a sharp redolence of cane and newly turned earth) came streaming in across his face through the open window.

Reaching New Bristol, he found the streets deserted, as he knew they would be by this hour. After spending the day since before dawn marching through the streets in the old clothes and costumes of previous carnivals (the custom on this first day of the holiday), the entire population of New Bristol had converged on the Sports Oval just outside town for the huge Carnival Monday night dance, a lesser version of which was being held in Bournehills at the social center in Spiretown. Tomorrow, Tuesday, people would don their new costumes and join the bands of their choice for the parade that would wind through the town till midnight.

As was his custom, Vere took his time, driving in a leisurely manner through the heart of the business district on Queen Street, then past the homes of the well-to-do in the large suburb adjoining the town. Tonight, whenever the dogs barked at him from behind the gates and the glass-topped walls he gunned the car's motor so it growled in answer. Describing the same circuitous route he took on foot, he then swung the Opel in a slow semicircle north, up to the vast swollen shantytown of Harlem Heights standing poised on its low ridge to come hurtling down on New Bristol below. He could scarcely squeeze the car through the Heights' rutted lanes, and he was stopped altogether at one point by a group of revelers on their way to the dance at the Sports Oval. At sight of the Opel looming fire-red before them in the darkness they broke out in wild shouts and surrounded it. "But, man, where you get this car, yes? You's a fireman or what?" they cried, their faces crowding the open windows. "Boy, you got yourself a real carnival car here, lemme tell you." "Ouch, this thing hot as max!" one of them shouted, snatching his hand from the fender. A heavy-set woman, her face gaudily painted in carnival colors and numerous strands of carnival beads roped round her neck, leaned in at the window beside Vere. "Sweetheart," she whispered close to his ear, "lemme tell you something. You could have any woman you see out here tonight with a car like this."

"I could have you?" he asked, returning her bold smile.

"How you mean!" Laughing, she chucked him under the chin and was gone with the others.

Finally reaching the ramshackle house where the girl lived, he parked the car some distance from it and walked the rest of the way—slowly, still taking his time, his back unnaturally straight. He had never for a moment doubted he would find her home. He knew her. She was as regular in her habits as he was. So that although this was Carnival Monday night and everyone had left long ago for the Sports Oval, she would not leave for the dance until her accustomed time. And she would go there by herself, for she was, he knew, without having to put it into words, as alone and lonely essentially as he himself, never mind the sailors and young officers from the tracking station she occasionally took home with her from Sugar's.

He saw the amber glow of her kerosene lamp behind the plastic curtains; and through the opening between the two halves he glimpsed her within the room. This time instead of waiting in the darkened lane across from the house for her to emerge, he climbed the square of pitted limestone that served as a stoop, rapped lightly once on the door and, without waiting for an answer, pushed it open and entered.

She was in the middle of trying on the costume she would wear in the parade of the bands tomorrow. It was an elaborate ball gown with silver dust sprinkled over the layers of pink tulle that made up the long skirt, and sequins glinting bright and iridescent on the sleeveless low-cut bodice. Paste jewels glittered at her throat, her ears, on her stringy arms and all through the towering blond wig she wore over her coarse, snuff-colored hair. And the strong red to her skin which Vere suddenly remembered, seeing her close-up, used to come surging dark and powerful to her face when they made love and she cried out and came beneath him, had been obliterated by a heavy stark-white pancake make-up that looked like grease paint.

She was busy applying the make-up to her neck and throat, having finished her face, when the door behind her opened, and as she saw Vere suddenly well up in the mirror to the makeshift vanity table at which she was sitting, her hand paused halfway to her raised chin. But she did not start. She made no outcry. Nothing crossed her eyes as they encountered his in the glass. Her chin remained at its high angle. It was almost as if she had been expecting him, as if at some point during the long weeks he had trailed her to Sugar's and back they had come to an unspoken agreement to meet this night. The hand poised, she quietly regarded his reflection over the toilet articles crowding the table, waiting, her eyes, her white mime's face, those of a sullen, intractable child.

Vere, oddly enough, was not looking at her but at the room, gazing curiously around him with slow-moving eyes. It was the room, more than her face which would, he seemed to feel, reveal her. There was not much to be seen there. Virtually every inch of space was taken up by her bed, the vanity table and chair and her clothes. Clothes hung everywhere, on the patchwork walls of scavenged wood and flattened five-gallon tin cans, at the head and foot of the old-fashioned iron bedstead, and on the back of the door Vere had just closed behind him—all the wide colorful skirts and frilled petticoats that would fuss around her knees as she mounted the stairs to Sugar's, which she would flounce disdainfully in his face those times when she turned to confront him in the night streets, challenging him to speak, and then at his silence swing away.

And dolls were to be seen everywhere in the packed untidy room—large, expensive boudoir dolls with deeply lashed, painted blue eyes and painted smiles and pink brushed lightly over their white cheeks. Vere had never seen so many of them at one time. They lazed amid the tumbled sheet on the unmade bed, where they obviously served as the girl's sleeping companions. They sat like queens with their limbs artfully arranged and their dresses spread out around them on pillows scattered about the floor. One doll was propped amid the toiletries on the vanity table where the girl sat, its dimpled arms opened as if to embrace her. And they were all dressed, even the ones lounging in bed, in an exact copy of her lavish gown; and their spun-gold hair, piled in the same elaborate tower of curls as her wig, was studded with fake jewels also.

Vere looked from the doll on the dressing table to the girl's reflection in the mirror, and as their eyes met, she said, very quietly, "You mean to say you've come to make trouble this Carnival Monday night?" Her voice was as level as her gaze. "Is that it?" she said.

He smiled, the same little cryptic expression of the lips he had given her the night she had screamed at him from behind the drunken soldier on Whitehall Lane.

"Here it is you had all these weeks to say whatever it is you have to say or do whatever it is you feel big enough to do and you mean to say you had to wait till Carnival Monday night when people are looking to enjoy theirself to make trouble . . ."

She waited; then irritably: "But what it is you want from me, anyway?" Her face swung toward him over her shoulder, but she didn't look directly at him. Her gaze stopped short, and she addressed a spot on the floor not far from his feet. "I got something belonging to you? I ask you, Vereson Walkes, I got something belonging to you anymore?"

Again she gave him time to reply, her gaze bent on the floor, then emboldened by his silence, she cried, "Well, you lie in hell, bo, because I don't have a blasted thing that's yours anymore. The few furnitures you bought when we was living together I left right there in my mother's house up Canterbury. You can go for them any time you want. And the little money you sent when you was in Florida spent long ago. Every penny gone. You think I still got some of it? Is that it? You think maybe I'm still spending it, that I used it to buy some of these things you see here"—she waved a skinny bejeweled arm toward the clothes, the dolls. "Well, you lie again. Not a thing here was bought with any money belonging to you.

"Or maybe you're looking for a woman now you're back," she said after a long pause and her voice had taken on a fine scorn, although her eyes still refused to meet his. "Maybe you're looking to play the man like before and want to start up with me again. Well, if that's the case you best find yourself somebody else. Leave me out, bo, because I don't have no time anymore for any small, poor-behind, country boys who don't have nothing to give you but some baby every time you look around."

Still Vere said nothing; the little bemused smile remained unchanged. His eyes, which at times gave the impression they had been cut in above the high bones long after the face had been completed, as an afterthought, continued to regard her reflection in the mirror almost impassively.

The girl waited longer this time. Then, finally, taking a deep breath that caused the shallow places within her collarbone to sink and fill with shadows, she said to the spot on the floor, "Oh, I know what it is. It's the damn child I had for you. It's what that obeah woman you've got for an aunt and all those liared bad-minded people in Bournehills told you I did to it. How I didn't care it good. How I killed it. The bitches. But I bet none of them told you that from the day that child born you could tell it wasn't going to live any time. It was a sickly something!" she shouted at the floor. "And t' besides," she cried at the same defiant pitch, all the silver dust and sequins on her dress shimmering amber in the dull amber light as she stuck her arms akimbo, "who told you the child was even yours? Who said you was man enough then to be giving anybody a baby . . . ?" She sucked her teeth in scorn.

But long before she had said all this, as far back as when she had first mentioned the child, she had caught out of the corner of her lowered eye the movement of his arm. Even as she had been shouting defiantly, he had been reaching back, his arm describing a slow graceful arc like that of an archer drawing an arrow from the quiver on his back.

She looked up, not at him (she had yet to do that) but at the foreshortened cane in his raised hand, and her eyes, huge and tobacco-colored in the artificial whiteness of her face, contained neither surprise nor fear.

"Yes." She nodded bitterly. "I thought so. All you Bournehills men can do is give blows. That's the only thing you all know: blowsing . . . "

The first blow caught her on the shoulder, silencing her, and she folded in like a bird, like some scrawny Bournehills hen bedding down for the night in a tree. Her shoulders hunched, her head drawn down between them so that her face, which she quickly covered with her hands, was doubly protected, she curved her body until it resembled that of a fetus. Only her back with the sharply canted shoulder blades like clipped wings and the long notched spine showing above the gown was exposed, and it, oddly enough, seemed to deflect rather than to absorb the blow. Nor did she once flinch or cry out, not even when the cane came stinging down a second time and its tip, as Vere brought it up, caught in her dress and, ripping through it, sent the sequins scattering like the rainbow-colored scales of a fish across the floor, and then, as part of the same upward movement, tore off the blond wig and sent it spinning like a bit of fluff after the sequins. Through all this she kept silent. And her silence—but even more so her lean humped back, said she had long grown inured to such abuse, that she knew how to take it. There was even a sense of acceptance and relief in the figure doubled over on itself before the cluttered vanity. She might have been glad he had finally come, relieved to know it would soon be over and done with.

And Vere, for his part, was wielding the cane with a dispassion that was in keeping with her stoicism. The two of them might have been carefully following the rules and practices of a strict code which they accepted without question. So that there was nothing vengeful or even angry about the blows he dealt her, which was odd, given the wrongs she had done him. Rather, he struck her—the cane coming down with slow regularity across her hard back, his face closed and impassive—in the same puritanical manner a father might a child, to chasten and reform it. It was the way the girl's father had probably chastised her as a child, and the way Leesy had thrashed him with the same Malacca cane when he was a boy.

And then suddenly he was angry. Perhaps it was the sight of that hardened back which sent the blows rebounding his way so that he almost felt he was whipping himself. Or the realization that no matter how long he flailed away at her he would never be able to convey to her what it was he had been seeking in having her as his woman and giving her the child, and how deeply she had wronged him by denying him both. She would never understand. His anger might have flowed out of his awareness of her profound ignorance. Whatever, all the bitterness and rage he had contained during his three years away came suddenly to a head, bursting in him like a huge boil that had long needed lancing, and he began striking at her with a kind of fury, missing badly in his wildness. Flinging aside the cane he searched the room for some more effective instrument. His eyes lighted upon the doll amid the toilet articles on the vanity, and reaching across the girl's humped form he snatched it up, sending the bottles and jars there in a wild spill across the floor. Holding it by one white dimpled leg he began slashing away at her with it.

She looked up then, her face emerging from the safe hollow between her shoulders like a bird's head from under its wing, and seeing the doll swinging by a leg from his hand, its gown already torn and hair in disarray, its blue painted eyes terrified, a look of horror came over her face, and she leaped from her stool, screaming, "Leave that! Put it down! God blind you in hell, leave my doll-baby. Put it down, you hear. You ain't got no calling with it. Oh, Christ, man," she pleaded, "give it to me, I beg you, don't you see you're hurting it. Give it to me, blast you. Take your damn hands off it. It's mine . . ."

An ugly red mottling her face under the white patina, she grabbed hold of the doll's other leg, seeking to wrest it from him, and a grim silent tug of war ensued, with Vere trying to free the doll so that he might strike her with it and the girl fighting for it with the strength of a mother who sees her child being murdered before her eyes. But neither of them won, and finally as they continued to pull and tug at the doll between them—tumbling the stool to the dressing table and crashing into the walls in their furious pantomime dance, the doll's body ripped wide, and all its sawdust and cotton innards exploded in a burst in the girl's face.

It was then that her cry broke—and it began at a high, with no build-up whatsoever: a sudden shrill atonal scream which rose and fell with the regularity of a siren in the tiny room, and which called to mind, in its almost ritualistic fluting, the high-pitched, tremolant keening of Arab women mourning their dead. It was a cry expressive of such sorrow and loss it could not have been simply the doll she was mourning, but all the things she had ever wanted and been denied. It caused the flame within the kerosene lamp to waver and the turds of gray dust on the floor to seek cover under the bed. Escaping the room through the cracks in the wall it traveled the length and breadth of the Heights, informing those few who had not gone to the dance of what had happened to her. And it continued long after Vere, with a gesture of disgust (she would never understand) flung the remains of the mangled doll at her and strode from the house, leaving the door sprawling open behind him. The loud ululation continued to rise and fall long after he had gotten into the Opel and driven away: ". . . *oh god Oh God oh god Oh God oh god Oh God oh god Oh God oh god Oh God oh god Oh God oh god Oh God oh god Oh God oh god Oh*

God oh god Oh God oh god Oh God oh god Oh God oh god Oh God oh god Oh God oh god Oh God oh god Oh God oh god Oh God oh god Oh God oh god . . ."

Later, back in Bournehills, he changed into the blue-and-white striped Osnaburg he would wear tomorrow, ate the balance of his and Leesy's noon meal which he found covered down in the larder, and then went over to the social center at the edge of the playing field where the Carnival Monday night dance was in progress. He passed unnoticed by Leesy and her ancient companions standing critical and aloof to one side of the large crowd outside the building. Forcing his way up the equally crowded veranda he found Allen waiting for him near the doorway where they always stood on Saturday nights watching the thronged dancers inside but too hesitant, both of them, to go in and dance themselves.

"Where the heck have you been?" Allen said as he came up. "I've been looking all over for you."

"In town," Vere said.

"In town? What'd you go there for? We don't go in until tomorrow," Allen said. He had also donned his Osnaburg costume, and with his thick, dark-haired arms and swarthy skin he looked, despite the rimless glasses, like a fisherman in some tiny village on the south Italian coast.

"I had a little business to see to," Vere said.

"Oh?" Allen waited; then, when Vere offered nothing more, he said with a shy, suspicious, and strangely worried laugh, "Wait a minute, don't tell me you've got a woman in town? Have you? That's what everybody's been saying is the reason for these mysterious trips of yours into New Bristol."

"No, man," Vere said with a tragic shake of his head. His gaze was on the couples dancing pressed close together inside. "I don't have a woman any place. But I tell you one thing"—his eyes shifted briefly to Allen; he gave a little determined smile—"come tomorrow I'm going to start looking around for one."

CHAPTER 2

Dawn found the Bournehills band well on the road to town. People had come straight from the all-night dance at the social center to join it, most without even stopping to take morning tea: the hot, overly sweet green tea and salt biscuits with which everyone began the day. All means of transportation were being used—the few cars in the district, including Merle's, Saul's and Vere's; the one or two small trucks, all the bicycles—and each of these carried a passenger on the frame; even donkey carts—Leesy had taken hers. The one old Bournehills bus, jammed inside with women and children, was festooned outside with little boys clinging to the widely spaced wooden slats which secured the vehicle's open sides. And more people, mostly the men, rode aloft the huge float depicting Pyre Hill in flames which had been attached to the rear of Delbert's pickup truck. The truck itself was piled high in back with the steel drums belonging to the idlers of the village.

It was a long, straggly caravan that made its way toward New Bristol that Tuesday. With the flaming hill in the lead, followed by the bus, complaining bitterly of its overload, and the string of donkey carts bringing up the rear, it crept along at a pace that would, it seemed, take it the entire day if not longer, to reach its destination. Yet, as slow and sorry-looking a cavalcade as it was, there was nonetheless something impressive about it with the float's garish flames licking high against the muted dawn sky and the young outriders spurring the bus up the hills with their shouts. And as the morning cleared, taking on the heat and vivid character of the day, and the risen sun, looking startled at the sight of the mass exodus below, hastened to overtake them, the hills almost appeared to level out and lie flat as the band approached, thus making the way easier for them.

They reached the ridge at Cleaver's by breakfast time at eleven, and calling a halt near the two tall royal palms which marked the highest point on the island, they unpacked a holiday feast of peas and rice, baked fowl, souse made from Leesy's pig, and rum which they had brought with them. And they took special care when drinking to make libation first. This after all was sacred ground, for it was here, along the narrow spine of the ridge, that Cuffee Ned and his men had put to rout the government force after raiding the arsenal, and then, three years later, where they had held off a full regiment for, some like Ferguson said, almost six months.

By the time they arrived in New Bristol, the carnival band contest at the Sports Oval, from which they had been barred because of their refusal to change their theme, was over, and the bands had taken to the streets for the mammoth parade which would not end until the midnight curfew and the beginning of Ash Wednesday. Queen Street and the winding maze of side streets, lanes, and alleys that led into it streamed with an unending procession of brilliantly costumed marchers, huge bedecked floats that could scarcely squeeze through the narrow corridors, rivalrous steelbands which would, many of them, clash openly as the day wore on, and banners, raised high on poles, announcing the subject of each band. This year, along with the usual large and noisy contingents of sailors and whooping American Indians, there were bands depicting Cleopatra's Egypt, Hiroshima—with a mass of twisted wreckage and corpses—The Garden of Eden, Wars to Come, The Fall of the Roman Empire—with a stout black Nero, a chaplet of leaves round his forehead, fiddling in the midst of a fake fire—Life on the Moon, The Twenty-sixth of July Guerrilla Band, The Parade of the Dolls—with Vere's former girl friend, her dress repaired and blond wig back in place, riding on top of the main float, surrounded by her dolls.

And everyone, including the girl, was singing the song chosen to accompany the road march this year, and those on the ground were dancing as they marched, their feet executing a slow rhythmic tramp designed to conserve their energy so they might last the day. But a few, the more exuberant among them, were already, despite the long day to go, dancing wildly, their ecstatic faces thrown back to the sun.

Viewed from the jumbled squalor of Harlem Heights the carnival band parade resembled a river with its main body along Queen Street and innumerable streams and tributaries feeding into it from the sides. And it was a river at floodtime, one swollen by the spring tides and upon whose surface had fallen blossoms of every color imaginable from the trees along its banks—bright crimson, oranges, hot pinks, yellows, violet, blues and fuchsia—each color sharpened and made more vivid by the water's darkness. That dark tide moved undeterred through the cramped town—slowly because of the colorful freight it bore, swaying heavily as it went, and everywhere taking its shape from the twisting streets. Carnival had flowed over and possessed New Bristol, and as one after another of the steelbands that accompanied each group of marchers passed down the line of spectators jammed onto the selvage edge of sidewalk and the sound of the deep-voiced bass drums swept through them, reverberating in the chambers of their hearts and overwhelming their senses, they, too, raised their arms as if possessed, and cried, "Beat the pans, man! Beat them! Play mass, yes! Play mass!"

Leaving their motley collection of vehicles at the Sports Oval just outside the town, the Bournehills band assembled under the direction of Delbert, who was in charge every year; and then, taking its time, made its way toward Queen Street.

"*Bournehills band coming!*" The word preceded them, traveling swiftly down through the ranks of both spectators and marchers. And beneath the din of song and dance and steelbands, a faint anticipatory hush fell. The crowd ignored the bands passing in front of them to crane their necks for a glimpse of the one from Bournehills. "Can you see them?" they called up to those watching the parade from the upper windows and balconies to the houses and shops lining the route. "Is it the same? Are they playing the same damn masque again this year?" And those above, catching sight in the distance of the familiar Guinea-blue banner with, dimly, the words "The Pyre Hill Revolt" emblazoned in white across it, called down, "It's the same, soul."

"But what the hell ails those people, yes? Why they got to come with the same foolishness every carnival, spoiling the fete? Why they won't change? The vagabonds! They ought to be banned from town."

But even the most vocal among them subsided into a silence that was at once bewildered, outraged, and helplessly curious as the Bournehills contingent approached.

The wide banner of coarse blue cloth which spanned almost the entire width of the street came first. Under the title were stitched the words "Best Local Historical," the name of the award given them the year, long ago, when they had first performed the masque, and which they still stubbornly laid claim to. Merle was among the dozen or so men and women holding the poles supporting the banner. Dressed in the Osnaburg, her wrists bound by the bracelets and the saints burdening the small lobes of her ears, she was staring straight ahead as she marched, seemingly oblivious to the crowd and noise. And while her left hand held the pole, her right, like all the others in this first line of marchers, was raised in the classic Bournehills greeting which always, even in the most casual exchange between two people passing each other on the road, suggested a meaning beyond the ordinary.

Immediately behind came the Spiretown steelband with the little daredevil boys from the bus pulling the heavy bass drums which were mounted on wheels. The idlers from the culvert wall were in charge. But they scarcely seemed themselves today. All the usual horseplay, the constant banter and jokes, all their frivolous wastrel ways had been replaced by a quiet studious air. In the midst of the gay roar around them they were sober and concentrated, utterly absorbed in the music they were shaping with their mallets on the tuned surfaces of their drums. And though they had been up all night playing for the dance at the social center and under the hot New Bristol sun the perspiration was already coursing down their bare arms in streams that followed the tracery of the veins there, they didn't appear tired. All the days, weeks, and months they had spent loafing under the tamarind tree, too lazy or caught up in their games sometimes to return the waves of those passing, might have been a storing up of strength on their part, a careful preparation for this one day when they would parade New Bristol's streets spelling out on their converted oil drums the story of Cuffee and the revolt. This was perhaps the only thing they deemed worthy of their energy, the one thing to which they were willing to give themselves.

In back of them marched what looked to be the entire population of Bournehills, including the whole of Spiretown as well as people from the tiny settlements between Westminster and the high ridge at Cleaver's, and ranging in age from Leesy and her crones to the baby the little girl in Harriet's "band of children" brought on her hip each morning to the beach.

The women and children, a long solid bloc of them, came first, with behind them the towering replica of Pyre Hill which was being propelled through the tight streets by the young lorry helpers and the like, Vere and Allen among them. To the rear of the float stretched an endless coffle of men and boys with Delbert, holding a large conch shell in his hand, trudging heavily in the lead. The majority of the men wore the loose Osnaburg over their trousers, but a small group to the very rear of the band were dressed in the red-coated uniform of the British soldier of the time.

It was a silent march in the beginning. Unlike the other carnival bands whose members were singing in an endless refrain the road march song for the year, the Bournehills band was silent. There was only the slow muffled beat of the steelband up ahead, not unlike taps being sounded; and above this, the steady, inexorable tramp of feet on the harsh asphalt of the roadway. They were doing, it was true, the dance called for at this hour, the restrained rhythmic two-step that scarcely brought the foot up off the ground and was meant to see the marcher through the day. But with them it was more pronounced. The slow dragging step that carried them forward was more stated, clearly audible and regularly punctuated by the loud ring of the bracelets the women and girls wore. With each slurred step they would half-raise their arms and then, together, bring them sharply down, causing the heavy silver to fall to their wrists with a stunning clash.

It was an awesome sound—the measured tread of those countless feet in the dust and the loud report of the bracelets, a somber counterpoint to the gay carnival celebration. It conjured up in the bright afternoon sunshine dark alien images of legions marching bound together over a vast tract, iron fitted into dank stone walls, chains—like those to an anchor—rattling in the deep holds of ships, and exile in an unknown inhospitable land—an exile bitter and irreversible in which all memory of the former life and of the self as it had once been had been destroyed.

And the members of the Bournehills band were as awesome a sight as they filed slowly past in the shapeless blue-and-white striped Osnaburgs. It didn't appear they would ever again be able to lift their heads or bring their bowed backs into line. The bones that served as the props to their spirit might have been broken. Nor would their half-hidden faces ever recover from the dazed look of defeat. It was almost as if—perhaps because they had performed the masque for so many years—they had actually become those they were depicting, or had been them all along, so that every detail of that long march and stern exile (all the horror of it) was still with them. And as though to confirm this, the entire body of marchers would from time to time, suddenly, without warning, raise their heads—all of them coming up together in response it seemed to a signal only they could hear—and stare out at the crowd with those eyes which always appeared to be regarding you from across a great vista of time.

It was an odd, unnerving look they bent on the spectators straining away from them against the buildings, one which insisted that they acknowledge them despite the crude silver at their wrists, the Osnaburg that was like a prisoner's uniform and the ignominious stoop to their bodies. And not only acknowledge them, but love them and above all act in some bold, retributive way that would both rescue their memory and indemnify their suffering.

But all down Queen Street the crowd fell back with a muted, unwilling cry, refusing. A stout matron in a yellow-print dress and carnival hat—the kind usually sold to tourists, with straw flowers sewn on the wide brim—raised a hand, palm out, to her eyes. "I can't look," she said. "They's too pitiful. Oh, God, what is it with them?" she whispered bewilderedly. "Why must they come dragging into town every year in the same old rags, looking s' bad and embarrassing decent people with some old-time business everybody's done forgot. Who wants to see all that? What's the purpose behind it . . . ?" Then, angrily: "The shameless whelps! The disgraces! I tell you, I'm hiding from them with tears in my eyes!"

But there was no hiding, because even as she cursed them the sound of the conch shell Delbert held in his hand could be heard, calling for the start of the pageant. The single deep note which had in it the lowing voice of the sea at Bournehills reached from one end of the band to the other, and at its signal the entire body of marchers came to a halt. The weary abject tramp ceased, the bracelets on the women's arms were stilled, the steelband boys up ahead completely silenced their drums and the giant float of Pyre Hill pitching along like a ship ablaze in a dark sea ground to a stop.

In the silence that reached out to embrace not only the crowds watching but those out of sight as well, including even the other carnival bands parading noisily through distant parts of the town, so that they, too, fell silent, a figure could be seen slipping quietly up Pyre Hill to the scale-model estate house at its summit. It was Stinger enacting, as he did every year, the role of Cuffee Ned. He was dressed according to the description of Cuffee in the old accounts at the library, in the standard Osnaburg tunic over a pair of homespun pantaloons. A blue kerchief, the same Guinea blue as the banner up front, was tied low over his forehead like a pirate's, and on top of this he wore a battered rush hat with a clay pipe stuck in the band. An obeah man's wallet (for Cuffee had been that also, both seer and shaman to the people, the intermediary between them and the ancient gods) hung at his waist and it was stocked with the farrago of his calling: the rusty nails and broken bits of glass, the bright-hued parrot feathers and small clay figures of his enemies, among them the planter Percy Bryam. Everything had been done to detail. Even Stinger's normally mild reflective face had taken on Cuffee's expression as described in the accounts and was suddenly shrewd, clenched and coldly purposeful as he crept up the float with the billhook that was like part of his hand flashing in the sun.

Meanwhile, above him at the top, the walls to the house had dropped open to reveal Ferguson as Percy Bryam stretched out asleep in a long nightshirt. An old-fashioned nightcap with a tassel covered his shaved head and his carved, elongated face was white with flour. He slept; Stinger, the blade poised, glided swiftly up, and all along Queen Street with its shops, offices and banks boarded up for the holiday, the crowd stood transfixed, their eyes on the float. Even those like the woman in the yellow dress who didn't want to look were looking. The afternoon sun that had been following overhead also paused to watch. He neared the top; there were but two more steps to go, and in the midst of the held silence a small boy in the crowd, believing what he saw on the float to be real, suddenly cried, his thin voice piercing the quiet, "Look sharp, Mr. Bryam, Cuffee coming!"

But Stinger was already on him, the curved blade at his throat. Ferguson awoke from his feigned sleep with a bloodcurdling scream, and a locked struggle ensued between the two men, the same desperate fight that was said to have taken place in the darkened bedroom between the man Bryam, who had owned all of Bournehills and everyone in it in the beginning, and Cuffee Ned, the mere chattel, who for years had been his trusted body servant. Ferguson, naturally, was overacting. His long ropy arms sawed the air, his fleshless legs kicked high, causing the full skirt of his nightshirt to snap and billow like a sail, and all the while he filled Queen Street with such howls, pleas, and gargling screams it appeared that Stinger, whose object, according to the story, was to take him alive, had changed his mind and slit his throat and he was strangling on the blood. But finally the cries and wild thrashing subsided, then ceased, and a triumphant Stinger as Cuffee led Ferguson as Bryam broken and defeated down the hill.

At that, and with a roar that shook New Bristol to the coral rock at its foundation, the entire Bournehills band broke rank. One group stormed the float, and again the screams reached from one end of the town to the other as the rebels, following to a letter the story, laid waste to the members of the Bryam household and set the house and hill ablaze. And so graphic were their movements as they swarmed over the slopes brandishing the make-believe firebrands, so authentic the perspiration pouring off them as from some intense heat, it did seem the painted wooden shell of a hill was burning. The fake flames, come suddenly alive, looked to be sending up great clouds of smoke and sparks, driving the spectators back farther against the buildings. And the mock battle that had broken out between slave and soldier on the ground, both using sticks carved to resemble muskets, seemed real also. You could almost hear the musket fire over the shouts and see the puffs of white smoke each time one discharged.

The pitched battle raged, the hill seethed, Stinger paraded his captive before the crowd, and far up front, under the raised banner, the steelband boys sent their mallets winging over their drums in a new song—a fast-paced, stirring hymn of jubilation and victory. Behind them the invisible fetters that had slowed the women's steps had fallen away and they were dancing in tune with the music, their bodies free and alive suddenly, the once-bowed heads flung back. Their feet rose from the ground in little joyous leaps and bursts that sent the dust of the road leaping also, and where their arms had been pinned down before by the weighty silver they lifted them, weightless now, to the sky.

It was a triumphal dance, and at another note from Delbert on the conch shell their voices soared in a triumphal song. And the effect of that sudden uprush of sound, coming as it did after the numbed silence, was of a massive shock wave upon the air, and once again, New Bristol seemed to reel at its base. Hurling their massed voices against the sky, the women began the long recitative that told the story of the Pyre Hill Revolt and Cuffee Ned—his deeds and exploits, his heroism. It was a song celebrating him.

And they went all the way back to the beginning, telling first of how he had spent years carefully planning and secretly organizing for the rebellion, and how, even when all was ready, he had waited until the main body of the regiment was out of the island helping to put down a maroon uprising in far-away Jamaica before striking. They sang then of what the crowd had just witnessed: Cuffee's daring surprise attack, the locked struggle between himself and Bryam in the white house at the summit, the firing of the hill which, legend would have it, had burned for five years, and the raid upon the arsenal atop Cleaver's followed by the sharp clash between the rebels, led by Cuffee, and the token force of government troops left on the island, which saw more than half of them killed and the rest put to flight.

Singing, performing the victory dance, the women started the band underway again, and their voices were taken to a new and powerful high as the men behind joined in—all of them: the incendiaries standing on the float with their firebrands raised, and both groups of fighters. Stinger, triumphant as Cuffee, was singing as he strode beside Delbert at the head of the men. He had claimed as a spoil of battle Ferguson's tasseled nightcap and was wearing it along with his blue kerchief under the rush hat with the long tassel hanging down. Even Ferguson's Percy Bryam was singing as he staggered along bareheaded under a heavy yoke which had been fitted to his shoulders to indicate how he had been shackled to the great horizontal ox-driven wheel at Cane Vale's old windmill, which had been used in those days to power the roller when the wind failed. It was a punishment Bryam was known to have meted out regularly to those whom he had considered no more than oxen, and he had soon collapsed and died at the wheel as many of them had also. . . .

They were singing, it was true, of Bryam, Cuffee and Pyre Hill, of a particular event, place and people, simply telling their story as they did each year. Yet, as those fused voices continued to mount the air, shaking the old town at its mooring on the bay, it didn't seem they were singing only of themselves and Bournehills, but of people like them everywhere. The struggle on the hill which had seen Cuffee triumphant and Bryam brought low was, their insistent voices seemed to be saying, but the experience through which any people who find themselves ill-used, dispossessed, at the mercy of the powerful, must pass. No more, no less. Differing in time, in the forms it takes, in the degree of its success or failure, but the same. A struggle both necessary and inevitable, given man. Arms outstretched, hands opened, the marchers sought to impress this truth upon the watching throngs.

And the band went on to tell the story of the revolt to its completion even though the crowd already knew it and would have preferred not to hear it again. They sang of how after defeating the small body of troops and sealing off Cleaver's, their forebears had lived for almost three years like the maroons of Jamaica and bush Negroes of Guiana—free, at peace, dependent only on themselves, a nation apart. For food there had been the yam, cassava and sweet potato grown in the fields. Breadfruit and mango had been plentiful on the trees. They had fished the Bournehills sea, casting their nets from the near reefs when the tide was out. For meat they had occasionally killed a pig. And to propitiate the gods, who were perverse beyond words and as jealous as they were kind, Cuffee would periodically spatter the earth with the blood of a cock.

"They had worked together!"—and as if, in their eyes, this had been the greatest achievement, the thing of which they were proudest, the voices rose to a stunning crescendo that visibly jarred the blue dome of sky. Under Cuffee, they sang, a man had not lived for himself alone, but for his neighbor also. "If we had lived selfish, we couldn't have lived at all." They half-spoke, half-sung the words. They had trusted one another, had set aside their differences and stood as one against their enemies. *They had been a People!* Their heads thrown back and welded voices reaching high above New Bristol's red-faded tin roofs, they informed the sun and afternoon sky of what they, Bournehills People, had once been capable of.

Then, abruptly, the voices dropped. You could almost see them plummeting through the bright, dust-laden air. They sang then in tones drained of their former jubilance of the defeat that had eventually followed: of how, as the example of Cuffee and Bournehills spread and others like them on the island sought to rebel, the government had decided to act, and with the return of the full regiment had mounted their attack. Cuffee and his men had held them for a time at Cleaver's, but they had been finally overwhelmed, utterly crushed. In voices that would never cease to mourn him, the singers described his death at the hands of his captors and the bloody suppression that had followed, for this, too, as painful as it was, was part of the story.

And as they told of how his severed head had been placed on the pike along Westminster Low Road to serve as a warning the crowd could see all the way at the very end of the band the lonely figure of Mr. Douglin, his wide-brim hat hiding the eyes that were like the empty eye sockets on certain statues which seem to draw you into the stone back to the age when the model for it had lived. He was marching by himself, slowly because of his great age, and carrying in one hand the cutlass he used to trim the grass at the one spot along the shoulder, and in the other a tall pike with a doll's head in a tasseled nightcap affixed to the top.

But Cuffee had died content, the band declared in a final coda. For he had seen his life and deeds as pointing the way to what must be. And obeah man that he was, a true believer, he believed that death was not an end but a return, so that in dying he would be restored to the homeland and there be a young warrior and hunter again. "Him feel joy," he was known to have said of himself at the end, "Him ready fuh to die now."

The voices trailed into silence. The steelband boys up front muffled their drums. The dust roused by the dancing filtered back down, and in the sudden quiet all that could be heard once more was the dull dispirited tramp and the intermittent tolling of the women's bracelets.

So it went the entire afternoon, the dead march alternating with the vivid scene on the float and the triumphal outpouring. The pattern was repeated throughout all of New Bristol's crooked streets, but as the afternoon approached evening, the time devoted to the numb procession and those parts of the pageant dealing with the revolt's defeat became less and less, until finally these portions disappeared altogether, and the only thing retained was the soaring tribute in song and dance to Cuffee, his victory on the hill and life in Bournehills during his reign.

With that the resistance of the crowd gave way, as it did every Carnival Tuesday when the Bournehills band reached its climax and in so doing seemed to lift the entire town onto its shoulders and take it marching with it. Here and there amid the packed spectators, voices could be heard singing along with the band, and some of the onlookers were actually dancing where they stood pressed up against the buildings. Even those who had cursed the marchers and declared they should be barred from town found themselves swaying as the Bournehills steelband passed and the music leaping off the surfaces of the drums to describe visible arabesques in the air entered them. "Well, yes," they said grudgingly, giving the lovely lift and shrug of the shoulder that was part of the dance, their bodies moving against their will, "you got to hand it to them, I guess. Those Bournehills fellas know how to beat the pans and those other brutes can sing."

Some in the crowd even began pushing their way out into the road to dance and march with them. An old man, who had had more than his share to drink over the two-day holiday, staggered out to Ferguson as he passed bowed down under the yoke, and shaking a black finger in his face cried thinly, his voice trembling with age and a long-suppressed rage, "It serve you right, Percy Bryam. It serve you right. You ain't had no business doing the people s' bad." His anger getting the better of him he swung at Ferguson, and the latter, forgetting himself, swung back, and they had to be parted.

Scores of barefoot children from the giant slum hovering over New Bristol, their carnival costumes the rags they wore every day, their faces a riot of carnival colors to make up perhaps for their lack of a proper outfit, had attached themselves like a string of noisy tin cans to the back of the Bournehills band and were singing of Cuffee as if he were their hero also. And soon members of other carnival bands began abandoning them "to jump behind" the one from the hills. Whole sections would come rushing down the side streets, their costumes of tulle and bright satin streaming behind them, to push their way in. A large contingent of the Twenty-sixth of July Guerrilla Band made up entirely of young people from the Heights joined forces with Bournehills. Dressed in olive fatigues, heavy combat boots and helmets camouflaged with leaves, the young men sporting beards and puffing cigars and all of them, even the women, brandishing cardboard machetes and grenades, the members of the guerrilla band came charging toward Queen Street and the Bournehills troupe, singing the praises of Cuffee as they came and firing toy machine guns and pistols.

Swollen to almost twice its size by the newcomers, the Bournehills band could scarcely make its way bay back up Queen Street to the Sports Oval where, now that dusk was falling, there would be a final "jump-up" before the last march, called the Last Lap, back through the streets and home. And more than ever now that dark human overflow, pressing its way through the choked street past Barclay's Bank and the air-conditioned offices of Kingsley and Sons and the department stores with their barricaded windows, resembled a river made turbulent by the spring thaw and rising rapidly—a river that if heed wasn't taken and provision made would soon burst the walls and levees built to contain it and rushing forth in one dark powerful wave bring everything in its path crashing down.

CHAPTER 3

By the onset of dusk whatever fresh air there had been earlier, when the parade began, lay trampled underfoot, and the only thing left to breathe—or so it seemed to Harriet—was the eddying dust and heat, the stench of the open drains running along both sides of the road and the almost overpowering exhalation of the black perspiring bodies crowded round her. This was what met her nostrils, that she tasted at the back of her tongue whenever she was forced to draw a breath. There was even, faintly, the smell of her own tired, overheated flesh drifting up through the wide neck of the Osnaburg dress and somehow calling to mind milk left standing in too warm a room.

It was more than time for her to quit the parade. She should have left long ago, in fact, she told herself, her head straining up in the hope of encountering a stray breeze as she felt the need to breathe again. She could have easily slipped away sometime back when the band reached the intersection to the street, sloping down to the bay, where the Cockerel Club was located, and there, as arranged, wait for Saul in the air-cooled American-style bar one flight up. She had even glimpsed the painted young cock on the sign across the turbulent sea of heads as she passed. And yet she hadn't left. Perhaps because stronger than her desire to leave had been the need—obscure, old, dating back to that quietly determined little girl in white stockings and a bow, who had welcomed all challenges—to see the parade through to the end, to prove that she could stay the course.

Also, in the beginning, before the air had been cut off, she had been too interested in everything to leave. Flanked by her two self-appointed bodyguards, Stinger's Gwen and the tall broad-shouldered woman from the road works, Hyacinth Weekes, who was also one of her regular visitors, and with Saul coming down from the line of men to check on her every so often, she had at no time felt in danger and had watched with interest as the Bournehills band repeatedly enacted the pageant. She had been moved on one hand by the silent downcast march, and vaguely unsettled on the other by the scene taking place between Stinger and Ferguson on the float (what little she had been able to see of it over the intervening heads), yet, as always, she had remained essentially out of it, removed, the spectator looking on from her seat near the wings. It had all seemed part of a somewhat busy drama which she could enjoy while only dimly understanding its meaning.

And she had also rather enjoyed—this, again, only at the beginning—the sensation of being borne along, almost without a body or will of her own, by that great swollen tide of humanity making its way through New Bristol by what seemed a slow but powerful protoplasmic action. She came to think of the Bournehills band, of the entire parade, as a huge, harmless, amoeboid mass that took its shape from the streets, changing as they changed, yet remaining intact, of a piece. At one point a woman spectator, spotting her amid the marchers, leaned out of the crowd and cried, amazed, "What, don't tell me you's a Bournehills, too, my lady?" Gwen had answered for her, shouting back, "How you mean! Of course she's one of we." And she hadn't denied it; she had even, strangely enough, found herself nodding. Just then, catching sight of Saul moving down through the band to check on her, she had smilingly waved him back, telling him she was all right.

But that had been more than two hours ago, before the saving breeze had died and her head began to ache, before the rough cloth of the Osnaburg had rubbed her skin raw. And before, moreover, things had gotten completely out of hand with the pageant being solely devoted to the riotous song and dance celebrating Cuffee, and the mobs of spectators and noisy masqueraders from other carnival troupes had come pushing their way in, eager to "jump with Bournehills" as it returned up Queen Street to the Sports Oval.

It was enough. She had more than proved herself. It was time now to seek the Cockerel Club, and there in the cool dimness, behind the drawn drapes shutting out the street below, slowly gather together her scattered parts over a drink. She would have a martini, although she didn't particularly like them. But she had need today of its chill, astringent, supremely civilized taste. It would burn away, like dry ice, the coating of dust on her tongue, in her throat, and cleanse her throughout.

And there, in answer to her wish, she saw up ahead the intersection to the street, where the club was situated. With a parting word to Gwen, who, in complete disregard of her condition, the swollen stomach Harriet couldn't understand, was doing the same strenuous dance as everyone else, she started toward it. Using her arm as a shield, her breath held, she forced her way through the moving tide of marchers, pushing a little angrily when they refused to yield, over to the thin strip of sidewalk along Queen Street. She reached the corner of the intersection and was about to start toward the club more than halfway down the long, slanted, painfully narrow side street when she heard what sounded like a massive war whoop well up above the sustained roar around her. She spun round, for the first time that day sensing danger, only to see the main body of the raucous green-clad guerrilla band from the Heights come ploughing across the ranks of the Bournehills marchers from the street above firing their noisy toy guns and sending up the earsplitting cry.

They were headed, she saw, in her direction and she quickly started back toward the corner and the comparative safety of Queen Street. But she wasn't quick enough. They were on her just as she started to make the turn, the first wave of them smacking up against her like one of those powerful Bournehills breakers which give the impression they have been gathering speed and force across the entire stretch of sea. She felt the ground pull away under her, and then as if she were no more than a pebble or bit of shell caught lying on the foreshore she was being swept down the street in their midst.

After the first jarring impact she tried regaining her balance. Again using her arm as a shield she sought to hold off the bodies crashing into her. Choking on the smoke from their cheap cigars, engulfed by the smell of their heavy sweat-soaked uniforms and the rum they had been drinking from the canteens at their waists, she began pushing and shoving toward the houses and shops lining the street, where she was sure to find a doorway to shelter her until they had passed and she could proceed on to the Cockerel.

But it was useless. Each time her foot touched the ground, the ground was unceremoniously snatched away, and the harder she struggled to cut across their lines toward the buildings, the more she felt herself being propelled in the direction of the bay spread wide at the foot of the street.

The bay! They would end in the bay! All of them spilling headlong into the water as they reached the edge of the land. She was suddenly convinced this was what would happen. Those in back would pile into those in front, unwittingly pushing them over, and then, just as blindly, follow suit, and the water would quickly swallow their startled screams.

And believing this she was more afraid for them than for herself, oddly enough. Because although she was still being buffeted along like a piece of driftwood, unable to gain her footing, her dress almost torn from her body, she was nonetheless certain she would reach the safety of the buildings before the street reached its fatal end. And so her concern was for them. For they were young—adolescents most of them. Tomorrow when they awoke (if by some miracle they were still alive then) the whites of their eyes would be clear, all evidence of today's dissipation erased. She envied them that. And being young, they were impetuous, headstrong, foolish. They needed direction.

"Do you realize where you're headed?" It was her voice suddenly shouting into the uproar. "Don't you see you'll wind up in the bay?"—and she found herself almost laughing at their wrongheadedness. "This way! Turn down here!"

And while still struggling against them, a raised hand staving off the black and brown faces charging into hers like images projected larger than life on a screen, she was pointing with her other hand to a small side lane just up ahead that would take them, she knew, by a series of devious twists and turns back up to Queen Street. "*Go this way!*"

But her voice couldn't carry above the furious clatter of their combat boots on the cobblestones, the insane rattle of the toy machine guns and the loud carnival songs, including the one extolling Cuffee Ned, which they were hurling, full voice, into the falling dusk. They hadn't heard her. Nor, she suddenly realized, her shock reflected in her eyes, had they really *seen* her. But how could this be? She was unmistakable among them with her hair (it was almost as blond now as Dorothy Clough's from the long months of sun) and her face, which despite her tan was still nonetheless white. But even those closest to her, the ones bumping into and pummeling her as they rushed past, appeared totally unaware of her presence.

Glancing bewilderedly around, she saw then that they were all staring with a strange fixity straight ahead, utterly absorbed in what seemed some goal or objective visible only to them. This had made them blind not only to her but to the bay at the foot of the street. On sudden impulse she reached out and waved a hand in the face of a girl stamping along at her side singing and waving a cardboard machete. The girl, who looked to be in her late teens, merely glanced her way. The look, chilling in its disregard, passed through her as if she wasn't there.

Harriet could have struck her. Not angrily, but the way one strikes an impertinent child, to remind it of its status. She suddenly wanted to give all those within her reach a good shaking. Her hand started out to snatch the fat, foul-smelling cigar from the mouth of a boy (he could have been no more than fourteen) who came barreling past her brandishing a cap pistol. They needed—the whole unruly lot of them—to be bathed, their mouths scrubbed clean of the tobacco and rum smell, and put to bed.

"This way!" She was pointing almost angrily now. For they had reached the small side lane and were about to surge past it, their helmets with the silly camouflage of leaves bobbing away. "Where are you going? Turn here! Turn here! You, can't you hear me? I said turn here!" she shouted up at a tall black-bearded youth, older than most of the others, whom she had been thrown against. The youth's gaze, fixed on the invisible goal, shifted briefly and he saw her: her white annoyed face, the imperious hand pointing. And he remained strangely unimpressed. He heard and understood her order, but paid no heed. Instead, planting himself in front of her, his arms holding off the crowd moiling and tumbling around them, he moved his body from the waist down in a slow lewd grind. She sprang back and he laughed, his mouth and tongue very pink within the black circle of beard and the lesser blackness of his face. Then he was gone, bulling his way through the mob ahead.

She was seized then by a revulsion and rage that was almost sexual in its force. And terror. For they just might take her down with them to the bay, after all! Because Queen Street, she saw, her head whirling round, had retreated far behind. They had plunged past the lane as well, and despite all her grim pushing and prodding she was no closer to the buildings to the side. And now to her horror she saw they were hurtling by the Cockerel Club. In a swift nightmarish sequence she glimpsed the cock on the sign, the bar's wide upstairs picture window with its drawn drapes, and faces, most of them white, peering down in amusement through an opening in the drapes at the scene below.

Her arm shot up, but even as she signaled wildly to them, knowing they would come to her rescue once they saw her, the faces disappeared in a blur behind and she was being hurled along down the last few hundred yards of the street.

It was then she started lashing out. In her sudden panic and hysteria she began slapping savagely at those closest to her, trying to beat them off. Her mouth twisting out of shape, she aimed for the faces that had refused to heed her advice, and the eyes that stared through her as though she wasn't there. Her own eyes turned a dense winter gray, all the blue in them gone; and her hair, swinging violently from side to side each time she whirled and struck, was like a short whip with which she was flailing them. She swatted away at them the way one would at a swarm of flies, and they, as indifferent to her blows as they had been to her insistent voice before, continued to sing and fire the guns and perform the reckless plunging dance. They continued to press toward the sea, bearing her with them.

The last building in the row loomed up, a scarred stone warehouse with vaulted double doors and boarded-over windows. Beyond this, and following the bay's deep curve, was the thin strip of road, scarcely big enough for a car, which served as a wharf; and then, abruptly, without so much as a guardrail along the edge, was the bay.

The last bit of cobblestone street vanished beyond the field of helmets ahead, and suddenly there was only the water in her view, very dark now that dusk was almost complete and rushing up to meet them at the same speed as they were racing toward it.

"Saul!"

The scream, torn from her throat, pierced the roar of voices and stampeding feet, and for a moment, less than a fraction of a second, the entire band seemed to freeze, pull back. But in the next moment they were surging forward again in a furious melee that saw her thrown from their midst against the warehouse door, and the guerrilla band, still dancing and singing lustily and firing the fake guns, charging en masse around the corner and then—moving a few abreast at a time so as not to fall into the water—up the narrow wharf road that would eventually take them to the Sports Oval on the outskirts of town.

Flung there against the high arched door that was like the entrance to a church, her bruised body flattened against it, she watched, terror-stricken, those green-clad hordes stream past her round the corner. And in her slowly drowning mind there appeared to be no end of them. She would never have believed there were so many—all with the same young, set black faces and farseeing eyes—on the island, in the world. Moreover, she suddenly realized, the thought occurring just seconds before a saving numbness came over her and her head dropped, that they wouldn't end, as she had believed, in the bay. There would be accidents, yes. In the crush some of them would lose their balance and fall in the water and have to be rescued. One or two might even drown before the wild march to the Oval had ended. But the vast body of them would reach the goal they had set for themselves: the thing she had seen in their eyes . . .

She was still slumped barely conscious against the door, her head fallen to one side and knees slightly bent under the weight of her sagging form—the victim, it seemed, of some casual crucifixion—when Lyle Hutson and Dorothy Clough found her. (They had been at the Cockerel Club having a drink when they had seen the band from the Heights passing and decided to follow it out to the Oval for the final jump-up.)

Harriet heard them before she really saw them, their alarmed voices reaching faintly down the dimmed corridors of her mind. She managed to raise her head halfway, and, her blank gaze slowly focusing, she made out the jaunty white sailor cap and uniform Dorothy Clough was wearing as her carnival costume, then the woman's frightened expression, and next, Lyle Hutson's anxious face (how odd it looked without the smile) and his hand reaching out to help raise her up. His hand, his face were the same as those in the band, the same color, and still in the grip of her rage and fear she would have struck at them had she been able to lift her arms.

With an effort, she took hold, and ignoring his hand, pulling herself straight by sheer force of will, she heard her voice (it seemed to come from a great distance) assuring them she was unharmed and explaining, as they anxiously questioned her, what had happened. She gave them only the barest details, describing with a somewhat shaky laugh that tried to make light of her ordeal how she had been swept into the mob on her way down to the club. "You should have seen them," she said using the laugh to cover her wavering voice. "They came swooping down on me like a pack of Indians and insisted on dragging me along with them down the street. For a while there I was afraid we'd all land right in the bay. But thank goodness, they had more sense than I thought and turned off just in time. They decided to drop me off here, a little the worse for wear as you can see but alive. . . ."

She couldn't go on. For it was as though it was all only now taking place. Something of the numbing shock that had caused her mind to go dark took hold of her again, so that she was only vaguely aware of what followed next. Dimly, she heard Lyle, joined by Dorothy Clough, suggesting, then insisting, that she let him drive her to his place and have his wife, Enid, who never attended carnival, look after her. As dimly, she heard herself saying, somewhat irritably, that she didn't need looking after and would prefer to go to the Cockerel where she and Saul were to meet. He would be worried when he got there and didn't see her. But Lyle was adamant. Promising to find Saul later and tell him her whereabouts, he left her with Dorothy Clough in the now empty street and went for his car, which he had parked in the same narrow side lane down which she had tried to direct the band.

He was quickly back and, too shaken and exhausted to protest further, she allowed them to help her into the car and minutes later was being driven through the maze of New Bristol's streets, and then up the private rise with its avenue of tall, evenly spaced royal palms (she could feel their coolness on her face as the Humber passed under them) among which his house stood.

And so she found herself at the end of the day alone with Enid Hutson in the huge modernized manor house overlooking the town. Behind where they sat on the veranda, the rooms inside were empty even of the servants, who had been given the day off. Below them, down through the black well of the night, the wind had taken the colored carnival lights strung along Queen Street and scattered their reflection over the water in the bay. And far to their left could be seen the egg-shaped ring of lights which marked the Sports Oval where the final jump-up was now at its height. The two women couldn't hear the noise at this distance, but they could see it. The din of voices, pounding feet and steelbands was a pall of brightly seething white dust hovering just above the Oval's open field and stands, and growing brighter as the darkness thickened.

Almost immediately after Lyle had dropped her off two hours ago Harriet had taken a shower in the gleaming turquoise-and-white-tiled bath adjoining the guest room where, at Enid's insistence, she would be spending the night. Stripping off the Osnaburg, flinging it along with her other clothes into a corner, she had remained for almost a half-hour under a near-scalding, stinging downpour of water inside the glass-enclosed booth. And she had made no effort to scrub herself, but had simply stood there, arms limp at her side, her head with the wet hair plastered over it bowed deep, letting the water beat down on her.

The shower done, she had then filled the bathtub on the other side of the room full of hot water and scrubbed herself until the cones of her breasts turned a dark ruddy pink.

She had completed the long bath and was sitting—wearing one of Enid Hutson's fussy sheer print dresses which was at least three sizes too large for her—on the veranda drinking coffee when Saul telephoned. His anxious voice sounded to her as if it were coming out of the dark roaring heart of the mob which she could hear in the background. He seemed almost part of the mob; and therefore lost to her. Still dazed, and overcome, now that her ordeal was over, by a lassitude that made her indifferent even to him, she assured him that nothing all that serious had happened and she was unhurt. (And she was never to tell him the full story. But how to speak of the terror that had seized her, or of the paroxysm of rage that had sent her hands slashing out like knives, making her a stranger to herself? How talk of this?) He said he was coming right up; and she told him there was no need. He must stay and see carnival through to the morning as he had planned. She would be going to bed anyway as soon as she had finished her coffee. She would sleep like a rock and tomorrow be as good as new.

"Harriet!" (She knew the tone: the exasperated, despairing note to it, which pleaded, almost angrily at times, for her to open to him). "Dammit," this is no time to play the tight-lipped WASP and keep your feelings to yourself. I'm asking you if you are really all right."

She sighed to herself, loving him, but tired, wanting simply to be alone; and again, before hanging up, she sought to reassure him, "Darling, believe me, the old WASP is fine. You'll see for yourself in the morning."

"You would think they would've had enough jumping up and flinging about themselves by now to be ready for their beds, but no, they're still down there carrying on. . . ." It was Enid Hutson, speaking in the voice which meandered, sluggish and uninflected, through everything she said. She was leaning forward in her chair looking out over the balustrade at the Oval with its welkin of lights. Her face in the glow from the rooms opening onto the veranda was whiter than Harriet's, which was deeply tanned. Her disapproving eyes were the same color as Merle's but with none of the latter's inner light. "And some of them won't even stop at midnight when they're supposed to," she was saying. "No, they'll keep right on spreeing till dawn. But then that's the way these people are, you know, especially that bunch from the Heights. They'll spend every cent they've got on carnival and then not have money even to buy a penny bread tomorrow. . . ."

A chair away, Harriet tried closing her mind to the woman's voice. She had thought several times of excusing herself and going in to bed, but greater than her need and desire for sleep was her fear that she might find herself reliving the day's horror in her dreams. And so she continued to sit there staring numbly down at a small black-and-blue mark on her left hand which she had gotten when in lashing out at the faces around her she had struck one of the helmets, and thinking—the thought stirring fitfully to life somewhere in her clouded mind—that Enid Hutson abandoned in the huge costly house was like her mother abandoned years ago outside the locked door to her father's study. For a frightening moment it was almost as if her mother had assumed the guise of Enid and come to sit beside her on the high-roofed veranda. It might have been her mother, and all she represented: her weakness, failure and utter ineffectuality, laying claim to her in Enid's voice.

CHAPTER 4

At about the same time, down through the great rift of darkness separating Lyle's house from the town below, Allen was searching the crowd inside the Sports Oval for a glimpse of Vere, who had deserted him to join in the dancing. They had arranged to drive back to Spiretown together, taking with them as many from the Bournehills band as Vere's car could hold. It was almost eleven o'clock by Allen's watch (the date in the tiny slot which had replaced the numeral three on the great moon face would soon change): time to go.

Just beyond where he stood near the main exit, the jump-up continued unabated, with the revelers, their arms linked and bodies welded in a solid bloc, churning round the field under the arc lights as if it were a huge, slowly revolving stage upon which they were dancing. And the dancing had taken on a kind of desperation now that the two-day celebration was nearly over, with the thousands upon thousands of stamping, pounding feet coming down with such force on the trampled grass that the ground shuddered. And the unflagging voices rose louder yet into the bright cloud of light and sound suspended above the arena as though hoping, by their very loudness, to forestall the midnight hour and the official end of the fete.

While waiting for Vere, Allen had amused himself by doing a rough, on-the-spot statistical analysis of the crowd wheeling past him in its gaudy panoply of costumes and floats. Scanning the faces from behind the one-way screen of his glasses, he had first estimated the percentage of poor; all those from Harlem Heights and the noisome back streets of New Bristol as well as the impoverished country districts like Bournehills. They would make up the largest figure. Then what percentage the struggling lower middle class of minor government workers, shop clerks, primary schoolteachers and the like. He also picked out those in the crowd who were clearly from the small New Bristol elite: the politicians (it was considered good politics to take part in carnival), professional and businessmen and senior civil servants—the younger and less conservative among them that is, those who couldn't resist the final Tuesday night jump-up at the Oval even though walking down Queen Street tomorrow they wouldn't so much as let their eye catch that of the clerk or carpenter they were dancing arm in arm with now. And finally, because he was Allen and thorough in his research, he tried gauging the small percentage of foreigners he spotted from time to time, the expatriates and tourists, soldiers and sailors, whose white faces occasionally bobbed up out of the dark throng with something of the luminous phosphorescence of fish in a night sea.

If he had had his notebook and pen he would have jotted down the figures, played around with them, perhaps even shown them to Saul tomorrow. But early that morning, just as he was about to slip the small spiral notebook and his pen into the pocket of the shirt he was wearing under his Osnaburg, Merle had walked over and snatched them from his hand. "Never no note taking today!" she had said—and her tone had sharply reproved him. "Not a bit of it. Whoever heard of anybody walking about with a pencil and paper at carnival? Why, people will think you're mad. If there's anything you want to remember today you're just going to have to jot it down up there"—and she had rapped him once with her knuckles on the temple.

He had been annoyed, but knowing there was no use arguing with her he had allowed her to take them. All day, though, he had missed the familiar light pressure of the notebook against his breast, over his heart. Without it and his pen he always felt not only unequipped for his work, but somehow personally unarmed, vulnerable.

Over in the center of town the bells of the Anglican cathedral began tolling eleven, and as the blurred echo reached the Oval an angry roar of protest and dismay welled up, followed by a wild stampede filled with the sodden pounding of feet on the stunned earth as everyone broke for the main exit and the hour-long Last Lap through the streets and home.

Moving out of the way Allen searched for Vere in the mob pouring past him. The muscles of his right arm stood tensed and ready to lift the arm high and wave him over the moment he spotted him. But although the masqueraders continued to flow past him for some time and he saw any number of faces from Bournehills among them he didn't see Vere.

He had just about decided to go and wait for him around by the Opel, which was parked with the other vehicles from Bournehills on the side of the stadium leading out of town, when suddenly he saw him burst from the very center of the Twenty-sixth of July Guerrilla Band which was charging in a violent group toward the exit. For a moment Allen didn't recognize him. He knew it was Vere. There, unmistakably, was the face with its pronounced bones, lightly sketched-in features and solidly dark skin. And he was wearing the Osnaburg which was soaked through. But he looked different, transformed. There was a boldness to his eye and smile which Allen had never seen before. And he was bringing his foot down in the reckless stomping dance as if laying claim to every square inch of ground he touched. And whereas Allen had never seen him with a woman, but was used to his always being alone, like himself (and this was one of the things that had drawn him to Vere in the beginning), he saw him approaching now with two girls from the guerrilla band on each side.

The three of them came dancing wildly toward him, the girls waving the cardboard machetes that were part of their costumes, and Vere with his arms around their waists.

"Man, I was looking all over for you," he said as they came up—and there was the same boldness in his voice and manner as in his eyes. "I got someone who wants to meet you." And turning to the larger of the girls he said, "Elvita, this is my friend Allen from America I was telling you about. Allen, Elvita."

The girl he drew over was no more than nineteen, but she had the full-blown body and bearing of a much older woman. Under the olive-drab uniform her hips curved wide from the waist: they would provide a strong cradle, a secure place for the children she would bear. Her thighs had stretched the cloth of her trousers taut. And her breasts, rising assertively beneath the army jacket she wore, had pushed the pleats on the high pockets out of place. Her face was broad, plain, and pleasant, and the same light buff color as Sugar's, the silent proprietor of the nightclub at the end of Whitehall Lane, so that like him, she seemed a blending, a coming together and canceling out of a whole spectrum of color.

"Pleased to make your acquaintanceship, Allen," she said, her smile, as she held out her hand, revealing a front tooth rimmed in gold. Gold-plated hoop earrings swung from her ears under her leaf-covered helmet, and the fingers of both her hands—the pinky, middle finger and thumb—were studded with rings of imitation gold. Gifts they might have been from an endless procession of suitors who had come seeking her favors.

Allen, flashing Vere a confused, questioning look, stammered a greeting, and the girl laughed—but gently, good-naturedly, a laugh which said she knew the effect she had on those meeting her for the first time, and sympathized with them.

"Come," she said, holding out a ringed hand, "let's not miss the Last Lap." And before he could object or, with his little diffident smile, excuse himself, she had drawn his arm through hers and was holding it firmly against her side, linking him to her and in turn to Vere and his companion, who were on her other side; and he suddenly found himself—he who had never danced before in his life—being hauled into the mob driving toward the exit while doing the exuberant jump-up dance.

He would have fallen any number of times and perhaps been trampled to death, had it not been for the firm grip the girl maintained on his arm. Stumbling along at her side, his feet in a tangle under him, he saw up ahead the tall gate standing open to the night. They reached it and were about to pass through into the street when there was a sudden massive shove from behind as those in back, catching sight of the gate, pressed toward it all at once, and he was thrown violently forward. Again he would have gone down had it not been for the girl. But his head pitched sharply forward at the impact, so sharply his glasses flew off. It was as though a hand had reached out and snatched them off, it happened so quickly. For a shocked second he didn't even realize they were gone until he heard, faintly, beneath the uproar, the sound of thin glass being ground underfoot and felt the heavy night air against his naked face.

He began yelling, then, and trying to force his way back through the crowd: "My glasses! Hey, wait a minute, my glasses! Vere, my glasses got knocked off! *Vere!*"

It was several seconds before Vere, on Elvita's other side, heard him and looked around. But by the time he took in what had happened and also, instinctively, made as if to fight his way back to the gate to search for the glasses, the crowd had swept them well down the path, away from the Oval.

"Man, it's no use," Vere said. "Those things are gone. We'd never find them back there. They're done mash up under all these feet. Do you maybe have an extra pair?" He had drawn them out of the hurtling throng and they were standing, the four of them, in the parking area outside the Oval's high curving wall, with a frantic, almost weeping Allen struggling to pull away from them and return to the gate.

"Of course, I've got an extra pair!" He heard himself shouting and didn't care. "But what good does that do? They're all the way in Bournehills." And the anger he felt with Vere, whom he blamed for the loss of the glasses (it was he, wasn't it, who had brought over the girl?), was heightened by the realization of how distant and inaccessible at the moment was that other pair.

"Well, the ones you had are gone, lick up, that's for certain," the girl Elvita said when he had calmed somewhat. "But at least you have a next pair, so there's no need to let it upset you and spoil what's left of carnival. Besides, you won't have any calling for spectacles tonight." She was still holding him firmly by the arm.

"Yes," the other girl, whose name was Milly, said. She was as strongly built as Elvita, but shorter and dark, Vere's color. "You mustn't let it spoil the rest of the fete for you. People are always losing things at carnival."

Vere also joined in urging him to forget his loss and enjoy the balance of the evening. He would see for them both, he said with a smile that sought to restore him.

It was then decided (Vere making the decision) that they would forgo the Last Lap and instead, taking his car, go somewhere quiet for the traditional last drink that ended the two-day spree.

And so, after what seemed a long time during which he was led, still completely unstrung, around to the side of the stadium where the cars from Bournehills were parked, Allen found himself seated in the back of the Opel (literally placed there like an invalid) with the girl's leg (those thighs that, locked around a man's back, would put him to the test) touching his and his arm still pinned to her side. He didn't dare open his eyes, not all the way at any rate, because without his glasses, the background—that is, everything at a distance—dropped out of his vision, and as it did, those things close to hand: objects and people, the whole bewildering welter of life, would come rushing in at him, everything blown out of proportion, distorted, inescapable; and he would be unable then to deal with the world in the way he preferred, in the abstract, at a remove. He swore silently at Vere and drew farther into his corner of the seat.

They drove to a board-and-shingle house in the squalid back streets behind the business district where the girl Milly had a room. It wasn't much larger than the room in the Heights where Vere's former girl friend lived, but it, in contrast, was neat and uncluttered and scrupulously clean. The floor had been scoured pale gray with sand and white lime, the sidings painted pink to hide the water stains and blemishes in the wood; and the only article of clothing to be seen was the maid's uniform Milly wore at the hotel where she worked, draped neatly, ready for tomorrow, over a folding screen that divided the room in two. Her bed stood out of sight behind the screen, while the front part of the room facing the road which she had made into a sitting area was entirely taken up by a secondhand Morris settee and armchair. Jammed in between them was the inevitable small mahogany center table with its vase of wax antirrhinum lilies set on a plastic doily. On the wall facing the settee hung a photograph of her two children, a boy and girl about the age of the Clough children, who she said lived with relatives in the country. She went to see them once a week on her day off, she said in answer to a question from Vere.

Under the sober gaze of the children, Vere and the two girls continued the carnival celebration long after the midnight curfew. Allen, huddled in one corner of the settee with Elvita beside him, Milly at the other end and Vere seated across from them in the armchair, only dimly heard their voices. Not even the loud bursts of laughter that rang out from time to time or the sharp rap of the rum bottle as they replaced it on the table fully penetrated the fog that had settled over his mind, brought on by his shock over the glasses and the accumulated exhaustion of the day which had finally overtaken him. And when he himself spoke, muttering he knew not what to the questions they asked him in their efforts to draw him into the talk, his own voice sounded muffled, distant.

He still couldn't get over Vere. Squinting painfully, afraid to open his eyes more than a crack lest their faces overwhelm him, he kept staring at him in numbed disbelief from under his drawn lids. Vere reared back in the armchair, his legs crossed and hands gesturing strongly, was regaling the girls with stories of his experiences in

America. His bold, self-assured voice filled the room, and his laugh when it broke, joining that of the girls, seemed to drown for a moment the light of the kerosene lamp. He was tossing down the small glasses of rum Milly handed him with all the expertise suddenly of the men at Delbert's. Where was the diffidence and uncertainty that had kept him—kept them both—standing outside the door of the Spiretown social center at the Saturday night dances?

Allen couldn't understand the change in him. It seemed part of the whole surreal character of the night. Vere, this changed, barely recognizable Vere, whose occasional smile his way urged him to relax and accept what the night had to offer; the cramped room in which they were sitting with the bed on the other side of the folding screen (Allen could feel its awesome presence behind the partition: it was like an altar which only those who had been fully initiated could approach); the girl at his side hedging him in with her thigh; and before, the swift ride through the darkened town with the sounds of the Last Lap—the roar of voices and steel drums—reaching them faintly from Queen Street, and the final unreality which had seen him being dragged along in the midst of the rampaging crowd and his glasses lost—it was all like part of a nightmare from which he could not awaken. He felt the protective fog over his mind deepen and a paralysis began to weigh his limbs; and as he sat there slowly giving way he told himself none of it had happened and he and Vere—the old Vere—were really alone in the Opel driving back to Spiretown over the dark friendly hills.

In his stricken state he was unaware of time passing. At one point he vaguely noticed through the top half of the door which had been left open that the moon had risen, a huge, pitted, round-faced moon with empty sockets for eyes. But he could not have said at what point Vere and the girl Milly disappeared behind the screen. He only discovered they were gone when Elvita beside him abruptly sat around and addressed him, alarming him so he roused and glancing up saw the two empty places. At that, a fear he had not felt since the last time he had been with a woman, sometime ago now, seemed to wind itself around his heart, binding it up, squeezing the blood from it as the thorns had done the sacred heart in the pictures which had filled his boyhood, and he fled, leaving his body behind.

"So you're from big America, eh?" Elvita was saying, the bit of gold around her tooth drawing the light to it as she smiled. "I tell you, that's one place I'd like to see before I close my eyes on this life.

I wish they had a farm labor scheme for women. Not that I've ever worked in a cane field. Oh, no, I'm strictly a town person. But I think I'd even be willing to head canes like any country woman for a chance to see the place. You hear so much about it, especially New York. I'd like to see there just once. Tell me, is it really as big-time and fast and pretty as they say . . . ?" She didn't wait for an answer, but musing aloud to herself, her eyes abstracted, continued, "Yes, just once, before breath leaves the body. You know, they're saying over here is getting just like New York—fast and with everybody out to make an easy dollar. But how could any small island be like New York?" She laughed scornfully, causing the gold hoops at her ears to tremble.

"I was to Trinidad once," she went on, "and even though that's a big-time place, and plenty fast, too, I know it's nothing like New York. Oh, yes, I was in Trinidad for upward to five years," she said as though he had asked her the question. "My mother sent me when I was fourteen to learn needlework with an aunt of mine lives there. I used to be all about Port-of-Spain . . . "

She spoke quietly then for some time about her life in Trinidad, telling him—her voice low against the murmurous voices on the other side of the screen—about her difficulties with her aunt, her dislike of needlework and the various jobs she had held after abandoning that. She had worked, she said, as a nursemaid for a number of well-to-do creole families in Port-of-Spain, then briefly as a stock clerk in Woolworth's. And she had had a child. "Yes," she said matter-of-factly, "I butt up on this boy friend over there and get a baby quick so. You know how it is. It's with his mother in Trinidad. But I'm looking to improve myself," she said with a strong nod. "Oh, yes. All I need is a chance, somebody to help me, and then watch Elvita move! You wouldn't know it's the same person. I'm hoping maybe to get a job at a hotel like Milly, because even though the pay is slight, I understand you can sometimes make good money in tips if the tourists take a liking to you. Tell me, do you know any of the people who run the hotels about here, Allen?"

This time she waited for an answer, sitting facing him on the settee, her eyes steady and expectant in the mild neutral beige of her face. Feeling the quiet insistence of that gaze, he slowly, after a time, shook his head.

"Well, that's too bad," she said, "because maybe you could have put in a word for me. You know it's all who you know in this life that counts." She laughed. Then, with something of the laugh lingering warmly in her voice she said, "You know it's a shame you have to wear spectacles because you have a nice set of eyes. They're the first thing I noticed about you when we was introduced. Some girl would be glad for them. What color do you call them?" She didn't seem to mind when he failed to answer. Instead, placing a hand on his hair which, brushed flat that morning, had rebelled over the course of the day and was now a tumble of dark curls, she said, "And you got some pretty Portuguese hair." With that she suddenly bent close and bringing her face up under his, kissed him on the corner of the mouth.

It was an awkward kiss, so that for all her boldness and experience she seemed as unschooled in these matters as Allen, as innocent. But she offered it, clumsy and inexpert though it was, in the same friendly manner in which she had offered him her hand upon being introduced. Holding him lightly by the shoulder, she kept her mouth on his, recognizing perhaps that it would take some time to rouse him. The kiss, the caresses that would follow, even the final embrace that would see their bodies joined and moving almost of their own will upon the settee's hard cushions were all, as far as she was concerned, it was clear, simply part of the carnival celebration, the fitting end to the two-day fete, nothing more. Her kiss said he should accept it in the same spirit.

In the place to which he had fled, far from the surface of his body, out of her reach, Allen scarcely felt the mouth against his or the hand on his shoulder. Rather, he was remembering, in the small portion of his mind that was still functioning (the memories coming in little fitful snatches that were like part of the continuing nightmare of the evening), other encounters such as this, all of which had ended badly, as this one would. Because greater than any desire he had ever felt for them (and not even desire so much as a passing curiosity) had been, first of all, his distaste: their bodies, it had always struck him, lacked purity of line with the up-jutting breasts and buttocks, the suffocating softness; and secondly his fear, borne of a recurrent phantasy of his as a boy, that once he entered that dark place hidden away at the base of their bodies, he would not be able to extricate himself but would be caught, trapped, condemned to a life-and-death struggle there for which he sensed he was ill-equipped.

Remembering how that fear used to seize him at night, driving him deeper under the bed covers, he shivered. Elvita, seeing in it another meaning, laughed softly, and getting up began removing the more cumbersome parts to her costume: the cartridge belt and heavy combat boots, the helmet, and loosening the uniform.

The kerosene lamp had died, and the moon, looking like a giant floodlight that in its sweep back and forth across the sky had come to rest on the house, was sending a broad band of molten light into the room through the top open half of the door. As the girl sat back down, half-reclining now beside Allen on the settee, the moonlight could have been a bedsheet she had drawn in sudden modesty over herself—over the breasts spread like gentle knolls, dark crested and carefully shaped, above the wide plain of her belly and the legs sheathed in the skintight trousers. Drawn up at the knee, the thighs slightly parted, those legs were like the portals to some imposing house.

She first talked to him for a time, again keeping her voice low in deference to the two inside. Then, when he made no move to touch her, but remained slumped in the chair, she took one of his hands and placed it within the open neck of her jacket.

Long minutes passed. They could hear Vere and the girl Milly laughing softly behind the screen. They sounded like children who had just, between them, invented an amusing new game.

Finally she spoke. "What's wrong, yes?" Her voice in the moonlit darkness was puzzled, solicitous. She tried to see his face but it was bent too low.

She again waited, and this time, holding his inert hand to her, she leaned up and once more sought his mouth. But it was like kissing someone dead, whose still warm but lifeless body had been brought and placed in a sitting position in the corner of the settee. An even longer period elapsed, and then in the sudden silence that had fallen in both halves of the room, the bed inside could be heard, an unmistakable sound which said that the time for the laughter and talk had passed, and the more formal rite had begun.

Had Allen been able to feel, if his nerve endings hadn't gone dead in the massive short-circuiting that swept him, he perhaps would have felt Elvita suddenly go very still and tense. And in the next moment she was flinging away his hand in disgust, and on her feet now, hissing furiously down at him, "But what the hell's wrong with you? You's a damn he-she or what?"

She began dressing then, stamping into the boots, clapping the helmet back on her head, and, savagely, in her anger and hurt, rebuttoning the jacket. And all the while she complained in an old woman's bitter, aggrieved and cruel voice, "But look at my crosses this Carnival Tuesday night, yes! Look what I let Milly get me into! A man that don't know the meaning of the word. Somebody that don't seem to have no uses a-tall a-tall for women; that acts like he's frightened for them or some damn thing . . . All you do the man wouldn't budge. Why, you'd think something was wrong with you the way he gets on, that you don't have no kinda looks or not little personality . . . I tell yuh—" she paused in the midst of buckling on the cartridge belt, "he's like somebody born without natural feelings. Or if he had any, something or somebody took them away . . . No feelings a-tall . . . But I wonder if all them in America is like him . . . Well, if so, I never want to set eyes on the blasted place. They can keep it!"

Fully dressed, cardboard machete in hand, she strode to the door, yanked the bottom half open, and then just before stepping out into the night swung back to face the room. Poised there, the helmet with its disguise of leaves like the silhouette of some fanciful crown against the moonlight, her many rings flashing, she started to shout some further insult at him. But remembering perhaps the two inside and respectful still of their pleasure, she stopped herself; and instead, suddenly raising the long knife very high, brought it sweeping down in a blow that severed in two the moonlight at the doorway, and was gone.

The angry martial tread of her boots in the empty street was a long time dying. And when, finally, the footsteps faded and the early Ash Wednesday morning silence returned, other sounds which had gone unnoticed by Allen before became suddenly, inescapably, clear: the sounds of the new lovers behind the screen—the soft, almost self-absorbed murmuring of the girl, Vere's silence, which was a sound in itself, the bed moving to their rhythm, by turns slow then swift; and somewhere in the darkness within the ticking of a clock.

Allen, immobilized on the settee, brought his arms up over his head in an effort to block out the sounds. But it was useless, because with his ears covered, they entered his body through the pores of his skin. So that all he could do while the paralysis held him was to sit helplessly by listening to the two inside with something of the wonder, rage and despair he had felt as a child watching the adults in his world perform feats that were beyond his small powers. Worse, he not only heard them but saw them after a time, the scene looming so clear in his mind's eye it was as if the moonlight flooding the room had burned away the panels of the folding screen to reveal them on the bed. The girl was faceless, unimportant, but he saw Vere clearly: his dark body rising and falling, advancing and retreating, like one of the powerful Bournehills waves they sometimes rode together in the early evening.

Suddenly, caught between that vivid scene and the sounds building swiftly toward a climax, he felt something as powerful well up in him, a wave of feeling and desire so awesome that before he could resist it, fight it off, it had sent him sliding face down onto the settee, where, on the lumpy cushions that were still warm from Elvita's body, he performed alone, with only his own sore and tormented body to hold, the act taking place behind the screen.

His cry at the end, which he tried to stifle but could not, broke at the same moment the girl uttered her final cry, and the two sounds rose together, blending one into the other, becoming a single complex note of the most profound pleasure and release—pleasure so intense it seems almost pain, a rending and effacing of the self.

Their cry held for a long time in the night silence. Even after he had leaped up from the settee and rushed from the house he heard it. It trailed him as he staggered without direction through the labyrinthine back streets and alleys toward the center of town. (And at each dark corner he thought he spied Elvita waiting with her machete poised.) Something of its echo even lingered when he finally reached Queen Street, completely deserted now except for the glass and paper refuse of carnival to be seen everywhere. And in his altered vision, to his overturned mind, the bits and pieces of glass lying amid the litter were the shattered lenses of his glasses glinting in the moonlight.

Much later that morning Saul and Merle found him asleep in the back of the Bentley over at the Sports Oval, his knees drawn up tight against his chest, arms wound around his head and his face buried in the worn cushion of the seat as though to shut out the sunlight pouring in at the window.

CHAPTER 5

"Well, what did you think of our little two-penny carnival?" Merle asked, turning to Saul in the dark street.

It was shortly after midnight and they were headed, just the two of them, over to Sugar's, where the celebration was scheduled to go on until dawn. Around them the streets were deserted, all the revelers, except those who had gone on to Sugar's, having disappeared almost magically as the bells of the Anglican cathedral struck twelve. But they might have left their ghosts behind to carry on the fete for them, because New Bristol continued to reverberate with the loud echoes of their feet and voices. The dust borne aloft over the course of the day still weighed the air. The two walking felt it suspended like a low cloud cover above the roofs.

After talking with Harriet on the phone Saul had gone in search of Merle. She would be remaining in town overnight, he knew, to attend a large breakfast party Dorothy Clough and her husband were giving in the morning (he and Harriet had been invited but weren't going: he had never forgiven the man for his article on the project) and he wanted to arrange for her to pick them up in the Bentley at Lyle's after the party. (His own car was being used to transport people back to Bournehills.) He had found her after the final jump-up outside the Sports Oval busy seeing off the Bournehills band which was about to start the long trip back, the line of cars, bicycles, donkey carts and the tired float being led this time by the bus with the noisy outriders of the morning asleep on the laps of the women inside. She had agreed to call for them after the Cloughs' party. They had both been on their way to Sugar's—Merle to pay her respects, as she always did, Saul to see carnival through to the end, so that when the last of the band had departed and the only vehicle remaining outside the Oval was her battered Bentley, they had set out together on foot across the empty town, leaving the car behind.

"I asked what did you think of carnival?"

"Yes, I heard you," he said, and continued in his abstracted silence. He had been thinking, as they slowly picked their way amid the shards of broken bottles and strewn trash on the streets, of the day's events and of Harriet. He was worried that her encounter with the band from the Heights had been more serious than she was admitting, and he was assailed by guilt. He should have kept a closer watch on her during the march; he shouldn't have allowed her to take part in the parade in the first place. And he was more than a little disturbed by her manner on the phone, the remoteness in her voice, her unwillingness to tell him in any detail what had happened, her definitely stated desire that he not come up.

"I don't know," he said, answering Merle's question finally—and he might have also been expressing his bafflement at Harriet, her essential secrecy, those things about her he would never understand. "I can't really say what I thought about carnival because I didn't get to see that much of it; the other bands, that is, and what was going on in the other streets. I was too busy watching Bournehills."

"Well, what did you think of our little show, then?"

There was another silence; then, his hands opening in a gesture which said he doubted he could adequately describe his impressions, he spoke. "It said it all. That's the only way I can express it, Merle. It just said it all. First, the long silent march at the beginning which told you better than all the words in the world what it must have been like back then for your people—and for mine, for that matter, all those centuries. Because it made me think of them, too. And then the scene between Stinger and Ferguson on the float. That really said it all. I must confess I felt a little uncomfortable watching it, its meaning for me and my kind was so clear, which only goes to prove I guess that one never really completely disavows anything." He made the confession in the same pared-down unembellished manner in which he was speaking.

"But that was it, today up there on the float," he went on. "The way it will probably have to be. It's sad a man can't win his right to live through reasoning with those on top, peacefully in other words. But it doesn't seem possible. History has more often than not proved that.

"And today said something else to me." He stopped short, and beside him Merle also came to a halt and turning, waited, watching him closely in the light of the moon which was rising very slowly, almost as if it were being hauled up by a pulley, above the jagged roofs of the Heights silhouetted against the sky like the remains of a bombed-out city.

"It's that people," he began, moving forward again, "who've truly been wronged—like yours, like mine all those thousands of years—must at some point, if they mean to come into their own, start using their history to their advantage. Turn it to their own good. You begin, I believe, by first acknowledging it, all of it, the bad as well as the good, those things you can be proud of such as, for instance, Cuffee's brilliant coup, and the ones most people would rather forget, like the shame and ignominy of that long forced march. But that's part of it, too. And then, of course, you have to try and learn from all that's gone before—and again from both the good and the bad—especially that! Use your history as a guide, in other words. Because many times, what one needs to know for the present—the action that must be taken if a people are to win their right to live, the methods to be used: some of them unpalatable, true, but again, there's usually no other way—has been spelled out in past events. That it's all there if only they would look. . . ."

"Well said." Merle spoke quietly, but without really committing herself. Her eyes hadn't left his face. "You're probably the only one in the whole of New Bristol today who saw more in our little show than just show."

It was so rare that she paid him anything even remotely resembling a compliment that he smiled, although he didn't feel like it. "I tried telling you once I wasn't completely hopeless," he said.

There was a silence broken only by the sound of their footsteps and the accompanying echo across the street. And then he was leaning down to her from his considerable height. "Another thing," he said—and in the light of the street lamp under which they were passing a frown could be seen cutting into the smooth stretched skin of his forehead—"which I haven't ever spoken to you about, although I've wanted to, is that for the past couple of months I've had the feeling I'm not seeing all there is to Bournehills. Something important seems to be eluding me. I've been more than a little troubled about it. Whatever it is has nothing to do with the research as such; it's just something I sense about the place, some meaning that suggests itself which I need to track down if only for my own personal satisfaction. Well, this today—the masque about Cuffee and the revolt—seemed in some way connected with that. For the first time I felt as though I might understand someday. . . ."

Reaching up, he passed a hand over his forehead as if to banish the frown; he gave an embarrassed laugh. "You know I'm beginning to suspect that what Bournehills needs is one of those old-fashioned soothsayers or diviners, somebody whose business is dealing in mysteries, not some poor half-assed anthropologist who's supposed to be concerned only with what's real."

Merle's eyes in the strengthened light of the moon were veiled, her expression as noncommittal as before. It suggested, though, that even if she knew what it was he was seeking she wouldn't say, that he would have to come to it on his own. So that with a laugh that made light of his suspicions, she said, "It's the sun. It's walking about in that Bournehills hot sun every day without a hat on your head. That's enough to start anybody imagining all sorts of things. If you know what's good for you, you'll take some of the multimillions George Clough swears you've got and buy yourself a hat."

He laughed in spite of himself, wanting suddenly to believe it was nothing more than the sun; and cheered unreasonably by the thought he took her arm as they crossed the street to Whitehall Lane, where Sugar's stood at the very end of the long finger of land pointing out to sea.

He was still chuckling to himself, his hand on her elbow as they mounted the dim stairs to the nightclub on the second floor of the old sugar warehouse and, some claimed, former barracoon. As always, the stone walls gave off a faint smell of muscovado and what could have well been the older, fainter exhalation of dark flesh, its essence distilled over the centuries and locked into the stone.

They were met at the top by Sugar seated on his high stool behind the bar facing the entrance, his shrunken form dwarfed by the enormous cash register he tended and his face hidden by the newspaperman's green eyeshade he always wore. Under the visor his gaze was trained on the nothingness that absorbed him utterly, making him oblivious to the carnival diehards packing the room and the celebration that was continuing unabated.

Someone had hung a string of carnival beads around his neck and Merle, as she leaned across the bar to kiss him, said, "Ah, Sugar, I see even you've got on your Juju beads tonight."

The eyes did not acknowledge her, but from somewhere within the blasted frame came the thrilling, deep-voiced monosyllabic "Yeah . . . !"—the only sound he ever uttered, which was charged with all meaning.

"What do you know about Juju?" Saul said when, after fighting their way through the crush inside the club onto the balcony, they found an empty table partially hidden behind one of the tall jalousied doors opening out from the room. Around them the overflow crowd from inside was doing the same unrelenting jump-up as at the Oval earlier, causing the floor to shudder under their chairs.

"How you mean!" she cried. "Remember I was once married to an African—still am, I suppose—and even though he was a scientist like yourself he nevertheless had a healthy respect for the unscientific. He knew man didn't live by technology alone, which is something people up your way need to learn. Besides, I told you I'm nothing but an old obeah woman myself."

She was suddenly in a gay mood, sparked probably by the high mood of the crowd dancing almost up against their table. Because she was going to the Cloughs' party in the morning she had exchanged the drab Osnaburg for one of her vivid print dresses, and with the light from inside the club heightening the colors and setting off a glow like that of the sun in her eyes and dark cheeks, she looked young.

"No," he said, entering into her mood, "you, Madam, are a confirmed Christian and faithful Anglican who never misses six o'clock service on Sunday mornings and tea with the rector on Wednesdays."

"Right," she said. "And before I go to this big breakfast do at the Cloughs in the morning I'll make it my business to stop in the nearest church to collect my share of the ashes. But then I'm a Jew, too." She grinned as his eyebrows went up in a show of surprise. "You didn't know that, did you? A better one than you probably. Because I'm also waiting on a messiah. No Jesus meek and mild though. No thanks. We've had enough of him. We need a tough somebody this time. Another Cuffee. And why do you think the guesthouse faces east?"

"Not Mecca!"

"What else but!" Their laughter rose against the background din, and a few people nearby glanced their way. "And what do you think I'm doing when I disappear for days at a time in my room?"

"I've no idea. I've often wondered, but I've no idea."

"Practicing a little Buddhism, that's what. Trying my best to achieve that peace which they say passes all understanding. And I'm as good a Hindu as any. At Holi you're likely to see me walking the roads sprinkling red water over everyone and ringing a bell. Oh, yes, I've got all the various Jujus covered. One of them, you see, might just be it; and I don't believe in taking chances!"

She uttered her familiar sharp hoot at the expression on his face, which said that although he was used to her by now, used to her way, he still wasn't quite sure how to take her at times. "No," she said, "there's no figuring me out. Let's just say I'm slightly daft. Mad-Merle as Enid and the ladies in town call me behind my back. And parading about in the hot sun all day has made matters worse. It's really set out my head. Carnival has gotten to me. Cheers!" She held up the drink one of the little bony, sullen-faced waitresses in the gossamer shifts had set in front of them as soon as they sat down.

"Oh, Merle," he said, and raising his glass touched it to hers.

She held up a warning hand. "Mind your tone," she said, "or you'll find yourself declaring your affections again."

He smiled, thinking of the Sunday morning that had just passed: the sodden bag of pork in his hand, the unbecoming hat she had had on, the children on their way to Sunday school who looked to be walking out of the round mouth of the sun. "I loved everyone that morning, come to think of it," he said. "I was full of love."

"And rum," she added. "You were good and salt. I tell you, you seem determined to become as big a rummy as anyone in Bournehills . . ." Then, a speculative note sounding in her voice, she said, "But maybe that's how it has to be." She was suddenly serious. "Maybe if someone like yourself, someone from Away, as we put it, ever really hopes to understand us, he has to become a little like us, slightly mad as people in town say we are and as you were sounding on our way over here; and taking his rum regularly. Rum's our elixir of life in Bournehills, did you know that? Oh, yes," she declared, and there was no telling now whether she was serious. "You might say we're preserved in the bloody stuff down there. The whole place. Preserved." She drank from her glass.

"You mentioned your husband's a scientist. What's his field?" he asked as they set down their glasses amid the ringed imprints of all the other glasses that had rested on the table. He had been waiting to ask the question.

She looked at him, then smiled. He imagined he could see the tiny muscles around her lips, beneath the dark skin there, slowly shaping the smile that usually came flashing out like a knife blade to hold him at bay.

"You don't intend giving up, do you?" she said. "You mean to get in my business if it's the last thing you do. But you're wasting your time because you'll never put me through one of your interviews. Oh, no, there'll be no data out of me tonight." She was still smiling though. She hadn't cut him off with the harsh look as at the almshouse that time.

"I'm not working," he said. "I've quit for the night."

"You're always working," she said. "Always collecting data. You think I don't know that. And you could get a stone to tell you its life history. I don't know how you do it." She thought about this a moment; then, her eyes narrowing suspiciously, "Unless maybe you're something of a Juju man yourself. Yes," she cried, laughing, her forefinger impaling him. "That must be it. You're an old obeah man, too, in your way. And don't think I haven't seen you up to your tricks. I've watched you work your magic. First you fix the informant, as you call him, with those eyes that look almost blind at times, then give him that half-sad smile of yours as if to say, 'Well, what to do, yes? We're all pretty much in the same boat, man. Life ain't shite,' and, by God, you've got his will. The poor fellow's willing to tell you his all. Oh, I've watched you operate. But that abracadabra won't work with me, bo, because I've got my protection against the likes of you. This for one"—she held up the cigarette she was smoking. The smoke, eating into the dimness behind the half-opened door where their table was situated, created a white wavering wall between them. "Smoke is one of the best protections against any form of obeah, we believe in Bournehills. These for another." She shook the noisy bracelets covering nearly her entire forearm. "Their racket is enough to keep the devil himself away."

"And I'm the devil, I suppose."

"Questions and more questions." (She hadn't heard him.) "You never run short. And yet scarcely a word from you about yourself. The poor informant must tell you his life story from A to Zed, everything—whether he actually owns the little cane piece he works on the side, if the woman he's living with is his lawful wife, what he thinks about government, when was the first time he had sex, everything, while you stay mum, your business to yourself. You know what," she cried, the finger fixed him again, "somebody needs to interview you for a change."

"All right, all right!" he cried, laughing, his arms raised in surrender. "Why don't you? You interview me. No, I mean it," he said as she started to turn away. "Interview me. I'm game. Ask anything you'd like. Who knows, if you're good I might add you to the team. We could use another researcher. Go ahead. Let's see how you'd do."

"All right." She declared—and she was prompt with her question: she might have prepared it months ago. "To go back, what made you take up this line of work in the first place?"

For a moment he could only stare at her in open-mouthed disbelief before the laughter convulsed him again. "Good God, woman, the way you put things! 'This line of work'? Why, you make me sound like a goddamn ladies-wear salesman. You have absolutely no reverence, do you know that. None!" He was almost shouting at her.

"But it's a good question." He had sobered. He remained silent for a time, his thoughtful gaze, his face with the singularly colorless skin reflecting the steady parade of varicolored lights from the globe-shaped fixture inside the club. Across the table Merle waited.

"Well, you already know," he began finally, "about my early disenchantment with my own country so I needn't go into that. And it's not that I gave up without a try. I was something of a radical in my youth, as were any number of people I knew then. We had committed ourselves either to reforming the system, really reforming it, or failing that, replacing it altogether. We didn't get very far with either, I'm afraid. The old juggernaut just kept going its way, committing its sins and crushing anyone foolish enough to try and stop it, as it did, in one way or another, many I knew. I certainly didn't want to be crushed. Nor, could I, for some reason, make the necessary accommodation, as did most of the people I started out with. Nor could someone of my temperament take living in a place where you felt so powerless to do anything all of the time. And so I knew—

not in any conscious way—but I knew I'd have to find work that would permit me to get out and stay out.

"But that was only part of it." He spoke after a pause, his gaze on the dancers walling them in, but not seeing them. "I didn't choose anthropology simply as an escape hatch, even though that's often said of us. But then we're not only the butt of many a joke but a convenient symbol, it seems, of Western man's alienation and disaffection. It's a hell of a burden. No, it's what I truly wanted to do—and especially my end of it, which insists on using research as the basis for practical programs to help improve people's lives. Maybe this means I'm just a wet-eyed do-gooder at heart—as has been said. Or, even less flattering, that I'm out to play God on a minor scale by thinking I can come into a place and do so much. And maybe there's something in that, I don't know. I don't pretend to understand all my motives. But it's what I wanted to do. And I'm good at it. In the field, that is. Not the classroom. I've never liked teaching. And I'm no great theoretician, even though I can throw around the jargon with the best of them if I have to. But I'm good in the field. I love the challenge of it. It gives me the sense of doing work which matters for something—if only for very little, given the present unhappy state of things, and I've always needed that.

"But I've left the more personal reasons perhaps for the last."

"And what're those?" Her voice was quiet. The solemn-faced saints framing her face reflected her stillness and attention.

"I don't know if I can say it so it sounds right."

"Try."

"Well, two things," he began. "First, from a boy I was always interested in that whole other world beyond mine. Maybe it was because my mother, who was something of a character, was forever talking about South America. Part of her family had come from there long ago, and she had a long story, most of it made up, that she used to tell all the time. Anyway, I wanted to know and be a part of that world out there—which I'm afraid very early made me something of a traitor to my own little closed-in world and perhaps in a way to my own people. My father's eyes, I remember, when he sometimes looked at me, said as much. But I was determined to break out, and he knew it.

"The other thing is that being what I am, a professional wanderer if you will, I've had the chance to live and be with people I would otherwise never have gotten to know, people of different colors and cultures. And to live and be with them on a decent human level, in situations where, by and large, the color of a man's skin isn't the first damn thing you notice about him, and the whole sick business of race doesn't infect the very air as it does in America. That's meant a great deal to me. Proof of it perhaps is that the most meaningful relationships in my life have been with people outside my own country. Why, just imagine"—he broke out in a smile—"if I had stayed home I probably would have never met one Merle Kinbona, and what a loss that would have been."

There was no answering smile on her part. She was the scrupulously objective, impersonal interviewer.

"Does that," he said, "answer your question as to why I took up this line of work?"

"In part," she said. "Now about Bournehills. Why did you decide to take the job here?"

His eyes met hers with complete candor. "Well," he said, "I had left off doing field work for a time for a number of reasons, and this was a way of starting in again. The other thing is that it sounded like the kind of large-scale, long-range project I'd wanted to do for years. But I don't know, now that I'm here, dear Merle, whether I'm up to it." His look teased her, but he was frowning slightly. "Not the way things are going with me looking for all sorts of obscure meanings to the place, seeing smoke where there's no fire . . ."

"You've met your Waterloo." It was both a question and a statement of fact the way she said it.

"It would appear so. But I don't guess I can complain too much," he said. "I've had some good years. We—my first wife and I—covered a good part of Central and South America in our time, mostly doing straight research, but occasionally getting the money to do a small project somewhere. It was a very exciting period of my life. I was young, enthusiastic, full of big plans. The doubts and disillusionments peculiar to middle age hadn't set in yet. Oh, not that I didn't make my share of mistakes. I was a great one for dreaming up all kinds of grandiose projects which I could never get financed, not back then. I had to learn to lower my sights. But everything considered it wasn't a bad time. . . ."

There was a pause; then, his head lowered so that his eyes were hidden, he said, "The only disheartening thing, of course, is the thought that if I were to go back to any of those villages I worked in during that period I'd probably find everything the same, if not worse. What I tried to do was so little in the face of what's really needed. . . . Is the interview over, I hope?" he said looking up, the sadness brought on by the thought filming his eyes.

"No," she said. "What about your wife?"

"Harriet?"

"No, the one you just mentioned, the first."

"Oh." His gaze shied from hers. "Why do you ask?"

"It's all part of the interview," she said. "What about her?"

"What d'you mean, what about her?" he said, with a laugh that didn't quite mask the sudden discomfort and irritation he felt with her for having asked the question.

But Merle said nothing more, only continued to look at him through the smoke and dimness and noise separating them with a gaze both patient and unyielding.

"All right," he said finally. "There's not much to tell though. She was Polish. A Jew. We met in Warsaw, where I had gone after the war was over to see for myself if it was really true: the gas ovens and the Black Wall and the rest. Sosha—my wife—had just been released from the camp where she'd been interned for years. We were married and she worked with me in the field. She was also, to use your term again, in my line of work, although she never got to complete her formal training because of the war. She had only just started studying anthropology when the Nazis arrived. You could say though, I suppose, she completed her study of man under them. There was the number 538724 stamped into her flesh—on the inside of her left wrist, to be exact—to prove it." He spoke in the detached manner of someone ticking off the facts in a case record, his gaze turned aside. "Anyway, we made quite a team for awhile. Unfortunately, she died following a miscarriage while with me on a research study in Honduras some six years ago. It was just one of those things."

She waited, her impassive gaze on his face, her arms folded on the table. "Go on," she said.

"What d'you mean 'go on'? What else is there to say?" he cried with the irritable laugh.

She smiled, unperturbed. "You haven't told me the half."

To escape those shrewd, undeceived eyes, he picked up his glass, almost snatching it up in his annoyance, and took a deep swallow of the rum. The liquor calmed him somewhat and he slowly set the glass down again, trying to gain time by carefully fitting it back into the wet ring it had formed amid the dried ones on the table. His face remained stubbornly bent over it; but when he did finally look up his annoyance had been replaced by a dim, resigned half-smile.

"I don't know if I like being interviewed by you," he said.

"I didn't think you would," she said. "Go on."

He didn't begin immediately, but for a time absently watched the crowd blocking their view of the sea with their bodies and drowning out with their boisterous singing and talk the gentle slap of the water on the rocks below the balcony.

Then, his face partly averted, he spoke. "It's just that the whole thing was my fault, Merle," he said. "I had no business, first of all, dragging her with me all over the place all those years, forcing her to live under the worst conditions imaginable most of the time, when I knew her health was almost shot from her long stay in the camps. Even more important, I should have insisted when she finally became pregnant after years of our trying (we had about given up in fact) that she return to the States for the nine months or go stay in Tegucigalpa, the capital, so she'd at least be near the big hospital there. And I suggested as much, but she would have none of it. She would go to Tegucigalpa, she said, in her eighth month, but not before. I should have packed her off right then though. But at that point I was all involved in the study I was doing and I needed her help, so I didn't insist."

There was a pause. He drew a deep breath to steady himself. He began again. "And then when she was maybe four months gone it started. She had been working—No!" he savagely reversed himself. "I had been working her much too hard, and it started. And never stopped. The blood never stopped coming"—he spoke in a hoarse amazed voice, the pupils within the pale centers of his eyes suddenly contracting as though to shut out that remembered sight. "We were all the way in the back country, where the roads at that time of the year were impassable from the rains, so that by the time we managed to get to the nearest town that had something of a hospital two days later she had not only lost the baby but had already practically bled to death. The doctor there tried his best but it was no use. . . ."

His head dropped and across the way Merle could see the small nerve at his temples, at the place where his hair had begun its slow retreat, slowly, visibly, pulsing.

"To have survived Birkenau only to die trying to have one little baby in Honduras. That's a hell of a note, isn't it?" It was said with a faint, ironic and deeply bitter smile, which scarcely had any shape to it. With his head bowed Merle could barely make it out. "And she had so looked forward to having the baby. Because her big fear was that she might not be able to conceive because of certain experiments the Germans had carried out on her and other young women in the camps. Toward the end when the fever set in and she began talking out of her head she thought the baby was still inside her, alive and ready to be born, and she begged the doctor to do a Caesarean. And when he told her, of course, that he couldn't, that there wasn't any baby there anymore, she really started raving. She cursed him, the hospital, Honduras, everything and everybody. She cursed life itself. Why had something like this happened to her? Why had she been made to suffer so? What had she done? That's what she kept asking me over and over again, screaming it at me. And what could I tell her? What do you say to such questions . . . ?" His hands, abandoned on the table, lifted in a gesture eloquent of the helplessness he had felt. "There was nothing, no answers—none I knew of at any rate that made any sense. And when she realized I couldn't even come up with a lie that might've made it easier for her she turned on me, telling me things about myself she'd held back all the years we'd been together. She died like that, screaming the questions at me, cursing me for not being able to give her anything by way of an answer, telling me about myself. And telling me behind it all that it was my fault. Even after she had died," he whispered, his stricken voice ebbing away, "her eyes, I remember, kept on saying it had all been my fault. . . ."

Bowed in the chair, his large bones awry and his own eyes, which sometimes gave the impression that he was quietly weeping inside, because of their reddish tinge, looking more so now, he was staring at Merle but seeing only his dead wife. And for the first time ever he was mourning her as he had never permitted himself to do before—openly, unashamedly, his guilt and anguish undisguised. On the other side of the small table Merle quickly lowered her gaze. Even the balcony and the crowded nightclub beyond the open doors seemed to pause and look away in deference to his grief: the whirling globe of colored lights, the festal ring of the steelband, the massed dancers all coming to a halt, observing a moment's silence, then starting up again at their furious pitch.

"It just made no sense, Merle." His numb voice was more a part of the long silence than a sound; and although he had addressed Merle and was looking at her, his eyes were screened with that other face. "No fucking sense at all. I think that's what got me more than anything else . . . And not only did she die, and the child, but also, it seemed, some illusion I'd always held about myself and how much I could do. That suddenly was dead, too. It had been foolish of me to think I could really accomplish anything in a world so fucking senseless and unjust. I had been kidding myself. Sosha said as much when she was telling me off at the end. Maybe, as she said, I did have some puffed-up image of myself as a latter-day Moses come to deliver the poor and suffering of the world, including her, only to fail them. Oh, she let me have it, talking out of her head but making sense.

"I couldn't take it," he quietly confessed. "Neither her death nor all the things that hit me as a result. So I went into hiding. Left Honduras—just broke off the study I'd been doing and left; I stopped doing field work altogether and started teaching. But that was really a way of just hiding out. And I'd still be in hiding, I guess, had not for Harriet who decided, for God knows what reason, to try and put Humpty Dumpty back together again, patch him up"—he could barely manage the frayed smile. Then: "I'm very grateful to her. And for the chance to try my hand at some real work again in Bournehills.

"And yet, goddamn it"—it was a fierce cry, low-pitched, directed at himself—"even though I'm halfway together again: married, back doing the work I love, I've had the strangest feeling in recent weeks that I haven't really begun again, and that I won't until I've made up in some way for what happened back there in Honduras. It's as though," he said, shaking his head in wonderment, "I'm only now beginning to feel it all."

His eyes cleared, the face superimposed there receding, and he saw Merle. And he looked genuinely surprised at finding her across the table from him. Under the swift procession of lights reaching them through the jalousies in the door her face was as tragic as the tiny ones of the saints on her earrings.

"Oh, hell," he said. "I've spoiled your evening with all this talk," and reaching across made as if to touch her cheek: "All your lovely carnival glow's gone. I'm sorry. I shouldn't be going on about such sad things on such a gay night. But it's your fault. You're the one who insisted. I've even made poor old Mutt and Jeff look more mournful than usual," he said with an attempt at a laugh, trying to restore her mood.

"Who?" she said.

He pointed to the earrings. "Those were the names of two characters in my favorite comic strip as a boy. Your guardian saints remind me of them. I've often wondered," he added after a pause, "why you wear them all the time. I can understand the bracelets. All the women in Bournehills wear at least two or three of them. But why the earrings?"

She looked at him, her gaze level, her drawn face reflecting the sadness he had evoked in her. And she weighed him for some time with the look; then, abruptly, in a flat expressionless voice, she said, "As a reminder to be always on my guard against Greeks bearing gifts, that's why. Especially when the Greeks happen to be Englishwomen in disguise."

"That's all very obscure," he said, when it became clear she intended leaving it at that.

"Is it?" she said. "Well, if you must know"—this after another wait—"they were a present from a lady friend I had some years ago in England. She had them copied especially for me from the saints on the outside of Westminster Abbey when I told her of our hill of the same name. It was very thoughtful of her, don't you think? But then she was forever giving me little tokens of her affection and I, idiot that I was, was forever taking."

He knew better than to press her, and there followed a long, seemingly final silence during which she continued to take his measure with the gaze and her familiar self-protective smile. But finally she went on, speaking too casually somehow. "We were very close, my friend and I. I even lived with her for a time. I guess I was what you might call a kept woman. But I'm sure you've heard. If not, you're the only one around here who hasn't. My past has long been grist for the gossip mills of the island."

"I've heard," he said quietly, and then could not help smiling. "I really can't see you in the role, though. But then, for some reason, probably my male arrogance, I've never been able to take that kind of thing between women very seriously."

"Ha!" The sharp cut-off hoot struck the air like a gavel. "My lady friend should have heard you! She took it seriously, I can tell you. Damn seriously. I wasn't to realize how much so until she had done her worst."

"How is it you got involved with someone like that?"

She shrugged. The gesture, her matter-of-fact tone still attempting to make light of it all. "It just happened," she said. "She was the ringleader of a wild crowd I fell in with after giving up on school, and for some reason she took to me. It was one of those typical London sets where every and anything goes. You know when the English decide to kick up their heels they can make even the French cry shame. Nothing's beyond them. And they're experts at making anything they do seem perfectly natural, and getting you to think so, too. Anyway, my friend was boss of the the pack I was in. She was much older than the rest of us and the one with the money. Her family was one of those upper-class types you hear of over there who don't seem to mind having produced a degenerate or two and they gave her whatever she wanted. She mostly used the money to buy foolish people like me. She collected people the way someone else might paintings or books, the bitch.

"But I won't lie," she said, meeting his eye. "She was a help to me in the beginning. When I met her I didn't have a penny to my name because Ashton Vaughan, the man I'm supposed to call father, had stopped sending me money when he heard I had left school. He wanted me to come home, but I had vowed never to set foot on Bourne Island again while he was still alive. Well, she told me I could come and stay at her place in Hampstead until I got on my feet. She needed someone to look after her mail and such and I could do that. I was grateful—and, yes, I admit it, flattered. Good little brainwashed West Indian that I was, I thought it quite something to have a rich Englishwoman taking such an interest in me, an almshouse child, who couldn't even remember her mother and whose so-called father had for years passed her by on the road without so much as a word.

"So I went to stay with her. And it was really quite pleasant for awhile. I never wanted for anything. I got to meet all sorts of interesting people at her place. The house was always full up. And she went in strictly for foreigners (the English bored her, she said) and students: she liked us young. During the time I lived there I met people from every corner of the globe: India, Asia, Africa, Canada, Australia, Gibraltar, all over the place. The sun, you might say, never set on the little empire she had going in her drawing room. There was even—to give you an idea how international it was—one big Polynesian chap from Tonga, I remember. My lady friend loved him. He could come and stay for weeks. . . .

"Most of them who came around were in my same boat," she said after a pause. "We had come out to study and then for one reason or another didn't want to go home. There were quite a few like that in London then. We were forever taking courses but never actually managing to take our degrees, or making out we were artists—anything so as not to have to leave. And my friend didn't mind helping us out a bit. What was a meal or a bed for the night or a little money to someone like her? Besides, she knew that would keep us in her debt, and that, my dear, was what she was after.

"Yes"— she gave a solemn nod—"it took me a long time to realize it, but that's what the lady was up to. All her supposed generosity and kindness, all those thoughtful little presents she was always giving you, were meant to do one thing: keep you dependent—and grateful. Because then, you see, you'd always be around to amuse and entertain her. And she loved being entertained. There was nothing she enjoyed more than sitting up like some queen bee in that big drawing room of hers while we buzzed and fawned around her and put on our little shows. And, of course, yours truly did her share of the entertaining. In more ways"—the rushing voice slowed; she tried to shrug off the thought but her shoulders didn't quite lift—"than I care to say.

"You know it's strange," she said—and she had been silent for a time, "I always used to think she was giving us so much by taking us in. But it was really the other way around. We were the ones doing the giving and she the one taking. The woman was draining our very substance. I'm ashamed to say it took me three years to understand that. And when it did finally dawn on me I knew I had to get out. I didn't know if I had the strength to do it but I had to try.

"And so one day I just said finish with that!"—and in a gesture Saul had seen her do from time to time she brought the palms of her hands sharply one across the other like two cymbals being struck. "Just so. I had had enough. Enough of all the things that went on in that house, and more than enough of the business between her and myself. That had me so I didn't know who or what I was. Besides, I needed to find out if I could make it on my own. Most of all"—and here for the first time she smiled: a thin wistful smile which recalled some hope she had held then, but which, from the tragic cast to the smile, had ultimately been frustrated —"most of all," she said, "I was curious to see if a man would maybe look at me twice. I wasn't any raving beauty but I had a way about me then."

"You still do, Merle."

"True?" Her short laugh held a surprised note. "You mean there might still be hope for me? I doubt it. So I left." The laugh had died. "My lady friend didn't like it, of course, but she didn't make a row. That wasn't her way. Instead, she helped me find a flat and gave me enough money to tide me over until I could find a job. Oh, it was all very friendly. I left with the understanding that I could come back any time I wanted. The woman was clever, yes! She knew far better than I how really frightened I was of being on my own.

"And I did go back from time to time. I know it's hard to believe, but I did. Even though I had made something of a new life for myself —had a job, my own place, other friends, even boy friends, I still went back every so often. It was the damnedest thing. But whenever things weren't going well or I'd lost another job I'd run back, stay awhile, and when I got up my nerve again, leave. And even though there wasn't anything between us anymore—she had someone else looking after her mail by then—she took me back each time. When someone like that knows how weak and dependent on them you once were they want to keep you that way. They need to feel they still own you.

"But I finally managed to stay away for good. And that's when my friend put into operation plan two, which was to be my undoing. She never telephoned, she never visited, but every so often she'd drop me a note, all very pleasant and chatty, and along with the note there would be a check. Just in case I might be short, she said. It wouldn't be for any large amount, but enough to tempt you. At first I thought of returning them, but then I said, what the hell, if the foolish woman wants to give away money why not take it? She's got more than she knows what to do with anyway. So I kept the checks. And each time one came I'd throw a party. I'd invite every half-starving West Indian student I knew in London and put on a big feed for them. We'd fete for days. I became famous for my parties. There we would be sitting up until all hours plotting the socialist revolution on our little islands and cursing the capitalists while eating and drinking off their money. Fitting, what!"

Her ironic laugh, the exaggerated English phrase, served as a double punctuation. But sobering abruptly, shaking her head, she said, "But I should never have gone on taking her money like that, because of course it meant I hadn't really broken with her. She knew it. That's why she kept it up. And I knew it; I used to worry about it sometimes, yet I kept on. It was as if I couldn't help myself.

"And then one day all that changed." She spoke after a long wait, and there was suddenly an awed note in her voice. "My entire life just changed . . ." She hesitated, once again weighed Saul with the look; then, almost shyly, explained, "I met my husband. He had come down from Leeds, where he was doing a special course at the university there, to spend his holidays in London and I met him, and everything changed for me."

In the silence that fell, her eyes became distant and soft as she relived to herself that first meeting.

"That was one beautiful black man, yes!" And she spoke only to herself, seeing her husband as clearly as if he had taken Saul's place across the table. "Oh, not that he didn't have his faults. He was a man once he made up his mind about something there was no changing it, and he had no patience with weakness of any sort. He could be hard, in other words. But still beautiful, you know. He was one of those people who are absolutely clear in their minds about so many of the things that leave most of us—especially when we're young—muddled and confused; who know, for example, exactly what they want to do with their lives. They've set a goal for themselves and they mean to reach it—and no nonsense about it. Ketu was like that. He knew, more than any man I'd ever met, what he was about.

"Take the field he was in," she said. "He had already done a degree in economics when I met him, but he had decided to stay on and specialize in agricultural economics because he believed, as you do, that the main job in these poor agricultural countries has to be on finding ways of improving the lot of the Little Fella out on the land. He used to talk about that all the time. It's the same thing we used to go on about at those parties of mine, but he was the first African, or West Indian for that matter, I'd ever met who was actually studying anything directly related to it. Most of the chaps in those days were doing either medicine or law. We needed the doctors, of course, but we could have done without all of those lawyers cluttering up the place. They were only out for themselves.

"Ketu was altogether different. He never said it in so many words, but he knew the work to be done and his own personal responsibility in seeing that it was done if the independence all of us were so busy demanding at the time was to have any meaning. He was one of those rare, truly committed people. And because he was, he hadn't been taken in, like so many of us poor little colonials come to big England to study, by the so-called glamor of the West. There was no turning his head, in other words. He had come for certain specific technical information and he wasn't interested in anything else they had to offer, either, as he once put it, their gods, their ways or their women.

"I wouldn't even try to tell you what it meant for me to meet someone like him." It was said in a voice so muted it scarcely carried across the table. "I can only tell you what I was able to do as a result and then maybe you'll understand. First, I was able at long last to break completely with that woman in Hampstead. One day I simply went over there and told her off. Another of her little checks had come in the mail and I took it along and threw it right in her damn face. But maybe," she paused, frowning, "I shouldn't have done that. Perhaps all the things that happened later wouldn't have if I had just quietly disappeared and left no forwarding address. People had warned me never to cross her. But I couldn't resist letting her know I no longer needed either her or her rotten money, that I had found someone. She never said a word, of course. She let me do the shouting. But I could tell how angry she was and that I wasn't going to be allowed to get away with such ingratitude. She could never permit it, not someone like her who had to feel they had the power of life and death over other people. She couldn't take someone she considered her inferior standing up to her.

"Anyway, I had my say and left, and scarcely gave her a thought after that. I moved up to Leeds to be near Ketu, found a part-time job and started reading history again at the university. And after awhile we were married."

Quietly, the words by virtue of their very stillness holding their own against the noise around them, she said, "We had only the two years together, scarcely any time worth speaking of, but in a way you know they made up for all the others before—and since. There's no describing them. Let's just say I became a different person with him. Softer, for one"—and as she smiled to herself, remembering, Saul, forgotten on his side of the table, glimpsed something of that softness in her face; it was the same softness he sensed at times lying just out of reach behind her defensive smile, her quick fending-off gestures and the torrent of words.

"And I didn't talk near as much," she said. "You wouldn't have recognized the old fire-eater." A hint of her old smile—but this time tempered by the softness—flashed and was gone. "But most of all, he made me know I was a woman. Yes"— she nodded quietly—"that, above all else, is what that man did for me. After years of not being sure what I was, whether fish or fowl or what, I knew with him I was a woman and no one would ever again be able to make me believe otherwise. I still love him for that.

"But I should have told him about myself!" It was a sudden harsh outcry that, catching Saul unawares, caused him to start. "About the way I had lived all those years and about the damn woman! I should have taken my chances and told him. Maybe he would have understood. But I didn't have the nerve. You know me." Her gesture said how deeply she despaired of herself; her voice had dropped. "All talk but no real nerve. Besides, I didn't see any point in it. The old life was behind me. I had seen the last of that woman and her money. Or so I thought. But she fooled me. She let me know, in no uncertain terms, there's no doing away with the past that easily."

"What happened?" He spoke only after she had been silent for a time.

"The bloody checks started coming again, that's what!" And she sounded almost impatient with him: he should have known, her tone said, without having to ask. "She had somehow managed to track me down all the way to Leeds and the blasted money started coming again. And she had chosen her time well, the bitch. Because I was pregnant and was going to have to leave off working soon. I held out for a while and sent the first two or three flying back to her without so much as opening the envelope. But then when the baby came we were really hard up, and I started cashing them. . . .

"I know," she said, her head bowed to avoid his gaze. "You don't have to say it. I should never have done it, bills or no bills."

"I'm not saying that, Merle."

She didn't hear him, nor had she really been speaking to him. "But I couldn't see turning away money when we needed it so badly. I told Ketu the money was from my father, that he had had a change of heart when I wrote him about the baby and wanted to help out. And I told myself I would start sending the checks back as soon as the baby was old enough to be put in a crèche and I could go back to work. And I did send them back once I started working again. But it was too late then. By telling off my lady friend that time and throwing the money in her face, I had, it seems, brought out the worst in her and she wouldn't stop now until she had destroyed me. And she would use every means to do it. Nothing was beyond her.

"So that when I started returning the checks the second time she simply went to my husband with everything. Right out to the university now! Oh, she didn't go herself, of course. No, she was much too great the lady for that. She sent one of the poor toadies she kept on the dole up from London to do her dirty work. And whoever it was not only told him everything but had brought along foolish letters I had written her years ago and pictures of the two of us together and, of course, the canceled checks—all of them, including the ones I had lied about and said were from my father. There was no lack of evidence."

Slowly then, her head came up and staring through Saul into that other time, she uttered a low sharp cry, full of pain, which caught violently at her breath. It was as if an old wound deep at her center that had never completely healed, but had, at least, remained dormant over the years, quiescent, had suddenly begun to lance her again. "If only you had seen him when he came home that day," she whispered. "His face, the look on it . . . I will carry that look with me to the grave.

"I couldn't even make out at first what he was saying he was speaking in such an odd jumbled-up way. He could scarcely get his words out. But finally he said her name and I knew."

Long moments passed, and then her hand, a deep burnt brown that became black in the dimmer lights from the globe, sketched a vague gesture of futility. "I tried explaining, of course, over and over again. But it was no use. He couldn't understand any of it. If it had been a man, he might have felt different. But carrying on with some woman! Taking money from her! He couldn't understand nonsense like that. And then there were the lies I had told him about the checks. There was no explaining them away. Nor was there any forgiving them—not for someone like him. . . .

"Oh, he tried to see my side of it. He really did. At times we both made as though it had never happened and our life together was the same. But that didn't work. Nothing helped. Something in him had turned from me and he just couldn't feel anything for me anymore. I can't tell you what a hell those last few months were. Every little disagreement ended with us going over the same old ground. And it wasn't only what he said then, but the way he would look at me . . ." A shiver passed over her, and she shrank back in her seat, seeing that look. "As though," she whispered, "I stood for the worst that could happen to those of us who came to places like England and allowed ourselves to be corrupted. I wasn't Merle to him any longer, a person, his wife, the mother of his child, but the very thing he had tried to avoid all his years there.

"It got so," the crushed voice went on, "that he wouldn't look at me, wouldn't so much as let his eye catch mine. And days would go by without his speaking. After a time he began acting as though he didn't even want me to touch my own child. I had hoped he might see his way to forgive me for her sake. She was such a perfect little girl and he was so proud of her. But not even having her helped. Sometimes when I was feeding or changing her he would jump up and take her from me like he was afraid I was somehow contaminating her with my touch. And at night when I tried touching him he would turn his back. I would beg him. Me, who never begged a soul for a thing in my life! And he would pretend not to hear. He stopped sleeping with me altogether after awhile.

"Do you know what living like that can do to you?" she quietly asked. "Loving someone who's lost all feeling for you? Have you any idea what it's like? No," she said with a bitter shake of her head that envied him his ignorance, "you don't have a clue. It can make you give up, so that you don't care about anything anymore, including your own child. It can make you want to prove you're as terrible as people say you are.

"That's what it did to me. I got so I didn't give a damn about anything. I began staying out, neglecting the child, doing all sorts of crazy things—just trying to prove, I suppose, that I was as rotten as he believed. Sometimes when the silence in that flat became more than I could bear I would take the bloody train to London and hang around with the old crowd for a day or two. And when he threatened to have done with me altogether and leave, taking the baby with him, I told him I didn't care, he could do what he damn well pleased. . . .

"So I wasn't surprised when I came back one day from one of my little jaunts to London and found them gone." She spoke in a detached, almost indifferent manner, but her voice was beginning to waver and break behind the words. "No, I wasn't in the least surprised. I had been expecting it, in fact. He had finished his course by then and had just been offered a post teaching and doing extramural work in agriculture at Markarere in Uganda, and he was eager to leave. And he was perfectly right to go without me, and to take his child. I certainly wasn't someone for him to take anyplace as his wife or to have raise his child. He did right. I was the one mistake he had made all his years in England and he was leaving it behind. You couldn't blame the man for that, could you?

"And yet," she said, trying to steady her voice against the tremor that was overtaking it, "even though I had been expecting it and knew in my heart he had done the best thing, the sight of the flat that day was too much. I had been slowly going out of my mind for months, I guess, from the way I'd been acting, but that really set me off. I was sick for a long time, just limp, like someone dead. And I might well have ended up in some state madhouse had not good friends of mine in London, an older married couple I had known for years, taken me in and arranged for me to see a doctor—some high-priced Juju man as I call them—they knew on Harley Street. And the talking to him helped. I slowly came round. But there was nothing to keep me in England once I was better, so when Lyle wrote saying that Ashton Vaughan was dying I decided to come on back. I thought being here might be a change for the better. I'd get a job, try to make a new life for myself, and maybe in that way get over it a little. But there's no getting over it. And time's been no help. These eight years back have been like a day.

"Oh!" It was the same sharp outcry as before, only more piercing this time. The old wound might have suddenly widened, sending the pain like a knife through her. "If only you had seen the flat that day! It didn't look as if they had gone. Everything was still there—all the furniture, his desk, the pull-out sofa we slept on, and in the other room the baby's crib next to the dresser where I kept her things, with the drawers closed as if her clothes were still inside. Everything in place, but empty. I've never been in a place that felt more empty. And yet I couldn't believe they were gone. I kept telling myself he had only taken her out somewhere and they would soon be back. All I had to do was wait. And I did. I must have stood for hours in the middle of that room waiting for them, unable to move. And in a way, you know," she said, her voice breaking finally and the tears gathering, slipping quietly in like mourners silently taking their places around a bier, "I'm still there. I'm still standing in the middle of that two-room flat in Leeds waiting for them to come back. . . .

"Brute!"

The charged word, hurled without warning into the midst of the long silence that had fallen, dealt the air a savage blow; and for an instant, as her enraged and anguished face with its tear-filled eyes came lunging across at him, Saul almost thought she meant him, that he was the one accused, and instinctively drew back. "Brute! How could he have just walked out like that? Without a word. With not so much as a note. Just gone. You come home one day and find the bloody flat empty. Everything tidy and in place, but empty. And to take the child with him! How could he have just run off with her like that? What right had he? She was as much mine as his. I was still her mother, no matter what I had done or how I had lived, and that gave me some say in what was to happen to her. And never a word from him all these years. He's never once answered my letters. . . . All right," she cried, "it's true: I did him a great wrong and it wasn't in him to forgive me; he wanted nothing more to do with me and he left, but oh, Lord, have some human feeling and write every once in a while and let me know how the little girl's getting along, how she's growing. But nothing. Not a word all this time. Oh, the brute . . . !"

Her eyes glazed over by the tears standing in them, her voice a barely suppressed shout, her face convulsed, wild, she cursed him: the old wound giving off its venom. Caught by the fury in her voice several people dancing nearby glanced over, and, seeing the angry face thrust close to Saul's across the table, quickly drew aside, thinking they were quarreling. A very drunk woman tourist in a jeweled gown, the unshaven blond hair of her armpits like corn silk under her raised white arms, wagged an admonishing finger their way.

". . . And what right had he to judge me, anyway . . . ?" The contorted face rushed closer, the low-pitched shout seemed louder than the riotous din issuing from the nightclub. "Was he God . . . ? Or was I the only person who ever lied to someone they loved or tried to cover up their past? I only did it because I didn't want to risk losing him. I couldn't bear to have him know what a botch I had made of everything before meeting him. I wanted him to think well of me. Is that so terrible? Does that make me the worst person in the world? Oh, damn him! Damn him! Damn him! Damn him for not understanding. Damn him for not giving me a chance. Damn him for leaving me standing there all this time waiting for them to come back!"

In the silence filled with the echo of that helplessly enraged voice, Saul saw her as she must have looked that day standing rooted to the one spot in the apartment: her dazed and stricken face, the eyes that refused to accept the meaning of the emptiness she sensed there, and then all of her slowly giving way to the paralysis, grief and collapse that had left her, as she said, like someone dead for long afterward. Not knowing what to say, he placed a hand lightly on hers, and found it lifeless, almost cold. Her private sun had gone into eclipse behind the film of unshed tears. And the faint lovely line from the wings of her flared nose to her mouth that, in arching wide, shaped her smile, had become deep tell-tale lines of age.

They remained like this for some time at the cramped table situated in the crook of the door: Merle, her anger exhausted, staring with the dulled eyes and drawn aging face into that other time, still waiting; Saul, his hand on hers, watching her from under his lined puckered lids that were too heavy suddenly for him to lift, and feeling helpless to do or say anything that might ease her. For a moment he found himself almost regretting that she had spoken. It was strange, but as much as he had hoped she would one day talk about herself, as important as he knew it was, in ways he could not even define, for him to get to know her, he still could not help experiencing a fleeting regret and even something akin to resentment. Perhaps it was because he knew that in loving her some measure of her sorrow and loss would be added to his own and he would carry it with him long after he had left Bourne Island and her face had dimmed in his memory. It would be yet another stone for him to roll before him up the hill.

Around them the postcarnival din continued to affront the night silence of the sea and the sleeping town, but the noise had dropped from its almost frightening high and people were beginning to leave. Their costumes soiled and torn, the heavy carnival make-up smeared and mixed in with their perspiration so that their faces, a melange of black, white, yellow, and brown, appeared to be dissolving in a wash of color, they filed slowly out of the club, first pausing to pay their bills and bid Sugar good night before groping their way drunkenly down the stairs. Beyond the balcony the sea had swallowed the moon which had greeted Saul and Merle from above the Heights earlier on, and the sea and sky had merged, becoming one in the darkness that would not last the hour. For it would soon be dawn, Ash Wednesday morning.

As if she sensed the morning stirring to life behind the screen of night, Merle roused, her mind traveling the distance from the tiny flat in Leeds back to Sugar's and the ring-scarred table at which they were sitting. And glancing around the balcony where a few holdouts were still doing the reckless jump-up, she closed her eyes. With the tears which she could not, even after all these years, bring herself to shed standing in them, she closed them. And in a way Saul understood only too well, that said she had seen enough of the world and had no wish to look upon it anymore.

"Oh, Merle!" he said.

"Yes," she nodded, her lids drawn shut, "say it like that. I need to hear it said that way."

Opening her eyes she gave him a wan smile and gently withdrew her hand from under his. Her gaze wandered out to the dark murmurous sea where the dawn waited, then slowly, after many minutes, drifted back to the scene on the balcony, and she said with sudden irritability, "I don't feel to go to any damn breakfast do at the Cloughs this morning, you know. I've had my fill of carnival and people jumping up as if there's something to be all that happy about."

"Stay with me, then," he said quietly, his eyes on her face, which was turned from him, watching the departing revelers. "We'll find someplace other than this to go. I know I don't have a right in the world to ask, but stay with me, Merle, for what's left of tonight." And strangely he was the one who sounded in greater need of comforting.

She slowly turned back and, for a long time, while the crowd around them continued to thin, they gazed almost impassively at each other across the table, her eyes narrowed because of the smoke from her cigarette, which she claimed was her protection against people such as him. Finally though she smiled, a sad fond smile that had something of the edge he had come to love to it. She lightly shrugged, saying with the gesture that she had done with love long ago.

"On one condition," she said.

"What's that?"

"That you don't make too much of it, meaning it goes no further than tonight."

He held back, then reluctantly nodded. "I don't know if that's altogether possible," he said, "but I'll try."

Downstairs, the brisk wind off the sea had driven the debris of carnival, the streamers, confetti and torn bits of colored crepe paper, neatly up against the sides of the buildings, so that Whitehall Lane looked as if it had been swept clean when they emerged. The dew, falling like a light spring rain now that it was nearing dawn, had borne the dust churned up over the two days down with it and packed it tightly once again between the cobblestones. The last of the carnival echoes that had lingered long after the midnight curfew had also finally died, and the old town, straining gently at its mooring on the bay, had recovered much of its accustomed tone; its ancient calm had been restored. The two of them sensed this as they moved through its close winding streets, past the shuttered houses and shops that would soon open to the day. By the time they reached the house where Merle had boarded as a schoolgirl, and where she still slept whenever she stayed in town, the sky was the color of the ashes that would be placed on the foreheads of the faithful later in the morning.

BOOK IV

WHITSUN

CHAPTER 1

The cassia was in bloom. Great clusters of pendulous blossoms the color of whipped butter or of the Bournehills sun when it first rises in the morning hung like Christmas ornaments on the old tree in the yard, their bright weight bearing the lower branches down almost to the ground, their fragrance scenting the salt air and the light from them reaching out to soften and warm the harsh landscape of sand-hill and sea. And it had all happened overnight, as Merle had said it would. Yesterday the tree had looked its usual self: shorn of every leaf, stripped of its bark even, dead to all appearances. No one had thought to notice the small, dark, tightly closed buds, mere nodules, that had quietly sprouted over the last week. And then during the night, under cover of the darkness, the buds had opened, the flowers unfolding, exploding full-bloom while those in the house and in the village slept.

"Talk about miracles!" Merle exclaimed softly. Wearing the long, shabby maroon-colored wrapper in which she began the day, she stood gazing up at the blossom-laden tree with a look of such wonder on her face it was as if she was seeing it for the first time. Behind her was gathered a small, equally awed crowd of onlookers: Allen, who had discovered the tree when he had come out earlier to tend his garden and had summoned her, Stinger, who had stopped off on his way to Plover Cliff with his one lean cow (the animal stood head bowed at his side, its breath a thin smoke in the chill morning air), and the small solemn band of children, Harriet's children, with the basins of sand and bundles of broom sage they came to gather each morning resting easily on their heads. The cassia had even brought Carrington out of her dim cave of a kitchen, and she stood off by herself in the bare pitted yard—a mute unsettling presence, her vast sloping bosom contained within the bib of her apron.

Saul and Harriet, though, weren't there. For they no longer lived at the guesthouse. Shortly after carnival they had moved to the house in the village proper which Stinger and Gwen had helped secure for them. But Merle had sent one of the beach children to call them so they might see the tree.

"I can't get over it, you know, no matter how often I see it," she was saying. "You're about ready to give up on the blasted thing and make firewood out of it and then, lo and behold, you wake up one morning and find all this waiting for you. All this in the space of one night now! It's enough to make you think some magician came along while you were sleeping and seeing how naked and sorry-looking the old tree was, took pity on it and touched it and it bloomed. Just so! At his touch. And the flowers this year are the largest yet. I tell you, it's enough to restore your faith in something or the other, right, Stinger? Allen?"

Behind her Allen shyly inclined his head, a little embarrassed as always by her exuberance and drama, while Stinger, his cap pulled low over his mild eyes, his billhook in hand, indulged her with a smile. "Is true, Mis-Merle," he said gently.

"Your old blaspheming friend, Ferguson, should be here, Stinger, to give us a verse," she said. " 'Consider the lilies of the field' or something so, because this is every bit a miracle. Better by far than the loaves and the fishes or . . ."

As she held forth, they heard Saul's car approaching, and turning saw it jolting over the unpaved road between the sandhills and Westminster's tall spur. Minutes later he was pulling up in the yard and walking toward them from the other side of the cassia.

"Behold the bridegroom!" Merle laughingly hailed him as he stepped, stooped over, from under the tree's low-hanging branches into their circle, followed by Harriet and the child who had been sent to call them.

He paused, and his back bent out of the way of the tree, laughed, as did the others.

"You're awfully cheerful this morning," he said, straightening up.

"And who wouldn't be?" She pointed to the tree. "Just take a look at our old friend here. Didn't I tell you she would surprise you one of these days? I'm sure, though, you never expected it would be anything like this."

"No," he said, looking not at the tree but at her, "you're wrong. I fully expected to be overwhelmed."

"True!" she laughed, and in the next moment swung toward Harriet, who had gone over to speak to the children after greeting Stinger and Allen. "And what do you think of the old girl this morning, Harriet?"

Harriet didn't answer immediately. Instead for a time she stood with her face raised thoughtfully to the cassia. It was almost as if she was waiting for the sound of Merle's voice to die and the air to clear before speaking. And she appeared strangely abstracted, remote: there yet not there.

"I must say I'm rather overwhelmed also," she said finally, keeping her gaze on the tree. "I would never have imagined it had this much life in it. It is lovely." Then, a memory transforming her eyes, erasing all the gray in them so that they were completely blue: "It puts me in mind of an oak tree outside a house I lived in some years ago. It was so ancient you never thought, seeing it in the winter, that it would be able to put out any new leaves come the spring. But every spring there the leaves were, all bright and new and green, a soft lovely green. More than anything else, that tree said it was spring."

Struck by the quiet in her voice and something else about her which they could not define, everyone had turned to listen, the children grouped around her looking up at her with their somber eyes.

"Where was this, Harriet?" Saul asked.

"At the house in Aberdeen. Haven't I ever told you about that oak?"

"No," he said.

"Really? Well, probably because it wasn't anything as spectacular as this." Then, turning with her even gaze to Merle, looking directly at her yet somehow giving the impression she wasn't seeing her (or any of the others there for that matter) clearly, but through the thin lingering haze of some thought or scene in her mind, she said, indicating the blossoms with a wave of her hand, "It's a pity, isn't it, all this finery can't last?"

Merle reflected on this a long moment, standing before the tree with the yellow glow of the blossoms warmly mirrored in her eyes.

She was suddenly as solemn as the children. "No," she said after a time. "It's only right they go their way. Let them fall. Otherwise we'd start taking them for granted and not even notice them after awhile. Besides, it gives us something to look forward to each year. You're right though. By this and next week all this lovely gold will be gone and my lady here will be her usual naked, half-dead self again. But what to do, yes? That's all in life, as the old people say."

In less than a week's time all the blossoms were down, the sharp salt wind sailing off with most of them before they could reach the ground, and once again the tree looked as though it had fallen victim to a hurricane, or as if an army of locusts had alighted and stripped it clean before passing on. With the cassia bare and carnival past, life in Bournehills resumed its established round. Stinger, Gwen, and the others returned to the fields scattered about the high slopes. Over at Cane Vale Ferguson again sounded the mournful horn that marked the change in shifts, and under his worried eye the worn-out rollers continued to grind the canes, screaming the while. Out along Westminster Low Road old Mr. Douglin could be seen lovingly trimming the grass at the one spot on the shoulder.

Shortly after carnival Vere got a job driving one of the heavy bulldozers in Bryce-Parker's soil-conservation program. All day, unmindful of the sun's envying eye, he sat with loose and easy grace at the controls of the machine, smiling faintly to himself as he gouged up tons of the parched useless earth and sent whole hills toppling. Back in Spiretown after the day's work he would wash and dress in the midst of Leesy's disapproving silence and then drive into New Bristol.

"Vere must be got himself a town woman," the once more idle steelband boys said from their culvert wall as the Opel Kapitän with its restored German motor and long menacing American-style body roared past them down the main road. The taillights glowed back at them like oversized fireflies in the dusk and the backfire, ringing out like pistol shots, lingered long after he had disappeared over Westminster. Much later, when he returned from the bed of the girl Milly, whom he had met Carnival Tuesday night, her warm singing bed behind the folding screen, the sound of the car in the darkness blanketing Spiretown was like his voice speaking with a new impressive authority and force.

"Vere like he's changing up," people said, and they not only meant his new manner but the physical changes taking place in him as well.

His face which had always, aside from the sharply angled cheekbones, appeared somehow unfinished, boyish, now had the character lines sketched clearly in; and there was an assertiveness, not seen before, to his walk, the set of his shoulders, and in the way he sat on top the bulldozer at work with his muscles gripping strongly under his skin as he manipulated the levers.

Some said it was the new job. Others attributed the change in him to the girl. A few declared it was politics—for it became known after awhile that Milly occasionally took him to meetings in the Heights, where the government was denounced and there was talk of forming a poor people's party. Still others claimed it was the car. "It's the car make him feel he's a man," they said, although they agreed, along with Leesy, that the car—this particular car—meant him no good. "That old wreck the white people in town din' want anymore! That they figured they could use to turn his head! That thing don't mean that boy no good!" Even Milly shared in the almost universal distrust of the Opel and urged him to sell it. She had a little money put aside, she said, and she would use it to help him buy a decent car. Whenever she brought up the subject Vere would give her that serene smile of his which said he had ceased listening to her for the moment.

On the evenings he didn't go to town, he could be seen out in the yard tinkering with the motor by the light of a tilly lamp, souping it up for the Whitmonday Race to be held in Spiretown some weeks hence. Under his patient hand the Opel soon developed the powerful growl of a sports car.

Out at the guesthouse Allen heard Vere every time he returned from New Bristol in the car. For the sound of that souped-up motor would roar out across the village and above the sea's voice to jolt him from his sleep. Even when he didn't awaken he heard him in his dreams. And not only heard him but saw him as well in his imagination, his dark face with the little pleased inward smile thrust forward intently above the steering wheel and his powerful hands skillfully guiding the Opel down the steep drop from Westminster. As Vere's face flowed out from his mind to fill the room Allen would draw the thin summer blanket farther around his head.

They seldom saw each other anymore. And when they did occasionally meet for a late swim in Horseshoe Pool on the evenings Vere didn't go to town, it was no longer the same. The old ease and intimacy was gone and they were suddenly as awkward with each other as at the beginning of their friendship. Their estrangement was due mainly to Allen who, following that Carnival Tuesday night, had taken to avoiding Vere. Neither of them ever mentioned that night, yet Allen was convinced Vere knew—knew not only what had transpired between himself and the girl Elvita, she of the cardboard cutlass and diadem of leaves, but also what had occurred after she had slammed out of the house cursing him: his lonely adolescent act upon the lumpy settee. Vere might even have been privy to the images that had rioted through his mind while he held himself. He knew all. What else could account for the pained, questioning look Allen thought he glimpsed at times in his glance—and which, each time he thought he saw it, filled him with such anger he could have gladly seen Vere dead at his feet, and the memory of that night dead with him.

With their friendship all but ended Allen had taken to spending most of his time working out at the guesthouse. He had completed the interviewing for the large sample-household survey he had been conducting over the months, and was busy now collating and coding the material for the report he and Saul were preparing to write. Using this as an excuse he had begged off from moving into the village with Saul and Harriet, although there was room for him in the house and they had both urged him to come. He would be able to work better on the coding, he said, in the relative peace and quiet of the guesthouse. And he was working with an intensity that rendered him blind to his surroundings and himself for the greater part of the day, and which sent him stumbling exhausted into bed at night. But nearly every night he was torn from that drugged sleep by Vere, the new Vere, speaking to him in the Opel's low-pitched penetrating growl from on top Westminster, and he would lie there assailed by the same inexplicable mix of anger and admiration, envy and longing, the same unendurable sense of abandonment, of having been left behind in some untried pupal state, as when his friend Jerry Kislak, eager to prove himself, had suddenly one day years ago joined the marines, only to die a month later in boot training.

Over in Spiretown during that same period Harriet was kept busy making the house they had moved to habitable. The house, old but solidly built and large by Bournehills standards (the husband of the widow who owned it had been a fairly prosperous shopkeeper), was in the heart of the village, halfway up the crowded rise that sloped up from the main road and led by a series of bare, sun-baked folds in the land to Cane Vale factory and farther north to the site of Bryce-Parker's reclamation scheme.

Surrounding the house on all sides were the small, pitched-roofed, unpainted board-and-shingle dwellings of Harriet's neighbors. Alongside lay their tiny plots of cane which were still, most of them, standing in the ground because of the decision, taken after Sir John's visit, to leave off grinding the peasant canes until the entire estate crop was done. Just above Harriet and Saul, in a little sentry box of a house poised, it appeared, to come crashing down on them at any moment, lived Leesy's friend, the old woman Mary Griggs who, even when she spoke, continued to hum the same loud cheerless hymn under her breath. The wordless song, borne down to Harriet in the old woman's penetrating, atonal voice, seemed to her a medley of all the rock-bound hymns she had heard in church as a child. Beginning at cock crow and lasting well past dusk, it was an endless, inescapable reprise that, until she was able to close her mind to it, evoked the dreariest of her memories.

Below lived Stinger, Gwen, and their countless children in their listing two-room house. At dawn Harriet heard the rattle of the chain as Stinger led forth the gaunt cow, and later Gwen on her way to work would sing out, "Harriet, I gone," standing in the dusty yard surrounded by her children, her fowl, and the dog, and with the crocus sack she used both as an apron and an umbrella when it rained in the fields, tied over her stomach which remained unchanged.

Farther down the rise stood Leesy's house, with its windowless wall to the road and Vere's fire-engine red Opel parked under the mango tree in the yard. Without being able to say why, Harriet didn't particularly take to the new Vere. She preferred him as he had been when they first came to Bournehills. She recalled the times she had glimpsed him working alongside Leesy in the latter's small cane piece adjoining the house or accompanying her somewhere on the donkey cart. Seeing them crawling along the road at a snail's pace behind the plodding animal, with Vere seated beside the straight-backed Leesy like some sleepy-eyed young primitive, with the reins gone slack in his hands, she had termed them in her mind a West Indian Gothic, and would have preferred to have them remain just that way.

Finding herself thrown into the very center of life in the village, with all its sights, sounds and smells, its turbulence, Harriet determined to make the house as pleasant and private a retreat as possible.

She had as help Stinger's youngest daughter by his former wife, whom he had lived with for many years before taking up with Gwen. The girl, named Loris, was eighteen, with a smooth, fine-boned face, three thick childish braids beneath an old woman's rolled-brim felt hat which she clamped on her head the moment she stepped outdoors lest, as she put it, the hot sun give her a cold, her father's solidly black skin and his deceptively slight but strong build.

Together she and Harriet put up curtains—bright cheerful cottons, hid the cracks in the walls with prints and colorful posters bought in town, scrubbed down the floors (Loris alone did this) with sand and white lime until the old boards assumed the look of bleached bone, reinstalled the medicine cabinet with its bowl of candies for the children on top, and to add a touch of green hung wire baskets of fern from the low roof of the small gallery out front.

Yet Harriet did all this with something less than the enthusiasm she had displayed in making over their wing of the guesthouse. But then the months had exacted their toll. Moreover, there had been carnival, and her encounter with the band from the Heights. A change, inexplicable but profound, had taken place in her, and, as a consequence, in her feelings toward Bournehills since that Tuesday. Not that the change was in any way discernible. She appeared her usual self as she moved around Spiretown on her various errands, dressed in her sensible walking skirt and shoes and wearing the white blouse that remained unwilted no matter how hot the day. Rising early each morning she still took her lonely swim, driving over to Horseshoe Pool in the car and changing into her bathing suit in a rude lean-to of wattle and daub that had been built as a kind of *cabaña* against one of the dunes. Nor did she seem any different as she went about the daily round of transcribing Saul's notes (and she found the rattle of the typewriter a convenient means of drowning out Mary Grigg's mournful voice from above), pouring fruit juice for the women who dropped in almost daily, or ministering to some child's cut finger or toe. In fact, they were making, she and the children, a large shellwork design of a palm tree, doing it on burlap stretched on a board, with the shells she had collected over the months; it was the kind of thing she and her two brothers used to do as children during summers at the seashore. And she paid the usual calls around the village. And whenever possible she went for her late afternoon stroll out to the cliffs beyond the guesthouse, sometimes stopping off on her way back to chat briefly with Allen or Merle—although with the guesthouse empty except for Allen, Merle had taken to spending much of her time in New Bristol and was seldom there.

Her smile seemed as effortless. And the special air she had when listening to someone, which gave the impression she had set aside herself for the other person, was the same. Yet from time to time, one sensed behind that clear, interested gaze her numb and still dangerously shocked mind. Sometimes in the midst of her attentive silence the memory of that Tuesday from which she had not, and would never, recover, would loom so vividly before her, crowding and obstructing her vision, that her eyes for all their directness didn't quite seem to be taking you in.

Saul tried repeatedly to get her to talk about that day.

"But what else is there to say, darling?" she said with a mildly exasperated laugh. It was late in the evening and they were sitting up over the coffee that was a nightly ritual with them. Outside their shuttered windows, the rise slept, the little houses battened down against the darkness as against a powerful tidal wave. In the silence they could hear the hard-backed beetles which roamed the night hurling themselves with almost suicidal force against the walls of the house.

"I've told you I don't know how many times," she said, "everything that happened. But for the very last time I'll repeat. I very foolishly, on the way to the Cockerel, allowed myself to get caught in an unruly mob of teen-agers who were playing soldier. They'd all had far too much to drink and didn't know what they were doing or where they were going. In fact, they looked as if they were headed straight for the bay—me with them. And yes, I was frightened. I tried telling them they were going the wrong way, but they refused to listen. Or maybe," she quickly added, remembering the unaccountable rage that had seized her at their refusal to heed her, and which welled up whenever she thought of them, "they just didn't hear me in all the noise. They didn't even seem to see me, but as I said they'd had too much to drink. Anyway, I finally managed to get away from them —not without having to put up something of a struggle, I admit. They went their way, and after awhile Lyle and Dorothy Clough came along and found me, and that was the end of it.

"Saul, I don't know why you're trying to make something world-shaking out of what was just a minor incident!" she cried after a long silence in which his eyes held quietly to her face. She had summoned a laugh to mask her annoyance.

He said nothing, but simply continued to look at her, waiting for her to tell him the rest—those things he sensed she kept hidden about the encounter, silently pleading with her to speak openly to him. Giving up finally, he sighed, and his worried, despairing gaze still reaching out to her where she sat across from him in a Morris armchair with her cup raised to her lips, partly hiding her face, he murmured, "Hatt. Oh, Hatt . . ."

CHAPTER 2

Saul, in the weeks between the ending of carnival and Whitsun, the next important holiday in Bournehills, took two steps that brought them closer to the second phase of the project. First, with Allen assisting him, he began writing the report on their findings to date, out of which the recommendations for this next phase would come. In preparation for the writing he completely reread his field notes, as well as Allen's. As he went over the mass of material they had accumulated between them over the months, part of him kept searching behind the events and conversations recorded and his own observations and comments, behind even Allen's impressive array of statistics, for the thing about Bournehills which he had almost felt within his grasp that Carnival Tuesday, watching the Bournehills band parade through New Bristol.

Second, and of greater importance than the report, as far as he was concerned, was the village council which he, with Delbert's support, managed to organize during the weeks leading up to Whitsun. The council, composed of those men who were the unofficial leaders in Spiretown (leaders not because of any position they held but by virtue of the respect and affection they enjoyed among their fellow villagers), men like Stinger and the cane cutter, Ten-ton, and of course Delbert, even Ferguson to an extent, would be fundamental, he knew, to the action phase of the project. Not only would the council, as he envisioned it, be directly involved in the planning (he would look to it, in other words, for ideas and suggestions as to future programs), but most important this core group of men would be the means by which he would be able to enlist the co-operation of the rest of the village. The council might well prove the first small step toward people in Bournehills taking charge of their own lives.

It began modestly. With Delbert, as the most influential of the unofficial leaders, serving as chairman, they started meeting informally in the back of the shop and at Saul's house on the rise. But as more people began attending, some only out of curiosity or to criticize, the meetings were moved to the social center at the edge of the playing field. There, under the burnt-out eye of the television, they discussed local issues and, as time went on, even began speaking out about what they saw as the main problems in the district.

Uppermost in people's minds was the question of their canes, which they complained were slowly drying up because of the delay in the grinding. And it was true. The canes, left standing too long in the ground, were beginning to take on a parched look. The tall flaunting leaves that, aside from the occasional breadfruit and mango trees and coconut palms, were the only bit of green to be seen in the unrelieved dun-gray of the landscape, were slowly turning brown at the edges, adding to the general look of blight.

As the end of the crop season neared, concern increased, and it was decided to send a delegation over to Cane Vale to speak to Merle's relative, Erskine Vaughan, in the hope of getting him to change his mind or, failing this, at least to find out the reason for the delay. Delbert, Saul, and one of the better off smallholders, a man with several acres of land, were chosen to present the village's case. But their mission proved futile. Erskine Vaughan, in an unusually obliging mood (even he, it seemed, sympathized with the smallholders' plight), declared he was powerless to act. And he insisted he was as much in the dark as they were about the cause for the delay. "They don' tell me a thing," he complained in an aggrieved voice of the Kingsley office in town. "I'm just here to carry out the orders they send."

Sometime later Delbert privately suggested to Saul that he go and sound out Hinds, the Kingsley representative in New Bristol. A dubious Saul agreed to give it a try and on the Friday before Whitsunday and the big Monday Bank Holiday which followed it, he drove into town. After the long trip over the hills, he arrived at the Kingsley offices in Queen Street only to learn that Hinds, who was one of the leading members of the all-white Bourne Island Yacht Club, had taken advantage of the long weekend and left on a cruise to nearby Grenada that morning. Feeling both thwarted and annoyed, annoyed with himself for not having telephoned from Westminster before setting out and then with Hinds for being unavailable, he left word he would return on Tuesday, and started the long trip back to Bournehills.

He was more than halfway out of town, headed for the winding corridor of a road that led out across the wide level breast of the island to Cleaver's, when he remembered that Merle was in New Bristol, staying at the house where they had spent part of the Ash Wednesday dawn together; and where, going back on his word, they had, always at his insistence, met once or twice since. And not wanting to return right away to Bournehills having accomplished so little, feeling discouraged, frustrated and at a low, needing her, he swung the car around. And in his despair at himself, to drown the loud condemnatory voice that immediately began within, he gave the steering wheel a vicious tug as he brought the Ford around, causing the tires to shriek wildly on the marl.

The house belonging to the old woman Merle called Aunt Tie was located in one of the many small, somewhat seedy enclaves in and around New Bristol, where the minor civil servants, primary schoolteachers and the like had their modest homes. This one, wedged in between the business district and the mazelike slums which eventually lead up to the Heights threatening New Bristol from above, was an old, once-fashionable section of one and two story Victorian houses with a good deal of gingerbread trim, steep tin roofs and bougainvillaea—strong purple, red and white—burdening their galleries.

Merle met him outside Aunt Tie's large, faded yellow house. She had heard the car pull up behind her Bentley parked out front and had come to stand in the trellised archway of the gallery which was completely covered over with a special strain of splashed purple-and-white bougainvillaea Aunt Tie had developed years ago. Silent, refusing to return his wave from the gate at the other end of the yard, she watched with expressionless eyes as he made his way toward her between the hedgerows of pink hibiscus bordering the path, and up the low steps to the gallery.

"I know you're avoiding me," he said. "But I've come anyway."

He had paused uncertainly two steps below her so that their eyes were on the same level, and for a time she silently inspected his dejected face and shadowed eyes. Then—and it was said with surprising gentleness, "It's not you. Or it's not only you, I should say."

"What's the rest of it?" he said, coming up to stand next to her. "What else besides me had you spending nearly all your time in town? Tell me," he insisted. "I miss not being able to catch a glimpse of you, if nothing more, when I go over to the guesthouse."

"It's Bournehills," she said, and looking equally as dejected went and sat down. In the shaded enclosure of the gallery, the abstract print she was wearing, its vivid color and design, rivaled the flowers screening out the sun. "It's Bournehills people. I can't bear to see how worried they are about their canes and how helpless they are to do anything about what's happened."

He dropped with a sigh into the chair beside hers. "I know," he said.

"And it's not, you know, that the few miserable canes they grow bring in any money to speak of," she said. "It's more the principle of the thing. It's important to Bournehills people that they have their own little crop which they can take over to Cane Vale and sell. It makes them feel they're somebody, too. And it wouldn't even be so bad if you knew what those people at Kingsley were up to, what was behind the whole business of having them wait. But nothing—" her voice dropped. "You don't have a clue."

"Yes, that is the worst of it—the not knowing," he said. "By the way, I've just come from over there. Delbert thought I might be able to find out something if I talked to Hinds. But I wasn't in luck. It seems the gentleman took off for Grenada in his yacht this morning. I'll go back on Tuesday, though."

"I hope you know you're wasting your time. You won't get anything out of Hinds."

"You're probably right, but I'll still go back on Tuesday."

Hearing their voices on the gallery, Aunt Tie had come to the door, and he went over to greet her. She was a tall, stooped woman with long fine hands misshapen by age and arthritis, and a face that was not only the exact color of an unblanched almond but had the same striated shriveled look to it. She insisted on wearing sunglasses even in the house to protect her failing eyesight. And she almost never came out on the gallery anymore in spite of the deep shade offered by the bougainvillaea. The light there was too strong, she said. Her sole interest was listening to the death announcements broadcast twice daily over the local radio station for the names of friends she could no longer visit.

Merle, whom the old woman treated as if she were still a schoolgirl, scolding and indulging her by turns, called over her shoulder for Aunt Tie to join them on the gallery, teasing her. The old woman, appealing to Saul to "teach that girl to respect her elders" hastened back into the dim heart of the house. Minutes later she sent out the servant with a pitcher of cold ginger beer for them.

"Dear Aunt Tie," Merle said. "She was Mother and Father to me."

"Didn't you and your father ever get along?" Sitting back down beside her, he placed on the armrest of his chair the glass of ginger beer the servant had poured him.

"Father? What father?" she cried, the bitterness which charged her voice whenever she spoke of Ashton Vaughan erupting instantly. "Ashton Vaughan was somebody to call father?" She glared, deeply offended, at him, and he regretted having asked the question. "A man who for years made out he didn't recognize his own child when he passed her on the road? And who when he did finally decide to admit she was his and take her to live with him scarcely spoke to her, and as soon as he could packed her off to some fancy school in town, where the half-white children there made her life miserable because she was black and her mother had been a common laborer who had had her without benefit of clergy at sixteen.

"Can you," she continued, her voice rising, "call someone a father who never said a word when the child's mother, who was supposed to be his favorite out of all the women he kept at the time, was murdered in cold blood? That's right. Just shot down in the house one day with the child standing there. You've heard the story, I'm sure. It was the biggest thing to happen in Bournehills since Cuffee set fire to Pyre Hill. And Ashton Vaughan never even tried to find out who did it. Maybe because he knew the Backra woman he was married to was behind it. No, bo, that man was no father of mine.

"He got his in the end, though," she said, her mouth a cruel line. "With all the land and houses he owned he died without a soul he could call family at his side. Had not Carrington been there there wouldn't have been anyone to even close his eyes. But his sort never end good. Take that woman in England who ruled me for years. The last I heard, her money had given out and she was sick unto death, and all her little wards had deserted her. How the mighty have fallen, eh? But then God, as the saying goes, doesn't love ugly."

There was a silence; then, with the tiny flecks of sunlight secreted amid the bougainvillaea playing over her tight face, she suddenly said, whispering it between closed teeth, "You would have thought the little idiot of a child would have at least remembered what the face behind the gun looked like."

"Oh, Merle, don't."

"No," she said, and her eyes as she turned to him pleaded with him to listen. "I need to talk about it. It'll do me good to say it out loud if only for once in my life. She should have remembered," she repeated. "All right, she was only two, but my God, even a child of two has some sense and should've at least been able to point to the person who shot her mother right before her eyes. That face should have been imprinted forever on her mind. But nothing. Just a blank."

"You know, of course, you're asking the impossible," he said.

"No, I'm not!" she cried, turning on him part of the anger and disgust she had long felt with herself for failing to remember. "She should have remembered something, the little idiot. Why some children can talk plain as day at the age of two. Even a half-wit like Seifert up at the almshouse would be able to point to his mother's murderer, I bet. Not me, though! Not your friend Merle! People say I was just standing beside her body sucking my thumb like nothing had happened when they found her."

"But you were only a baby, for God's sake," he said. "How could you possibly have known what was going on? You're being unreasonable."

"I don't care," she said. "Something, some little thing, should have stuck in my mind. I've never told anyone this, but once when I was attending that high-priced Juju man in Harley Street I asked him to put me under hypnosis to see if I could remember anything about that day. He wasn't very keen about the idea but he finally agreed. But a lot of good it did! He said that as soon as he started questioning me I woke up. Again, nothing!"

"Forget it, Merle, forget it," he urged her. Leaning across he placed a hand on her arm. "You can't hold yourself responsible for what happened to your mother. Because you know as well as I do that her death, as well as her life, the way she was forced to live, her relationship with your father, even the way he treated you when you were little, all go back to the whole goddamn inhuman system that got started in this part of the world long before you were born—the effects of which are still with us, sad to say, both in Bourne Island and in my country—more so there. You know that. So how can you blame yourself for her death? That's like blaming yourself for the entire history that brought it about.

"Don't get me wrong," he said quickly as she started to pull her arm out from under his hand and rise, "I know what you're trying to do. This with your mother is all part of your attempt to come to terms with the things that have happened in your life. To go back and understand. And it's a good thing you're doing. More of us should try it. It's usually so painful though: looking back and into yourself; most people run from it. I know I did for a long time. But sometimes it's necessary to go back before you can go forward, really forward.

"And that's not only true for people—individuals—but nations as well," he added after a reflective pause, the heavy lids coming down over his eyes. Next to him, Merle followed their movement and was still. "Sometimes they need to stop and take a long hard look back. My country, for example. It's never honestly faced up to its past, never told the story straight, and I don't know as it ever will. The juggernaut's going too fast for that. It's not likely to make it though.

"But do you know something . . ." The creased lids suddenly lifted and he was smiling. "Mis-Merle's going to make it. She's going to come through."

"You think so?" Her tone sought to disparage this, and thus herself.

"I know so."

And, slowly, under his steady gaze, she, too, finally smiled—a thin, unwilling but tentatively hopeful smile. "You're just trying to make me feel less hopeless about my damn self," she said.

"And why not? Even I've begun to feel less hopeless about myself since coming to Bournehills."

As they continued to sit there, silent for the moment, a clock inside the house struck three, its gently whirring notes conveying a sense of the cool dim rooms inside with their polished wood floors and crocheted antimacassars. Shortly afterward they saw through the archway with its overhang of bougainvillaea scattered groups of students passing on their way home from the nearby girls' high school. All they could see of them above the waist-high fence outside Aunt Tie's house were the tops of their regulation navy jumpers, the white blouses they wore underneath and their wide-brimmed boaters of soft straw. These rode jauntily on the backs of their heads, the round brims haloing their dark faces and setting off the large bows some of them had tied to the ends of their braids. Their busy voices, the girlish laughter they pretended to suppress behind their palms carried easily across the yard to the gallery.

"You used to turn in at this gate," he said.

Merle nodded. "And glad to get here." But she was smiling. It seemed that as a result of their talk, as brief, really, as it had been, something of the hurt she had long felt because of the abuse and taunts she had suffered at the hands of her schoolmates years ago was gone, and she could smile about it for the first time.

Saul, leaning close to her chair, his hand passing lightly over her arm, was thinking as he watched the straw hats float by that if he were blind and knew her only by the feel of her skin he would imagine her to be no older than the girls passing. And there was something of the young girl in the uncertain, almost cautious way she opened to him when they were together, and in her insistence, at those times, on pretending that he was not who he was but one of the people from up Canterbury with their fair skin, light-colored eyes and reddish hair. But there was the woman also. The faint, self-absorbed, self-congratulatory smile he sometimes caught on her face at the height of their embrace said she knew her woman's power to move and delight. And there was a woman's unmistakable, almost frightening authority in the way she had once, to spell him and delay the end, taken his face between her hands and lightly joked with him.

"Three o'clock gone," she said, and started up.

"I'm not going yet if that's what you're hinting at." His hand on her arm, he was smiling up at her, but his eyes on hers were very still.

Reading their look, she laughed. "What, love in the middle of the day with children coming home from school! Never heard of it," she teased him. "No," she said as he tightened his hold. Then, softening somewhat, "But I like you a lot, you know. Even though I'm using you."

"Really?" he said, and dropped her arm. "How?"

She bent on him a fond, sad smile. "Why you're my new Juju man from Harley Street, don't you know that, love?"

"Oh, Christ, Merle," he said. "Let me stay."

Later, in the room in which she had slept as a girl, high under the pitched roof of the house, she said, "You don't really mind, do you, my making use of you? People always do in one way or another, you know . . ."

He didn't answer but, his face against hers on the pillow, his mouth opened against the lobe of her ear from which he had removed the earring she wore as a reminder of her long subjugation, he shook his head, saying no.

CHAPTER 3

The sun was gazing down on Spiretown with its usual fiery midmorning detachment when the first of the excursion buses from New Bristol appeared at the top of Westminster that following Monday. The buses, packed with those people from town and the flat cane country on the other side of Cleaver's, who continued the old custom of spending the Whitmonday Bank Holiday in Bournehills, crept slowly, looking like so many clumsy mastodons, down the steep drop into the village. A vanguard of taxis and hired cars, filled with the overflow from the buses, led the way. These would take part in the car race to be held later on.

The visitors were deposited outside the social center at the edge of the playing field, and as they stepped out into the sunlight, nearly all of them paused, and, raising a hand to shade their eyes, looked curiously around them. Spiretown, which was only a scant fourteen miles from town, the whole of Bournehills in fact, might have been alien country, another island, and its people strangers, from the expressions on their faces. Like Saul they, too, seemed to sense something about the place they could not define. "Lord, this place far, yes," they said with an uneasy laugh, and hoisting the heavy baskets of outing food onto their heads, calling to their children to come, they set off to encamp upon the playing field.

Ignored by the villagers, who tolerated their presence for the day but kept aloof, they laid out their holiday feasts on tablecloths spread on the ground, milled among the hastily erected stalls offering sweet drinks and penny games of chance, and after a few rums crowded into the social center to dance in the close sunlit dimness there. Outside, their children raced in dark streaks across the grass that was brown and sere from the long months without rain.

As the heat brought its full weight to bear, many of them strolled over to swim in Horseshoe Pool. The bolder ones even braved the open sea, venturing out beyond the surf line, and laughing when the breakers caught and flung them back onto the shingle. Others, the old people, simply stood in the boiling white water at the edge, breathing deep the Bournehills sea air which was said to cure all ills. As they lingered there, the women with their dresses gathered up out of the way of the eddying water, the men's trousers rolled up around their stringy legs, they seemed to be puzzling over the sea in front of them which was so different from the mild Caribbean on their side of the island. Their wondering faces raised, they appeared to be asking the reason for its angry unceasing lament. What, whom did it mourn? Why did it continue the wake all this time, shamelessly filling the air with the indecent wailing of a hired mute? Who were its dead? Despairing of finding an answer they would turn away eventually and, leaving the young people romping in the surf, make their way slowly back to the village in time for the car race along the main road.

The Whitmonday Race had started informally a few years before Vere went to Florida. A number of the young taxi drivers from New Bristol who drove down those whom the buses could not accommodate had taken to racing their cars along the main road to impress the girls and while away the time till departure. These were only excuses, though, because something about that pure stretch of road which pierced Spiretown like an arrow whose head lay buried in the sandhills at the end had long excited their imagination, all the way back to the time when they had been little boys riding on their mothers' laps in the cramped buses to spend Whitmonday in Bournehills.

And so in the early afternoon, when the sun looked as if it would not budge from its high seat overhead until it had dried up the sea and turned the land to ash, they would pull their raffish hats low, adjust their sunglasses, and with considerable ceremony drive out to the foot of Westminster where the race both began and ended. At a signal they would be off, charging crowded together down the road past the cheering lines of spectators; then, just short of the sea, where the road swung left toward the guesthouse, they would turn back, their tires streaking the marl as they fought to negotiate the U turn in the narrow space. This done, they would scramble back toward Westminster, all the while viciously trying to shoulder each other into the open drains to the sides.

The race had become the high point of the Whitmonday excursion, and even the residents of Spiretown came out to watch or looked on from behind the jalousies at their windows and doors if their houses faced the main road.

Like them, Vere had kept aloof from the visitors, although just before noon he and Milly, who had come down for the day, had gone over to the playing field where they had strolled amid the stalls and danced once in the social center. But he had done this only to please her. Even now as he joined the fleet of cars on their way out to the starting point, the race about to begin, he drove somewhat apart from them, his souped-up motor growling confidently, eager to demonstrate its power.

All the heat and glare that had built up over the day was concentrated on the road. Above, the afternoon sky had been completely drained of its blue and resembled one of those three-paneled aluminum reflectors used in northern regions to draw the sun's rays in the winter. It was filled with the same blinding artificial-looking yellowish-white light, and seemed made of the same metal. The sun held to its vantage point directly overhead.

As the cars passed in a slow processional out to Westminster's broad foot a hush fell over the waiting crowd. The faces that would run together into an indistinguishable blur once the race got underway stood out separate and distinct now. Vere picked out those familiar to him. Delbert, by his sheer mass, caught his eye first as he drove past the shop. Wearing the Panama hat and hot shirt, he sat enthroned on the limestone stoop to the bar with Stinger, Saul, Ferguson, Collins, and the others gathered nearby in the trodden dust of the yard. Returning their solemn Bournehills wave, he thought with a smile of the noisy toasts they would drink in his honor later, to celebrate his victory—and although he had seldom before ventured into their midst (he had never felt quite up to them), he would join them today for a rum in the masculine intimacy of the shop.

Farther on Merle, standing next to the Bentley which she had parked off the road, held up two fingers in a victory sign. Milly was with her, seated in the car, where she had gone to shelter from the sun. Only this morning she had announced she was pregnant for him.

It would be a son, he was certain; and one, this time, who would live no matter what. Nothing, no one, would be able to kill him. Because he would, this new son, possess almost Herculean powers. Moreover, he would be free of his defects. He would not, for example, be someone who was easily taken in, as Leesy often said of him, nor be as trusting. There would be no turning his head, another fault she attributed to him. At the thought of that son who would possess the qualities he lacked he gave Milly the smile that was like a gift and drove on.

Out near the starting line, he glimpsed Allen far back in the crowd which had gathered to watch the take-off. His face, what little he could see of it, appeared tense, strained. Vere hadn't seen him in some time, but this morning as he was washing down the Opel Allen had suddenly appeared in the yard. He had come, he said, to wish him luck. Then, his eyes avoiding Vere, he had started to blurt out something, only to hurry away with it unsaid.

Swinging the car around in line with the others at the starter's direction, Vere wondered, as he had from time to time before, at the change in Allen since carnival. But in the next instant all thought of him vanished as the flag signaling the start of the race came down, and with a few expert motions of his hands, his feet performing a quick little dance on the pedals, he sent the Opel leaping cleanly forward.

It was exactly as he had imagined it would be in the daydream that had sustained him his three years away. The long white ribbon of road with the sea at its head. The heat, the stinging dust and the smell of the tires on the hot marl whipping across his face at the open window. The sun racing to keep up with him above. And below, at the roadside, the forms and faces of the crowd rapidly merging into a dark featureless frieze shot through with the molten colors of the clothes they were wearing. Even the amazed and somewhat apprehensive glances his competitors darted his way from behind their sunglasses as he gradually began to pull ahead were as he had pictured them in his mind. They brought a smile to his lips.

As for the Opel, it was outperforming all the cars he had driven in dream. It responded to his slightest touch, obedient to his will; its performance was a reward for the months of hard work he had put into restoring it. Moreover, as his foot bore steadily down on the accelerator and the speed began to build under him, he felt the combined power of that supercharged German motor and long, low-slung

American body which, in motion, looked like an animal lunging forward to strike, flow up through the floor and through the shaft of the steering wheel and enter him, becoming his power. His smile widening, he spurred the Opel ahead, and the surprised roar that went up as he took the lead and left the other cars scrambling in the dust behind, was the same stunning hosanna of his imagining, a sound like the roaring of his own blood in his ears.

The sandhills at the end of the village loomed close, mirages created by the shimmering heat and the salt drift off the sea, and the road took its abrupt turn southeast to the guesthouse. Gearing down as he approached the bend, Vere easily swung the car around in the tight corner, the wheels holding to the road under his careful maneuvering. Then, deftly sidestepping his competitors charging desperately toward the cut-off, with the difficult turn still to negotiate, he swept up the road again, headed back the way he had come on the second and final lap of the race.

He was more than halfway to Westminster, the race his (the crowd was already proclaiming him the undisputed winner) when he felt the first tremor. It was like a horse grown restive under too tight a rein, and treating it accordingly, he eased up a little on the pedal, still smiling to himself. And his smile—that beautiful but too trusting Vere smile which was like a light illumining his face—held even when the first of what was to be a series of massive shudders began deep in the chassis and, quickly spreading up, shook the entire frame. His foot shifted then from the gas to the brake pedal only to find—and here his expression took on a slight note of surprise—that although he was pressing it all the way to the floor nothing happened; the brake did not hold.

With that the car seemed to fall completely apart around him, disintegrating, all of it, into so many separate parts, the wheels moving out from their axle, the steering device becoming unhinged from its mooring under the dashboard, all the bolts and nuts and screws which he had so painstakingly and with such love secured over the months coming loose at once. The collapse was so total it seemed deliberate, planned, personally intended. It was as if the Opel, though only a machine, had possessed a mind, an intelligence, that for some reason had remained unalterably opposed to Vere, so that while doing his bidding and permitting him to think he was making it over into his own image, to express him, it had also at the same time been conspiring against him and waiting coolly for this moment to show its hand.

Or perhaps it had nothing to do with Vere. The collapse taking place around him, which he was helpless to stop, flowed perhaps out of a profoundly self-destructive impulse within the machine itself, and Vere, in foolishly allowing himself to be taken in by what he had believed was its promise of power, was simply a hapless victim.

Whatever, the Opel, weaving and lurching like a drunk, completely out of control, carried him on an insane course back up the road toward his goal at the foot of Westminster. And the crowd that only moments ago had been wildly proclaiming him the victor (their shouts still reverberated in the air) and pressing forward for a glimpse of him as he sped past, fled screaming from him now. Vere neither saw nor heard them. There was only himself and the thrashing, careening car, and he fought it, all the while checking in his rear-view mirror to see that his competitors were well behind: for in the midst of it all his mind remained fixed on the finish line ahead. Struggling grimly to straighten the front wheels he swung the loosened steering wheel sharply to the right. At that the Opel did a violent half-spin in the middle of the road, and as though helplessly committed now to its own end headed in a straight, swift line for the waist-high culvert wall over the dry riverbed, where the idlers of the village passed the day.

It struck the wall with such force its rear lifted, the back wheels kicking up like the hind legs of a bucking horse, and the entire body went pitching forward headfirst over the culvert. For a few seconds the car was actually air-borne, upside down, before it crashed in the riverbed with a sound that was to be heard echoing in the folds of the surrounding hills for many days to come. When the first of the spectators reached it the wheels were still spinning like someone kicking up his heels in glee.

They sent for Leesy, who always made it a rule never to leave the house on Whitmonday until the last excursion bus had departed. Today, knowing that Vere was entering the race, she had lain since morning on the wooden day bed in the drawing room where she sometimes napped, her face to the wall and the shutters in place over the windows. She hadn't once spoken or looked at Vere, but the hard dry back she had kept turned to him had given off her disapproval in a powerful voltage that had charged the silence between them. Now, as the boy who had been sent to call her started up the dirt road toward her house, he found her waiting on the slight elevation above the yard. And she had already put on her late husband's fedora over a fresh headtie. Before he could speak she said, "It kill him, yes?" and at his nod she stepped down, and taking her time followed him as he ran ahead to tell the others she was coming.

By the time she reached the culvert, walking slow and frail and unutterably alone down the middle of the road with the dust set in motion by the cars drifting lazily above her head, they had brought Vere up and laid him on the ground in the shade of the tamarind tree that stood to one side of the culvert. With something of his smile lingering and his eyes open, he was staring like Seifert at the almshouse straight up into the sun through the fernlike leaves of the tamarind. Beside him in the dust, holding his head with its broken neck between her hands knelt a distraught, loudly weeping Merle. Milly stood closeby crying without a sound, one hand hiding her tears, the other clenched in a fist on her stomach as though to defend the child there from the thing that had killed Vere. Beyond them and filling the roadway were gathered the shocked and silent crowd.

The crowd parted to make way for Leesy, and without looking to either side, and ignoring Merle, who lifted her tearstained face to call her name as she came up, she went to stand beside Milly. She glanced without expression at the girl, at the hand covering her face, then turned her gaze on Vere.

Quietly and for what seemed a long time to those watching, she studied his inert and broken form. Leaning closer, the brim of her raffish hat hiding the upper half of her face as she bent over him, she inspected his face. She might have been making certain it was really Vere. You almost sensed her checking off his individual features: the upswept bones that gave the face its essential character, the stretched skin that was either brown or black depending on the light, the lips whose faint trace of a smile appeared to be teasing her gently, the nose with its broad arched openings through which it seemed the winds of the world could pass.

Satisfied apparently that it was Vere she straigthened up, and still ignoring the crowd, in the silence broken only by Merle's unrestrained lament, she traced the tire marks the Opel had left on the marl in its suicidal drive toward the riverbed. Her head turning slowly, her gaze down, she followed those black angry scrawls over to the culvert a few yards away.

Allen stood there with his back to them all staring down at the smashed car. Its wheels had stopped spinning by now. No one could see his face, but from the way his head hung down and his hands were gripping the culvert ledge so that his knuckles stood out tense and white, from a tremor passing in slow regularity over his shoulders and back, it appeared that he was also weeping—but silently, to himself, like Milly.

Leesy's glance scarcely took him in. Instead, turning back she brought her gaze to rest on Merle, kneeling in the dust beside Vere, her entire self given over to her grief. Leesy studied her. Her head cocked critically to one side and each breath she took shaking the light hull of her body, she listened to her. And it was clear she understood the meaning of those loud sobs racking the silence, knew that Merle as a woman of vivid feelings which she gave vent to without shame was weeping not only for herself but for her as well, crying the wild tears which she, being Leesy, could never have brought herself to shed. Yet, it was also clear she didn't quite know what to make of this open show of grief. It was too alien to her. Moreover, she wasn't even sure she approved. Not knowing what to do she suddenly, for the first time, turned to the crowd who had been waiting for some sign from her. With bewildered eyes she scanned the faces before her, searching for her neighbors amid the strangers from town. But she appeared utterly confused, unable to distinguish one from the other.

"But what's wrong with you, Leesy Walkes? Why you don't close that boy's eyes, yes, and see he's there looking back to take somebody else with him!"

It was her friend, the old woman Mary Griggs, calling to her from the heart of the crowd in a voice that was both harsh and tender with reproof. And recalled to herself, Leesy quickly bent down and averting her face from Vere's lest his dead gaze reach out to claim her, she passed a hand lightly over his eyes—scarcely touching them—and they closed. Then, taking the nearly hysterical Merle firmly by the arm she raised her up, whispering to her as she did, "Come now, Mis-Merle, it's enough. You'll only set out your head again."

With a brusque wave of her hand she ordered the women standing nearby to take Merle and the girl Milly away; and as they hurried forward she signaled to the men to bring Vere home for her.

Later, alone with him in the house she sprinkled water and a few drops of rum at the foot of the bed, her bed, upon which he lay. Going outside, she did the same around the exterior of the house. She next washed and dressed Vere in the powder-blue suit he had worn home from Florida, and afterward carefully arranged his limbs in the proper attitudes. This done, she drew over a chair to the bed, and sitting down, folding her hands—those disproportionately large, work-scarred hands with the ring on the left middle finger to mark that she was a widow—in her lap, she began the wake that would last the night.

The funeral the following afternoon was the largest seen in Bournehills in some time. "Ah, Vere," people were to say afterward, "he had a short life but a sweet funeral." The entire district turned out, the women in white, "bare white" they called it, the color of death and mourning in Bournehills; the men in the one dark suit they kept for such occasions, which were rusty with age. The young taxi drivers from town who had lost the race to Vere despite the way it had ended returned, as did many of the excursionists, along with scores of the curious from New Bristol who wanted to see "the boy who got his neck popped in the Whitmonday Race" as he came to be referred to by people in town.

Led by an antiquated hearse, with Leesy in her white missionary dress walking alongside, the long line of cars and mourners on foot formed a cortege that stretched the length of the main road. And it moved at a pace set by Leesy, who had refused to ride in any of the cars, so that by the time it reached the cemetery behind the Anglican church on the road leading to Cane Vale, the sun had reached its final station of the cross between Westminster's spires.

At the end, with the pine box resting on two planks above the raw gash in the earth, Leesy left where she was standing between Milly and Merle—a drained, silent Merle today, and stepped up to the graveside just as the men in attendance began removing the cheap silverplated ornaments used to decorate the crude coffin. She waited, her face lifted so that her filled eyes did not encounter the box. The cords in her throat, which seemed made of catgut, quivered slightly beneath the black worn skin as though they had been plucked once and quickly released like strings on an instrument. Then, as one of the attendants unscrewed the silver plaque inscribed with Vere's name and the dates that had begun and ended his life, she held out a hand, and without a word the man placed it in her palm.

CHAPTER 4

. . . It was awful, Chessie. His eyes stayed open for the longest time before the old woman who was his aunt thought to close them. And they seemed to be looking straight at you, singling you out of the crowd. It almost made you feel you were in some way responsible for the accident. And for some odd reason, I kept thinking, seeing him there, of Alberta's nephew, the one you remember who was found murdered at the bottom of the pond that time. It was as though her nephew was the one lying dead under the tree and not Vere, the name of the young man. Or that it was both of them in one body. I don't know why I should have thought that. Allen was terribly upset by the whole thing. I don't think I ever mentioned it to you, but he and Vere had been quite friendly for a time. And our landlady, Merle, who was also very fond of him, as we all were, just broke down completely, as you would expect. Saul and some of the others tried to get her to leave the body when it was brought up from the riverbed but she refused. She insisted on remaining beside it, just kneeling there on the ground and crying. Everyone else was more restrained, but you could tell they felt it as deeply. I myself don't know when I've been so affected by anything.

As you can imagine, the death has added to the general state of gloom in the village. Nothing has changed since I last wrote. People are still waiting for some word about their canes, and although Saul has been to see the Kingsley representative in town twice he's been unable to learn anything. There's a terrible sense in the district of waiting for the worst to happen. I somehow even feel it in a personal way. And the weather isn't helping any. It's the height of the dry season and the sun's become so unbearable it's impossible to go out except in the very early morning and late afternoon. I don't know how the people who work in the fields manage. You have no idea, Chessie, nor did I until I came here, what life is like in the Bournehills Valleys of the world. I don't think I will ever recover from the experience of these past six months. Six months? It's more like six years! I can't tell you how much I'm looking forward to the trip home we're planning to take once the report Saul and Allen are working on is done. Saul, by the way, is going to insist that Allen come along with us. He's not only been working much too hard but seems troubled about something, and Saul feels he needs a break before the second phase of the work begins. And Saul and I desperately need some time away from here. He warned me that field work was a hazardous undertaking even with the best of marriages, and I'm afraid he was right. We aren't as we used to be with each other for some reason, neither of us, because I sense a change in myself as well. I can't pinpoint what it is that's gone wrong or whether it's in any way serious. One thing I'm sure of, though. This place is to blame. Bournehills seems to have a bad effect on everyone and everything. It's even made me start questioning whether Saul should stay on with the project once the preliminary study is done, and this is something I want to talk over privately with you when we come up to Philadelphia. Right now I somehow have to manage to get through the next month or two. If only it would rain it might help. . . .

CHAPTER 5

Merle, holding a cold bottle of beer in one hand and, in the other, a glass containing a finger of rum, her drawn face still reflecting in part her grief over Vere's death, quietly came and stood in the doorway of the room Allen used as a study. Inside, Allen sat working at the large trestle table which served him as a desk, his back to the door. For a time she watched him from the doorway which opened onto the veranda, standing there poised uncertainly between the noisy darkness of the sea and night behind her and the overly bright room within. Her eyes narrowed against the glare, she studied the dark head bent over the papers, the hunched concentrated back, and under the thin summer shirt he was wearing, the subtle stir of the muscles across his shoulders as he wielded his pen. He must have sensed her behind him after awhile, because his back stiffened, fending her off. He bent closer over the work in front of him.

And he continued to work even when she crossed the room with a loud rustling of her maroon-colored wrapper on the floorboards and, drawing up a chair, sat down at the side of his desk.

"I'm looking for someone besides myself to talk to around this place," she said. Then, as he continued to stab down the figures in a statistical table he was preparing for the report: "I know you're busy, but you've been at it all day and almost half the night and it's time you took a break. Had something to drink." She placed the bottle of beer on the desk and waited.

Finally, with a small show of irritation, he put down his pen and looked up. The face he raised to her had changed profoundly since carnival. Not only was it drained of all the warm coloring he had acquired over the months but the hazel eyes had retreated farther behind his glasses. He hadn't spoken yet.

"Well, how's it going?" she said. "The report and all."

"All right."

"When do you think you'll be finished?"

"In another couple of weeks maybe."

"And then it's home for the three of you, eh? For awhile anyway."

"I don't know about the three of us. I might stay and Saul and Harriet go. It hasn't been decided yet."

"I see," she said. Then: "Where's the big boss tonight?"

"Saul? At a meeting of the council."

"I might have guessed. You can hardly catch up with him these days for that council of his."

"He was over here earlier working on the report but you were up at the almshouse. He said to tell you the man from Harley Street sends his compliments—whatever that means."

She laughed, brightening somewhat, and raising her glass, said, "Cheers."

They drank, but Allen merely tasted the beer, and quickly putting it aside, once again picked up his pen. He began searching for his place on the rather elaborate-looking table he was working on, a demographical analysis of the population of Spiretown by age, sex, occupation and the like.

"I'll be glad when the Mathersons come," she said.

"Who're they?" He was about to jot down a number.

"My two most reliable customers," she said. "They're an old retired couple who come out from England every year about this time on holiday. You missed them your first time here. They're an odd pair. They could well afford to stay over at Crown Beach Colony but for some reason they prefer Bournehills. And they're great dog fanciers. As soon as they arrive they adopt every stray on the beach. The money's turned them foolish, but at least they'll be somebody to chat with in the evening. . . ."

There was a long silence, which she again broke by suddenly, without warning, leaning toward him across the desk. "What's it, Allen?" she asked quietly. Her eyes, fawn-colored against her blackness, searched the face bent over the paper. "What's troubling you? What's wrong . . . ?

"Is it Vere?" She spoke after some moments. There was no response. His head bowed, his pen poised above the page, he made it clear he was waiting for her to have done with her questions and leave.

"Is that it? Are you still grieving over him? Oh, I am, too, you know"—she sat back in her chair. "I haven't gotten over it either. Sometimes at night I can hear him coming back from town in the damn stupid car, burning up the road down from Westminster the way he used to and waking us all out of our sleep. It's as though he's not dead, as though as hard as that car tried it couldn't really kill him. Yes, it's Vere, isn't it . . . ?

"Yet come to think of it you were like this before he died," she said reflectively when he failed to answer. "You haven't been yourself for some time now. You've gotten so quiet and keep so much to yourself—just staying shut up in here all the time working. Oh, I know you're eager to finish the report, but my God, you could take a break once in a while. Why, I don't know the last time you've gone for a swim. You scarcely want to stop long enough to eat. You've even lost interest in the garden. I had to run the other day and put down some poison for the crabs. They were eating everything. I don't know, you've just changed up altogether. Your face even is different.

"What's it, love?" she cried softly, reaching a hand across to him. "You can tell me. I don't understand it, we used to talk all the time before. We were close good friends. But you hardly have a word for your old friend Merle anymore. Tell me," she urged him. "It'll help to talk about it, whatever it is."

She waited—longer this time than before, but finally as his gaze remained stubbornly fixed on the long columns of figures, she drew back across the desk with a sigh, and picking up her glass, rose. "All right," she said with a parting look at his hunched, rigid form. "I'll let you get on with your work."

She was almost to the door when he said, very softly, the words barely audible, "It's just that I feel like shit most of the time, Merle."

Her long skirt made not a sound this time as she recrossed the room and sat down again. Nor did her glass as she replaced it on the desk. And she was utterly still, her hands clasped in her lap and her face turned discreetly aside. It was as though she wanted to give the impression she had left the room, simply disappeared into the darkness of the veranda, so that he might feel free to speak aloud his thoughts.

"That's right," he said. He had not glanced up to see if she had returned. "Like shit. I know that sounds odd coming from me. I'm not one for the four-letter words usually, but that's the only way I can describe it. It's not so bad when I keep busy. I can forget then. But otherwise that's pretty much how I feel."

"Why so, Allen?"

Issuing out of her stillness and neutrality, the question seemed not to come from her, but from him, put to him by a voice speaking from a remote turn in his mind.

"I dunno," he said, shaking his bowed head. Then, running a hand over the hair which he brushed flat each morning: "Oh, it's a lot of things. Some of them too . . . too personal to talk about even to you, as close as we are. And we are close, Merle." He stole a glance at her averted face. "We're still good friends. I know I haven't been acting like it lately, but we are.

"In fact," he said, "I feel closer to you and people in Bournehills than to anyone else I know, including my own family. That's right. In a way Bournehills is more home than the States to me. That's strange, isn't it.

"But something's happened since I've been back this time." And knowing he could trust her not to look at him, he raised his head slightly. "I feel the same closeness, even more so because—" he paused—"because of Vere, but it's somehow different this time. For one thing, I've found myself thinking a lot about what my life's been like, remembering things from all the way back when I was a kid. Not that I had a particularly bad childhood as they go. It was just kind of lower middle class and dull. And Catholic. My father was an all-right guy but he never stood for anything, and never really did anything except sell fifty-cent life insurance, and my mother was, I'm ashamed to say, a very narrow, bigoted woman. She disliked all kinds of people, especially Italians, never mind she was married to one and had a son who was one, half one anyway.

"But I went along with them, did what they wanted, although they still can't figure out why I became a social scientist or just what I do. And for a long time I was able to tell myself I didn't dislike them. They couldn't help being what they were or living the way they did—so frightened and anxious all the time, always wanting to be the 'right' people, especially my mother. It wasn't their fault, I told myself. And it isn't, I know. But I'm no longer so charitable. Something's happened since I've been back here this time and I can't forgive them. I'm even afraid when I go home again they'll be able so see in my face what I really feel about them, how much I almost"—he hesitated a second, watching Merle—"hate them.

"And not only them!" he followed with an angry burst that brought the color surging to his face. "But that house with those fake Austrian shades my mother puts to the front windows to make it look like we're somebody. And that block where all the houses look alike, and everybody thinks alike. And that miserable town. And Jersey. It's gotten so I'm not sure how I feel about the whole darn country anymore," he declared. "And I used to be so patriotic. Oh, I knew there was a lot wrong with it, but I was still a red-blooded American all the way. I wanted to join the marines with my best friend, I remember, and I must have marched in the Columbus Day parade with my father up until I was sixteen. Now, I just resent the hell out of all of it."

"Have you asked yourself why, Allen?" It could have been the inner voice speaking to him again.

He didn't answer her right away, but for a time sat gazing down at his hands which he had placed palm down on the desk. Broad, strongly shaped, with the black hair sprouting between the knuckles, they looked capable of a powerful grip. Yet they were far too soft in appearance and as overly white as the papers they were resting on.

"Because I know now," he said, "that all that took something from me, something important that I needed if I was ever really to make it. That's gone, missing. I can't tell you what it is, there's no way to describe it. I can't even spell out what not having it has done to me . . ." There was a pause; then, abruptly, with a quick glance her way: "Well, for one thing, I'm not much with the ladies. But I'm sure you've suspected as much by now. They don't take to me or I don't to them—something. Anyway, I've generally had a bad time with them. . . ."

"But any woman could love you, Allen, don't you realize that?" she said gently.

"Ha!" It was his own mild version of her sharp sardonic hoot. "Maybe I can't love them. Have you thought of that?"

She almost broke their unspoken pact and looked at him. But she caught herself and keeping her head bent sat frowning down into her lap. "No," she said slowly. "I don't guess I have."

"Oh, it's not even the darn women so much." He spoke harshly.

"That doesn't bother me half as much as it should, I guess. It's more the feeling I've always had that I've never really done anything."

"How's that?"—and without thinking her head came up and she looked at him.

"Just never done anything."

"But how can you say that? What's all this?" The wide, kimonolike sleeve of the gown swept out to indicate the piles of charts and graphs and statistical tables on the desk. The loose sheets of paper scattered on top stirred lightly in the breeze she created. "All these figures. Why, Saul tells me there're not many who can match you at this type of thing, young as you are."

"Oh, this," he said and fanned down the work before him. "I can do this with my eyes closed. I'm a walking IBM machine, don't you know that? Always was, even as a kid. Mine's just one of those freak talents. But this isn't what I'm talking about. What I'm trying to say is that I've never done anything that was a real challenge, that didn't come easy like the stuff here. And I'd like to. Just for once I'd like to try my hand at something that would really test me. And it might not turn out right. I might go all out, risk everything on it, including even my life, and it still might fail. It's crazy I know, but can you understand that, Merle? Something that wasn't so safe and sure all the time . . ."

"Yes," she said, "I can understand that. But why not go ahead? Whatever you feel to do, do it. You're young."

"I couldn't," he said quietly. "Even if I knew what that something was, I couldn't."

"But why?"

He hesitated, searching for a way to put it so that she might understand. Then, slowly, after the long pause he began, his voice groping, his gaze averted. "Because of what I said before: that something important is missing with me. Call it guts, daring, what you will—I don't have it. And without it you don't go around taking on dragons. You don't try anything that's not a sure bet. You never even live halfway."

"But how can you be so sure you don't have whatever this thing is."

The eyes behind the glasses met hers fully for the first time. "I know I don't," he said, "when I meet people who do." Then: "You, for instance, Merle. You have it. I've always thought of you as someone who was never too afraid to live, who took on life. Oh, I know the rough time you've had and the terrible things that've happened. But in a funny way those things, bad as they were, are to your credit: proof that you haven't held back. I almost envy you them . . ."

"Envy me!" It was an incredulous cry.

"Yes," he insisted. "For someone like me who's always felt so out of it—the kind of guy who does his work and gets by but knows he doesn't have what it takes to live fully—I envy you. And Saul has it—this thing I'm getting at. For a long time after his first wife died everyone in the profession swore he was through, and here he is back again. And so, in a way, does Harriet, even though you might not think it. But she does, because as you may know, in the States people like Harriet—the ones my mother would love to be like, the pure WASPs with no Italian thrown in—don't as a rule go around marrying Jews or come to live in places like Bournehills. And an uncle of mine had it, the one I told you just decided one day to switch over to the poultry business—took a chance—and lost everything. And so did Jerry, my old friend Jerry, who upped and joined the marines when he was seventeen. And Vere. Vere had it."

He was silent for a long time, and when he did finally speak again, his voice, muffled by his bowed head, could scarcely be heard. "I was jealous of him, Merle," he whispered. "I can't tell you why, but I was, so much so I've had this crazy feeling since his death that in a way maybe it's what I wanted to see happen. Isn't that horrible, when I liked him so much and for awhile there, before carnival, we were such good friends. Really friends . . .

"Oh, God!" he cried, his head coming up violently: an invisible hand might have reached out and grabbing him by the hair, yanked it back. His eyes, which Merle likened to the rose window in the church, looked as if someone had hurled a rock at them, shattering all the mild lovely grays and greens, the tawny yellows and browns that made up the small color wheel there. And his voice was as shattered as he said, whispering it hoarsely: "Have you ever noticed that it's the guys like Vere and Jerry who die while the ones like me who play it safe all the time, who never take a chance, go on living. Taking up our cubic foot of space, breathing our share of the air, living—if you can call it that, because I swear in a way, it's the same as being dead. No different."

The silence which followed had a final, almost deathlike quality to it, and for a long time they simply sat there, Allen staring down at the various charts and graphs in which he had always sought to contain the whole formless bewildering sprawl of life, Merle gazing across at him with that helpless look—part sadness, part shying away—that comes from seeing too deeply into a friend.

Inside the room the few moths that had wandered in from the veranda noisily circled the lamp, dying, some of them, when they ventured too near the hot chimney. Outside, the sea kept up its steady dirge.

"I bet you're sorry now you asked," he said finally. He did not look up.

She thought of this for some moments, her gaze shifting from his face to a large area map of Spiretown on the opposite wall which he had drawn up, showing in meticulous detail the houses and shops and small plots of cane. Finally, she nodded. "Yes," she said, "in a way I am. Because I know there's probably nothing I can say that'll help. I'm not even sure, dear Allen, I understand all that's troubling you. It seems to go so deep. . . .

"Maybe the best thing would be for you to do like most of us—just go ahead and make a start at life. Find yourself a nice girl someplace for instance—and you shouldn't have any difficulty because as I said any woman could love you—and get married, have some chil—"

But the word was lopped off in the middle, her voice struck down by the look on the set white face he raised to her. It was a look bitter with disappointment. It said better than any word how deeply she had failed him.

"Thanks," he said quietly, "for the suggestion. How did you manage to figure out what I needed so well without cards or a crystal ball or tea leaves, without even reading my palm. That's pretty good . . .

"A nice girl and some children, eh?" It was said with a contemptuous snort. "And why didn't you add while you were at it a nice job teaching at some nice Midwestern university like Michigan State or Wisconsin—that goes along with it, after all. Or better yet, a nice job making a lot more money in private industry doing research in cybernetics and the like. They're eager for guys like me, the computer minds . . . A nice girl!" He turned away.

"But what's so wrong with that?" she asked. "Why sound as if it's the worst thing that could happen to you?"

He swung back. "What's so wrong with it?" he cried, his voice at an angry high, his trembling, bled-white face thrust at her across the desk, ready to hurl at her all that he found wrong.

"Yes, what?" She spoke boldly into the center of his rage. "Everybody needs someone, whether they want to admit it or not. Love in some shape, form or fashion. It's only those like myself who've gone through two or three lives in the space of one who can stick it alone and even we give way from time to time."

At the reasonableness of her argument his anger collapsed and he sank back in the chair. "Nothing's wrong with it," he said in a spent voice, "except that a wife and children have little or nothing to do with what I'm talking about, that's all. Nor would they solve anything. In fact, they'd just make matters worse."

"Then what is it you want to do, I ask you?"

He waited until the sharp, almost impatient echo of her question died and then said very carefully, each word separated from the next by a clear measured pause and his shattered eyes pleading with her to understand if only this once, "I told you, something different—and difficult. Not just some nice girl and children. That's the easiest thing in the world to come by, I suspect. I'm talking about a real challenge, something that would give me the feeling I was—how to put it?—out there in the center of life and not just looking on from the sidelines all the time. And it might even be something people didn't approve of so they no longer thought of me as such a nice, respectable type. In fact," he said, a thin vindictive smile taking shape, "I'd rather like that."

"Well then do it, I say, and the world be damned!"

He gazed at her for a long moment, the look eloquent of the despair he felt with her and most of all with himself. "It's obvious I haven't made myself clear, or you haven't been listening, one," he said. "Because what I've been trying to tell you is that even if I knew of something to do I couldn't bring myself to it. That I don't have *it*. Haven't you understood that? I guess you haven't. But then I suppose it's impossible for people like you who've always been out there in the center to understand my kind, the ones who just look on. . . .

"Look, I don't want to talk about it anymore," he cried savagely. "There's no point."

She started to speak, perhaps to make apology or to tell him that she understood but could offer no help. His manner, though, as he turned aside, the hopelessness and fury in his face, kept her silent.

A full minute passed before she spoke again. "Would you like me to leave," she said, "or can I sit with you a bit longer? I'd like to."

He didn't answer and she stayed, her helpless gaze on the large map opposite and her small, square, absurdly childish hands fallen open in her lap. Across the way Allen, his head sunk on his chest and his hair tumbling forward, was staring with a strange fixity at a graph amid the papers spread before him, staring at it almost as though he saw a human form trapped behind the crosshatching.

At the end of a silence broken only by the muted hiss and roar of the tilly lamp, the insects and the sea, he picked up his pen and began jabbing down the numbers in their long columns, and Merle, gathering up her cigarettes, her empty glass and the beer he had scarcely touched, rose to leave.

"I'm sorry I blew up," he said as she reached the door. "It wasn't you."

"Don't you think I know that, Allen?" she said, and stepping out into the warm night left him to the harsh white sanitized light in the room.

CHAPTER 6

The following morning their conversation of the night before seemed forgotten as they stood, just the two of them, out in the yard facing the road that led to the village. They were listening with puzzled expressions to the sound of Cane Vale's horn reaching them clearly through the early morning quiet and over the lowing of the sea on the other side of the house. For it was not the usual hoarse foghorn blast that signaled the change in shifts, but a deep plangent cry that rode the air like the sound of hundreds of conch shells being blown in unison. It brought to mind the vast dim underwater world from which life had come and to which, perhaps, what was left of it would return. There was the same note of finality to it, of things having come full circle and a long cycle at an end.

"But I wonder what the devil's wrong with Fergy this morning?" Merle cried as the horn continued to desecrate the dawn quiet. She stood with her arms akimbo and the full sleeves of her faded wrapper hanging down. "Has he gone daft or what, waking people out of their sleep with that horn. He must have had one too many at Delly's last night."

"No, something must be up," Allen said. "Erskine would never let him go on like this for nothing."

"But what could it be?" she said. "The only time they blow the horn this way is at 'the blowing out' when they've finished grinding all the canes and are about to shut down the machines. It's their way of letting people know the crop season's over. But how could that be when the smallholders still have their canes—" She broke off; a look of foreboding crossed her eyes like a shadow passing over the face of the sun which stood newly risen nearby. Her voice a frightened whisper, she said, "Allen, make haste and go over to Cane Vale and see what's up. Take the car."

When he returned sometime later with a visibly upset Saul seated beside him in the Bentley, she was standing in the same spot in the yard. She might not have moved but for the fact that she had exchanged the robe for a dress and, in place of her slippers, had put on the rather fanciful open-back shoes with the raised heels she always wore.

She took no notice of them as they drew up. Her set face and apprehensive eyes remained turned in the direction of the village, and although the horn had ceased blowing, she appeared to be hearing it still. Even when Saul came over and, taking her arm, informed her that the main roller had broken down and Cane Vale would be closing, she didn't appear either to see or hear him. But she said, her voice short, peremptory, "Let them fix it."

"They say they can't. Not right away, at any rate," he said. "I managed to talk to Erskine, who had just been on the phone to Hinds, and it seems that Hinds feels it's too late in the season to bother with it. That shrewd bastard Sir John must have seen what was coming that time he was here. Anyway, Erskine's been ordered to send what's left of the estate crop over to the Brighton factory all the way on the other side of Cleaver's. And he's saying the small farmers will have to do the same. How the hell they're supposed to get there without proper transportation I don't know. No donkey cart will ever make it over these hills with a load of canes. . . ." He paused, his distressed eyes reflecting the morning's tragedy. "I don't know what to say, Merle"—she still hadn't looked at him. "There doesn't seem to be anything we can do. Erskine's gone and shut himself up in his house, and Ferguson, poor guy, has just disappeared. He probably feels it's all his fault. I thought on the way over here of going into town and asking Hinds if he would at least allow the small farmers to use one or two of the estate lorries for their hauling. I doubt he will, though. I'll have to see what Delbert and the others think of the idea. Merle . . ."

But she continued to stare beyond him. Then, abruptly, she slipped her arm out of his light hold and without a word walked over to the car and got in beside Allen, who had remained at the wheel.

They drove in silence over to Cane Vale, Saul in the back seat, Allen driving and Merle at his side gazing stonily ahead. They arrived to find the tall iron gates leading into the huge compound closed and a hastily written notice up announcing the shutdown and barring all trespassers. Beyond the shut gate, across the dusty expanse of yard, where the excess canes from yesterday lay piled in the storage nest called the hive, the run-down mill and its outbuildings loomed silent and empty, their doors yawning open. Nor was any smoke to be seen rising from the great chimney, and the special silence which reigned over Cane Vale during the off-season, which gave the impression Kingsley and Sons had finally made good their long-standing threat and closed the place, was already in force.

Virtually the entire population of Spiretown stood outside the gate and down the long stretch of road leading to it. Silent, impassive, their arms folded loosely at their waists, they were all, even the children, caught in that stillness of body and gesture only people in Bournehills were capable of; which, at times, seeing them on a road or in a field with their hands raised in the immemorial salute made them almost resemble statues that had been placed on an abandoned landscape to give it the semblance of life. And today, more so than usual, their deep-set eyes appeared endowed with a two-fold vision: of not only being able to see backward in time so that, unlike most people, they had a clear memory of events long past, but, by some extraordinary prescience, forward also. They knew, you were certain, what the future held and that, despite all they had undergone and had yet to endure, it was assured. Perhaps this was why standing there before the barred gate they appeared largely unaffected by what had happened.

Stepping back onto the brown, sun-burnt grass of the shoulder they made room for the Bentley to pass, and as it moved swiftly down through their ranks and they glimpsed Merle beside Allen at the wheel, they quickly dropped their gaze—embarrassed, knowing that Merle, who lacked their restraint, would surely do or say something rash. But their downcast gaze also expressed solicitude and love: they knew the toll that outburst would exact and would have spared her the pain if possible.

From under their lowered lids, they watched her get out of the car as it pulled up in front of the gate, and refusing, with a curt wave of her hand, Saul's offer to accompany her, her face tight, her eyes fixed ahead, push open the gate (it was not locked) and ignoring the posted sign enter the yard.

She went first to the small weighing office, where Erskine Vaughan could usually be found hovering over the bookkeeper as the latter recorded the weight of the loaded trucks on the scale outside. Finding this deserted, the door locked, she immediately proceeded to Erskine Vaughan's house, a large plain bungalow with scaling walls and louvered shutters situated behind a sandbox tree at one side of the yard.

It seemed a long walk to those watching, but she covered the distance quickly, her heels raising little flurries of dust and cane chaff each time they struck the ground and the large flowers on her dress coming full bloom as the breeze sent it billowing out around her legs. She vanished out of sight behind the tree which hid the entrance of the house. But they soon heard her knock on the door—an imperious sound that carried easily in the silence; and then her voice, faint but very clear and ominously pleasant, addressing the servant: "Would you call Mr. Vaughan here for me please, Ilene."

It was a long wait before the servant—a young girl from her voice—returned to say through the jalousied panel of the door that Erskine Vaughan was busy and couldn't come, and though her voice was no more than a thin frightened whisper to those at the gate it nonetheless conveyed a picture of the shuttered house within and of Erskine Vaughan, his wife and their numerous freckled sand-colored children cowering out of sight in a room to the back.

Merle called him herself then, shouting his name repeatedly through the jalousies, hurling it like rocks she had armed herself with against the walls of the house. The crowd across the yard saw in their mind's eye the tensed-forward body, the angry face pressed to the door and the saints at her ears quaking in fear.

Then, when he still did not answer, she cursed him—and as her rage erupted those at the gate further lowered their eyes. Not knowing anymore what she was saying, not caring, she called him a coward, a lackey and a conniver, and accused him of having broken the roller on orders from Kingsley. It had been purposely done, she cried. With the estate canes almost done, they had seen no point in keeping the mill running, and had ordered him to break the machine. She challenged him to deny this to her face. She disowned him, declaring he was no family to her. She cursed his mother for giving birth to him, his father, a distant cousin of her father's, for having sired him, and finally the long-dead planter Duncan Vaughan for having, she said, spread his seed like a disease from one end of the island to the other, contaminating them all.

But in the face of the unassailable silence of the house, the abuse she heaped on him sounded hollow, ineffectual, even pathetic. As quickly as the curses rose they fell. Those outside could almost see them falling like downed birds through the air. She, too, must have finally realized the futility of her harangue because her voice suddenly ceased. And as quickly the off-season silence returned. She might not have spoken.

She reappeared after what seemed a long wait to the crowd at the gate and they could immediately see the change in her. The determined stride that had borne her swiftly across the yard was gone and her steps dragged. The dress hung limp on her body, its printed flowers wilted. Pausing in the middle of the yard she slowly looked around her with a dazed, bewildered expression. It was as if she suddenly didn't know where she was and had, moreover, forgotten what had brought her here. In its slow confused sweep round the mill her gaze encountered the silent throng out on the road and she still didn't seem to remember. And then she spied the men who had arrived for the day shift just as the horn had sounded. They were crowded to the front of the others, directly behind the tall iron bars, and they were holding, as if they didn't quite know what to do with them, the chipped enamel kits containing their eleven o'clock breakfast of rice and saltfish. At sight of them she shivered once in the early morning heat; her head dropped and her body went as limp as her dress.

She remained like this for some time, a small, slack, bowed figure in the middle of the empty yard, under a sky that due to the dry season was also empty except for the single glowering eye of the sun. Then, as though she could not as yet bring herself to confront those at the gate and see in their faces the reflection of her own powerlessness, her sorry failure on their behalf, she turned and, catching sight of the opened door of the mill at the far end of the yard, started toward it, walking slowly, the dust scarcely stirring at her heels this time, and disappeared inside.

She was gone for close to a half hour when Saul, realizing that no one in the crowd around him would dare venture past the notice posted on the gate and go to her, and that perhaps only Allen and himself by virtue of their status as outsiders could risk it, left where he was standing beside the Bentley, and stepping into the yard followed her same path across to the building.

He entered the factory to find her—once his eyes adjusted to the dimness—standing in Ferguson's place on the platform above the roller pit, staring numbly down at the silent machines over the guard rail. Ignoring the inner voice that cautioned him to remain near the door until she had noticed him, he made his way toward her through the ship's-hold gloom of the mill, with its brown light and close, sickening sweet smell. The cane chaff which had whirled like a minor sandstorm around his head on his previous visits hung motionless in the air, and although the metal floor with its raised studs was warm underfoot, he knew the fires were out in the huge furnaces below. But strangest of all was the silence. Coming in the wake of the unrelieved drumming and pounding of the machines and the human shriek of the rollers, it was so absolute it seemed no amount of noise could ever fill it again.

Merle, standing with her back partly to him, gave no sign she heard him approach, and he paused midway up the short flight of steps to the platform. A hand on the railing, the Saracen nose probing the air like an antenna, he studied her rigid back and what little could be seen of her face, trying to assess her mood; and again part of him said it would be better for him to return as silently as he had come and wait at the door. Above all, it cautioned him not to speak. But he did, after holding back for a time. Bracing himself as he always did, almost instinctively, when he wasn't sure of how she would receive him, he softly called her name across the distance separating them. She didn't respond and he repeated it, somewhat louder this time, thinking she might not have heard him. He called her again and was about to take another step up when she slowly turned his way. And the sight of that face, which at times appeared to contain in ever-shifting and elusive forms all the faces in Bournehills, drove him back to the lower step.

She didn't speak. With her arms dangling limp at her sides, she simply stared quietly at him with the utterly blasted and enraged eyes. Finally, in a deceptively calm voice, she said, "Is that all you can do, stand there and call my name?" She waited; then, in the same even tone: "Do you think maybe if you call it often enough this roller might start working again? Perhaps you've heard that my name is some magic word people say over broken machines and before you know it they're fixed. Is that it? Well, you heard wrong, bo. My name never fixed a thing. *Merle!*" She spat it at him, the bitterness, the cruelty even, which were never very far behind her smile, which had always from that first night at Sugar's held him and all like him accountable, rising swiftly to the surface of her voice to sweep aside the false calm.

"Is that all you can say—or do, for that matter: stand there rehearsing my name, I ask you?" she cried, and the old decayed building, which the silent machines had turned into a huge echo chamber, rang with the words. "Can't you maybe try to fix this thing? You said you came to help, didn't you? That's the reason you're in Bournehills, isn't it? All right, here's your chance. And you don't have to do anything big. We're not asking for any million-dollar schemes just now, no big projects. You don't have to play God and transform the whole place into paradise overnight. All we're asking is that you fix one little machine. That'll be enough for now. And that shouldn't be difficult for you. After all, you're from a place where the machine's next to God, where it even thinks for you, so I'm sure you know how to repair something as simple as a roller. Machines come natural to your kind. Well, then, show your stuff and fix this one.

"Go on, get down there"—a slashing hand ordered him over to the ladder leading down from the platform into the deep pit—"and fix it so those people out at the gate can get their few canes ground before what little juice there is in them turns to vinegar. If you like them as you say you do, if they're your friends—Stinger, Delly, Fergy and the rest—if you feel for them, fix it. If you love me, fix it. That's the least you can do. Or is that asking too much? Perhaps all you can do is walk about asking people their business. Collecting data. And writing reports. Is that all you're good for? And sitting around worrying about something you say you can't understand about the place. Well, open your eyes, damn you, and look. It's there for a blind man to see. Look at those poor people standing out there like they've turned to stone, afraid to set foot inside the gate when they should be overrunning this place and burning it the hell down, or better yet, taking it over and running it themselves. Talk about change? That's the kind we need down here, bo. Look at this damn roller which was broken on purpose. That's right, on purpose. You couldn't tell me different. The estate canes were in and they didn't see any point in bothering with those belonging to the smallholders so they had their lackey break it. That's how it was. It was purpose work. Look at me," she screamed, but her face was so distorted by her rage she didn't resemble herself, and Saul, stranded on the stairs, lowered his gaze, refusing to look. "What more answer do you need? Does somebody have to draw a picture for you, so you'll understand? You know what your trouble is? Do you know?" She took a menacing step toward him, but he held his ground. "You can't see for looking, that's what. Or maybe deep down you don't really want to see. But I don't give a blast, just fix this bloody roller or don't ever call my name again. Or, if you go down there and see it can't be fixed, then take some of the multimillions the newspaper said you're planning to spend on us and go out and buy a new one. Buy two because the other one probably doesn't have long to last, either. Order them today from England or America. The jet can have them here tomorrow. Do it, I say. Do something, but oh, Christ, don't just stand there with your head hanging down doing nothing. Oh, blast you. Blast all of you. You and Sir John and Hinds and the Queen and that smooth high-toned bitch of a wife you've got and that other bitch who tried to turn me into a monkey for her amusement. Look, don't come near me, you hear. I don't want to see not a white face today. Not one! *Fix it!"*— and the scream shearing off the top of her voice set the cane chaff hanging motionless in the air moiling again. "You're a so-called scientist, aren't you? Well, what's the good of all that science and technology they teach you in that place you're from if you can't fix one little machine? Great is the magic of the white man? Well, then, let's see some of it. Get down in this pit and start this damn wheel turning. Come on. Form yourself here for me." Once again she ordered him over to the ladder, the gesture loud with the crash of her bracelets. When he again failed to respond, her scorn knew no bounds. "Look at him, yes. He's supposed to be a big-time scientist and can't fix a simple wheel. Why, Vere would have had this thing working by now I bet and he never had a lesson in science or mechanics in his life. But he's not around anymore, is he? He went to America and you people turned his head with a lot of nonsense about cars and he's dead. Just so. Cut down just when he was coming into his own. His young life spread out on the road for everybody to see. Oh, God, to kill the boy one month and shut down Cane Vale the next! They must really be trying to finish us off down here in Bournehills. . . ."

At the thought of that double tragedy, something in her, the last vestige of her reason perhaps, gave way, and a darkness, as complete as on those nights in the village when there's no moon and the oversized Bournehills stars are hidden by clouds, seemed to close over her mind, over her eyes, snuffing out all the light and sanity there. "Kill! Destroy!" The words issued shrill and incoherent out of the darkness. "That's all your science and big-time technology is good for. Don't think I don't see it for what it is. Why, you've even smashed the rose window in the church. Everything and everybody blown to bits, the whole show up in flames because you couldn't have it your way any-more. Everything flat, flat, flat. No—wait!" She paused, her demented eyes filling with another image. "No, they'll use that other one I read about someplace that they call the neutron or some damn thing, that they say only kills off the people—the people, everybody, just vanish into thin air, but everything else, the buildings and so are left standing right where they are. Yes! That's the one the brutes will use. All the buildings will be there but there'll be nobody inside them. Empty. The cars and buses right where they were on the roads when it dropped but not a driver in sight. No passengers. Not even a dead body to be seen on the streets. The houses with the curtains at the windows like people are living in them but not a soul inside. Every living thing just gone from the face of the earth. Oh, God, the silence! You can hear a pin drop the world over. Everybody gone. All the poor half-hungry people who never had a chance. The little children. The baby's gone. Everything in place but both of them gone. Oh, how could he have done that to me? I see it, you hear, I see it. The whole world up in smoke and not a fire to be seen anywhere!"

Her eyes were so filled with that apocalyptic vision, her words, re-echoing endlessly through the empty building, had made it so vivid, that Saul, struck dumb on the steps, could almost see that flameless fire raging between them on the platform. And just as it reached up to snatch away her voice and consume her utterly, a faint light glimmered for an instant within the darkness that had engulfed her and she saw him, and even as her eyes went dead and the raving once more took possession of her, she cried, screaming it like one drowning, "Saul, oh, Saul, take me out of this terrible place!"

He did not see her again until much later that night. When he led her, distraught and crying out in the broken voice, over to the door, he found Gwen and several other women from the crowd at the gate standing waiting in the drenching sunlight outside. They must have heard her screams very faintly across the distance and had come. Without a word, they drew her from him, and forming a protective circle around her slowly guided her back across the yard.

He left for New Bristol almost immediately afterward, only stopping off in Spiretown long enough to confer with Delbert, who had remained behind in the village, and to pick up his car which was parked outside the house on the rise. Harriet was there. Besides Delbert, she was perhaps the only other one who had not gone over to Cane Vale when the horn sounded—which was odd since she could have easily taken the car. But she had remained behind with the solid wood shutters they used at night in place over the windows facing the road. When Saul told her about the shutdown she expressed her concern—but in a vague, detached manner. On his way back out she called to him to make sure and close the door behind him.

Allen and Stinger accompanied him to town, and while they waited downstairs he went up to see Hinds in the Kingsley offices above Barclay's Bank. Hinds, his large good-humored face flushed and hot despite the air-conditioned chill of the office, repeated with a philosophical shrug what Erskine Vaughan had said before barricading himself in the house: simply that it would be impossible to repair the roller before the end of the crop season. It might be broken beyond repair, he said—he would be sending a man down in a few days to look at it—and if so, they could only hope the London office would decide to replace it and not just (this in his pronounced querulous white Bourne Island accent) "shut the damn place down once and for all 'cause they're only losing money keeping it open. But I don't have any say in the matter. It's the people in London."

To Saul's request that he allow the smallholders to use the estate lorries to haul their crops to Brighton, Hinds declared he had no authority to do that and all the trucks were needed to transport the remainder of the estate canes. "Besides," he said, "Bournehills people don't know how to care anything. They'd lick up the lorries the same as they did the roller."

And when Saul, his voice rising, insisted that something had to be done, Hinds merely gave his bluff laugh. "Why, Dr. Amron," he said, "you're getting on like they're your canes. But don't upset yourself. You don't know Bournehills people. They'll manage to get those few dry sticks they grow over to Brighton if they have to head them the distance there."

At that Saul left, and as he stood cursing out loud in the heat and noise and blinding glare of Queen Street with Stinger and Allen looking on, his outrage was a bitter-tasting phlegm that had gotten lodged in his throat and was choking him. And he suddenly knew, in the deepest personal way, all that Merle had felt standing on the platform in the silent mill: her frustration and rage, the sense of utter powerlessness that had sent her lashing out at him.

They next went to see the head of the labor union, hoping there was something he could do, but he was in Washington attending a conference of Caribbean trade unionists being held under the joint sponsorship of the largest of the American labor unions and the State Department. His assistant said he had no authority to act on his own. Besides, what could be done, he asked with something of Hinds' resigned shrug. The workers in Bournehills had never been properly organized: the place was too out of the way and the people unreceptive.

At Allen's suggestion they then went in search of Lyle Hutson, only to learn from the clerk in his chambers on Upper Queen Street that he was also out of the island. He had left a day or two ago for Antigua on government business, taking Enid with him (Dorothy and George Clough, with his tour of duty over, had returned to England shortly after carnival), and they were planning to stay on, once his affairs were concluded, for a brief holiday.

Finally, although they knew it would do little good, they drove over to Legco to see Deanes, the Member for Bournehills who, in all the months Saul had been on the island, had only visited the district once. The lower house was in session and as they waited for Deanes in the vaulted antechamber which boasted the names of the island's former rulers, the long line of kings and queens, carved into the thick stone, they could hear the voices of the legislators inside. They were heatedly debating the question of the gambling concession for the mammoth hotel the Hillard chain was scheduled to build under the new development plan.

Deanes emerged, round-faced and flustered. He had heard of the breakdown. "They woke me out of my sleep this morning with the news," he said, his eyes not quite meeting theirs, his glance darting over his shoulder in that nervous habit of his. "It's a serious business, yes. Lord, what are the poor people in Bournehills to do? I feel for them, you know. They have it too hard. But these things will happen. Kingsley and them are going to fix it, though. I telephoned Hinds first thing this morning to demand what they intended doing—oh, yes I did; after all, I have to see to the welfare of my constituents"—his heavily accented voice was loud amid the echoing stone—"and he told me they're going to fix it. Of course, it'll take time. A roller is a serious business, you know. But at least they're going to fix it if they can, so all Bournehills people can do is wait and hope and try to manage as best they can. It's not easy. But tell them for me, Dr. Amron"—the eyes which reflected the almost poignant uncertainty he lived with as a largely uneducated, self-made man, briefly appealed to Saul—"that I'm doing my best for them over this side. Stinger"—he turned in the same breath to Stinger standing with his cap pulled low to hide his face—"tell the people I'm coming down to see them soon. They've been keeping me so busy over this side I haven't had the chance, but I'll be down soon, tell them, to speak to them personal and seek out their grievances. Tell them," he cried, backtracking toward the tall double doors to the council chamber, "that I have them in my thoughts the whole time." He disappeared inside.

They quickly left town after that, with Saul driving with something of Merle's recklessness once they reached the open road. The morning's defeat was like alum on his tongue, in his dry mouth, and he scarcely heard what Stinger and Allen beside him were saying. Back in Spiretown—and it was late afternoon by the time they arrived, the day almost gone—they conferred with Delbert and the other men who made up the core of the village council. It was decided, as the only possibility open to them, to try hauling the canes jointly, using Delbert's pickup truck and any other vehicles they could find.

Later, near dusk, at a hastily called meeting in the social center, Delbert put the plan to the villagers crowding the room and overflowing onto the playing field outside. He didn't begin right away. Rather, standing silent and immense on the platform where the steelband boys played for the Saturday night dances, his stance favoring the leg that had been broken, he studied them from under the battered hat, his eyes moving in benign authority over the massed faces before him, then traveling slowly out the door to those on the field whose dark forms were already beginning to blend with the onrushing dusk.

"We know we're not a people famous for helping out the one another," he began flatly—and there was an uncomfortable stir. "Not anymore at least. Years back when Cuffee was alive and we was running things around here ourselves we did different, maybe because we knew then that if we had lived selfish we couldn't live at all. Well, it's the same now. Kingsley and them has shut down Cane Vale, saying the main roller's broken, and leaving our canes standing in the ground, and we must needs get them out and over to Brighton before they develop red-eye and are no use to anybody. We're faced, in other words, with a grave emergency down here in Bournehills, and we're going to have to see whether we can't work together, help out the one another, as we did back in Cuffee's time, if only for this once. Because if we don't, if it's going to be every man for himself and to hell with the other fella, not one, but all of we are goin' to lose out. . . ."

Under the plan as he went on to describe it, each man would reap his crop in the customary way, either doing the cutting himself or hiring help, but this time he would do so according to a schedule worked out by the council which would undertake to transport them to Brighton. (Allen had already brought over his large area maps with the peasant holdings clearly marked, and was busy, along with other members of the council, drawing up a schedule that would co-ordinate the cutting and hauling.) Each man was to contribute toward the cost of the hauling, but no more, Delbert said, than he normally paid to have his crop taken the short distance to Cane Vale on someone's cart. The bulk of the money needed to hire whatever trucks were available, buy gas for the long trips back and forth over the hills, make repairs and the like was to come, he explained, from Saul, who had offered to provide the money out of the funds he had on hand for the first part of the research. They would have to move quickly, though, he warned, because word had reached them that Brighton, with most of its grinding done, was due to close soon. At the end, after other speakers including Saul had urged them to accept the plan, Delbert asked for a show of hands; and with the exception of Leesy and a few like her, all over the large room and out on the darkened playing field the hands quietly went up—black with the light-colored palms—to signal their assent.

There was still the matter of the additional trucks, and Saul, along with Stinger and Ten-ton, spent the rest of the evening driving around Bournehills in search of these. Bryce-Parker, the soil conservation officer, agreed to let them use his dump truck after working hours. They managed to hire a van from a fairly well-to-do produce farmer in the village just beyond the high cliffs that walled off Bournehills to the southeast. Driving back through Canterbury they spotted an ancient lorry with two missing tires parked in the yard of a rumshop. The owner, who had been to America with Ten-ton on the labor scheme many years ago, offered them the use of it if they would buy the tires needed, which they agreed to do. These three, along with Delbert's pickup and the Bournehills bus which they were planning to convert into a truck by removing the benches and tarpaulin roof, would perhaps be enough. If not, Stinger said, and "push came to shove," they could always add the hearse.

Returning to Spiretown, they stopped off at Delbert's to give account of their finds. The shop was more crowded than usual tonight, yet as soon as they entered, Saul's eye was drawn to the far corner where the jukebox stood, and to a dim figure sitting alone at the table there to which the butcher Collins and a partner would sometimes retire for a game of dominoes when things got too noisy at the counter. He saw it was Ferguson, who had gone into hiding following the breakdown. The story went that when he had reported for work at about two o'clock in the night (he sometimes left straight from Delbert's, walking alone and a little salt over the dark roads, his long sword of a stick assaulting the air as he declaimed aloud about Cuffee) and found the roller broken he had spent hours down in the pit trying to repair it, near to tears and cursing as he labored over it. But it had been no use and giving up finally, he had, openly crying by then they said, sounded the horn and shortly afterward disappeared.

Leaving Stinger and Ten-ton to tell about the trucks, Saul went over to him. He had drunk more than half of the quart bottle of white rum in front of him and behind his thick glasses his eyes were blank, glazed over; and his head, that long, beautifully sculpted Benin head which he kept shaven clean as though to call attention to its shape, was weaving imperceptibly from side to side, almost like that of a woman heading a load of canes down a slope.

Saul started to greet him, but confronted by those eyes and that tremulous head he could say nothing and, dropping into the chair opposite, his face sank into his hands. They sat like this for some time at the small table, which had been battered smooth in the middle by the dominoes Collins slammed down with savage emphasis whenever he was winning. Beside them the garish jukebox from America played its silent tunes. At the counter the thick crowd of men kept their backs discreetly turned and their voices low.

And then suddenly Ferguson spoke. Staring with unseeing eyes into the terra-cotta dimness of the shop, his hoarse voice wavering like his head, he said—and he spoke more to himself than to Saul, "I was goin' tell him that time. As God is my witness, I was. Sir John and Hinds both. I was goin' come right out and tell them straight to their damn face the roller din' have long to last, that it was old and tired out. After all, I'm a man knows a thing or two 'bout machines. I could tell. But what was the use. They wouldn't have taken my word for it. Or they would have said I was trying to run their factory for them and maybe get rid of me. You know what these white people give. It's a rare one comes like you. But I was goin' tell them all the same."

There was a long pause. Then, quiet-voiced: "Cuffee woulda done different. He would've spoke up."

And again after a silence, his voice all the more subdued but confident, his huge sheened eyes filled with the belief that sustained him: "He's goin' come again. For all such as me, Cuffee's goin' come."

Across the way Saul nodded, although he knew Ferguson had yet to really see him. He stayed awhile longer, drinking in silence with him at the scarred table, and then left.

As his last act of the long day he set out across the village in the car to see Merle. He had learned upon returning from town that after Gwen and the women had taken her, still dangerously overwrought, back to the guesthouse, they had sent for Miles Wooding, the medical officer for the district. Wooding had been up at the almshouse clinic, which he visited twice a week, and had driven over to see her. But he never got near her because as soon as she heard he was coming she had locked the door to her room and turning her fury on him had accused him of being in league with Kingsley and Sons, and had shouted at him through the door to go and repair the roller. Only Leesy, whom they had then summoned, had finally been able to quiet her.

Driving out now toward the guesthouse along the main road he came to the unpaved turnoff that led to his house on the stony rise. He could see what must be their lights shining like a row of small square stars set high in the darkness. Harriet was up. The water for the coffee she would start to prepare the moment she heard his car outside was, he knew, already standing on the unlit kerosene stove. The two cups they used would be turned down in their saucers to protect them from the tiny winged insects that somehow gained entry into the house each night. . . .

Suddenly, as if he saw an impending accident just up ahead: another car coming directly at him or a figure he had failed to notice because of the darkness, he swerved sharply to the side and, his left wheels narrowly missing the open drain, his screeching tires rousing the dogs under the houses, pulled up on the shoulder. His arms came up to fold over the top of the steering wheel; his head, his entire body dropped to meet them, and for the longest time there on the empty road, with the darkened houses on each side already settled into their long sleep, he sat bent to the wheel, his hands gripping its hard scalloped form against the sudden overwhelming sensation of falling that swept him. And as the thoughts that he had fended off for weeks found their opening and rushed him, setting upon him like the dogs who had rushed out and were furiously circling the car, his shoulders, bulking up in the darkness, were seized by a light steady tremor—not unlike Ferguson's just now—which he was powerless to control. He remained in its grip for long minutes, falling helplessly into the dark endless well, and when the tremor finally passed and he raised up, his head struggling up with such an effort it might have weighed more than all the other parts of his body taken together, his eyes held Ferguson's look. They were screened by the same colorless opaque glaze that was designed to shut out both the world and the fact of himself.

It was some time before he was up to starting the car, and when he did the dogs who had retired back under the houses sent their howls trailing him down the road.

He arrived at the guesthouse to find Carrington on guard outside the closed door to Merle's room which stood off by itself in a part of the building he had seldom been in before. Carrington—her face, her tall figure, her massive bosom—was indistinguishable from the shadows filling the passageway leading to the room, and he would not have seen her but for the white high-bibbed apron and cap she wore at all times, even on her day off (as a reminder perhaps of some long and bitter servitude), and for the inescapable force of her presence which, when he and Harriet had lived at the guesthouse, had always reached out from the kitchen to pervade every room.

She rose, towering, maternal, and mute as he came down the hall, and for a moment he was afraid she meant to bar his way. But perhaps his determined step dissuaded her, because as he drew near she wordlessly moved aside to let him pass. He asked her how Merle was, and touching her temple just below her cap she gave the little eloquent gesture that said "out": "the head's out," meaning Merle had sunk into one of her long, frightening, cataleptic states during which she was more dead than alive.

Opening the door he caught sight of her on the bed across the room, and his first thought was that she had fallen asleep while sitting propped up in an awkward position against the raised old-fashioned headboard, and he almost started to withdraw. But crossing to the bed he found that her eyes were partly open. There was no indication of life in them, though. Like Sugar on his high stool behind the bar she appeared to be staring, with his same flat quiet intensity, into all-absorbing nothingness.

"Merle . . ." he said, bending over to bring his face into line with her vision. But nothing happened in her eyes. There was not the slightest hint of recognition or awareness. It chilled him and he quickly straightened up. It was as though she had fled completely the surface of herself for someplace deep within where nothing could penetrate, leaving behind a numb spent face, a body which looked as if it had been thrown like a rag doll, its limbs all awry, on the bed and left there, and the dead eyes.

And standing gazing down at that discarded body, unable to reach her in that numb center to which she had retreated, he was suddenly overwhelmed by a sense of *déjà vu*. He was positive suddenly that he had stood feeling the same helplessness at this same bedside before. The scene, himself, Merle, was a fragment broken off from a life he had lived at another time but had forgotten. And then he remembered his first wife lying in almost the same comatose state on the hospital bed during the brief lulls amid the delirium that had ended her life. In Merle's empty stare and lifeless form he suddenly saw that other woman he had loved, whose death he had brought about, the faces merging, becoming one, before his eyes.

But hadn't he, now that he thought of it, sometimes glimpsed Sosha looking out at him from behind Merle's sunlit gaze? Hadn't he, thinking back on it, heard her screaming at him in Merle's voice this morning from the high platform? Behind the latter's angry demand that he fix the roller had been Sosha's anguished plea that he give her a reason for her suffering. In the abuse Merle had hurled at him for his ineffectualness had been contained the curses his wife had scourged him with at the end for his silence. And it fleetingly occurred to him, the thought merely glancing his dazed mind, that perhaps in Merle he was being offered a chance to make good that old failure. Perhaps this, more than anything else, was what bound him to her. What had she said that time at the old woman's house in town about the uses to which people put each other?

The faces separated, his dead wife's receding, Merle's coming into focus again, and he saw that her eyes had closed. But it was no different than when they had been open. The blank quiet stare was unchanged, he sensed, behind the drawn lids, and he could still feel her huddled like a child overwhelmed by a world it had found too complex and unkind in that inaccessible corner within. And afraid that she would remain there, permanently out of his reach, and he would fail her as he had that other woman years ago, he leaned over and very carefully straightened out her body in the bed and then drew the top sheet over her. This done, he sat down beside her and taking her hand, which felt muscleless and cold, began chafing it between his.

It was then he became aware of the room, her room which he was seeing for the first time. Because although they had met the few times in town, they had never met here. She hadn't permitted it. Once, right after Vere's death, when she had locked herself in for days, he had come and knocked on the door, worried about her, but she had refused to let him in. Curious now, he looked around him.

It was a large room, nearly as large as the long rectangular seldom-used drawing room opening onto the veranda on the beach side of the house; and, like it, it was filled with furniture taken from the old estate house built by Duncan Vaughan generations ago—heavy ornate pieces with little style or grace. Dominating them all was the bed, an ugly massive antique of stained mahogany with cherubs trailing garlands of flowers carved on the tall headboard. It might well have been the bed in which old Vaughan had sired the forty-odd children before retiring for the night on his planter's chair.

Gleaned also from the original house probably were any number of faded prints and drawings depicting life long ago in places like Bournehills, which Saul saw hanging on the walls. The old prints offered beguiling scenes of the planters' wives and daughters out for their late afternoon drives in the horse-drawn buggies of the day, taking high tea and playing lawn tennis in the cool of early evening. One showed a plover shoot on a cliff which looked very much like the one just down from the guesthouse, with the planters, sporting knee gaiters and guns, imbibing great quantities of coffee mixed with rum while awaiting the birds. A number of prints pictured the rowdy nightlong feasts in the manor houses which saw whole calves consumed by the diners while their liveried slaves, some of them no more than sleepy children, stood in attendance at each chair.

And there were other scenes as well, these mostly of black figures at work in the fields that looked deceptively pleasant in the old prints, and filing in long columns up the ramps to the sugar mills with the canes on their backs bending them double. There was even a print showing them bound to the millwheel along with the oxen used to turn the giant wheel whenever the wind fell. In the midst of these, and overwhelming the wall upon which it was hung, and even somehow the room, stood a large, very old and probably quite valuable drawing of a three-masted Bristol slaver, the kind famous in its day. It had been meticulously rendered in cross-section to show how the cargo, the men, women and children, the babies at breast, had been stowed away on the closely tiered decks to take up the least room on the journey.

To all this Merle had added her more personal belongings. Books on West Indian history from her student days in London were scattered everywhere. There was her sewing machine, an antiquated affair with a foot treadle, which had been a present from Ashton Vaughan to her mother. Beside it on a chair lay piles of the colorful cloth with their abstract tribal motifs which she used for making her dresses. On a crowded vanity table nearby he saw a large tin of the talcum powder she was forever dusting on her face and neck, along with the cruel iron-toothed comb she heated to straighten her hair. And pushed out of the way in a corner, almost swallowed by the deep shadows there, were a number of large steamer trunks, their battered flanks covered with stickers. These contained the remains of her life in England. They stood open but only half unpacked.

It appeared she had brought the memorabilia of a lifetime—and of the time that reached beyond her small life—and dumped it in a confused heap in the room. The confusion was rampant, although there were, to her credit, a few signs that she had tried to impose some order on the chaos. Several books stood neatly ranged on a shelf. She had made a half-hearted attempt to create a small sitting area near the door with a few of the heavy baronial armchairs. A family photograph taken before the disintegration of her marriage, showing her, her husband, and a baby who gazed out at the world with her eyes, had been unpacked and placed upright amid the clutter on a table. But overwhelmed apparently by the enormity of the task, she had given up, and most of the furniture and other effects had been left unarranged, unsorted, so that the room resembled more a furniture warehouse than anything else, or an antique shop—or, considering the age and history of some of the pieces, a museum.

It expressed her: the struggle for coherence, the hope and desire for reconciliation of her conflicting parts, the longing to truly know and accept herself—all the things he sensed in her, which not only brought on her rages but her frightening calms as well. He almost felt as his gaze wandered over the room that he was wandering through the chambers of her mind.

But the room expressed something more, it suddenly seemed to his own overtaxed and exhausted mind, something apart from Merle. It roused in him feelings about Bournehills itself. He thought he suddenly saw the district for what it was at its deepest level, the vague thoughts and impressions of months coming slowly to focus. Like the room it, too, was perhaps a kind of museum, a place in which had been stored the relics and remains of the era recorded in the faded prints on the walls, where one not only felt that other time existing intact, still alive, a palpable presence beneath the everyday reality, but saw it as well at every turn, often without realizing it. Bournehills, its shabby woebegone hills and spent land, its odd people who at times seemed other than themselves, might have been selected as the repository of the history which reached beyond it to include the hemisphere north and south.

And it would remain as such. The surface might be jarred as it had been by the events today. People like himself would come seeking to shake it from its centuries-old sleep and it might yield a little. But deep down, at a depth to which only a few would be permitted to penetrate, it would remain fixed and rooted in that other time, serving in this way as a lasting testimony to all that had gone on then: those scenes hanging on the walls, and as a reminder—painful but necessary—that it was not yet over, only the forms had changed, and the real work was still to be done; and finally, as a memorial—crude in the extreme when you considered those ravaged hills and the blight visible everywhere, but no other existed, they had not been thought worthy of one—to the figures bound to the millwheel in the print and to each other in the packed, airless hold of the ship in the drawing.

Only an act on the scale of Cuffee's could redeem them. And only then would Bournehills itself, its mission fulfilled, perhaps forgo that wounding past and take on the present, the future. But it would hold out until then, resisting, defying all efforts, all the halfway measures, including his, to reclaim it; refusing to settle for anything less than what Cuffee had demanded in his time.

As he groped his way across the room to the door his eyes had the same look as on the day, months ago, when he had stayed too long out on the slope with Stinger and his crew, and had been overcome by vertigo on the road: as if he had been struck down and temporarily blinded so that he might see in another, deeper, way. Blind, his mind beseiged by revelations and visions which, in days to come when he had recovered, he would put down to his exhaustion and the crises that had marked the day, he stumbled from the room and down the hall past Carrington. But she didn't notice him, for she had dropped off to sleep on her chair outside the door, her chin fallen onto the great breasts that had been used, it seemed, to suckle the world.

CHAPTER 7

The next hectic two to three weeks in Bournehills were spent transporting the peasant canes to the factory at Brighton on the other side of Cleaver's. From before dawn until late into the night and sometimes all night, the small fleet of trucks which the council had rounded up, together with the Bournehills bus which had had its roof and benches removed, could be seen struggling, loaded down, over the hills toward the high ridge. Perhaps about three hours later they would return, only to leave immediately with a fresh load.

The council's plan was working, though not without its problems. There were frequent breakdowns due to the condition of the trucks (at Saul's suggestion Ferguson was put in charge of repairs; and silent, sober for the most, hardly sleeping, he labored over the vehicles without letup), sometimes the schedule Allen and the others had set up went hopelessly awry, especially when the smallholders failed to have their canes cut and ready at the appointed time, and there were one or two serious disputes over the weight of the load and the payment received at Brighton which threatened to bring the entire experiment to an end.

Then, there were those like Leesy who remained hard-set against the plan and insisted on transporting their crops the long distance by donkey cart. These invariably broke down well before reaching Cleaver's, and the loads had to be rescued and taken the rest of the way by truck.

Yet, in spite of all the difficulties the canes were being hauled, and perhaps for the first time since that time long ago when Bournehills, under Cuffee, had been a nation and its people a People, one could almost sense something of that same spirit moving in the district again.

One night during this period the weighing office at Cane Vale was set on fire. It wasn't serious and Erskine Vaughan was able to put it out before any real damage was done. No one in the village could say who had started it; none had witnessed it, yet everyone, even the children, could describe in detail how Erskine, clad only in his nightshirt, had rushed cursing and crying back and forth from his house to the office lugging buckets of water—the water sloshing over his bare feet as he stumbled on the long skirt of the gown. The men at Delbert's added a ribald touch to the story, saying, "And did you hear how when Calamity fell down once and his nightie flew up so you could see his all-in-all, that he didn't have any you-know-what? Nothing at all there, I hear. But I wonder how Calamity got all those many children? I tell you, he best ask the wife a question."

Two days after the fire Deanes came down to Bournehills as he had promised and held a meeting in the evening on the Spiretown playing field. Standing in the back of the small sound truck he used during election campaigns, and from which, at those times, he dispensed free rum and beer, bags of rice, used clothing and the promise, made every election but never kept, to run a water pipe up Canterbury, he spoke of his efforts on their behalf. For one, he said, searching nervously for the faces drowned in the darkness beyond the reach of the light bulb dangling over his head, he was urging government to set up a commission of inquiry into the shut-down at Cane Vale, and he was keeping after Kingsley and Sons to repair the roller or, failing that, to replace it: "Oh, yes, every day God send I'm on the telephone to them. I'm not giving them a moment's peace." He congratulated the villagers on having found a way to save their crops—and he said it almost as if he were partly to be credited for it. He knew how hard life was for them, he said; after all he, too, he reminded them, had once cut canes on Bournehills steep slopes—and he held up a hand on which all the old calluses had been rubbed smooth. He was a self-made man, he declared with bitter pride, nobody had ever helped him.

Then, as he mentioned the fire at Cane Vale, telling them that although their grievances were just, they still "had no right setting fire to the white people property," someone in the faceless throng that scorned the light he stood in let fly an overripe mango. It caught him on the small V-shaped bit of white shirt above his vest, and bursting upon impact sent the saffron-colored juice and pulp streaming down the shirt, his tie, and over the hard little paunch he kept tucked guiltily up under the vest. Deanes, his mouth opened to shape the next word he had been about to say, the hand with which he had instinctively sought to ward off the missile raised halfway, stared down at the spreading yellow smear as though it were his life's hopes and ambitions lying squashed and dripping there on his chest. After what seemed a long time he slowly lifted his stunned, incredulous eyes to the silent crowd (they had not uttered a sound when the mango struck), and the fruit smeared over his shirtfront he gave them a look so eloquent of his hurt and bewilderment, so filled with gentle reproof, it seemed almost possible to forgive him. They should have known how it was with him, the look said, his smallness, his terror, his dream and desire for high office; they, of all people, should have understood. It lasted only a few seconds, and then, amid the dark roar of laughter which suddenly erupted, he was scrambling down from the truck and across to his new Rover parked nearby, glancing back nervously over his shoulder in his characteristic way as he ran. He quickly disappeared up the main road, leaving the sound truck for his aide to drive back to town.

Saul recounted the incident to Harriet later that evening. She had not gone to the meeting. She had intended to, but overcome at the last minute by a profound reluctance she had stayed behind and watched it from their small gallery out front. She had been able to see down through the darkness the lighted sound truck in the midst of the black faceless sea, and she had heard, very faintly, the sound of Deanes' voice over the loud-speaker and the roar of laughter at the end. She had gotten up then and gone into the house to await Saul.

Harriet was perhaps the only one in the village to remain untouched by the excitement that had swept it now that the canes were being hauled. But by this time, late June, she had almost completely given way to the enervating sense of waning interest and weariness with Bournehills, with the island, that had come over her since carnival.

Part of it, as she told Chester Heald in her letter, was the weather, the long season without rain. She had come to find the unvarying perfection of the days with their cloudless blue skies and never-failing sun unimaginably wearing. The ruinous Bournehills heat to which she had at first appeared immune was such now that she seldom went out. (When people in the village commented on this, asking why they didn't see her "abroad," as they put it, as much anymore, she blamed it on Saul, saying with her light laugh, "It's that husband of mine. He's been keeping my nose to the typewriter these days getting out the report." And they accepted it without question, the women saying, "Well, yes, these men'll turn you into a workhorse if you don't watch yourself.") And although there was usually a cool wind at night she was denied its relief, because here of late she had taken to barricading the windows as soon as dusk fell, against a bat who had taken to flying boldly into the house from the darkness outside.

But far more disturbing than the weather was the feeling—which became more intolerable with each passing day—of having been thwarted, utterly frustrated, in some fundamental way in her relations with people in the village, even with those like Gwen whom she genuinely liked. It seemed that all her efforts over the months to ease life a little for them had come to naught. In spite of the gallons of vitamin-rich juices she served, and the aspirins, cough syrup, dewormer and the like, which she freely dispensed, with all the cuts on the children's splayed toes which she personally cleaned and bandaged, afterward giving them a hard candy from the jar on top of the medicine cabinet, there had been not the slightest change. She hadn't been looking for any dramatic overnight improvement. She was not so foolish or unreasonable. Hers, after all, had been only the most token gestures. Yet, she had hoped for at least a small sign on their part that she had had some effect to the good. But nothing. They remained, perversely, as they were. The children continued to present her with the balloon-shaped bellies and thin scrofulous limbs. Gwen, to her exasperation, went on selling her eggs to the postmaster instead of feeding them to her children as she had repeatedly advised her, and despite all her pleading she had been unable to get her to go and see the doctor about the tumor which kept her looking pregnant. (Harriet was utterly convinced by now it was a tumor; no baby could be that long overdue.) To prove it, she offered to drive her into New Bristol to the hospital. But Gwen, who insisted it was nothing more than another child, refused, saying with the smile that banished the premature lines of age from her face, "Whoever heard of making such a big to-do over a child that's not born yet. It'll come when it has a mind to, Harriet, so stop worrying up yourself." She followed this with a mischievous laugh: "It might decide to do me a favor and not come at all, who knows . . ."

And there was—Harriet became convinced—something deliberate in the failure of Gwen, the children and everyone else in the village whom she sought to help, to respond in even the slightest way to her efforts. She sensed in it a subtle but firm rebuff. She knew better, but it was as though they had agreed in secret to remain as they were as a kind of judgment on her. She suspected a conspiracy. Or perhaps they felt she was not doing enough and, in their refusal to respond, were holding out for some greater effort on her part, demanding that she do and give more. *What was it they wanted?* She could not have said. But it was too much, of that she was certain. She could not give it, whatever it was, without being herself deprived, diminished; and worse, without undergoing a profound transformation in which she would be called upon to relinquish some high place she had always occupied and to become other than she had always been.

She would never agree to this; and so, in the face of what she felt to be their unreasonable demand, for the sake of her own self-preservation, her sanity, she had turned from Bournehills, slipping into an indifference which made everything going on around her, including the present excitement over the hauling, seem remote, unimportant, having nothing to do with her. While her body went through the motions required of it, her mind remained centered on the trip home they would make once the report was done. She found herself more and more considering the possibility of Saul's not remaining with the project once the first phase was over. She even caught herself hoping, when the days were too much, that something might happen to prevent his staying on.

The strain of all this began to show after a time, in the form of a faint, barely perceptible shading around her eyes, as of some cosmetic she had applied to set off their grayish-blue clarity. A worried Saul, sensing the slow, irreversible collapse taking place within her, urged her to go on to Philadelphia ahead of him: he would join her as soon as the hauling was over and he and Allen had completed the report. But she was adamant against this. She couldn't tell him, there was no way to say it, but for her to leave before him would be the same as an admission of defeat on her part, proof that Lyle Hutson had been right after all and Bournehills had shown itself too much for her.

So she stayed, confining herself as much to the house on the rise as Merle, sunk in her long, near-lifeless depression, was confined to the cluttered room at the guesthouse. Both women received their share of visitors. The children continued to come and go in Harriet's case, and in the evenings the small group of women which included Gwen would drop in to sit and gossip—although they no longer came every evening.

As for Merle, there was a virtual pilgrimage each day from the village out to the guesthouse to inquire about her from Carrington. Some of the visitors brought gifts—a dozen cashews with the kidney-shaped nut attached to the fruit, a few specially selected mangoes, a chicken to be made into soup for her, a freshly baked loaf of coconut bread which they knew she liked. Coming up to the top open half of the kitchen door, they would ask, "And how's she today, Mistress Carrington? Has she come to herself yet?" And Carrington would give the mute sign that said she was unchanged.

Saul was usually part of the small crowd gathered in the pitted limestone yard before the kitchen door. Although he and Allen were busy supervising the hauling, along with the other members of the council, he nevertheless made a point of stopping by the guesthouse almost daily to check on her. He would have gone and sat with her for a short while some days, but Leesy Walkes had replaced Carrington outside the door and she refused to allow anyone in.

Soon, people meeting him on the road and knowing he was one of those who regularly went out to the guesthouse to see about Merle began asking him for her. At first he somewhat apprehensively searched their faces, worried that in their shrewd way they had seen through to the larger feelings that prompted his concern: his love—the affection and friendship which shaped it, and the wistful hope, obscure and unacknowledged, that in seeing her through this crisis he might in some way make up for having failed that other woman six years ago. But though he probed their faces and distant eyes he could detect nothing. Indeed, something in their manner said it was only right that he should go over to the guesthouse and wait humbly with the others out in the yard for Carrington's terse report. This, they seemed to feel, was no more than a small act of obeisance—like the kiss Merle demanded of everyone—due someone like her.

He was relieved on one hand at not finding himself under suspicion, but certain, on the other, that they knew about himself and Merle—knew in the way most things were known in Bournehills, at that deeper level of consciousness one sensed moving beneath its static surface. Moreover, they had known all along, he was convinced; before it had happened in fact. Why then did they withhold their censure? Perhaps because they had long understood something he had dimly come to believe; namely, that in his desire to know and embrace Bournehills, it was inevitable, indeed necessary, that he first know and embrace Merle. And again, as on many occasions before, he felt surrounded by a mystery that would never fully yield to his understanding.

Only once did someone make what could have been taken as a veiled reference to himself and Merle, and even then he wasn't sure. It was during the third and final week of the hauling, and he and Stinger were driving a truckload of canes over the hills to Brighton. (They were Stinger's canes, grown on a parched half-acre plot which he rented from the Kingsley estates for a few dollars a year.) The two men, seated side by side in the truck's cramped overheated cab, had been conversing quietly about the events of the past three weeks, when Stinger suddenly, as they were passing the blackened ruin of Pyre Hill in the near distance, changed the subject and began speaking of Gwen and himself, something he had never done before. In a voice touched by the inexplicable sadness and remorse always to be seen shadowing his face, he talked about how they had first met. It had been, he said, at a small Pentecostal church in Spiretown, where he had gone one night with the woman who was his legal wife, the mother of the girl Loris, who worked for Saul and Harriet. A revival meeting was being held, drawing people from all over Bournehills, and Gwen, who was then living at a place called Drake's some miles away, had come with members of her congregation. He had seen her there and immediately taken a liking to her, had wanted her.

"Just so," he said, his eyes which the sun out in the fields had stained the color of brandy over the years abstracted under his pulled-down cap. "That's how it was. I saw her sitting in back of the meeting hall that night and took to her right off. I din' know who she was or where she was from or whether or not she had a man already. I din' care about none of that, though, because my mind was made up to have her if I could. But that's a man for you. He sees a woman someplace and takes a liking to her and has to have her even though he knows he shouldn't, that it'll only bring trouble.

"Because what right I had with Gwen?" he cried with sudden intensity (and it was obvious he had put the question to himself many times before, in the privacy of his heart). "What right, I ask?" he repeated, his despair and disgust with himself deepening the lines etched in a careful, precise design (time exercising great skill) around his eyes, across his sucked-in jaw. "She was a young young woman and I was already an old man then, my body done lick up from the lot of hard work, my children near grown. I had no business putting myself with no young woman. Besides, I already had a woman, and a good one at that. I had no fault to find with Vi Stinger. She was a good hard-working Christian woman and we was living good together. She never did me a wrong. . . ."

He paused, and his head bowed he stared down at the bill-hook he was never without, lying across his knees. Beside him Saul waited, moved that Stinger had at last confided in him, yet fearful that the story was in part directed at him. He was grateful that he was driving and had to keep his eyes on the road.

"I don't have to tell you how Bournehills people talked my name when Gwen and me first started living together," Stinger said quietly after awhile. His face with the blackness that seemed to reach clear through to the bone remained bent over his knife and he was swaying lightly to the jolting of the truck. "They said I din' know shame, that I was only trying to make like I was a young sports again. And upward to this day Vi Stinger won't let her eye as much as meet mine when we pass on the road. But the thing that really hurt my heart, Saul, man"—and for a moment he couldn't say it: the hurt was still so fresh—"was that she turned the children against me. Stopped them from speaking to their own father! My oldest boy is a big man in Canada today, but he has never written me a line because of the mother, and it's only since I got Loris the job with you that she has a word for me now and again. The others still don't speak.

"But what to do," he said, his face coming slowly up to reveal not only his profound and lasting regret, but a tragic acceptance of himself as well, his faults, his human frailty. "I had to have the blasted girl, yes. A man can't help his feelings sometime. He don't even understand his damn self half the time and there the trouble starts."

In the silence that followed Saul turned hesitantly toward him, and in the sunlight pouring through the windshield his own face reflected the strain of all he was living under. He started to speak, but Stinger, who had been gazing blindly ahead with the resigned tragic expression, suddenly leaned forward. "Brighton yonder," he said, pointing with his billhook. They had scaled the high ridge at Cleaver's and could see the sprawling factory waiting below on the wide level sweep of plain. Stinger immediately began speculating about the amount of money his small crop would bring.

CHAPTER 8

The last of the canes were in. The stony lands in and around Spiretown, where the smallholders had their plots, had been stripped of all their little eye-saving green. The crop season was over. And just as generations ago, the horns of the bullocks that pulled the long spider carts used for hauling then had been adorned with flowers to mark the end, flaming orange and scarlet flamboyants and jasmine, so now the council's five decrepit trucks made their final runs decorated with a few wild flowers picked from the roadside and the long slender leaves of the canes gathered and tied to their radiators like palms for a Palm Sunday. "The last of the canes gone down today," had been the saying in the old days. And it hadn't changed, this being Bournehills. Leesy, standing with Mary Griggs on the embankment above her yard, watching the empty, decorated trucks returning for the last time along the main road below, gave the sharp little nod that was like a tic. "Well, yes," she said, "the last has gone down."

With the end of crop, a stillness that was like the cessation of life itself descended upon Bournehills. And time, which in the district had its own laws: on one hand lengthening weeks into months and months into years so that Saul could no longer say for certain just how long they had been there unless he consulted the calendar; and on the other, telescoping whole centuries so that events which had taken place long ago and should have passed into history and been forgotten seemed to have occurred only yesterday—time had had a stop.

During the dead season (for this was what it was called in Bournehills, this period between the end of crop and the beginning of the rains), people moved slower than usual along the roads. It took them longer to execute the solemn stiff-arm greeting. Now the bar half of Delbert's shop was crowded both day and night, the men idling away the empty hours over a finger of rum, a game of dominoes, and the never tiring talk of Cuffee Ned while awaiting the August rains. For the rains would bring the tender new shoots springing from the stumps buried beneath the thick mulch of leaves in the fields, and there would be a few days' work each week clearing the ground and weeding. Outside the opened door to the bar the shorn land looked too exhausted ever to bear again.

Over at the guesthouse the old retired English couple, the Mathersons, who came down on holiday every year at this time, had arrived. Each day dressed in bathing suits and rubber swim shoes and carrying a large straw beach bag stuffed with combs and brushes and special dog powders and chunks of beef which they purchased in New Bristol, they would set off for a section of the beach near Plover Cliff and there spend the day grooming and feeding the stray dogs of Spiretown. They would comb and brush them until the animals' eyes became glazed, their bodies limp, and they fell into a sensual stupor; and until the perspiration stood out in bright pustules on the old man's crumpled flesh and his wife's glasses misted over.

Just beyond where they sat surrounded by the dogs, the sea was undergoing its seasonal change. Every year at this time the water darkened, the tide rose to the point where it was difficult to withstand the undertow even in Horseshoe Pool, and the cry of the swollen breakers as they moved in over the reefs, that loud unremitting sob of outrage and grief, was taken to a new high. Moreover, each time the giant waves hurled themselves against the land now they left behind great masses of seaweed dredged up from the bottom, dumping it like mounds of rotting refuse along the length of the beach. The sea, Bournehills people said, was cleaning itself, and they stayed away from it.

By the time the Mathersons arrived Merle had more or less recovered, and most days she could be found sitting on the veranda in the familiar faded red gown. Her eyes had not as yet regained their accustomed light and her body still remotely called to mind a catatonic in that it seemed capable of maintaining the same painful position for days on end. But you could nonetheless sense her groping her way back to the surface of herself. Drawn deep in the chair, the sweeping skirt of the gown wrapped around her legs, she would gaze for hours out at the changed sea beyond the railing. Her head resting against the tall slatted seat back, she listened to the heightened roll and crash of the waves. Not long after her recovery she announced she would be closing the guesthouse once the Mathersons left and going away for awhile, possibly to Trinidad, where she had friends.

The first time Saul came and found her outside she had slowly turned at the sound of his footsteps and watched him approach down the veranda's long, sunbleached floor which sloped gently with age, like the deck of a ship. She had been told of his almost daily visits during her illness, and as he drew over a chair and sat down beside her with an uncertain smile, she bent on him an odd, faintly suspicious look. She appeared to be asking who or what aside from herself had made for his devotion. Then, without either of them having spoken as yet, she turned back to the sea, and for a long time they sat in silence.

Finally, without looking at him, she said, "I guess I really performed over at Cane Vale the other time. Called you everything but a child of God."

"Just about," he said, and he could laugh now. With the season ended, that day seemed long ago and forgotten. "You gave me one of those tongue-lashings you usually reserve for Lyle. But never mind, it's all over. The canes are in, the Kingsley people apparently mean to repair the roller: they sent a man down again last week to look at it, and you're yourself again. How do you feel? I tried getting in to see you any number of times but there was a little tigress at the gate in the person of Leesy Walkes and she wasn't letting anybody in. Tell me, how's Mis-Merle?" Reaching across, he gently turned her face toward him and found she was wanly smiling.

"You know me," she said, "I'll live."

"Oh, you will, you will!" he cried, and his laugh held not only relief but a note of personal triumph also.

With the smallholders' crops in and the season over, he had resumed writing the report which he and Allen had had to put aside during the emergency. And he was working on it now with a desperation born of two things. There was the crisis in his personal life he tried not to think about and the need for himself and Harriet to get away. (He was reluctant to leave, though, at this point because interest in the council had begun to wane with the end of crop and he feared the organization might disintegrate altogether if he was gone for any time.) Then there was the experience (he could think of no other word for it) he had undergone in Merle's room that night, which had somehow suggested that Bournehills was, in some profound and inexplicable way, irredeemable. If this was so, the project would be of little use. But he was being absurd, he told himself. What had occurred that night was nothing more than a hallucination brought on by the accumulated physical and emotional exhaustion of the long traumatic day. His hunger had made him lightheaded—and he reminded himself that his sole food that day had been a can of Libby's corned beef which he had wolfed down straight from the can, crumbly yellow fat and all, in Delbert's. He had nodded off while sitting beside Merle on the bed and fallen victim to a bizarre dream. . . . Yet despite the explanations he offered himself he found, mysteriously, that the vague questions which had nagged him for months appeared to have been laid to rest. No matter, he told himself; he had taken hold and from here on would confine himself only to what was real. That was more than enough to deal with.

As proof of this, he was making only the most practical recommendations for the second phase of the work. He was calling first of all for a much larger research team of experts and technicians drawn from both CASR in Philadelphia and the Bourne Island government (he had already started interviewing people in the various ministries in town), and then, to match this, one or more demonstration projects.

One such project had already been suggested by the council. Almost to a man they had urged that the hauling operation be made permanent so that the villagers would no longer be totally dependent on Cane Vale for getting their canes ground. Saul agreed. If this could be done, it might, he found himself dreaming, lead to a time when people in Bournehills might be willing to work their tiny fields together, as a co-operative venture, to the greater benefit of them all; he even—perhaps dreaming too wildly—envisioned the day when they would demand that Kingsley share more of the land with them. Or, they might well someday take over one of the estates as he had seen happen once on a hacienda in Peru.

As a second project he was considering—at the request of the people on Canterbury—running the long-promised water pipe up the hill. Also, his hope was to strengthen the council by setting up a leadership-training program among the younger men in the village. He saw this as perhaps the most important part of the work ahead, and said as much in the report.

By early August it was done, and Harriet had been given the final sections to type. She had come to think of each word she struck on the machine as a step taking them closer to the day of departure, so that although she had found the typing a wearisome job in the heat (she had to keep a handkerchief nearby for her perspiring hands), her spirits had lifted somewhat as the pages began to accumulate and she saw the end in sight.

And then only yesterday, as she was about to start on the very last section, an utterly dejected Saul had come in from a meeting of the council to say that as important as he knew it was for them to get away, they might have to delay the trip. Things had reached a low at the council; hardly anyone had come out to the meeting, and he just couldn't risk leaving.

She sat this morning with her hands gone slack on the typewriter keys. Outside the window, in the teetering sentry box of a house just above theirs, Mary Griggs' drone gave voice to the hot, still, dusty gray monotony that was life in Bournehills during the dead season. Above the village, the exasperatingly perfect blue sky seemed to be mocking the human imperfection below. Then, even as she sat idle at the machine with the old woman's toneless hymn and the sky, the sun, adding to all she was feeling, she heard far down the rise the unmistakable sound of Lyle Hutson's Humber—its powerful motor effortlessly negotiating the sharp road up to the house, its horn putting to rout the sheep and chickens and small children in its path. The windowpane near her worktable caught the car's silver glint and sent it streaking like white fire round the walls, and seized by a sudden unexplained panic she turned to call for Loris to come and head him off on the gallery.

Only to remember that Loris wasn't there. She would not be there until late in the afternoon when she returned to prepare supper. Because lately Harriet had started letting her go home once her morning chores were done. She had found it disconcerting having her around all day. Her quiet presence out back, where, her duties over, she would squat in the sunlit kitchen doorway with the dowdy cast-off hat perched above her childish face, seemed to Harriet to be making the same unreasonable demand of her as everyone else in the village.

With no Loris to come to her aid she turned back to her worktable and, being Harriet, by the time Lyle Hutson stepped onto the gallery her face was composed, her eyes clear and, her head bent over the papers next to the machine, she was briskly typing.

"Ah, I see they have you slaving away."

He stood in the doorway, his surface smile calling to mind Andrew Westerman, his tall figure and face eclipsing with their blackness all the sunlight in the room. He had obviously just come from court because he still had on the lawyer's white bands at his throat and the flowing black robe which, like most barristers of his standing, he wore in a faded threadbare state as a mark of his long years at the bar.

He saw the look she gave it and laughed. "I've just come from court in the district west of here. Once in awhile I like to take one of these country cases if it's big enough and they can pay my fee. They help to keep me on my toes. Since I was so near I thought I'd give you people a shout, see what you're up to over this side. I haven't seen you, you know, since all the excitement down here. I understand your husband and the little group he started worked something of a miracle while I was away. People in town are beginning to take a second look at the professor. They're saying he might be the first to actually do something with this place. I needn't tell you some of the big boys on Queen Street like our friend Hinds are getting worried. Where's the good doctor? I'd like to congratulate him."

He had crossed the room and was standing gazing down at her from the other side of the table she used as a desk. The worn, rusty robe hung casually off his shoulders, revealing the Savile Row suit underneath.

"I'm afraid Saul's not here," she said. She spoke with her fingers in position on the keys. "He's in town interviewing people for the new research team."

"Oh, well, I won't stay then," he said, but made no move to leave. "I'll probably run into him there. And is the younger professor in town also?"

"Allen? No. You should be able to find him over at the guesthouse."

"Good," he said. "I intend looking in on Merle as soon as I leave here so I'll see him. . . .

"How is Merle, by the way?"

She didn't understand the little pause that preceded his question or his slightly altered tone, and she puzzled over them to herself.

"I hear she really took to heart the unpleasant little business at Cane Vale," he said, "and was in a very bad way. I hope she's over it by now. I've been so busy since I've been back I haven't had a chance to come down before this."

"Yes, she's much better," she said, and nothing in her face, her voice, in the clear equable gaze she directed at him betrayed the sudden uneasiness she felt. "I'm afraid I'm as bad as you, though, and haven't been over to see her since she's been up I've been so busy —slaving away, as you put it. But Saul tells me she's pretty much herself again. She had everyone worried for awhile though."

"You could have spared yourself some of the worry," he said. "After all, you know that Merle is given to these little—what to call them?— attacks, bad spells, what you will. They're to be expected with someone so high-strung. And, yes, they can be frightening, but she always manages to snap out of them. There's no keeping her down, you know. Dear Merle." The veiled eyes softened momentarily. Then: "So, the small farmers' canes are in, thanks to the professor and his group; Merle's her own self, thanks, in part, I'm sure, to the solicitude of all concerned. Things are as they were, in other words."

"Yes," she said, "back to normal, and I had better get back to work." Her head started down toward the typewriter.

"And what of you, my dear Mrs. Amron?" he said, and although he had not moved, she felt that he had suddenly leaned forward in the black robe and was studying her close up. "How have you held up under these multiple crises? Aren't you about ready for another brief holiday over our way? It's been some months now."

She didn't answer, only continued to gaze up with amused patience at the affixed smile, thinking to herself that he must put it on each morning the same as he did his shirt and socks and shoes, his suit, carefully adjusting it before the mirror as he did his necktie.

"You know you really are amazing," he said. "I don't see how you've managed to stick Bournehills this long. It's quite a feat. Anybody else would have been brought raving down from the place ages ago. You must be made of stronger stuff than I thought. But I do think you've more than made your point and it's time you relaxed, come to town once in awhile, permit yourself a few harmless pleasures. Because I'll tell you something"—and again without moving he appeared to bend closer—"I learned while in the RAF and saw good friends of mine, chaps I had gone to school with, go down in flames over Europe, simply, that those of us who have been fortunate enough to survive the various bloodlettings man indulges in from time to time have, as I see it, an obligation to live as fully as possible, if only to make up for those who are gone. We ought to take advantage of every pleasure that comes our way, deny ourselves nothing within reason. Perhaps you would call mine a frivolous attitude . . ."

"It's certainly a convenient one, I'll say that for it." She laughed.

He bowed. "However, I hold to it," he said. "So come out of your cloister, Mrs. Amron. Come down from your mountain monastery. This is not a Catholic country. Not any longer at least. Stop denying those of us in town the benefit of your cultivation and charm, and stop denying yourself whatever we might have to offer by way of diversion.

"But seriously, we'd like you to come." His manner softened a shade. "Enid's always asking for you. She remembers the pleasant time you two had Carnival Tuesday night after Dorothy and I rescued you from that rowdy bunch from the Heights. Dorothy, by the way, asked me to say good-bye for her. As you may have heard she, George, and the brood left for home shortly after carnival."

"I'm sure you were sorry to see them go."

He laughed, and with his head thrown back she could see a faint touch of pink high within the nostrils that branched wide and deep from the shaft of his nose. "Yes," he said. "Especially Dorothy. She was a very decent sort. They both helped to brighten things up with their little breakfast parties and the like. We shall miss them. The truth is, Mrs. Amron, life on the island is so dull most of the time—one sees the same faces at every party and makes the same idle talk—that the few of us with any measure of sophistication find ourselves having to look to the occasional visitor for some relief from the tedium. That's why it's almost unkind of you to deny us the benefit of your company just because we happen to live on the wrong side of Cleaver's.

"But there's a more important reason why I think you should come and spend time with us occasionally."

"And what's that?"

His smile widened, becoming very white against the burnt umber of his face. Gathering up the badly frayed, dusty hem of the robe he draped it over his arm which he held bent at the elbow, close to his body.

"Simply this," he said after making her wait. "That in addition to its white coral beaches, warm blue waters, happy natives, its three hundred and sixty-five days of sun"—his tone, the grandiloquent gestures with his free hand turned it all into a mockery—"Bourne Island also offers its visitors the chance to—how do you say it up your way?—let their hair down. People feel somehow freer here, liberated from their inhibitions, especially those like yourself from North America. I've actually heard them say as much, these Americans and Canadians who flock to our shores on holiday. They love the place, mainly, I suspect, because it provides them with the opportunity, usually denied them at home, to test certain notions they hold about people of a different color, to satisfy certain curiosities about them in an atmosphere that is both tolerant and permissive. Nobody raises an eyebrow on Bourne Island. And if someone should, what do our visitors care? They'll be going home sooner or later."

He paused, frowned, suddenly serious despite his joking air. With the hem of the robe over his arm he looked to be addressing a court. Across the table from him Harriet had steeled herself.

"They are, of course, these notions they hold about people other than themselves, only notions," he said. "Fantasies, myths, old wives' tales. But they've been with them so long, my dear Mrs. Amron; they've achieved such a hold on the imagination, they've become almost real. I was never more convinced of this than during a trip I made to your country not long ago. I had something happen to me while there which, though insignificant in itself, did point up what I see as some of the interesting psychological aspects to the question of race in your country. Your Justice Department had invited me and a number of other barristers from the Caribbean to tour some of the courts in your federal system. It was one of those small plums your government occasionally tosses to those of us in the area who behave ourselves. One night in Chicago I went to a reception at the home of a lawyer I knew there—a very well-to-do chap, white, who lived in one of those posh high-rise apartment houses in an exclusive section of the city. It was a pleasant enough evening and I left about midnight. I rang for the lift, it came, the door opened, and as I stepped in, an elderly woman standing inside with a small dog in her arms took one look at me and screamed, not loudly but scream she did, and her dog started barking. The two of them created quite a row for a moment. And it was more than that she had been startled. The woman looked at me as though I was some sort of monster who had suddenly appeared before her, a beast of a lower order even than the dog in her arms. I've never seen such naked unfounded terror in anyone's eyes. . . ."

He paused again and, his own eyes changing, drifting back to that time, he stared down at Harriet almost as if he saw, superimposed on her upturned face, that of the old woman's in the elevator. Across from him Harriet's expression remained unchanged.

"I don't know who she thought I was or what she supposed I intended doing to her," he said quietly after a moment. "Perhaps she mistook me for some thief off the streets—although I assure you I wasn't dressed like a thief, or one of those mad-dog rapists one reads about in your newspapers. But one look at my black face (she saw nothing else) and something wholly irrational took place in the poor woman's mind. It was most odd. She apologized of course, said she suffered with her nerves, and we even stood and chatted for awhile in the lobby. She seemed relieved to learn I was from the West Indies and told me she had once spent a very enjoyable holiday at Montego Bay in Jamaica.

"A minor incident, you say? Hardly worth mentioning . . . ?" He waited, peering down at her from his height, but she refused him the satisfaction of commenting. "Perhaps." He shrugged. "But it did seem to me part of the peculiar notions I referred to before, those deeply rooted, almost mystical beliefs that appear to lie at the heart of your racial dilemma. I've always found them the most interesting part of the problem. They seem to suggest a terribly dark and primitive side to your troubled countrymen.

"Yes," he said, drawing more of the robe's hem over his arm. "Yours is a most unfortunate country, Mrs. Amron, as regards this question of race. Not that we in the West Indies have escaped the problem altogether. We like to think we have, and talk a great deal about having achieved a truly multiracial society, but it is with us also. One thing, we have escaped the more barbaric practices your countrymen, especially those in the South, are given to: the murders, drownings, burnings and the like, and we do take comfort in that. The last lynching to take place on Bourne Island, for example, was Cuffee Ned centuries ago, and from the way Bournehills people still go on about him, the old fellow scarcely seems dead.

"But enough!" he cried and clapped his hands once, the way he did when summoning a servant. The hem of the robe slipped from his arm with the movement and fell with the soft rushing sound of a curtain being lowered back down to his feet. "Consider all that nothing more than an aside. The only point I'm trying to make is that since we find ourselves, black and white alike, caught in this web of notions one about the other and are a long way from seeing each other as we really are: poor forked creatures all, not endowed with any special prowess or beauty or any special evil either, as my elderly friend in the lift assumed I possessed, we might as well try to derive whatever enjoyment we can from the situation; and when the opportunity offers itself, as it does on Bourne Island, to do what we will, with whom we will, to take advantage of it.

"Enter into the spirit of life on the island, Mrs. Amron!" he exhorted her. He was his mordantly playful, ironic self once again. His empty laugh rang through the room. "And that shouldn't be too difficult for you. You've obviously overcome much of the narrow thinking to be found up your way. After all, you've married into a group that has long been the most persecuted in the world. And you've come to live amid the alien corn of Bournehills, among people I'm sure you wouldn't think of associating with at home. You're not, in other words, unalterably opposed to the strange and different, like so many Americans. Well, then, it's time to take yet another step forward and enter fully into the fold—embrace yet another brother, so to speak. It might well be"—all trace of his laugh died and he was suddenly, briefly, serious—"to the good of your salvation. What say you?"

She was ready with her answer. "I say it's been a terribly long speech for someone who said he wasn't staying, and that it's kept me from my work."

For a long time he looked silently at her, standing over her at the table like some judge about to pass sentence in the black robe. The muscles that held his sealed smile in place hardened. "You're very cool under fire, aren't you?" And as quickly the tightness around his mouth eased and he was laughing, "You win. I'll let you get back to work. I see you're determined to play the part of the martyr despite my efforts to spare you that fate."

"Martyr?"

"Yes. What else can you call this show of constancy and devotion on your part"—the wide sleeve of his robe swept out to indicate the typewriter with, to the left of it, the neat pile of finished copy and to the right the hand-written draft of the report—"but a form of martyrdom in the light of events since carnival."

"Whatever are you talking about?" And she found herself laughing, a mild bewildered laugh which said she seriously questioned his sanity; but the uneasiness she had felt earlier had returned.

"Oh, come now." He was growing impatient. "Surely you don't think some of us in town haven't realized by now how matters stand between the professor and Merle. After all, they've been seen once or twice out at the house of the old woman she calls her aunt—not recently, it's true, but they've been seen; the two cars parked right in the road out front. It's hopeless trying to hide anything in a place like New Bristol where everyone knows everyone else's car and license number. And I myself caught a glimpse of them leaving Sugar's together before dawn that Ash Wednesday morning which, I suspect, is when it all got started. That sort of thing is always happening at carnival. You've obviously decided to regard it as nothing more than that, a little carnival fling, and look the other way, but I would warn you not to take it too lightly since these things have a way of getting out of hand. . . ."

He must have noticed finally the change in the quality of her stillness, her listening silence, because his voice with the clipped Oxonian edge to it she found so annoying suddenly faltered and then tapered off. And the smile that was a permanent fixture vanished. (Without it he seemed as vulnerable as the next man.) Starting forward he stared with a shocked expression down into the face raised to his. It was still composed. And the eyes which had never once wavered continued to regard him with their even, unperturbed gaze. Her chin remained at its attentive slant. Nothing he saw there gave a hint of the upheaval that had brought her heart, her breathing, all the complex, delicately balanced workings of her body to a standstill inside her. But leaning over her he felt the stillness, the almost deathlike suspension, and with a look of dismay and apology he stood up and stepped back from the table.

"I was never one to tell tales out of school, Mrs. Amron. I was certain you knew."

She said nothing, but for the first time since he had crossed the room to stand over her, she dropped her eyes.

"Mrs. Amron . . ." Then: "Harriet . . ."

She responded finally, glancing briefly up at the black robe which had turned him into a huge version of the bat that occasionally invaded the house at dusk, and said—and it took all she had to hold her voice steady, "I don't see how you can wear that ridiculously heavy robe in this heat."

He started, looked down at himself, at her, then half-smiled in grudging admiration. "And you, as I said before, remain cool under the most intense fire. We'll make a good match. Here, take this." Reaching inside the robe to his suit pocket, he withdrew a small card and held it out to her. "It's a number in town where I can always be reached." When she made no move to take it he placed it on the carriage of the typewriter, in front of the sheet of paper on the roller. His hand lingered on it.

She stared numbly at the hand holding the card in place, at the fingers—the scrupulously clean, trimmed nails, the ridged blackened flesh of the cuticles that had been pushed firmly back, the crescent moons all of a size; and she remembered that hand touching her in the hotel bar that first night and the dark stain, as of some unknown part of her rising to the surface, it had evoked.

The hand was withdrawn, leaving behind the card with the telephone number. Seconds later the sound of his footsteps could be heard receding across the room. If Harriet could have managed it, she would have started typing, keeping it up at least until he had gotten into the car and left. But try as she did, she could not lift her hands, which lay as if broken in her lap; nor could she really see the letters on the keyboard although she was looking directly down at them.

By the time Saul returned from town late that afternoon she was calmer in mind than she had been since carnival. For it was suddenly as though all the vague, exasperating things about Bournehills which had made for her disenchantment and indifference and now, at times, her outright hostility toward the place, all the intangibles about the district which had slyly over the months set out to defeat her, had finally assumed visible, tangible form. She had been presented with a flesh-and-blood foe. And one who was in no way formidable. A hopeless compulsive given to emotional outbursts, periodic breakdowns and dramatic retreats; someone who had been unable to stand up to life. Harriet found herself almost being grateful to Lyle for having spoken.

"Lyle Hutson dropped by today," she said.

"Oh? What did he want?" He was standing in the same spot as Lyle at her worktable, leafing slowly through the finished sections of the report, his head bent. His wilted shirt, the perspiration that was like an oil slick on his face bore witness to the fatiguing trip to and from town.

"He came to congratulate you on the success of the hauling and to urge me to enter more into the spirit of life on the island."

"What'd he mean by that?" He glanced across to where she sat in front of the typewriter. His tired eyes were scribbled red.

"He was referring to the opportunity the island offers its visitors to form liaisons across all sorts of lines. I guess he was thinking of himself and Dorothy Clough. He feels I'm missing out on the fun and offered to do something about it. He left a number where he could be reached in town." For the first time she touched the card lying against the carriage of the typewriter. Picking it up she held it so he could see the number.

"The bastard." He spoke between anger and laughter. "I hope you threw him the hell out."

"According to him," she said, holding up the card, "practically everyone takes advantage of the opportunity, even you have it seems. He was genuinely shocked when he realized I didn't know."

In the long silence that followed they continued to regard each other with the expressions of moments ago—when it had all been just casual talk—still on their faces. He took note, absently, of the way she was holding the card lightly between her forefinger and thumb and the exact, carefully measured lift to her chin. And he thought, as he waited to say what could no longer be avoided, of how everything that had gone into making her: the careful disciplining in the small arts that had marked her well-bred Protestant childhood, the parental schooling in the proper use of the hands—things which the Jew in him both envied and resented, which had always both intrigued and irritated him, lay behind each unerring gesture of hers.

"This is no time to talk about it, Harriet," he said quietly.

"No," she said, "it isn't. You've had a long hot day in town and I have the last section of the report yet to type. But it won't do any good to wait." She had replaced the card on the machine, and for a time, before going on, stared down at it, frowning slightly.

"Lyle seems to feel it's nothing more than carnival," she said.

"Fuck Lyle."

"Little things like that are always happening then, according to him." Her eyes hadn't moved from the card. "People get carried away with all the drinking and dancing and start swapping husbands and wives—a little like what's supposed to go on in suburbia back home. It's harmless enough, I guess, and certainly nothing to make a fuss about. . . ."

She paused, then drawing a breath to steady and prepare herself, she raised her eyes. "I tend to agree with him," she said. "I don't think it's anything more than carnival, either, even though he did warn me these things can sometimes get out of hand and become—what?—what the French might call a grand affair of the heart. . . ." She spoke lightly; she was close to smiling. "But no, I'm sure it was just too much carnival."

She waited for him to confirm this, poised there with her face quietly raised to his, her faint smile lingering.

And for a moment it seemed he would give her what she asked and declare it had been nothing more than a minor indiscretion brought on by the holiday. Something in the eyes that had seen through to the hurt, bewilderment and rage behind her shield said as much. But he visibly checked himself.

"It's neither, Hatt," he said. "Neither a grand affair of the heart nor a little wild postholiday fling. Both are beyond me at my age. It's true Merle and I spent part of that Tuesday night together. After you made it clear over the phone that you didn't want me to come up to Lyle's, I went along with her to Sugar's to see the rest of carnival out. We talked. I told her about the bad time I had after my first wife's death and before I met you. She spoke—and I suspect for the first time ever—about the breakup of her marriage and some of the things she went through in England. It did us both good to talk as we did. I felt very close to her. What followed was simply part of that feeling of closeness. . . .

"And it's true," he went on, his gaze meeting hers without apology, "that we met once or twice afterward. But that was before Vere's death. It's also true I'm very fond of her and will continue to be even when we leave Bournehills for good. She's one of the real friends I've made here—or anywhere else for that matter, and she'll always mean something very special to me. I tell you all this"—he had not paused—"not to be cruel, although I know how it must sound, or to excuse myself, but I can imagine how Lyle must have distorted it and I won't have that.

"It'll be all right, Hatt," he added as she continued to sit at the table as if he hadn't spoken, her expression unchanged and the trace of a smile intact.

"It's ironic," he said, "but in a way we're talking about something that's over. Because I think I told you Merle's going away soon. She was never very happy about the turn of things and after the bad time she's just been through she really wants to get away. And as soon as I'm a little more sure about the council we'll take a long break. This first period hasn't been good for us. And ever since carnival you've been acting so strange it's made things between us worse. Maybe it's that you've had your fill of Bournehills, which is understandable. It's not an easy place to take. Anyway, we'll come right again, Hatt. We will. If you'll just give us a chance and not keep everything to yourself so much. Everyone, it's true, is entitled to his privacy but with you it's almost a total withholding. It's something that's always bothered me. Never mind, though. It'll all come right. Hatt . . ."

She might not have heard any of it. The moment she realized he would not give her what she asked and agree that it had been nothing more than carnival, a slight matter, at that moment someone, a protective spirit perhaps, might have slipped a caul over her head, some tough transparent sheathing through which nothing could pass. So that while giving the impression of attending to him, she hadn't been able to hear him. Nor did she appear able to see him as he waited, uncertain and suppliant, across the table from her although her gaze was trained on his face.

"Yes, I'm sure that's all it was: one of those small things they say happens at such times. . . ." She spoke from behind the thick caul in a muffled faraway voice. Behind it her eyes were very wide and empty. "It's even understandable considering the circumstances. But what puzzles me is why anyone would want to make something so trivial seem important. Usually something like this is quickly over and done with and no one's the worse for it. . . .

"Oh, why are you like that? Why must you take everything so seriously?" Behind the invisible shield her voice had risen. "Why must you always get so involved? And I don't mean Merle. I really can't take that seriously. It's not her. How could it be? A poor disturbed woman like that who, from what I gather, had led an unbelievably messy life, and who seems helpless to do anything about herself. I can understand how someone like you, who goes around taking on the problems of the world would pity . . ."

"It wasn't pity. It wasn't just carnival. It wasn't trivial," he insisted doggedly.

". . . would pity"—she bore down hard on the word—"someone

like that, and in trying to help, find yourself involved. That's not hard to understand. I mean this place. It's this place, can't you see that, where nothing you do seems to matter. It's this place!" She spoke wildly, irrationally, her eyes dark gray, suggesting that the mind behind them had gone dark also. *"This place!"*

The outcry, which didn't sound like her at all, contained the weight of everything she had come to feel about Bournehills, and as it struck, causing the sunlight in the room to recoil, the protective caul fell away, leaving her for a moment utterly exposed. And in that moment Saul glimpsed that part of her which had always remained a stranger to him, the profoundly troubled self she kept carefully disguised behind the impressive exterior calm. And shaken by what he saw there, frightened for her and for them both, he quickly said, "All right, Hatt, we'll leave when we said we would and not wait. As soon as the report's in and the Center lets me know what they think about it, we'll go." He had come around the table to stand beside her chair.

"What good will that do?" she cried angrily, her eyes the dark dangerous gray. "I know that's what I've been asking all along, but what good will it do really, a short trip home? We'll only be coming back. And if I know that hopeless woman over at the guesthouse she won't be able to stay away any time. That's if she even goes anywhere."

"Well, what would you have me do, for God's sake?" His voice matched the anger in hers. "Should I tell them up in Philadelphia to get themselves another director? Is that it? Is that what you want me to do? Well, that's out. I won't do it. This is the first real work to come my way in years."

"You know you're probably right and things will work out." She spoke after a silence, and her voice held something of its usual calm. And she almost seemed herself except for the overcast eyes, which continued to stare, unseeing, out the open doorway to the gallery opposite her worktable. "After all I didn't marry you thinking you'd never sleep with another woman. I'm not that Victorian. Even though I must say I didn't expect it'd be this soon. But then I should have remembered your lady colleague out at Stanford whom you continued seeing almost up until we were married. . . .

"Please," she said wearily, glancing up at him, "don't stand over me like that. People have been standing over me all day talking down at my head. Go away. Go in and rest until dinner. Something like this isn't going to be resolved in the space of an afternoon and you look exhausted."

But he remained, gazing silently down at her, his face reflecting his guilt and despair and the deep fear he felt at what he had glimpsed in her just before. His tired body gave the impression it was about to collapse in a heap of large bones at his feet. He saw the natural parting at the crown of her head, where the hair sprang strongly from the root to form the pale wheat-colored cowl that framed her face. Each strand was, as always, in its assigned place, and to add to his sadness he could see secreted among them, scarcely distinguishable from the rest of her hair which the Bournehill sun had turned several shades lighter, the first few signs of gray. His hand started up, then dropped back: he would have touched them if he dared.

"The last thing I wanted to do was to spoil things for us, Hatt," he said. "To do wrong by you. I think you know that. I've managed to disappoint so many people, I didn't want to do the same with you."

Looking out into the late afternoon sunlight at the doorway, she said—and her face had tightened in a clearly perceptible grimace, "I think," she said, "of your touching someone like that and I can't understand it."

She felt him go stiff. "You mean because Merle's black, don't you?"

She didn't answer.

"Yes," he said, "I thought you'd get around to that. It's probably been the thing most on your mind." (She felt the cold breath of his anger on her head, and knew that the pale irises of his eyes had the look of harsh metal.) "Well, for your information that particular aspect of it presented no difficulty, perhaps because I've always been somewhat eclectic in my tastes as far as women go. The first woman I ever loved was Peruvian, a mestizo—part Indian, part Spanish in case you don't know what that means. My first wife looked exactly like a Russian muzhik, broad Slavic cheekbones and all; and here you are purebred Anglo-Saxon which, frankly, I find equally as exotic. So for a man like me, someone with such wide tastes, Merle's color presented no problem. She was the one. She couldn't bear the thought of my being white and insisted on pretending that I was really one of the red people from up Canterbury.

"And just think, someone could ask you the same question. They could ask how is it that you, a Philadelphian blue-blood, could bear to have me, a long-nosed Jew, touch you. They might not be able to understand that, either."

He was gone only a short time to his workroom at the back of the house, leaving behind the ugly ring of the words on the air, when

Loris, returning to cook their evening meal, appeared in the doorway. And for an instant, seeing her silhouetted against the sunlight, with the absurd felt hat which obscured her face perched on her head, Harriet thought it was Merle in the unbecoming hat she wore to church on Sundays standing before her. And not only Merle, but everyone in the district, every man, woman and child. After the long weeks she had spent in the beginning carefully separating out the individual faces from the all-engulfing blackness that had at first made it impossible for her to distinguish them one from another, the faces had begun to merge and blend again, moving together to form a solid bloc against her.

CHAPTER 9

The following day she went to see Merle. She timed the visit to coincide with her late-afternoon stroll out to the high palisade of Plover Cliff. Taking her time she first walked in a leisurely fashion out to the cliffs. But today, instead of going by way of the beach as she usually did, she took the narrow potholed road to the rear of the guesthouse: Merle was certain to be on the veranda at this hour. Reaching the cliffs, she sat for a long time on her favorite rock gazing emptily (her eyes had recovered only a small portion of their accustomed blue) out at the sullen thrashing sea which was still in the throes of its seasonal change, and half-listening to the hollow boom and suck of the water in the inaccessible caves below. She had spent the entire day in this manner, sitting idle for hours, her gaze off in some distant place.

On her way back—along the seaweed-strewn beach this time, she passed the elderly couple from England sitting in the lee of a sandhill surrounded by the village dogs whom they were busy grooming—rubbing them down with long loving strokes of the brush. It was past their four-thirty teatime, the hour when they usually quit for the day. But the number of dogs had increased since their arrival—the strays having been joined by those who had homes—so that it took them longer to attend to them all.

Nearby, looking on, stood a large group of children also come over from the village, among them Harriet's early morning visitants from the days when she had lived at the guesthouse. The children, she knew, had been hunting turtle along the beach, a favorite pastime with them. On certain days they would claim to see a sign in the sky telling them that one of the huge female hawksbill turtles had come ashore to lay her eggs, and they would rush over in a ragtag band from Spiretown to hunt it down. (Harriet had never been able to get them to explain just what the mysterious sign in the sky was.) The children would comb the beach from one end to the other, searching for the turtle in the shallow burrows under the thick sedge and grape leaves covering the dunes. If they were lucky and found one, several in their party would race back to Spiretown for help while the others kept the creature at bay by pelting it with stones and wet clods of sand. They knew better than to try and kill it themselves. For the great webbed limbs slashing out savagely from under the shell and sending up the sand in a blinding whirl could knock them unconscious; the turtle's powerful jaws could easily crush an arm or leg. When the men came and killed it, there would be meat at the evening meal—meat the dark red of dried blood—instead of the customary salt cod.

But today, like most days, the sign in the sky had deceived them and they had found no turtle; and on their way back to the village they had paused to watch the old couple and the dogs. Their flat expressionless eyes said there was little in the world that could amaze them.

Harriet tried to slip unnoticed past them all—the barefoot band of children and the Mathersons. She succeeded with the latter who, absorbed at the moment in feeding the dogs the last of the meat they had brought with them, were unaware of her as well as the onlookers gathered nearby. The children, though, spotting her passing far down near the water's edge, turned in a body to wave. But something about her step and the slant of her body, something in the brief tight smile she gave them caused their arms to falter midway. At her step the tiny land crabs, indistinguishable from the sand but for their black antennae, scuttled into their holes and the sandpipers took wing.

As she had expected, Merle was on the veranda. While still some distance away she made out the tired red of the familiar housecoat, the smoke trailing up from her inevitable cigarette and the dark feet with their outrageous tan-colored soles planted firmly against the posts of the railing (they made her suddenly, for no reason, remember the song, a spiritual, her mother's maid Alberta could often be heard singing long ago: "I shall not be moved"), and finally the face, very dark and grave and spent-looking against the driftwood white of the lawn chair with its high back.

"I see you're up and around again," she called from below—and she was surprised at how easily she managed the light tone and the smile. "How are you feeling?"

"I'll live, they tell me."

Merle's answering smile over the veranda railing made Harriet think of a pocket mirror being held up to the sun. It gave off the same harsh splintered light. It seemed hard with the knowledge of something. Perhaps, she told herself as she continued on around to the stone steps leading up to the house, the woman had known it would eventually come to this and had been patiently awaiting her. Perhaps she even knew her mission in coming. It didn't matter. It would make what she had to say easier.

"Good Lord, you tend to forget how really noisy the sea is living over in the village," she said, crossing the long veranda and taking a seat one away from Merle. "Just listen to it."

"I know," Merle said. "It's been lecturing me the whole bloody afternoon."

"And the beach has become an unsightly mess with all the seaweed."

"Yes," Merle said. "And it's no use trying to clean it up because as soon as you clear away one load of the damn stuff the waves come along and dump another. But what to do, the old sea's cleaning itself. It's worse this year than I've ever seen it though. The water's rougher—you don't even dare go near Horseshoe Pool, and the noise is enough to stun you. People are saying it's grieving over Vere. But it'll be done soon, and then—ah, then"—she smiled to herself—"it's like a new sea altogether, the water's as blue and clear as in those fancy swimming pools over in Crown Beach Colony. You get the sweetest sea bath in the world then. The beach is always mobbed on Sunday mornings. Even our large friend Delbert, who never goes near the water as a rule, comes and sticks in a big toe."

"It must be quite a sight to see him taking a swim," Harriet said.

"More than a sight." Merle laughed. "He makes Horseshoe Pool look no bigger than a bathtub. There's scarcely room for anyone else when he's in."

She had said all this with her face to the sea, but she turned now to Harriet with something of the smile she had given her minutes ago over the railing. Her eyes reflected its hard-edged knowing light. Under the worn wrapper her body waited.

"Care for a drink?" she said—and in that way of hers, which Harriet always found so irritating, she had already turned to call into the house without waiting for an answer.

"No, I won't be staying long," Harriet said, although with her legs lightly crossed under her oatmeal-colored linen skirt and her slender, somewhat angular form settled easily into the chair, she looked in no hurry. "I still have a few pages of the report left to do," she said. "I meant to finish the whole thing yesterday, but Lyle Hutson dropped by, as you probably know: he said he was coming over here afterward, and threw me off schedule. But I'd like to get it done by this evening if possible so we can mail it off tomorrow."

"And then it's 'off' for the three of you also, isn't it?" Merle said. "Back to America for a nice long holiday."

"Yes, if that impossible husband of mine doesn't change his mind again, which he's subject to do!" she said with a laugh that again surprised her with its effortlessness. "I don't know whether he or Allen has mentioned it to you but things haven't been going well at all with the council and Saul's uncertain about leaving right now. So that if we do go it will probably be only for a short time, and we won't leave until the Center's written and told us what they think of the report. I must confess I'm more than a little disappointed. I was looking forward to the two of us being home for at least two months. But I'm learning," she said with a philosophical sigh, "that being married to a field anthropologist is as bad as being married to an old-fashioned country doctor. Somebody's always having a baby in the middle of the night, meaning it's one crisis after another so that you can never plan.

"But if Saul feels it's important that he get back to Bournehills right away, then, of course, that's what we'll do," she declared. "Or, if he changes his mind again and decides he had better stay and go right into the next part of the research without a break, then we stay. Because I know"—and here her voice suddenly slowed and the words became more pointed—"how much the project means to him. . . ." There was a slight pause: "I think you do, too," she said quietly.

Their eyes met across the empty chair—Harriet's with the gray overcast that had not as yet lifted completely, Merle's reflecting the harsh light of her waiting smile.

"Not only," Harriet said, "is this the first real field work he's done in years, but this particular project is the kind he's always wanted to do but never got the chance to before. So you see it means a great deal to him, almost too much I sometimes think. He's gotten so caught up in the work and in Bournehills he hates leaving here for a day. Anyway, he's very anxious naturally, and so am I, that nothing go wrong. I think you are, too."

Again there was no response aside from the imperceptible smile that in its set, cold fixity called to mind Lyle Hutson.

And again, after waiting a moment, Harriet calmly continued, her voice placing careful stress on the words, forcing them to carry the full weight of her meaning. "I'm not speaking, I should explain," she said, "about things that might go wrong in terms of the project itself, such as the trouble Saul's run into trying to keep the council going. That's to be expected. I'm thinking more of situations that might arise apart from the work which might create problems. Not very serious problems perhaps, but problems nonetheless.

"I wouldn't want to see that happen," she said firmly. "I—" Suddenly without warning, the firmness gave way and she lost voice. It lasted less than a fraction of a second. With an effort that caused the flat white bone at her knees to press hard against the tanned skin, turning it white also, she quickly rallied, and said—but in a somewhat changed voice, one that contained what could have almost been an appeal, "I—I just don't want to see anything spoil this for him, that's all—nor would you, I'm sure, were you in my place."

They looked across at each other for much longer this time. And this time as Merle's gaze which had the power, some claimed, to penetrate a person's innermost being and read his life at a glance, read deep into Harriet, a change came over her also. All trace of the hard-edged smile died and was replaced by something close to compassion. She knew, the look said, what it meant for her—Harriet!—to have to come and plead for him like this. The love, desperation and need that had driven her to it. And because of this she, Merle, regretted her part in it, that softened expression said. Perhaps if she had not been a forty-year-old isolate with nothing to show for the years but a white elephant of a house and a room filled with the miscellany of a broken life and history, none of which she could reconcile; perhaps if she were not someone almost consumed by self-pity and guilt, too shamed and fearful even to go and demand the right to see her own child; if she wasn't someone driven nearly insane at times by the long punishing exile she had imposed on herself, the whole thing might never have happened. Or, if it had she would have seen to it that it went no further than the one night. But she had been impelled by a need as complex and enormous in its way, as awesome, as the one she glimpsed in Harriet. So that in spite of all the things which set them apart and the fact that they sat drawn up like two armies about to do battle on each side of the empty chair, they were essentially the same, the look declared: two women who had long been assailed by the sense of their uselessness, who had never found anything truly their own to do, no work that could have defined them, and so had always had to look outside themselves to the person of the lover for definition, a sense of a self, and for the chance, in their relationship with him, in helping to shape his life, to exercise some small measure of power.

For a moment, seeing that look, understanding its meaning, Harriet was afraid the woman would do something truly foolish, such as reach across and place a hand on hers to seal what she saw as the bond between them; and offended beyond words, she felt her body brace to spring out of the way of that touch.

"I'm thinking of going away, Harriet." It was a subdued, compliant, sympathetic Merle who spoke.

"Yes, so I understand," she said. "In fact that's what I came to ask you about. I was wondering just when you were planning to leave and where you were going."

"Well, I've pretty much decided on Trinidad," Merle said in the mild, conciliatory tone. "And I'll be leaving soon as the dog lovers down on the beach go home and I either close up the house or let you people use it for the others you say will be coming down from the States. They'll need someplace to stay."

"I see." She appeared strangely dissatisfied. There was even the suggestion of a frown. She said, "I'm a little surprised you've decided on Trinidad. It's so close, right around the corner, so to speak. It's hardly like going away."

"I've friends there," Merle explained, "and a good chance of a job, which is important since I intend staying for awhile, for good perhaps if things work out."

"Oh, well, of course, it makes sense then," she said, but the slight frown remained. "Somehow I always had the impression from the way you talked that you were eager to live as far away from the West Indies as possible, in someplace completely different. I could be mistaken but it seems you always indicated as much—and frankly, I think that would be best."

Merle gazed at her for a long moment, seeing not her face so much with its precision-cut features and surface show of calm, but the angry hurt and woman's pain behind it. And compliant still, she said, "Yes, that would probably be best, but you know as well as I do, Harriet, that I don't have the wherewithal to be making any big moves right now. I'll be lucky if I can scrape together the plane fare to Trinidad."

"Yes, I know that," Harriet said. "That's why I thought that if you were interested in really getting away you might consider letting me advance you enough money, not only for your fare but to tide you over until you found a job. You could set the amount."

If she was at all aware that Merle had suddenly grown very still she took no notice of it.

"And there wouldn't be any need to repay it," she said. "You could consider it a gift or, if you like, a token of appreciation on our part. After all, you were very helpful in the beginning in seeing to it we got settled in. So that it's only right we should return the favor. Anyway, I hope you can see your way to accepting it. Because then . . ."

"Harriet." Her hand had come up in a mute gesture of warning and something in her voice as she called her name almost pleaded with her to forbear.

"Because then," Harriet repeated, the firmness restored to her tone; what little blue there was in her eyes had hardened, "you'll be able to go wherever you'd like and not have to settle for just any place. There's Canada, for instance . . ."

"Harriet."

"I understand quite a number of West Indians have gone there to live. And there's the whole of Europe, of course. And I hear you have a husband and child somewhere in Africa. I don't know what the situation is with your marriage but you might like to live somewhere near your child . . ."

"Harriet!"

"Or if you wanted, you could return to England."

"England?" It was barely a whisper. "Did you say England?"

"Yes," she said. "I've heard you express the desire any number of times to return there. I assumed you meant it. For one thing, you'd have a much easier time getting settled since I understand you have very close friends in London.

"So," she said, looking at Merle but ignoring her stricken face, "if you'll let me know the amount you think you'll need, I'll get it to you.

And I'll see to it personally. No one else, not even Saul, need be involved. I'm sure you understand that. And it might be best if you could arrange to be gone by the time we return from our trip home."

She had no sooner finished when Merle's feet, propped up against the railing posts, slid heavily to the floor. The muscles supporting them might have suddenly gone limp. As part of the same stunned move she turned and, leaning out across the arm of her chair, stared at Harriet—and though the empty chair and about two feet of space on each side of it stood between them, it seemed her face was only inches away.

It was the familiar look she bent on Harriet, which went back to the first night at Lyle Hutson's when, during their conversation on the veranda, she had repeatedly leaned close and openly, brazenly, peered into her face as though she spied someone she knew lurking there. She was looking at her now in the same way, searching intently for that other face in hiding behind hers. And she had grown very quiet again, her entire self given over to the search. Only her earrings moved, and these only slightly, the saints shivering a little as though the mild wind off the sea had turned cold.

Across from her and disregarding the look as she had always done, Harriet sat waiting for her offer to be accepted and the amount named so that she could leave.

And then Merle suddenly gave a violent start. And in the same moment her eyes squeezed shut—her face contracting painfully with the effort—and with a choked cry of fear, horror and dismay, her hand coming up to fend off that other face which had at last, after all these months, revealed itself, she fell back in the chair. She lay there for a long time, her eyes tightly closed and her face frozen in the painful lines; utterly exhausted, defeated: some long chase, like those which occur only in dreams, might have ended for her with her pursuer having closed the gap. And then in that abrupt change of mood that was so much a part of her drama, she once again brought her feet up to the posts with their scaling white paint, and throwing her head back she laughed.

It was an ugly anguished scream torn from the very top of her voice, and as frighteningly empty and ironic as the huge gut laugh which, unprovoked, convulsed Delbert from time to time. And she let it come. Her head arching back against the wooden slats that made up the backrest of the chair, bracing herself on the posts, she forced it out, sounding like a woman in labor with a stillborn child, who screams to rid herself of that dead weight. Merle might have also been trying to rid herself of something dead inside her, that face perhaps which had attached itself like an incubus to her mind, sapping her strength and purpose over the years, debauching her will. In what seemed some ancient exorcistic rite she gave vent to the laugh, and as it rose in a shrill steady line the sea beyond the railing appeared to fall silent in deference to its greater power.

Harriet ignored it, just as she had the disconcerting look before. Poised in the chair, her legs lightly crossed, her instep arched, she patiently waited it out. Idly, her gaze wandered over to the feet pressed up against the supports to the railing. They were darker than the woman's face, black almost, with childish toes that curled in and the ludicrous bisque-colored heels and soles. (As a child, looking at the maid Alberta's pink palms she had often wondered how this had come about; why had this part of them been spared?) But the feet were surprisingly well-shaped as were the legs she glimpsed in the opening to the long skirt of the robe. Harriet had always considered those legs something of an anomaly in view of the rest of the woman's rather short, altogether undistinguished body. Her glance reached up to the throat bent all the way back, and came to rest there. She could almost see the screaming laugh which she had closed her ears to rushing up through the arched ribbed tube. She saw the darker line where the skin met in a natural crease and, in the crease, what looked to be a lingering trace of the talcum powder she was forever dusting on herself. And gazing as if transfixed at that too short and, to her mind, totally unaesthetic throat with its powdery remains, she wondered—the thought causing sudden chaos in her—whether Saul had ever paused during their embrace and, as he often did with her, trace with his fingers the line of that throat from the chin down to the small hollow at its base, and then down to the breast. . . .

Her head swung sharply away. A tiny nerve near her mouth gave a savage pull, drawing her lips into a hard line, and as if to spare her the full brunt of the feeling that swept her, a saving numbness, the same dense gray her eyes had suddenly become, closed over her mind.

And it remained for some time, so that she wasn't really aware when Merle, her body convulsed by the laugh that was more a scream of pain, her face distorted by it, struggled up from her chair and came to stand over her. She couldn't have said just when the laugh finally subsided and the woman started shouting. Only gradually did her mind rouse to the sound of that voice and the sight of her in the maroon gown standing over her with her hands struck at either hip.

". . . England now!" she was shouting, her voice at a scathing pitch. "Did you hear her? Does she have any idea of the hell I saw in England? Why, that's the last place in this world I want to see again. Canada. Africa. My passage paid to the ends of the earth. Get thee gone, Satan, and here's enough money to stay gone. Oh, God, this woman must be trying to set out my head again coming over here this afternoon talking about money.

"Money! Always money! But that's the way they are, you know," she cried, informing the sea, the long, wearily sloping veranda, the house with its ancient ghosts, of the fact. "They feel they can buy the world and its wife with a few raw-mouth dollars. But lemme tell you something, m' lady"—her face, streaked white from the tears brought on by her laugh, dropped close; it was only a dark featureless blur in Harriet's remote gaze—"I can't be bought. Or bribed. I'm not like some of those thieving politicians we've got in Legco. And I don't accept handouts. Not anymore at least. I used to. You might not have heard about that, but I did. And for the longest time. And because of it lost the two people who meant life itself to me. But not anymore. I've grown wise in my old age. And proud. Poor as the devil, but proud."

She raised up, trembling with her rage, unable to go on for the moment. But slowly the trembling ceased as a thought took hold of her, and her tears, those left over from her laugh, slowly hardened to emit a cold light. Below her in the chair, an outwardly unaffected Harriet was looking past her out to the beach.

"And lemme tell you something else, m' lady," she said, and her voice was as cold as the changed light her eyes gave off. "I don't think I'm going anyplace. I've changed my mind. Because you're right, you know, it doesn't make a bit of sense for me to go dashing off to some island which is practically right next door and pretty much the same as here. That wouldn't be any real change. And, although you didn't say as much, it wouldn't solve anything. I'd still be too close for comfort. All anybody who wanted to see me would have to do is catch a plane and he'd be there in no time flat.

"No, I had best stay put until I can see my way to make a really big move. Besides"—the derisive note dropped out of her voice, leaving only the hard anger—"I don't like people ordering me about like I'm still the little colonial. I've had too much of that. So when they say gee now, I haw. When they say go, I stay. And stay I will. Right here in Bournehills where I belong. My mind's made up. And it'll be just between the two of us why I suddenly changed plans. You don't have to worry I'll tell a soul. Yes, my lady, you'll be able to find me sitting up big as life on this veranda any time you like. And when you and Saul take your little trip home and come back I'll be right here, waiting for you. *England!*"

With that her head went back and the earsplitting laugh erupted once again. And this time it was more a laugh and less the anguished scream that had sought to rid her of the dead weight. She might have been delivered. Turning, she started toward the door of the drawing room, staggering a little under the force of the laugh, stopping to hold onto the backs of the chairs along her way each time it seized her afresh. She entered the house and the suddenly free ringing laugh routed the stale silence in all the rooms and dim stone halls through which she passed, setting off echoes which found their way out to the veranda long after she had disappeared.

Left behind, Harriet continued to contemplate the beach beyond the railing. Seated there with her skirt draped quietly across her knees, an unhurried serene look about her, she appeared to be calmly waiting for Merle to return—for the laugh to spend itself and a penitent Merle to re-emerge from the house, take her seat and in a sober tone accept the offer and name her sum.

But the chair one removed from hers remained empty. The last stubborn echoes of the laugh died, the children passed on their way back to the village, the Mathersons trailed up from the beach carrying between them the large straw bag containing the combs and brushes, and disappeared inside (they were staying in the wing she and Saul had occupied) and still Merle failed to put in an appearance.

Finally, as the last of the sunlight withdrew and the darkness began its rapid build-up far out to sea and she as yet hadn't come, Harriet's face also darkened, reflecting in part the changing light, but more so her suddenly changed inner state. When had she felt this way before? Like an enraged, thwarted child who would bring an entire room—everything in it!—crashing down? And then she remembered the green-uniformed horde with their cheap cigars and noisy toy guns who, spurning her advice, had insisted on going their own way down toward the waters of the bay. A resolve quickly taking shape, she rose and, leaving the guesthouse, returned to Spiretown the way she had come, along the cratered road between the sandhills and Westminster's spur.

The rest of the evening passed pleasantly enough. Back in the village she quickly completed the final pages of the report, and when Saul—a subdued contrite Saul who was afraid to meet her eye—came in, accompanied by Allen, they proofread it together. And for the time the three of them sat working at her desk, it was almost as though nothing had gone wrong: there might have been no Merle, no Bournehills even.

Later, when the two men left for Delbert's, first stopping on the way down to pick up Stinger in his house below, and she was alone, she wrote to Chester Heald and then read. But she had to force her eyes across each sentence on the page and fight to retain the sense of what she was reading.

CHAPTER 10

The report had been in only a short time when they received a cable informing Saul he was being replaced as head of the Bournehills project, and that the project itself was being suspended until such time as a new director could be found. He was to conclude his affairs in Bournehills as quickly as possible and return to Philadelphia where, due to a number of staff and organizational changes within CASR, he was being put in charge of the entire program-planning and development section at the Center. Allen, who would be continuing with the project once it resumed, was also to return home for the present. The long cable ended by praising the report they had submitted and congratulating Saul on his new appointment.

As with most people when they receive some devastating piece of news: word of a fatal illness or some other reversal, neither Saul nor Allen, who was with him and Harriet in the house on the rise, could react at first, but stood as if struck dumb.

Even when Saul finally found his voice and said in a stunned whisper, "Pulling me off the project . . . dropping the whole thing just like that . . ." it was clear his mind hadn't as yet taken it in, could give no credence to the cable's message. "I don't get it, Al, do you?" He turned with a dazed look, a little boy's bewilderment almost, to Allen. "What the hell are they talking about?"

And an equally incredulous Allen could only numbly shake his head.

Even when his disbelief exploded in an angry roar that shook the frail walls of the house and brought Mary Griggs' hymn, drifting in at the window, to an abrupt halt, it was still as though he couldn't believe any of it. Shouting now, he began charging up and down the room, his unstrung body and plunging step, the wildness in his eyes calling to mind one of those caged animals who remain unreconciled to captivity.

". . . What the hell are they up to, will you tell me?" And it was the stung, enraged cry of an animal. He strode past Harriet's restraining hand without seeing it and back and forth past the confused and silent Allen. "How could they do something like this? Just pull me off the project and switch me to some job behind a desk without so much as asking me first. What kind of high-handed business is that? I'm no goddamn administrator. I can't go around playing office politics and kissing the backsides of those bastards on the Institute's board. I've spent my life running from all that . . ." Then, his outrage mounting, he cried—and again the walls threatened to give way under the impact—"And to drop the project just when the real work was about to begin!

"Drop it!" he repeated savagely, momentarily turning his fury on Harriet who, speaking for the first time, quietly sought to remind him that the cable had said it was only to be a temporary suspension. "You don't know these goddamn research outfits the way I do. Once they start talking about temporary suspensions and the rest of it, it means one thing: the end. They'll never come up with a new director. I know them. One minute they're all fired up about a project and the next they're ready to drop it. They think nothing of behaving in the most cavalier fashion possible with other people's lives. That's what power is all about to them . . .

"But they're not going to get away with it this time, the bastards," he said grimly, his shout subsiding all of a sudden. He had come to a halt in the center of the room. "I'm not going to stand by as I did once before and see them abandon Bournehills or use me like I'm a pawn in some little game they play up there in Philadelphia to fill in the time.

"Besides," he cried, his eyes narrowing suspiciously, "I don't buy their explanations about staff changes and needing me up there. Why me all of a sudden?" He turned with the question to Allen.

"I don't get it either, Saul," he said.

"No, the whole goddamn thing doesn't sound right," he was saying to himself, his pale gaze indrawn. "Something else is behind it. Something's going on up there I don't know about . . ." Then, his loose-jointed body fusing with sudden purpose, he declared, "But I intend finding out. Come on, Al, we're going to town."

He made for the door, with a puzzled but obedient Allen behind him, and Harriet rose sharply from her chair. Her voice as she called to him, asking him what he intended doing, was also sharp, anxious. Without breaking his stride he hurled over his shoulder that he was going to the cable and wireless office in New Bristol and put through a call to his friend Barney Cole at the Center.

And then he was out the door and moments later the car was pelleting the late morning silence with the sound of the small stones exploding under its wheels as he sent it hurtling down toward the main road below.

Harriet, too taken aback at first to move, had started after them across the room once she recovered. But by the time she reached the door they were already pulling off, and the violent sound of the wheels on the unpaved track brought her up short inside the doorway.

She stood there for some time, her legs poised to carry her out onto the gallery and the words she had intended saying to dissuade him from the wild trip remaining unsaid, still part of her shocked silence.

Outside, the Ford sent its loud echo floating back long after it had started the steep climb to Westminster. When this finally died Harriet slowly retraced her steps to the Morris armchair in which she had been sitting. She didn't sit back down right away, though. Instead, for awhile, she paced the floor in front of the chair, following without realizing it Saul's angry path of minutes ago. And when she did finally take her seat again, sinking into the chair as if the frame which supported her flesh and all her slender, strong, well-articulated bones, had suddenly buckled, her eyes—very large now and a shocked, apprehensive blue—held his same dazed look.

She was seated only a short time when the old woman in the house above resumed her fateful drone.

Because of the time difference between Bourne Island and Philadelphia and the difficulty involved in placing an overseas call (Bourne Island shared a single cable with several other islands and had to wait its turn), it was nearly dusk when Saul and Allen returned. The sun had burned away all the jagged edges from Westminster's twin peaks, turning them into smooth cones that might have been shaped on a potter's wheel, and was about to drop behind. The sandhills had undergone their magical transformation from the burning white of early afternoon to gold glittering with mica as the sun began its decline and were now a deep rose that would soon shade into mauve. The sea was the color and texture of burgundy that contains its own light. And all along the stony rise lying north of the main road, the smoke of the evening fires drifting up through the slatted walls of the shed-roof kitchens could have been wraiths seeking the darkening air.

Loris, having returned from her long midday break, had prepared the light meal they took in the evenings and, at Harriet's instructions, had laid a place for Allen at the dining table which stood to one side of the large front room. The serving dishes containing the food stood neatly grouped in the center of the table under hoods of wire mesh to keep out the flies. As her last act before leaving, she had filled the three tilly lamps used in the room (two lamps would have been enough, but ever since the bat had taken to flying in at dusk Harriet had insisted on three) and put them unlighted in their assigned places. Then, the felt hat on her head and wearing a pair of Harriet's shoes which the latter had given her when they became slightly worn, she had departed, carrying with her in a basket her portion of the meal to share with her mother and two sisters at home.

She had been gone only a short time when the men returned. They might have passed her in the car on the road. Saul, the wild anger of the morning passed, moved heavily into the room, his unsteady gait and glazed eyes giving the impression he had been drinking during the long wait to put through the call.

He lurched past Harriet (completely blind to her standing there), and while she turned questioningly to Allen, who had paused in the doorway, reluctant suddenly to come any farther into the house, he wandered aimlessly about the room, stopping from time to time to look around him as though he didn't know the place and nothing about it was familiar to him.

Finally, he stumbled to a dazed halt at the worktable in the far corner, where he sometimes wrote in the afternoons if there weren't any visitors and again at night after coming back from Delbert's. His loosely hanging head gave the impression it was connected to the rest of him by a single frayed tendon as he stood staring down at the various items which Harriet always kept neatly arranged for him there: the long canary-yellow legal-size pads he used for making notes, the freshly sharpened pencils standing at attention in their ceramic holder, the ashtray for the occasional cigarette he smoked while working, with the cigarettes themselves lying in a box made of small, perfectly matched sea shells which she had bought him as a present at the Handicraft Center in town (she had placed a folder of matches beside it), and finally the desk calendar with a notation in her handwriting made several days ago that there was to be a meeting of the village council this evening. His eyes came to rest there.

Harriet spoke his name after several minutes, but her voice, perhaps because it was pitched too low, didn't seem able to penetrate the distance between them. She called him once more in the same low hopeful tone, and when he again failed to respond she turned back to Allen drawn up ill at ease at the door. "What happened, Allen?" she said. Her voice sounded as usual. "Were you able to get through?"

"Yes." He shifted uneasily. Behind his glasses his gaze reached nervously across to Saul, then back to her, containing an unformed question. "We had to wait nearly the whole day, but they finally managed to put through the call."

"You actually spoke to Barney Cole?"

"Yes. Saul did."

She was standing at the dining table near one of the chairs and she pulled it out and very slowly sat down before speaking again. "What did he say?"

Allen sighed, shook his dark rumpled head. "The whole thing's as much a mystery to him as it is to us, it seems," he said. "He says there has been some reorganizing going on—people being shifted around and new people coming in—but he didn't think Saul was in any way involved, and he certainly didn't think he was being considered for any desk job up there no matter how big. Everybody assumed he would be staying on in Bournehills with the project. But that's the way they do things in these operations, I guess. Everybody, of course, thinks it's a great break for him, but they're still as surprised as we are."

"Does Barney know whose decision it was?"

"It could only be Ted Neilson's as head of the Center," Allen said. "Either he recommended Saul to the board or they did to him. Barney says Neilson's not talking about it for some reason. In fact, according to him, they hardly see Neilson these days he spends so much time over at the Institute consulting with the board. But then he was always their boy."

"Was anything said about the project itself?" Her questions

scarcely carried across the less than twelve feet between Allen at the door and herself. Over in his distant corner Saul had not moved. His stillness made him almost seem one of the inanimate objects with which the room was furnished: a life-size statue done in pale stone to convey a theme of desolation and defeat.

"That's the first thing Saul asked about," said Allen—and again his gaze flew swiftly between them, vaguely troubled by something he sensed but could not define. "He wanted to know whether they meant to drop it. But Barney couldn't say. He and everybody else thought the project was definitely set to continue until they got word it was being delayed and Saul was being switched. The staff at the Center was kept as much in the dark about the whole business as we were. But Barney promises to do some snooping around and see what he can come up with. He doubts he'll be able to find out very much, though, since both Neilson and his friends on the Institute's board are a pretty tight-lipped bunch, but he's going to try. He also thinks Saul should get up to Philadelphia right away and see if he can't get them to change their minds—although he said he's heard the decision to pull him out of Bournehills is final. So I don't know how much good it'll do. I don't guess those big shots on the board could possibly understand why someone wouldn't want a nice fat job behind a desk."

"I don't guess so, either," she said. "But I think Barney's right and the best thing to do is for us to get back as quickly as possible."

Allen resisted this a moment, all of him visibly opposed to the idea of leaving. But finally his thick unscholarly shoulders lifted in a resigned shrug. "Yes, I don't suppose there's much point hanging around Bournehills now that it appears we don't have a project." Then: "Gosh, I'm beat"—and his face, looking more boyish and bewildered than ever, showed both the strain of the long day and the effect of the news. He stepped back. "I think I'd better go rest if I'm to make the council meeting tonight."

Harriet quickly rose. "But you must be starving," she said. "Stay and eat first. I had Loris set a place for you."

He shook his head, already edging out the door. "No," he said, "I don't have any appetite. All I want is some rest." Then, just before stepping back onto the gallery he called across to Saul. "Saul," he said, his voice gentle with solicitude, "do you think you'll be coming to the meeting tonight?"

For a moment it didn't look as if the numb figure in the corner would answer, or that it was even capable of speech, but finally a low muffled sound could be heard. "I'll get there, Al. You go rest."

Allen left, and he might have taken the last of the daylight with him. Because the moment he stepped out onto the gallery and the sound of his footsteps could be heard on the shaky steps leading down to the small yard and then amid the noisy stones of the road, night fell—that swift primordial Bournehills night which each evening rushes in to embrace the land like some overardent lover, and out of whose seed comes each morning a world that, before the sun rises and destroys the illusion, looks wholly new, freshly created.

The darkness came pouring into the house: smoke, it seemed, from the final conflagration set off by the departing sun atop Westminster. Entering by the windows, through the thin walls and under the door Allen had closed behind him, it quickly filled the room, and Harriet hastened to light the lamps. She had become expert at this over the months. She knew just the right amount of pressure to apply when priming them, and after putting a match to the wick would work the piston in strong measured strokes until the mantle with its delicate filigree glowed white-hot inside the chimney and the overly bright, caustic light sent the shadows ducking for cover under the furniture.

She moved about the room, through the marathon silence, past the stone figure at the desk, attending to the lamps. And she took more time than necessary with them this evening, needing something not only to fill the time until one of them should speak, but to fill and occupy her hands as well. Because today, while sitting immobilized in the Morris armchair waiting for them to return, she had suddenly, for the first time in years, experienced the odd sensation that had plagued her toward the end of her marriage to Andrew Westerman, the terrifying feeling that her hands, no matter what she was holding in them, were empty.

She had just finished priming the third lamp, the white candent light had rushed out to reinforce that already in the room, when she was startled by what almost sounded like one of the shadows addressing her from where they had gone into hiding under the tables and chairs. For his voice—drained, flat, distant—came, it seemed, from a source other than himself.

"I never really told you, did I, about the Moran Research Corporation out on the coast . . ."

There was nothing in his tone she could place, no meaning there she could identify, and for a moment, puzzling over it, she remained silent. "No," she said.

"They rounded up a whole bunch of us some years back, offered us more money than we could make in a lifetime teaching or doing ordinary research, set us up in a suite of fancy offices with our names on the doors, and said, 'Go to it, boys, any project you decide on, anywhere in the world, and money's no object.'

"And we came up with a good project," he said in the painfully slow, remote, dead voice, his lips scarcely moving beneath the deeply bowed head. "We planned to rebuild a small village in Chile that had been almost finished off by an earthquake. And our hope was to rebuild more than just houses, but the very life of the people there. And we would have been able to do it given the time and money. But no sooner had we completed the preliminary study than the powers-that-be at Moran, the big boys on the board, decided no. They never bothered giving us a reason, although it seems they felt the project didn't really serve either their interests or those of the State Department, where they got most of their money. Or maybe it was that they realized we weren't going to spy for them. Anyway, they cut off our funds, left us high and dry down there having to tell the people in the village that we weren't going to be doing any of the big things we had talked about . . ."

It was then he looked up, and where his eyes had always spared her before, the worn lids coming thoughtfully down over the mirrorlike iris to hide her reflected image from her, they didn't now, but remained wide-open and intent, unsparing. For a long time the only sound in the room was the lamps which burned with the muted gaseous roar of a blowtorch.

"You couldn't have said anything to your friend Chester Heald, could you, Harriet?"

She had had the more than six hours while they were in town to prepare herself for that question, but although her eyes as she returned his look were marked by their usual candor and her voice when she spoke was steady and even-toned, she nevertheless felt herself falter now that it was actually being asked.

"Saul, I know you're very upset—and understandably so, but perhaps it won't prove such a bad thing. You've . . ."

"I'm asking you whether in writing to Chester Heald you might have said anything to him that might have prompted all this?"

"You've always wanted, haven't you"—there might have been no interruption—"to be in a position where you could design the kinds of programs you feel are really needed. This will give you the chance to do that."

"I've asked you a question."

"I know you hate the thought of leaving Bournehills, but in a way you'll still be supervising things here, since the director of programming, as I understand it, is also the person who oversees all the projects the Center has going. You'll still be in charge in other words."

"Answer me, Harriet."

"And they're not abandoning Bournehills!" Her voice rose a shade. "I don't know where you got such a notion. They're not dropping the project. It seems to me they made that perfectly clear in the cable. It's only to be a temporary delay until they find someone else. Why not take them at their word instead of thinking the worst and suspecting every . . ."

"Did you say anything to Chester Heald, Harriet?"

"Oh, Saul, the change will be to your good! To our good! Everything will work out, I know it will, once we're home, away from this—this place!" The tiny muscle near her mouth gave its involuntary tug and the dangerous gray which attested to the damage done her by the long months in Bournehills began to seep into her eyes. "You'll see," she said. "It'll all work out."

"Because if you did say anything to him"—he had continued despite her; and something in his manner now, a cold implacable note struck aside her voice and she fell silent—"if, when we return, I should find out that you and your blue-blooded friend on the board were in any way involved in what's happened—and I'll find out, make no mistake about that . . . in a way," he said, "I already know, you've already told me; but when I find out for certain I think you know what it will mean for us. We'd be through, Harriet. It would be finish for us. I hope you understand that."

And she saw the truth of this in the haggard face and inflamed eyes. She heard it in the coldly calm, detached voice that was more ominous than his shouting earlier in the day.

"And it doesn't matter why you did it, what your reasons were," he said. "They could have been the best in the world—as I suspect they were; we'd still be through." It was said quietly, the voice that was hardly recognizable tolling out the hard truth in dispassionate tones.

"Because I won't have you running my life, Harriet. You're not going to shape and direct my career—what little there is left of it—from behind the scenes, as you might have done with your first husband. That's out. I'm not going along with whatever master plan you have in mind for me. I run my own show. Maybe badly in your eyes, but I run it."

"Oh, Saul, can't you see it's for your own good! You would have ruined everything the way you were going on." But her cry went unheeded. Nothing she said mattered anymore.

"I tried telling you as much before we came here," he said. "I made a point, in fact, of begging you not to interfere. Because somehow I was afraid you would. That you almost couldn't help it. That's part of the reason I didn't want you to come along in the first place. But no, you had to have it your way. . . ."

His gaze dropped to the desk and to the calendar with its notation of tonight's meeting, and again for a long time he stared silently down at the words written in her neat hand.

"Oh, God!" It was a choked cry which brought his head up with a sharp, wrenching movement, and across the way Harriet saw what could only be tears standing like very still clear water in the pale wells of his eyes. "What am I going to say to people here? That's all I've been thinking of all day. To Stinger, Ferguson, and the rest. To Delbert, who's gone out of his way to help me so much, who's been working harder than me these past few weeks to keep the council going because he realizes how important it is to anything we might try to do later.

"And not that I thought we could accomplish any hell of a lot," he cried, speaking aloud to himself about the work, needing to get it out. "For once in my life I wasn't kidding myself I could perform miracles. I wasn't dreaming up all kinds of grandiose plans that I knew didn't have a chance. I didn't want to fail this time.

"Nor was I kidding myself about how much difference any one project, no matter how big, could make in Bournehills. Because it's true in a way what everyone's always saying about the place, that it's not going to change—at least not on any terms but its own. I've come to believe that also. But I felt that if we went about the project the right way we might do some good, if only in helping Bournehills people to feel a little less powerless and forgotten. Then, hopefully, they'd take matters into their own hands. And we had made a good start. The success we had hauling the canes and before that in setting up the council were steps in the right direction. We could have built from there. That's why I kept praying nothing would go wrong."

He had said all this to himself, but now the eyes, flecked red behind the tears standing in them, returned to Harriet. "How could you have done it, Hatt?" He spoke almost softly, too drained by this time for anger. But it was unlikely that Harriet would have heard him even if he had shouted, because a strange rigidity had come over her while he had been talking, and this, along with the winter gray of her eyes, gave the impression her mind had closed on his voice, and that she was both there in the room and not there.

"And not to me so much," he was saying in the spent voice. "But how could you have done it to Bournehills people, who've been so decent to us: strangers coming to lord it over them whether we mean to or not, with our white skins and our money. How could you have interfered with something that in the long run might have perhaps made life a little easier for them? You've not only taken from me the one thing I've wanted to do in years, but worst of all you've done a terrible thing to people here. I hope you understand that, and understand something else: that I can never forgive you for it."

The still form remained unchanged. She had become the stone effigy now.

"What is it with you and your kind, anyway?" The question, hurled at her across the intervening space, jarred the room and everything in it, but had no effect on her. "If you can't have things your way, if you can't run the show, there's to be no show, is that it?" His voice shook and the face thrust her way across the desk was quivering. "You'd prefer to see everything, including yourselves, come down in ruins rather than 'take down,' rather than not have everything your way, is that it . . . ?"

He waited, trembling, but he no longer looked for any response from her. He knew better. For in the woman with the stone lips and drowned eyes standing across from him was contained the quietly willful child who had always acted secretly, in concert only with herself; and who, moreover, had always refused, even when it would have saved her from being punished, to admit either innocence or guilt.

But even if, by some miracle, she could have spoken; if, for only this once, she had been able to open to him, it wouldn't have changed matters. For she would have told him, speaking in that carefully modulated voice of hers, that her view, her concerns were far narrower than his, and all she had seen or cared about was that their life together was in jeopardy, and she had acted. It had been as simple as that. And presented with the same threat again, she would behave no differently.

"All right, have it your way," he said. He had straightened up and his voice had steadied. "But let me say for your information that I might not be leaving Bournehills, after all. That's right," he said as he thought he saw something stir in her darkened gaze. "Fuck the Center and the Institute and the board. I'm going to refuse to leave, that's all, and if they cut off the money because of it, I'll get it somewhere else. I'll find another agency or foundation to sponsor the project. There's plenty of money around nowadays for this kind of thing. It's not as it used to be. So, in spite of all your wheeling and dealing I may still be around and there may still be a project. I'm going to do my damnedest to see to it.

"As far as you're concerned"—he had moved away from the desk—"you can go or stay. It doesn't matter. Because I'm done with you. As I've heard people here say, you come like a stranger to me from now on."

And as he passed her on his way to the door, his closed indifferent gaze moved across her face as though she was, indeed, someone he didn't know, a mere passer-by on the street whom he never noticed.

Harriet heard from a great distance the door close and then his footsteps repeating the same sound pattern as Allen's on the gallery, the shaky steps going down, and amid the stones of the road. But his step was heavier than Allen's, made ponderous and groping by the weight of his sorrow. And each heavy sorrowful step jarred his body, she knew. She felt them jar hers standing there. A voice called softly to him. Stinger. Instead of coming up to call for him as he usually did whenever there was a council meeting he had, sensing there was trouble, discreetly waited below, outside his crowded house. She heard them greet each other. Stinger's tone was hushed, gentle, that of someone sharing a friend's distress without having to know the cause; Saul's, hoarse, difficult, barely audible. Then, quickly, the darkness closed over the voices and the sound of their retreating steps.

It was then she realized she hadn't boarded up the windows after lighting the lamps and that the night was staring boldly in at her from under the shutters standing open on their long poles. At that her seeming paralysis vanished and she began moving swiftly around the room lowering the long slabs of wood into place over the windows and fastening them to with the latches on the sills.

Following this, she started clearing the table of the uneaten meal and straightening the room, going about it as if there was to be a tomorrow for her. Perhaps, like many women, she held to the belief that the small rituals of life—the lighting of a lamp, the closing of the curtains at dusk—somehow had the power to restore the life of two people when all else failed. So that if she now replaced the unused dishes and glasses in the old-fashioned cupboard people in Bournehills called a press, taking them there one by one to gain time, and the silver and napkins in their drawers, and stored away the food, putting the meat and other perishables in the kerosene-powered refrigerator in the kitchen, the bread in the larder with the wire-screen doors, all this would somehow, magically, set everything to rights between them again. He would continue to be upset, true; but by the time he returned later that night his anger and suspicion would have lessened somewhat and he would drink the coffee she had prepared for them. By the next two or three days he would have calmed considerably (she knew him to be incapable of remaining angry for very long) and certainly by then have abandoned his wild scheme to find another sponsor for the project. And once she had induced him to return to Philadelphia and he realized the possibilities of the job at the Center, the power that would be his, he would even be grateful for what had happened.

And then she thought of the way his eyes had passed over her at the end, as if she was simply one in a faceless mob through which he was passing, and, hastily, she had to put back on the table the large platter of meat she was about to take out to the kitchen lest she drop it. And as hastily she had to sit down, her legs giving way under her.

She could not have said how long she remained at the dining table in what was, after the first moments of her collapse, almost a pleasantly anesthetized state, one impervious to all thought and feeling. But around midnight, the time the council meetings usually ended, she heard Stinger again, the sound of his unaccompanied footsteps feeling their way up the rise, his bare feet stirring the loose stones. And she wasn't surprised to hear him returning alone.

The footsteps came to a halt on the roadside opposite his yard: he had paused, she knew, to look up at their house. The boarded-over windows would give the impression she was peacefully asleep, and although it no longer mattered she was glad of that. Then he was leaping lightly over the low embankment into his yard. His cow, tethered out back, lowed a soft welcome, and a voice called to him from within. It was Gwen. She never slept until he came in at night. And then, once more, there was the silence, that absolute Bournehills night silence which somehow suggests that everyone in the district, every man, woman and child, has deserted it for the night and gone to spend the hours till dawn in some distant place to which they are also native.

Harriet passed the entire night at the partially cleared table, sitting there the long hours with her hands fallen open in her lap and her dull stare and slack body giving the impression she was asleep with her eyes open. Only when the light in the tillies began to fail and the shadows she had banished under the furniture came creeping slyly out, did she get up and, moving like a somnambulist around the room, prime the lamps. But she went about this listlessly, her old efficiency gone. There was scarcely any force behind the hand driving the piston in and out.

The shadows, escaping the moment the light dropped, played little tormenting games with her. Stealing close to her chair they would assume the forms and faces of people she had known over the years, mostly members of her family, all those whom she had always excluded from her thoughts for fear that she might one day be the one held to account for them. But there was no barring them tonight. Under guise of the shadows which she didn't even bother chasing away after a time, they circled her chair, re-enacting long-forgotten scenes, pantomiming the past.

She saw in vivid snatches that were without sequence or order, which could have lasted hours or merely seconds, the old woman in the dim portrait at the Historical Society which she had been proudly taken to see as a child, the shrewd widow in her frilled cap who had trafficked in moldy flour and human flesh; then suddenly there was her father in the years before he retired to his study, when the talk between him and Chester Heald and her great-uncle Ambrose Shippen (he who had been dubbed the robber baron of the family) had been money and mergers and manipulating the market. The blue scrawl of their cigar smoke in the downstairs rooms had been the signature of their power. Out of the smoke, which she not only smelled but saw again, its blue haze drifting lazily about the poor room in which she was sitting, another figure emerged. And as clearly as if she had come to stand over her at the table, Harriet saw that hopeless, unreconstructed Southern belle who had been her mother; who, in her unwitting and indiscriminate cruelty, used to touch her as though hoping to remold her into some more pleasing, less angular form; and whose tone when speaking to the maid Alberta had casually assumed her to be a lesser person.

Alberta, whom Harriet had once believed the fairies had turned black because of something naughty she had done when little! She saw her gathering together their used clothes and toys—hers and her two brothers'—to send to her nieces and nephews in Virginia, and she saw herself, the child she had been then, clinging dry-eyed and adamant, unyielding, to the toy she had refused to send them that time. What had it been? Sitting at the table waiting out the darkness she became obsessed by the need to remember. For what might have been hours she searched her mind, trying to discover what it had been, believing obscurely, beyond thought, that if she could but recall the toy this would in some way serve as a reprieve. But her mind, clouded over, numb, already anesthetized against the final pain, refused to offer up its secret.

All the long search brought finally was Andrew. His shut face and flat distant eyes. Standing there before her like some Frankensteinian form of her creation. And he was to remain with her for the balance of the night. So that for what seemed an eternity she was back with him in the house near the Proving Ground, seated across from him at the breakfast table, asleep just beyond him in their separate beds, and dreaming once again of her hand on top of his on the lever and together the two of them, perversely, as if driven by an excess of power, committing the monstrous act that could only bring about their own end.

Toward morning he touched her. And at the same place on her arm where Lyle Hutson's hand had rested that night months ago. And his touch brought the same dark splotch like an ugly bruise or one of those Rorschach inkblots that would reveal her, surging to the surface. Only this time it did not confine itself to the one spot. But as the shadows in the room increased, closing in around her, it spread, and in the spreading stain which soon covered her entire body, she saw (no longer able to shut her mind to them) all the things she had denied the years with Andrew: her secret desire, for one, to have done with him and move on once her plan for him was fulfilled; for another, her shattering realization that morning upon awakening of her complicity in the destruction planned, and the feelings of guilt and horror at herself which she had sought to flee by leaving him—only, she had to admit, her head dropping heavily and the shadows howling the truth at her, to seek out a Saul with whom she could repeat the pattern. . . .

The admission aged her. The face that was impressive, even beautiful in its unshakable composure became worn, haggard, old, as the night neared its end. All the small, carefully arranged muscles that shaped its characteristic expression might have suddenly lost their tension and fallen, and in so doing brought the face down with them.

Dawn came but she couldn't see it because of the boarded-over windows. She felt its coolness, though, through the thin walls, and she could tell the moment the first light appeared. She sensed it, that dawn light, blossoming with the opalescence of a pearl and moving slowly, with all the stateliness of a royal barge, into the heart of the darkness outside. They embraced—the darkness and the light, so that when she finally rose and opened out the shutters she had the impression that the night, bedding down in the great folds of the hills, contained the dawn, and the dawn the darkness. It was as though they were really, after all, one and the same, two parts of a whole, and that together they stood to acquaint her with an essential truth.

Moving numbly about the room, her will gone, she extinguished the lamps and finished clearing the table. This done, she left the house as she did every morning at this hour, taking with her in a beach bag her bathing suit, cap and a towel.

Around her the rise still slept, the tiny gray-board houses tightly sealed against the night, temporarily abandoned, by the look of them. Only the shutters to Leesy's house halfway down the stony track stood open on their poles, and as Harriet passed she thought she glimpsed the old woman's time-yellowed eyes peering impassively at her from between the slats of the shed-roof kitchen. Or they might have been Vere's eyes singling her out that fatal afternoon on the road. Or Alberta's nephew, whose weighted body had been found at the bottom of the pond. Watched by them, borne down by their gaze, she continued on her way to the sea. And as always she heard it—the sea—long before it came into view. The massive detonation set off by the breakers on the reefs. And then the spray rising in the dazzling white toadstool of a cloud.

~ ~ ~

Later that morning the children, coming for their daily supply of broom sage and sand, found her clothes inside the tiny bathhouse of wattle and daub just up from Horseshoe Pool, the clothes—the plain linen skirt and white blouse she donned like a uniform each day—neatly folded on top of her underthings on the bench, the towel beside them, her beach bag hung on the wall hook and her shoes arranged side by side on the hard-packed sand which served as a floor.

The body was never recovered. Those who knew the Bournehills sea well said it had probably gotten lodged on one of the outlying reefs when the breakers sought to return it to shore, or that with the sea still going through its violent seasonal change, it had been swept south into the inaccessible caves under Plover Cliff, or, simply, that the sharks had gotten to it. But a tearful Gwen rejected all three theories. She swore that the body had been borne back to America. And she insisted on holding a wake, saying, "It's the least we can do, yes."

CHAPTER 11

As Merle had said it would be, it was like a new sea. The water, a clear, deep-toned blue that absorbed the sunlight to a depth far below its surface, looked as though it had been endlessly filtered to remove every impurity. And all trace of the unsightly seaweed it had sloughed off like so much dead skin over the weeks was gone. Most of this had been gathered up and buried under the dunes, but some was being used as fertilizer and a small portion had been carefully washed and boiled into bush tea to be drunk as a tonic. Even the sand, that rough, brown, coarse-grained detritus peculiar to Bournehills that could so bruise the foot, appeared to have been passed through a giant sieve that had sifted out the larger, more cutting pebbles.

And a marked change had taken place in the several voices of the Bournehills sea now that the yearly cleansing was over. For one, the roar of outrage the huge breakers sent aloft as they flung themselves, exhausted from the long cross-Atlantic run, onto the outer reefs had lost some measure of its fury; and the high-pitched ritual keening of the lesser waves and the wind which never ceased had been taken to a slightly lower register. And though the sea continued to hurl itself in an excess of grief and mourning onto the shore, sending up the spume like tears, it did so with something less than its usual hysteria. Above all, the powerful undertow that had been felt even in Horseshoe Pool during the period of purification, and which everyone assumed had swept Harriet out over the low barrier of rock into the open sea, had dropped, and the water within the enclosure was manageable again.

A silent Merle sat in her familiar pose at the veranda railing, her feet up, her head resting against the slatted back of the chair and her gaze on the bright scales of afternoon sunlight adrift on the waves. Beside her, in a chair turned away from the beach, sat an equally silent Saul.

It was their first meeting in the three weeks since the drowning. Because after the futile search for the body Saul had gone to stay in town, taking a room at a small guesthouse where no one knew him. And he would not have returned to Bournehills yet if Allen—who had visited him from time to time—hadn't told him this morning that Merle would be leaving the island shortly, going finally to Uganda to see her child. He had driven back with him then to say good-bye.

No mention had been made, though, of her leaving in spite of the fact they had been together for some time on the veranda. But by way perhaps of silently confirming the news, Merle had taken out the folder containing the plane ticket and placed it on the armrest of her chair.

As if to avoid having to look at it, Saul sat hunched forward in his seat, his elbows on his knees and his back at a sharp slant. It was the same numb pose he had maintained for days on end on the edge of the bed in his small room in town. Then, his dazed filmed eyes and limp body, his head hanging loosely down, had called to mind an exhausted prizefighter, some aging heavyweight who had never been particularly good at the game but had stuck with it, and who had now just lost yet another round in a fight that was clearly going against him and sat badly winded and near-insensible with pain on his stool in the corner of the ring. His opponents during the three weeks had been his grief and remorse, his anguish over the never-to-be answered question as to the true nature of Harriet's death, how it had actually happened. These had detached themselves from his mind to become visible foes who had flailed away at him without letup in the room and on the blind walks he took through the streets of New Bristol at night. And they had followed him back to Bournehills to assail him as he sat beside Merle.

Finally, still in the hunched-over position, he reached back for the ticket lying between them. He held it in his hands without taking it from the folder.

"My traveling papers," Merle said quietly, both pride and sadness sounding in her voice. "I had to sell almost everything I owned to raise the money, but I managed. You should see my room. It's as bare as a bone. Everything gone—all that old furniture and junk I had cluttering up the place. I sold the whole lot week before last to an antique dealer in town. He'll make a fortune reselling it to these rich expatriates we've got round the place who love collecting stuff from the old estate houses on the island. I even sold the very bed from under me and I'm sleeping on a cot these nights. I haven't slept better in years. And the wreck of a car is gone. Some millionaire American over at the Crown Beach Colony whom Lyle knows bought it off me when he heard it had belonged to the last English governor we had here. I guess he thinks he'll feel like him riding around in it. And the earrings I've worn all these years? Gone! A jeweler in town paid good money for them. Haven't you noticed how different I look without them?"

And he saw then, really looking at her for the first time since his arrival, that the earrings with the piously suffering saints were gone, and that without them she looked as she had the few times they'd been together at Aunt Tie's, when, as part of the small rites between them, he would remove both the earrings and the heavy silver bracelets on her wrists: unburdened, restored to herself. He saw, too, that she had left off the talcum powder she was forever dabbing on her face and throat as though to mute her darkness, and that her hair which she normally kept straightened flat with the iron-toothed comb he had seen in her room that night now stood in a small rough forest around her face, framing it. She looked younger, less scarred, with it that way.

"Yes," she said, "I've been busy these past three weeks. Nearly everything gone, sold, and my ticket bought. What do you think of that? I'm not so hopeless after all, am I?"

He didn't answer. Instead, replacing the folder, which he hadn't opened, on the arm of her chair, he said, "When are you leaving?"

"Saturday week."

His gaze dropped, and Merle, after waiting a few moments, said, "I thought you'd be pleased to hear I'd finally gotten up the courage to go."

"I am, Merle, I am," he said but kept his eyes down to hide from her the sense of utter desolation that had suddenly swept him.

"It's as both of us have said any number of times," she began. "I'll never get around to doing anything with what's left of my life until I go and look for my child. You know that"—he nodded, his head bent—"I'll just go on as I am," she said. "Doing nothing but sitting out on this veranda all day or down in that damp cave of a room feeling sorry for myself and blaming everyone and everything for the botch I've made of things. And talking. Oh, God, going on like some mad woman all the time but doing nothing. And letting the least little thing set out my head, but doing nothing.

"Finish with that!" she cried strongly. "I'm going to get up and give it a try again. I made up my mind to it these three weeks I haven't seen you. But before I can think of making any kind of a start I have to go see my little girl. That before anything else.

"And I'm not going there to make trouble," she added hastily. "You wouldn't recognize me I'm going to be so calm and reasonable. No raving. All I want if possible is for her father to agree to some arrangement that would allow me to see her from time to time. Maybe, if she takes to me, she'd like to come and spend her long school holiday over here every two years or so. He might be willing to agree to that. After all, it's been a long time and he's older now and maybe a little more understanding. Anyway, I'm going to take my chances and see."

"Have you written to let them know you're coming?"

"No," she said, and she was suddenly worried. "You think I should have, don't you?"

"That might have been best," he said. He was looking at her now.

"Oh, I thought of it," she said. "But I was afraid he wouldn't answer the letter. He's never answered any of the others I've written. Or that if he did answer it might be just to say no. So I thought the best thing would be to simply go there. And I won't have any trouble finding them, because I know for a fact he's still teaching at Markarere." Then, with a strained smile: "I'm hoping that when he sees how old and harmless I've become he'll relent and not be so set against me. . . ."

But the faint smile quickly gave way to the worried frown again, and turning from Saul, her eyes with their odd almost tawny cast sought the sea, and for a long time she gazed somewhat apprehensively at what seemed a point far beyond the horizon.

"I'm being selfish," she declared suddenly.

"No, you're not."

"Yes, I am. Interfering in the child's life after all these years. That's what some people would say . . ."

"To hell with what they say. She's your child, too."

"Oh, she is!" she cried, turning back to him with a grateful look. "And that gives me some rights, doesn't it! Why, maybe for all you know she thinks about me sometimes, wonders what her mother looks like, what kind of person she is. She might even be happy to see me, who knows . . ." Then, her uncertainty returning: "That's if her father hasn't turned her against me."

"He won't have done that, Merle," he said. "And no matter what, she'll be glad that you've come to see her."

She looked at him for a time, wanting to believe him but full of doubt. "Well, let's hope you're right," she said. Then: "Even if she doesn't take to me, I'll try not to mind. I'll understand. After all, you can't very well expect a child of nine to welcome with open arms some woman who suddenly appears out of the blue claiming to be her mother. It'll take her a little time to get used to the idea. But even if things don't work out, it will be enough for me just to have seen her . . .

"And what of you, Saul Amron?" she asked gently, after a silence. Sitting around in her chair she placed a hand on his arm. "What of you? What will you do now that this"—she searched for a way to say it—"this terrible thing's happened?"

Slipping his arm from under her hand he again leaned far forward in his seat, his elbows on his knees supporting the body that had become sodden with the tears that had accumulated over the three weeks. It felt waterlogged. Part of him might have also drowned, part of him died with Harriet. And in a way, this was how he had come to see his death, as a series of small ones taking place over the course of his life and leading finally to the main event, which would be so anticlimactic, so undramatic (a sudden violent seizure in his long-abused heart, a quick massive flooding of the brain) it would go unnoticed. It was the small deaths occurring over an entire lifetime that took the greater toll.

"It's no use saying, I know, that you mustn't hold yourself entirely to blame," she said, when it became clear he didn't intend answering her. Her hushed voice scarcely intruded upon the silence. "Because you're going to, anyway. It's hard not to, I guess, in a case like this where you don't know how it all happened and never will. Even I feel in some way responsible. I never told you, but we had words the last time she came over here. It doesn't matter about what anymore, but we did.

"You keep asking yourself why something like this has to happen . . ." She spoke to herself. Her gaze had shifted back to the sea. "It's a foolish question I know, but you do. What would drive a person to do something like that . . . ? Oh, I still can't believe it," she cried suddenly. "I keep expecting to see her strolling along the beach in the afternoon taking the breeze or out at the crack of dawn swimming in that cold sea. Harriet. She wasn't an easy person to know."

She thought she saw him slowly nod. "Not even for me, Merle," he said. "I never really got beyond her surface, I've realized these past three weeks. To the other Harriet you could sometimes sense there. Maybe it's that I didn't try hard enough. Or that all I wanted from her was that calm controlled front of hers. I don't know. Anyway, I never really got through. I somehow never found the way . . ."

And in the face of that mystery which had been Harriet, which he had been unable to penetrate even with his love—that awed, somewhat uneasy love he had borne her—his hands dangling lifelessly between his knees opened in a gesture of despair and he fell silent again.

Nothing was said for some time. Seated there, their chairs arranged like one of those old-fashioned S-shaped sofas, with Saul's turned from the sea and their armrests touching, they appeared close, intimate, of a mind. But their separate thoughts—his of Harriet, hers of the journey ahead—had already taken them far from each other.

"But you haven't answered my question."

His head lifted questioningly. He thought back. "You mean about me?"

"Yes, what're you going to do?"

He let his body slide back into the lawn chair's deep slanted bottom. From there she could see his face. "I haven't thought about it," he said. "But I'll make out, I guess. Once you've hit bottom as often as I have you either stay down or start finding it easier to drag yourself up again. I don't know which it'll be for me. It doesn't much matter.

"One good thing"—a little life stirred in his voice—"it looks as if they mean to go ahead with the project. I've heard from my friend Barney at the Center and he tells me they're not going to drop it altogether. They haven't changed their minds about me, of course. But then I couldn't stay on in Bournehills, anyway, after what's happened. Nor could I have anything more to do with that outfit. Maybe Barney could be persuaded to take over as director. I'm going to talk to him when I get back. He and I worked together in Peru years ago and he's a good man in the field. And Allen—who absolutely refuses to go home for some reason—will be here, which will give a sense of continuity to things."

"What about you though?"

"I told you I'll manage." His indifference to his own fate was reflected in the slumped body and lightless eyes. "There's always teaching. And there was some talk, I remember, at the place where I taught before coming to Bournehills, about setting up a program to recruit and train young social scientists from overseas—those in my specialty—to work in their own countries. I'd like to be part of that maybe if they've gone ahead with it. I'm more than ever convinced now that that's the best way: to have people from the country itself carry out their own development programs whenever possible. Outsiders just complicate the picture—as you and I know only too well. . . .

"But whatever I do, one thing is certain: I'll be staying put this time. And I mean that. No more field work. No more—what?—odysseys, for want of a better word. And it's not just a matter of giving up and wanting to hide out as it was the last time I quit. It's that somehow, in a way I can't explain, after Bournehills there aren't any places left for me to go. Don't ask me why I feel this, but it's something I've come to understand these past three weeks."

"You'll get over it," she said with the same gentleness as before. "And be up and about this part of the world again."

"No," he said, and the look he gave her left no doubt of his decision. "No, not after Bournehills."

His gaze dropped to the armrest of her chair and for a long time he studied the folder with the plane ticket. "I suppose," he said, "you might be staying over there if things work out . . ."

"And what would Africa want with me?" she said with a sad laugh. "A slightly daft, middle-aged woman with history on the brain."

"Perhaps your husband will have had a change of heart."

"Ha!" It was her familiar hollow hoot. "I wouldn't bet on it," she said. "If he just doesn't look at me as he used to toward the end as if I were the worst person in the world, or worse, if he doesn't chase me from his door, I'll be more than content.

"But you're right," she went on. "I might stay over there for awhile, travel about, see the place. I've borrowed some extra money from Lyle and I can always get more from him if I need it. It's odd," she added after a pause, her eyes seeking again the invisible point beyond the horizon, "but I have the feeling that just being there and seeing the place will be a big help to me, that in some way it will give me the strength I need to get moving again. Not that I'm going expecting to find perfection, I know they have more than their share of problems, or to find myself or any nonsense like that. It's more what you once said: that sometimes a person has to go back, really back—to have a sense, an understanding of all that's gone to make them—before they can go forward. I believe that, too.

"But I'll be coming back to Bournehills. This is home. Whatever little I can do that will matter for something must be done here. A person can run for years but sooner or later he has to take a stand in the place which, for better or worse, he calls home, do what he can to change things there."

Her tone, the eyes which fixed him clearly sought to impress this upon him, and in the face of it he said, "I take it you're suggesting that I also mount the barricades when I return." She didn't answer, and with a sigh he turned aside. "I suppose you're right. I'll have to, as you say, take a stand, do something toward shaking up that system. It's odd, but whenever I've thought of living back in the States it's always been as a stranger almost, someone on the sidelines, out of it, who's simply awaiting either the return to sanity in the country or the end. But that won't do, I guess. I'll have to get involved as I once was, although God knows I've little heart for the fight anymore. But that's the only way I'll be able to take living there permanently, I know. Despair," he said, "is too easy an out. Anyway, we'll see." Then: "What about you? Have you thought about what you might do when you get back?"

"A little," she said. "I might try to get a government loan to fix up the guesthouse and see if I can't make a go of the hotel business. But that's not certain. Or, I might try teaching again—and this time make sure to slip in Cuffee on the sly, when the headmaster isn't looking. Or, don't laugh"—and she suddenly laughed at the thought—"I might go into politics. Start a political party of one, strictly radical. How's that?"

"I'd vote for you."

"Then," she declared, her eyes coming to rest fondly on his, "I couldn't help but win. And so would Bournehills people. They'd give me a vote. Lord, Deanesie would shed tears of blood. And I can hear Enid and the ladies in town now: 'Oh, God, have you heard the latest? Mad-Merle's in politics!' " Her laugh rose, only to fall abruptly. "Not that I'd be able to do much as things stand. But I bet that if I was in Legco we would at least get the water pipe for up Canterbury and the gabions and asphalt for Westminster Low Road so it wouldn't wash away at the least drop of rain. Because by the time I let loose a . . . a . . ." She turned to him. "What do you call it again in your country when those Congressmen from the South try to talk to death any bill that's to help the black people there?"

"A filibuster."

"Yes, that's it. Well, by the time I let loose a filibuster on those rascals in Legco they'd be only too happy to run the pipe up Canterbury and put some asphalt on the road, if only to stop my mouth."

Then, with a thin threadbare smile she might have copied from him, she leaned close to say, "And when I get to be a big shot and your government invites me up on one of those good-will tours they hand out every so often to us down this way, I'll come look you up. How's that? I'll drop in for a visit."

"I look forward to it."

But his tone was too serious and she backed off. "No," she said, "I doubt I'll ever come to America. Too many terrible things go on in that place. And somebody seeing the two of us together might make some nasty remark. We'd see the ugly thoughts in their eyes. I know what these white people give, you know. I got to know them only too well those years in England. No, we wouldn't do there.

"Maybe," she mused aloud to herself, "it's only in a place like Bournehills, someplace the world has turned its back on and even God's forgotten, that we could have met and gotten on so well together, been such good friends.

"But not in that damn place you're from!" she broke out, sudden anger splintering the sunlight in her eyes. "Where they treat the black people, the very ones who made the bloody country rich in the first place, so badly; a place where, oh, God," she cried softly, "you read in the newspaper sometime back how they bombed a church killing four children, four little girls now the age of my daughter; and where, every time you look around, they're warring against some poor, half-hungry country somewhere in the world . . ."

"Merle," he said. "Merle."

"Yes, I know." She nodded wearily. "There's no use my upsetting myself. Such thoughts, as Lear said, lead only to madness. Oh!" She again uttered the soft cry, but differently this time as she was caught in the hold of some memory. "I loved that old king nobody wanted around anymore. I used to read that play over and over again as a girl. He was an almshouse child like myself.

"You're to promise me something," she said with sudden urgency.

"Of course."

"Not to leave here till I do," she said. "Because if you go before me I just might not make it on the plane. With all my guff I'm really nothing but a coward, you know. Scared. Why I might never have gotten around to buying this ticket had not for you. I wonder if you realize that?"

"And have you any idea what you've been for me? Done for me?"

"Yes," she said promptly. "I've let you know you don't fail everyone."

"Oh, Merle." And in that gesture of obeisance he had seen others pay her, he brought his lips to rest briefly on her cheek, and then down on the dark hand lying on the chair arm.

"You don't know it," she said over his bowed head, "but I started to come and see you any number of times these past three weeks. I just wanted to come and sit quietly with you, the way you did with me that time I took in so badly over Cane Vale. One night I even drove as far as Cleaver's, but lost my nerve and turned back. I was afraid you didn't want to see anybody."

"How I wish you had come," he said, lifting his head. "Or I had come to you. I wanted to. It was all I could do some days not to get in the car and drive down. In the midst of everything I was feeling about Harriet I wanted to see you. . . ." He numbly shook his head, remembering how he had sat in the small room mourning Harriet and wanting Merle, his grief and desire one. What had Stinger said that day on the way to Brighton about a man not understanding himself?

"How much are they charging you at the place you're staying in town?" she asked abruptly, with a hint of a smile that was both playful and sad.

"Why do you ask?" he said, puzzled.

"Just tell me."

He told her.

"Those thieves!"

"You think it's too much?"

"Too much! It's far too much! Why you could have all this"—her sweeping wave took in the decaying guesthouse behind her, the listing veranda upon which they were sitting, the perennially sorrowing sea out front—"for half that amount."

"But they have lights and hot water," he said entering into the joke.

"Yes, but they don't have Merle."

He smiled wanly for the first time. "You have a point."

"We have," she said very quietly, "these few days before I leave."

And as quietly he nodded.

She left a week from that Saturday. And with the exception of Saul, whom she asked at the last minute not to come, it seemed the whole of Spiretown accompanied her to the airport. Dressed in their town clothes, the women with their faces powdered near-white, the childrens' legs and the small ashen knobs of their elbows shiny with Vaseline, they crowded into the Bournehills bus that had had its benches and roof replaced and into the trucks and vans that had been used for the hauling. Some even pooled what little money they had left over from the crop and hired taxis from town. Merle was in Saul's small English Ford, seated in front between Allen, who was driving, on one side, and Leesy, in her austere white dress, her hand clutching the window ledge, on the other. Carrington, Gwen and Vere's girl, Milly, whose stomach was as large now with his child as Gwen's had been all along, rode in back.

The cavalcade set off down the main road, the car with Merle in the lead. Saul, standing with Collins and a few others outside Delbert's shop, caught a final glimpse of her as the Ford passed. Silent, painfully tense, she was staring straight ahead. Her gaze was trained so intently on the moving stretch of road just in front of the car that she failed to notice the scattering hands raised to her in the traditional Bournehills salute along the way. She had, it was clear, already made the transition. Bournehills and everyone there were already behind her, and her eyes, her mind were fixed on other scenes, other faces, on all that awaited her.

And she was not taking the usual route to Africa, first flying north to London via New York and then down. Instead, she was going south to Trinidad, then on to Recife in Brazil, and from Recife, that city where the great arm of the hemisphere reaches out toward the massive shoulder of Africa as though yearning to be joined to it as it had surely been in the beginning, she would fly across to Dakar and, from there, begin the long cross-continent journey to Kampala.

Saul left a few days later, feeling as he sat squeezed in among Delbert, Stinger, Ferguson, Ten-ton and one or two others from the shop in the Ford like someone being exiled permanently from all that he loved. And as if they also sensed this the men were silent for the most, the only sound for long stretches Delbert's labored breathing. With Allen again at the wheel the car moved swiftly, complying with Saul's wish to be gone now that the lifetime (and he saw it as such) he had spent in Bournehills was over.

Old Mr. Douglin, faithful keeper of the grave, hailed them with his cutlass from his fixed station along Westminster Low Road, at the place where Cuffee's severed head had been left on the tall pike. Much farther on they passed Pyre Hill off in the distance and, with the waves of afternoon heat rising visibly from its blackened hull, it looked, as always, to be smoldering still, the fire that Cuffee had started, which legend would have it had burned for five years, refusing to die. It would flare again, full strength, one day.

They were within sight of Cleaver's when they saw the first rain of the season high on the ridge. It stood suspended there like a sheer drop curtain rung down from the sky, all golden with the sun riding unconcerned above it and gently ruffled by the wind. As the men in the car watched, the blown curtain of rain moved securely down the precipitous drop from the ridge, then, spreading out, over the parched shabby hills that made up Bournehills, staining them dark as it swept over them. And it was clearly gathering strength all the time it came —and speed, until soon it was advancing to meet those in the Ford at an even greater speed than they were traveling. And as it slammed up against the car, almost stopping it in its tracks, Delbert loosed his great gut laugh and said, "Well, yes, we can look for the old road to take a walk any day now."

Grenada, West Indies. New York. Yaddo.
1963–68